CW01433132

A Man Was Going Down the Road

***in the original Georgian*:**

Gzaze erti k'atsi midioda (Tbilisi, 1972, reprinted 2010)

Otar Chiladze

A MAN WAS GOING DOWN THE ROAD

translated by Donald Rayfield

GARNETT PRESS

LONDON

first published in Great Britain in 2012 by

The Garnett Press,
Dpt of Russian (SLLF)
Queen Mary University of London,
Mile End Road, London E1 4NS

Printed and bound in Great Britain by
TJ International, Padstow, Cornwall

FRONT COVER ILLUSTRATION:

Woodcut illustration of the escape of Jason with Medea and the death of her brother Absyrtus, from a German translation by Heinrich Steinhöwel of Giovanni Boccaccio's *De mulieribus claris*, printed by Johannes Zainer at Ulm ca. 1474

ISBN 978-0-9564683-0-7

CONTENTS

Translator's Introduction

Otar Chiladze (1933–2009) is by consensus the most important novelist of the 20th century in Georgia: his six novels and other works (two plays and a body of poetry) consistently reflect his philosophy of life, his interest in myth and history and, although most of his creative life was spent under Soviet rule, his defiance of the ruling ideology. We publish in English his first novel, of 1972, *A Man Was Going Down the Road*, because it is the key to his later work, and because, its point of departure being the Greek legend of Jason and the golden fleece, its appeal is more obviously international and general. To this day, this novel has been a favourite of readers of all ages in Georgia and in Russia: it is almost the only Georgian novel still in print in Russian translation.

It is a bold as well as magical work: on the surface, it deals with the consequences for the obscure kingdom of Colchis after the Greek Jason comes and abducts Medea. To a politically aware reader, though apparently not to an inattentive Soviet censor, it is an allegory of the treachery and destruction that ensued when Russia, and then the Soviets, annexed Georgia. (Chiladze's drama *Tsate's Red Boots*, which also deals with a historical precedent to Russian conquest, did attract the ire of Soviet censorship.) This novel can be read as Chiladze's interpretation of life as a version of the ancient Anatolian story of Gilgamesh, or as a study of Georgian life, domestic and political, in which women and children pay the price for the hero's quests, obsessions and doubts. Chiladze's later novels explore later Georgian history; the last two (of which the Garnett Press will next year publish *Avelum*) are set in contemporary times. But in all of them, the situations and predicaments of *A Man Was Going Down the Road* recur: Orphic redemption, children doomed by their parents, executioners and victims tied by blood and marriage.

This translation aims at fidelity, no easy task given the extraordinary richness and range of Chiladze's syntax and vocabulary. I have taken liberties only with characters' names. Chiladze names some — Ǣëtes, Medea, Jason, Phrixos — as in the Greek legends; others, such as Chalciope, Absyrtus, he renames as Charisa and Aphrasion, but in this version the Greek originals are restored. Georgian names are transcribed in a simple system, but two names are translated: Popeye's Georgian nickname *Kusa* is given him because of his popping eyes, while 'Hey-Boy' translates *Imano*, the nickname of the vintner's assistant. Other Georgian names also have meanings: Oqajado means 'kilo of magic', Ukheiro 'awkward', Kama 'dill' and Tsutsa 'catkin', but it was thought better to leave them untranslated. One other note: the main hero of the latter part of the book, Parnaoz, bears the name of Georgia's first king, a figure perhaps no more real than King Arthur, but just as resonant in national mythology.

I thank Tamar Chiladze, the author's daughter, for her help, the Chiladze family for their generosity, which has made it possible for this translation to appear, and Shukia Apridonidze for materials and much helpful advice.

PART ONE

ÆËTES

CHAPTER ONE

THIS is a story of the time when Vani was a city by the sea; when the first Greek set foot on Colchian soil and humbly asked for asylum. That very day the sea took courage and, after much hesitation, took its first step back. The first step was the most important: everything afterwards happened of its own accord: who could have stopped it? Even if every inhabitant of Vani, big and small, had tried to hold the sea back in their coat-tails, it would still have slipped away: no force can oppose anything nature has planned to do. Sooner or later this had to happen: the sea had plucked up courage and had begun to carry out this truly treacherous plan.

Vani's inhabitants were so alarmed and shocked that they didn't even try to seek and recover what they had lost. They were deeply convinced, and ever more deeply as time passed, that the sea had abandoned them because they had committed some great sin; it had abandoned them as a breadwinner might abandon his family, or a husband his wife, once he could take no more of her frivolity and flirting. The husband had just got up and left. But, before he left, he had been so cautious, deliberate and patient that nobody guessed what he was planning until everything was revealed and he was out of reach.

Abandoned by the sea, the land was as moist and wrinkled as a newborn baby: it gradually grew and spread all along the shore like a black mourning ribbon. Then an enormous marsh appeared between Vani and the sea, as green, bubbling and slimy as a dragon's poisonous vomit. The city that was once famous, the pride of the country, became a remote, inaccessible place in the back of beyond. The time had gone when everyone in Vani could see the sea from their window, when in every house you could hear the sea's constant, endless breathing. Nobody in Vani had ever thought of opening the window just to look at the sea, or ever woken at night and sat up in bed just to listen to it. Everyone sensed that the sea was always right there.

What woman believes her husband is going to abandon her? Neither did the people of Vani believe that the sea would abandon them. Roofed with tiles shining blood-red, the city had boldly reared up over the sea, like a beautiful girl over a love-stricken Goliath.

The people of Vani used to love going down to the port, to chat with foreigners, to have a good gossip and find out all the secret goings-on in the world. They took an interest in everything, they knew everything: they knew where every ship was docked, what it had brought, what it was loading, whether it was arriving or departing. Seen from the port, the world appeared wider and more interesting. Vani was part of this wide, interesting world, and ships were happy to make for Vani. Everyone remembered the time they spent here as one extraordinary, dizzy dream.

Anyone who had never visited Bakha the vintner's cellar with its forty steps had no idea of what wine really tasted like. One bowl of wine drunk here was worth more than whole amphorae. Like a mistress enjoyed for one night, this wine could make a man suddenly, at any moment, feel such a longing that he would drop whatever he was doing and head back to Vani. Likewise, anyone who had never heard black-eyed Malalo and her six daughters sing had no appreciation of song.

Black-eyed Malalo was a woman from Babylon and for any stranger she would sing in his native language 'I was born in Babylon, but grew up in Vani.' This was how Malalo introduced herself to distinguished visitors, and if you'd asked her which she loved most, which she preferred, Babylon or Vani, she probably couldn't have answered. Her six daughters, who had identical hair and dresses, were so much like her that you'd think you were seeing black-eyed Malalo in six mirrors. The girls looked their mother affectionately in the eye, like good pupils at their teacher, and parroted — repeating and learning by heart — her words, her responses, her swaying movements.

Black-eyed Malalo also had a real parrot which she had brought with her from Babylon; it was her only compatriot and the only witness to the youth she had squandered on her journeys. The parrot's expression implied that it was standing guard over itself, as if it was both a forlorn prisoner and a watchful warder. Its amphora-shaped reed cage hung from the ceiling by a long chain; anyone who passed by would be sure to hit it with his hand, as if worried that the warder might fall asleep and the prisoner escape. 'Hostess!' the parrot would shout, as it and the cage swung, its splendid black hooked beak grabbing its tail, tucked between its legs, and it would spin like a wheel on its perch. Then the parrot would squawk 'Hostess!' once more and angrily flash its yellow, daisy-like eyes at the world, at everybody and everything outside the walls of its cage. 'Hostess, hostess,' the guests, uncaged prisoners of freedom would then repeat, smiling vaguely, after the parrot.

Visiting black-eyed Malalo really was sheer pleasure. Many, foreigners and natives, felt the urge to be there, but not everyone proved worthy of the attention of the seven songstresses. Black-eyed Malalo could know a man just by glancing at him. 'He'll turn nasty when he's drunk,' she would decide instantly when she saw tiny close-set eyes or unnaturally red wet lips. Anyone who turned nasty when drunk was banned for life from black-eyed Malalo's house. 'My house is a temple,' black-eyed Malalo liked to say, and although most of her guests were men, the whole house was dominated by exemplary tidiness and tranquillity, thanks to seven pairs of hands and seven pairs of eyes. Guests gathered in a big room where the talking parrot's cage hung, and the six girls with identical hair and identical dresses tirelessly explained and advised the visitors where to go, what to see, what to buy and try out in a city they still found strange. That was how time passed in the world that swung in the shade of the reed bird cage. As well as the big room, black-eyed Malalo's house had many little rooms: we needn't say what happened in those little rooms, or what went on anywhere in black-eyed Malalo's house when the singing was no longer audible. But those were the times when the city recalled black-eyed Malalo and her daughters. When the song was suddenly put to bed, for a minute it excited the whole city, as the thought of a field lying fallow excites the peasant.

Everyone who by chance or on purpose set off for Vani was eager to see for themselves what they had only heard about and what really justified undertaking such a long journey. A man knew before he came that he would find ten girls prepared to marry him in exchange for jewellery from Vani, that half his home town would grimace with envy if he wore a dagger from Vani or put his baby to bed in a cradle from Vani. That wasn't all: dying man, told that he'd be laid to rest in a sarcophagus from Vani, would be overjoyed, and dismiss his fear of imminent death, so that you'd think a sarcophagus from Vani shielded one from dying.

There were many other things in Vani considered worth seeing and wondering at: Dariachangi's garden was in itself something for a man to contemplate and long for. When buds were unfurling at one end of these gardens, fruit was already ripening at the other end. The scents that wafted from Dariachangi were enough to knock a grown man over. The people of Vani used to say that anyone who plucked and ate an apple in that garden would beget a golden-haired boy. Anyone who wanted could pluck an apple; anyone could roll about on its velvety cool ground, but the tiniest branches were sacred and mustn't be broken, or the garden, big as it was, would instantly vanish without a trace. Ships travelling to Vani could, while still at sea, catch the scents of the gardens: it embraced them invisibly, drew them on and then it was hard to escape from this scented noose which made you a thousand promises and excited hearts and minds in countless different ways. 'We've arrived and here we are,' sailors would say the moment the scent of eternal fruitfulness spread over the sea.

This was the city's characteristic scent, as Vani, gleaming white, fierily topped with red tiles, slowly rose from the sea to meet the speeding ship.

In fact, every district of Vani had its own peculiar atmosphere, but the goldsmiths' quarter was special. Not a single foreigner left Vani without visiting that quarter at least once. You have, as they say, to see things with your own eyes, so who would miss out on such a good opportunity? From morning to evening you could hear the tapping of little hammers, the humming of lathes and the snipping of pliers from the goldsmiths' quarter; from morning to evening gold leaf was pressed, cut and stamped; from morning to evening the noble metal tinkled, giggled and took on flesh and colour, like a girl turned into a woman in the course of one night. This quarter was also called the magicians' district, and there was in fact something secret, bewitching, daunting in a goldsmith's satanically screwed-up eyes and his wrinkled lips' secretive smile. At the entrance and exit to the quarter stood mirrors so enormous that a man and his horse could be seen in them. And who would have the courage to turn away from this mirror, when they were given to understand that anyone who came to this quarter, whoever they might be, would turn into a man of gold? They didn't just take a casual look, they forgot about leaving, they felt the mirror's surface with their hands and smiled as awkwardly as the golden man in the mirror looking at them.

In their little workshops, as narrow as wine-presses, the goldsmiths were hunched like squirrels; they seemed not to give the amazed strangers a glance, but they knew in advance what their visitors were doing, and when. 'He's going to look at his hands now,' they would say to themselves, and the stranger, as if complying, would inspect his own hands, as if he'd found them on the road. The goldsmith's experience told him, 'The stranger will now test out the mirror,' and instantly the stranger's quivering fingers would carefully, timidly feel the mirror's surface, like a blind man feeling the face of his deceased twin. Everyone was overcome by the same mixture of fear, embarrassment and awe in the face of a mystery. But there was little mystery: the tight row of workshops emitted so much gold dust that even an elephant passing by would have been gilded from head to foot.

Such was life in Vani when it was a sea-port, until Goliath, offended by a flirtatious girl's disdain, gathered his belongings and cleared off, fearing that his generosity had been mistaken for stupidity. Everything began the day that Bedia was out in his boat and dragged from the water a boy more dead than alive, and a ram. Nobody had any premonition of disaster, the whole city was in a festive mood. Even nature didn't sound the alarm. The sea still ebbed and flowed. Just one fluffy cloud made the bright sky seem more peaceful and closer. Sheltered from view, a woman was washing her hair in sea water. Children had dragged a goat kid, for fun, onto a roof. The frightened kid turned and twisted, its hooves slipping on the tiles, bleating pathetically, but the children wouldn't leave it alone: they were throwing stones at it, shouting, waving their arms, until the loudly bleating kid leapt from one roof to another.

The unconscious boy was still clinging to the ram, so that Bedia was forced to drag both of them together into his boat. Bedia dried his wet arms on his chest and couldn't help looking towards the city, as if the city would tell him from where and how this Tom Thumb of a boy and this extraordinarily large ram had turned up in the open sea. Far off, in the blue and rosy mist, the red roof tiles glimmered. Bedia smiled. The boy and the ram he had rescued were recovering in his boat. Its oars left hanging in the water, the laden boat was revolving and pitching as if it intended to throw Bedia and his booty into the water. Other fishermen were speeding towards him. They were up to their ankles in their catch, but nobody cared about the fish, everyone was trying to close in on Bedia's boat and take a look inside. What now met their eyes in the boat was a supine reborn boy. A smile of joy and pride, like a colourful bird roosting, suddenly fluttered over the fishermen's sun-tanned weathered faces. But Bedia was more excited by this event than anyone else. This strange boy, as nameless and as unprecedented as a new-born baby, had come back to earth thanks to him. It seemed to be inscribed on fate's tablet that the boy should undergo an ordeal but should escape and be born again in the boat of a fisherman from Vani.

Bedia could not hide his wild smile; he felt as if he was carrying up the alleyway a baby in a cradle embellished with colourful rags.

The oars creaked in their locks. The boat was gently slipping towards the shore, filling this great wide-open space with domestic cosiness. This space was Bedia's home; here he had been born, had grown up and grown old, too. The walls of this house had moulded, shaped and trained his soul and flesh to their liking. Only in this house did Bedia feel at home; all around, from the day he was born, everything was familiar and close to him. When he was at sea Bedia always felt at ease. The fishermen had chosen him as their chief for good reason: he knew like the back of his hand where everything was in this house, where the sun would rise, where the rain would come from; he had explored a thousand times every nook and cranny, cellar and larder. It was an unforgettable sight when Bedia, leaning forward on the prow of his boat, his arms bare to the elbow, holding a harpoon over his head with his bronze-coloured arm, pursued a shoal of cod. Then Bedia the hunter was like a god; in vain the wind blew against his chest or the waves, enraged by the boat's passage, rocked him, as they were overcome, calmed and sent back behind Bedia, to the depths that created them. Bedia was an inseparable part of the boat, its offshoot, its branch, its fortress and its beauty. For just an instant the three-pronged harpoon that Bedia threw vanished in the green, foaming waves; almost instantly, like a beam emerging from the dark, it would shine in the sun, victorious, wet with tears of victory. A black blood stain oozed around the wretched cod, struck by sudden death, and in vain the cod tried to get back to its round slippery vessel from which Bedia's harpoon had irrevocably removed it.

News of the event at sea reached the shore before the boats did. The whole city was spread out along the shore. Everyone wanted to see the boy who had been rescued. The boy and the ram, both quivering like full wineskins, were gently carried out of the boat, laid on the sand and revived. The ram was the first to come round: it instantly leapt to its feet, belched several times, shook its fleece and, like a man who has been offended, looked sideways. Soon the boy, too, opened an eye. Bedia put his knee under the boy's head and gave him wine to drink from a jug. The boy grimaced and let the wine pour back. 'Can't be one of our people,' Bedia joked. The women, their cupped hands over their mouths, howled continuously. The boy, conscious and with his eyes open, made the death which he had miraculously escaped seem more horrific. A stream of blood-coloured wine flowed down the boy's neck and formed a strange flower-like pool on his chest. The boy stood up unaided. He wore a short tunic, edged in gold. He had lost one of his sandals, the other was attached to his shin by criss-cross laces. With great difficulty he relaxed his tightly clenched fist and proffered it to the crowd; in his palm he had a crumpled, faded, broken-edged olive leaf. Bedia took the leaf, turned it round and round in his hand for some time and, when he was sure that it really was a leaf and couldn't be anything else, he held it up high and called out, 'It's an olive leaf, he's asking for asylum!'

They immediately took the boy and the ram to King Æëtes. By evening everything was common knowledge. The latest information flew out blindly from Æëtes's palace, like fledglings from a nest, straight into the mouths of the expectant city. Whatever quarter of Vani you might find yourself in that day, everywhere the extraordinary story of the boy and the ram had everyone gossiping: the old women sitting outside their houses, the men gathered in Bakha the vintner's cellar with its forty steps, the girls and boys promenading endlessly up and down and, you can imagine, black-eyed Malalo's guests, too.

The story of the boy and the ram really was extraordinary. The boy turned out to be a king's son: his name was Phrixos. Apparently, he had a sister, but she perished on the journey. The boy's father, as they say, had taken a new woman to his bed, but the stepmother had taken a dislike to the boy and girl, saying, 'Why should I wear myself out for someone else's orphans?' She kept this up so long that she made her husband see things her way: she gave him donkey brains for supper and urged him to have the children slaughtered. Harvest failure provided a useful pretext: she said that it was the children's fault that the wheat was not setting ears; in fact, she herself had dried and ruined the seed corn. She nagged so much and exhausted her husband, asking why he had married her when he didn't know how to support a wife, that at last he gave in. But just when the priest had the sharpened knife in his hand, out of the blue a ram came flying in — not running, but flying — and seated the wretched brother and sister on its back, and left the executioners empty-handed. The stepmother, apparently, pursued them, hurling stones, but to no avail. The little girl perished on the journey. The poor child had long golden curls and cheeks as rosy as apples. The ram flew on much further, but in the end it was exhausted and splashed down, with the boy, into the sea. Æëtes took a great liking to the boy and was very angry, asking what sort of people could deem such a boy inauspicious. Then he summoned his own children, Chalciope and Absyrtus, and said: 'From now on there are three of you: see to it that he does not feel himself a foreigner.'

After the boy and the ram were brought to the palace, the people quickly dispersed. Only the fishermen remained on the shore. The catch had to be seen to, the boats had to be brought ashore. When Bedia heard the screech of boats being dragged onto the sand, he recalled again the anxieties of the morning. That morning, when the fishermen dragged their boats to the sea, Bedia found the sea was further off; his back was covered in sweat and he was amazed, but he said nothing at the time, he thought it was probably an illusion, or that he really had aged, and that was why. But he clearly couldn't altogether quell the gnawing suspicion, because now, when the people had dispersed and the boats were screeching over the hot sand, sounding like slaughtered buffalo, he was again overcome by his anxiety that morning. Until then he had forgotten about it, for he had had no time for worry. The morning's catch had filled the nets with bounty; then he had seen a far-off black object bobbing up and down and he sensed with his body that something out of the ordinary must be happening in his life. He immediately headed his boat towards the object. True, he had lost his fish and his nets, but he had never come back from the sea with a catch like this. But for him, a great misfortune would have happened. Wouldn't it have been his fault if the boy had perished? Isn't the master of the house accountable for all that happens in it? That is what Bedia believed. But now the first excitement was over and the boy and the ram were safe and sound, Bedia again remembered the suddenly extended distance between the sea and the boats' resting place. No, the sea really was plotting something. The fishermen were now dragging their creaking vessels over the sand, while he squatted down, his grey, restless eyes looking now at the sea, now at the brightly shining shore, where the soles of his feet knew every grain of sand. The fishermen slowly gathered: they trod heavily, proudly carrying baskets full of shining white fish. Once or twice they called out to their chief, 'What are you doing, aren't you coming?' But Bedia just waved to them, and then they immediately left him in peace.

Bedia could not leave so easily. Without asking him, someone had entered his house and moved not just the furniture, but the walls. It might be insignificant, but if it weren't seen to in time, things would change little by little, and one fine day nothing at all would be there any more. Bedia knew that staring at the sea couldn't make it tell him anything, the sea could outdo his eye and his patience. He was looking at his own suspicion, he was assessing whether it was worth raising the alarm or not, whether people would appreciate such vigilance, or whether he would become some joker's laughing stock: 'Our Bedia's like a broken-backed donkey, scared of a magpie.' That was very likely. More patience was needed, and his suspicions needed proof. The suspicion was small, as slippery and elastic as a fish's scales, it slipped out of your hand, but it never ran far, it lay shining brightly just a couple of steps away. Bedia chose what was probably the best solution: several times he used a rope to measure the distance from the boat station to the sea, then he rolled up the rope and put it round his neck, so that it was always to hand should he need it. As soon as he'd wound the rope round his neck he calmed down, as if this rough rope could tether such a great sea and stop it from moving an inch without his say-so.

Bakha's cellar with the forty steps was now full of people. Here too the talk was of the boy and the ram. It was cool in the cellar, the swell of quivering voices, the walls, stained with smoke and damp, and the dim daylight that crept halfway down the steps, gave one the impression of a secret gathering of believers in the abode of some forbidden god.

Bakha the vintner was listening attentively to the people who had gathered in the cellar, but he was not altogether pleased to find his servant, the boy Hey-Boy, standing idle, his arms folded, leaning casually against a wine barrel; Bakha the vintner loved watching a feast, drunken guests interested him more than the money he earned from them and he would rather have died than water his wine. He considered it a great sin to put these two incompatible elements in one and the same vessel, for the result of this unnatural coupling could only be a feeble, cheerless child. If anyone ordered just one bowl of wine, Bakha served him two, to stop him leaving too soon, to make him gabble, then mumble until… until he was finally able to go up the forty steps again, to return to a world that was as sober as a hare and just as timid.

Bakha the vintner was enchanted by the godlike power contained in the wine barrels. Set free, that power could give the whole world whatever new colour, shape and appearance it fancied. In fact, whenever Hey-Boy dipped a pitcher into the barrel Bakha the vintner was overwhelmed by the feeling that some god had taken refuge in his cellar and opened a vein, gushing out this magical fluid, as inexhaustible and eternal as the god. Bakha the vintner could not watch without emotion the wine pouring from barrel to pitcher, from pitcher to ewer, from ewer to bowl, from bowl to stomach. Released from the barrel, the wine needed this magnificent festive progression from one vessel to another in order to breathe, to stretch its limbs: as it progressed, the wine rejoiced, giggled, shone, sparkled and doggedly pursued its final goal, to its last drop to give its strength and joy to all, without distinction, who wanted it. When this strength and joy had passed on to everyone, then Bakha the vintner felt happy. Happy and proud, he sat down on his favourite chair, as the master and director of this strength, as if this all-transforming force, which embellished, emboldened and enriched everybody, actually came from him. Bakha the vintner sat on his favourite chair, a round-headed cornel walking-stick between his knees; his bloated hands, chapped by the sun and the wind, were placed over the stick like roof tiles, and his chin rested on his hands, as if he was afraid the tiles might slip off. What could compare with the noise, roar and jangling of those carefree voices, the sound echoing down vaults crumbling with the damp and the murk, to disintegrate into a mixture of songs, oaths, promises and threats? Bakha the vintner was happy that life was continuing, that every morning daylight crept down the forty steps of his stairs, and until evening shut its eyes to the voices and smells that rose up from the cellar's secret depths: he was as indulged as a golden-furred cat, and so he should have been, because he had been, ever since he became the owner of the cellar and was installed there, like an idol in a temple.

As soon as he reached the steps, Bedia shouted: 'I'm the boy's father, I'll stand a jar of wine.' The cellar echoed with loud laughter.

'Hey-Boy, take it from the middle one,' Bakha the vintner called to his servant, whom he never addressed by his real name, so that others also called him Hey-Boy. Hey-Boy was well aware that Bakha the vintner put the same wine in all the barrels, but nevertheless he dipped the pitcher in the 'middle' one. Designating a particular barrel had a magical effect on customers, it raised their spirits, made them prouder, because they thought they were friends of the house, drinking 'special' wine. A simple word did the job in this fabulous cellar.

People were quite tipsy when the butcher said, 'I've slaughtered rams and ewes, lambs and hoggets, stud rams and castrated rams, but I've never come across one with wings.'

'Have you looked under its tail?' asked the blacksmith. His face was beetroot-red, as if he had been staring at a piece of red-hot iron; he had two white patches on his cheekbones, which may have made the rest of his face seem unnaturally red.

'Under its tail?' asked the butcher in amazement.

'That's where it keeps its wings,' said the blacksmith. He was clearly forcing himself not to laugh at his own joke. But the others couldn't hold back and a burst of laughter hit the walls like a smashing plate. Even the butcher smiled, nodded and, for some reason, began wiping the table with his elbow.

Success emboldened the blacksmith. Next he singled out Bochia, the cradle-maker, the tubbiest man not only in the cellar but in all Vani. The blacksmith insisted, 'I bet one night ten years ago you made a secret trip to Greece.' He added, 'Knowing you, one night was more than enough.'

Again the whole cellar laughed, the butcher more than anybody.

Bochia had a white face and his arms were just as pale, covered with golden down. In sunny weather, and it was mostly sunny in Vani, he had only to stop briefly in the street to have a word with someone he knew, when he would suddenly redden, as if he'd been dipped in dyer's madder. He was kind and shy, and if he was offended by anything he would go and stand under the trees to clear his mind quickly. The cradles he made rocked by themselves and even crooned: they only had to be pushed once and the baby's parent could then safely go to sleep. Nobody knew how old Bochia was: everyone, his many fellow-citizens, even his own children, remembered him as he was when they first encountered him or when they departed from him. His numerous offspring were constantly increasing on the earth and beneath it. They were born, they grew to adulthood, aged and died, but Bochia remained unchanged. Bochia was the same when Potola gave birth to his first child. Since then the squeaking of cradles and cooing of babies had never ceased in their family. This strange couple was not subject to time. Perhaps Bochia and Potola worshipped the ground each other walked on because they were united by undying love and couldn't imagine the world without each other. Bochia constantly longed to be with his sleek, cheerful and diligent Potola. Nobody could recall how long they had been married.

Bochia married Potola after the death of his foster-father, on the day that his foster-father fell asleep for ever, his head lying on a cradle he never finished making. The foster-father was also a master cradle-maker, so imbued with the smell of wood that woodpeckers would perch on him. Bochia arrived just seconds too late to express his gratitude to a man who was as truly noble as a tree. When Bochia came into the workshop, his father's head was on the cradle, while his arms, bereft of strength, hung down, mingling with the wood shavings. The unfinished cradle was gently rocking. Bochia had often been told by his foster-father that rocking an empty cradle was wrong, so he stopped the cradle. Bochia brought Potola into his foster-father's house, put on his foster-father's leather apron, sat down to his foster-father's lathe and plunged his legs up to the knee in fragrant lime-wood shavings. Then they had so many children that they lost count and treated every child, theirs or someone else's, as their own son or daughter. 'Well it might have been our child,' was Bochia's first thought when he saw Phrixos, sprawled helpless on the sand in front of so many people, as weak as a seaweed stalk, and lifeless. Bochia himself was a foundling, which may be why he was so fond of children. True, he no longer remembered how old he was, but he could still see the sunny morning when his foster-father cautiously removed the colourful kerchief covering the basket and looked inside. Bochia was lying in the basket and opened his eyes just when his foster-father removed the kerchief. The first thing that he saw and that was permanently imprinted in his memory was his foster-father's face, amazed, smiling and lit up by the morning sun. Afterwards in Bochia's eyes the whole world had the same face — amazed, smiling and lit up by the morning sun. Now he was thinking of Phrixos. The blacksmith's joke reminded him of the child with a face as pale as mistletoe and blue lips. Bochia had been on the point of stepping out of the crowd and saying, 'It's my child, leave him to me, I'll see to him myself.' But he lacked the courage, he was so moved that he could not get his tongue round the words, but he decided without a thought to adopt this foreign boy if a better foster-parent wasn't found.

The blacksmith, meanwhile, was in distress, unable to find a way of ending his joke which had now flopped; he felt this, became irritated, and even more confused.

'Does Potola know about all this? Does she?' asked the blacksmith, anger entering his voice, as if Bochia really had slipped off for one night to Greece ten years ago and been unfaithful to Potola. Apart from the butcher, nobody else was laughing at his worm-eaten joke. This annoyed the blacksmith so much that he didn't know whether to turn to the butcher or to finish his business with Bochia. He now seemed to be squabbling, rather than talking, and this made the silence of his fellow-drinkers even more fraught. So when Bedia called out, 'Stop it, let's have a drink,' the blacksmith came to his senses and, like a drowning man, clutched the rope round Bedia's neck.

'Just explain to me why this man is hanging himself,' the blacksmith shouted and jerked the rope so hard that he hurt Bedia's neck.

Bedia was startled: he felt as if the sea had shaken its dishevelled white head at him and stared at him with blazing, salt-coloured eyes.

'I know those Greeks, they'll dump a sheep on you and demand a whole flock in return,' said Bakha the vintner.

The people of Vani would have forgotten the story of the boy and the ram earlier, if that was the end of it. But something utterly unforeseen happened. The next day the whole city was filled with children riding sheep. The children were obsessed with the idea of flying and were making thc sheep, their mouths foaming and their eyes bloody, gallop up and down the streets. But, to the children's amazement and dismay, not a single sheep tried to rise even an inch into the air: they would rather die on the ground. The meek animals could not endure for long this totally unnatural galloping and, swollen like giant blisters, collapsed under the thighs of their remorseless riders. The streets were strewn with sheep with rolling eyes and rasping breath. Men came running with knives, women sprinkled earth over the pools of blood, but the children had no intention whatsoever of giving up their obsession, which had claimed so many victims. 'Ram-riding', which they themselves called this game, blotted out everything else for them. Soon, the people of Vani couldn't bear the sight of mutton. But there seemed to be an endless supply of sheep: they didn't know they had so many of them. The bleating of sheep drowned out every other sound in the city. People smiled awkwardly, like deaf-mutes, and waved their arms about senselessly; men avoided the eyes of their fulminating wives. But, like it or not, they had to intervene and make the children forsake, for once and forever, this game: it was not just truly idiotic, but ruinous, breaking up families, putting asunder wives and husbands, wrecking homes… In fact, during this period there were no dinners, husbands never had time to be alone with their wives, cooking pots and beds were set aside by the blood-curdling pleas of bleating sheep being sacrificed. 'Thrash him, I say, before it's too late,' wives wailed biliously to their husbands, but the husbands continued for some time to scratch the back of their necks instead, so much did they love their children. There was fear in that love: they were sure their arms would wither if they thrashed a child. This belief had been passed on down the generations, and everyone blindly adhered to it, because nobody wanted to challenge it. What reason was there to doubt it, anyway? Why take unnecessary risks?

Meanwhile, Vani looked like a city at war. The streets were strewn with loose paving stones, fences and hedges were smashed, broken branches hung in tatters from the trees, all the children were covered in grazes and bruises. Now they didn't even rest at night: 'ram-riding' had got into their dreams — they dreamed of mounting and flying on rams, but their souls were gripped by fear, not pleasure: the rams had slippery backs, and the horns were thorny. They had to hang on, and below them roared the foaming sea, rearing up like a hungry wild animal trying to grab both ram and child rider. Gasping for breath, the child lost its grip on the ram's slippery back and flew, himself roaring, down to the roaring sea. Heartbroken parents leapt out of bed and woke the child, gave him a drink of water, poured more water over him and pleaded, 'Wake up, look around, it's your mother and father.' Soaking wet, the trembling child gnashed its teeth like a madman and pushed its parents away, 'What do you want, leave me alone, can't you see I'm sleeping?'

Whatever the parents tried or devised, this weird mania would not quit the children. When neither kindness nor threats had any effect, they tied their children hand and foot and floored them, like oxen to be gelded at the blacksmith's. But this changed nothing, for the children's mania was stronger than any rope: like martyrs, the children silently put up with everything and waited for the right moment to gnaw through the ropes and run outside to begin the game again.

One day what everybody feared and what everybody expected finally happened. A father thrashed his son. The whole city echoed with the sound of whacking, of doors and windows knocked out of their frames, of crockery being smashed, of wine jars cracking in the ground; cattle in the stables and sheepcotes bellowed, even the heaviest objects were displaced. The father who had thrashed his son came out on the main square of the city and showed everybody his withered right arm, which hung from his shoulder like a broken branch.

Then the people of Vani decided not to allow any sheep into the city until the children grew up, and everything had calmed down. Not a single sheep was left in the city: just one was kept tethered at Æëtes's palace, in a stall specially built for it in the courtyard. The ground around it was strewn with thumb-sized droppings, it never stopped chomping its lips and, above all, it was radiant. When this ram was led past the goldsmiths' quarter, its curly fleece attracted, absorbed and retained so much gold dust that it was weighed down by its unusual burden and could hardly walk. When it was brought to its stall, it lit up its surroundings, as if it were not a sheep, but a bonfire lit in order to dry clay walls.

The children of Vani, like children anywhere, easily adapted to anything. Once the sheep had disappeared, 'ram-riding' was forgotten, but at every city gate and, of course, at the port, guards were placed for some time to come, lest anyone try to smuggle in this utterly meek and yet very useful animal.

By now it was summer. The palace began to prepare to move to its country seat. Nannies bustled about, causing a fuss, as if an enemy was attacking and they didn't know what to take with them, or what was most essential for refugees.

As always, the children were initially reluctant to leave, they claimed to have stomach ache, they clung like thorn branches to everyone and everything, and it was in fact as hard for their nurses to get them into the boat as to stuff dry Jerusalem thorns into a sack. But the bare-chested boatmen had only to dip their oars into the water for the children to forget everything except the sea, the boat and the boatmen. The boat headed north, until it reached the mouth of the well-watered river, then it turned up river into the heart of the country, followed overgrown banks, covered with trees as trance-like as temples, with resplendent orchards and vineyards, and villages wrapped in the smell of smoke and charcoal, with brightly-dressed lads and lasses in their alley-ways and courtyards.

The boat with a baldachin was now carrying three children: Chalciope, Absyrtus and Phrixos.

Phrixos was now used to his new 'brother and sister'. When Chalciope, unseen by her nurses, bent over the boat and dipped her hand in the water, Phrixos imitated her. If Chalciope asked him to change places, he agreed without hesitating, as if the two simultaneously felt the urge to change places. Chalciope could outdo both boys in wilfulness. She could not stay long in one place, she was constantly giggling, whether she had cause to, or not.

Absyrtus sat on his own, watching the branches that hung down into the water, the dragonflies hovering in the air, listening to the birds hidden in the velvety bushes. Absyrtus was three years younger than Phrixos, two years younger than Chalciope. His unnatural calm and his unchildlike talk annoyed his nurses most, because they were by nature prepared to deal with children's naughtiness, restlessness, whims and stubbornness, and although they constantly snivelled, complained and cursed their lot, this was still their life: were it not for 'difficult' children, their nannying would have no point. But Absyrtus didn't meet their expectations: he never got lost, he never drank cold water when in a sweat, he'd never turned his nose up at food, he never went to bed without washing his hands and feet. What was the point of being a nurse if you never had cause for anxiety or anger, for weeping or complaining?

'It's his aunt's fault, she's made a fool of him,' said the nurses. Although they were afraid of this tall, tight-lipped woman, who was as dry as a stick, they never missed a chance to gossip about her behind her back. 'Nobody's ever seen her bring someone back from the dead or make an old man young again,' they said, as if this could cast a shadow on their grim rival, who had far more influence on Absyrtus than they did, even though she never washed his face or made his porridge. When she walked the streets, the whole city was filled with the scent of medicines which vanished only when the breeze wafted it away. Aunt Qamar taught her nephews and niece to tell healing herbs from poisonous ones, but she soon gave up on Chalciope. Chalciope liked flowers with big petals which would stay in place in her hair, she couldn't recognize or take an interest in any others. 'You'll never be anything but a wife,' Aunt Qamar once told her, but Chalciope didn't mind: she was in fact pleased to be left in peace so quickly and escape her aunt's mentoring so easily.

But Absyrtus was capable of watching from morning to evening a thousand different sorts of roots being pounded in an enormous mortar; he constantly sampled the fragrance of savory bark, dill, plantain, horse fennel and spurge. His happiness knew no bounds when he was allowed to take a long stick to the bubbling cauldron boiling up, according to his aunt, a medicine that was a matter of life and death. Absyrtus learned a lot from his aunt, but unfortunately he, like his sister, was not cut out to be a priestess-healer. He was a boy, and no ordinary one: he was heir to the throne. 'But I'll never become king,' Absyrtus used to say, and not because he preferred priesthood to kingship, but because he was clairvoyant and could see what would happen to him in the future. Nature had endowed him with the gift of foresight and had thus for ever distinguished him from other children, for ever depriving him of the tension of experiencing the unexpected. His other, and main misfortune was that nobody, not even, indeed particularly, his aunt, believed him, because she was a soothsayer herself and knew better than others how much knowledge and experience was needed just to predict tomorrow's weather, let alone a man's fate. But Absyrtus still won himself the reputation of being a strange child.

Æëtes didn't like his heir growing up a dreamer, he would rather have had a little devil with grazed knees, covered in sweat and always hanging on to a horse's mane; for the time being the king left well alone, and Absyrtus belonged to the womenfolk, while Æëtes bided his time. 'He's a child, he'll get over it,' the palace people said in the king's hearing, but Æëtes wasn't listening and didn't want to, as though his son would grow out of this childishness if he paid no attention. Æëtes didn't know what his son had to get over, what strangeness the heir to the throne was suffering from, but he realised that 'strangeness' was too mild a word for it and, on reflection, could have countless different meanings. That may be what Æëtes afraid and why he let well alone. In any case, Absyrtus was growing up for the time being under the women's care. The nurses preferred the restless Chalciope, who was preoccupied with playing, to the quiet and obedient Absyrtus. At times Absyrtus would say something to them which left them at a total loss, whereas Chalciope was a normal child, naughty, tireless, full of laughter.

Once, when he was barely five, Absyrtus fell ill. He was restless with fever and for whole nights turned in his bed like a spit. His nurse sat drowsing by his bedhead.

'The plane tree says…' Absyrtus suddenly began.

'Did you say plane tree?' said the alarmed nurse.

'The plane tree says someone should pluck a leaf and put it on Absyrtus's brow, then he'll get better instantly,' said Absyrtus.

What could the nurse do: she could hardly climb a plane tree at midnight, and she didn't know which plane tree the fever-stricken child meant in his delirium.

Absyrtus was a kind boy. He felt pity for everything. He couldn't even bear the sight of a chicken being slaughtered. Tears would well in his eyes when the budding twigs crackled as the bread oven was heated up. 'If he's going to be like that, how will he live?' Æëtes asked in anguish. If he had known that people in the palace amused themselves by making fun of the heir to the throne, there would very likely have been bad trouble. As father and as king, he would not have put up with this.

'Tell me, if you're a good lad, where the black-handled knife I lost last year is, and what it's doing,' the idle courtiers who surrounded Absyrtus would ask. Absyrtus was upset, bit his lips and his brow sweated because he didn't know such a small thing. He understood what a bird, a herb or a cricket hidden in a cranny, or the rain dripping on the leaves was saying; he had a premonition if any joy or sorrow was in the offing for him and those close to him, but he didn't know and couldn't guess about that business about the knife lost by someone last year, and it might even not have been lost. So Absyrtus was upset and stood there, his head bowed, as if guilty, before the owner of the 'lost knife', as if he himself had stolen the knife and was too ashamed to show that he had stolen it. But he had such an odd way of speaking that nobody could be blamed for finding it fun to accost this pale-faced boy who wandered the palace corridors like a soothsayer. 'Every butterfly is blind,' Absyrtus would say and, when asked why he blinded butterflies, what had they done to him, he replied in all seriousness, 'I don't blind them, they're born blind so that their two days of life seem longer to them.'

'If a butterfly weren't blind, it would take too long to choose which flower to fly to, every flower would seem equally delightful and alluring, and it would suffer pain, would hesitate and would even die of pain and hesitation. As things are, it has time to find more flowers, because it's blind and can't choose,' Absyrtus used to say: it was hard not to be astounded by such talk coming from a Tom Thumb of a boy.

'There's nothing childlike about him,' said the nurses, who continued to prefer the 'wildcat' Chalciope to the calm and meek, precociously wise or congenitally silly Absyrtus.

Now Absyrtus was sitting with the others in the boat and gazing at the banks of the well-watered river. He knew the route by heart, but what to others was an ordinary tree, bush or flower, like any of a thousand trees, bushes or flowers, every one of them had, as far as he was concerned, a unique soul and appearance. A rain-scoured river bank or a fungus-eaten stump could become any sort of extraordinary vision. He knew in advance where a leopard might leap out and, in fact, at the next bend in the river, azaleas would burst out of the bare hillock, like a pouncing leopard. 'Leopard, leopard, leopard,' Absyrtus yelled, his eyes shining as he smiled because nobody could see his 'leopard', though Chalciope and Phrixos spent the journey looking round bewildered, sticking out their necks, hoping to recognize in the ordinary undergrowth a herd of deer making for the river, an eagle about to take off, or outlaws having a feast. But whatever Absyrtus saw did not exist for them. The boatmen couldn't help but listen to the children, smile at their silliness, and row ever more cheerfully.

'Well, tell us what that bird is saying,' a boatman asked Absyrtus.

This was the boatman nearest to the children and, when he smiled, he showed his crumbling teeth. Chalciope had noticed the boatman's crumbling teeth and kept looking to see if he would show them.

'This bird is saying how big Chalciope has grown, and how it would like to raise fledglings that big,' Absyrtus immediately replied.

Everyone looked at Chalciope: she was embarrassed, but to hide her embarrassment jostled Phrixos so hard that he fell off the bench and hit his face on an oar handle. The nurses rushed forward, the boat rocked, and passengers and crew all fell against each other. Phrixos's nose was bleeding, he'd turned pale, but he still smiled. He wiped away the blood with his fist, smearing his face even more. When she saw this, Chalciope burst into peals of laughter. That may be why nobody heard Absyrtus's remark: 'The bird said that Chalciope will be Phrixos's wife.'

Ten years later the bird's, or rather Absyrtus's, prophecy came true.

CHAPTER TWO

THE marriage of Phrixos and Chalciope put the whole city in the mood for love. Within a year most of the women in Vani were about to give birth. Either a ploughshare or a spinning-wheel would be put on the roof, depending on whether a boy or a girl was born. Chalciope barely noticed her pregnancy: her face wasn't coarsened, her legs weren't swollen, her belly was not very prominent — pregnancy even suited her. Her maternity dresses hung loose on her as always, and from all corners of the palace, simultaneously, you could hear her peals of laughter. Chalciope could have danced with happiness, she couldn't admit or believe that her transformed nature was now saying goodbye for ever to a youth that had been free of sorrow and care. When the midwife laid the newborn baby in her bed, she was even a little astonished, and took some time to understand what linked her to this tiny creature that insisted on turning its sweaty and slightly downy head towards her, like a flower towards the light. She had never before seen this absurd animal, worn out by its long journey, only now coming to its senses, its eyes closed by its inherited experience so that it could get used to its new surroundings while slumbering and not be horrified when it finally woke up. The first feeling Chalciope had for her own child was one of estrangement, but her whole body was so scalded the first time the baby cried that she suddenly realised what this ugly, feeble tyrant demanded of her, and immediately put her breast in its mouth, as if it had been lying by her side all her life and there had never been a time when Chalciope did not own it. Chalciope was now a mother.

Even the queen was no exception to her fellow-citizens' obsession with love. Æëtes's wife gave birth at almost the same time as her daughter. But the queen gave birth a little later, and her breasts were dry. Chalciope had so much milk that she fed both her baby and her mother's.

One after the other, Chalciope gave birth to four children, all of them boys. Because of their father, the boys were given Greek names: Argus, Cytisorus, Melas and Phrontis. Although they weren't twins, they were like twins, for they all wanted at the same time to eat or to cry. Phrixos lost patience, would stand over them and shout, 'Acco, alphisto, mirmo; acco, alphisto, mirmo,' and the children would instantly fall silent.

Thus everything seemed to be going well, the population was increasing and so was joy in life. But one day Phrixos became downcast, and melancholy took over his mind. That day he wouldn't get out of bed, but lay on his back staring at the ceiling. Chalciope brought in one of the boys, then another, and finally all four surrounded their father's bed. The boys, as hefty as bear cubs, performed somersaults, but Phrixos went on frowning, lying there and staring at the ceiling.

This went on for a whole week, then a month, and a tearful Chalciope fell at her parents' feet and begged, 'Help me, I'm losing my husband.'

'Perhaps he doesn't love you any more?' asked Æëtes, after listening carefully to what she had said.

'If he doesn't love me, then I hope he dies today,' yelled Chalciope.

Her father's words had momentarily disoriented her, but she instantly made up her mind, shook her head stubbornly and said, 'If he stopped loving me, my body would have felt it.'

'He loves me and the children, but something evil is on his heart, keeping him away from me,' Chalciope went on lamenting.

The next day the king and queen went to visit their son-in-law. He was lying on his back, staring at the ceiling, on a bed that hadn't been made for a month. His face had lost colour, his skin sagged, his eyes had sunk and turned dark; his weakened hands, the colour of candle wax, lay on top of the blanket. When he saw his father- and mother-in-law he tried to smile: he grimaced so pathetically that the queen averted her gaze.

'Well, son-in-law, tell me how you are,' said Æëtes tenderly.

Phrixos looked Æëtes in the face and gave him a lingering look; then a large teardrop rolled down his cheek.

'There's nothing we can do for him,' Æëtes said quietly to his wife.

The palace filled up with soothsayers, seers and palm-readers. The whole area smelled of medicine, the servants walked about holding their noses. But it had no effect on the patient.

Ever more doctors, soothsayers, and clairvoyants came: everyone had heard about Æëtes's son-in-law's illness. Soon there was no more room left in the palace: tents were set up in the courtyard. Æëtes strode, distracted, among the tents, like a general who had no idea when the enemy might appear, or where he might attack from. Wherever you looked, fires were lit, everywhere medicine was being boiled up. Reconciled with his fate, giving up without a fight, the patient, his eyes closed, swallowed bees and scorpions, swallow's nest ash and locust legs, partridge's spleen and fox dung. From the ragged tents, all day long, you could hear the constant mumbling of soothsayers. Chalciope now knew all the bad signs: if the patient wanted to be in the dark, if his head slipped off the pillow, or he began talking to the wall, or his breath began to stink, or he didn't want to see anybody, if one eye became smaller than the other

— there were a thousand, ten thousand bad signs which Chalciope had now learnt by heart, and she was worn out because every day she had to run so many times to the patient's bedside to check on the effect on his face of the soothsayer's mumblings. It seemed to Chalciope that the patient showed all the bad signs, but she still couldn't accept the idea that her husband was dying, abandoning her just like that, so ruthlessly. 'What right has he got to die?' thought Chalciope, and she was overcome with horror when she imagined being a widow.

Chalciope had been brought up freely: whatever she wanted was done and she came to believe that nothing could possibly distress or dismay her. But now this accursed inexplicable illness was challenging her and was even about to get the better of her.

Phrixos's death would have changed a lot of things in Chalciope's life. Apart from anything else, she would be compelled to mourn her husband, to wear black, to lock herself up in the dark and, for God knows how long, hide from life, from her own self. But Chalciope couldn't do this: couldn't and wouldn't. Who could compensate her for time wasted in the dark, who would laugh instead of her, who would fix the flowers with the biggest petals to their hair? 'What could you tell me, when you don't know anything yourself?' she once shouted at her aunt Qamar, who put her hand over her withered lip to stop herself from cursing her niece. Chalciope threw black-eyed Malalo and her daughters out of the palace, kicking them as they went, because even their singing failed to help the patient. The whole palace was despondent when it saw Chalciope in this mood. It is hard to say whom they most pitied: the doomed husband or the young wife who was hanging on by her teeth to her husband's vanishing life. People stood permanently in the square outside the palace. Every now and again a servant would appear in the tower and shake his head as a sign that there was no change.

One day the queen went in to see Æëtes and told him, 'You're the king, never mind about our son-in-law, we're going to lose our daughter. Is there some sin you might have committed?' the queen asked him, adding, 'I'm as pure as the day I was born, before you and the gods.'

This made Æëtes think: he plaited a rope of thought, dropped it into a bottomless well and lowered himself down. He got to the bottom and his heart sank: the bottom of the well was full of people waiting for him. 'Thank God, you've remembered us,' the inhabitants of the well cried out. Æëtes had one good look, then another. He knew them all: they were Colchians he had exiled, defeated and dispossessed; they had grudges against him and were as dangerous and ruthless as naked wolves.

The loudest shout came from Oqajado, his cousin, the former king of Colchis: 'Watch out, Æëtes, that you don't let go of my throne, because being my cousin won't help you.' Others joined in, and the well became nothing but loud guffaws and howls of rage. For some reason Æëtes recalled his childhood, or rather one day when he thrashed his cousin (his father's brother's son). Æëtes had a violent temper: his eyes would go dark and he himself couldn't remember what he did. That day Oqajado had done something to infuriate him. In his rage Æëtes, for want of anything else to hand, grabbed a lamb by the hind legs and beat his cousin mercilessly with it, still holding the lamb as he pursued him. After that day Oqajado was careful not to anger Æëtes. He behaved as if nothing had happened and he himself laughed when his father and uncles called him 'lamb-basted'. Æëtes had long forgotten this incident and was himself amazed to remember it, lowered into the well, after so long a time. 'He's hated me ever since then,' thought Æëtes.

For a long time Æëtes put up with Oqajado's kingship, but when he realised that his cousin's wasteful nature might ruin the country, he lost patience and one fine day removed Oqajado and his hangers-on from the throne. But such deeds can't be done without bloodshed and enmity: however just you may be, you can't share your sense of justice with everyone as if it were bread. So it was with Æëtes: the well filled up with so much bile and desire for vengeance, getting fuller every day: like a ripe carbuncle, it was bound eventually to burst open and ooze fluid.

People bolt the stable door when the horse has fled: this was Æëtes's case. At the time he forgot that only a dead dog doesn't bite. The ex-king and his followers got on a ship and fled their homeland. Æëtes didn't stop them: let them go and keep out of my way, he thought. He didn't miss any of them, except for Ukheiro. Ukheiro was a real warrior, he ate his bread with a dagger and, while still a beardless youth, had no peer in strength or dexterity. When he threw a javelin, it could bring down twenty men, if you lined them up in front of him. Oqajado had spotted him and brought him to the palace. Then, when everything fell apart, Ukheiro joined the ex-king on the ship.

Æëtes emerged from the well of memory with his mind poisoned. Immediately, he went into a tent and told a soothsayer, 'I have these sins on my soul, they're the reason for my son-in-law's illness.'

'Can that be a sin?' the soothsayer retorted.

The prolonged incurable illness had gradually made everyone indifferent to the patient's fate. Time had made the stench of the medicines and the ragged tents familiar, as were the endless squabbling and disputes between soothsayers and seers, healers and palm-readers, the howling of the confined dogs on which the medicines were tested, and which gulped down with canine gullibility and greed a swill mixed with drugs, dozens of them sacrificing themselves every day for the life of an unknown human being.

One soothsayer, without telling the others, poured Phrixos's dirty washing water on a black dog: when the dog failed to shake itself dry, the soothsayer quietly dismantled his tent and crept away from the palace. The soothsayer's disappearance was soon noticed, because on the patch of trampled earth, where his tent had been, a pile of bones appeared, as if the soothsayer had done nothing but eat. Others soon followed the runaway soothsayer, on various pretexts. Nobody tried to stop them. Everyone had given up in the face of the incurable disease: they agreed to anything that might cause a change, even if for the worse. This mass desertion by soothsayers and healers was a precursor to imminent change. Every time a tent was dismantled, a pile of bones was left where it had stood, and now the starving abandoned dogs that had survived hungrily and noisily went for the bones. The cauldrons were of no further use, for the burnt herbs stuck to the bottoms were impossible to scrape off, however hard they were scrubbed. The paving stones of the courtyard had cracked under the constant camp fires and were marked for ever with ash-coloured, indelible outlines of those fires.

And then, one fine day, a hitherto obscure healer, now that he saw he had no competition, gathered his courage and loudly declared, 'This is an illness which neither knife nor ointment can touch. This illness is called homesickness and just one pigskin filled with the air of the motherland will be more effective than all our medicines.'

'God bless you!' groaned Phrixos and turned over in bed.

These were the first words Phrixos had uttered all the time he had been ill. Soon the whole palace was repeating them: 'Have you heard, Phrixos said, "God bless you!"?' they rejoiced, as if an inability to speak these three words was Phrixos's illness, as if the words had been stuck in his throat like bones and, because he had finally spoken or spewed them out, there was nothing else wrong with him.

Diagnosing an illness doesn't mean, of course, curing it, but this seemed to be enough for Phrixos to look better. Soon he was out of bed. The palace celebrated: all their efforts had not been a waste of time. Chalciope's peals of laughter echoed down the corridors, and Æëtes forgot his well-dwellers as if they were a nightmare. The healer, hitherto neglected and left in the shade, prospered and bought a new house. 'He outdid us by being patient,' said the other disappointed healers who had abandoned the patient's bedside too early.

Although on his feet, Phrixos was still ill. He no longer lay motionless in bed, he came down to the courtyard, patted his boys, who stood around him, on the head, but his thoughts and mind were far away, still half-asleep. Out walking, he would suddenly go into a trance, dig his heels in like a donkey, lift his head and stare into the empty air until his wife or a watchful attendant gently poked him into action. Now he would stare at herbs and grasses, then pick some of them, sniff them, chew them, sniff again and say, 'This plant grows in our country, too.'

While others considered Phrixos more or less cured, Chalciope knew that something bad was happening to her husband.

Hitherto Chalciope had feared only that Phrixos might die and leave her a widow with four children. From the start she had convinced herself that Phrixos had been sent to her by the gods, that he was destined to love Chalciope, that this was his duty and therefore he had no right to die. That was why Chalciope had never completely lost hope, although she could read on her husband's face all the bad signs that the soothsayers had muttered about. Now, however, she wondered if being a widow might not be better than being a wife to such a husband. Phrixos seemed not to notice Chalciope, not to want to see her or hear her voice. At first this dismayed Chalciope, so hard was it to imagine or to believe that her husband was tired of her, that he no longer loved her. She even thought that soothsayers and seers might have put a spell on him to stop him loving her, but as time passed it became clear that Phrixos was deliberately avoiding her. Then Chalciope became furious, but when she looked at Phrixos, withered by his illness, she felt a burning pity and restrained herself; but she didn't know how long her patience would last. They still didn't share a bed: Phrixos was silent, but Chalciope's pride would not let her offer herself first. But now she sat up later by her husband's bedside, although he, as motionless and inert as a carved wooden doll, was far away, flying in the clouds: he was no longer able or willing to see Chalciope's beauty. Chalciope felt insulted but, at the same time, her husband's indifference set her pondering. She sensed that by being indifferent Phrixos had become more attractive, more significant and more interesting to her. But this was a secondary, relatively trivial aspect; she could not rest until she understood the reason for this indifference. Her nature couldn't accept for even one day being forgotten, undesired, found tiresome. No, Chalciope couldn't put up with that; better that death should take away her husband, than that her husband should leave of his own free will. But for the time being, it was better to be patient, she had to act as if she didn't notice anything, as if there wasn't anything to notice. Sitting at her husband's bedside, as enchanting and joyful as life itself, she would whisper until dawn broke to her drowsy and listless husband, who found her enchantment and her joyfulness the hardest thing to bear. Chalciope realised this, she was herself irritated by it, but she wouldn't show it and in a voice coarsened by repressed anger she reminded him of their childhood, their first kiss, the birth of their first child… as if she was telling a fairy story to send a capricious child to sleep. Perhaps she herself couldn't feel any more that every word she said was a badly disguised threat, a woman's threat which forbad anybody to make a mockery of her happiest days.

Chalciope was a proud woman who stood on her dignity, but she still had a child's naivety: she thought as she saw, and she saw what she wanted to see. She belonged to that class of women who decide in advance who they will fall in love with: one day they are convinced, 'We are in love,' and without hesitation or doubts they get entangled in a net of imaginary love. This belief can sometimes last a lifetime as their substitute for real love and, compared with other women, they feel any defeat much more painfully, because they subconsciously sense that they are the ones who initiated everything. Defeat annoys them as much as a physical defect which they don't want noticed but can't hide. Self-deception is for such women a means of self-defence: they always behave as though they had no worries. In fact, they are afraid of people, of being demeaned in the eyes of others, and they hide their personal life as carefully as they would hide hairs growing in the wrong place.

Chalciope was still a child when she firmly decided, 'I have to make Phrixos fall in love with me.' After that she could never be sure what was more important for her, the decision she took as a child, or Phrixos. This decisiveness made Chalciope an adult and a woman, and on it alone depended how she would be when she really did fall in love with a man: bold and direct, or cowardly and calculating. Chalciope was both cowardly and calculating. She needed love, if it really existed, as an ornament, not as a source of suffering. She wasn't born to suffer, she couldn't stand pain: in fact, if she only scratched a finger, half the palace had to come and blow on her scratch, while the other half had to swamp it with kisses and presents. Chalciope wanted whatever would enhance her, what would make her more noticed and make her happiness and beauty even more enviable. That was why she made Phrixos fall in love with her. The foreign king's son was growing bigger and more handsome with every day, and with every day was attracting more attention from girls. Chalciope made him fall in love because she was better than any other girl and had to love the best boy.

But this was all in the past now and the 'best boy' was planning to get away: he no longer wanted Chalciope and it was very likely, should this happen, that tomorrow Chalciope would be mocked by the girls whom she had once disdained and who were heartbroken by envy of her. 'Let's have another baby, the others have grown up now and are too old to cuddle, you can see they won't let us come near them,' Chalciope murmured to Phrixos. When Phrixos replied that they shouldn't have had the other children, she couldn't understand why her children shouldn't have been born and felt her patience running out: she was on the point of grabbing her husband by the throat and with her fingernails gouging out his eyes, which were already half out of their sockets.

'What sort of men are they going to be, when they've never had their own bread in their stomachs?' said Phrixos.

Her husband's words hurt Chalciope to the quick; that moment she loathed the sight of him, for what he was saying was not what troubled or interested her. Above all, Phrixos had no right to be ungrateful to anyone. Who would dare grudge Chalciope's family their bread, and how could Phrixos even think of saying such a thing, unless it was just another trick to enable him to escape from her? Chalciope's smile, half amazement, half loathing, died on her lips.

'Whether people grudge it or not, that's how it is,' Phrixos insisted.

These utterly pointless and futile nocturnal conversations irritated them both still more; gradually, like a spurt of water, the conversations spewed out and muddied the little courtyard which Chalciope had once fenced in for her imaginary love. Now they attributed an exaggerated meaning to every word, and chewed it over a thousand times: they were in torment and they tormented each other. Husband and wife encased themselves in their own shells, from which they now kept an eye on each other. The beds, separated after Phrixos's illness, stayed separate. Life became hard and colourless, like a lame sheep lagging behind the rest of the flock that moving on, all white, to graze on the sunlit hills.

The autumn rains had begun in Vani, thrushes attacked the berries on the nightshade which clambered over the walls. Red leaves were strewn over the greying paving stones. A fog came down from the mountains, passed over the city and hung over the sea. The firewood wept sap, but there was nothing better than sitting by a fire.

Phrixos found this a pretext to shut himself up again in his room, sprawl on a divan and stare at the ceiling. But one day, to everyone's surprise, he summoned his sons. Chalciope had forebodings of something bad, but how could she stop her children being alone with their father? While the boys were in their father's room, Chalciope couldn't relax; at first she tried to get on with her knitting, but she was soon sure that her shaking needles were dropping stitches, so she then opened her jewellery box, scattered the rings and earrings on a table and put them on one by one, as if she hadn't seen them before. But she couldn't keep this up for long and with one sweep of her arm swept them off the table as if they were cucumber peelings. Finally she was so angry that she snatched a broom from a servant, saying 'You don't sweep properly, you've left dust in the corners,' but she soon smashed the broom on the wall and rushed out of the room. She walked up and down many times past her husband's locked room, hoping that she might catch some encouraging word from it, but she couldn't hear a sound, as if they had all been killed or had slipped away. The five persons closest to her and most loved by her were now in this room, but not one at the moment remembered that she existed. Chalciope felt rejected, and such sadness filled her heart that she lamented, 'God, how forsaken I am.' She found pleasure in gulping down her bitter tears. Chalciope was carved of special wood: she wouldn't let others see into her ravaged home, and nor let her doubts creep out for others to see. So she quickly came to her senses, sobered by her tears, and she smiled biliously at the emptiness around. She took up the challenge from her husband and sons and prepared to do battle.

Thus autumn, and then winter passed. Only when the first swallow dived under the gate arches did Chalciope feel how much time had been spent on pointless vigilance. 'Yet another spring,' she thought sadly.

The earth was still damp, snow still lay on the distant peaks when Phrixos loaded a pack-mule with spades and shovels, gathered his boys and set off for the mountains. Asked where he was going, what he had set his mind on, Phrixos said, 'I have a debt to repay.' Chalciope personally prepared her husband's and sons' food for the journey. They didn't say where they were going, and she didn't ask. She told others, 'They're going off, they'll walk about, they're men, and with their father there they'll be all right.' Her husband and sons were going outside the palace walls for the first time without her, but she kept smiling.

For three months Chalciope stood by the window, for three months she fended off forebodings, for she was sure that all five would come back, that they wouldn't abandon her so treacherously, without saying a word, that they wouldn't dare dupe her. The trees came into blossom, then unfurled their leaves. Old cobwebs flew through the air. After three months the sound of spades and shovels reached the city, and soon the people of Vani saw Phrixos and his sons again, standing up to their waists in a ditch. Behind them a wide-mouthed, winding ditch stretched back to the mountains made pallid by mist. The five men had hurriedly dug the earth; dry bread and a drinking vessel stood at the side of the ditch. The people of Vani were upset to see the king's son-in-law and grandsons in this state, but Phrixos would not let anyone come near.

'The gods ordered me to bring water down to the city, so that I can at least give you thanks for giving me, a homeless boy, asylum,' he said. 'This is my and my sons' business only,' Phrixos declared firmly, wiping the sweat from his face with his hand; a blue vein pulsed in his neck, his hunched, weak shoulders were sun-tanned.

It was harder to continue the ditch into the city, the sides of houses had to be negotiated, streets had to be crossed before they reached the main square. Felled trees were laid across streets torn up by the ditch so that people could cross. On the main square Phrixos erected a masonry tank, put in an arch, installed a spout on the arch, and one fine day muddy, unfiltered water, like a dragon tamed, came down the ditch to the city from the mountains made pallid by mist: on the way down the water wriggled as if it was trying to get rid of an invisible and troublesome burden. Finally, from the spout in the arch the water gushed forth, its first spurts bringing last year's leaves, dry stalks of grass, and silt. Phrixos, naked to the waist, mud-stained, was perched on the water tank's wall; he was holding a bowl and inviting the people, 'Come and try my water!' Phrixos was happy, as were his four sons, who were at his feet, breathing heavily from exhaustion. The water roared, spraying out droplets and creating a cool, silvery mist that hung over the entire city. Enveloped in this mist, Phrixos had the feeling that he was back in the home he had lost twenty-five years ago.

Meanwhile Chalciope was standing by the window, listening to the clamour of the people gathered on the square. She sensed how much her husband and sons had distanced themselves from her. True, they had come back, but not the same as when they had left three months ago. Three months of life in the open, unsupervised, sleeping in a ditch and drinking water from the same vessel had brought them closer to each other and made them even more alike. Chalciope had not yet seen any of them, but she could feel that recognizing them would be hard. Those five men were united by something other than blood, as if the ditch had cut them off and left Chalciope on the other side. Nobody was inviting her to cross to the other bank, and she suddenly feared meeting her husband and sons: they seemed to be more powerful, and there were five of them: if she wanted to be with them, she had to overcome on her own the strength of five men. And she was alone. Yet she wasn't: she had Medea, who was both sister and daughter. When she remembered Medea, she felt there was help at hand; Medea was not yet fifteen, but she was Chalciope's, one of her own people!

Medea turned out to be fertile soil in which Aunt Qamar could easily sow the seeds of her knowledge. Aunt Qamar stubbornly clung on to life, held her head high and until the very end walked as upright as a rod, because she felt in her heart that sooner or later she would find someone worthy to inherit the vocation for which she had toiled so hard over God knows how many years. Chalciope and Absyrtus had disappointed her. The first had been excluded from the role by female frivolity, the second by being male. Aunt Qamar believed that handing knowledge of nature's secrets to a man was like putting a dagger into a maniac's hand. So that when Medea was released from her nurse's apron strings, Aunt Qamar immediately took her toddling into her secret world. At the age of ten Medea already knew how to make the rabid meek, and the meek rabid. The clever, intuitive girl found the road to knowledge and its deserted corridors easy to follow. The whole world, from grass roots to the stars, was an open book to her and if she took her eye off it for only a minute, Aunt Qamar would tap on that book with a finger that resembled a bird of prey's talon, and she would go back to studying it. This book of wisdom, enhanced by its cloud of secrecy, gradually took under its wing the child's questing soul and mind, as a hen shields the sole egg on whose hatching depends the survival of its race. In that book's sweet and sour, warm and cold aura Medea gradually grew and was enlightened; every day its light extracted new wonders from eternity's darkness. While her nephews hung about in alley-ways, getting their feet dirty, Medea, startled and hunched by the sting of knowledge, listened to and committed to memory what her aunt was instilling, followed her aunt into the most remote forests and ravines, gorges and gullies, collecting in her skirts a thousand different flowers, herbs and mosses.

'Herbs contain the secret of men's life and death,' she was told by her aunt, as dry and erect as a stick.

It was said of Aunt Qamar that if a man looked at her he would be turned to stone on the spot. This was not, of course, true, but she did have uncanny eyes, green, fiery, and her eyebrows and eyelashes seemed to be scorched by the heat of her eyes. Medea experienced the force of those eyes, and a strange tremor ran through her entire body when Aunt Qamar fixed a testing gaze on her and said, 'If I wanted to, I could turn myself instantly into a whippersnapper of a girl like you.'

Medea believed that her aunt really could turn into a whippersnapper of a girl. In fact, she fancied she could see two identical freckled little girls with delicate shins, gathering herbs and grasses in their skirts. Her head bowed, Medea followed her aunt, thinking in her heart that it would be good if her aunt really did decide to turn into a little girl like herself, then they could roll about together on this meadow. Medea's aunt had told her that such thoughts were wrong: they took up room in the mind needed for knowledge. Medea knew that silly, ignorant children rolled about on the meadow, but at times she was so overcome by an urge to play that she would have agreed to be the silliest, most ignorant child in the world if only she could have, just once, all the fun she wanted.

Aunt Qamar could read others' thoughts; suddenly she would stop and give a look like a wild animal growling in the bushes, and say, 'Stop dreaming: am I talking to myself?'

When Aunt Qamar died, Medea was neither surprised or very upset, because she considered this was something that her all-powerful aunt had wished for: it was probably necessary, she probably preferred dying to becoming a whippersnapper of a girl. And Medea wouldn't have been surprised if one fine day she saw her come back from Elysium.

Aunt Qamar's temple was in Dariachangi's garden. Medea went there every day and the whole city knew when the carriage, pulled by mules, would appear. Medea stood in the carriage, holding the reins in her right hand and a whip in her left. Twelve handmaidens, with their skirts tucked up to their knees, ran after her. A little later, thirteen girls, all of the same mind, each more beautiful than the other, were as radiant as a bonfire in Dariachangi's garden. This was their world and realm, closed to outsiders' eyes, sheltered by the nearby temple. But the other, wider, less protected and bolder world, which they fled from every morning, covered in dust from the mule-drawn carriage, would give them no peace even here, and made its coarse, passionate voice heard this far. This voice made leaves tremble, grasshoppers leap, and bees buzz; the girls felt, not admitting it in so many words, that this voice was to blame if they too trembled like leaves, buzzed like bees and leapt like grasshoppers on the grass. They didn't run away from this voice, they had sought isolation to be with it so that they could get a deeper sense of it and even get used to it.

'Scattered millet see-ee-eed…' one girl would begin, and the others would then join in: 'Who but a chick picks up? And what else apart from dea-ea-eath Will tear me from your love?'

They sang and smiled ambiguously, they looked each other in the face like conspirators, frightened and excited by their own boldness. The secret hidden in the words enveloped them in a sweet fog of wrongdoing.

What Medea liked most about this song was the chick, yellow and downy, pecking at the millet seed.

Through the hanging branches the sea's blue, pensive eye flashed now and again, and they were now drawn to the sea. They had a favourite sheltered and convenient place for bathing, where only the sea could see their nakedness. Because they hid, they probably knew why they were hiding, what had to be hidden. The sea was dazzlingly bright: a rosy thigh, or a belly as white as a marble slab, or a furrowed nipple occasionally emerged from the splashing water. Then they flung themselves on the burning hot sand and confronted the sky with their eyes half shut. The sounds that came from the other world now throbbed in their temples. With baited breath they listened, and an exciting, almost uncontrollable joy took hold of them, like children expecting a present.

When Chalciope came in, Medea was combing her hair. She hurriedly fastened it at the back and put the mirror aside.

'How beautiful you are,' Chalciope told her.

Medea smiled back, but couldn't help stealing another glance at the mirror. Chalciope sat next to her sister, kissed her on the forehead and repeated, 'You're very beautiful.'

Chalciope was good at ingratiating herself, and had plenty of praise for others. She never had the slightest doubt that she was more beautiful than anyone, but this beauty had to be made bearable for others, others had to concede it. So Chalciope never forgot to give people tiny bribes. Grudging a kind word seemed to her as wrong as visiting the sick without bringing them something.

Medea was not an ugly girl, but she could not be called a beauty: her appearance was as changeable as the weather. Not just her facial features, but her whole body would change, even the colour of her eyes. A minute earlier she might be as tender and rosy as a blossoming branch, then suddenly she would resemble a trapped wild animal, when her eyes expressed both sadness and rage.

'Your future husband will imagine he's dreaming and then be frightened when he wakes up,' said Chalciope.

Medea smiled. 'What's this dress you're wearing?' asked Chalciope and ran her hand down Medea's side. Medea looked down at the dress. 'I'm everybody's nanny. I get no time for myself,' Chalciope continued: now she smiled.

Then they were both silent for a good while. Chalciope suddenly became downcast, and focused on something on the floor. Medea didn't know what to say and felt a sudden relief when she heard her sister's voice again: 'To hell with anyone who doesn't need me, husband or sons. You have to take out his chamber pot, because he's embarrassed by the servant girl, but not by you.'

Medea became tense. Chalciope was talking about something different, unusual, which she had never discussed before. Medea knew that when women married they idolized their husbands, and ran around like temple handmaidens looking after their families, but this happened in another world, a world of which Medea understood nothing, knew nothing, except for the silly verses which her handmaidens sang in Dariachangi's garden. That was Chalciope's world. True, she and Chalciope were sisters, but they were as different as water from wine. Medea belonged to a god, Chalciope to a man. From the start Aunt Qamar had initiated Medea as a handmaiden to the moon, which may be why she had never thought of any other kind of life. Her childhood, too, was different from others' childhood. Medea still hid the only doll, which she herself made, under her pillow, as if it were an illegitimate child, because she sensed that it had been sent from the other world, forbidden to Medea, and was drawing her back there. But Medea was frightened even to look in that direction. Instantly she had a vision of Aunt Qamar's fiery eyes and finger, hooked like a bird of prey's beak. The knowledge she had inherited from Aunt Qamar weighed on the womanly core of her being like a lid, blocking out light and air, preventing her from holding her head high. But she didn't yet know that this tiny, forcibly repressed, still embryonic shoot of womanliness would take control of her life, thus compensating nature, instead of the knowledge of the secrets of that nature, which she had acquired from Aunt Qamar. This was a different sort of knowledge, still slumbering in the dark, although it was now beginning to squirm in her sleep, like a sleeping prisoner hearing the sound of a warder's steps. Those steps were coming closer, hovering over the prison and getting louder. Medea had a feverish shiver and curled up. Chalciope burst out in a peal of laughter.

'I expect I frightened you so you won't look at a man again,' said Chalciope, with another peal of laughter. 'No,' she continued. 'There's a lot of pleasure, too, in family life; if you love someone, you bring them both water and a chamber pot.'

Medea didn't know what to say, how to react. She did feel that she was being asked to understand something, something that upset her elder sister badly. Medea didn't even know what worm was gnawing at Chalciope and that she needed a woodpecker to remove it. All she wanted was woodpecker to peck out this worm with its sharp beak. Several times Medea tried to say again, 'Tell me more clearly what's bothering you, you can see I haven't understood,' but she held back. If Chalciope didn't speak 'more clearly', that was probably as it should be. Medea herself was in the wrong, it was because of her lack of understanding that she tormented herself and her sister, too. Quite unexpectedly, Chalciope asked her an even more embarrassing question: 'Do you know how a sick man's bed stinks?' Fortunately, Chalciope didn't wait for an answer and went on: 'It doesn't matter who's lain there, it makes you want to vomit and you'll hold your breath as long as possible until you find an excuse to get out and make yourself scarce.'

'If I wanted to I could instantly turn into a whippersnapper of a girl like you,' Medea for some reason recalled Aunt Qamar's words. This was a remark Aunt Qamar frequently repeated and Medea was always astonished why Aunt Qamar wouldn't turn into a little girl, at least for a short time. 'Perhaps this is why,' Medea thought, because she suddenly sensed some obscure, elusive link between every whippersnapper of a girl and what Chalciope had said. What Chalciope was saying seemed so loathsome that Medea couldn't wait for her to go away. Chalciope, without meaning to, was banging at a door behind which Medea's real nature was still sleeping, but the sleeper could hear this unpleasant and irritating sound that was trying, deliberately or not, to wake her up.

But sitting there so resentfully would have been unconscionable. Chalciope's eyes were begging Medea to speak out, to say something to calm her, support her, take her side. At any moment she might frown, lose her temper and take Medea's silence to be betrayal.

'I'm so pleased Phrixos is on his feet,' Medea suddenly said.

The mention of Phrixos's name startled Chalciope, as if a snake had bitten her: her face showed amazement. It was clear that Medea had misunderstood her, or was being devious and deliberately averting her eye from the pain that Chalciope was trying to show her. The only reason Chalciope had come was to get rid of this pain, an object of unknowable destination, unintelligible and of no apparent purpose. And she had chosen Medea deliberately. Whatever happened, unlike other women,

Medea wouldn't celebrate when she found out that her elder sister had been rejected by her husband, who was avoiding her, hiding from her, like a capricious child hiding from its nanny. What Chalciope had come to complain about was her fear of being lonely, and so she fled to be with her sister. But she sensed straight away that it would be hard to be totally frank with her sister. She didn't doubt that Medea would sympathize, but sympathy was now what she feared. If she deserved sympathy, one way or another, she would be demeaned in Medea's eyes, and her pain would be all the greater. Because two would now know what hitherto only one knew. Another person, whoever she was, would start looking dubiously, trying to identify the defect which made this truly beautiful and always smiling woman repulsive to her husband. Pretending was better, and Chalciope decided to pretend. She seemed to be pointing the finger at Medea's non-existent husband, warning, even threatening him should he behave bestially or look at anyone else after taking Medea's virginity.

'I don't intend to get married,' Medea told her in a tearful voice, but Chalciope still persisted, so as not to return to her main topic, her reason for coming, for starting a conversation.

'Having a wife makes a man proud and happy,' Chalciope raged, but when Medea suddenly mentioned Phrixos, she shuddered and gave Medea a look as if she had knocked a cup from her hands as she raised it to her lips. Medea felt dispirited, a bad premonition poisoned her mood, because she suddenly sensed with her whole being how pitiable and unhappy her elder sister was, and at the same time sensed how powerful and oppressive was the idol which Chalciope had chosen to worship. In the abrupt silence that followed Medea could hear a strange rustling, and she couldn't help covering her chest with her hands, as if someone might see her heart expanding like a bud struck by sunlight.

'But you're going to be happy,' said Chalciope.

Phrixos's boys now gathered round their father every day. And when they came back, their faces made it seem that had been doing something very bad. They avoided everyone's gaze. All four had the same reddened faces. Their eyes blazed with heat. Chalciope felt that some secret had come between her and her family, and that she had no share or place in it. She suffered, but her pride stopped her from humbling herself and asking her sons to explain what was going on.

The sons still loved their mother deeply and tenderly, as they always had, with their hearts, but this was no longer their only love. Chalciope now had a rival, but she didn't know her rival's name or face, which made her all the more frightened and reluctant to meet this rival.

Like all secrets, however, this secret was revealed unexpectedly and very simply. One day when the whole family was dining, Phrixos's eldest son Argus sipped some wine from a chalice and said, 'Our sea is the colour of wine.' The other three boys stared so hard at their mother, that Chalciope couldn't help becoming tense: something had been said, something important which would have explained a great deal, if she had been more attentive. Chalciope gave Phrixos a look. Phrixos felt his wife's gaze, his cheekbones turned bright red, but he didn't raise his head. Then he too sipped some wine, thrust the chalice aside and told Argus, 'But not the colour of this wine, our wine has a different colour.'

It was then that Chalciope understood which sea and what wine they were talking about. Suddenly she slumped, put her hands in her lap and smiled bitterly, like someone who has been deceived, who has been tricked into carrying a burden to the wrong place. 'How long it is since I last changed my dress,' Chalciope thought and suddenly felt how angry she was, as if a hot wind had struck her from the roots of her hair to her toenails. Not because she expected some horror and had been let down, but because she was sitting there with her husband and sons, hunched like an exhausted man, her hands folded in her lap. Chalciope banged the table, knocked a chalice full of wine ringing and clattering to the floor.

'Why are you so cross with me: have I fed you on roasted snakes?' Chalciope yelled.

Phrixos left the dinner table and slipped off to his room. The sons didn't dare get up from table, they forced themselves to choke down each morsel, as if they really were eating snake meat, then they thanked their mother for dinner and dispersed. Phrontis dragged his feet, but still found it too hard to approach his mother, whose expression was thunderous, and followed his older brothers out. She was left on her own, considering she had won, but instead of celebrating, she became more and more angry. 'What's wrong with me?' she wondered, but crockery was still noisily falling off the shelves and smashing at her feet. She now knew her rival's name, but, unfortunately, she couldn't drag it by the hair or scratch its eyes out. The rival was very far away, and thus seemed all the more powerful and formidable. All she could do was to gather her wits and thank the gods that her rival had turned out to be not an ordinary mortal woman, born of woman, whose rivalry, or even just existence, really would rub her womanly pride and self-respect in the dirt.

Frankly, Chalciope didn't even have the right to destroy her sons' love for their father's homeland. Probably such a thought would never have occurred to her if Phrixos and the boys had not wrapped everything in a fog of secrecy. Chalciope's womanly pride was still intact, unsullied, but she was more furious than ever, perhaps because she thought herself out of danger. Now her husband's and son's endless whispering took on another appearance: 'Why are they hiding things from me, they must be afraid of me,' she explained to herself, and decided to attack these conspirators, to make them really feel her power and her rights, so that once and for all they would understand whom they were dealing with. First of all, however, she went to see Medea, clasped her tenderly to her bosom and said, 'If you love me, forget what I said and how I behaved that day: I hadn't slept, and I tormented you, too, my little, beautiful and silly darling sister.' Who knows what Medea thought? Although her expression implied that she couldn't understand anything, she may well have been pretending. She was not as naïve as she seemed. At her age Chalciope already had a child.

Chalciope never forgave her husband his betrayal in life or even after death, but their relationship more or less recovered. The family was again a family, or seemed so from outside: outsiders didn't see the separate bed and Chalciope could calm down.

One evening Chalciope was sitting in an armchair, knitting. A cat was playing with the ball of yarn, rolling it over the flagstone. Phrixos was sprawled on a divan, staring at the ceiling. The boys sat in a corner whispering to each other. The cricket in a crack in the pillar lamented desperately. Its incessant chirruping made the cosy atmosphere that reigned in the room tense. Suddenly Chalciope lifted her head and said for all to hear, 'Before I die I'd like to see my husband's and sons' homeland.' Nobody expected to hear this from Chalciope, neither her husband nor her sons, not even the cricket, for it too fell silent. Phrixos sat up on the divan and started groping for his slippers with his bare feet.

'Do you mean that?!' Phrixos asked, leaning forwards, his palms pressing on the edge of the divan.

'I do,' Chalciope confirmed and went on knitting as though nothing important had been said. Phrixos and his sons couldn't sit still: they moved away and then, after talking, gathered around Chalciope. She went on knitting, smiling and nodding her head calmly. The boys were bursting with joy to see their mother smiling, nodding and approving the country which their father's tales had told them about and taught them to love. They all talked, interrupting one another, because the magical maternal and conjugal power of Chalciope's smile was coming back.

'Mama, hey, mama,' Phrixos's sons twittered. 'In father's city there's an old woman who used to sell pumpkin seeds. Father and our unlucky aunt used to slip away to buy pumpkin seeds. They tasted so good, father can still remember the taste. They had to give their nurse the slip because they were king's children, nobody would let them eat pumpkin seeds.'

His own face round with happiness, Phrixos looked his wife in the face, as if she too should be drooling at the mention of pumpkin seeds. But Chalciope went on knitting, smiling and calmly nodding.

That night Phrixos tossed and turned in bed for a long time, unable to sleep: sleep would not open its doors. Phrixos was missing something, some part of his body, without which he could not keep his balance, and that was why he was banned from the realm of sleep. Finally his mind cleared and he grasped that this 'something' was Chalciope, his bed partner and the mother of his sons. This revelation alarmed Phrixos, because he was now aware how all this time he had become used to doing without his wife. Now, if it cost him his life, he could no longer simply pull the covers off her bed. The journey to possess Chalciope from which, for better or worse, he had been exempted from travelling, now stretched out endlessly with all its difficulties and hazards. Phrixos was now at the start of the journey, but she was at the end. The sudden appearance of this distance cut the ground from under his feet. The worst misfortune was that his wife made him feel ashamed. 'How can I look her in the face?' he thought angrily, for he felt the desire becoming more and more unbearable. He felt the woman's power and the fact that this woman no longer belonged to him. The woman he had married, who had borne him four children, now turned out to be inaccessible to him. It was female power that tied and paralysed Phrixos's male power and urges. 'How can I be a man,' thought Phrixos, 'if I suffer like a child? She treats me, in fact, as if I really were a child. I should have made her wash my feet before I go to sleep, then things would have been different. If you give in to a woman, she'll bully you, and you'll deserve it.'

This was the first time that Phrixos's being had experienced a conflict between youthful shyness and masculine desire. He knew he had rights over a woman, he believed that she was his property and was duty-bound to carry out his every wish. Who knows, perhaps a woman would have had great joy carrying out 'his every wish', but Phrixos didn't dare reveal his wish, he could in no way overcome the barrier that had suddenly appeared, his shyness or embarrassment that barred him from everything natural and possible for a human being. There has never been an occasion when anyone failed to overcome this barrier: it has to be overcome if you want to live, but there are various ways of overcoming it. Some do so roughly, blindly, stubbornly, without caring, hesitating, thinking, or a backward glance: like beasts set free, they trample down the vulnerable flame flickering in the human soul, trampling it until there is no trace left. Phrixos was on the point of deciding to enter his wife's room and demand, not ask — no, just possess, not demand her as his property. Only thus could he properly punish his wife, who was probably peacefully sleeping just two steps away from him, for her indifference and neglect. Phrixos egged himself on to break the last shackles of shyness and embarrassment, for the woman he now meant to punish was for him the most desirable and unattainable of women, and yet was just two steps away, under the same roof, between the same walls, breathing the same air. Yet despite their having so much in common, she did not remember Phrixos, as if he didn't even exist. But her heat hit Phrixos in the face and blinded his eyes, like a bird caught by the leg flapping its wings at him; his whole body shuddered as if he had just planned, in fact, committed, the most evil of acts and was still trampling the scene of the crime, unable to run away, detained by his conscience. Phrixos was in torment, his morbidly inflamed desire really seemed criminal to him, because it was concealed, drawn out and tedious.

Phrixos imagined that Chalciope must be asleep and would wake up only when he clasped her in his arms, when it would be too late. But the moment he was about to get up, he instantly thought she might well be awake. The thought was like a bucket of cold water; what would he say to his wife if he came across her awake? He hadn't thought of that because all he wanted was for everything to happen silently, without a word spoken. If a word was spoken, his desire would seem demeaned and defeated. Now Phrixos began thinking differently, to cover up his own timidity and cowardice: 'She'll come herself, she can't fail to understand and come.' He then trusted this thought so much that several times he even fancied that someone had crept into his room. The illusion was so clear that he held his breath and got into bed. It seemed more natural to Phrixos that the woman should come to him, the woman must surely be aware of his desire and have heard his heart pounding. If she was a woman who called herself a wife, she had to come, to come and to say, 'Look, I've come to satisfy your every desire.'

'Why not?' thought Phrixos, 'She can't possibly calmly go to sleep, can she?' Phrixos's mind was so tense that he wasn't in the least surprised when Chalciope entered the room.

'I am your property,' said Chalciope, 'haven't I always carried out your every wish?'

Chalciope was wearing a translucent white shift. Phrixos had seen this shift only once and had long forgotten about it. Chalciope had worn it on their wedding night. Her hair, which she had combed out straight, was tied in a knot and fell over one shoulder. The thin, airy shift clung to her barely moving breast and belly as if someone invisible was breathing air under it. Her weak wheaten shoulders drooped helplessly. 'Why not?' thought Phrixos, finding it hard to swallow his saliva and automatically slipping into bed. He was ashamed of his involuntary movement, but put on a brave face, threw back the covers and exposed himself to Chalciope.

'Forgive me, forgive me,' Phrixos was muttering a little later, kissing his wife's breasts which she thrust towards him. She was weeping silently. Phrixos couldn't see her tears, so the teardrops seemed astonishingly large to him. Appreciated and humiliated at the same time, he was subconsciously aware that his nature had painlessly accommodated two mutually incompatible feelings, because he felt that this was the freedom he had longed for, which the scent of a woman and the sadness of tears made clearer and more palpable. A woman's calming hand was crawling over Phrixos's back like a harmless millipede looking for food. These two bodies were unable, and had no right to deny one another. They needed each other, they complemented and enhanced each other: perfect harmony reigned between them and separation infringed this harmony only because a complete body, split into two parts by nature's inventiveness and enthusiasm, was made by their union.

'Suppose I've been unfaithful, have you thought about that?' the woman suddenly said and wiped her damp cheek against his shoulder.

No woman ever entirely surrenders to a man. She always keeps back a small, unattainable, inaccessible territory where no force on earth can conquer her. What the woman knew was that she was for Phrixos the most important woman, and knowing this gave her courage. No other woman could ever take her place, nobody could take away her prior right. In fact, not just Chalciope but Phrixos thought so, because he gradually came to his senses and now a feeling of emptiness and dampness was irritating him. Flabbergasted, Phrixos smiled awkwardly in the dark. He reacted bitterly to his wife's remark: 'Suppose I've been unfaithful, have you thought about that?' He reacted so bitterly, that not a speck was left of the unbounded joy he had experienced a moment before. He now knew that everything was the ephemeral fruit of his overwrought imagination, as damp and loathsome as a squashed toad.

But his wife's voice as still ringing sharply in his ears. If he'd only shown a little courage and somehow got to his wife's bedroom, then everything would probably have happened exactly the same way, as it always did. So perhaps his wife had said in truth what his inflamed mind had prompted her to say. ‘So it’s gone as far as infidelity,’ thought Phrixos. Imagining his wife’s possible infidelity scared and demeaned him so much that he leapt out of bed with youthful deftness and this time really did run to Chalciope’s room. When Phrixos reached the door the first cockerels started crowing in the city, bringing movement and pallid light to the darkness cradling the house. Chalciope was not asleep; she was sitting up in bed, as if waiting for her husband. This was such a surprise to Phrixos that for one moment he thought of turning back. He had the impression that her smile was mocking, as if she knew the reason for Phrixos’s tension and constant blushing and was pleased, because she was a woman, a triumphant woman who could perturb a man and walk all over him. Phrixos sensed he was defeated. He was shackled by the sudden feeling of having wronged this woman and the weakness that ensued; she was inhibited by female dignity, by self-respect and a sense of superiority from offering herself to this ridiculous and pitiable man, who called himself her husband and was probably now incapable of accepting such an offering. Phrixos suddenly saw his reflection in his wife’s smiling eyes: frightened and confused, stark naked, like a beggar hunched in the doorway, like a child caught thieving. And the woman was sitting in bed, seeing Phrixos like this, of course, even though she behaved as if the darkness stopped her from recognizing who was standing at the door to her bedroom.

Quietly, almost in a whisper, for at the time everyone in the house must still have been asleep, Chalciope asked, ‘Who is it?’ Phrixos’s throat was so dry with emotion that he rasped, coughed nastily and replied, ‘It’s me, I couldn’t sleep and I got up for a walk.’ Chalciope was worried and called out to her husband, now in a normal voice, ‘All right, if you don’t feel well, I’ll get up.’ Now Phrixos realised that there was no point in carrying on the struggle. He had lost the fight, shamefully and irrevocably, and the reason for his defeat was, again, his own timidity and weakness, which he had suffered from ever since his childhood as a poor relation, and which, like people envying him his luck, never let him forget them. Phrixos suddenly hated everything, above all himself, and he could barely mumble, ‘Don’t get up: there’s nothing wrong with me.’

He hadn’t moved two steps when he heard his wife laugh. He found the sound of this laughter so unexpected and shocking that he froze to the spot in astonishment, wondering whether he had imagined it or not. Chalciope really was laughing: in short bursts, nervously, provocatively.

After this unpleasant night Phrixos changed completely; he seemed to be more cheerful, more talkative and active, but like a man about to set off on a journey, he couldn't settle to any lengthy conversation or job. In any case, he no longer hid his plans: he said for all to hear, 'I mean to return home, some spendthrift may be squandering my father's property.'

'It's all very well,' said Phrixos whenever he found all his family around him, 'it's all very well, but if a man doesn't look after his patrimony, he's not a man. I'm no ordinary man, I'm the son of a king and the lawful heir to the throne. This throne, I'd have you know, is as good as any other. I want to take my wife and children, if, of course, they agree.' Saying this, he always looked and smiled at Chalciope. 'My sons ought to see where their father was born. Who knows, my wretched father may be watching the road and seeing his son and his grandsons may prolong his life a few days.' Finally, Phrixos always added, 'What breaks my heart is that my unhappy sister hasn't lived to see this day.'

Phrixos started to pack. He would call out, 'Come and see, I'm only taking what I've got by my own hands and what I need for such a journey.' When asked how he planned to go, he would smile and reply, 'My father-in-law will let me have a ship, or at least hire one out to me.'

'I'll let you if you ask, but I don't advise you to ask,' Æëtes told him, frowning.

'I'm not a child any more,' replied Phrixos.

Æëtes bit his lip; a thin trickle of blood, like a frightened earthworm, ran down to his beard. For his daughter's sake, however, he restrained himself. Chalciope declared, 'Wherever my family goes, there I must go,' and she, too, began to pack. Phrixos was taken aback by Chalciope's decisiveness: he had expected this least of all. He had long thought of returning home, but it was Chalciope's fault if he was now in a hurry: he was running away from Chalciope, she made him feel ashamed, even afraid. After that night, he found living under the same roof unimaginable, and this was what gave him the courage to carry out what he had long planned, to go back to a distant, secret past. But Phrixos did not dare openly say no to his wife; he merely grunted, 'It's up to you.' On the other hand, Phrixos's sons were out of their minds with joy; all day they ran down Vani's streets, shouting, 'We're going. Goodbye, we'll always be grateful for everything.'

But Phrixos's sudden death turned everything around.

CHAPTER THREE

PHRIXOS was found dead in bed. He lay there curled up, as if he had thrown off his bedcovers in his sleep and then felt cold. If Phrixos had died a little earlier, nobody would have been surprised and they might even have shrugged and thought nothing of it. But now, when he seemed to be in good health, to have started to enjoy life and was planning to set off on such a journey, his death set people wondering. That day they recalled again his extraordinary arrival, how fishermen brought him and the ram to shore, how Bedia poured wine into his mouth and how they all laughed when he brought up Bedia's wine. Only now did the palace servants remember that Phrixos's ram, which was still standing trance-like, like a golden idol, in its own light, was butting the walls with its horns until dawn on the night that Phrixos died.

Bochia felt Phrixos's death more acutely than anyone. All night he tossed and turned in bed as if he lay on an ants' nest. Potola's cradle was next to the bed and when their latest baby started to mewl in its sleep, Bochia would rock the cradle with his foot. 'It's as if my own child had died,' Bochia sighed. Bochia meant what he said: when he first saw Phrixos sprawled on the shore, like a splinter of wood drifting from the ocean depths, exhausted and drained of colour, he was so upset, as if it were his own son lying, wretched and innocent, on the sand. If Æëtes hadn't done so, Bochia would have adopted and reared him. Bochia and Potola had reared so many children that it would have been no hardship. Their sons and daughters also multiplied so much that a new city might have been needed, although there were a few years when not a single child came to see them. They were now bearing life's yoke, had acquired families and had no time to go and see their eternally youthful parents.

'If they needed anything, they'd remember us,' Bochia reassured Potola and smiled, for he knew his wife was counting her children in her head: some had died, some had grown old, some were still in their prime, following life's course. Maybe the children were even embarrassed to look more aged than their parents, and for that reason avoided them. It was indeed embarrassing for a grey-bearded child, hunched with age, to complain about his troubles to a father who was as straight-backed as a young lad. 'That's why,' Bochia used to say, 'some of our sons have married women who are no better than donkeys, others — women who yap away like dogs.' Potola was quite different: you would search the whole world in vain for a woman like her. She would walk through fire for her husband's sake, even if pregnant (and she was pregnant very often). She never even asked for a drink of water, ignored her pregnancies, not letting go of broom and cleaning rag until the last moment. She swept the house three times a day, went to the attic ten times, and saw to the hen-run and the kitchen garden a hundred times; she never questioned her husband unnecessarily, nor did she tell him too much, either.

Only once did Potola wake her husband up: she had a customer who came and pestered her, 'Wake up your husband this instant.' Finding no way to get rid of the customer, Potola got her wedding shoes out of the cupboard, as if wedding shoes entitled and emboldened her to go to her husband. Potola put on the shoes and walked up and down Bochia's room. The tapping of the shoes, in fact, woke Bochia up: he was pleased to see his wife. But the next day, when he looked in the mirror he saw he now had one grey hair. Bochia pulled out the grey hair, showed it to Potola and said, 'Look what your shoes did.' After that Bochia could sleep in peace. Potola would rather drop dread on the threshold than let anyone disturb her husband.

'It's as if I'd lost a son, it's as if I'd lost a son,' Bochia lamented all night: Potola, lying with baited breath in their eternal marital bed, didn't know what to do, how to help her husband.

This premature death left both wife and husband at a loss, disconcerting them both: their life was just one battle against death, they resisted death by one bed and mutual love. They had no other weapon to fend off this mighty and sly enemy; they were heartbroken when this enemy turned out to have helpers and collaborators. Death was invincible, it always had its own way, but if you didn't do battle with it, it would be even more arrogant and unbridled, and would ravage the entire world. If there were any justice, death should take a man only when he was no longer fit to live, when old age withered him on the stalk and he had only the strength to tumble into the earth and walk on his own feet into the realm of death, as into a refuge: nobody should push him from behind, or hurry him on: thus he can slowly get used to the cob-webbed gloom of a secret world which has frightened and allured him since the day he was born. Man should be ready for death, not forced to fall into it, as a panicked mouse falls into the first hole it sees; he should be stored, like dried fruit in the attic, so that the dead can do the living good, and his fragrance, as noble as a teller of fairy tales, imbued with the earth's moistness and the sun's protracted heat, should reach halls cheered in the long winter nights by the sound of human voices. Death can take a man when Bochia's and Potola's bed has replaced him.

But death, devious and insatiable, often broke the rules of engagement, because it had many helpers: murderers and criminals, disease and bad luck — all of them death's comrades. Still, Bochia always found it hard to believe that anyone or anything could take away a man's life before his time, to take away what it couldn't appropriate. Even if a murderer still held a bloodstained knife, Bochia couldn't have accused him or 'charged' him with such a sin. He had been against death all his life, he couldn't accept or come to terms with it, and his wife's perpetual fertility was the result of this intransigence.

Phrixos had died prematurely. Bochia remember his arrival on the scene, as if it were yesterday, and the forty odd years which nature had granted Phrixos flew past for Bochia like a single day. To Bochia nature's meanness and unfairness was heartbreaking, devastating and outrageous: as if a temple, which an architect had spent years building, were instantly destroyed by an earthquake. All night long he groaned and lamented without stopping. Only when Potola took the crying baby from the cradle and gave it her breast did he come round: his wife felt sorry for him and said, 'There's no way you can get up today, poor thing.'

Phrixos was buried in the traditional way. They wrapped him in an bull's skin and hung him from a tree in the grove of the deceased. When the leather coffin, weighed down by the corpse, swung on its hooks, Phrixos's sons howled, 'Our father has flown away.' But Phrixos could no longer fly anywhere or see that longed-for country which he remembered all his life as a dream, which caused the sadness that had in fact, at least apparently, sucked him dry.

Vani mourned its adopted son with all due ceremony. For a whole week a series of famous keening women kept up a wailing and lamenting that never stopped for a minute in Æëtes's palace, draped in mourning black. Vani's inhabitants streamed constantly to the palace. All this time nobody left their house without holding a branch of laurel or willow. In the courtyard facing the palace people walked round Phrixos, who was lying in state, and threw the branches over the body. The ram was tethered by Phrixos's head, and the single sandal and the short gold-edged white tunic from his childhood was laid by his feet. The whole city was in mourning. The people had not forgotten even cripples and the infirm elderly, saying, 'If they didn't see him alive, then at least let's show them his corpse.' They brought them tottering along, or laid them on carpets and dragged them there. People came in through the main gates and left through the back ones, so that they could then give condolences to Bedia who stood hunched to one side, hiding his tear-stained face in the tangled loops of the rope round his neck.

Phrixos's sons huddled under an arch: one day's bereavement had made them paler and smaller, but the four of them were excited, as if they had suddenly found an urgent task, or a hope they had stopped expecting. It is odd, but a man finds hope just when almost everything is decided, and stubbornly clings to that hope to the last moment, and prefers to think about the best, rather than notice the worst. That is human nature, and if there is any way of doing so, a man will not believe in his own misfortune, because belief is the last rung of misfortune, and at that point the ladder breaks and there is nothing left, except for biting cold, darkness and loneliness. He can put his ear to the beloved corpse's chest, wondering if he's mistaken, and therefore delay the burial; hope makes him drag his feet and put off as long as possible looking the truth in its cruel and unfeeling face.

Phrixos's sons, straining their eyes, stretching their necks, watched the endless trudging procession which, albeit slowly, softened and almost dispersed the general sadness that their father's death had brought upon the city. 'All those people coming!' they thought, standing on tip-toe, as if trying to see the head of this strange river. The youngest, Phrontis, was more captivated than anyone by the spectacle: tension made his jaw gape and poked out the pink tip of his tongue, like a squirrel looking out from a hole in a tree. While his older brothers furtively jostled each other and whispered among one another, 'There are more coming,' he looked up at his brothers and a restrained smile of pride ran over his face.

Chalciope was placed between Medea and Absyrtus. Like her sons, she too was proud that the people of Vani were mourning her husband in this way. She was now reconciled and attuned to things, and even believed that Phrixos really deserved everybody's love and respect. She couldn't have chosen an unworthy husband, could she? 'Phrixos was a good man,' she thought, 'but he still got away from me.'

However sinful, it's better confessed that Chalciope was a little bit pleased by her husband's death. Even widowhood was better than being half a wife, than constant pretence and emotional turbulence. She believed that a husband should die before his wife: it made little difference if this was today or a year later. Deep down, she even liked being the mother of four orphans and the widow of a man respected by the whole country. Her husband had taken with him the secret of their bed: now there was now way he could tell anybody.

54

On the day of the funeral the whole palace was like a military camp: some were scrubbing cauldrons, others chopping wood, others putting bellows to the fire. Ash got everywhere. Death requires a lot: there were barrels of vinegar, bowlfuls of salt, pounded coriander and fennel leaves, all shining like hills after the rain. A chef standing on a chair was stirring a gigantic pot with an oar. In the central courtyard, where the deceased had lain in state, only the ram remained. Bathed in its own light, it was tethered by a rope to a block of wood, as torpid as a golden ram. It was thinking: it had a lot to think about, for unless there was a miracle, this was its last day. 'They came together and they will go together,' Æëtes had ordered. Whatever happened, who was going to stick out their neck to save a superannuated ram?

'What's astounding is that I'm being killed because of the person I saved,' thought the ram. A long-bladed, fish-coloured, grooved knife lay on the block: an ant was crawling up the groove. The butcher threw a branch over the ram and scratched the back of his neck, as if first asking forgiveness. 'You watch out he doesn't fly off,' someone called out to the butcher. The butcher utter a muffled broken laugh, as if he had a cough, and scratched the ram's neck again. The ram understood it all: during his long life he had learnt human language. He even laughed inwardly: 'I'll fly when the gods want me to.' But he believed to the last minute that something would happen and he would certainly survive. Although he didn't know how, he must differ from an ordinary sheep: he understood human language and had even flown, true, only once, but the memory of his flying and his lightness still made him feel dizzy. In fact, compared with an ordinary sheep, he had really undergone and experienced an unimaginable amount. He resented nothing, he did not fear death, it was shameful for a sheep to outlive a human being, but he really shouldn't have his throat cut like an ordinary sheep, he should be killed some other way, he should before he died at least be freed of the mud-encrusted rope; the wooden block that stank of rotten blood should be removed. He wasn't going to run or fly away: just moving his legs, let alone flying, was difficult, so saturated was his fleece with gold.

Right to the end the ram could not believe the gods would forget him, the gods who had once, after all, chosen him for an ordeal that none of his fellow sheep were worthy of. Suddenly, the ram seemed to feel again the ground falling away from under his feet, and a rough wind blowing fiercely in his face. But the ram was mistaken: this was another sort of flying, chilling and deadly in another way: it came crawling with the ant that had squatted on the knife and whose finger teased him as it went up and down the groove in the knife. True, the ram was no ordinary sheep, he would accept death rather than mediocrity, although only death could at a stroke annul the superior status he had in life, a status which set him permanently apart from the woolly, bleating breed that can give man only milk, flesh and wool. He, however, understood more, he had taken part in realising a human idea and although he could not fully understand the essence of this idea, he always felt with pride that he was involved in a cause greater than the beasts. If he had been exiled, then his being here must have seemed necessary. Someone, not just someone, a human being had needed him and, instead of being slaughtered, eaten and skinned, he had been saddled with a boy and made to fly like a bird, to leave his homeland for ever: yes, his homeland, for where you first open your eyes is your homeland, whether you're a sheep or a human being. But he was apparently no longer needed by humanity, what had to be done was done and now they were going to slaughter him like an ordinary sheep. 'Like an ordinary sheep,' thought the ram as the butcher slashed his neck with the long-bladed, fish-coloured knife and black blood came gushing from his gaping throat. This thought froze permanently in his dead head, the bent horns dipping in a pool of blood like elbows. With the indifference of an object, his still open, pallid eyes reflected everything — the keeners, staggering from the wine they'd drunk, the damped-down fire, and the copper cauldrons where his body and feet would be boiled.

Phrixos's death was followed by a series of strange events. The city, hitherto free of fear or sorrow, had food for thought, even anxiety. At the wake Æëtes accidentally knocked over the salt cellar, and salt spilled all over the table. The guests were dumbstruck: this augured quarrelling, and with Æëtes of all people. The blood drained from Æëtes's face. 'I should not have slaughtered the ram,' he thought again: he forced himself to smile, swept up the spilt salt in his cupped hands and ate it all like a horse. That day, in various parts of the city, at the same time, as they found out later, pigs keenly rooting through the rubbish suddenly fell upon each other so furiously that they could be calmed down only by scalding them with boiling water. A little later, as if nothing had happened, the pigs returned happily grunting to their rubbish heap. Before the pigs' sudden attack of rage had been forgotten, a weird dream perturbed everyone. Bedia had the dream: it was peculiar to him, but he couldn't keep it quiet and went to the cellar with forty steps and told it to Bakha the vintner, so that soon the whole city knew about it and the dream was public property and was talked about as if everyone had dreamt it at the same time. Soothsayers found the dream hard to interpret, but they were interested and asked for time, collected countless different magic objects and talismans and stared like owls into the impenetrable darkness of the inexplicable. The dream really was weird: two bald men, looking like brothers, came to the city; each had faces of which one side laughed and the other side cried. They thrust a bunch of grapes at everyone they came across, old or young, man or woman, although they were carrying no baskets, neither on their backs nor in their hands. Wherever you looked, everyone was eating grapes, all smiling on one side of their face, crying on the other. The grapes were large, the size of a thumbnail, but they had no flesh and tasted only of bitter salt tears. But people ate them, and as soon as they finished, the bald brothers offered them more bunches and guffawed as if the heavens were falling. 'What the hell does this mean?' the people of Vani asked, unable to settle down.

The sea took advantage of the general confusion and retreated a step more, so cunningly that it escaped the notice of Bedia, who was watching it so alertly and persistently, with his rope wrapped round his neck. Not that Bedia can be blamed: Phrixos's death and then the dream had for a while knocked him off balance, and when he noticed the sea's treachery it was too late to be worth raising the alarm: Bedia was compelled just to lengthen his rope.

Everything began with the slaughtering of the ram. When the butcher hung the ram by its hind leg and skinned it, he strained his arms and tensed his knees, but still couldn't stay upright and fell under the fleece, which flopped on top of him. 'Help me, it's crushing me,' the butcher yelled, as red as a radish. The ram's fleece really had become as heavy as a gold ingot. Twenty men could only just lift the edge and drag the butcher out by his feet, which were sticking out. 'Perhaps I shouldn't have had it slaughtered,' Æëtes thought for the first time. Everyone without thinking took a step back, as if the fleece, spread out on the ground, had a magical force. Perturbed, the people fixed their gaze on the king. Æëtes laughed, more to calm the people, and said, 'Now at least you'll be certain that this was no ordinary sheep.' Then he became thoughtful, frowned and stood up to look at the sky, as if he was keeping an eye on Phrixos's ghost. After a short while a forced smile relaxed his face and he continued, 'This is a gift from Phrixos, we must accept it and look after it, we can't let a dead man down.' The fleece was carefully carried into the palace. Æëtes's court became even more resplendent. The king had a niche cut in the wall behind the throne and hung the ram's fleece there. A door was fixed to the niche, and a carpet was hung over the door, and the throne placed against it. 'Rest assured, my son-in-law, that not a hair will fall from your gift,' said Æëtes as he sat down on his throne.

Vani resumed its old life, everyone went back to their usual business. The workshops became as noisy as ever, the port bustled as before, people came and went, unloaded and loaded ships; the streets and squares were full of carefree strolling girls and boys. 'What have you seen, what have you heard?' their elders asked them when they came home, while the young just shrugged and replied, 'We haven't seen anything or heard anything, we just went for a walk, and then came home.' In fact, when they thought about it, they themselves were amazed that they'd seen, said and heard everything a thousand times over.

But things weren't quite as they seemed. Everything was changing, albeit slowly, imperceptibly. There were changes in the people and in the city that people had built to protect themselves from the outside world, so as not fear wild animals or to live quivering in fear and cold in damp dark caves, so as to yield their place peacefully to their progeny. Time had left its mark on the city walls. The plaster was peeling, cracking and falling; carriage wheels had rutted the paving; sun and rain had faded the roof tiles; trees had grown too tall, too large, and their desiccated, eroded bark was peeling off the trunks. Furniture and crockery was worn out, on its last legs, faded, but people didn't notice, for it all happened under their noses, they themselves were part of this degeneration. They didn't even notice changes in their own nature, because today they knew more than yesterday, they had added to their forebears' knowledge, but this knowledge had taken away the alertness which their forebears needed so much when they crouched in caves, anxiously heeding the mysterious voices of the outside world. Humans had now lost the feeling of fear, or rather they had acquired the ability to suppress their fear, for they were now sure that death was inevitable, sure that this world was nothing but a strictly defined alternation of death and life: one gave rise to the other, bringing it out of mother nature's inexhaustible depths.

Man, involved in this eternal cycle of alternating death and life, had only one concern: not to fall out of it. Time's and nature's eternal, constant alternation had covered its face with a mask of monotony, so as to complete its job unnoticed and in peace. Life was a puzzle and would remain a puzzle, because this puzzle's complexity and simplicity lay in the fact that everything happening on earth seemed to be because of, due to and for the sake of man, yet it happened independently of him… Yet, wherever he looked, a god was looking back at him. There were so many different gods around him, carved from wood, moulded from clay, cast in gold or bronze, that he could stop racking his brains trying to solve the eternal puzzle. The gods were as stern and as loving as parents, and they knew when to punish men and what to protect them from. Man was like a loving child whose parents had been killed before he could reward them for their goodness, and was now obsessed with devoting himself entirely to looking after their graves. And he took great care of these faces, tense with eternal silence and wisdom, of these breasts, swollen with eternal maternity and these arms and thighs, whose muscles expressed manliness and a force that dominates the elements. For them, man fattened poultry and cattle and, sweating from sun and toil, his skin shrivelled like dry wheat chaff, dedicated the first sheaf to them and brought the first grape-laden vine branch from the vineyard to them, as well. Men revered all the gods equally and always stood aside when the gods, for his sake, but likewise independently of him, destroyed or multiplied, impoverished or enriched, weakened or strengthened one another. His reverence, submission and service were eternal, unshakable, unstoppable, indiscriminate, because, old or new, defeated or victorious, they all incarnated one and the same god, just a little transfigured, more powerful, more adult, beautiful and wise.

At this time yet another weird dream came to Vani. If, like Bedia's dream, it didn't become everybody's property, that was only because the dreamer didn't dare tell the dream to anyone. The dreamer was Æëtes's younger daughter. What had happened in the palace and in the city had given Medea, too, cause for alarm and thought. True, Medea had her own particular world: she had little understanding of the world where these happenings occurred, but as time passed that world became more noticeable, noisier and more interesting. As from a suddenly opened door in a house of merriment, Chalciope's carefree peals of laughter used to burst out, disturbing everything outside that door for a moment. Medea was standing outside that door, her sister's laughter alarmed her strangely, striking her like the scent of a non-existent flower. Medea had never had the slightest wish to walk, or even look through that door; she was too embarrassed and she thought everyone would greet her with laughter, asking what she was doing there. Medea also felt awkward because she never understood what her own sister said. Her sister would pour her heart out, but Medea couldn't see inside it. Yet Chalciope helped Medea discovered her own heart. Afterwards Medea could find no peace, she couldn't move a step without asking her heart, she couldn't utter a word. If her heart disapproved of something, it would give her a hard time, worse than Aunt Qamar: her head buried in her pillow, she would sob all night, 'All right, ask your lovely sister whether she feels like crying,' but her heart would not relent, and Medea no longer knew what she should do to hide from this truly ruthless being. 'Why shouldn't she feel like crying, her husband has died,' Medea shouted to her pillow, but her heart had other ideas, other beliefs: because it was hidden, it allowed itself to do as it liked.

Medea believed that Phrixos was Chalciope's god, her idol, who had given sons, each one better than the other, to his faithful and beautiful handmaiden. But Medea also sensed, especially lately, especially after her last conversation with Chalciope, that something had happened to disrupt this obligatory harmony which should exist between a god and his handmaiden. Medea knew well that the gods are capricious, but no good handmaiden would let the gods' capriciousness exhaust her patience or make her forget her obligations. Often Medea's god had frowned on her, it had often hidden from her in the clouds, but she never stopped praying to it and serving it. True, Chalciope and Medea had different gods, but they were like each other, if only because both gods required handmaidens. Of course, Phrixos had died, and Medea was as distressed as anybody else, but for Medea this was the death of a god, a hopeful sign. Didn't gods die? But they were gods because they could rise from the dead, be born again to return to earth even mightier and more beautiful. Her heart pounded, fluttered, like an embryo in its mother's womb, reminding the earth of its existence by muffled, quivering jolts, 'Perhaps I've had enough, it's time I was born.' Medea felt as if her heart was becoming visible, that, if she took her hands off her chest everyone would see it, a heart as big and as scarlet as the flower that Chalciope plaited into her hair. Her heart really was behaving as if it felt cramped and embarrassed in a virgin's weak, slender body; it was trying to escape from captivity and, like a fish washed ashore, it would give up the ghost, and leap about absurdly, or it would take its owner with it into the whirlpool of real life, into the dust and mud, braving the wind, like a race-horse, taking the bit between its teeth, its chest covered in foam, carrying a rider who has collapsed on its back.

Her heart invented all sorts of things to frighten and confuse Medea still further, being more powerful, farsighted and omniscient than its bearer. 'Look out, I'll feed you to the dogs,' Medea threatened it angrily, but her heart, safe and sound in its dark nook, persisted and embittered the girl who was deeply upset by the painful, deep-rooted and shocking transformations. 'Why don't you ask your dear sister if her husband just died or if she killed him: did he died, or was he killed?' her heart echoed, like a drum heated up by the fire.

Of course, her heart was exaggerating, Phrixos had not died by poison or by the dagger: death had killed him, selected him, that was all, but Medea crept into the hall where Phrixos's corpse was kept at night. 'Now can you see? Have you calmed down?' she appealed to her heart, but her heart wouldn't back down, still insisting that there were other ways than poison or a dagger to kill a man. All that Medea felt sure of was how dangerous, ruthless and hard to adapt to was the world, her elder sister's world, which her heart was drawing her into, every day more insistently and stubbornly. Chalciope's world was more dangerous and more interesting. Every minute something was happening there, was being created or destroyed every minute, crashing with a bang to the ground, with a feeling of challenging pride in its inevitable perdition and in its ability to wrap everything in its own dust in one minute.

Medea still lived her old life. Every morning she would get into her mule-drawn carriage, holding the reins in her right hand, a whip in the left, and, accompanied by her twelve handmaidens, she set off for Dariachangi's garden. But once there, in the splendid temple of the gods, she could no longer forget the passionate, excited and unavoidable voices which now penetrated more freely, shook her more violently, as if intending to wake her and pull her into their camp, so as to become even stronger and more manifold. Her heart was to blame for everything, it gave her no peace and pulled her away with pleas or tears, as a child clutching its mother's skirts drags her home when she stops to talk to a neighbour. 'You'rc playing, while others are living,' her heart wailed and, however much Medea turned a deaf ear or a blind eye, she saw everything around her in a changed light, as if the constant beating of the second, invisible being housed inside her was gradually cracking the clay mask hiding the world's real face. Medea had the feeling that the garden and the temple used to be bigger. Either they had become smaller in the twinkling of an eye, or she had grown bigger, grown so much that she now felt cramped in the space in which she had hitherto been able to lose herself, like the downy yellow chick in her handmaidens' song. 'Scattered millet see-eed, Who but a chick picks up?' Medea found herself humming, and she smiled sadly.

Like the chick, she had a hard task: she had to come to terms with her surroundings until the world, now perturbed by Phrixos's death, gradually calmed down, became peaceful and left Medea in peace. Medea had her own world, inherited from Aunt Qamar, built with the bricks of Aunt

Qamar's knowledge and held together by the mortar of Aunt Qamar's patience. But Aunt Qamar's knowledge and patience were, evidently, enough to build only three walls, because here in Dariachangi's garden the winds from Chalciope's world were playing freely. In fact, they had flown in before Medea noticed or paid attention. A long time ago, seeds scattered by these winds had settled and, cunningly biding their time under the sun, had copiously strewn their intoxicating pollen and fluff, making the twelve girls prance naked, like fillies, grow sad or cheerful without cause, wrapping their actions, speech or songs in an atmosphere of play, like any childish secret. This went on until time drove the fillies back to the stables, to the world where playing becomes living and dreaming — reality. In the stable these scented garden and sun-blanched banks became objects of desire, but they could never go back to what they were, and the garden and banks, when they encountered them, would be different, colourless, much diminished and more remote, because every day the grumbling of husbands and the wailing of children would tighten their bridles.

The little world shaded by apple trees had only an exit, while the big world had only an entrance. They, too, had to come out of one world to enter the other. Medea's heart was right, but this rightness still alarmed and irritated her, although she herself could sense that even she lacked the knowledge and patience to build the fourth wall which Aunt Qamar had left, deliberately or not, unbuilt. Medea would rather destroy the other walls, as thoughtlessly and ruthlessly as a child destroys its toy house of sticks when nurse calls it in for dinner. 'Scattered millet see-ee-eed, Who but a chick picks up?' Medea hummed, not understanding what was happening to her. She had inexplicable, distressing expectations, and suffered all the more because there was no way she could explain what she was expecting. When she had the dream, she felt a little relief, thinking it must have been what she was expecting, but now the dream's boldness and fear-arousing bliss left her confused. The dream itself was confused: the sisters had been interchanged and Medea had dreamt it instead of Chalciope, because, in Medea's opinion, it was more Chalciope's dream. The hero of the dream was like a resurrected god, returning from the underworld, striding the earth with godlike calm and firmness, recovering what he had temporarily lost.

After dreaming this, Medea thought all night about Phrixos. The hero of her dream actually was in some ways like Phrixos, but he seemed more handsome, bolder and stronger. Not that this was surprising, for death kindles life in a god even more than wind in a fire. But if this really was

Phrixos, transformed and enhanced by death, why had he appeared to Medea and not to Chalciope, which would have been more natural? Or had Medea perhaps been transformed and taken Chalciope's appearance? How often she had wished and imagined herself as beautiful as Chalciope, how often her heart nearly stopped when a speck of dust or ash got into Chalciope's eye and she raised a shriek, 'God, I've gone blind, I can't see a thing!' Medea broke into a cold sweat just imagining Chalciope one-eyed and waited, as if paralysed, for Chalciope to take her hand off her eye. Then, smiling with happiness, she looked ecstatically at her sister, whose painful eye was just a tiny bit red and who blinked her long, moist eyelashes as fast as a black butterfly landing on a flower.

Perhaps, though, Chalciope had taken on her sister's youth and virginity so as to be immaculate and unsullied when she met her resurrected, rejuvenated husband? Torturing herself with such thoughts, confused and ashamed, Medea was mortally afraid of leaving the house, and when she got home found it hard to cross the threshold, as if she were going to be scolded or mocked. Her dress made her uncomfortable, as if she had bathed in it and it had dried on her body. She felt at ease only with her nephews and couldn't wait to see them and sit among these four bold, strong lads. Their rough movements and loud uninhibited talk was balm to Medea's distraught nature. These lads had the strength she lacked, but which she needed, like railings, as she stood on the last rung of the ladder of youth, made dizzy by the height and unfamiliarity. After Phrixos's death the boys came to see their aunt more often. They jokingly called her 'auntie' and Medea laughed heartily, so odd did it seem to be an aunt to boys of her own age. They would spend whole nights chatting endlessly about nothing in particular, they themselves were amazed and happy not to be dragged off to bed by their nannies. They felt they had grown up and this perception encouraged them and gave them more rights than they wanted or needed, for they wanted to have everything, and at once, too.

Sometimes Chalciope would knock at their door, asking 'What are you talking about all this time?' She hesitated to enter, as if feeling that now the sons were adults there was no place for her, as her tired and pleading voice confirmed. Before, Chalciope would bark at them, take all four by the scruff of the neck and drive them off; none would have dared protest. But now they laughed when they heard their mother's voice; they called out, 'Leave off, mama, it's too early to sleep, we're not children.' They'd finished with childhood: they weren't children any more.

'Until I've eaten pumpkin seeds, life won't be worth living,' Argus would say and all four smacked their lips with such relish as if they had roasted salted pumpkin seeds in their coat-tails. 'Don't our pumpkins have seeds?' asked Medea, surprised, and stared with animation at the brothers' curly-haired heads, which harboured thoughts she could not comprehend. The brothers sensed Medea's animated gaze and all four were overcome by an even stronger urge to show off and boast in front of this unique woman who was both sister and aunt to them. 'Who knows if some wretch is squandering out father's property? When we get there...' Phrixos's sons threatened, talking like this to spite their grandfather, because in their hearts all four resented Æëtes for declaring, for all to hear, in the grove of the departed, 'That's the end of it, everyone is to stay as they are.' Phrixos's corpse was already swinging from a tree, but his boys were drying their burning tears with their clenched fists and thinking of running away. Actually, they began thinking about running away when Æëtes said, 'That's the end of it, everyone is to stay as they are.' 'They'll go, all the same,' thought Absyrtus, afraid lest he blurt out aloud what only he knew. True, Phrixos's sons were at that moment thinking of running away, but it was more a threat than a decision. Once Phrixos had died, Absyrtus kept his head bowed, as though it was his fault that Phrixos had died, as though he was the reason for his sister's being widowed and his nephews orphaned. Absyrtus thought this feeling not entirely baseless, for he had been the first to foresee Phrixos's death and Phrixos was dead to him at the time when he was getting better and had got out of bed, and when, naked to the waist, he was digging the ditch. Death settled first in Absyrtus's mind and from there reached out to grab Phrixos. Of course, Absyrtus was powerless and had no way of blocking death, but, knowing in advance that it existed, he seemed guilty, death had made him an accomplice, a fellow-conspirator. Even though Absyrtus had revealed the conspiracy, he had done harm and made his nephews hate him. 'You were thinking about our father dying because you wanted him to die,' his nephews told him.

Absyrtus used to slip off to the forest, lie face down on the grass and weep for the sadly smiling Phrixos, for happily laughing Chalciope and his nephews, with their grazed knees and sweat-smoothed curls, leaping one after the other off the castle walls. Then, his head bowed, he would walk, not letting anyone see his tear-stained and dirt-spattered face. Phrixos was going, slipping away, like water from a cracked vessel. Absyrtus was so horrified by Phrixos's sons' lack of concern that he couldn't refrain from telling them, 'Your father is going to die.' All four went pale, they could barely avert their eyes, flashing with hate, from their sobbing uncle, who was awkwardly wiping his tears; they span round, and left; tears dripped on Absyrtus's trembling face, because he loved both Phrixos and the boys.

When Absyrtus in the grove of the deceased thought, 'They'll go, all the same,' Argus looked round and scowled at him, as if he had guessed what his uncle was thinking and was warning him to keep his mouth closed. In any case, Absyrtus confided in nobody, because experience had many times taught him that foretelling something was pointless: it would still happen as it had to, as the goddesses of fortune had decided. What was life seemed a dream to Absyrtus: he knew everything but couldn't actually do anything as he wanted to. Knowledge weighed heavily on him, it had a grudge against him. Nobody found it pleasant to have foreknowledge of what awaited them, whether it was joy or sorrow. Absyrtus's only consolation was that he, too, was not fated to live long.

On the day that Medea had her dream, Absyrtus was strolling on his own in the courtyard, which had been swept and sprayed with water: he smiled so oddly at his sister, who was standing by her mule-drawn carriage, that Medea couldn't help being alarmed, for Absyrtus's smile expressed so much warmth, love, and regret. Medea smiled awkwardly back at her brother, and for some reason lashed the mules with her whip. The mules took offence and, jerking their heads up and down, moved off through the gates. Medea was now ready for her dream which crowned, albeit heavily, her inner turmoil, confusion and unconscious flight towards the unknowable.

That day the girls spent a long time splashing about in the sea. Then Medea went off on her own, lay down on the hot sand and gazed at the setting sun. Fluffy black and red clouds were piling up on the horizon. Medea was so tired by the water and the sun that she did not want to move, although she knew that it was time to go. The evening breeze rippled and furrowed the surface of the sea. All the time, little white waves crashed onto one another, like lambs rushing out of a sheepfold, the sand slowly cooled, giving Medea goose pimples, but she still didn't get up, as if she'd been ordered to lie there and wait. What she was to wait for, she didn't know, but she felt that something was about to happen, which made her inwardly alarmed and intrigued.

And lo and behold, Medea's expectations came true: a man came up out of the sea. Her fellow maidens' voices were barely audible in the distance. So far Medea could only make out a black outline, because the man coming from the sea had the setting sun behind him. It suddenly turned dark. Medea felt much colder and gazed with amazement at the man coming towards her. She didn't even try to get up or reach out for her dress, as if she had to lie there in full sight of the stranger who was striding towards her. Medea was lying on her back with her hands spread out. The man kept coming. The sand crunched under his feet, his bronze-coloured body shone as if it had been greased, his wavy hair was fastened by gold braid. The stranger held a three-pronged harpoon and approached, as if he knew both that he was expected and who was waiting for him. He went right up to Medea. Medea shut her eyes and shuddered as if a rough fig leaf had been placed on her naked body. When she opened her eyes again, the man was kneeling by her feet, the harpoon's haft was stuck into the sand. The three sharpened prongs shone like a constellation. The man cautiously lifted Medea's foot with both hands, as if he was picking up a chick, and kissed its pink sole. A wave of warmth ran through Medea's whole body, as if the sea had suddenly washed the shore. This wave completely subdued and weakened her and made her lips part in a blissful smile. The stranger then gently bit her thumb, and his hot palm slowly stroked the length of Medea's leg and he laid his hand on the mound of her belly, as curly as lamb's wool. Medea thought there would never be an end to the extraordinary bliss drawing her on, absorbing her, softening her and about to devour her. All Medea could do was unconsciously clutch the stones at random, trying to resist this mighty gravitation. But the stones uprooted themselves from their resting places and flew up as she flew. Medea's barely open eyelids let her see just three big stars: red, green and blue. The stars were spinning dizzily above Medea, making coloured circles in the air. The sea was making a strange groaning as it came closer, as if everything — the entire universe — was trying to break into Medea's being. Medea felt a hot and endless, bold and rapid torrent of molten stars cut into her entranced being.

Medea woke up. The twelve girls were standing over her, and their expressions suggested that they had been watching some strange animal which had chanced to be washed up on the shore. When Medea opened an eye, they shouted with one voice, 'You've been asleep!' and burst into such peals of laughter that they sounded just like a flock of birds startled into flight.

The sun, as sinewy and crimson as wild honey, had half set over the sea. In between sun and shore the sea stretched as a belt of the same colour. The sun glistened on the girls' bare shoulders. Medea hadn't yet shaken off the dream and couldn't understand why the girls were looking at her so strangely. Then it all came back to her and she instantly got up.

She turned her back on her fellow maidens and quickly put on her dress, because she felt so clearly those hot kisses all over her body. The marks of three kisses appeared like three stars on her chest: red, green and blue.

Medea plaited her hair, wound the plait like a thick rope round her head and fixed it with an ivory pin. The girls then rushed to get their dresses, they too hastily twisted their wet and heavy hair on their heads; in a minute everyone was ready to leave. Soon, in single file, like geese, they took the path leading to the temple. Behind them the sea moaned. In the lead was Medea: now a woman, both perturbed and happy. A smile spread over her face, which the chill air made pale. The smile was like a letter from a foreign land, which she had hitherto known only from Chalciope's words, and which had always frightened and irritated her, as the stage does an actor until he sets his foot, shaking with nerves, on it. But the actor also knows that the fear and nerves are trivial compared with the magical force which comes over him and enables him to do what he would never dare do otherwise.

This was now the force felt by Medea, like an actor going on stage, her knees trembling and her face smiling as she went into life, where she was expected and where room had been made for her. Medea was sure that this was what Chalciope wanted, Chalciope had tried to win her over, to lure her into her own world so that Medea could undergo what she had undergone and endured. Medea knew that her elder sister was unhappy, but this unhappiness seemed enticing and alluring, like everything else connected with Chalciope. 'Let it be as you want,' Medea thought, 'I can do even this for your sake.' Medea had become as pliable and generous as a child clutching her favourite toy to her chest. This 'favourite toy' was the dream. She would never, as long as she lived, let anyone see or know about this dream, it was hers, hers alone, and she felt happy to have had such a dream. Now she had to resist temptation, to control herself and not tell anybody, or what happened to a poor boy who couldn't be patient and told his stepmother his dream, could happen to her. 'Mummy, mummy,' Medea mockingly imagined the poor boy saying, 'the sun sat on one side of me, the moon on the other, and the stars washed my face.' The stepmother felt jealous; inevitably, how could anyone tell such a dream? In fact, the boy would not let his stepmother or even the king have his dream, but in the end he and his dream ended up in a dungeon.

CHAPTER FOUR

AFTER he ate the salt, Æëtes's mood became grim. He drank a hundred jugfuls of water, followed by a hundred jugfuls of wine, but nothing dissolved the rough lump of salt. Utterly downcast, Æëtes was plunged in thoughts. Once again he went down the bottomless well. The well responded with shouts and yells. 'What are you so pleased about?' Æëtes asked, astonished. 'Whatever makes you sad,' the well called back.

'Come on out, if you've got the courage!' shouted Æëtes, his face white with anger.

Æëtes was so angry that his hands almost let go of the rope and he nearly went to the bottom of the well with a great crash. The bottom of the well was wild with joy. There was more joy to come. If Æëtes was angry, that meant he could find no peace. This was a first, unmistakable sign of a crack appearing in his firmness and stubbornness: water was attacking him, the water brought to his capital city by the Greeks, spurting like a dragon through a pipe the diameter of a man's arm, and covering the whole city in a bright shining haze.

Æëtes crawled up from the well and ordered his war chariot to be rolled out and the most lively horses to be yoked to it. The palace was horrified: what had come over him? But who would have dared to question him? His word was their command, the chariot was waiting by the gates, the horses were foaming at the mouth and chewing their bits. They were pawing the ground, impatient to rush off. Absyrtus stood up in the chariot, the reins wrapped around his wrist and, bending backwards, was holding back the horses. Æëtes took the reins from his son, saying he wanted to drive on his own, and the carriage moved off.

In the twinkling of an eye the thoroughbreds had left the city behind, raising a cloud of dust in the streets that made people start to cough. The chariot got to the ever-flowing river and followed it upstream. The thoroughbreds fought back many times, and kept turning their sinewy necks, but they couldn't get away from a driver who was even more furious than they were. Midnight had passed when covered in dust and mud, its wheels falling apart, the chariot was brought back by Æëtes to the city. The exhausted, sweating horses' hooves skidded on the paving, their swollen bellies rumbled, and if they were not so terrified of their driver, they would have collapsed in the street. Æëtes handed the reins to his stableman and told him, 'If you like horse meat, you can have these horses as a present, they're no good for anything else now.'

'I'll rest them, wash them, feed them up and sell them,' the stableman instantly thought. Æëtes's anger had ebbed away. He went back into the palace, his head held high as before, snatched a wood torch from a servant and, in its bright light, stood over his sleeping wife.

But doubts persisted. They gnawed at the wall from quite a different direction, as if they were not at all interested in Æëtes. But every now and again they would swing the rope of thought under his nose, as if to say, don't you need us? Æëtes averted his eye, but he knew in his heart of hearts that he could not long resist the temptation to descend the challenging shaking rope of thought again and revisit the accursed well. The rope of thought both allured and alarmed him, like offal left to lure a hungry lion. But Æëtes bided his time: he had to, while he could, for anything was better than that descent. 'Why are you looking so hang-dog?' he would call out to his family, but his forced merriment was so obvious, that nobody felt like singing and dancing, although nobody refused to drink wine. Phrixos's sons drank like oxen, keeping up with their grandfather, and they boasted, too, 'This wine can't make us drunk, it only swells our bellies.' But they only said that because they were tipsy: it was the wine talking.

Once Cytisorus called out, 'My father's just walked past.' The mention of Phrixos startled everybody, and all eyes were on Cytisorus's outstretched arm. Æëtes frowned, he was sorry for his son-in-law who had died so young, but he didn't want others to see his softheartedness. Æëtes had started to keep an eye on his family, watching each one of them, as if he hadn't seen them before. When his gaze, as sharp as a sword, fell on Medea, he was astonished and flabbergasted: instead of a freckled little girl, a woman was sitting in front of him. He did not know this woman, he had never seen her, but a father's tenderness suddenly came over his heart, he felt a painful rush of blood, he nearly stood up to put his hand on his younger daughter's honey-coloured hair. To stop himself leaping up he banged his fist on the table as hard as he could, and made a toast to his enemies.

'They give me strength!' shouted Æëtes.

Phrontis had laid his reddened cheek against the moist belly of the wine jug and his eyes were unfocused. 'Stop drinking!' Medea called to him. The wine had gone to Æëtes's head, too, but he still couldn't forget what he wanted to forget. The rope of thought was dangling under his nose and he felt again its dry, stinging hairs tickling him.

'No, you didn't like my father,' Argus insisted. But Æëtes wasn't listening now, he was suddenly fed up with everything, but didn't feel like leaving, for something was holding him back and he kept his hands between his knees like a lion's paws in a snare, to stop them grabbing against his will the rope dangling under his nose, because now he was in no state to descend into the well. 'She has grown!' every now and again it occurred to him, as he look in confusion at Medea who was smiling, her head bowed, at the drunken uproar. This honey-haired creature, who wafted all around a comforting scent of cleanliness and purity, aroused in her father's heart, for some reason, a feeling of both pity and fear. She was not like Chalciope, nor like Absyrtus. In a way, she resembled both of them, but had something extra which made her very different from either. This 'something' was in her hands, which lay calmly on her knees, and the moment Æëtes noticed them he averted his eyes, because their unnatural calm and self-sufficiency alarmed him.

It was not long after this that Phrixos's sons disappeared. First, the cook came rushing in to see the king, and turning away his face, said insistently: 'Punish me, punish me.'

'But I need to know what to punish you for,' Æëtes retorted, although he felt instinctively warned that he shouldn't ask, for he would hear nothing good. He waved his arm at the cook and said, 'Go away.' The cook slipped away without a sound.

'I hope that's the last I hear of it,' thought Æëtes.

But no sooner had the cook left than the harbour-master entered, bowed to the king and with military brevity and clarity reported, 'There's a yacht missing from our port.' Æëtes said nothing. He went on: 'It was an old ship, it needed recaulking, but I thought it my duty to report it.'

'Perhaps the waves swept it away,' Æëtes tried to avoid the truth of the matter.

The harbour-master felt insulted. A seasoned sailor to his bones, all he needed was to lose a ship to the waves.

'For the last two weeks the sea's been as calm as a bowl of porridge, there could be cobwebs between it and the shore. Thank the gods, I can still tell the difference between a rope that's broken and a rope that's been cut,' the harbour-master declared and, for some reason, like the cook, he turned his face away.

'So much the worse for you,' Æëtes muttered, his hand indicating that he wished to be alone, meaning 'You and your ship can go to hell.'

When the stableman found out that the pantry and the port had been burgled, then he rushed to the stables and counted the horses: he found they were all there, with their heads in their nose-bags eagerly munching their oats. They lifted their heads only for a moment, looking round with surprise at the stableman. Overjoyed, the stableman ran to see the king and reported than everything in the stables was in order, not one of the king's horses — indeed not a single grain of oats — was missing. Æëtes then burst into a rage, his eyes popping and his hair and beard dishevelled; he smashed whatever was to hand against the wall and had the stupid stableman spread-eagled on four stakes in the central courtyard like a drying hide, and lashed from head to toe with leather thongs as thick as a snake: they hissed through the air like a snake. 'I can't take any more, forgive me,' bellowed the stableman.

By now the flight of Phrixos's sons had been discovered, but the news didn't surprise Æëtes: he was expecting it and he suddenly calmed down, because his expectations had been realised. Only he told his distressed wife and daughter, 'They haven't vanished, they've run away.'

Phrixos's sons' escape gave rise to a lot of agitation and gossip in the city. People gathered round the Greek's source for unending discussions and arguments. Everyone disapproved of Æëtes's grandsons. Nor, of course, did they forget Phrixos. The saying is, nothing about the dead except good things, but the living are especially fond of talking about the dead and don't leave out the bad things. This happened now. The story of Phrixos's strange appearance and his equally strange adventures, once believed by everyone without protest, now appeared in a different light, covered in a fog of suspicion and, after so long a time people found it hard to believe what they had once seen with their own eyes. 'Tell us what happened,' they ordered Bedia, dragging him out, still wearing the rope round his neck, to tell them the same old story for the thousandth time. 'When we went out to sea, may it have mercy on us, there was something bobbing on the water, not a fish, not a boat, but like rags thrown overboard I thought, but how could rags stay afloat so long, I wondered…' Bedia said.

Something unusual only had to happen in Vani for the sea to take instant advantage and retreat further. Bedia was well aware of this and that was why he had recently measured again the distance between the boat station and the sea. The sea had retreated this time, too, and Bedia, with cause for reflection, lengthened his rope, but said nothing for the time being. In any case people were, he thought, agitated, and he wound the rope round his neck and wore it like a strait-jacket. In fact, as soon as he felt the rough hair of the rope touch his skin, he became calm.

The flight of his grandsons reminded Æëtes of his rope of thought. This time even he could not resist the temptation and went down the bottomless well again. He could swear by his life that not a sound could be heard from the well. Æëtes was initially relieved, wondering if they'd all been killed, but when his eyes got used to the darkness, he couldn't help being afraid: the well's inhabitants were smiling as they watched Æëtes dangling on the rope of thought. They seemed to have noticed his fear, because they were jostling each other and exchanging meaningful glances. But they didn't utter a sound. Æëtes hung there for some time. The inhabitants of the well had obviously secretly agreed not to talk to him, but how could Æëtes go back up without exchanging a word?

'Are you going to say something?' Æëtes called out to the well.

'Say something,' echoed the well.

'You're good sons and daughters,' Æëtes began, and, to his surprise, his voice was trembling. Æëtes coughed. The well laughed. 'You're good sons and daughters' Æëtes went on, 'but as for me, I can't take this throne with me… What use is a throne if the man who gets on it is no use to the country? Shame, shame and shame again on that throne and the person sitting on it. I need this throne for the good of the country. Now look at the state the country was in when you left it to me!' Æëtes let one hand slip from the rope and wiped his face clean of the sweat which his agitation had caused. 'You have to do a man justice. Nowadays not a crow can fly over us or an ant crawl about for fear of me. We're recognized as a country, people have pride, they walk about with expressions to gladden your heart.' Æëtes said, waiting for them to respond, but when the well stayed silent, he laughed and continued: 'When people catch sight of each other, they don't lay hands on one another, a good life has made people good. You can't just shake off everything, as if it were a dinner you'd had and forgotten. Anyway, what does it matter that we've quarrelled? Peace and quarrels are like brothers and sisters, they have the same mother, and they're lame without one another. Together they're beautiful. Am I right?' Æëtes again questioned the well, but his question now dropped like a stone. Æëtes didn't know what else to say, how to tackle the inhabitants of the well who were made stronger and more frightening by their silence and indifference.

'The country will perish, people!' Æëtes bellowed to the well, because he sensed that his hands were losing their strength and he couldn't hang on much longer, dangling on the rope of thought.

Then the dark damp depths of the well began roaring, shrieking, jangling and shrieking. 'Let it perish, let it perish, and we'll be avenged on you!' shouted the well's inhabitants in general discord.

Æëtes spat down the well and clambered up. That moment Chalciope entered the hall. She was in mourning, her hair was combed up and piled on the crown of her head like a sheaf of wheat. She was holding an over-ripe melon, which was dripping juice.

'You know I don't eat melon,' Æëtes told her, but took it all the same to avoid hurting his elder daughter's feelings.

Chalciope was badly shaken by her sons' disappearance, which she hadn't expected, although one glance should have warned her, because they were Phrixos's offspring and Phrixos had probably passed on his poison to them before he finally managed to escape his wife's clutches. But Chalciope had other ideas. While she had the four boys by her side she didn't consider Phrixos entirely lost, because he was part of those four boys and in each of the boy's eyes or movements something remained which moved Chalciope's heart. Now that they had made their escape, they had eluded Chalciope too, as if there was really no place for anyone, either husband or sons, other than her in this enclosure which she had made with her own faith, pride and love: Chalciope had spent so much time fencing in this area, and with such devotion and enthusiasm, that if anyone had broken just a single stake in this fence she would have scratched out their eyes. But her husband and sons had broken the stakes, or rather dug under them like a herd of pigs, in order to break out, as if the ground outside the fence was better, easier to root about in and better-tasting. That's why Chalciope's heart was on fire: not so much because she was perturbed by her son's flight, which would have been more natural, but she felt insulted and angered, like a trader by the stupidity of a customer who has chosen someone else's inferior wares in preference to his good wares. She instantly remembered those sleepless and endlessly long nights when she gritted her teeth in her deserted bed, as harsh, remorseless and unfeeling as death, because she was then longing for her husband to die and was deeply convinced that only her husband's death would save her from shame and humiliation. She was driven mad just by thinking about her husband no longer wanting her, avoiding her, standing aside and, instead of himself, putting in his wife's bed an insulting patience. Thank God, her dream, which had pained and shamed her like a physical defect, had come true. But if Phrixos hadn't died, if the gods hadn't heard Chalciope's prayers and pleas, then she would have died, because she could have borne such a life: the anger would have been enough to kill her. Yet it turned out that her husband's death was not enough. He was nicely wrapped up in a bull's hide, the breeze cradled him, birds perched on him, in spring so many flowers were scattered around him that he was no longer visible from afar; but he had left poisonous seeds on earth and now the seeds were about to disgrace her and make a laughing stock of her. No, she was not the sort of woman to be laughed at or to sob away from others' hearing and swallow the unpalatable tears of an abandoned wife and despised mother.

Chalciope now bitterly regretted choosing Phrixos as a husband, first choosing and then falling in love, for she believed she loved him, because she wanted to and therefore at the time overlooked, failed to notice or foresee what existed anyway, independently of herself, and beyond the limits of her wishes or knowledge. It not only existed, but was stronger than Chalciope. But she did not think deeply about her belated insight; she was interested in the enchantment of the mistake, not its causes, which were deeply and secretly rooted in her impatience and lack of foresight.

People are mostly blind to their mistakes. But if they discover them, they feel just pleasure, and the misfortune that befalls them because of a mistake is halved: this is true of women, but especially of a woman like Chalciope who looks to her mistakes to justify her own paths and feelings. And so it happened. Realising her mistake brought Chalciope a lot. First of all, she was relieved of the unpleasant sensation, as far as her husband was concerned, of being in the wrong, because she had firmly believed that her ardent prayers and pleas had put Phrixos in that hide coffin covered in bird droppings. Now she could justify her hatred, which was attached to an invented love like a flower to a lifeless stalk. Moreover, discovering her error meant discovering her own personality, not just discovering, but valuing, and she was inspired by the fact that she was so indomitable and could grab with both hands life which had once let her down, but had not been able to break her or bow her proud neck. True, she had always had this personality, but it was not a personality until its peculiar features came to the surface, just as a mistake was not a mistake until Chalciope had discovered it. 'How much time I've wasted in vain!' she thought, feeling distressed that the mistake had lit up so much of her path all at once. The mistake illuminated, and had its own light and, like all luminaries, had the power to transform and stir up everything. However horrific, terrifying and destructive it might be, it left the being it had frightened an escape and a refuge. It helped to find the refuge where its victim could rush to, like a hunted animal to its hole. This refuge was the mind, in this case a woman's mind, Chalciope's, which had no intention of dropping its sword and shield and smiled, challenging life with the slogan, 'We'll fight on to the end.' Her mind was the only place where she could once again be in the right and beautiful, but neither being right nor being beautiful had any value as long as she was still in her 'hole', if only she knew about its existence. Like mineral ore, it had to be brought to the surface. It was with this in mind that she held an over-ripe melon and, a carefree, flirtatious and beautiful woman, approached her father, although she knew as well as anyone the black pitch seething and boiling over in his heart.

'It's rotted on the stalk and it's not edible,' said Æëtes, who automatically bent over to stop the melon juice falling on his chest, then changed hands and licked the sticky fingers of his free hand.

'I didn't bring it for eating,' Chalciope replied.

Æëtes fixes his eyes on his daughter, while she watched him with a smile, her hands on her hips, bending at the waist as only women of her breeding did. Æëtes suddenly realised that his daughter had outwitted him: she was standing there, hands on hips, thrusting the melon into her father's hand and preventing him from moving. Æëtes imagined how pitiful he must look and smiled, 'My elder daughter is as beautiful and sly as a goddess,' he thought to himself.

'I am rotting on the stalk like this melon,' said Chalciope.

'What are you saying, woman, you've got four marriageable sons, what stalk are you talking about?..' Æëtes said with genuine amazement.

'I have no husband and I have no sons,' said Chalciope in a singing voice, 'I'm as free as a maiden.'

Æëtes looked feebly around, not knowing what to do with the melon which was dripping juice over him. He couldn't be angry any more, as if he had no right to be while he had this soft, scented fruit in his hand.

'For heaven's sake, control yourself!' Æëtes pleaded with Chalciope, lowering his voice for some reason.

Æëtes generally found it hard to talk to women, especially his own daughters, and on such subjects. Chalciope was a mother of four, but Æëtes couldn't imagine a daughter of his getting pregnant like other women. 'It's hard, I know, but what can we do about it, that's how it's happened,' he muttered like a guilty child, avoiding his daughter's eye, as if it was nothing to do with him and he had been forced to listen to this conversation. 'I could kill my wife,' Æëtes thought angrily, because he was utterly convinced that this was women's business and only his wife's stupidity had forced Chalciope to come and complain to her father. He said aloud, 'Your husband's hanging from a tree, you've got sons to care for, don't let's make ourselves the country's laughing stock.'

'If I have sons, show me where any of them are!' Chalciope said, refusing to back down. Her voice failed and she put her fist to her lips.

Æëtes felt heartbroken: like an abandoned child, his daughter's misery clambered onto his knees and he couldn't help freezing, lest he hurt the child with any careless rough movement. Suddenly he felt that his daughter was fleeing from a fire and, if she was still smiling, it was because of her royal pride and resilience. Æëtes put the melon on the floor and wiped his sticky hands on his thighs.

'They'll turn up, child, what else…' he said in an affectionate but cracked voice.

Chalciope smiled at him again, with her usual coquettishness, as if she hadn't noticed the momentary flash of weakness in her father's voice and eyes, forcing him to remove his mask of contentment, to be open and boldly to put his hand on the sore point. She now found pretence hard to keep up, because her father had offered her sympathy instead of violence. She hurriedly told the king that she believed him, bowed to Æëtes and, swaying as she went, left the hall.

Æëtes had a prolonged search made for his grandsons, but there was not a trace of them at sea or on the ever-flowing river. They couldn't even find out if the sky or the earth had swallowed them up and only when nobody expected to see Phrixos's sons again did all four come home, alive and unharmed, of their own accord. The people of Vani had now said so much good and bad about the king's grandsons that they didn't know whether to be displeased or glad at their return. Everyone shrugged their shoulders. But the palace was out of its mind with joy. Again, Chalciope's peals of laughter sounded out, untrammelled, challenging, triumphant and therefore, perhaps, improper for a mother glad to see her lost sons. It seemed that Chalciope's laughter was tailored to this happy event, rather than provoked by it. So it sounded wrong and made people take notice: it lacked only the blindness of a newborn baby.

After seeing her mistake, she again became a prisoner of her own mind, or rather clung to its skirts, because she was sure that her mind was the only strong, severe protector, guaranteed against all weakness, which could restore her wasted time and well-fenced enclosure. Now she didn't care whether it was love of their mother which had brought back Phrixos's sons, or something else had made them act in this way. The point for her was that they were back.

However hard Chalciope pretended, she couldn't face the fate of a rejected woman, she couldn't bear to see sympathy in another woman's face, for it oppressed and demeaned her and, she thought, mocked her. Her sons' return meant her husband's, too; whatever he intended, he remained Chalciope's husband, at least in strangers' eyes. The main thing was that nobody should suspect that Phrixos had tried to run away from

Chalciope, that he had died before his time because he could see no other way of getting out of the clutches of a wife he no longer loved.

Even dead, Phrixos was dangerous, and could fight Chalciope. His memory rested on four solid pillars, the love and loyalty of four men, which Phrixos had ensured all the more by his premature death. At times Chalciope actually thought that Phrixos had not died, but had split into four, to make it harder for her to watch and control him. In fact, which of them should she chase after? Either she had to leave all four to do as they liked, or she herself had to split into four. But there was another way out on which she could rely: somehow she could win over her sons or quadruple husband, become their ally, move heaven and earth for them, even flatter her own children, so long as everyone had the impression that she was in the know. If they intended to run away again, then they would take her with them and not abandon her so shamefully. A mother was entitled to do that, wasn't she? Really, after the umbilical cord is cut, no child belongs to its parent, just as a ship, once it weighs anchor, no longer belongs to the land. But aren't children obliged as long as they live to protect their mother's name and not let it be sullied? She asked for no more than that, but this seemed a lot even to her: when she looked at the four boys together, all sun-tanned, muscular and dishevelled, she found it hard to believe that these four men, coarsened and tempered by risks they had taken, were her sons.

In those two months Phrixos's sons had become men, they were more insolent and challenging, as if it was the fault of anyone they encountered that they had come home with their tails between their legs, that they had failed to carry out the first plan they had independently conceived. They were taciturn. 'Don't get carried away, we've only come back for a while,' they snarled at everyone, and even kindliness annoyed them, like wolf cubs forcibly dragged out of their den, because they were frightened of being laughed at, of someone considering their firm, masculine decisiveness to be childish silliness.

Phrixos's sons sensed in the grove of the deceased that, like their father, they were losing a fabulous country which they knew about from him, losing it for a long time, if not for ever, because now, after Phrixos had died, Æëtes was less likely to let his grandsons leave for a foreign land which might very well not even exist. Perhaps it was nothing more than the fruit of his son-in-law's morbid imagination, but they had now tasted this fruit and caught their father's disease. It didn't matter now whether this land existed or not, they were still going, hoping for the best, relying on just the sea and their oars. And if they ended up empty-handed, if this fabulously beautiful land and their royal origin turned out to be a fabrication, it would still be a relief to them that they had travelled the route which their father's dreams had roamed. Maybe Phrixos really had imagined it all, had invented and then bequeathed this invented country to his children, because that was all he could do or think of. But as well as an 'invented country', hadn't he had instilled hope in his children? Hope is a possession! They lived more boldly, they wouldn't let anyone get them down: they had 'somewhere to go'. But it all ended the opposite of what was intended. He had deprived his sons of peace of mind with this 'somewhere to go', for if a man thinks he has somewhere to go, he is certain to go there, since anyone would rather be where they are not. Naturally, Phrixos's sons left, preferring the imaginary to the real: they left without a thought the home where they had been born and raised. What Phrixos's sons then knew was that their grandfather's house was their only real home, which no other home could ever replace; the smell of the walls of their grandfather's house, over time, imperceptibly but persistently permeated their pores, wrinkles and souls, and had crystallized as an indelible memory from their very first step, word, tear or smile, their first fright or joy, just as honey crystallizes an insect, flower pollen or a splinter in its golden depths.

What happened to them here could never have happened in any other house: it would come back as a memory, a bitterly depressing one, if they ever decided not to return. But Phrixos's sons could not yet know this, they had the instinct, like newly fledged chicks, that the time had come for them to fly off and, excited by this feeling, they blindly obeyed the dream they had inherited from their father, a dream that was driving them with a mother-bird's ruthlessness from the nest. It was instinct that made a mother-bird act to stop grown-up heavy fledglings from upsetting the nest and to teach them to fly in good time if they wanted to live. Are human beings all that different from birds or any other animal you care to name? They are governed by instinct, but they need a mind to evaluate a life which is utterly impossible to retrieve, repeat or put right.

Phrixos's sons' escape had ended in failure, but they had digested the bitterness of failure, undergone the ups and downs of homecoming and, above all, learnt what they most needed to know: the other land existed. True, this time they hadn't managed to get to this other land but they now knew for certain that their father had told the truth and, that being so, they too were in the right. This truth justified their actions and this may be why they held their heads so defiantly high instead of falling at their grandfather's feet and apologizing to their mother for the distress and anxiety they had caused. The joy of people they met increased their boldness, dispersed any feeling of wrongdoing, and not one of them had any doubt that their crime was limited to the damage done by their futile flight to their grandfather's port and pantry. They were sincere when they told their grandfather that they would pay for every single thing as soon as they got their father's inheritance: they took pride in being able to say so. 'Off with you, you villains,' said Æëtes, unable to be angry, smiling all the time, his eyes gleaming with joy. The grandsons felt their grandfather's joy, which kept his tempestuous nature firmly in control, and this, of course, only made them bolder and more arrogant.

'There's no problem jumping out of here, look how low the wall is,' said Melas, pointing at the window.

The brothers looked out. The city's battlements, lizard-coloured, dried and hardened by the sun, could be seen from the window. The brothers used to compete by jumping from them.

'Yes,' said Æëtes, his lips parted in a smile, 'but you should have asked before you just got up and went.'

'We knew you, that's why we didn't,' Phrixos's sons replied, almost as one. Æëtes understood perfectly that his grandsons were saying they didn't trust him. But he wasn't, or rather refused to be angry: a wave of joy swept over him, his smile gradually lost its warmth and tenderness.

'If your ship was wrecked, how did you get back? Or did you fly here like your father?' Æëtes asked with a touch of venom, because his joy had now gone and he had his grandchildren close by.

Phrixos's sons turned surly; Chalciope gave Æëtes a worried look.

'If I didn't respect your mother, I'd... Look at me!' Æëtes suddenly yelled at Melas who was looking out of the window again, examining the courtyard and walls with the casualness of a guest.

The brothers' faces flushed as they exchanged glances. Now Æëtes was angry, as if he realised for the first time that these four milksops had made him the topic of common gossip, but what a happy grandfather, father and king he would be if this was the end of it all. But worse shame and misfortune was awaiting him, and bringing about this misfortune had been entrusted by fate and providence to his grandsons.

In the reed-beds of the ever-flowing river there was already anchored a twelve-oared Greek ship. From his grandson's evasive and vague remarks, he knew that this ship had rescued them from shipwreck; otherwise the fish would have long ago sated themselves on their flesh. So Æëtes was obliged to a ship that had invaded his country without permission. But he wanted to pay his debt. 'It's amazing,' Æëtes thought, 'that these sons of bitches knew they would be rescuing my grandsons.' In fact, it was hard to imagine setting off on such a journey just for that purpose. It now had to be established whether this ship knew at the start why it was sailing to Colchis, or whether such a plan arose after rescuing the grandsons of the king of Colchis. Perhaps they had just heard of the existence of the golden ram from Æëtes's grandsons. Perhaps the lads had promised the golden ram as a reward to their rescuers, because, after nearly drowning and being terrified, they couldn't think of anything better. True, his grandsons insisted stubbornly that the captain of this ship was a relative of their father, that he intended to take back the throne for its lawful owner and had come to ask for Æëtes's help, but countless different thoughts were mingling in Æëtes's head, mercilessly devouring each other, like hungry fish. Quite possibly, these Greeks were ordinary pirates, and they had simply captured, not rescued his grandsons, then taken fright and were now asking for a ransom, albeit in a roundabout way, so that nobody would suspect them of piracy. If that turned out to be true, their ship was not going to last much longer. But if his grandsons were telling the truth, it would really be unimaginably ungrateful and harsh on Æëtes's part if he summarily burned the ship and its captain. On the contrary, royal dignity obliged him to receive the people who had rescued his grandsons and shower them with appropriate gifts. But suppose they asked for the ram's fleece? Phrixos's sons had an answer ready, but it was all hard to believe. If he was to believe his grandsons, their father's ghost had travelled to his homeland and pestered his kinsfolk, 'If you want me to give you rest and cleanse you of sin, then, like it or not, you have to bring back the fleece of the sheep which helped me escape from your knife.' This is what Phrixos's sons said, swearing it was true, but the stench of doubt persisted in Æëtes's flared nostrils. Too many lucky coincidences had occurred: trusting and distrusting seemed equally ridiculous. Why then should his grandsons be rescued by the very ship that had set off for Colchis and which at great cost found a reliable guide and mediator? Why then should a relative of the rescued turn out to be the rescuer, if the gods did not themselves will it, or could the imagination of a frightened child or a greedy pirate think of nothing better? 'If they're good people,' thought Æëtes, 'why are they hiding in the reed-bed, after all my port is open to all.'

Æëtes listened carefully to everything, then raised his head, noisily sniffed the air like a horse, and said, 'There's a smell of treason in my palace.' Yet he agreed to receive the foreigner and, as his grandsons asked, 'just hear him out'. By now Æëtes himself was interested in seeing this foreigner: if he didn't order him and his underlings to be pulled like kittens out of the twelve-oared ship, that was only to avoid an unpleasant misunderstanding if the stranger really turned out to be a relative of his son-in-law.

Meanwhile, on the twelve-oared ship they were impatiently waiting for Phrixos's sons to return, or rather they were all in a state of vague, nameless, unspecified waiting.

The return of Phrixos's sons might well decide their fate. The sons might end up as guides to Æëtes's men and reveal their hiding place, and then… Then they would be beyond help, they would have to express their gratitude and kiss the earth at Æëtes's feet three times if he let them return home. The decision they had taken in their own country no longer seemed so right or so easy to carry out. The saying goes, measure your feet before you order the boots. But their feet turned out to be too big for the boots they had ordered without proper measuring. And the cobbler either has to throw away what he's made or somehow appease the angry customer and keep him happy until he's made another pair to fit. There was no point arguing and quarrelling, the customer was in the right, and in a strong position, too. Making a run for it wouldn't help: where would they run to, who would compensate them for the time wasted, the material used, their worn-out eyesight and the awl punctures on their fingers? Thus the twelve-oared ship waited in the reed-beds of the ever-flowing river. The waiting was unbearable. The alien surroundings wrapped everything — their plans, too — in a haze of secrecy and unattainability. Perhaps it was the hidden plan which induced a feeling of wrongdoing, in turn arousing and aggravating their fear and caution. They were so far from home and had no hope of getting help. And the Colchian ships were at least as fast as their twelve-oared ship. So luck and a lucky chance would decide everything, and they waited.

They spent the first night on their thoroughly camouflaged ship sleeping, or rather staying awake until dawn, because now, when they were just a step away from their goal, everything got back its real colour and smell. The pleasure of travelling to an unknown land and the desire to experience danger had vanished without trace. After breaking in like thieves into Æëtes's country, they began to think bitter thoughts. The alien surroundings, the pitch-dark night and the constant croaking of frogs made it impossible to rest. Horrific ghosts prowled all round, rustled in the undergrowth, flashed their red eyes, whispered, clattered about, wailing and guffawing. Even the usual splash of the water and rustling of the reeds aroused horror in them. They didn't dare light a fire that night.

Nobody even undid his sandal laces, as if they had to be ready to flee. They sat there, as if sulking, not knowing what awaited them. If only it could all be over soon, especially the torment and agony of waiting, the only reality that connected them to the outside world.

'What came over me to trust them and let them go?' Jason agonized. He sat on the deck, his arms around his calves and his chin resting on his bare knees. From a distance you might have thought he was asleep, but something only had to rustle for him to raise his head and stare into the darkness, like a dog waiting for its master. Jason had deliberately acted as he had, releasing all four, because he didn't dare keep a hostage. His 'relatives' had told him so much about Æëtes's anger that they had given even this fearless fortune-hunter food for thought. True, before he had departed, he had been told a lot of things and had asked a lot of things about the king of Colchis, but there, where he was safe, it was different. He had liked, even taken pride in setting off to meet such an angry and manly king. At home, where you have only friends around you and a chalice full of wine in your hand, it's a pleasure to talk about a lion, especially a lion whose viciousness and ruthlessness is legendary and the talk of the whole country, but you have to be a fool if this feeling still persists when the smell of the lion's den hits your nose. Jason didn't rely on force, nor could he. Only by underhand cunning could he get hold of that lousy ram's fleece on which the lion lay, its yellow eyes just now and again giving a lazy, appropriately lordly glance at a foreign visitor. Jason should have worn a sheepskin, bowed low to the lion and timidly bleated out his plea, then perhaps he might have won over this wrathful king, who may already have known about his uninvited guest and, perhaps, the evil plans he was harbouring. But Jason had no alternative: if he had kept any of the grandsons hostage he might have enraged Æëtes more. Jason's request would have dressed him in a pirate's sheepskin. Jason was a king, the lawful heir to an unlawfully stolen throne and he had come to see another king in order to ask for help. In doing so, he conceded Æëtes' superior status and expressed unbounded trust in his royal power and nobility. Wasn't a king, especially one as powerful as Æëtes, obliged to support another king, especially one as weak as Jason, if the latter's name and reputation were being unjustly sullied and if that name and reputation could be restored by just one lousy fleece, which for Æëtes, so rich in gold, really was nothing more than a lousy fleece? 'Well, think about it, if I didn't believe in your kindness and generosity, would I set off on such a journey into the unknown, unless I was mad?' Jason prepared to say to Æëtes, but he was displeased: the more he polished, softened and sweetened the words, the more false and unnatural they seemed. He was sure that, if he could have a calm conversation with the king, the latter would detect his cunning and stop him before he finished, or would tear out the truth together with his tongue. Fate was clearly preparing a great test for Jason. He had to see it through, remain fearless, or else immediately dive into the water without his men noticing or understanding and swim off breast-stroke until he was well away, while he had the strength, until he was safe. Suddenly Jason had such a desire to get away that he could barely stop himself diving into the water like a frog. To free himself of the temptation, he bent forward, got onto all fours on the wet planks and called in a whisper into the darkness enveloping the ship and hiding his men, 'Are you asleep, brothers?' The sound of his whispering in the dark startled them, as if a washed-out sand dune had fallen onto them. Ragged shreds of darkness crept towards Jason, like beetles from a smashed nest. The captain's whisper reawoke the fear which had abated and they all rushed automatically to the place where the unpleasant whisper seemed to come from; it was as if a leak had appeared in the ship and water was pouring in to sink them.

'Brothers!' Jason whispered again.

Then he coughed into his fist and, for some reason, looked all round.

They then saw a light; an unsteady yellow patch was leaping about like a hunted animal in the thick undergrowth, moving among the centuries-old trees, slithering like snakes over the twisted roots, coming closer every moment, but unable to stay in one place for any time: the whole land, as if covered in grease, was slipping from under its feet.

Phrixos's sons were coming with the light. 'It's us!' they called out to the ship from a distance, as if sensing how unbearable it was for those on board to watch a leaping, dazzling light, until they realised what the light was bringing and concealing. Now the faces of those on board were visible in the light, and Argus was so shaken by seeing so many scared faces that he threw his torch into the water. The flame went out with a sizzle, sending a smell of burning pine into the air.

That morning Jason and Phrixos's sons set off together for Æëtes's palace. Daybreak had given everyone more courage. Once seen, the land seemed less frightening that they had imagined when it was almost erased and transformed by the darkness. The nightmares, too, vanished, as if morning had licked the land clean, as a snake licks a stone on which it leaves its poison. The news brought by Phrixos's sons somewhat calmed the forebodings that beset everyone. Æëtes had agreed to receive the foreign guest, which meant, if nothing else, that their lives were safe.

Once their fears were assuaged, they were now in a mocking mood. 'The price for this night has gone up: you'll have to add your grandfather's skin to the sheep's, or I won't take you to the homeland,' Jason told Phrixos's sons, who smiled with delight as they watched their fellow Greeks roaring with laughter at the captain's joke.

Daylight came with agonizing slowness, but nothing could stop it from emerging out of the boundless depths to be born. They were still all up to their waists in milky fog. Only the prow and mast of the twelve-oared ship broke through the mist. Somewhere a bird whistled at them and this feeble, almost insignificant sound was more proof that the earth existed. Everyone paid heed to the bird, twisting their necks as if the bird could be seen, as if nothing bad could happen while the bird whistled. Then the earth, unevenly broken up by the mist's creeping hands, came into view. The mist extracted itself from the endless tangle of shrubs and trees, like a mother slipping away from her barely sleeping child, while the child, before it falls asleep, hangs on with both hands to its mother's lapels and headscarf. Seeing the trees and earth made everyone rejoice, as if their surroundings had become familiar, as if they had now returned home. Here too, the earth was the earth, with the same furrowed face and movingly numbed by the pain of eternally giving birth.

Jason stood on the ship's railings, lifted his tunic skirts and leapt ashore. 'Hey-y-y!' the crew shouted at the sight of their captain's bronze thighs. 'That's how we do it,' Jason called out, pulling out one foot after the other, ankle-deep in the soft, boggy ground. Then he looked proudly back at his men who were laughing out loud at his nimbleness. He was the captain and never missed a chance to show off in front of his men.

'While I'm away, collect raspberries and blackberries so you don't die of hunger,' Jason called to the ship and with exaggerated casualness took his first step in this country, so foreign and fateful for him.

The bird kept whistling, as though encouraged by seeing the land emerge from the mist. The broad luscious leaves dripped juice, like a full udder dripping milk. The sharp smell of birth and renewal spread over the whole country. The snails left slimy trails that shone on the rocks. Tiny shells buried in the sand crunched underfoot. The sand-coloured water of the ever-flowing river, every now and again, as if by accident, would lap against the twelve-oared ship, leaving a palm-like imprint on its convex flanks. The constant breeze over the river bent the reeds as if someone had just lain on them. The earth gave a sigh and wafted a smell of rotten fungus and tinder to the men who were shivering in the morning cold, as they stood on the ship's railing waving at their captain who was walking so casually into the unknown.

Jason was holding an olive branch. As they approached the palace, he ran forward and sat on the envoy's stone. At this time Medea was still in her room, getting ready to go and see Chalciope. She had no forebodings, nothing perturbed her, although Jason's heart, as he sat on the envoy's stone, was pounding. Phrixos's sons stood back, as if they had caught Jason's hidden anxiety; because they had all come together to their grandfather's palace, they too felt they were foreigners. The guards soon noticed the stranger sitting on the envoy's stone, and when they saw Phrixos's sons nearby, they quickly realised who the stranger must be.

By now the whole palace was talking about the twelve-oared ship which had brought back Phrixos's lost sons. Æëtes ordered the guests to be given a proper reception. He emphasized the word 'guests' because he already considered his grandchildren 'foreigners', too; he behaved as if he hadn't seen them before. Jason, pallid, but proudly erect, entered smiling ahead of Phrixos's sons. Medea had not yet opened the door of her room when her maids rushed down the corridor and her ears couldn't help catching a tiny, almost meaningless fragment of their conversation, like a fence tearing off the edge of a headscarf. Medea's mind seemed not to take in, not to pay any attention to the word or words she chanced to overhear. But she had still, apparently, managed to catch something, for shortly afterwards, seeing the stranger approach the palace, she instantly recalled with full clarity the oddly twittering voices of her maids as they rushed down the corridor. For some reason only now, on seeing the stranger, did it all make definite sense. Medea saw the edge of the headscarf caught on the fence, fluttering helplessly in the wind, like a one-winged creature no longer able to fly. The whole palace had assembled in the courtyard and Medea was afraid she might cry out. But fortunately everyone's attention was fixed on the foreign guest.

When Chalciope saw her sons, it pained her heart that they seemed so insignificant next to the enchanting guest. They walked up as if they themselves were foreigners, and there was not a trace left of yesterday's self-assurance; their eyes moved from side to side as if this was the first time they had been in their grandfather's palace. Chalciope felt that her sons were looking for her, and she automatically stepped forward. The sons were glad to see their mother, smiled at her awkwardly, which pained her heart still more. The real foreigner, however, behaved proudly, slapping the olive branch against his shin, smiling enchantingly. Chalciope was at first confused, then angry, then heartbroken, because this was the first time in her life that she had sensed so painfully, with a hatred bordering on pleasure, a man's attraction, now hidden behind an ingenuous smile and, above all, making her own sons seem underlings, colourless, diminished. Chalciope would rather the ground opened under her feet than see her sons like this. She already knew whom they were emulating, what the source was of their self-assurance yesterday, their rudeness and coarseness that both astounded and enthralled her. 'So this is what my rival must be like,' Chalciope thought, herself amazed that she was putting up with this creature so calmly, so submissively, with such compliant weakness, perhaps because she had never thought that her rival would be a man. Now, calmed by the unexpected, she refused to rebel against what she had been born for, what she instinctively gravitated to, trusted and even submitted to without saying a word.

Medea was overcome by a feeling that her whole body was slumped and emptied, as if she had fainted and was slowly, gradually coming round from weakness and non-existence. This morbid sensation was made worse by everybody smiling. Absyrtus laid a careful hand on her, as if taking her pulse. The man who had been the hero of her dream was, however, slapping his shin with the olive branch; Medea could hear only the swish of the branch and her heart was racing to bursting point, for she couldn't understand and couldn't have grasped why he didn't come up and put his hand on her shoulder, as if it were his property. Medea was, after all, his property. Everyone knew that, probably: that's why they were smiling at her. They knew what the foreigner had come to ask for and what he had discussed with Æëtes. But what was there to discuss, what could talking alter, when the gods had already decided her fate?

Medea could only hear the swish of the branch and see the stranger's reddened shin — not so much see as sense the stranger's shin reddening as it was being whipped by the branch. Then she caught the smell of fire and saw an ox, which had its throat cut, rolling its eyes. Now she heard the butcher's voice as he said something while he dried his hands, red from washing in cold water. The butcher smiled at her, took off his apron and covered up the ox's bloodstained head with it. The edge of the apron had fallen into a pool of sticky blood and soaked it up on the spot. Medea didn't know when he had come, or what he was doing here; she couldn't even understand what the butcher was saying to her, but smiled at him like a deaf-mute apologizing first for everything and agreeing to everything. 'Is this the man I dreamt of?' Medea worried, unable to understand where the stranger had disappeared to, why she couldn't hear the swish of the olive branch any more, and why she couldn't see the reddened skin of his shin. When she was climbing the stairs, one slave girl called to another, 'Our boys are having a bath.' Medea felt weak at the knees. The stranger really had come, he was here, within the walls of her father's palace.

While Jason and Phrixos's sons were shrieking with pleasure and splashing about in the guests' bathroom, Æëtes was walking about in the courtyard supervising the banquet preparations personally.

'You ought to take a rest for a while,' the queen called to him from the top of the steps.

'What nonsense, woman, this is no time for resting, my grandsons have come for a visit,' he replied sullenly and went off to the wine cellar.

It was dark in the cellar. A smell of wet earth and wine embraced him like an expectant woman and clung unpleasantly to his lips. Æëtes wiped his lips. By the amphora ghost-like figures were bustling: they froze and two pairs of eyes stared at Æëtes from below. 'How can you see in this darkness?' said Æëtes. 'We're used to it,' the ghosts replied, and Æëtes heard the wine being poured from the ladle into a pitcher. Then he saw a bundle of yellow saffron on the wall and thought, 'It's not that dark here.' 'Would you like to try some?' said the ghosts. Æëtes took the wet ladle in the darkness and lifted it to his lips. He drank very slowly. When he had drained the ladle, he saw again a yellow bundle of saffron hanging from the ceiling. 'It's getting light,' he thought for some reason and laughed at his own silly thought, handed back the ladle to the darkness and came out of the cellar. He seemed to bring darkness with him from the cellar, for it was already evening. Æëtes crossed the courtyard, left through the back gate in thc wall and went up the steps. Suddenly he was covered in sweat and his heart began to race. As he walked he wondered, 'What's wrong with me?' A narrow, single-file path wound up, twisting through the bushes, as if it was hiding from him. Æëtes couldn't help quickening his pace, as if trying to catch the path's tail before it succeeded in finally becoming invisible in the bushes.

Suddenly, from nowhere, a solitary pointed star fell from the sky and hit Æëtes between the eyes. It made sparks fly from his eyes and blinded him for a time. Cold sweat was now streaming from his face. His body shuddered unpleasantly. The star that had just struck him between the eyes was back in the sky, twinkling as if it, too, was getting its breath back. Æëtes, without thinking, covered his face with his hand. A hobbled horse was crunching the grass under the fig trees. Suddenly he clearly sensed the smell of the horse and the dry grass and had a strong, heart-rending desire to mount the horse. The breeze brought someone's relaxed voice from afar, 'Watch out you don't let it burn!' 'I'm dying,' thought Æëtes and suddenly felt relief, as if the terror of death was only a terror of admitting it. Æëtes felt as if not just he but the entire country was dying, including the star that was staring fixedly at him. And Æëtes couldn't understand what the star wanted, why it stared at him. 'Is it death, perhaps?' he thought again. The man's voice that had said 'Don't you let it burn', was dying, too: it was his parting word to somebody, and he went off where he wanted to go; the fig trees and the horse sheltering under them with the buzzing mosquitoes in the dark were also dying. 'Everything's dying,' Æëtes concluded, 'Do you know now why you're dying?' he asked himself, and a bitter smile distorted his face. 'I know,' he answered the question, 'because… because I don't want to die.'

Æëtes stumbled and automatically leant against the rocks that were lying nearby. The rock was warm, like an animal fast asleep, it even seemed to have a pulse.

The next day all Vani was talking about Æëtes's foreign guest. The people were not yet well informed on the subject and, as always happens at such times, they confused truth with lies, rumours and inventions. Some said that the Greek had asked Æëtes for his throne, others — the contrary: he had lost his throne and had come to ask for Æëtes's help, he was a relative of Phrixos and Æëtes was his only close kinsman. Others said that the throne was nothing to do with it, that he had come to ask for a daughter, as had Phrixos, so as to be a kinsman of Æëtes. There was a little bit of truth in all this, but the truth was still quite different: Jason asked Æëtes for the ram's fleece and nothing else. That was it. At the same time, Jason had told his life story to Æëtes and given his reason for coming here in the form of a fairy tale, no doubt thinking that it would thus be easier to understand.

'Once upon a time,' Jason began, 'there was a city called Iolcos. The king of this city had a stepbrother: they had the same mother, but different fathers. The stepbrother decided he wanted to reign himself, and one fine day he seized the throne and overthrew the lawful king. You yourself will be only too aware that two kings cannot share one throne, just as two women,' (Jason smiled), 'cannot share a kitchen. The poor ex-king was beggared, but what could he do, he had no help from above. But the gods, it seems, hadn't entirely abandoned the ex-king: they gave him a son.' (Jason put his hand on his heart and smiled again, as if to say that he was that son.) The father was afraid that his stepbrother would not spare the son either and hid the newborn baby with shepherds in the mountains. He spread a rumour among the people that he had a stillborn child and held a wake.' (Jason paused and looked at the people in the hall; they were all listening closely.) 'When the boy grew up,' Jason continued, and suddenly saw Medea, or rather Medea's hands, which she had laid on her knees and was looking at, as if reading a book. Jason stopped: his right foot, which he had put forward, twitched as if he was standing on a fallen animal and about to kill it. Suddenly he could hear the sea's roar, muffled, restrained, as if someone with a blanket over their head was murmuring or lamenting. 'When the boy grew up,' said Jason hurriedly, 'he decided to return to his city. He went to see the king and told him: "This is who I am, so give me my throne back." He was wearing only one sandal, but asking for a throne,' laughed Jason, but this time the laughter sounded forced, as he himself realised, before continuing, chastened: 'The king was aghast, wondering how this wretch had turned up, but he was clever and resorted to cunning. "I agree to give it up to my stepbrother's son," he said, "but I have a condition which you have to fulfil."' (Æëtes lifted his head and fixed his eye on Jason. Everyone sensed that the condition was the key to this fairy tale. Jason was anxious, but made an effort to control himself and enounce clearly every word of the condition.) 'The king told the boy, "I had a dream in which the ghost of Phrixos, your uncle and your father's cousin, appeared to me and asked me to get back the fleece of the ram which flew him to Colchis. I'm now too old and too weak to undertake such a task, but you're young, so go, bring it back, lay your uncle to rest and take away the sin from our race." What could a young man do: so off he went,' Jason ended his fairy tale and smiled again, disarmingly, naïvely.

'I've understood everything,' said Æëtes. 'A man is divided into two, one half is on the throne, the other is looking for it.'

'We don't want anything other than to leave here,' Argus replied.

Compared with his brothers, Argus acted more boldly, but it was still obvious how mortal pain each word cost him. 'This fleece belongs to my father; my father is this man's uncle. How can we refuse a relative of our father some lousy fleece?' said Argus, blushing to the ears. 'Lousy fleece' was Jason's expression and he couldn't help repeating it now.

The people of Vani claimed that Æëtes became so rabid that he said, 'If you weren't my guests at dinner, I'd cut out all your tongues, but for the time being, I'm forced to put up with it.' There was a grain of truth in this, for at one point Æëtes had decided to slaughter everyone at the dinner table, to tear the heads off his grandchildren as if they were little chickens, because all the talk they and their kinsman had concocted was choking him with rage.

Æëtes suddenly felt on his cheek the touch of a rough, dry lion's tongue and he lurched to one side. 'Could it still be alive?' Æëtes wondered and he asked, 'What do you want?' 'And what do you want?' the lion retorted, then yawned, licked its black nostrils with a red tongue as long as an arm, and continued: 'I'll deal with that lot later.'

The lion was clearly in a mood for a fight, it just needed a pretext. 'Should I set it on them?' Æëtes thought for a moment, and his eyes blazed so much that everyone froze. The queen warned him with a smile and Æëtes grabbed at that smile like a man who has been robbed grabs a belt, not knowing what he will do with it. 'No,' Æëtes whispered to the lion, 'I'll bide my time now: let's see if these lads are good for anything, the bird may not be worth the plucking.'

'You know best,' the lion growled and lay down on the withered grass of Æëtes's soul.

When Jason got back to the twelve-oared ship hidden in the marshes of the ever-flowing river, he said, 'Things are bad: instead of just giving me the ram's fleece, Æëtes is going to put me through an ordeal and oblige me to do something which not even a demon could do.' He added, 'I hope you don't have to take home just my bones.'

There was no point in hiding now: all Vani knew that they were there and what they planned, so that it was better to dock the twelve-oared ship openly on the bank. Jason's men slowly dipped their oars, thinking, 'They've probably got a man hiding behind every reed. A cloud of fear and uncertainty lay over the twelve-oared ship, which was more used to victory and merriment. The cloud took everyone under its indolent, slippery belly and drenched them from head to foot. Midges and mosquitoes swarmed. The frogs croaked even louder, drowning out every other sound.

At night the banks of the ever-flowing river were again covered in fog. An ash-coloured, sticky mass moved like some invertebrate monster among the willows, indiscriminately devouring everything in its path. The fog penetrated the body. The men lying on the deck huddled, so as to be close to one another if anything happened. Every now and again a little owl screeched, so unexpectedly and eerily that everyone's blood froze. But they could do nothing: screech owls are screech owls and at night they let the world know of their anger and pain. In the Greeks' country the owls screeched exactly the same way, but there it was different, and only a child would be frightened by a little owl's sudden screech, and only women would then curse the bird that was hiding in a hole in some rotten tree.

Jason was now sitting alone on the stern, his arms round his calves and his chin on his knees. 'If only I had a dog,' he was thinking. The large ship was filled with his loyal men, but he still felt lonely, because Æëtes had singled him out for the ordeal, and he was the only one who would be tested. But that was how it had to be, because his men had come on such a journey only for his sake. Yet he could in no way reconcile himself to the idea that he alone was in jeopardy. He had often been in life-and-death situations, but his stubborn nature had never accepted the idea of death. Jason could not believe that he, such a deft and strong, well-built and charismatic man, could die like anyone else. Thinking about death made him so perturbed and disoriented, he found imagining his own death so difficult, that he would rather believe an alluring falsehood outright and shut his eyes to the awful truth. He believed that the gods would make an exception for him and wouldn't let him leave the world of the living. Anyway, why should he leave when he felt so well here? This was his place and so he would do anything, crawl through the eye of a needle, because here, in this world, he wanted everything that others had or could have. True, as today, he had often been disappointed, but he had always come out victorious from the unpleasant sensations which disappointment brings. This was what he was now thinking about, seeking an escape, and his heart was full of anger at being alone. This time Æëtes had politely kicked him out, but it could all have ended worse. He still had the right to choose: he could leave as he had come, or he could accept Æëtes's challenge. What he had to decide concerned only him. His men had nothing to worry about: coming or going, they were free to roam about and have a good time. But he was after more than a good time and demanded more than having a full belly. He had been entrusted with a task for posterity. That was what the greatest of kings, King Minos, had told him, 'A task for posterity.' His men really had nothing to worry about: if Jason fulfilled Æëtes's conditions, which he very much doubted, they would all go home safe and sound. If he didn't, then they would return with a sack containing Jason's bones that Æëtes would probably put on board as a leaving present. Nobody was going to stick out their neck for a dead man; in fact, to while away a long journey, they might even start playing dice with his bones and remember their cheerful captain with gratitude for entertaining them even after his death. 'Ugh!' said Jason, mentally spitting and then cursing the living and the dead who had sent him here. The screech owl called again somewhere. Jason shuddered and now became really angry that he had not taken a dog on board a ship as large as this one.

Then he saw in front of him his uncle's age-wrinkled face, as crumbling and desiccated as vine bark, and he spat again. When his uncle found out that Jason, who had a claim to his throne, was setting off for Colchis, the old man became like a child with joy. What made that toothless old man so happy? The prospect of Jason's death, of course. Jason didn't know what his uncle knew: what his empty-headed nephew was getting himself into. 'That son of a dog knew,' said Jason bitterly, his teeth chattering with the cold. He would ascend the throne in any case after his uncle's death, but there was no likelihood of his uncle dying soon, nor had Jason the patience. In any case, King Minos had intervened and Jason did not dare to refuse the Supreme King, the patron and supporter of every claimant to a throne. 'If you want me to get you back your throne, then go to Colchis, have a good look round, explore it and find out the nests where our kinsfolk were born and the graves where they are buried. That's where your father's nephew, the heir to the throne of Beotia, is buried; his four fledglings are in the nest with their beaks gaping, waiting for food from their parents. You should know that for every Greek king feeding those four fledglings is a matter for posterity. And, as proof, grab and bring the fleece of the ram which flew your father's nephew out of here. The rest we'll discuss later,' Minos told Jason. Jason understood everything: Minos's task seemed so easy to him that he was even surprised why just for one lousy fleece (that's when he said 'lousy fleece') he would be put on the throne, but he had his wits about him and bit his tongue: Minos never spoke idly, nor let anyone else say more than was needed, although he only ever heard agreement.

Jason immediately ran to see his uncle, but the first thing he saw in the eyes of this truly decrepit old man was his own death, in fact undisguised joy at his probable death. Jason then decided not to spare his uncle and told him to his face, 'While you're still alive, I'll shake you like dust off this throne.' His uncle flung at Jason the bowl he drank milk from. He never drank anything but milk, which was probably why he wasn't going to die soon. Now Jason smiled as he remembered his uncle's frightened face: there were fatty drops of milk on his beard and moustache, as if his mother, fed up with his gluttony, had only just tugged her breast out of his mouth.

'Brothers!' Jason called out with a groan and looked over towards where he thought his men were. The ashen mist was swirling round in puffy clouds round the ship, as if raising smoke from a bonfire of rotten leaves. Jason was alone, and could see this loneliness, it was crouching like a faithful dog, in front of him. 'O-o-o-h' Jason howled like a dog at the darkness, listening to his own voice. His voice couldn't break through the thick wall of fog: it just stuck to it like a wet leaf. Nor did anyone on board the ship respond: they all seemed to be fast asleep after the previous sleepless night. This now made him despondent. 'Perhaps I should fall upon them and wipe out the lot of them,' Jason thought, although he knew full well that this was idle boasting, just to bolster himself, to ward off fear, the fruit of anger and envy: now he really felt envious of anyone who could calmly go to sleep. No, Jason was not such a fool as to attack Æëtes; he and his men were too few for that. And who would follow him, and would he let them, anyway? He knew from experience that baring a sword, like baring a woman, for no good reason was just shameful: it was disgracing oneself. And now Jason recalled Medea, or rather her hands, unnaturally calm and self-sufficient, beautiful and fearful at the same time. He remembered being lost for words in Æëtes's hall when he saw those hands. Then, when they were dining, Jason could see only Medea's hands. Nothing had moved him so much, neither Æëtes's splendid palace, nor Æëtes himself, his eyes blazing like a dragon's, nor Chalciope, who kept turning her head and pouring him wine personally, nor Absyrtus, the dragon's heir, who had nothing of his father in him and who talked a lot of nonsense, such as 'If you want to be happy, don't cause my sister any offence.' Jason couldn't understand from Absyrtus's mumblings why he should offend anyone. As it was, he was on tenterhooks, not knowing if he would succeed in leaving this palace alive.

Medea reminded Jason of somebody, but he couldn't think of whom; perhaps because now, in Æëtes's palace, he was thinking only about Medea; although he did manage to survey the women in his memory, none of them had anything in common with Medea. Now, crouching on the deck, lost in fog, his mind suddenly lit up. Medea was like the sea. Now he remembered that he constantly heard the sound of the sea when Medea was sitting in the hall. At the time he paid no attention to this sound: he wasn't surprised, he knew the sea was nearby, but as soon as he remembered Medea, he heard the roar of the sea again, heavy, restrained, almost eternally pacified and eternally reconciled with the banks in which nature had enclosed it. This sound was Medea's voice. The point about the sea is that it will never be pacified or reconciled by anything. It was simply recovering, letting its waves, scratched by the rocky shores, calm down so as once more to smash against the monotony and immobility. The sea was really roaring in Jason's ears when Medea sat with her head bowed between her father and the foreign guest and put her hands, palms open and upwards, on her knees, like… like a murder weapon which is put for all to see on the table during a trial. Of course, that's not what Jason was thinking, but he was oddly struck and disturbed by the sight of those hands, he became lost for words and his leg started to tremble as though he were standing on an animal to be slaughtered. 'There's someone who might help me,' Jason now thought. He might possibly appeal to Medea and even make her fall in love with him. Hadn't such things happened quite often? More often than you think. How many times Jason had been told, 'On such-and-such a day you were in such-and-such a place and such-and-such a woman fell in love with you: if you lift a finger, she'll lie down with you in the public square.' Why couldn't things happen like that now, why should Colchis girls not like Jason? Of course, in this impenetrable fog it was foolish to build castles in the air and dream of Medea's love, but Jason could in no way stop thinking about Medea: he knew in his heart that he could forge something out of this thought. He had a particular taste for tasks done by a woman's hands: this was no alien fruit for Jason, but those women were different women when they slaved for him, being in love with him. Love made them shut their eyes and lit up their minds. But why should Medea slave, why should she take risks for this foreigner whom she had seen just once, when it was questionable if she had really seen him at all? Jason couldn't recall Medea lifting her head or even looking towards him: she sat there looking at her hands. You can rely on a woman only when she loves you. So Jason had first to make Medea fall in love with him, and then ask for her help. 'She may not be stand-offish, but it's nothing but gossip,' the words of a song ran through Jason's mind. He knew very well how unapproachable such silent girls with lowered eyes could be. If you had the strength of a yoked buffalo, you still couldn't even make her open her tightly clenched knees. Still, it was pleasant to think of Medea, it gave him hope, it calmed and reassured him, especially when the cold was getting to his bones, his lungs were saturated with the sticky fog and somewhere, as if to annoy him, the little owl was screeching its heart out.

CHAPTER FIVE

FOREIGNERS appeared on Vani's streets the next morning. For two days now the people of Vani had been expecting them: nobody was surprised to see a group of men armed to the teeth. They greeted them like old acquaintances. 'Phrixos, Phrixos!' they called out to the slowly moving group, this being the only Greek word they knew. Vani was in a good mood: it was a sunny day and people found this unusual spectacle very entertaining. So many specially polished helmets, buckles, shields and swords, long and short, drew all the sunlight and were so dazzling that it took time to re-focus one's eyes. Moreover, that day the people of Vani had concluded that Greeks always walked about so heavily armed, at war or at peace, abroad or at home. 'Every nation has its customs,' said the inhabitants of Vani. The Greeks made no requests or enquiries, they didn't stop anyone and didn't stop to look at anyone. The only sign of life they gave was that they moved about. The children were the first to be bored with watching them. For some time they grimaced at their absurdly distorted reflections in the big copper shields, then, when they realised that this was all to be had, they left the Greeks alone. When the midday sun made everything baking hot and the city shut itself up in cool rooms, the Greeks stopped by the source, thinking they were alone, for the heat had become unbearable for them. But even here the group stuck together: they only came out one at a time, stuck their helmets under the stream as thick as a man's arm, drank, used the rest of the water in their helmets to wash their faces that glistened with sweat and then went back to the group. Thus the group stood almost without changing position or moving behind its shields, like a miniature tower. When it had quenched its thirst, the miniature tower marched off, with heavy measured steps, left the city and headed for the ever-flowing river.

Soon the sight of the miniature tower became familiar on the streets of Vani. It now behaved more boldly, spent longer at the Greek's source, drank all the water it wanted, put its heads and necks under the splashing torrent, laughed and, the people of Vani supposed, expressed its satisfaction in Greek. The Vani girls who wracked their brains to get the best view of the foreigners and tried to stay in view as late as possible, now eyed them with unconcealed delight and greed, probably recalling days spent on an island where women were desperate to find a man. But this couldn't happen here. The Vani girls tried to make themselves attractive, but the Vani boys grimly watched their every step and sought any pretext for a fight, as the father of ten girls awaits the birth of a boy. But the foreigners were behaving decently for the time being: they gave no pretext for a fight or quarrel. It wasn't their fault if the Vani girls preferred charming foreigners to anything else. But women and fights seem to go together, and there was a little unpleasantness.

The midday sun was baking hot, as usual in Vani; the miniature tower was resting by the Greek's source. One of the Greeks started talking to a Vani girl. The girl had come to fetch water, smiled warmly at the foreigner and waved her arms about to say she didn't understand a word. The Greek said something more to her. The other Greeks burst out laughing. The girl took offence and frowned. Out of nowhere a Vani boy appeared, rose up like a pillar and asked the Greek, 'What do you want with this girl?' The Greek then smiled and waved his arms to say he didn't understand a word. The Vani boy gave the Greek a slap in the face that sent him spinning round, shield, lance and all. Whether because they were sensible, or manly, the other Greeks kept out of the fight, but they shouted encouragement to their comrade and egged him on. They brought him round, and he angrily attacked the Vani boy. Then a row broke out, with both Vani men and Greeks applauding and yelling. The two champions rolled about in the dirt, biting each other, twisting each other's arms, tearing hair and panting. Finally the girl calmed everything down, filled a fallen helmet with water and poured it over the brawlers: drenching the two champions made both Greeks and Vani men feel like laughing. The quarrellers stood aside and shook down their clothes.

This incident brought the foreign guests closer to their hosts. The miniature tower was now greeted everywhere with joyful shouts. 'They're just ordinary people,' said the people of Vani.

No day passed without the miniature tower turning up at least twice in the goldsmiths' quarter. The humming of the lathes, banging of metal, tapping of hammers and snipping of cutters would stop for some time when the fingernails of so many gilded warriors scratched and scraped off one another the shiny dust that had wafted onto them.

The miniature tower's endless strolling through Vani's streets finally brought them to Bakha the vintner's forty-stepped cellar. It descended the forty steps with such caution and awe, as if going down to some eternal resting place. The cellar's depth or the smell of wine that had accumulated inside it made it giddy as those depths disappeared, like a happy child, into the damp cool of eternity.

Bakha the vintner still sat on his favourite chair, with his round-headed cornel stick placed between his knees, and his two hands, like roof tiles, arranged on top of the stick. Seeing so many thirsty men longing for wine excited him, too. There was no more room in the cellar. They all stared at him, their eyes popping with desire, nostrils flared like hounds that have caught a scent. 'They know my power,' thought Bakha the vintner and almost immediately his short, but divinely generous order resounded, 'Hey-Boy, use the big barrel: they're foreign guests!'

The wine drawn from the 'big' barrel made the guests merry. Someone stretched out to touch the bundle of garlic and sank his teeth with relish into an unpeeled head of garlic, and shortly afterwards just a plait of dry, stiff stalks was dangling from a beam.

'Open the door, let the whole world see inside!' called black-eyed Malalo, when the sound of a formation of steps was heard in the street and she caught the smell of wine and garlic. The day that black-eyed Malalo heard that the Greeks' twelve-oared ship hand had entered the ever-flowing river, she ordered her daughters to get the house nice and tidy. After that day she waited for guests. A guest, especially new and foreign, is the best medicine for old age, which was black-eyed Malalo's greatest fear. True, old age was still passing her by, but it was getting closer every day. It was lurking in every shiny object, from which it would suddenly call out 'Gotcha!' and break the heart of a woman who loved life. Black-eyed Malalo really did love life, but time was doing the inevitable, taking away what it could, without asking, pitilessly: her six daughters, who looked more like sisters next to their mother, only confirmed this. What black-eyed Malalo lost, her daughters gained. That was why she tried to look like her daughters, or make them look like her, so that an outsider had difficulty telling which of these seven women might be the mother of the other six. 'How many people I am! I can jump from one to the other, from the second to the third… from the third to the fourth, from the fourth to the fifth, from the fifth to the sixth… Old age can chase me until it gets bored,' black-eyed Malalo used to say, but just the mention of old age saddened her, so that she swept her six daughters like goslings out of the room and wept, wept bitterly, but wiped the tears as soon as they reached her eyelids, so as not to wash away her ceruse and rouge. Six daughters were not enough to keep old age at bay: black-eyed Malalo had to think of something better.

'Hostess!' called the parrot, but after that she heard nothing more except the sound of her youth gradually walking away, becoming more remote and then swallowed up in the world's sounds. 'You shameless traitor!' called black-eyed Malalo, on the verge of tears, to her youth that was slipping from her grasp, running off without a backward glance, as if it was escaping from some great ordeal. But even her sadness could not last long, because black-eyed Malalo also knew that even if you couldn't get your youth back by being carefree and merry, you could still attract other people's youth and this 'other's' would become hers, at least for a little time. Only she had to promptly strike at life, as colourful and noisy as the parrot in the cage, and never let it sleep, never let the unity, coexistence and unanimity of the colour and artless simplicity, tears and smiles, prisoner and warder be spoilt.

While the Greeks were learning about the city and its customs, Æëtes was conferring in the palace.

Æëtes now realised that he had made a bad mistake in accepting Phrixos, who had been abandoned by his parents, into his palace as one of the family, and then adopting him. Now an entire ship had come on Phrixos's traces, and tomorrow the whole of Greece could well be at the gates. No, he had no intention of even talking about concessions: concessions were a sign of weakness. True, the foreigner seemed to have a right to ask for what he was asking, and what after all should not be hard for Æëtes to give up, but who could guarantee that the foreigner wasn't lying? Do wolves hesitate to wear a sheep's skin if they want to get into the sheepfold? Æëtes didn't trust the foreigner, he seemed to be too charming to trust. He had another reason to be mistrustful. Wherever the ships that visited Vani came from, whatever they brought or took away, not one of them had ever steered clear of the port and hidden in the reeds of the ever-flowing river. Bringing back his grandchildren, looking after them and taking risks for them: none of this seemed natural. Possibly, his grandchildren had only the most noble motives when they went to such lengths to do their rescuer a good turn (if that man really had rescued them), especially as the rescuer was their kinsman (if he really was), but it was also possible they had been intimidated, or promised something to win those four milksops over against their grandfather and country. In short, Æëtes trusted neither the foreigner nor his own grandchildren. 'Fear your own people,' his father had always rightly warned him. It had come true; when Æëtes mentally surveyed his own people once again, it was only Chalciope's offspring who aroused suspicion. He disregarded Medea, because an unmarried daughter can have nothing more dear to her than her parents. Absyrtus angered Æëtes for other reasons. The years passed, Absyrtus grew up, but he remained the same secretive and 'weird' person. 'He ought to be involved in something, he needs to learn how to be king,' Æëtes kept telling the queen, but in his heart of hearts, where the father superseded the king, he rather liked having a son so reserved who didn't poke his nose into everything on the pretext that he was heir to the throne. In any case, Absyrtus really was no traitor, he seemed to want to stay just the heir and, who knows, perhaps he was praying to the gods to let his father live many more years and not to have responsibility for his country shifted to his shoulders. Absyrtus was genuinely fond of his father, and Æëtes knew it. Once he had asked as a joke, 'If you really are clairvoyant, tell me when I'm going to die.' A tear welled up in Absyrtus's eye, his chin trembled and he barely mumbled, 'I don't know, this will happen after I'm gone.' Æëtes felt a pang of pity and never asked such a question again. One way or another, to his father Absyrtus was above suspicion, and Æëtes apologized for the thought: 'Forgive me, son: thrones are something you need to keep your ears and eyes open about.'

Æëtes waved away the rope of thought that was dangling under his nose, because he knew anyway what rejoicing there probably was in the well, and he declared, 'In my opinion, the Greeks' twelve-oared ship should be burnt…'

While Æëtes was conferring, Medea went to sleep, without taking off her clothes, and had a dream. This dream was unlike the first; it was a horrific nightmare, tormenting and remorseless. The poor girl groaned, and was drenched in sweat, but there was no way she could escape or get away from the nightmare.

It really was a frightening dream: everyone seemed to have gathered in Æëtes' banqueting hall, including the foreigner, who was smiling at Medea so pitifully that the smile could have melted a stone. 'Why have you come?' Æëtes asked the foreigner, stealing a look at Phrixos's sons as he did so. 'You have to give me your daughter,' the stranger replied, looking at Medea. Æëtes seemed not to hear his reply and said to him, 'If you want me to give you the ram's fleece, then dance over a cauldron of boiling water.' 'I don't want the ram's fleece,' the stranger yelled and smiled a heart-breaking smile at Medea. The water was already boiling in an enormous copper cauldron. This cauldron was used for boiling a whole cow, it took ten men to put it over the fire. A plank was placed over the cauldron. Such thick steam came from it that people could hardly see one another. 'Dance, go on, dance!' people shouted at the stranger. The stranger no longer knew what to do, he couldn't make his views heard. Only Medea understood him, but she dared not say a word for fear of her father. Like an ox for the slaughter, the stranger stared now at Medea, now at the rejoicing Æëtes. 'If he gets up onto the plank, then he loves me,' Medea thought. Yet her heart was breaking, hoping he wouldn't get onto the plank; she was thinking, 'What stupid ideas come into my head.'

But the stranger did get up on the plank, spread his arms out piteously and moved his feet up and down as if to say, 'I'm dancing.' Æëtes burst out into loud laughter and knocked the plank from under the stranger's feet. Medea shrieked, the stranger fell with a splash into the cauldron and was boiled to death. 'Pour out the water,' ordered Æëtes, and the banquet continued. Ten men picked up the cauldron, took it outside and poured the foaming water, together with the stranger's bones, onto the ground. 'This is no banquet for me,' thought Medea, and also went outside. Steam was coming from the ground where the boiling water had been poured. A dog and a pig were attacking the scattered bones. Medea gathered up the bones in her skirts, took them to her room and emptied them onto the bed. 'If I bring him back to life, I'll regret it; if I don't, I'll regret it,' said Medea. Then she took from her medicine chest a Caspian sea shell in which she stored magical medicine, and she sprinkled it over the bones. Brought back to life, the stranger sat on the bed, rubbed his eyes and said, 'What's happened to the golden fleece?' Then, when he was more himself, he leapt up and ran back to Æëtes's banqueting hall. He ran in, shouting, 'I've won, I've won!'

When they saw the stranger, they all laughed. He'd been boiled alive in that cauldron, so where had he turned up from now? 'The ram's fleece is mine, isn't it?' the stranger asked Æëtes. 'But you came to marry my daughter,' Æëtes retorted. Then he called Medea over, 'Come, woman, you've got to settle our argument.' 'Why don't they leave me alone, what do they want of me?' thought Medea. What she said, however, was, 'Let me say a word.' 'Ten, if you like,' came the reply from all around.

'The stranger has done what was asked,' said Medea.

There was then such an uproar that nobody could hear anything. 'Wait, let her speak,' the stranger yelled, raising his shield as he did so. 'Now let my father dance over a boiling cauldron, and then they'll be quits,' Medea managed to finish what she had to say, and her heart was gripped by fear. 'I'm raving, what a catastrophe for me.' Another inner voice, however, told her, 'You must want this if you say it.' Fear was gripping Medea's heart, but at the same time she was pleased by her own boldness, both fired and delighted at acting so freely, as if she was flying in the sky and had no intention of coming back to earth. 'So be it,' said Æëtes, shocked and confused: he then got up onto the plank. His expression was such that, if Medea hadn't covered her lips with her hand, she would have shouted out, 'What are you doing, father, where are you going, is this worthy of someone like you?' It looked as if Æëtes was in no mood at all for dancing, but he spread his arms and his feet danced.

Medea ran up to the cauldron and removed the plank from under her father's dancing feet, saying to herself, 'What am I doing, why don't my hands wither?' Her inner voice, however, replied, 'You're doing it because you want to.'

Æëtes fell into the boiling water and was boiled to death. Ten men lifted the cauldron and carried it outside. 'I've won, I've won,' the stranger yelled, crouching behind his shield in case all these people should trample him. Medea rushed out of the hall to get to her medicine chest. But she found that the Caspian sea shell was empty. The medicine inside had all been poured over the stranger's bones. Medea was so distraught, so distraught, and then woke up.

When she opened her eyes she found herself in rose-tinged darkness. She leapt to her feet in fright and inspected the walls of the room. When she had recognized everything, she slipped her hand under her pillow and, finding her doll in its usual place, breathed a sigh of relief.

'No, my dear friends.' Medea whispered, on the verge of tears. 'How could you be so silly as to think that? It was a dream, a bad dream, but this is our home, my father's house. What business has a stranger with us? You understand, you understand…' she said, banging the doll with her fists. A jet-black eye fell out of the doll, but Medea kept on hitting it and shouting, 'Why are you so deaf, why can't you understand?' Then she lifted her skirts and dried her face in one movement. 'You'll be getting no help of any kind from me, even if Chalciope asks me,' she said, her face hidden in her skirts, and suddenly her heart started to race. 'Why didn't I think before, my sister might really ask me to help the stranger.' After all, the stranger was a kinsman of Chalciope's sons and, if any misfortune happened, Æëtes would see to it that Phrixos's sons suffered too, for bringing the stranger here. Medea thought it through, and opened the door, for she suddenly decided to go and see her sister. But she stopped in the doorway: how could she go, dishevelled and barefoot? She went back into her room, but could find no peace. She wondered what had happened, who might be looking, and then rushed to the door again, but couldn't cross the threshold. Three times she tried to go out and three times she held back, then she staggered to her bed and collapsed onto it, as if onto the corpse of her beloved. She lay there, her face pressed into the pillow, weeping silently. Without a sound and alone. Her constant tears had left the first stain on a virgin's bed: Medea now felt guilty, although she had done nothing wrong. She could never get rid of this bitter feeling of guilt, it followed her like a devoted dog, it dipped into the waves when she did and would follow her to alien lands, because this dog could not be scared off by sticks and could not be killed by poisoning its swill. It was predestined, sent by the gods. Medea didn't yet know this and, even if she knew, it is very hard to say whether that would have changed anything in her life.

If a woman cries, even in a sealed wine jar, another woman will always find out. This 'other woman' turned out to be Chalciope's maid. She happened to be passing Medea's room, but something bothered her and she turned back. Taken aback, she looked around and put her ear to the door. She did so because she couldn't work out what the sound was she could hear in the room, a child sobbing, or a dog whimpering.

The maid didn't dare enter Medea's room, so she ran to see Chalciope. 'Forgive me, God protect you, but I think there's something wrong with your sister.' The servant's appearance was just what Chalciope needed: her four sons were besieging her and snarling at her from all sides, like wolves, 'You can see what your father is doing to us, you're our mother, so help us, before we burn the whole place down.' She certainly wanted to help her sons, but what could the poor woman have achieved, when she was suffering defeat after defeat in the struggle to live, always because of her proud character. Her castles of dreams had turned out to be in reality sandcastles which she herself had cobbled together on the seashore as a child and then flattened. She and her sons were far apart. Her morbidly overdeveloped pride wouldn't let her show even a mother's tenderness. And her sons didn't understand their mother. They were men and would sacrifice everything to assert their masculinity. Was it worth going on with the struggle? Chalciope was alone again, alone against five. Against five men. As soon as she saw the stranger, she was sure that she could no longer control her sons. Perhaps this stranger really was Phrixos's kinsman, but he wasn't like Phrixos, there was a different light in his eyes, the light of a wild animal which is more dangerous when captured than when released. Adolescent boys imitate men like that, and women give in to them, because there is no point fighting them. Chalciope, too, was ready to join the five men's side, but this was no easy matter, she had to earn the right to do so, she had to make her contribution to the kitty if she was to become a full member of today's enemy camp.

Chalciope didn't delay long in running to Medea's room. Her maid followed her, but Chalciope waved a hand to dismiss her.

When Chalciope saw Medea with her face pressed down on the bed and her shoulders quivering, she was horrified: she supposed that Æëtes had sacrificed her children and that Medea had heard before she did. 'Woe is me, my children: why doesn't this accursed house collapse?' Chalciope wailed. Medea got onto her knees and, amazed, stared with tearstained eyes at her sister. 'You silly woman, there's nothing wrong with your children that's worth weeping about: why are you cursing our father's house, what's he done to you?' Medea wanted to say, but her mouth was paralysed, she couldn't part her lips. All Medea knew was that she was in love and no magic medicine could cure her: she would die of it and, until she died, this is how she had to be: distressed, perturbed, carried away. 'I want to die, sister, to die,' she wanted to yell, for she really wanted to die, and perhaps even thought that love meant wanting to die. Medea was utterly convinced that if anything happened to the strangely smiling foreigner, she wouldn't want to live a day longer: either she would jump into the sea, or hang herself from a tree, or drink some poison brewed by her aunt. For the time being, while she supposed this strangely smiling foreigner to be unharmed, she could not die: she wanted to, but couldn't, and that was the whole paradox of love.

'I want to die, sister, to die!' Medea yelled through clenched lips, genuinely wondering why the whole palace couldn't hear her, why nobody was running towards her. The word 'love' made Medea tremble so much that she found it hard to enounce it even to herself. This little word, so harmless at first sight, comprised so much resistance and unhappiness, and implied such terrible visions, that Medea felt she was gasping for breath, drained of strength and dissolving in the air, becoming as light and insubstantial as air. Saying the word and feeling guilty were the same thing, as if falling in love meant you had to commit a crime, and if you wanted, you had to express and assert your love.

'Did you go through that? What crime did you commit?' Medea wanted to ask her sister, but when she finally managed to open her mouth, she said something that amazed her own self. However, instinct dictated to her that it was better, having chosen a path, to follow it to the end. Medea did so.

'I fear and weep for your children's fate, sister,' said Medea.

She had taken the first step in committing a crime, but a step is not a journey: a second step would have to follow, and then a third, and so on for Medea to learn and be able to travel on her own in that mysterious and vertiginous field called love.

Your children's fate worries me, sister,' Medea went on. 'They are my brothers, after all. How many times my mother has told me that my real mother is Chalciope.'

And now a gap had appeared between the toddler and its parents, who squat, holding out their arms, feeling both fear and delight as they watch their first-born.

All that Medea needed now was someone to support her and approve of her actions. She wanted her heart's desire, which she would in any case follow, to be confirmed by some outward obligations, so that it would be a compulsory wish: now compulsion was coming of its own accord. Could anyone let down a sister who'd come with a plea? Certainly not, especially if the anyone was an elder sister, a substitute mother whose breast raised you and without whom you might easily not exist and might never have experienced this feeling, as intoxicating as wine and as emboldening as drunkenness.

'I want to die, sister, to die!' Medea howled to her sister.

Extremely perturbed by what Medea was saying and doing, Chalciope embraced Medea's knees, put her head on Medea's belly and began to sob. Medea already knew what Chalciope would say to her: she would rather sacrifice her father than her sons, and this wasn't because she preferred her sons to her father, but because she needed them more now, she preferred to appear to others as the protector of her sons, rather than a weak woman with no family, dependent on her father. Medea's cheeks blushed, a feeling of shame upset her, because she knew that she was forcing her sister to betray their father, she was obliging Chalciope to help save a stranger. 'I'm weeping for my children, too, my clever, golden-haired sister,' Chalciope sobbed and kissed Medea's belly. Then she lifted her head, with one sweep of her hand she pushed back her hair, which had fallen forward, and looked at Medea with such eyes that Medea was a little frightened: Chalciope looked capable of murder.

The sisters looked each other in the eye for some time, as if this was the first time they had got to know each other and they found it impossible to overcome the feeling of alienness and mistrust which is innate to every human being from their mother's womb. There was no need for Chalciope to torment herself: Medea now knew what her sister was going to say and was waiting anxiously for the words to come from her sister's lips and become law, a law which would be a cover for her own passion and desire.

'Commit it to memory, when you're awake or asleep…' Chalciope murmured.

'What are you saying?' asked Medea.

'Even when I'm dead, I'll give you no rest and I won't believe that you couldn't have saved my children,' said Chalciope.

Medea was distressed, kneeled down and threw herself about as if she wanted to fly, but couldn't. She was amazed and angry at herself, because she felt that her nephews, or brothers, for whom she once would have given her life without hesitating, were no longer close to her heart and, at the moment, she wasn't at all concerned by their fate. She herself needed all the supply of pity that her being could provide. She couldn't share this pity, least of all with four men who could, like the wind, rush off anywhere they fancied. 'I should look after myself, myself,' Medea silently lamented.

'It's raining,' she said suddenly.

Chalciope looked at her sister in amazement, but then she, too, heard the sound of rain. The rain forced a gust of hot air through the window. The air in the room became stuffy. The two sisters listened to the rain. Medea saw the stranger walking off, drenched, in the grove, holding his shield with both hands over his head. Medea smiled and said to him, 'You really are drenched!'

'What?' said Chalciope, surfacing from her thoughts.

'You really are drenched,' Medea repeated.

Chalciope used the hem of Medea's dress to dry her tears, and she then saw Phrixos. Phrixos was running towards the house, holding two children under each arm. The children were kicking their legs in the air and shrieking with joy. Chalciope also smiled, with sadness and regret.

They say that if you want something very much, it will come to pass. This is true and at the same time not true. Untrue, because not even the strongest wish comes to pass by itself. This is not hard to prove. And it's true only inasmuch as human beings act entirely under a wish's influence and effect, and conscientiously do all they can to carry out everything dictated, or rather ordered, by their wishes. The wish forces a man to do only what is necessary to make it happen, what he would never do, but for that wish. It also forces him to find in his own being the necessary strength, firmness and boldness and, if it is absolutely required, a capacity to deceive, insolence and ruthlessness, too. And resisting all-powerful desire involves serious difficulties, because any kind of desire is equally captivating and demanding.

The sisters were now captives of desire: both were being devious and both were right in their own eyes.

The moment Chalciope entered her sister's room, she instinctively sensed that Medea was in love. This discovery so perturbed her as if she was being deprived of something which belonged to her alone and which she couldn't spare, even for her sister. The sound of the rain reminded her of yesterday's alarm. 'How stupid I am,' she thought. 'If it's true, then there's no need for me to ask Medea.' Chalciope stood up, walked up and down the room aimlessly, then sat on her sister's bed again and whispered conspiratorially into her air, 'The stranger said, "If anyone can help us, then only Medea."' Medea blushed to the ears and couldn't help covering her face with her hands. She had expected anything but that. Chalciope took advantage of the surprise: she was silently triumphant: her instinct had not let her down, now she had to behave as if she didn't understand, and had to let her sister go on pretending.

'He said, "Ask her on my behalf",' Chalciope whispered.

'I don't need other people's requests,' Medea automatically whispered back. Then she knitted her brows, as if offended by what her sister had said, and continued in her usual voice, 'Isn't it enough for you to ask? For you I'd throw myself into the water, into the fire, or be buried in the earth. No, Chalcïope, I can't think of anything more precious to me than your children's lives. That foreigner needn't trouble himself: the sooner he leaves and gives us peace, the better.'

Chalciope flew out of her sister's room full of hope that her sons were no longer threatened by any danger, because Medea would stop at nothing to save her beloved. Nobody knew that better than Chalciope. Against Medea's magic drugs even Æëtes was as helpless and weak as a new-born baby. Above all, Chalciope could now go and see the five men, who had become one ball of thorns and had been trying to get away from her for so long, wrongly, because they had misjudged, mistrusted and disbelieved her. Now Chalciope too had got something to put into the common kitty. She was as happy as she used to be!

She spilled the beans, word for word, to her sons who were impatiently waiting for their mother to come back and were really attacking the walls like captive wolves. When she saw delight and thanks in her sons' eyes, Chalciope proudly straightened her shoulders. Even though the rain was still pouring down, Argus set off straight away for the ever-flowing river. He told his brothers to keep an eye on Medea, because the 'silly girl' could easily change her mind and at the last moment take her angry father's side. 'Don't worry about that,' Chalciope told them. But they were men and had no understanding of women.

There followed a bitter night for Medea. She didn't notice the palace gradually quietening down, the stars twinkling in the sky, the dogs ceasing to bark and the country, the water, even the mother of a stillborn child going to sleep. Only Medea was still awake: how could she sleep when this dark, stuffy and all-embracing night was the last night of a happy, beautiful and peaceful maidenhood? From tomorrow a new life would begin. At dawn an enormous iron door would rumble open and an invisible, rough, mighty hand would drag this little girl into a crevice of an unknowable world. God knows what she would find the other side of the door. One thing, though, was clear: she would never be able to go back. Cursed and excommunicated as a traitor to her parents, who had tenderly brought her up like a fledgling in their hands, she would have to forget forever the road back. And for whose sake? For the sake of some stranger whom she hadn't even spoken to, who would take what was his and casually set off, because he was expected, he had his own road, roof and hearth. But from tomorrow Medea would have nothing other than love, unrevealed, unrequited, unwarranted love. True, without Medea's help that stranger would die, but it was hardly her fault, or her business. Her father knew best who was to be saved and who wasn't. These were things for men to sort out, so why should she suffer? Because she loved him more than herself. Didn't she love her parents? Parents are parents, but he was different… he was in danger!

Who knows what ordeal Æëtes was preparing for the stranger. He might make him do battle with his black and red bulls, which he kept locked in a dark cave, sticking burning brands into their nostrils from outside. These bulls, their eyes squinting with madness, became so enraged at the sight of a human being that if they got the chance, they would gore him to pieces, trample and batter him. Medea could see the stranger skewered on a bull's horns. Her father was a wrathful man. He carried everything, trial and punishment, to extremes. But, nevertheless, there were ways of turning aside his wrath. Moreover, he was not the only danger awaiting the stranger. The moment Medea set eyes on the stranger coming into the palace courtyard, she sensed and was stunned by the enormity of the ordeal which was hanging over this captivating youth, even though the stranger acted proudly and his face was wreathed in a carefree smile. Medea not only sensed, but saw that his life was hanging by a thread. Someone horrifically powerful and ruthless held the thread of his life in their hands and could break it at any moment. Medea saw this invisible monstrous ghost standing over the smiling stranger. The danger which threatened him from her father, from Æëtes, famed for his cruelty, was trivial, compared with the indefinable, but irrevocable danger which the strong-shouldered, courageous young man was running away from. Yes, running away. Because there really was something of the refugee, the poverty-stricken, the distressed, the destitute and the desperate in his face. Possibly, Medea was imagining things, and it was the carefree smile, which suited the stranger so well, that gave her this feeling, but one thing was clear: he was walking a tight-rope. After this, Medea never stopped having forebodings, and this is why she nearly decided to throw herself at her father's feet and beg him to protect the stranger, to keep him in the palace, not let him out, because here in her father's palace he might possibly survive the main ordeal which someone somewhere across the seven seas had planned for him.

The poor girl thought of everything. She felt as if her head was getting ugly and enormous from so much thinking. Now it worried her that now the stranger wouldn't even look at her: how could she show herself with such a swollen face? If he had to die, so be it, she would kill herself and that would be the end of it. 'That would be better, of course, it would be better,' the thought clutched Medea not by the hand but by the throat, and she rushed around the darkened room like a blind man, hitting the walls: it was as if a bird had accidentally flown in and couldn't find the way out.

Now she caught the sound of young women gossiping and laughing. Her blood curdled. She clung to the wall, as if she wanted to be plastered on it like mortar and stay there for ever. The women were laughing at Medea, 'You can't bear to look at her, that quiet modest girl is raging with passion. She's abandoned her father and her country for the sake of an oaf. Why did she need to do that? Shame on our men!' The women were saying countless such stupid and vile things: in reality, they were sleeping like the dead and not even thinking of Medea. Medea was thinking and speaking for them. 'Child, wait a little, I'll marry you off myself,' her father now opened his eyes, shining with sadness. 'O-o-oy!' groaned Medea: nobody could hear her, nobody wanted to understand.

'I want to die, to die!' Medea shouted and rushed to her medicine chest, sat on the bed and put it on her knees. The chest reminded her of her dream, and she leapt up, as if bitten by a snake: was she sitting on bones, she wondered. For a long time she stared at the bed which was covered, as by a fluffy blanket, by the moon's bright, golden light. Medea cautiously ran her hand over the bed, and suddenly wanted to live, even if it meant suffering and torment, fear and confusion, because life was unfurling the bud which had been tightly closed, and this little room was now too small for it. This was no longer her place. Medea didn't know this, which was why she suffered so much. Life was moving up just one rung at a time, dragging Medea with it, because it was Medea's own life and it couldn't take a step without her. Medea didn't know this, either, but she went along with life because she could not do otherwise, she had no right to refuse to follow this mighty hand that filled her little body with pain and bliss.

By the time dawn broke Medea knew that she was going to help the stranger and, if he just beckoned, she would stick to him like a dog.

First of all, Medea looked at her wash basin to see if her head really had grown bigger. It hadn't, but her reflection in the basin was a girl with tousled hair, swollen eyes and a washed-out face. Medea dipped a finger in the basin and when the cold water rang out like glass shattering, she was pleased, and smiled. 'Today I have to be beautiful,' she thought and with two cupped hands took water from the basin. After washing her face, she stripped naked and rubbed her whole body with rose oil, washed her armpits with scented water and loosened her hair, which was tied at the back of her neck. Her cool, light hair poured over her bare shoulders. Medea couldn't help being startled. Her own hair seemed alien to her. Outside the birds were chirruping somewhere. Somewhere, at the other end of the city a cock crowed and Medea suddenly felt ashamed to be standing naked at the window, as if the whole country was watching her. The cock crowed again, a prolonged and hoarse call.

Medea changed into a turquoise dress with gold buckles. The room filled with morning voices, and she could smell the paving which had been sprayed with water. 'Now I'm ready,' Medea thought and she saw the world, Chalciope's world that was luring her out, making her lose this little room for ever, promising her nothing in return, for she now had to find everything herself. This was what Medea feared and, looking in the gold-framed mirror, instead of her own face, she saw what was happening outside these walls, outside a virgin's cell. Slave girls were sweeping the palace courtyard with long-handled brooms. Every sweep of the broom showed the sharp contours of their strong thighs and the shiny whiteness of their calves when they bent down to pick out the grass lurking between the paving slabs. Their every movement, their freshly washed faces and simply combed hair were imbued with the warmth of the beds they had left and with a secret, making the morning's cleanness and tranquillity more palpable, intimate and pleasant.

Kindling was crackling as it burned in the bread oven, and sparks like small red berries showered the jutting oven ends. The bakers were bringing a kneading trough covered with linen, as if someone was asleep in it, and the dough under the linen really breathed like a living creature.

Twelve maidservants hand-fed oats to the mules that were harnessed to Medea's carriage. This carriage was now the only thing linking Medea to her old world. The mules knew no other path. Medea had only to get into the carriage, hold the reins in one hand and the whip in the other, for the mules to head straight away for Dariachangi's garden. Today was no different. For some reason Medea had arranged a tryst with the stranger there, in the realm of her goddess, in the country she had inherited from Aunt Qamar. Perhaps this was a final, self-sacrificing battle of her virgin soul which could already sense the danger awaiting it, and was ready to meet that danger, yet still sought a path to retreat, not because it shunned danger, but because it was once more and finally convinced of the danger's power and inevitability. 'If my goddess is more powerful, then let her kill me on the spot. If Aunt Qamar really can come back to life, then let her come to life. I am helpless,' Medea was thinking when she was anointing her budding breasts, round which a girdle was stretched, with 'Prometheus's ointment'. Fire could not burn, nor dagger pierce anyone who anointed their body with this preparation; it gave added strength and courage, but only for one day, after which it lost its strength. Only one day was required of Medea, she had in one day to deal with treason and love, because there was no next day. 'I've been born for this one day,' she thought and was very intrigued: would the gods and Aunt Qamar allow her this one day, or not? Their skirts hitched to their knees, their heads bowed, the twelve handmaidens followed the carriage.

The minutes of waiting dragged intolerably. The girls now knew everything. They'd cast lots to see who'd stay behind in the temple that night and whose place the stranger, disguised as a woman, would take to follow the mule-drawn carriage to Æëtes's palace. 'We're women and we always have to be on the side of the weak,' Medea told them. Time dragged, it dawdled, it hung on to everything, like a prisoner being led into the daylight to be beheaded, but still advancing to the square where his sentence is to be carried out. Walking to the square is hard, because up to then he still has some hope, but after that, when he sees the executioner's block and hears the roar of the crowd that has come out for the spectacle, he quickens his pace of his own accord, runs to the block and lifts his pleading eyes up to see the executioner who will quickly put an end to his torture and martyrdom.

The thirteen girls simultaneously saw the stranger coming towards them. His golden, streaming hair was tied by a braid band round his head, he was wearing a short white tunic and silver-laced sandals, and he was girded with a broadsword. He had turned pale with anxiety, but was still smiling, although he himself couldn't see anyone. Medea, however, had now seen her execution block and heard the roar of the crowd. She managed to wave to her handmaidens to indicate that they should keep their distance. For a moment she lost her sight and wondered if she had imagined him, then she looked back to where fate had hauled her from. The sound of footsteps was steadily getting closer. Medea stood alone in the square. Everyone was pointing at her, talking and interrupting one another, and Medea couldn't understand whether they were pitying or cursing her. Neither the goddess nor Aunt Qamar could be seen. The sun dazzled her. 'Why, for what reason?' Medea thought once again, and by the time the dark haze in her eyes gradually lightened, the stranger was already standing in front of her. For a long time they stared at each other. The whole world seemed to be struck dumb, except for a dry twig broken underfoot by one of the maidens hidden in the bushes, or a branch suddenly dropping from someone's hand and swishing through the air.

'Don't be afraid,' the stranger finally said: for the first time Medea then felt what fear was.

Fear had eyes with no eyelashes, a mouth with no teeth and a jaw that dribbled. It put a hand into Medea's chest and grimly gripped her left breast, so that her whole back suddenly perspired with the pain. 'Be quiet, not a sound,' fear warned Medea, and bent over her as if it meant to kiss her. Medea didn't dare avert her face, but fear did not so much kiss her as wipe its dribbling jaw against her lips. Medea didn't even dare wipe her lips; she couldn't help thinking, 'Why should I be afraid?'

The stranger talked and talked and talked, but his coarse voice was barely audible to Medea. His voice tried so hard to penetrate Medea's mind: it was like the overturned beetle on its back by Medea's feet trying to turn over, feebly waving its desiccated, furry legs in the air. Medea watched the beetle and listened to the stranger's voice. The voice made her dizzy, just like a spell cast on a snake, so that Medea couldn't help the beetle. In fact, it only needed a push from her finger. 'If only I had a stick,' Medea thought irrelevantly and her eyes began searching for a stick. 'Then it can go wherever it wants.' Medea suddenly bent down and turned the beetle over. The panicky insect fled from the human hand. 'Wives and mothers… stretched out along the shore… walk and weep for us…' the stranger was saying, and Medea automatically, like a pupil, heard these words without understanding their meaning at all. But if she couldn't understand them, she couldn't escape this strange entrancement.

'I'll be grateful to you until my dying day,' said the stranger before falling silent.

As soon as his voice stopped, Medea came to her senses. She boldly looked the stranger in the eye and smiled at him. She was no longer embarrassed, because the duty she now firmly intended to carry out caused her no embarrassment. She would help this man in his trouble.

'And then go wherever you feel like going,' Medea said, and for some reason visualised the beetle running in panic through the grass.

Medea picked up the stranger's heavy, hot right hand in both of her hands and went on, 'Tell me, what's the maiden waiting for you like?' Medea was amazed that she said this so calmly and casually to the stranger, as one asks a visiting child something unimportant, among other things, to make him feel at ease and at home.

'My darling,' the stranger said timidly, because he suddenly sensed that the girl loved him, to be precise, he sensed it after he had said this word, which is why shortly afterwards he repeated more boldly, 'darling' and held Medea's hands in his cupped palms.

A cold breeze blew in from the sea. The handmaidens hiding in the bushes were excited by the sight of the couple on their own, perhaps because they were looking furtively. In any case, it would soon be time to leave. When the stranger, wearing a woman's dress, came out of the temple, the girls couldn't control themselves and came rushing out of their hiding places shrieking and squawking. Embarrassed and confused, the stranger spread his arms out and smiled. Seeing a man in a dress made the girls forget their embarrassment: he seemed to have become one of them, a member of their camp, once he had put on a dress. They span round like stones sent skimming over water, they tugged him from all directions, they pulled his dress down a little, saying, 'We can see your shins.' The stranger, his face as red as a poppy, spread his arms out, turned round and round, smiled and… put up with it.

CHAPTER SIX

WHEN Medea went in to see her father, Æëtes was on his throne, staring at the floor and lazily scratching his bared chest. Recently, Æëtes had often sat up late, perturbed by forebodings; what kept him up was that everything was turning out to be his fault. 'How could I push away an orphaned boy whose country was hunting him down for the kill?' Æëtes worried. Now he thought about Phrixos more than anyone else. In fact, whatever he might think about, it always ended with him facing Phrixos and hearing with every gust of wind his son-in-law's bones rattling ominously. 'What do you want of me, what quarrel do you have with me, what are you threatening me with?' Æëtes would snarl at Phrixos's ghost. The ghost stood huddled in the doorway, as miserable and grateful as a whipped dog, and it actually sneaked out like a dog every time Æëtes snarled at him, coming back a little later.

This is how Æëtes remembered Phrixos: meek and grateful. When he'd first been brought to the palace, he came running up and kissed Æëtes's hand. Æëtes was deeply touched. The touch of the child's lips sent a shiver running down his whole body and left in its wake a bewildering, somnolent weakness. All the king could do was to put the boy between his legs and sniff the top of his head. The scent of Phrixos's hair softened this lion-hearted man even more, it released distant childhood memories in him, but he still couldn't recollect what smelled just the same, so tender, touching, stunningly familiar, but now forgotten. After that he stood Phrixos between his legs several times, and sniffed the top of his head, but he utterly failed to establish what the smell of the child's hair reminded him of. Æëtes was in torment: 'It's on the tip of my tongue, but I can't say what it is,' he childishly complained to his family, but Phrixos took the secret away with him to the grave. Either this strange scent or the whole sad story of Phrixos's life was the reason why Æëtes had loved him from the moment he first saw him, his heart going out to him with pity. He had insisted on giving this royal child a royal welcome; of course, he did this to spite another king, Phrixos's real father, because he was most angered by the existence of that real father, an invisible rival who had the right to doom his son to die. Æëtes was able to protect the little boy only by interceding, nothing else. The real father would always mean more to Phrixos than Æëtes did, even if the former held a knife over him and the latter a pastry. At the time Æëtes hadn't given it much thought, but he was instinctively alert and angry, and when he said, 'This boy really is too good for his parents,' this was an unconscious, blind battle with an invisible but powerful rival to make him release for ever this frightened and pallid boy whose hair gave off a mysterious, soul-stirring fragrance.

Time quietened everything down. Now there were three uneven staircase-like sets of marks scratched into the wall of the children's room, showing the three children's vital growth leaping ever higher. Phrixos grew taller, his looks changed, he became one of the family, and Æëtes watched all this happening. So Æëtes soon forgot about the existence of Phrixos's real father. He relaxed, because he didn't know the truth. The truth was as bitter as gall: Æëtes had a taste of it twenty-five years later, when Medea came in to see him, bringing a bunch of cherries. Without thinking, Æëtes plucked a cherry off the bunch, thinking it might clear his mouth.

The truth was known only to Phrixos: the twenty-five years in Æëtes's palace were spent hiding it. Phrixos was ten years old when he crossed the threshold of his father's house for the last time. He may have been only ten, but this child raised in poverty had an adult's wits. He immediately guessed what would be demanded of him, what he would be obliged to do: to be precise, what would induce the men working for the Supreme King to pay most money to his parents. Until the day he died, Phrixos never forgot one of these men: even when he had grown up, he would dream of this man and leap out of bed in fear and panic, covered in sweat. This man wore a neckband made of jet and his nails were dyed black, too. He had the habit of falling asleep while he was talking, and then Phrixos and his parents would wait with bated breath for him to wake up and open his marsh-green eyes. These sudden sleeping bouts terrified everybody. People thought he would slip away when asleep and be unable to recover consciousness and that the Supreme King would then blame them for this man's death. Phrixos's parents, pallid with fear, communicated by hand gestures to tell Phrixos to sit still, not to utter a sound, not that Phrixos needed any warning, for he was so frozen with fear that if you'd set a dog on him he still wouldn't have been able to move. Fortunately, the Supreme King's messenger always woke up, first smiled and then opened his eyes. He seemed even when asleep to see everything and, in his sleep, found it amusing to watch people struck dumb by terror. The man who worked for the Supreme King always resumed a conversation with the word at which he had fallen asleep. 'Colchis is a good country,' he would say, as if he had only just come back from there. 'Every single child that's born there can be happy with their fate. Yes indeed, Colchis is the land for children, a child's word is law there and, would you believe it, their children are cleverer than our old men, because they like to learn. The Supreme King has decided that Greek children should get their learning and education there. There's nothing bad about that, the child will understand a thousand things, will become a man and be useful to the motherland; and you will be looked after to the day you die, you won't ever go short of wine and bread, because the Supreme King is generous. There's no reason to ponder or delay: if you love your child, hand him to the king, you don't want to have him drown himself, too,' said the man who worked for the greatest of kings, smiling at Phrixos. Phrixos's parents spread their arms out, opened their mouths wide, but not a sound came from them, as if a piece of food they had been grudged had stuck in their throats. But the moment the Supreme King's messenger left, they went for each other like rabid dogs: 'It's your fault, you've destroyed my children.' It could be said, in fact, that in the ten years Phrixos had spent with his parents, he had seen nothing but quarrels. Phrixos knew that his mother and father loved each other, but life gave them no chance to exchange affectionate words, every day they were struck by new disasters, and when Phrixos's elder sister Helle drowned herself life in this hovel with its rotten walls became unbearable. True, Phrixos was terrified by the man who worked for the Supreme King and by what he had said, but he quietly prayed for his parents not to refuse, because he was sure that he couldn't be taken anywhere worse than this house. His parents' endless quarrelling and whining had left Phrixos so distressed that he was sorry for them, for he felt that it wasn't their fault if they hated each other, if betrayals and endless misfortune made them set about one another. 'If not today, tomorrow; if not today, tomorrow,' Phrixos thought all day and all night, but the next dawn brought no relief. On the contrary, every new day brought new torment and new misfortune.

Phrixos was seven when Helle drowned herself, but he never forgot that terrible night. He had just got off to sleep when Helle came to bed. At first he couldn't understand what was going on, that it was Helle: he realised that only when his eyes got used to the dark. Helle was kissing him like a madwoman on the face, the neck, the arms, she ripped open his shirt to kiss his chest. Phrixos gasped for air, he burst into a sweat, because Helle was as hot as if she was on fire and had thrown herself on her brother for help. At that moment, Phrixos hated her, he pushed away with his knees, he grabbed her by the neck and refrained from shouting only because he was reluctant — in fact he was afraid — to wake their parents: they might start complaining and give him no peace until morning. 'Leave me alone, leave me alone,' Phrixos whispered. But Helle went on kissing him frantically, telling him, also in a whisper, 'Goodbye, don't forget your unhappy sister.' Phrixos couldn't wait for Helle to leave, for her to leave him in peace; he angrily wiped away the traces of his sister's kisses, but Helle seemed unable to see or feel anything, she just went on kissing him, her boiling-hot chest lying on top of him: Phrixos was strangely shaken and frightened by this restless, strong and burning-hot body, which really was his elder sister Helle, but was not like Helle, perhaps because she now belonged to death and would not be seen ever again after tomorrow. The next day Phrixos sensed the extent of the disaster that had struck him: Helle had left him on his own with two embittered antagonistic people fighting to the death, and they were as much Helle's parents as his, but Helle had vanished, Helle who only had to smile to stop her father picking up a broken paving stone to fend off her mother.

Helle was found in the river; she was wearing a green dress, her head was on the river bottom and she was naked to the waist, and her slender white legs were just perceptibly swaying in the water. Both banks of the river were suddenly crowded with people. Phrixos's head ached from the constant howling and the heat; for some reason, he thought Helle wasn't dead, perhaps because her bare legs were moving a little. The divers found it hard to attach a noose to Helle's legs. Because the water was extraordinarily transparent, you could see everything happening in it. Several times, the people forced Phrixos back, but he pushed himself forward, butting and jostling with his head and elbows through the hot, sweaty wall of people. 'It's my sister, let me through,' Phrixos pleaded, but nobody could hear him. In fact, someone punched him in the back of the neck, 'Where do you think you're going, you son of a bitch?' Phrixos was crying, tears and sweat were streaming down his face, but he stubbornly pushed himself forward, searching for the thinnest and softest part of the wall, so he might break through and see Helle, or at least Helle's beautiful legs that were gently rocking in the transparent water, as if to anger, provoke and attract the divers. As long as Helle's legs swayed, Phrixos could not believe she had died. The current kept carrying away the roped lads, who were shivering in the cold water, but they came scrambling up the bank and got back into the water, where the girl in the green dress, her legs swaying, still had her head in the silt. The divers attached the noose several times, but it always slipped off the girl's gleaming white leg at the last moment. Phrixos was distraught, he prayed silently for the rope not to grip her leg, as if this was now the main thing for saving Helle, whom so many people had set about catching. Not just Phrixos, but everyone was carried away and distressed by this extraordinary spectacle and, when the rope suddenly slackened and, coiling like a snake, slipped off back towards the bank, a groan was heard from both sides of the river, as if from people gathered at a horse race when the winning horse unexpectedly stumbles. Helle seemed to prefer to be in the water, giving the divers no means of fixing the noose properly to her leg. Finally, however, the divers succeeded, carefully pulled the rope, attached to the leg, towards the shore, and Helle's whole body gave a start, as if she was awaking from sleep or only now understood that she'd been snared. Both banks of the river gave a groan of relief. Phrixos turned his back and looked up with amazement at the gathering. Everyone's face was red with the heat. Helle turned over in the water, as if she had fought to escape from the noose. Now her hair spread over the surface of the water, and almost every hair spread out separately and quivered. Soon Helle came up to the surface and stopped movement, as if she was embarrassed by the gathering, whom she had caused such agony and suspense. The divers had come ashore, pulled the rope more, and Helle slowly, without resisting, drifted towards the bank. The leg to which the noose had been attached stuck, up to the knee, out of the water. Water streamed off the rope and off Helle's exposed leg.

After that not a day passed without Phrixos's father telling him, 'Grow up quickly, I have to go and join Helle, I'm sorry for the girl, she's alone.' But his wife would immediately shut him up, as if a living father no longer had the right to say this about a dead daughter.

'Be quiet, don't say it!' the wife would yell as she looked for an object to hit him with.

Sobbing, Phrixos clung to one or the other of them: he thought it better that his parents, inflamed by the loss of their daughter, should take it out on him, that the ruthlessly flung mortar, dough scraper or bowl should hit him. Phrixos felt sorry for both of them. They were both his parents and had suffered a common disaster. 'If not today, tomorrow; if not today, tomorrow,' Phrixos still said as he went to sleep, although he didn't know what could happen the next day that might make him forget his raging parents, Helle's death and his own helplessness.

Now the only day the whole family looked forward to was the Day of the Dead. Though they had almost nothing, they saved up the last scraps so that on that day there would be a pot full of stew standing by the door of their rotten hovel. That day they stopped shouting at each other, they swept and scrubbed everything, as if a potential groom was coming to look at their daughter: and what better visitor than that could anyone expect? 'Today my darling daughter's going to come!' Phrixos's mother kept calling out and fussed over the pot hanging over the fire as if she was going to feed the whole city, not just a slip of a girl. The day before all three would have a bath. The mother washed all the clothes, darned, stitched, mended to such an extent that they looked like new, so that the sight of her parents and brother in rags would not frighten or dismay Helle: that was the reason she had left them. Nobody slept that night, they waited in silence for the dawn, because only in the morning would they find out if Helle had come or not. If they found the pot empty, they would be so happy that they did not know what to do, they embraced and kissed each other, as if they had never argued. 'Our girl's come back,' the father would say and put a hand of his wife, who was sobbing with happiness. Mother was weeping a stream of tears, but smiling, and then they both were so beautiful and lovable that Phrixos felt a shudder run through his whole body. Then his mother would leave the pot and go outside and deliberately stop by the door until some neighbour, bereaved like her, noticed and called out, 'Mine came, what did yours do?' Phrixos's mother would joyfully turn over the empty pot, which had been licked clean by a beggar or by stray dogs, and would call back, 'Mine came, of course, the darling.'

Phrixos's father had a little plot of land fenced in by thorn bushes. This was his hope and his despair: Phrixos's father watched over this plot from morning to evening, devoted himself to it, exhausted himself working it, but it was all wasted effort: the lifeless ash-coloured earth couldn't nurture the seeds and didn't even give a tenfold harvest. Unable to get anything out of the infertile soil, infuriated, one day he set fire to the thorn hedge, but the land did not forgive this rebellion by a man who had shown it so much respect for so long. A snake rushed out of the burning thorns and, before Phrixos's father caught sight of it, slithered onto him and wrapped itself around him like a frightened child clinging to the first person it sees: the snake's blunt mouth kept striking his chest and belly until he fainted and fell. His whole body swelled up, his mouth foamed, his flesh, torn by the snake's bites, was covered in sores. In that state he was carried indoors. His eyes were still wide open with horror, but he was losing consciousness. Seeing her husband like this, his wife raged, 'He wanted to get away from me, that's why he got himself bitten by a snake.' What did he think his family was going to do? Dying is all very well, he could get a rest, but he'd landed a woman on her own with everything he was supposed to do. Anyone who has a child to raise has a hungry basket, and he had two to support, his rotten basket was twice as hungry. 'No, man, I'm not going to let you die yet,' Phrixos's mother shouted in his father's face and bustled about so much that she managed to snatch his swollen, stinking corpse from death's clutches. When Phrixos's father finally got out of bed, his wife and son found him changed beyond recognition. Death had hung on to parts of him: he was so drained that he could only stumble about, he could have been knocked over with a feather. He could not stand for long on his match-like legs, he couldn't rely on them: they would start shaking if someone didn't immediately give him a hand, and collapsed like twigs under his weight. His tongue, on the other hand, had swollen up and was too big for his mouth: it was such a loathsome sight that even his children avoided him. 'The reason you're in this state is the foul things you say,' his wife told him, her hand on her hips. But the sight of her husband feebly mumbling shocked her badly and she would then say affectionately, 'Don't be afraid, we'll get your tongue better soon.' One way or another, the poor man was now no good for anything, yet his wife still needed him. Apart from anything else, he was her outlet for her insane anger and bile. Not that he was idle for long: she found a task even for his useless state. Every morning Phrixos would now take his father to a street corner and put him on a chair, place a bowl of roasted pumpkin seeds by him and leave him there until evening. Phrixos's father sold the pumpkin seeds, and Phrixos, Helle and their mother cleaned and roasted pumpkin seeds all day long. They were all stained by the yellow, slimy, viscous liquid, their frayed bedclothes and floor rags were permeated with its smell: the bread and water of their poverty tasted of pumpkin seeds.

But even this could become an unattainable dream for them. It was then that the Supreme King's messenger appeared, and said, scratching his chin with his black-dyed fingernails: 'Your plot of land has been given to the temple of Demeter, because the goddess has been angered by your setting fire to it, and we are now threatened with harvest failure.' Everyone was too shocked to speak. Then the man saw Helle, smiled and went on, 'You can get enough money for this girl to win the goddess's heart and get your land back.' Shortly after this Helle drowned herself. Distressed at being parted from her family and by her unknown future, Helle got into her brother's bed and wept for everyone, for herself, for her brother and for her parents. 'It's because I've grown up,' she told her brother, who gasped for breath as she embraced him with crazed affection. Then, when she was found in the river, Phrixos was afraid that he too would grow up, sooner or later, if not today, then tomorrow.

When Helle was buried, the Supreme King's messenger reappeared. 'Your sorrow has softened Demeter's heart: she has given you back your land,' he explained to the parents, plunged in gloom by their daughter's death; he then put some olives into Phrixos's cupped hand.

Three years passed. Of those three years Phrixos remembered nothing except the messenger with the neck-band of jet and the black-dyed fingernails. His parents were so used to this strange visitor that they would be restless if he was the slightest bit late and would keep sending Phrixos into the street to see if he was on his way. The messenger had a truly odd way of speaking, inspiring both fear and calm, as if he were dreaming aloud. He sat and talked without end about some distant country where golden-haired boys and girls were born, where magic trees blossomed, where milk, wine, and fragrant oils and waters came gushing through copper pipes. Colchis was apparently not like other lands where people had to endure a thousand sorts of misfortune until their bodies, reduced to skin and bone, finally made it to Elysium. 'The people there are enlightened and gentle,' said the Supreme King's messenger, and when he suddenly fell asleep in mid-sentence, Phrixos, half fearful, half blissful like most timid people, couldn't help thinking about this fairy-tale distant land. This man had one strange habit: every time he came (and he came often) he was bound to ask how old Phrixos was: when Phrixos's father and mother replied, 'He's not yet eight — but you came only a month ago,' he would smile and say, 'If I was here a month ago, then he's a month older, he'll soon be eight and then ten.' Then he always added, 'He's a fine lad, our boy!'

In fact, the three years flew past, perhaps because the family no longer suffered poverty in that period. The Supreme King's messenger never came empty-handed, and when the lady of the house felt awkward at accepting his offerings, he would cry out, as if one of the family, 'I'm not a stranger, we ought to help each other out.' The endless, dreamlike conversations and the frequent little gifts made the man with the black-dyed fingernails like a kinsman to Phrixos's family. Three years earlier this man had said that as soon as Phrixos was ten he should be sent to Colchis to get an education. The three years had flown past. All this time the only subject of conversation in Phrixos's parents' hovel was Colchis, and they were so used to the subject that when the time came, they were paralysed by fear: how could they now refuse, they'd been letting the Supreme King's messenger encourage them? Family quarrels and rows started again; Phrixos's parents, once again let down by life, turned on each other.

'We've got no alternative; who knows, perhaps he'll make his fortune and won't rot away in a crumbling hovel,' Phrixos's father would say, but it was again the dream of a helpless man, deceiving himself, trying to justify his disgraced existence. He himself felt that he no longer had any right to do so, once he had let his son be sold.

When he said this, he shuddered and looked at his wife. His wife seemed to be expecting this, for she silenced him, 'You'll sacrifice us all; snake venom couldn't kill you, because you've got more venom in you than a snake.' Then they went for each other and there was no stopping them. The father's jaw gaped with hatred; the mother gabbled faster and faster, as if she feared she might leave something out, and so much spittle and dribble came with every word that the earth floor turned to mud. Phrixos stood between his parents and watched out, in case they threw things at each other. While his parents hissed at each other like two venomous snakes, he shivered to the very bones from fear. Every day was like this, every day was the same: it seemed the gods had granted them one endless day and tomorrow would never dawn. Phrixos was up to his neck in the venom his parents spewed out. He was imbued with this venom, choking on it and afraid to go outside. He thought he would be stoned, or have dogs set on him, that nobody would let him come near. Three years ago he had been horrified by the thought that he would be parted from his parents; now, after three years, he was desperately impatient, he even feared that the man with the black-dyed fingernails might have changed his mind about taking him to Colchis. 'Colchians are gentle people, they cut off the arm of anyone who beats a child,' his father used to reassure him apologetically. But Phrixos no longer needed reassurance, he couldn't wait to escape from his parents' hovel, poisoned by venom and hatred. He would agree to anything, in order not to be like his parents, not to share their fate. The only thing that weighed on him was Helle's fate. He had the feeling that as soon as he left the country, Helle's grave would be dug up. Phrixos now knew the Supreme King's messenger's real condition: he was to settle in Colchis for good, to live there and die there too when the time came. He had to make his nest and his grave there ('nest and grave' were the words of the man with the black-dyed fingernails, when he got hold of Phrixos so that his parents wouldn't hear what was said), for this might some time be required by somebody, probably the person who had ordered the purchase of Phrixos. Phrixos didn't understand this condition very well, but one thing was clear: he would no longer be hearing his parents' rows, he would no longer go to bed on an empty stomach, or wake up broken-hearted to find himself still alive, and, above all, he would be helping his parents, because the Supreme King was paying a lot of money as compensation. Thus, his throat dry with excitement, he immediately nodded his agreement to the man with the black fingernails, when the latter put his mouth to Phrixos's ear and whispered, 'You're no longer a little boy, you yourself must decide.'

Then Phrixos was put on a ship and sent off on his way. He was given new clothes, embellished with gold braid; the bundle his mother gave him, with which he'd wiped the tears from his eyes, was thrown into the sea as soon as the ship had left the shore.

When the ship left the shore Phrixos understood that his good luck would be short-lived. He didn't want anything any more, not the new clothes, nor all the different things to eat and drink, nor sailing the seas: he preferred his hovel with the rotten walls, he loved more than his own self that raging, dispirited woman wearing a headscarf with frayed hems, who stood in the bustling port and had fixed her suspicious gaze, like a stick — in fact, like a hand —, on the ship, stopping it setting out to sea, as if she sensed that she was being deceived and being deprived of her only child: her mind was about to see clearly, she would shriek out something so dreadful that it would empty the whole port, make the oarsmen leap out of the ship with a clatter, and the man with the black-dyed fingernails take Phrixos by the hand and deliver him at a run to his infuriated mother. She would then fling the purse stuffed with gold in his face, and herd back to their hovel with its rotten walls her rescued son and snake-venom enfeebled husband, who was crouching at her feet and thus could not see Phrixos leaning over the ship's rails.

But nothing like this happened. There were countless different people in the port, it was impossible to hear anything, the oarsmen were already straining as they dipped their oars, the ship shuddered, Phrixos couldn't see his father, but he was sure his father was weeping: withered up, his jaw drooping with hatred, this man was sitting, weeping, at his wife's feet, because that was all he could do. Phrixos could tell this by his mother's face, as grim as pitch, and he wept burning tears. This is how the child, bound by the terms of his agreement to silence, left his motherland; he was quite certain that this was the only possible way of prolonging the life, if only by a few days, of his parents, for they would be waiting for a child lost for ever: Helle at least visited his parents' hovel once a year and ate the food her mother put out for her, whereas nobody would be putting out a pot for him, because he was one of the living dead.

'Remember, you're the son of the king of Beotia, your stepmother tried to kill you, and a flying ram saved you. That's all you remember, and all you know is that you're the son of the king of Beotia, the son of the king of Beotia,' all day long they drummed into Phrixos on board the ship, but the 'son of the king of Beotia' could see his parents in their rags, living in mutual hatred and thus deterring a bigger, more ruthless enemy, the world all round that threatened to trample them down.

The 'flying ram' meant to save the 'son of the king of Beotia' was tethered to the mast; it constantly chomped its jaws and scattered cherry-size droppings all round.

When someone shouted, 'Land in sight: it's too dangerous to go nearer,' the ram was released, the boy was put on its back and they got ready to throw them into the water. Overcome by the prospect of splashing down into the freezing water and by the immense fear of water which imbued all his breed, the ram was so terrified that it sent everybody flying off, battered everything around it, sending a stack of barrels rolling down, and the screams of a man crushed by a barrel drove it even madder. Now it had to fight to the end, since nobody would forgive it for this sort of fury. The ship was shuddering, the sailors were chasing rolling barrels over the deck, while the ram ran up and down with its rider, already regretting that it had upset so many people. The ram had nothing but good to say of the men: he had been given all he could eat and all the praise he could take. 'There's not a ram in the world as handsome and brave as you,' they kept repeating all through the journey, and the ram was puffed up with pride, so pleasant was the praise from human beings. His eyes popping with fear, Phrixos flew about on the ram, clinging to its horns, feeling sick from galloping in a circle. 'All this time I could have got used to the water and got to the shore,' the ram thought with regret. It was then that someone shouted, 'Hit that damned sheep with a burning brand!' In no time at all there was a smell of singed fleece and burnt fat in the air. Pain gave the ram wings; with a clatter of hooves, it ran down the deck, kicked both hind legs against the side of the ship and flew off with its rider. But it couldn't reach the shore and splashed down into the water.

Flying through the air, Phrixos lost consciousness; only on land, sprawled in front of alien people, did he come to.

Phrixos was ten when he was reborn. As fearful and amazed as a baby, he studied the alien surroundings and faces which bent down, smiling at him; they were saying something, but Phrixos did not yet understand their language, he wasn't yet one of them. His legs were shaking like his father's, but he timidly stood there: if he wanted to live, he had to learn all over again to walk and to talk. What he knew was no longer any use and he had to forget it for ever, eradicate it, because so far he had only been in the process of being born: the real Phrixos was born aged ten, after sleeping for ten years in the womb, having terrible dreams. The land into which Phrixos was now born had nothing in common with those dreams which had constantly beset him for ten years, the ten years when his blood had been sucked by gigantic leeches and he had been trained to fear, to fear and obey.

But however hard Phrixos tried to forget these things, they still existed, they were still inscribed on the other side of the stone on which Phrixos now tried to stand. The stone only had to turn over under his foot for the hungry freezing past, nothingness, non-existence to come back. It all depended on Phrixos, on his behaviour, on his choices: dream or reality, his parent's destitution or foreign luxury. And Phrixos chose: as soon as he was brought to the palace, he pulled himself together, ran forward and kissed the hand of the king sitting on the throne. He couldn't help looking at the king's fingernails, but the man sitting on the throne had ordinary nails, undyed. For some reason, Phrixos was surprised: because he had been sent here by the man with black-dyed fingernails, it seemed that everyone should have black nails here, too. Now Phrixos had to keep up a lifelong pretence, all his life he had to keep up a lie which fate had devised for him at birth. What did fate want, why had it sacrificed him like this, sending him flying through the sky like a dandelion head, and blowing from below to stop him coming back to earth? How long did he have to stay suspended in the sky for all to see? Until the downy seeds fell off him? But when only a bare stalk was left of him, he wouldn't be allowed down, he would crash to earth. This is what Phrixos felt, and all day and all night he anticipated the painful blow, he was afraid of the end, but a lie recklessly spoken was driving him down a road of falsity, deception, submission and concealed hatred.

From the very first day Phrixos felt how far away his parents' hovel, his ragged mother and father, and Helle's grave were. All this was now so distant, that he occasionally thought he must have dreamt it, but then he would be struck by the musty smell that reigned in the hovel, and could see his mother's surly face, his father sitting on a little chair at the corner of the street with a bowl of roasted pumpkin seeds in front of him, and Helle's legs, barely swaying in the transparent water: this alone was enough to bring a lump to his throat, and he would creep into a niche in the wall and there, in constant damp and darkness, weep his heart out because he was an orphan and alone. No, Phrixos could not forget everything; on the contrary, as time passed, he became more convinced that he had neither the strength nor the desire to cross out, scrape off or uproot those ten years which fate was making it his duty to deny. By all means, let things be as fate wanted, he wouldn't break the condition, he would not reveal the truth to anyone, but it was nobody's business what he thought at heart, what he dreamed of, what he remembered and whom he chatted to at night when he lay on his bed of thorns. He felt happy only when he was left on his own, when the palace quietened down and the yawning nannies took their last look at the children breathing imperceptibly in their beds. Then Phrixos, as much as he wanted, could roam his own land, which was like his father's barren plot fenced in with thorns, or rather by fire that rose to the sky and roared loud enough to petrify his enemies. But whenever Phrixos went up to it, the wall of fire would part and let him through without a word, because the king and queen of this land were his parents: 'Hey, our lad had come,' the queen would applaud, running down the throne's gilded steps. The king, wearing his crown, followed her, holding a three-headed snake and smiling regally. Then Helle would come running and place a full bowl of stew before him. Her wet dress clung to her body and while Phrixos ate with appetite, she gave him no peace, 'Eat quickly, I know a good place to bathe.' Their parents smiled, glad to see their children together, but their mother deliberately knitted her eyebrows and told Helle off, 'Give him time, girl, you can see he's hungry.' Phrixos went on enjoying his food, his heart swelling with joy, because his mother had cooked a stew for him. Then his mother turned the empty pot upside down and called to the servants with black-dyed fingernails, 'My lad has come.'

Every night was like this; time passed and the land that the child's fancy had invented and embellished gradually grew, as did Phrixos. Now he sincerely believed that this little barren plot of land, fenced by thorns, was really a whole kingdom, his father's kingdom, and later, when he told his children about this kingdom, he had not the slightest doubt that everything he said was true. Only one thing tormented him, that he had to talk secretively with his children about his father's land, as if he was doing something very wrong.

In fact, everyone treated Phrixos well, but their attention, their concern and kindness were always obvious, exaggerated and therefore irritating. How often they had allowed Phrixos to hear them say he was a foreigner and allowances had to be made. O how bitter and hurtful such support was: they stood up for him, not because they accepted him as one of them, but because he was an outsider. He would always be an outsider, to give his supporters a means of favouring him and showing their kindness and generosity. He would always be an outsider, because he had a past which didn't exist for them. Phrixos was an outsider, given refuge, obliged, even forced to endure everything, even affection. At night he wept bitterly, like an orphan, for he had nobody beyond the wall of fire to whom he could freely complain of his sufferings.

The unmerited title of king's son and the equally unmerited respect shackled his soul, but he couldn't reveal this to anyone. Phrixos put up with it, for he had no choice, there was no other way he could now live and, although he talked all night to the wall, he swore an oath that he wouldn't stay here any longer, he would slip away the next day, he would go to the hall smiling, greet everyone respectfully and smile a broad smile of joy when one of his elders said, 'Look, Phrixos has already washed his face, Phrixos is better than any of you.' And when Chalciope shouted out, 'I'm fed up hearing about your Phrixos!' he would be so frightened that his heart would stop beating, because he was afraid that others would look down on him as did Chalciope. He was afraid of her and even hated her, especially after the day that she jolted him and made him bang his nose against an oar. But he still didn't want Chalciope to look down on him. He did everything to win her heart: he caught grasshoppers for her, he gathered flowers with the biggest petals for her, he shook mulberries off the tree for her, he wouldn't let anyone else carry the basket with her lunch when they went for a walk. He did all this to win her over, to make Chalciope notice his 'loyalty' and never again say in anyone's hearing, 'I'm fed up hearing about your Phrixos!' He was afraid of her and this fear kept him constantly close to her.

In fact, all his life he was running away from Chalciope, even when he married her and then begat four sons one after the other. The more time passed, the more loathsome the hidden lie became, the greater the weight of the punishment he expected. That was why he was afraid of Chalciope, and always tried to stick close to her, because he suspected that she had always been doubtful about his royal origins, and that was why she kept saying, 'I'm fed up hearing about your Phrixos!' Surely, if he really was a king's son, he wouldn't dare come, like Chalciope, into the hall without washing first? Would he put his clothes under his pillow? Phrixos used to keep his carefully folded clothes under his pillow until Chalciope noticed. To his dying day he never forgot Chalciope's mocking voice as she hopped around him on one leg, while his face blushed red as a poppy, and called to him like a magpie, 'Country oaf, country oaf!' She was the only one to notice his unroyal habits, but for some reason she was merciful and didn't let everyone know, probably so as to make him a dogged slave and dominate him all his life. It was no accident that Chalciope fixed her cunningly smiling eyes on him when they were going to the country by their canopied boat, passing villages where the country children standing on the crumbling river banks waved and called to them, 'Princess and princes, hey, princess and princes!' It is hard to say what the village children wanted, to annoy the people in the boat, or whether they were just envious and heartbroken that they themselves weren't gliding along in that fast, beautiful boat. Phrixos was drenched in sweat, his face burned and he tried to hide behind somebody, as if the children on the crumbling river bank might recognize him by sight and then yelled out to him, 'He's not a king's son, he ought to be standing with us on the bank.' This fear of being exposed as a liar made him go, his knees trembling, up to Æëtes and ask for Chalciope's hand. He stuck closer, he clung harder to the person he feared and tried to escape from, because he thought that this would make it harder to expose both him and his lie, which coiled round him as a snake does a rabbit, in order to devour it the moment it awakes. Meanwhile the rabbit was waiting, unable to go anywhere, hypnotized by the snake.

Then the children were born and the hidden lie grew bigger, fourfold, because his sons were in fact the fruit of this lie. It was then that Phrixos felt the extent of the sin he had committed: now he had to deceive his four offspring for the rest of his life. Worse, they must never ever realise that they were eating the bread of charity, that they were foreigners, interlopers who had been swept by fate's broom out of a hovel with rotten walls.

Phrixos could not go on living like this. What use was he, what was he doing? He was doing nothing, and nobody was interested in him. It wasn't him, but his nest and his grave that interested everyone. No wonder he'd been told, 'We don't want anything of you except your nest and grave.' He'd already made his nest, or rather the hand of the man with the black-dyed fingernails had, like a cuckoo's egg, laid him in someone else's nest, so that he would think from the moment he hatched out about the grave whose owner would one day turn up there and clear away the thistles. But Phrixos already had those thistles on his soul, and he had to clear them away himself, or else be buried alive, and for how long? For whose sake? But it was not easy to break a silence of twenty-five years, to forget twenty-five years of submission, to clear a twenty-five-year debt. But he decided to have it out with reality, which had put him out, like a sheep, to graze on someone else's pasture, had made him tell lies for so long, and had made him as deceitful as a shop assistant. Somehow he had to make his sons loathe the world around them, he had to redeem himself somehow and, together with his sons, return to the 'fairy-tale country' that smelled of pumpkin seed, that was covered with mould, steeped in the poison of hatred, but really was theirs, their property. That's why he spent three months digging the ground from the mountain to the city, bringing spring water, because that was the only way he could redeem himself and his sons. He was happy standing in the ditch, because he had his sons by his side, he could hear their heavy breathing and he was sure that they would never abandon him. But he ran short of time and died before he thought he would; although he hadn't given death a thought at the time, death was the final item in the terms and conditions, and he hadn't intended to carry out that item, and after twenty-five years his entire being had rebelled against this particular item. But the rebellion obviously came too late, or he was simply not fated to leave this country as a breaker of promises. Everything happened as had been agreed between him and someone who needed only to have his 'nest and grave' in this faraway country. Unintentionally, Phrixos had conscientiously fulfilled the conditions, but he died happy, because he thought before he died that the money earned in his 'nest and grave' would allow his mother for some time to come to cook Helle her annual pot of stew.

Bitter, then, was the truth whose taste Æëtes came to know after twenty-five years. When Medea came in, Æëtes was sitting on his throne and thinking about Phrixos. He had now realised that Phrixos was the first wave coming from the enemy camp to test the shores, a wave as gentle and quiet as silk, ebbing out on the sand and leaving on the shore foam as white as damson blossom. Phrixos's head smelled of the foam on the waves, and his hair smelled the same, as Æëtes now remembered twenty-five years later. Ever since childhood Æëtes had loved this smell, he would lie face down on the seashore, pushing his face into the wet sand, letting the crashing wave come over it, and when the wave passed, Æëtes could hear the foam sizzling on his bare back. The sea attracted and drained Æëtes's suntanned body, washing the sand away with a crunching sound, but he still managed to hold onto the moving sand. He played with the sea that wanted to carry him off, but the boy's sinewy, well-built body always left the mighty element empty-handed. This small boy, his nose pressed into the sand, already knew the sea so well that he could tell just by the sound of a wave where it would collide with the ebbing water and thus he always managed to get his body out of the way in time, so that the disappointed wave took away nothing but sand and dry sticks. Ever since childhood Æëtes knew that one wave was always followed by another wave; he knew that the following wave would be stronger than its precursor. Thinking constantly about Phrixos reminded him of the waves. Phrixos was the first wave, his sons were the second, the third wave came after the second in the shape of the smiling stranger, and the third, of course, had to be followed by a fourth, because nature's ordained custom demanded it. Æëtes was now trying to identify this fourth wave: the fourth would be stronger, bolder and noisier. Æëtes was flustered, as if an enormous wave, rearing up, topped with turbid foam, was creeping up on him, a boy with his face pressed down in the sand.

Medea had a bunch of cherries in her hand. Æëtes thought, 'What's happened to my girls to make them bring me presents?'

'Have a cherry, father,' Medea said, smiling at him.

'If I take a cherry, what have you got to tell me?' Æëtes asked: he actually wanted a cherry, because he had a bad taste in his mouth.

'I liked the bunch, so I broke it off for you,' Medea told him. Æëtes plucked a cherry off the bunch and put it in his mouth, looking critically at his smiling daughter, in case she had come on some other business.

Medea withstood her father's intense stare and her ingenuous smile didn't leave her face until Æëtes fell asleep. Æëtes fell asleep without taking the cherry stone out of his mouth.

'My father really has aged,' thought Medea, heartbroken.

Æëtes slept: the drug Medea had concocted for him knocked him out, and his grey, tousled head slumped to his chest. Sleeping, he seemed bigger and more terrible.

Medea straightaway found the keys to the wall cupboard, because she knew that Æëtes had plaited them into the hair on the back of his neck. Then she had to push the throne out, because it stood exactly in front of the cupboard, protected by a carpet, in which the ram's fleece hung. Medea put her weight against the throne, but couldn't move it. 'Help me,' she called out angrily to the stranger who was hiding behind a marble pillar. The stranger came up at a run and effortlessly slid away this heavy object, the throne on lion's feet together with its no less heavy royal occupant, for the stranger had saturated his body with 'Prometheus's ointment'. When he was sliding the throne away, Æëtes jerked his head as if he had fallen asleep on horseback. Æëtes was asleep, but he could still hear and see, because this was an induced sleep and it couldn't entirely switch off his mind. Æëtes felt his daughter searching his head, as if he had a plague of fleas or lice; he felt himself being slid on his throne to the middle of the hall, he heard the door of the secret niche cupboard being opened and all the bustle as the ram's fleece was rolled up and allowed to flash for the last time and dazzle Æëtes's hall. 'Quick, quick,' the stranger kept shouting, and Æëtes wanted to say, 'Hey, you cissy, you should have a woman's thimble, not a sword in your hand.' But he had no more control over his voice than over his limbs. He was out of this world. Only one thing gave him hope: because he saw the stranger was wearing a woman's dress, he thought that it all might be a dream, 'Well, if a man puts on a dress…'

As soon as the sleeping drug wore off, the king bellowed 'Medea' in a horrible voice and rushed from the throne. But Medea was by now far away. Beating his head with his fists, letting his eyes blaze came too late: the mistake had been made long before, now he was merely reaping the fruit, bitter and slimy, of that mistake. His trust and generosity had been ill rewarded by the offspring of alien seed, by those fed on his bread and raised as his grandchildren. What had to happen had happened. As soon as an opportunity came, they took the side of their fellow-countryman, although they had never seen this fellow-countryman before. His foreignness had enchanted them and their blood had sensed that they too could have been like him, were their fate different. This uncanny revelation made Phrixos's sons instantly forget the care and concern which had let them be 'like that' and, without thinking, they joined the pirates, as if this were the only way to assert their Greek origins.

Asylum seekers are like that. Of course, they're grateful if you share your bread with them, shelter them under your roof, keep them a place by the fire, but at the same time they are filled with envy, because they don't have their own bread, their own roof or their own fire. True, it's not your (their protector's) fault in the least, but you remain the chief object of their concealed hatred, because you have what they could have. And if that is so, then it is natural for their disturbed mind to raise the question, 'Why you and not me?' What irritates them is having to be grateful to you. The feeling of gratitude is demeaning, for it automatically, quite unintentionally, increases and emphasizes your superiority. The more generous and soft-hearted you are to your refugee, the more full-blooded and unbridled is his bile. Your generosity oppresses him and increases the size and weight of the debt which you don't even expect to be paid off. But 'debt' implies the inevitability of repayment. Such 'debt' is usually repaid, however, as Phrixos's sons repaid theirs: in malice, treachery and bloodshed, so as to leave you, and only you, the noble and compassionate you, in no doubt that they stand for something and have not become entirely an object of charity. In fact, they turn your cause on its head so that you'll need to ask for charity. And if it comes to that, they themselves know, and will show you, how to give charity. They've learnt from you and experienced personally what evil pointless, reckless kindness and generosity can bring about. After all, they've always been laughing behind your back when you've divided up your bread equally between them and your own children; when you punished your own children more severely if they unintentionally hurt the feelings of an offspring of alien seed, an eternal displaced person. By doing so, of course, they were doing evil, not good. For one thing, a foreigner, whoever he may be, brought into a family will never be your life-long devotee, because he prefers his pumpkin seed to your life and, before he came to live with you, he had his own devotions and the devotee, who still exists somewhere, because of distance and unattainability, becomes a hundred times more loved and desirable. Devotion to you can never replace devotion to the other, just the mention of the other makes him sadder and more malicious. He looks at you and he sees the other, the object of his devotion before him, he eats your bread and longs for his own, he drinks your water and hears the babbling of his own source, because this is human nature, or rather refugee nature.

For another thing… your endless sermons on philanthropy have given your own children, who are forced to listen to them, many wrong ideas not only on philanthropy, but on life in general. They have come to believe that anywhere, wherever they happen to be, they will be received as generously and as gladly, as selflessly and wholeheartedly as you received Phrixos. The fact that this was wrong, your own offspring, your younger daughter has most bitterly become aware. But a fifteen-year-old girl cannot be sceptical about a feeling which she was born to experience and which she will have to serve all her life, like a warrior his banner. Medea has acted the same way and now for her whole life she has to lie spread out like a corpse on love's bed, shouting through clenched lips, 'because I loved him, I loved him, I loved him.' Through clenched lips because she won't dare pronounce the name of her sole and eternal goddess, all-creating and all-destroying.

Now Æëtes knew that he had made a mistake, because it was Phrixos's offspring who had turned their mother and their aunt, his own daughters, against him. They had tricked, as if he were born yesterday, a man whose awesome voice and strength made him like the god of war. But Æëtes's nature still prevented him from admitting this mistake, from calling a mistake what he considered to be a human being's duty, from seeing what he had perceived as kindness to be malice. But he couldn't learn anything from the mistake, because even now, deceived and disillusioned, he would not hesitate to receive any homeless pauper who turned up at the door and would feed him before asking any questions. That was his nature and there was no way he could change, and old age was no time for changing one's habits. So he walked the palace courtyard, his arms spread out, amazed and smiling stupidly. He couldn't and wouldn't believe it. What he had seen clearly when he had been drugged into sleeping, seemed a dream to him when he was awake.

Medea was now far away: they found in her bed just a lock of hair she'd cut off. Perhaps she had left it as a souvenir of her irrevocably lost virginity.

The whole city was up and about. A row of ships bristling with weapons and soldiers was leaving the port, and Æëtes's son Absyrtus was standing on the prow of the leading ship. He would return on the same ship, or rather his corpse would be brought back on that ship, together with the other ships. Absyrtus already knew this, but he still went, because fate wished him to.

Æëtes, however, still hoped that his fast ships really would overtake the pirates: he was pondering whom to punish, and how. When he looked in his heart of hearts, however, nobody except Medea interested him any more. Compared with Medea, they all seemed small and banal. In any case, they all had some justification, except Medea, who had betrayed her father without cause, which stunned him most of all. Her betrayal was so unexpected that he didn't even try to seek any explanation for it. Æëtes felt pain in his blood, which was why he prowled the palace courtyard like a breaking storm, bellowing, 'Bring me Medea, Medea!'

Chalciope, who felt guiltier than anyone, was no longer mentioned, let alone blamed, by anyone. When she was sure that nobody despised her like some dog, she felt she loathed all those whom she had tried to mislead, whom she had been afraid of, in case they guessed that her husband and sons had rejected her. She feared humiliation. But nobody seemed to take any interest in her, nobody at all. 'Medea,' her father was bellowing. 'Medea,' every nook and cranny in the palace whispered. But she couldn't have done anything wrong, because she was nothing, just an empty space for fixing a flower to, that was all, a moving talking doll, a child's toy, a plaything. No, she was not even a doll, she didn't even exist: her shoulders hunched, like a sulky child that won't eat, like a candle that burns out and drips wax in the night, she aimlessly wandered the palace corridors and felt, like a painful wound in which someone has rubbed salt, how invisible she had become. The panicking servants, endlessly running up and down, kept knocking into her, jostling her, pushing her out of the way. Either they were blinded by the disaster, or nobody could see or recognize Chalciope any more. Who needed a woman whose husband preferred death rather than her, and whose children had treated her as deceitfully as if she were a whore? They had used deceit to get what they wanted and had hurriedly stolen out of her chamber. 'Perhaps I don't exist now,' Chalciope thought, but she felt, or rather feared that she was alive, for her whole being was filled with indiscriminate, limitless, unrelenting hatred. She had never felt life so acutely, because she no longer wanted it, it made her feel sick, it stank, it had a loathsome smell of dead flesh, rot, misery. She loathed everybody and everything, most of all she now loathed Medea, because Medea had outwitted her, had turned out to be what she had spent her whole life pretending to be, dreaming of being, but never capable of being, because she had never been able to give anything up. What she had not been able to do, she had asked others to do. That's why they had all stolen off. But they had abducted Medea; they hadn't run away from her, they'd taken her with them. Who'd done it? A real man who had the light of a wild beast in his eyes, who didn't drag his feet like Phrixos, because he knew what he wanted, and why and for how long. Chalciope had never known a real man, she hadn't deserved to, because she was too eager and too stupid. Wasn't it her own stupidity that put a jellyfish, a fish, a toad in her bed? Her own stupidity, her own stupidity, nothing else. And a toad that dishonoured her bed, a toad that jumped out of her bed?! 'Oh, I wish the earth would swallow everything up, that the water would sweep everything away,' Chalciope cursed, and from somewhere in the depths of her soul a chill came and penetrated her flesh and bones, making her shiver, turning her blue, as if her abducted sister had pulled the bedclothes off her and she lay naked — the abandoned, humiliated and defeated Chalciope — for the whole world to see.

After two weeks a ship appeared on the horizon. It was moving slowly, as if reluctantly being dragged by someone's invisible hand.

The city had fallen still. Everyone just watched, Æëtes went up onto the battlements to watch the sea, or rather one black point which gradually grew like a storm cloud, moving at snail's pace towards the city. He bit his lower lip with tension, his broad, crooked teeth red with blood. Meanwhile the ship slowly, as if under compulsion, approached the shore.

'It's Absyrtus's ship,' someone said, recognizing it; Æëtes held his breath. Soon they could make out a man climbing the mast. The man was twisting round awkwardly, like a dragon's tail tied to the mast, hitting his head with his hands and shouting something. Finally they could hear his voice: 'Vani, put on mourning, put on mourning,' the man shouted from the top of the mast.

The ship was laden with the corpses of the pursuers. Corpses were piled in a heap; some had their stiffened, horribly bent arms, or legs, or heads with clenched jaws and staring eyes, hanging over the bloodstained sides of the ship. Absyrtus's corpse was brought ashore first. Then the crowd gave a roar and rushed aboard, like chickens looking for millet grains in a dunghill. They were seeking their dead; their faces suggested that their hearts would burst if they didn't find them.

Absyrtus had a horrible, ugly wound in his side: it looked like a toad's mouth forced open. Blood had clotted over the wound. Æëtes knelt down by his son's corpse and looked for a long time at the pallid face, as if the corpse might say something. Absyrtus's face seemed to have been calmed by some ghastly equanimity, and he seemed to sprawl at his father's feet with indifference, as if he had distanced himself from everything and was equally uninterested in everything.

Æëtes cautiously put his hand into Absyrtus's wound, dipping his hand in black, clotted blood, and smeared his face.

'We were betrayed, people, we were betrayed!' yelled the man on the mast. 'They slaughtered us while we slept, people, while we slept!'

When the ship was unloaded, he stayed on the mast, with no intention of coming down, as if so many people had been slaughtered that he now feared vengeance. He madly rolled his eyes, which were half out of their sockets. For two days and nights, still mad, he stayed up at the top of the mast, ceaselessly lamenting out loud to the city those sad and horrible events which he had witnessed and which had driven him insane.

'Absyrtus was deceived by his sister, people, by his own sister! And the foreigner pierced his side with a sword!' wailed the madman.

After two days and nights the people of Vani lost patience: they took an axe and cut through the bottom of the mast. The top of the mast came crashing down on the shore and crushed the man tied to it.

Not long after this another ship appeared. This was the flag ship. Soon the whole horizon turned dark with pitch-black Cretan ships. The fourth wave was making haste for the shores of Colchis. The Supreme King had been building up this wave for some time, long awaiting this day. And now it had dawned! This day was to put an end to, draw a line under a task begun a long time ago. Everything was ready now. There was no point delaying. Ever since Jason was sent to Colchis, there had been crowds standing in the port of Knossos. The ships, washed clean and black as pitch, slowly rocked on the bridled, immobilised waves, pointing their sharpened prows into the open spaces like javelins to ward off the enemy. The people wondered where in particular the sharpened prows of these fighting ships were heading for. In general, it was all too clear, the Cretans were accustomed to this sudden mobilisation of their invincible fleet, they were glad to see it depart and arrive, because it had never come back empty-handed. It took weeks to unload the ships whose bellies were stuffed with booty: out of them came bellowing cattle, of many colours, dusty, covered in dried mud, with burrs from their native meadows still stuck to their tails and dewlaps; barrels of wine and olive oil were rolled out; wooden trunks and cloth bales were dragged out; tear-stained, pale-faced boys and girls, like ruffled chicks, came sobbing out; women, after sleepless nights, dishevelled, their dresses torn by their captors to show off their exotic flesh, came tottering out. 'Glory to Minos!' shouted the spectators, excited by the sight of these trophies; they threw flowers, anything that came to hand at the victorious, puffed up soldiers back from war in their heavy armour, as they crawled like monstrous beetles through the narrow streets of Knossos. The soldiers smelled of wounds, sweat and conquered lands.

The people of Knossos were, as usual, not mistaken: again they were preparing ships for war: nobody knew against or for whom Minos was sending them. But this only increased their craving and aroused greater curiosity. 'Tell me, if you're so bold, where Minos is going to get the wine we'll get drunk on, and where is the woman coming from that I'm saving up to buy?' they joked, spoiled by victories, sure that it would always be so.

Minos had known for twenty-five years where his black ships would be going today, today in particular. True, not all had gone to plan, but there could be no further delay. One instant's delay would waste twenty-five years' patience. The net he had been weaving for twenty-five years might tear and everything would have to be started all over again. This was the day that Minos expected to hear news from Colchis of Jason's death, good news, for he had planned it and was sure Æëtes would have this wilful youth torn apart into four pieces after he rudely went up to him and said, 'I've come to take away the ram's fleece.' 'Ha, ha, ha,' Minos would laugh heartily when he imagined their conversation, such stupid nonsense did it seem. In the end, it was nonsense: the ten-year-old boy had understood what was wanted of him better than that big oaf who would be king. Phrixos had done his duty conscientiously: he had made his nest and a grave: fledglings loyal to Greece had hatched in the nest, while in the grave the remains of a Greek king, yes, a Greek king, rested.

Nobody could stop Greece in mourning from coming to sit by the grave. But Jason had bumbled about and messed up everything, because he would rather be a hero than a king. Instead of Jason's bloodstained tunic, which Minos had intended to hang from his flagship, Jason himself turned up, bringing both the ram's fleece and Æëtes's daughter. Who needed Jason, the fleece, or the daughter? Poor children! The goddess of love had snatched them from Æëtes's clutches. Minos had every reason to say, 'Poor children!' when he was informed that Jason had returned from Colchis with Æëtes's daughter. He instantly realised why it hadn't gone to plan. He had made a mistake that was altogether unforeseen and unforgivable for a king like himself. He had failed to take Medea into account. Medea! Minos knew that Jason would do anything to save his own skin. He was like a wolf: there was no cranny he wouldn't sneak into, no nook he wouldn't sniff at. But Minos didn't know, or had forgotten, or omitted to think that in one of those nooks Jason might possibly come across Medea, his doll and his saviour. A stupid girl had interfered and overturned a business that a wise man had planned, pondered, measured, assessed and calculated for twenty-five years. Medea existed in order to save, whatever it cost her, someone a wise man had sacrificed. And it had happened. Jason had not turned out to be a hero. But Minos needed a hero, or rather a hero's blood which, thanks to a stupid girl, had not been shed and had therefore lost its value. Minos had specifically told Jason what he wanted of him. He said many other things, but if Jason really was as clever and sensible a youth as he seemed, he should have pricked up his ears at the very first word and acted as that short, two-syllable, but very significant word obliged him to. When Minos first summoned Jason, he paid him no attention for a time, as if he didn't notice him, he deliberately spoke to others, but kept an eye on Jason, studied him, tested him to see if it was possible to say to him the short two-syllable word. In any case, Jason had a real hero's looks: he was handsome and young. If he perished, many hearts would be touched. Suddenly Minos turned to Jason and asked him, 'who are you?' 'I am the son of the ex-king of Iolcos and nephew of the present king,' Jason replied without hesitating.

'No,' Minos almost shouted, 'you're a hero!'

The hero had gone and abducted a girl and, for the sake of a lousy fleece, had made an enemy of Æëtes. Jason had been as stupid as Medea, neither had understood where their duty lay, but Minos couldn't now reject these poor children. It is hard, really hard, to be 'auntie' to everybody. Minos could not now hang Jason's bloodstained tunic from his flagship, but he still had a handy pretext for a quarrel: there were people pursuing his envoy; they had not let him take the sheep's fleece, they had forced him to steal it, a lousy sheep's fleece, such as any shepherd, beggar or pirate wore; they had not let him have the girl and had forced him to abduct her, when every country longed to have as a citizen a son-in-law of the king of Greece. Luckily those poor children had someone to intercede for them. The Supreme King intercedes for all the oppressed. There was no point settling accounts with Jason now: it just wasn't worth it. Jason, or Jason and Medea, had done at least part of what they were obliged to do. Not in the way they were asked, but as best they could. Jason was a wrongdoer, but his crime could be forgiven. At least the wild animal had come out of its den, shown itself and become weaker, because one of its cubs had been captured alive and the other had been thrown back dead. O Jason, O Jason and Medea! The things that the goddess of love will make a man do! There had been a pretext for war, but it lacked finesse, the finesse typical of Minos. A pretext has finesse when it is coloured with the blood of your own people, not your opponent's, whose blood now has to be shed for that very reason. Anyway, everything was now clarified, everyone involved in this business knew what portion was theirs, who had what to gain.

Even in the thickets of the ever-flowing river, on the twelve-oared ship, wrapped in the mists of Colchis, Jason sensed that he was just a stone thrown to lure a wild animal lurking in the bushes — a stone or a clod of earth, dispensable, unwanted, whose life nobody gave a damn about: if he escaped alive from one king, he'd be torn to pieces by the other, because both needed the sight of blood in order to attack one another. But Jason wanted only to escape alive, then and now, only to save his own skin. But to do that blood had to be shed. This blood of the brother of the girl who had saved his life, in fact made a gift to him of it, who had given him rebirth. But wasn't this the best course for Jason and the girl, too, if she really loved Jason? It was better, better for everyone this way, besides so much blood would soon be shed that the blood of Medea's brother would be a drop in the ocean: everyone would be equally just, or equally sinful in the eyes of the gods. What had to be done would happen and had in fact happened. Minos's black fleet was already visible from Vani. It was led by Oqajado.

This was the son of Oqajado the elder, Æëtes's cousin. He was the last hope, the bastion for avenging his father, whom Æëtes had once thrashed with a lamb and who had become dust and ashes, after living in hope and despair at the other end of the world. But from these ashes, which were now almost cold, a spark had flared up to light up the night of his unavenged injury, his ineluctable old age and endless waiting. When his wife became pregnant, Oqajado senior could hope that the gods had not wholly abandoned him, but had put by his side a vessel free of cracks, so that he could pour into it his dreams, his bile and his ambition. When his wife gave birth and said, 'Congratulations, you have a son, what shall we call him?' He thought and said, 'There should always be an Oqajado on this earth.' But he didn't live to see the day he longed for. His son was still spinning tops when he gave up the ghost and set off for Elysium. It was for the best: reassured and hopeful, he shut his eyes to the fortuity, cruelty and treachery of this world.

When Oqajado the younger grew up, the Supreme King, everyone's foster-father, told him what his father had said, 'You are the heir to a throne, but your throne is a long way away.' Then Minos looked him in the face and kept staring until what he'd said produced the first signs of unbridled animal joy on Oqajado's flat, immobile face, as a stone thrown on the water makes gradually increasing circles that swallow each other up. Then Minos asked him, 'Do you want to be king?' What could Oqajado do but agree, although he was too excited to say so. Minos realised anyway that Oqajado agreed. After that Oqajado never set eyes again on the Supreme King, but one sighting proved enough to imbue him with Minos's majesty, a regal quality that was eternal, intangible, overshadowing everything else, irradiating his whole being. After conversing with a superhuman majesty (true, Oqajado hadn't said a word during his encounter with Minos, but somehow he had a lifelong impression that he had never had such a heartfelt, businesslike and pleasant conversation with anyone) he again became a bit puffed up: 'I'm valued and I deserve to be.' That same day Oqajado set himself to learn how to be king, a really complicated, but useful skill. He had already firmly decided his future status, to mount a throne, no matter whose, wherever it was, even if it meant crossing nine lands and nine seas. The word 'Vani' had no meaning to him except as a future kingdom. If he lived ten lives, he would never once have wanted to go there, although, before Minos, his decrepit father had often told him about its existence: 'We're from Vani, son.' When his father said this, he would stroke his mossy beard with trembling fingers, as if counting the years of waiting which had dried on his beard. 'I know, papa,' Oqajado would respond and look for an escape so he could go and spin his top, or ambush a girl coming to fetch water from the spring and smash the pitcher she was carrying on her shoulder with a well-aimed stone. Oqajado was a child then and can't be blamed for ignoring the words of a father old enough to be his grandfather. But when Minos looked him in the face and curdled his blood, confused and stupefied him for ever, like a snake with a sparrow, Oqajado now wanted only to hear about Vani. In Vani a kingdom awaited him, he could reign there as silent as a great king, not uttering a word, not making a move for hours, weeks, months without end. His only worry was, if he went to Vani to be king, what would he do if he missed this country? But this worry was nothing, just a way of passing the time — it made the time spent waiting to be king gallop by and speeded it up, as a little dog hurries a herd of cattle homewards after a whole day idling in the meadows.

Meanwhile the Supreme King was silent, delaying, as if he had forgotten his promise. Oqajado's mother had told him that kings tend to be forgetful; frightened and saddened by this indefinite wait, like a caged fox-cub, he paced up and down his room, and when his mother called to him, 'Stay in one place, damned child!' he would stare at his mother, waiting for a response or a word of comfort. At the sight of her son's flat, immobile face Tsutsa (as Oqajado's mother was called) would burst out chuckling, cover her face with one hand, then both until she regained control, would chuck Oqajado under the chin and chuckle. His mother's chuckling was balm to Oqajado. As long as Tsutsa wasn't frowning, he had nothing to be alarmed about. Nobody knew better than Tsutsa what was happening in the Supreme King's palace, and she even knew what was about to happen in the near future. 'I've given you birth and the king will put you on the throne which your father's bottom slipped off,' Tsutsa used to tell Oqajado: he believed her, as prisoners condemned to death believe any word of comfort. Oqajado loved his mother and was even in his heart of hearts a little afraid of her, because she occasionally beat him. In Tsutsa's opinion, a stick was by far the best teacher, and she used to beat Oqajado, when he was a child if he childishly damaged something, and later when he grew up if he took any hasty step without asking his mother, or without her agreement. When, after a thrashing, Oqajado thought about his behaviour, his mother always turned out to be right, although he wasn't capable of great thoughts either as a child or an adult. But he had enough wit to see that his mother was right and to admit it. So the thought of becoming king gradually, with the help, of course, of canings and slaps, instilled into him limitless awe, reverence and above all trust in his mother. But the terrifying silence of the Supreme King, and the endless waiting made him take one more unconsidered step. This time, too, he failed to ask his mother and now bitterly regretted it, although he gained a great advantage from it: it made his mother an ally and a fellow-conspirator, and their alliance, fortified by wrongdoing and murder, was after this never ever broken.

Oqajado's tiny mind had not managed to make any sense in the cloud of confusion that buzzed round his head like a swarm of bees: one fine day he went to see Knossos's famous soothsayer, taking a sack of wheat and one black and white lamb as an offering. The soothsayer thought hard, but was unable to read anything in Oqajado's flat, immobile face — not so much a face as a terracotta mask. The soothsayer threw a snake's tooth and an owl's eye into boiling water, added some fleece from the black and white lamb Oqajado had offered, and a handful of wheat and stirred them in the pot with a crooked stick, until they all sank to the bottom of the pot; meanwhile, she mumbled something. Oqajado patiently waited, thinking what his mother would say if she could see him. Finally the soothsayer's voice brought him to his senses, 'Pick up the pot and pour the boiling water down my throat!'

'It's too hot,' said Oqajado, worried.

'So it should be,' the soothsayer replied, opening her mouth and throwing her head back. Oqajado did as the soothsayer had instructed him. Then he sat down on his chair and stared with inexpressive, well-trained eyes at the soothsayer who was bubbling like a geyser. A haze and a puff of stinking steam came from the soothsayer's mouth. Oqajado waited patiently, for a long time, and finally could wait no more: he asked her: 'Hey, tell me the good news, woman,' The soothsayer spat out the stinking stew, which had now cooled, from her mouth and said, 'There's human blood in this grain, that lamb was raised on dog's milk, and you can't possibly be a king's son.'

Oqajado's cheek was suddenly burning, as if his mother had just slapped him. 'Serves me right, why did I come here without asking mother?' was his bitter reflection as he turned back sourly. It seemed that Oqajado had to believe this soot-stained old crone, who had held boiling water in her mouth, swallowed a snake's tooth and an owl's eye and was still unharmed, but the moment he left the soothsayer's stinking hovel, doubt pursued him, grimacing like a beggar, 'Test me out! Throw me alms: it'll do you no harm.' How could Oqajado test out what he'd been told: where would he find the ploughman who sowed that wheat, or the crazy dog that had suckled a lamb instead of its puppies? The only thing that Oqajado could do, and which horrified him most, because he didn't give a damn about the grain mixed with human blood or the lamb raised on dog's milk, was to establish whether he was a king's son or not. This secret had just one key, and the key was entrusted to his mother, or, to be precise, both the secret and its key belonged to her personally. It had been put in time's box and, who knows when she had swallowed it down, box and all, deeply convinced that it would never be needed again. If Oqajado wanted to know the truth, he had to overcome his fear, set aside his diffidence for a while, and somehow force his mother, a woman received at the Supreme King's palace, a queen worthy of the throne of Colchis, his father's noble consort, to spew up the secret, conceived even before Oqajado was born, of his conception. How could he dare ask this of a mother, what's more a mother like Tsutsa. But doubt gave Oqajado no rest, it clung to his coat-tails and followed him home and even threatened to disgrace him publicly if he didn't give it alms. The prospect of public disgrace thanks to that wretch frightened Oqajado: for a moment he thought that the Supreme King, too, knew about this story and that was why he never summoned Oqajado. This was too much for him: he trotted up to his mother and gabbled at her, as if he was passing on a message, 'Mummy, I was told in a dream last night that if you let me suck your breast I'll live until old age.' Tsutsa gave him a searching look, but she too failed to read anything on her son's flat and immobile face, except that sweat was dripping from his spotty brow. 'He's become a man,' she thought: touched by her son's stupidity, she felt maternal affection. Oqajado couldn't wait for his mother to undo her tunic: he fidgeted and rubbed his hands.

Oqajado didn't remember what happened next: when he saw the white breast with its flattened tip, his eyes stopped seeing and his teeth gripped the breast, and he had no idea what he was saying. But Tsutsa understood, and was bitterly hurt: would she ever have thought that she would be reminded of her sins in old age, and by whom? The person for whom she had committed the sin, the fruit of the sin, the creature conceived amidst horses' whinnying, the smell of hay and dry dung, a creature with a face as flat and immobile as the boarded floors of the stables. Tsutsa forcibly tore her bleeding breast from Oqajado, who was even more worked up by his own boldness and by what he had heard: dribble and his mother's blood were dripping onto his chin and he didn't even try to get his face away from his mother's angry fingernails. Tsutsa was scratching her son's face as madly as if she was sliding down a wet mountain side and trying to cling on. When her arms wore out, she once again struck out at him, 'You're the son of a stableman, your place is in the manure heap,' and rushed out of the room.

Oqajado stayed there for a long time, staring fixedly, covered in scratches, his face washed in his and his mother's blood. His face didn't even twitch, but his eyes gradually began to shine and a smile, budding at the corners of his lips, soon unfurled over his whole face, as if the sun had looked through the tiny holes in the ceiling of the stables and shone on its newly washed floor. Oqajado burst into loud laughter. He rolled on the floor and jerked his legs in the air, as if fending off someone: he wouldn't let anyone near, so that he could guffaw alone, and be alone on the floor to enjoy tumbling like this. Oqajado was grateful to fate for entrusting kingship to the son of a stableman. Now he could go not just to Vani, but beyond it: he would fight to the death to keep what he had found without lifting a finger, thanks to the foresight of fate or Tsutsa, 'My mother's a great woman,' Oqajado thought with delight.

The next day the stableman was found in a stall with his head cloven in two. The horses, frightened at having a dead man near them, were huddling in a corner, whinnying with their necks stretched out and teeth bared. Only Tsutsa knew where to find the criminal, but she put her homicidal son above one night of stolen love which was already consigned to the past, because she needed this son for the future.

True, Oqajado had the Supreme King standing behind him, and victory was guaranteed in advance, because it only needed a small child, let alone Minos's army, to subdue Æëtes. But he didn't dare enter Vani's port, and, choosing the pirates' route, led his fleet to the ever-flowing river. He immediately disembarked the army on shore and it was here, between Vani and the ever-flowing river, that he awaited Æëtes's final battle. Æëtes was defeated, he knew that he was going to be defeated. But he didn't want to give up Vani without a battle. This new traitor made him even more fiery and wretched. Most of his commanders, who had only yesterday sworn on their lives to be loyal to Æëtes, turned up to everyone's surprise in Oqajado's camp. Resentment harboured so long, added to catastrophe, got the better of Æëtes, and his bodyguards were forced to tie up this man, who was raging like a lion, and carry him, still shackled, out of the city, in which he would henceforth not set foot again, and where fate or ill fortune made him chew so many bitter herbs and bite so much blood-saturated earth. As feeble as a child, whimpering like a child, Æëtes was forever removed from his native city. Those who heard his last sobs never forgot them to their dying day: who would have thought that this Goliath, this wrathful man could weep? But what amazed everybody was that Æëtes was weeping not over his defeat, his treacherously killed son, his ravaged home, but over his younger daughter who had contributed to his every misfortune. 'What will you do without me, my poor child?' Æëtes sobbed like a woman.

The battle on the ever-flowing river was still going on, the blood had turned the willows' bright white roots as red as doves' feet. Although Æëtes was no longer there, his loyal fighters would not retreat and they were slaughtered to the last man.

When Oqajado entered Vani, the inhabitants and the people he sent in advance (who they were was never established) spread carpets along the streets leading from the city walls to Æëtes's palace, and then scattered bright flowers over them. With bated breath the city awaited the victor, as if it had suddenly lost its ability to resist as well as to enthuse. But one Vani man stood on the roof of his house and urinated on the carpeted street; when Oqajado's soldier struck him in the neck with a javelin, he spewed out both blood and the words, 'Long live Æëtes!'

The ever-flowing river had no more room. Ship after ship kept coming, bringing, apart from the army, the families of those exiled by Æëtes. Vengeance was coming back up from the well. Those returning to the homeland couldn't wait for the ship to be moored: they leapt straight into the water and swam for the shore, then, up to their waists in water, stumbled along, then clambered and got onto the longed-for shore on all fours, kissing it crazily and eating the silt and mud.

It is said that a mosquito can defeat a horse if a big wolf helps it. This is what happened. The banks of the ever-flowing river were crowded with vengeance-seekers. Many of them had been born far away, on the island of ninety cities in the wine-coloured sea, but ever since they were children their parents had instilled into them love for their lost land. Now they were competing with each other to demonstrate that love.

Mothers were dipping thc heads of babies at their breast into the turbid waves, rinsing them like dirty rags and laughing heartily when the sandy water came gushing out of the nostrils and ears of the whimpering babies. 'Bathe, bathe!' yelled the excited mothers; when they came out on shore, their wet unbleached linen dresses clung to them and they had such trouble walking, that it seemed as if they had only just been moulded from clay People gathered to sing under the willow trees, although it was not so much singing as yelling in order to hear the sound of their own voices. Everyone had tears in their eyes, but nobody could tell whether it was tears or the river water from which they only just emerged. Gradually the bank became so crowded that there was nowhere let to stand. As it was, many were standing up to their waists in water, and from there their voices sent out a song, or a cacophony, about returning to the homeland. All these homeless people had turned into one condensed, quivering, whimpering, singing and grumbling mass, but they were all under one roof: joy! It was hard to define, it was chaotic, elemental, but it was joy. It was impossible to say where this mass began and where it ended, because it couldn't move, it trampled the ground under its feet, it shifted from one foot to another, while brothers fought in a ruthless, bloody, endless hand-to-hand battle between this enormous colourful mass and the city they longed for.

The banks of the ever-flowing river were a sight both moving and horrifying. The surface of the river, from bank to bank was entirely covered with garish rags, with dolls stuffed with hay, pitchers with reed stoppers, headscarves, broken oars which people had lost or got rid of when they were crossing to the bank; the river water was swirling this useless offering, herding it as an experienced sheepdog herds a flock, and then rushing it off to the open sea.

PART TWO

UKHEIRO

CHAPTER SEVEN

UKHEIRO lay on a stretcher. His copper-coloured muscular right hand drooped over the edge of the stretcher, swinging as if to say goodbye forever to its bloody and stormy life. At least, that's what the warriors, whose tempers were poisoned by the heat and by having to haul such a heavy man. The closer they got to Vani, the heavier their load became, and the more pointless their exertions seemed. Ukheiro was already lost to this world. What difference would it make if he reached Vani and, before he died, cast an eye over a city his heart had spent thirty years longing for? It was doubtful whether he would even recognize it.

Ukheiro was a real warrior: weapons enabled him to support a family. He no longer recalled when it happened, when after practising on a dummy stuffed with straw, he first pierced a real human being with a javelin, and saw with his own eyes a man die: the dying man tried to say something, but his pitifully contorted mouth emitted only blood. After that, Ukheiro never let go of his javelin. Even when lying with a woman, he would put the javelin nearby, at his bedside, within easy reach. Ukheiro had killed many men, he had many near escapes from death, but he didn't give up this profession, for he knew no other. 'You're a man as long as you can kill another man,' he used to say.

Disaster befell him so unexpectedly that everyone was shaken. Especially as the battle was already over.

Striding over the corpses, Ukheiro had gathered up on the battlefield an armful of the finest javelins, as if they were kindling for a fire. Chariot horses, maddened by the loss of their drivers, were racing wildly round the quietened battlefield, and a chariot shaft struck Ukheiro on the back of the head as he strode about, after which the horses dragged the overturned chariot over his legs. This bolt from the blue made Ukheiro, dazed and stunned, think that he had been shamed in front of everyone. Then he tried to get up, but his body, broken at the waist, refused to obey. He smiled bitterly, 'There's your Vani!' and supporting himself on his hands, he looked around in bewilderment. Somewhere a horse was neighing, but he could see nothing. 'What's happened to my javelins?' he now thought, and his hands, supporting his gigantic body like pillars, suddenly began to tremble, forcing him to lie down. Ukheiro closed his eyes, and when he opened them again he was lying on a stretcher, and his daughter, ten-year-old Popina had shouldered her father's javelin and was following the stretcher. The javelin was torture for the child, it seemed that it had a soul which had awoken and wanted to play. The javelin felt it could do as it liked in a child's weak, inexperienced hands: it wouldn't have dared do this to its master. Ukheiro knew where and how to handle it. His hand's casual, painful, yet agreeable touch made the javelin shudder and roused it for battle. But now it felt like clowning. Its new bearer had to know whom she was dealing with. When the child first tried to pick it up, the javelin couldn't help tensing up, expecting the familiar pain: it held its breath, it got ready, but nothing familiar happened. The child lifted up one end, put it on her shoulder and only with great effort managed to free its proud tip from the earth. 'She's put me on her shoulder like firewood,' thought the javelin. At first it was angry, then it was in the mood for clowning. For a minute or two it held its breath on the child's shoulder, as if saying, 'I've accepted my fate,' and just as the child, lost in thought, was forgetting about its existence, it suddenly slipped forwards, toppled over, and stuck its tip in the ground, tripping up the dreaming child. 'Now you see, you can't manage,' someone called to the child. The javelin was laughing, its whole body shook and shone with laughter. The child wouldn't give up, as if she realised that the javelin was being cunning, and she gripped the happily swaying javelin with both hands on her badly bruised shoulder, even though her sinews were on the point of tearing.

'My father's died,' the child was thinking. 'That javelin's not going to be used again,' thought Ukheiro, quite unable to understand the heavy weight his wife was carrying as she followed behind Popina. Finally he realised and smiled: she wasn't carrying anything, she was pregnant.

They were just entering the gates of Vani when Marekhi went into labour: she was to dic giving birth, but in her stead presented her permanently crippled husband with a baby boy. Thus Ukheiro's family still numbered the same. In the new house, vacated for Ukheiro in recognition of his bravery in the field, the same number of people entered: Ukheiro and his two children, the ten-year-old Popina and Parnaoz, who still had not been washed or had his cord cut.

When Ukheiro fainted, the first to run to him were his loyal servants Shubu and Kaluka. Shuba fell straight on his knees and put his ear to Ukheiro's heart. 'He's alive!' he called to the crowd who had gathered round, and then felt the whole of Ukheiro's body, 'It's all right, it's all right, man,' Shubu muttered. But things were bad. The chariot wheels had smashed both thigh bones, and torn the muscles: blood was gushing from the wounds. The flesh was ripped off in so many places that there was no point bandaging it. 'Let's shovel earth over him,' someone said.

When Ukheiro's pregnant wife and ten-year-old daughter arrived, they had already buried him up to the waist. Blood oozed through the earth. The porous mound of earth gradually absorbed the moisture, sank and subsided. When they changed the earth, the flow of blood was stemmed, but Ukheiro had changed colour: he was drained, crumpled and blackened. 'It might be better…' someone ventured again, but Shubu immediately interrupted, shouting: 'Ukheiro has to see Vani!'

As soon as the gates of Vani came into sight, Marekhi had labour pains. Kaluka led Marekhi, who was grimacing with pain, off the road and sat her on a rock. 'Go away,' she called to the others, but the warriors put the stretcher on the ground and slowly, probably to win time and give their limbs some relief, turned towards the women.

Marekhi sat on the rock, her daughter standing over her and Kaluka's hand on her head. Bent double, Marekhi clutched her clenched knees, while thick shiny beads of sweat settled on her brow.

'Get lost!' Kaluka growled at the warriors.

Kaluka was hoping that Marekhi's pangs would pass and they would manage to get home in time. But Marekhi contracted even more and slipped off the rock. Her eyes showed fear and despair, she didn't recognize anybody. She smiled pathetically as if she was going to be beaten, her lips were blue and clenched tight, she turned over to lie prone and covered her eyes with her hands, as if she was doing something so shameful that she no longer had any right to look at the world. 'Take the girl away,' Kaluka called to the warriors, who had turned away, and she pushed Popina off. The warriors shouldered the stretcher again and headed almost at a run for Vani.

Ukheiro was aware of none of this. When he opened his eyes he was indoors, lying on a divan, a flame was flickering in the oil lamp. But Ukheiro still could not make anything out, except for enormous spherical shadows roaming round the room, colliding, merging and separating again, with agonizing slowness, as if they were covered in glue. The house was full of weird sounds. The shadows seemed to be pursuing these sounds, trying to catch them or drive them out. The roar of the river, the howling of jackals and whinnying of horses all mingled. It was these sounds that brought Ukheiro back to consciousness. At first he thought he was in camp, but almost immediately, somewhere very close, a baby cried. This sound cheered him: Marekhi's been delivered, he thought, and tried to stand up: he tried again, but someone's invisible hand stopped him; the invisible hand was stopping him from raising his head and putting him back on the bed, while the person whose hand it was, also invisible, said to him in a false, unnatural voice, 'Lie down, Ukheiro, lie down: Marekhi is past any help.'

Ukheiro immediately believed the hand and the voice: he believed and understood. This new knowledge was easily and quickly absorbed by his being, because he had been made to swallow the whole bowlful of medicine in one go, without any dilution or subterfuge: he got through it instantly and was cured of uncertainty, of hope, of terrors, of futile dreams. Marekhi had died! The objects and bodies in the room took shape. Ukheiro recognized them all. In fact, except for Marekhi, they were all here; Marekhi, naturally, couldn't be here, because she had died. Ukheiro wasn't interested in details which he had missed because he had been unconscious. Did it matter? Death took advantage of his exclusion and snatched Marekhi. If he had been on his feet, it wouldn't have happened, so that Marekhi's death was his fault. 'How strange it is,' thought Ukheiro, 'that Marekhi isn't there any more and never will be. While I was unconscious, death recruited her and had her taken off instead of me. I've got my mind back, but I've lost Marekhi for ever. Wouldn't it have been better?.. Hey, death, why have you left me behind, eh? You can't blame death, a man shouldn't faint, he should fight, endure, overcome, or if he does faint, he should never come round. If a woman ever spends a night away from home, she can't be trusted any more. The mind is the same. Marekhi isn't here any more, she'll never suddenly jerk awake when she's asleep, she won't smile at me, she'll never ever say to me, as she used to, "We can't complain, as long as you like the sight of us." Marekhi has gone and, instead, has left this bawling bundle of rags which Kaluka is holding tightly to her chest, looking at me, as if she expects me to call out and tell her, "Come, Kaluka, show me my child, thank God we've been allowed to keep him, at least."'

'That child is not going to live,' Ukheiro suddenly shouted.

A little later, he resumed his normal voice, as if assigning a servant a domestic task, 'Kill him quickly so he can join his mother.'

Kaluka's face fell: frightened, she look round at the people gathered in the room: 'Don't let me carry such a burden on my own, help me!' But nobody dared answer Ukheiro back.

The new-born baby began life in a strange way: his mother immediately abandoned him without even looking at him; his father sentenced him to death for murdering his mother. His mother was laid out on the floor in the next room, her body covered with white canvas the size of a sail. At the corpse's feet Popina squatted with her head on her knees, sobbing piteously like a hungry puppy.

Marekhi's funeral was silent and dull.

On the day of the funeral Marekhi was laid out on a divan in the middle of the room, and the canvas as big as a sail was removed. The smile of relief and regret had frozen for ever on her washed-out face. In the next room Ukheiro was shouting, 'Let my daughter kiss her mother so that she will always remember her.' The womenfolk kept bringing Popina up to her mother's body. Dead, her mother was beautiful, but death had changed her. It seemed to Popina that this motionless and beautiful woman was not her mother, but a dummy that looked like her, who'd been put there to trick her, while her real mother had been taken away by death. Popina was neither surprised nor afraid. Hadn't her mother told her that death took whomsoever it fancied and considered worthy? She was even a little proud that this time death had chosen her mother, but couldn't understand why this beautiful dummy, which was so very like her mother, had to be laid out here. The disagreeable feel of the dead woman's chill skin sickened her. 'They're trying to frighten me,' she thought, but she couldn't have understood who needed to frighten her, and why. When Ukheiro shouted yet again that his daughter should kiss her mother and the women once again brought her to the corpse, she couldn't stop herself being sick. Vomiting made her dizzy and her eyes stopped seeing. She didn't feel her face being washed. Her chest was wet. She now avoided looking in the direction of the corpse, and she tried to think of something else, if only of the butterfly pinned to the wall by someone who had lived in this house before her, to whom everything around was familiar and close, but who had been forced to leave the area to escape death, which pursued Ukheiro's family like a treacherous dog.

Death had made everything around yet more alien. Popina knew, and was even glad that she was coming back with her parents to her homeland, but it hadn't come up to her expectations: she had followed two stretchers into a house which, like overwintering swallows, they had been so anxious to reach. On one stretcher lay her father, crushed by a chariot; on the other, her mother's corpse, and she felt she had set foot not in her home, but in the kingdom of death. She herself felt she was too little for that. Not for a moment had she felt a desire to run away. Where would she go, in any case? Here she had everybody; even her mother would return if she was desperate to see her children. After all, Parnaoz was alive. True, his father had ordered him to be killed straight away, but Popina knew that Kaluka had hidden the baby somewhere. Kaluka had said, 'If I were to kill him, how could I look his mother in the eye?' Then Popina began to hope: she suddenly believed that her mother really would come back.

She just had to be patient and wait; above all, she had to keep a look-out and not miss her mother's return.

After that she dreamed almost every night of her dead mother, or rather the dummy that looked like her mother, with a butterfly fluttering over her. She was afraid to go to sleep. She was sure that the dream was watching out somewhere for her to feel sleepy. In the dream everything was repeated so exactly and so logically that you could hardly call it a dream. Her father yelled, the women wailed and caressed her, telling her, 'Don't be afraid, it's your mother,' and dragged her towards the divan. A butterfly was fluttering over the divan and shedding shiny black powder. 'That butterfly is my mother's soul,' Popina thought in her dream. The moment she woke up she rushed to the wall where someone had pinned the butterfly. When she saw it was where it should be, for some reason she felt calmer and, shivering from standing on the cold stone floor, she ran back to bed.

This was repeated every night. Thoughts of her dead mother gave the little girl no rest: it was frightening to be motherless, to feel that she needed an older woman to emulate, in order to learn what she absolutely needed to know. All she knew was that she was a girl: that was all that her mother had managed to tell her: 'You're a woman, and don't you forget it,' her mother used to say, but Popina was in no hurry to understand the meaning of these words: why should she, when her mother was at her side, and she could look at her all the time; she was dizzy with happiness when she imagined becoming herself just as beautiful a woman, smiling at herself in the mirror. Now her mother's words were as silent as stones, as if they too had died. Popina now felt with her whole being that she would remain for ever as weak and ignorant if she didn't get to the heart of this impenetrable and oppressive silence. 'I'm a woman, I'm a woman, a woman…' she repeated before she fell asleep, sprawled on her back, her eyes wide open. But when the feelings which these words produced took shape, Popina curled up, because they were feelings of fear. 'I'm a woman, so I have to be afraid, I have to be afraid of everything, because I'm a woman. That's what my mother meant to say, but she couldn't tell me. Or I didn't understand, because I wasn't a woman yet,' Popina thought. The thought was hard to fight free of, and she kept on repeating the same thing: 'What has a woman got to be afraid of? Her father? Her brother? Everything? Well? Does she have to be afraid of her father? Yes. Of her brother? Yes. Why? Because she's a woman. God, don't make me dream of mother tonight, at least,' Popina murmured as she lay there, sleepless. 'Or let me dream of my real mother, the one death took away.'

But the dummy-mother's frozen face erased for good the image of Popina's real mother. This was how she had to remember her: however hard she worked her mind, she could not manage to imagine the face of the mother that death had taken. Who could she ask what her mother looked like? There was nobody she could ask, or who would tell her…

Kaluka had hidden her brother in the most remote room in the house to stop him falling victim to his father's sudden wrath. Ukheiro never asked again about his son. Instead of the baby, Kaluka dropped a rock wrapped in rags down the well. The well accepted the offering, and responded with a belch: there was now a secret in the house. Ukheiro in a state of anger was capable of anything. But everyone swallowed the secret, as the well had swallowed the rock wrapped in rags. First of all, Kaluka told her own son, Philamon, 'I'll kill you with my own hands if you blurt it out to anyone.' And who would let Philamon, a mere child, get close to Ukheiro: he was just a little pitcher; but Kaluka told him, because little pitchers have big ears.

The secret brought everyone closer, but it made them more frightened, tense and devious. They took turns to spend the night at the baby's bedside. The moment he cried, they stuck a frayed rope-end dipped in milk into his mouth. It was easier to keep the baby quiet in the daytime: everyone was deliberately noisy, Kaluka banged the pots and saucepans with a stick and there was such an uproar in the house that you couldn't hear thunder, let alone a baby crying. Ukheiro never asked why there was so much noise. He had long ago guessed that his household was deceiving him and deliberately turned a deaf ear, because his initial anger had passed and he was now even glad that his order had been disobeyed. Staying silent and turning a deaf ear was the only way he could preserve his son's life. So he went deaf. Everything else in the house went on as before. Everyone was nervous and alert, covering each other's lips with their hand. Popina found all this more difficult to bear than anyone, she couldn't understand why her father shouldn't love Parnaoz, she couldn't accept this horrific attitude to a baby, and her little heart was worn out with fear and sadness. 'If he doesn't love Parnaoz, then he doesn't love me either,' thought Popina. This thought loomed larger and larger, and grew until it took root in Popina's heart and soul, until she decided, whatever it might cost her, to test her doubts. She was now old enough to believe that nobody had ever thought or noticed what she was thinking and noticing. It was natural for her to want to share her impressions with someone, or rather the person closest to her. But where would she find that close person? One was dead and not likely to return. The second was lying stretched out in his room, covered to the knees by the sail-sized canvas in which Marekhi's corpse had been shrouded: he was embroidering the canvas with flowers made from coloured threads. The third person had a frayed rope-end, dipped in goat's milk, stuck in his mouth and couldn't even cry. All that was left was her own self. Popina could always chat to herself, and whatever she wanted to say, she would listen to: she and herself weren't afraid or shy of each other, and they had plenty of time, because they were almost always alone, and when they were alone they forgot about everything else. So Popina got into the habit of talking out loud to herself. She was gradually more enthralled and carried away by these talks, which at first were inaudible to others, so that she no longer noticed if she was alone or not. At first, everyone assumed that she was talking to them and questioned her. 'No, I wasn't talking to you,' Popina would reply and then fall silent until her anger had passed and she could resume her conversation with herself. Once she scared Philamon. It happened when Popina took it upon herself to supply her father with coloured threads. Popina was stirring a pot of boiling dye, while Philamon squatted nearby, blowing on the fire.

'Stupid Philamon,' Popina suddenly said.

His jaws gaping, Philamon looked up at Popina, but she was stirring the pot with a stick and pushing back her hair with her free hand, stopping it falling into the pot of dyed threads.

Time passed. The children grew. Ukheiro went on with his embroidery. Sitting up in bed, his back against the wall, the sail-sized canvas over his legs, on it he depicted with coloured threads the story of his stormy life. He began the embroidery the day that he was fully convinced that he would never stand up again, never set foot on the ground, because no doctor on earth could set or knit the bones crushed by the war chariot's wheels and enable them to support the weight of Ukheiro's enormous body. However hard it was, Ukheiro had to reconcile himself to his fate, and he did. A warrior's will power, tempered over the years, stood him in good stead in his illness. Life was over for him, but he now had to wait for death, and that was no easy matter. One day death would get round to him, a cripple confined within four walls, when there were so many men and warriors in good health walking around. Even dying took time, and Ukheiro had to pass that time somehow, if idleness wasn't going to make him strangle himself with his own frustrated hands. Embroidery dispersed and lessened a little the bile and melancholy that had accumulated in his heart; instead, he learnt to think, he looked within himself and he was so badly clawed by remorse that in mid-work his hand would suddenly freeze, his eyes stare at the ceiling and stay fixed there for some time while a venomous smile slithered over his cruelly clenched lips like a broken-backed snake. So it was. Then he would touch his face with his hand, as if wiping away the venomous smile, and go back to his embroidery.

As time passed, so did the number of lines on the rough surface of the canvas, and it became clearer to Ukheiro how senseless was the life he had lived. Every day began the same way, was burdened with the same adventures, and ended the same way. People were almost always the same, everyone resembled everyone, because they died the same way: the last unspoken word came from everyone's mouth as blood and spittle, just like the first human being whom Ukheiro, trained on a dummy stuffed with hay, pierced with a javelin. The dying man tried to say something, his eyes rolled piteously but instead of a word, his contorted mouth produced black blood. After that, Ukheiro speared so many men with his infallible javelin, that anyone else would have lost count. But Ukheiro remembered every single one, despite their amazing similarity. He realised this again when he had the sail-sized canvas spread over his shattered legs and became forever reconciled to his fate. The reason he began embroidering was that his memory, full of corpses, bothered him. He had somehow to drag those corpses around and look after them until he died. Because he couldn't kill any more, he had to show respect to those he had already killed, to bury them and lodge them. That was the only thing he was good for. He didn't waste time, not until morning did anyone blow out the flame constantly flickering in the oil lamp, even though it begged in vain, 'Put me out, I'm exhausted.' Ukheiro didn't spare himself until tears clouded his eyes, until his back ached intolerably: he went on frantically digging a grave in the sail-sized canvas so that he could inter yet another man he had killed and thus be freed of him. The graveyard embroidered in coloured threads was getting bigger and bigger. But he still had a lot of men to bury. 'How long I have lived!' he kept thinking with amazement. Every seemingly insignificant incident or story, in fact, brought up so many memories that Ukheiro kept bustling like a poor housewife, not knowing how to lodge so many unexpected guests. Disability had made Ukheiro wiser. When he read the inscriptions he had embroidered the day before, he was surprised: 'I fell and I saw!' he had stitched in black thread at one point, and it was true. A fallen man could see what a man still standing carelessly walked over.

At the time he couldn't see, he couldn't see anything except the place where his javelin had to strike. He couldn't see, because others saw him and were running away, or they thought they were getting away, that his infallible javelin might miss them. That is how time had passed, like a piece of cloth ripped when transfixed on a javelin tip, laying bare a country, leaving it shattered like a woman widowed at her own wedding, and then dying itself. 'Perhaps it's all a dream,' Ukheiro sometimes thought, perhaps there had never been that time whose ashes he was now raking up on the sail-sized canvas. But when he set eyes on his highly polished javelin he saw it all clearly. He really had a special javelin, with a heavy body and a light head, like himself. The javelin had a decorative inscription. Ukheiro liked to boast, 'There are only two javelins in the whole world with inscriptions of that sort, and one belongs to me.' 'My master conquered me, but in his hand I've become invincible,' was inscribed on Ukheiro's javelin. When Ukheiro pressed it down on the earth, its golden tip rose a whole hand span above his crest-like hair, and Ukheiro was a tall man. 'Your height is the only kingly thing about you,' his wife, the unsmiling Marekhi, used to tell him. Ukheiro knew full well what his wife was getting at, but he was not in the least angry, because he was sure that Marekhi loved him and was even proud to be his wife. Marekhi's older sisters thought the same, because they envied her, the youngest sister, for being head over heels in love with her husband, 'an ordinary warrior' allowed only rarely to leave the camp to visit his family. Covered in blood and dust, he would come rushing like a storm, to turn everything upside down and drown everything with his loud guffaws and roars. Perhaps Marekhi was so envied by her sisters because their husbands were worn out and exhausted by endless waiting and one and the same worries. Marekhi always sat with her head lowered while her sisters talked about her maniac of a husband, but she always recalled what they said, in order to use her sisters' pointed remarks for her own protection and survival when she found herself face to face with Ukheiro: this truly manic river, overflowing with love, made her giddy and swept her away bodily.

Marekhi's father was Oqajado's vizier. When Æëtes overthrew Oqajado, the vizier did not abandon the ex-king, but reaffirmed his loyalty and, with his many daughters, also fled the homeland. He was a clever man, but he hadn't thought a quarrel between cousins could grow so violent. When the Supreme King went to the trouble of putting on a solemn reception for the refugees, the vizier's heart missed a beat, for he realised that they would not escape unscathed from Minos's hospitality. 'We're trapped,' he wanted to tell his king, but Oqajado was so patently over the moon, so flattered by the attention and respect, that the vizier felt sorry for him and bit his tongue. Instead, he resigned his post. He resigned of his own free will: nobody needed him as vizier, and he had no time for kings. Now he had to see to his children who had lost their homeland. At first they had no complaints and even liked being refugees: everyone was interested in their vicissitudes, everyone showed them sympathy. But, apart from anything else, sympathy is the forerunner of contempt; what is extraordinary today is ordinary tomorrow, and soon becomes tedious. He had been appointed vizier because he had a sharp mind, and thinking about his homeless family made it even sharper. So he wrote fewer decrees and charters and made more frequent visits to the heirs to lost thrones. He didn't need to go far: if you threw a stone at the palace of Knossos you'd hit an ex-king, a pretender, a supposed king, a usurper, or all four at once. Soon he had married all his daughters off, except for the youngest. He was helped by the fact that he always struck while the iron was hot, and got to work quickly. He never let anyone forget about the news from Colchis, he told people about the fairy-tale riches and magnificence of this faraway country, so that marrying a woman from Colchis, especially a noblewoman, seemed something to boast about. 'All these kings and queens, so how can I be vizier to all of you?' he would joke to his daughters and sons-in-law. 'We need just one more king,' the married sisters would burst into peals of laughter, while Marekhi the youngest dreamed of her prince, as she sat by the window, watching the road. The vizier was extraordinarily fond of his youngest daughter and planned a exceptionally good match for her. As he had placed the elder daughters, he could think more calmly about Marekhi's future: there was no need for hurry or to make a grab: he could look for the best of the best. But Marekhi let him down by marrying, admittedly extraordinarily, an ordinary warrior. At first the vizier disliked his youngest daughter's choice, but after pondering countless times, thinking deeply and taking a closer look, he became convinced that Marekhi was in a safer pair of hands than his older daughters. Apart from anything else, Marekhi and her husband were compatriots: it was easier for them to adapt and get used to one another. They had the same fate: both of them were set on returning to their homeland.

Ukheiro was in the street when he fell in love with Marekhi: he happened to set eyes on her and from that day he knew no rest. When he got back to camp, his friends didn't recognize him. He looked frightened, his eyes rolled senselessly as if he didn't believe he had escaped from some ordeal. Ukheiro had seen plenty of women, women and war were inextricably linked in his mind. Willing or not, women filled their camp after every battle or raid. Where these women appeared from, where they had been hiding, Ukheiro couldn't understand and wasn't, in any case, interested. They came when he waned them to come, when he had the time. Many times he had woken up in bed drunk, with a woman by his side, unable to remember if they'd gone to bed together, or whether his friends had later put her there as a joke. In short, he didn't know much about women: he knew only what he didn't have to learn. But Marekhi was different, she didn't remind him of any woman, she didn't arouse the usual desire, although ever since he first set eyes on her everything seemed unusual. Ukheiro started strolling in that street more often and soon established that Marekhi lived at the end of the street, in a house painted bright red, and at the other end of the street there was a temple where Marekhi went to pray. So she wasn't hard to pursue. The only walk the young girl took was from home to temple and back again.

Not daring to do anything else, unable to think of anything, one fine day Ukheiro rolled an apple into the temple where the now nubile Marekhi was praying alone. Marekhi spotted the apple straight away and picked it up. The apple had something carved into it with a knife. As the inscription was hard to read, Marekhi was forced to read it out loud and syllable by syllable: 'I swear I won't mar-ry any-one ex-cept U-khei-ro...' Marekhi pursed her lips, shrugged her little shoulders, to say that she didn't understand any of this nonsense; then she gave a sudden shriek, clutched the apple with both hands to her chest, as if hiding it from somebody, and looked round the temple in fright. But it was now too late. This 'nonsense' was like an oath sworn in God's hearing. There was no way of going back on the oath, which the temple vaults had parsed and repeated together with her. Now they were silent, but the silence was meaningful and expressive. Statues of the gods were looking at her as if approving her decision and promising support in this venture. Marekhi left the temple, barely able to walk. Where was her birdlike nimbleness, cheerfulness and twittering? Her face that had shone with youth was washed out; her body, once on springs, slumped, as if she had been locked in this temple since birth and only now been allowed to come out into daylight. She found herself in an empty street, which, once turned red by the early pomegranate flowers, had now suddenly wilted. She still had the apple clutched with both hands to her chest.

After that day Marekhi took to her bed. The vizier, his hair turned grey in the shadow of the throne, wrung his hands with despair, for he could not understand what pained his daughter so much, until his eldest daughter found the apple under Marekhi's pillow and they read the inscription the knife had carved. The vizier grieved, but the sisters couldn't stop laughing about Marekhi's choice. 'She's not just the youngest of us, she's the silliest,' they told their pensive father. Marekhi said not a word; she lay on her back staring at the ceiling. She seemed to be waiting for a secret sign to appear on the ceiling.

After a great deal of thought, her father gave up: to save his daughter from dying, he sent a messenger to Ukheiro, 'I have a matter to discuss, come and see me.' When the vizier, or former vizier, saw Ukheiro, confused, his eyes flustered, his face pale, he thought, 'They've already settled it between them.' What most upset Marekhi's father was, 'How can I offer my daughter to this beanstalk raised in a tent?' But now he saw Ukheiro's fearful, confused face, he was pleased: 'I'll make him beg for her, though.' Ukheiro stood there, his head bowed. He fidgeted with his fingers, not intending to ask for anything, as if he couldn't wait to be allowed to leave. 'The goddess of love has driven both of them equally mad,' Marekhi's father thought. What he said was, 'You're one of us, you seem to be a good man, so ask me for whatever you want.' Ukheiro was startled, his eyes opened wide and he stared at his prospective father-in-law for some time. Then he coughed, cleared his throat which was blocked by emotion, straightened his shoulders and said, 'Let me wrestle your sons-in-law.'

Ukheiro had by now embroidered this story on his sail-sized canvas, and whenever he re-read it, he smiled at this stupid request. Fortunately, Marekhi's father didn't listen to Ukheiro's request: his reply struck the beanpole warrior dumb with happiness and surprise.

'I know everything,' said Marekhi's father. "We can't go on like this. You're not a child any more; you should have come earlier and sorted out this business before. We're not cannibals, are we?'

Ukheiro sat radiant at the wedding, he felt the world was his oyster. He squashed gold and silver chalices in his fist, he guffawed so heartily that soon the whole wedding party was guffawing with him. Marekhi, red with embarrassment, hid her face in her hands. This was a habit she acquired on her wedding day and kept until the day she died. Someone had only to mention Ukheiro for her to cover her face with her hands. It is hard to explain why she did this. Marekhi loved her strange husband heart and soul. Once, when Ukheiro was on yet another campaign and Marekhi was about to give birth, she admitted to herself, 'I loved Ukheiro even before he rolled an apple at me in the temple.'

Love is always followed by fear. As soon as she was alone, when she shut her eyes, Marekhi could see Ukheiro dead. She broke into a cold sweat and tried to think of something else, although whatever she thought of always brought up Ukheiro's face, as lifeless as stone. 'He'll be killed, he'll be killed,' she worried all night long. By day she took ground chalk and a piece of leather and polished Ukheiro's javelins. When she had the javelins shining, then she shook the dust off his letters and would read absolutely every one from beginning to end. When least expected, a slave sent by Ukheiro would appear, panting and moaning as he dragged an enormous stone and laid it at her feet, as he had been ordered. The scrawled letters scratched in the stone told Marekhi of her husband's adventures. 'Instead of such a big rock he could have sent a couple of words by messenger,' Marekhi would tell the sweating slave, as the latter, like a wild animal, tore at a roasted leg of mutton, belching freely. She said so to conceal her joy: her heart swelled with bliss that her husband should send her such heavy letters. It took a lot of time to carve so many letters in stone, so that all that time Ukheiro could not have been thinking of anything else. This letters on stones made it easier for her to wait for her husband to come home from the wars. When the day dawned on which they would go back to the homeland, Marekhi first of all had the letters stored in trunks, had the trunks put in the hold and only then got on board the ship heading for her motherland.

When Ukheiro was brought home to Marekhi wounded for the first time, she was appalled: it took her a long time to realise that she would spend her happiest days at the bedside of her husband whose face was burning with the fever of his wounds. Then Marekhi became mother, nurse and servant as well as wife to Ukheiro. She was happy to hand-feed a man as big as that, hiding medicine in the food, while he never guessed. Then she would tell him strange stories to make Ukheiro lie quietly and stop his barely closed wounds from opening again if he carelessly tossed about.

The stories that Ukheiro was told by his wife he now transferred to the sail-sized canvas, not in order to show them to others, but to have Marekhi always close to him. Marekhi's tales were for him the same as Marekhi. He put his hand to the embroidered lines as tenderly as if he were caressing Marekhi's little head pressed against his shoulder.

We have to admit that Ukheiro in his heart of hearts was proud to have such a noble wife. Although, as he used to say, if he'd picked her up in the city market, he'd have loved her just as much. Marekhi told such strange stories — 'They're nothing but fairy tales,' Ukheiro used to exclaim. But Marekhi went on telling them with the patience of an old nurse so as to get her husband off to sleep. Ukheiro could be as difficult as a child: he would interrupt, make her go back and repeat the same thing over and over again. There were a great many things in his wife's stories which Ukheiro found doubtful, but one he did enjoy and believe, although this story was no more plausible than the others. Yet Ukheiro liked it, perhaps because it was hard to believe. Who knows how many time he made Marekhi, who was by now yawning, tell him about the winged twins who she claimed were born to her great-grandmother's great-grandmother? He would put his hands behind his head, smile and see something then which exceeded any truth in strangeness and beauty: Ukheiro could see the winged twins. The spectacle both saddened and pleased him. For some reason he remembered his own childhood and the city where he was born, and which he would love to fly over just once, more than life itself. It was now like a fairy-tale, non-existent land, lost through carelessness or stupidity, and now forgotten. Flying in his distant memories, Ukheiro genuinely believed that in 'that land' everyone was born with wings, everyone, including Ukheiro. But he couldn't understand why he had left, or had been made to leave 'that land', which, if recalled just momentarily, filled him with such sadness and joy. And when had his wings been cut off? Back then, a long time ago, he really did have them. Now he didn't have the slightest doubt: so convinced was he that he interrupted his wife's tale and told her, 'Why don't you put your hand on my back?' His wife thought his back had a bed-sore and tenderly stroked it.

'Is there nothing there?' asked Ukheiro.

The winged twins were swirling in the air like swallows which had flown in by accident, they chirruped, they played, and their light wings made the vibrant air tickle Ukheiro's face.

Ukheiro had killed many men, but earlier, when he was on his feet, he never had any pangs of remorse, he wasn't bothered, because he considered this to be his trade, a man's trade which needed to be carried out conscientiously. It didn't need any explanations, everything was clear as it was: if you didn't kill, you'd be killed. But incurable illness changed and displaced a lot of things in Ukheiro's mind. Now he had more time to think. Thought, like a prudent woman, never visited anywhere alone, and always took sadness and regret with it. Sadness and regret made his feelings, already sharpened by endlessly lying in bed and by prolonged pain, even sharper and refined them. So obscure sentiments, rather than rational reality were most important for him. Diving deep into this darkness, he naturally found weeping natural, and somewhere in the most inaccessible and intangible depths of his being, he would weep the copious tears of all those he had slain, because they were all united by identical deaths and he was equally sorry for all of them. The only way in which some differed from others was so insignificant that it eluded definition: Ukheiro's infallible javelin had speared some earlier, others later. Now Ukheiro was living in their world and didn't intend to come back from it, because he had permanently forgotten the way back. The only thing that brought Ukheiro back to everyday reality were the coloured threads. Whenever he ran short of a thread, he would raise such a thunderous uproar that anyone who happened to be passing in front of his house would look up at the sky. His domestics would come running in flustered, and woe to them if they didn't provide the thread in time. Sitting up in bed, his eyes popping, Ukheiro would hold above his head his infallible javelin.

After a number of such incidents, Popina took it upon herself to ensure her father was supplied with thread. Her child's intuition told her that coloured threads were her only means of getting into her father's world. And that was what she dreamed of. All she knew was that the man whom people were so afraid of that they tip-toed around the house, who spent whole days like a girl waiting for a bridegroom, doing nothing but embroidery, was her father. Her child's nature needed, longed for, sought the smell and warmth of a parent, and surrounded him with affection. Many times had the motherless Popina wept, hiding her head under the blanket; many times she felt anguish and wished that she were dead and pitied her dead imaginary self. After her mother's death Popina was constantly afraid: she felt that she was not growing up properly, that her arms were shorter than they should be. She had a flatter chest than other girls her age, who were in every way like women. 'That's because I don't have a mother,' Popina thought, and any changes in her growing, still temporary shape, however natural, normal and necessary, terrified her. Popina longed for a parent's hand even if that hand caused her pain, tore her hair, bruised her flesh, as long as she was sure that this hand really was there and belonged to her parent.

His wife's death had distanced Ukheiro from his family even more, because his whole nature had reacted by rebellion to the loss of Marekhi. He linked even his own invalid state to Marekhi's death, as if she were the fairy-tale bird, the guardian of his vitality.

Ukheiro had accumulated so much that his illness had no noticeable effect on the family for some time. But his wife's death and his withdrawal gradually made the household somewhat peculiar, a shelter where orphans and homeless cripples could get all the care they needed, and children would not feel orphaned, or cripples abandoned.

The children gradually grew up, became aware and now realised that their life was on the wrong path, that they had lost for ever the inner comfort derived not from others' concern but from a parent's scolding. Very often Popina lurked in the doorway of her father's room, hoping he might look up, see her and call to her. Her persistent stare breached the thick barriers of self-absorption that protected Ukheiro so well from the outside world, but Ukheiro would just glance, take a look and a meaningless, insignificant smile would run across his face, before he went back to his task. Every day the sail-sized canvas covering his smashed legs grew more colourful and beautiful and excited the child's curiosity, as the smell of carrion excites a hungry cat. She could go on watching without end, albeit from a distance, this magical canvas, which in the candlelight seemed like a verdant meadow strewn with white blossom. That may be why Popina took it on herself to supply her father with threads. Nobody helped her because she wanted the thread which her father was using to pass through her hands alone — perhaps, she thought, it might pass on to her father what she had said to it. Popina would lift the threads, once they were dyed and rolled into balls, to her lips and whisper her longing and her wishes to them: 'Tell father I love him very, very, very much. There's a little boy with a lump on his head the size of a fist: he'll know who I mean. And also tell him that…' she would whisper endlessly to the ball of rough thread until she fell asleep.

In a small wooden shed Popina set up a dyer's workshop: she had Philamon clean out the shed, take away, pile up and burn chairs with shaky legs, barrels with broken hoops or falling planks, and baskets with no bottom or with broken handles. She made a fireplace in the scrubbed and tidied shed, hung sparkling clean pots across the walls, heaped up a thousand different sorts of plant roots, bulbs, stalks and leaves on the shelves so that they would always be to hand. Popina mixed and boiled the dyes herself. Soon she became so skilful that you could wash a thread she'd dyed in water ten times and the colour still wouldn't fade. She dyed the thread herself, spread it out herself on hazel laths to dry and personally guarded it with a long stick from the hens, which stuck their heads out, looking with amazement at the strange carpet of colour and cackling to express that amazement or their wish to poke about in it.

Popina would wind the dried thread onto bits of branch-wood and would arrange the shaggy balls of yarn, like fat hedgehogs, in a basket. A pungent smell of wild flowers came from the basket full of coloured threads; intoxicated bees buzzed all round it. Popina's labour and devotion did not go without a response: when, frightened to be so near her father, yet with a feeling of pride, she first brought the scented and dazzling basket to Ukheiro, he put his mighty hand, like the blade of a spade, on her head and said, 'You've got your mother's kind heart.' Then, suddenly overwhelmed by, and unable to cope with a wave of emotion, the best he could think of was to put his hand on the sail-sized canvas and add, 'If you want to, have a look.' That was all Popina wanted. No sooner had she looked at the sail-sized canvas than she had dots in her eyes: the sail-sized canvas was really as radiant, verdant and intoxicating as a spring meadow full of the smell of honey and fire. Popina could clearly hear bees buzzing and streams trickling. Soon her eyes focused on a stream shining in the sun's rays: it was running through the flowers, as lithe and fast as a snake.

'It's beautiful,' said Popina.

This remark made Ukheiro shiver. He hadn't expected it. First he looked at his daughter to make sure he had heard right, then he himself stared at the canvas, as if he wanted to find the link between it and his daughter's remark. But he apparently failed to find the link, and now he muttered in his usual otherworldly voice, 'You're a child, that's why.' Silently he went on, 'You won't understand what horrors happen on this "beautiful" canvas.'

This is how Ukheiro's and Popina's friendship began, how little Popina's ball of coloured thread helped her break into her father's secret and fairy-tale world. Popina acquired the right to be in her father's room. The household, too, settled down, because a full basket of balls of coloured yarn was always there at the head of Ukheiro's bed. Popina also sat there, on a low three-legged stool. The crochet needle had given Ukheiro a blister on his index finger, but he still embroidered quickly and Popina could see the canvas's rough surface become more colourful as it filled up with more and more new flowers. Father and daughter didn't understand one another. For one, everything was strange and enchanting, for the other familiar and horrible. Ukheiro was burying time, or a friend's corpse, but Popina could only see flowers sprouting from the rotting corpse. She sat and watched, and when she was so tired she began to have spots in her eyes, she herself, without knowing how, felt she had walked out onto this colourful meadow. Everything else — the walls, the flickering oil lamp, the bed and her father — had vanished somewhere. All around, as far as her eye could see, was a verdant meadow full of wild flowers, and she was standing in the middle of it, not knowing where she was, so similar were all four sides of the meadow. Her dress, wet with dew, clung to her thighs. The sound of her footsteps made vultures lazily rise up from the tall grass, turn their bald necks towards her and then descend to the spot they had just flown up from. The bees, swollen with nectar, swarmed suspiciously round this alien animal who had wandered into their kingdom. The stream had also seen her and ran off with such a rushing noise that the flowers were knocked against each other and dropped their pretty coloured crowns into the foaming water. Popina could see only the tail end of the stream, in which the laughing sunbeam shone like a metal burr. On a grass stem a green grasshopper was crouching, watching Popina with its big popping eyes. Red ants were attacking a white bone which had been gnawed out. Popina felt that she was alien, or rather superfluous to this meadow. Everybody and everything had their proper place here, and if any of them, or any part, however insignificant, were to be changed or displaced, everything would be all mixed up. But Popina was ready to disturb and breach the regulated peace and order which reigned in the meadow, unless it conceded her too a place, unless it accepted her as one of them. With the stubbornness of a child rejected by her friends, Popina tried to hold her end up. But she failed to realise how far the temptation had lured her, how genuinely alien and powerless she was in a place where everything belonged to a dead time. She was wandering about not in an imaginary meadow but in her father's memories, her father's past, and she couldn't change anything because everything had already happened: it had been ordained and buried before Popina was born. She herself was the fruit of all this dead time, and the only thing she could do was to break away promptly from this gnarled and thorny tree.

Popina was tearing out flowers by the root, exterminating the bees, who were sluggish with their rich food, pursuing the stream, treading on its tail and laughing spitefully when the pain caused by her footsteps made the stream twist its foaming body from tail to neck; she tore the wings off the green grasshopper with popping eyes and laughed spitefully again when the wingless grasshoppers crawled piteously through the trampled grass. The only thing that could assuage Popina's anger and lure her back from the meadow was age, but time did not exist on the magic meadow. But Popina had her own time which, when she crossed over to the meadow, she had left on the three-legged stool. Popina may have left time behind and forgotten it, but it went on doing what it always did: it grew and added to Popina's age and, when she was again standing on the stone floor of the room, she was no longer a child. On her low three-legged stool her younger brother, Parnaoz had nestled.

'What do you think you're doing, creeping in here in the dark? Go away and play!' Popina shouted at her brother and left the room so as never to remember again her disillusioned childhood, that had slipped so pointlessly between her fingers.

After that Popina seldom went to see her father, only when Ukheiro was running out of thread or an ulcerating wound opened up and had to be rebandaged. As well as pus and blood, tiny sharp shards of bone came out of the wound. Popina was expert at this task, too; when she bandaged Ukheiro, he was filled with relief and bliss. These were the relief and bliss which only a sick man can experience, when his pain abates. At times, when an ulcerating wound became inflamed, then swollen and hardened, making all his skin painfully taut, Ukheiro would be upset, restless with fever and would look with such pleading eyes at his daughter bustling at the foot of the bed, as if he was asking her for forgiveness for some inhuman crime. Popina felt a heart-rending pity and realised then how wretched and helpless her father was, how alone and simple. Pain was persistently, mercilessly shattering and annihilating the stern frowning mask of this hermit of a man, and giving him instead the face of an ordinary mortal, frightened and ravaged by illness.

Popina didn't like this face, because it aroused pity and demanded sympathy. That was too much like her. A long time ago she had lost that ability or desire to resist, a desire which wandering over her father's sail-sized canvas had aroused in her. Faster and more thorough than nature, the sense of her own helplessness had changed her whole being, not just changed it but had burdened it with intellect and shown it its place. Popina armed herself with this sense, as a frightened traveller takes a stick to arm himself against the dogs in an alley-way. Popina had only one obligation: despite her fear, she had to get through the alley-way full of dogs, because the other side of the alley-way was the goal for which she had left home: the realm of eternity. Popina imagined life to be as severe and surly as her father's mask. When she became, or forced herself to be convinced, she became calm again, because it was easier for her premature mental pain and sadness to fit in with life seen thus. But a very tiny sensation of human weakness, softheartedness or compassion left her confused. This is why Popina disliked her father's unmasked face, washed out and frightened, confessing the fear and the unbearable pain of being alone. Popina experienced this transformation of her father as a betrayal, as if she had been abandoned on the battlefield.

'You're alone, too, and you're in pain, too,' thought Popina, upset and trying to avert her gaze from her father, as if she was ashamed of finding out his secret. Wasn't the colourful canvas with its straggling letters just outright self-deceit? Could thread overcome the weight of loneliness and pain? Wasn't her father weaving a refuge in which to hide from life? If not, then why didn't he do embroidery when he had the use of his legs, when he wasn't in pain, when he wasn't alone and when he used to send his wife enormous rocks instead of beads and earrings? Because he was then as strong and awkward as a rock, as heavy and as deadly dangerous as a rock. Now being aware of his own helplessness or nothingness had so unmanned him that he put a bird or a flower at the beginning and end of every line. Who needed his bird and flower and what for, who would find them touching? He was just deceiving himself because he was afraid of the truth. Pain had instilled fear into him, pain and loneliness. Why did Popina have to stand alone fending off life, as if it was a bellowing herd, and why did she have to defend this stone hovel which was called their house, their family, their common refuge? No, he ought to be standing shoulder to shoulder with her and listen from afar to the sound of paving slabs breaking under the hooves, the pillar rocking and bending, the walls being stripped of plaster and wrecked as the cattle rubbed their flanks against them.

CHAPTER EIGHT

TSUTSA led her son up to the throne. Oqajado's face was burning with excitement; he slowly, timidly lowered himself onto the throne as if some joker were about to remove it from under him. 'How odd you are,' Tsutsa told him. She crossed her hands on her breast, bent her head to one side and looked with delight at her son as he sat on his throne. Oqajado was embarrassed, he swivelled his eyes to remind her of the courtiers constantly bustling about in the throne room, but Tsutsa was unable to notice anyone, and her cheeks, too, burned with excitement. It was hardly amazing. Everything had turned out for the best, her dream had come true, the long awaited day had dawned. No! She had made it dawn, she had torn it by force from life's hand. It belonged to her, that was why. She had put herself out, she had sacrificed herself for it, she had wracked her brains, shed blood, drained herself of everything she had. That's why she deserved it. Her dream was now on the throne. True, her dream had a flattened face like a stable floor, with red pimples on its sweaty brow and was smiling with confusion, but he bore the title of king. This king was the fruit of her mind, rather than passion. He had burst forth from her brow, because her mouldy old husband had refused to help her, smiling with embarrassment, as if he were a father with his daughter. From that day on Tsutsa had no rest because she was now sure that her husband, chaste in his old age, could no more see a throne than his own ears, whereas she could not live without a throne, couldn't manage without a throne: going without a throne would wither her like unrequited love. Tsutsa had spent her whole life in palaces and would die if she breathed a different air even for one day. The throne's cold, majestic splendour enveloped her in a listless peace and somnolence, as fire does to a cat. But she never let her vigilance drop for a second. Tsutsa knew every cranny of the palace by heart, she could keep watch from every cranny simultaneously and be the first to notice what hole the mouse crept out of, or what hole she herself should dive down so as not to be seen by a ruler who had got out of the wrong side of the bed.

Tsutsa didn't care who sat on the throne, where that throne was, as long as she was in the dazzling light shed by the throne. Tsutsa knew even the bacteria of that light, she knew like the back of her hand who annihilated or fertilized whom. She knew that on the other side of that light another life began, not so much a life as a trap in which anybody could be caught whose willpower fails or who is duped and just for a moment lets go of the throne's hard and heavy corner-stone. She would know this better than anyone. Tsutsa had sensed many unexpected dangers in the offing when her spineless husband ruled. She didn't have the right to remain a frivolous woman like those queens who sit next to real kings, inviolable until death. Tsutsa was different. Clouds of danger were always gathering over Tsutsa's head. She had to swallow countless different things, endure humiliation, she had to keep smiling and even dancing, in order to preserve her title of queen. It was this title that allowed her, the wife of a refugee king, with no throne and no heir, to circulate in the palace. Tsutsa's intuition warned her in time of the dangers to be expected: her husband was fading away as she watched, and after her husband's death who needed the widow of a childless overthrown king? The sound of the trap snapping shut was so close that Tsutsa was fraught with fear. Just a day's delay might be fatal. 'Save yourself,' someone shouted in Tsutsa's ear when she was stunned with fear: she moved into action.

Fortunately, everything was now over. The past had swallowed up the sleepless nights, when Tsutsa's head roared like a well-stoked stove, when, spread out in the murk of sin, she listened tremulously to the pulsing fruit of her womb, so as to convince herself once and for all that she really was pregnant, that her offspring, her dream, her future was coming, breaking through an abyss of darkness and nothingness. Anybody who hadn't experienced this personally could not grasp what Tsutsa had endured until the day she could stand with her arms folded and her head on one side, watching with delight her son's pimply face. 'First of all, I've got to find him a wife,' thought Tsutsa.

There was someone else who was heartily glad of Oqajado's accession to the throne. Glad is not the word: ecstatic! 'Justice has triumphed,' he cried out to the ceiling and punched his chest with his fist. This was Æëtes's stableman. After his flogging, the stableman could not rest, he was overcome with melancholy, he could forgive neither himself nor Æëtes, although he never said a word against the king in anyone's hearing. On the contrary, he loudly insisted that the flogging had brought him to his senses, had been as good as medicine. When he said that, he laughed, bared his crooked teeth and added, 'Now I and my horses understand each other better.' But his heart was swelling and bursting with anger, he couldn't sleep at night and kept his family awake with his groans and moans. This hidden resentment and anger became more unbearable with every day. He would lock himself up in the stable, would stick his head, like a horse, into a bag of oats and sob. The more he loathed Æëtes, the more he feared him. The horses would watch him with amazement, they snorted, and stamped their hooves on the floorboards, frightened by seeing a man sobbing. But the stableman had no alternative, nowhere else to go, nobody else to complain to. He was used to the stables, it never occurred to him to leave them. In any case he had never reconciled himself to sleeping elsewhere. Before he married, his bed was in the stable and he heard horses whinnying as he fell asleep Then his wife insisted that he either sent her back to her parents or let her live a normal life. After some argument she got her way: the stableman couldn't resist the female attractions and picked up his bedding that was permeated with the smell of hay and horse manure. 'This is your stable,' his wife told him, and the stableman liked his wife's joke, he felt more cheerful, and he smiled from ear to ear. He soon got used to living in two stables; in one he would expect to find his horses, the other he would enter like a horse, his teeth bared, neighing loudly. 'At least light the oil lamp, or I'll think I'm kissing a horse,' his wife used to joke.

'Justice has triumphed!' the overjoyed stableman cried out when he heard of Æëtes's defeat. He felt as if Oqajado had come from Crete just for his sake, to avenge him. Of course, he was exaggerating, but one thing he was sure of: Oqajado must have known about what happened to him, how Æëtes had stretched him out like a drying hide on four stakes and made him the laughing stock of the whole palace. Every king needed a loyal man in his palace. Oqajado would probably take a good look, and the stableman would be one of the first he'd notice, and he'd be right. It wouldn't be so odd as some might think for a lowly stableman to offer his thanks and pay back his saviour and helper. The stableman would pay his respects to Oqajado, bow down and say, 'Here, lord, is my loyalty: a poor stableman can offer you nothing more fitting.' Oqajado would straight away understand how wretched the stableman was, his stableman who knew every little detail about Æëtes's household, knew in advance who would say what, or think about the new king. 'That's how it is, man, you avenge yourself, debts have to be repaid,' the stableman thought as he started planning. He was sure that the new king would keep him in his old job. Where would he find a better stableman? Who would value the good deed more than a man abused by Æëtes? He might keep him on as stableman, but… no, no, no, the stableman would refuse everything, would fall at his feet, would make him change his mind, would urge him, 'I prefer to be in the stables, that's my place, I can serve you best there.'

The stableman was thinking all this when he heard the call, 'Quickly, you ass, to the king!'

'At last it's happened!' the stableman thought and entered the throne room, his face radiant. He found such confusion in the hall that he was taken aback, he forgot everything he wanted to say, the words of greeting which he had rehearsed on the way there froze on the tip of his tongue and hung there like a padlock. Courtiers were coming and going, the hall buzzed like a bee-hive and it seemed to the stableman that the buzzing was coming from the trunks that had been opened and were scattered all round. The bustling courtiers kept bumping into the stableman who was sidling awkwardly through. The stableman knocked himself against a trunk: a silver bowl fell out of it and went bouncing with a ringing noise over the floor. The man sitting on the throne looked grim, knitted his brow and that very moment caught sight of the stableman. 'I'm finished,' thought the stableman for some reason and bent down to pick up the still spinning bowl. Suddenly he burst into a sweat. His heart began to pound loudly. He would have rather died than look at the throne. Now he was clutching the bowl with both hands to his chest; not knowing how to act, to give it to a courtier or to put it back in the trunk — but which trunk, when they all looked the same? 'Why did I have to look at him?' the stableman thought again, and suddenly the whole hall froze, fell silent and bated its breath. The stableman sense he had been called: he hadn't heard, but his body sensed it and he smiled bitterly. A woman took the bowl from him.

'How old are you?' asked the man on the throne. The question brought him to his senses. 'If he knew his job, he'd ask my name, not my age,' he thought. His spine was dripping with sweat and he couldn't decide whether to add or to subtract from his age. Time was passing with such dizzy speed: if he delayed his answer, he would certainly be kicked out and then have to say goodbye to the stables for ever.

'I'm not forty yet,' said the stableman with a toothy grin.

He had decided to understate his age, because the new king seemed much younger than the old one.

'Do you like women?' asked the man on the throne, not giving him time to breathe.

'Mercy, for heaven's sake, ye gods!' the stableman replied, even more alarmed. 'What does this wretch want of me, what a question to ask me, what's on his mind?' He suddenly decided to say frankly, 'I'm not a stud stallion, I'm just a poor stableman, if you don't want me, I'll keep out of your sight,' but then bit his tongue and decided to be cunning, instead. What else could he do? He had to try his luck. He smiled humbly as if he had been praised, put his hands on his hips, wriggled his shoulders, described a semicircle on the floor with the tip of his sandal, and said, 'I'm quite an expert in that subject.'

'What do we do with this man?' Oqajado called to his mother. Tsutsa covered her face with her hand and giggled. Only now did the stableman notice that the woman who had just taken the bowl off him was old. He was amazed how much time had passed, or rather, how suddenly it had passed. He breathed a sigh of relief: the feeling that his fate had been decided instantly brought him peace. He consented to everything, he was free from everything, he accepted everything. Acceptance brought him relief and peace of mind. He now looked boldly at the new ruler; he no longer averted his gaze, because his conscience was clear; acceptance had annulled the feeling of guilt which had been bothering him, although he didn't know what he might be guilty of. He now thought of nothing, he stood there waiting to hear what they'd say, what he would be entrusted with. He would soon find out, very soon, as soon as that toothless old woman controlled her giggles.

'Have him castrated!' ordered Oqajado.

The stableman didn't quiver; he seemed to ignore the king's order. It was as if it didn't concern him, as if this word, which was just like a stone hurled at him, bounced off his hearing, off his entire being, like a stone off a wall. For some reason he remember a day long past when he and his father had taken a pig to be slaughtered; he was a little boy at the time, and not much cleverer than the pig. 'It's getting dark, bring the damned pig,' his father called to him. The stableman could still see the pig, its hairs bristling, trotting about through the puddles.

'Hey, piggy!' the stableman called out loud.

Soon the whole city heard about the stableman being made a eunuch. The people of Vani found this event to be really odd: many of them didn't even know what the word 'eunuch' meant. What he'd now be like, whether he would go on living, how could you tell, and many similar questions could be heard on the streets of Vani. The more knowledgeable and intelligent would reply, 'He'll be fine, he'll live, but…' 'Well, personally, I'd spit on a life like that,' said the people of Vani angrily, for some reason. The stableman, however, wasn't much disturbed by it all. Manhood is all very well, but at least he'd kept his life and his job. Oqajado had no intention of throwing him out of the stables. He told the stableman that this was for the best, for now his entire attention would go on the horses. But the horses had a different opinion: the wolf had leapt out from the place they least expected it. After he recovered, when he first went into the stables, the horses failed to recognize their master; they bared their big crooked teeth at him, they lashed their tails in his face and, if he hadn't jumped back in time, they would have kicked him, too. The horses were alarmed by the stableman's changed voice. The stableman, however, was puzzled. He was deeply perplexed: the same horses were tethered there, he knew them all by name, and he called them again, but the horses went even madder, lifted their heads up high, neighed and bared their teeth and stamped their shapely quivering legs in the dung. They wouldn't let him come near and he couldn't even sweep the dung out. He got up and scratched the back of his head. The next day the same thing happened. Soon the horses' rebellion became the talk of the palace. The horses only had to catch sight of the stableman for them to try and smash their way out in any direction; foaming at the mouth, rearing up on their hind legs, the horses bit each other, banged their heads against the walls and rolled their eyes, white with fury, horribly. The stableman dared not try to enter the stables any more, he called to the horses from outside, cajoled and pleaded with the crazed animals, but the violent shaking, the clatter of hooves and the neighing and whinnying from the stables became even more frantic. Then the stableman himself banged his head on the wall until he had scraped the skin off his brow and people who had gathered to watch the spectacle forced him to leave. Finally the stableman realised that his sacrifice had all been in vain: the horses no longer wanted him. This was a great injustice, a shameful act, an insult, a thorough humiliation, it was robbery, murder. The only thing that he considered to be his property was his profession, and he had now lost that. He needed his profession more than his manhood. For him his profession was not just a livelihood, it was the air he breathed, it gave him a soul, it made him a man. He had spent his whole life in the stables, in the smell and warmth of horses, he himself was permeated with that smell and warmth and he had become like a horse by living with them all the time: he ate standing up, he neighed rather than laughed, he held his head high, bared his teeth, flared his nostrils and whinnied. 'My good times are over,' the stableman thought: his bones were crumbling, his heart was broken like a mother whose baby has died; he wanted everyone to pity him, but was ashamed of the state he was in. Meanwhile the stables shook violently, there was loud neighing and banging of hooves. He had no choice: he had to try his luck once again. The stableman hung a knapsack round his neck and, for the first time in his life, crossed the threshold of the palace walls forever.

The appearance of the king's stableman in the streets of Vani caused a great commotion. As soon as the rumour got around that the stableman was coming down their street, sharp-tongued women, emboldened by his impotence, lined up on the roofs to flirt and call to the stableman, who was walking past, his head bowed, with a knapsack, 'Come on up, lad, my husband's out.' Then they nearly killed themselves laughing at their joke and dissolved into cackling and peals of laughter. Packs of children followed him and mocked him with children's ruthlessness. 'Gelding, gelding!' they called out a word they had heard from their elders, and threw stones, too: they wanted to madden this harmless man with the knapsack round his neck, his head nodding as he went down the street, harnessed like a horse to an invisible shaft. Very rarely, really upset and driven beyond endurance, the stableman would suddenly spin round to face the children and, when the frightened children disappeared like lizards hiding in the cracks of a wall, he would lift up his head, bare his teeth, turn round, stamping his feet, and whinny.

At first, the men were angry with the children and told them to leave him alone, that he had enough misery to cope with, but they themselves smiled as they spoke. That was all the children needed: there was nothing but uproar, whistling and loud laughter to be heard.

It was the stableman who put an end to this endless mockery. When this former stableman first held out his hand and begged for alms, the people of Vani were taken aback. This was more amazing to them than a man being castrated. They had never seen or heard of such a thing: a man asking for alms. 'What has Oqajado done to this wretched man?' the people of Vani wondered in distress, and they all tried to persuade the stableman to take some bread from them; the stableman put away the bread he'd been given in his knapsack, and he calmed the people of Vani, who were so disturbed by the strange spectacle, 'Be patient, I'll accept it from everyone, I'll need it tomorrow, too.' Now the people of Vani got bread ready in advance to give to the stableman and if he was just the slightest bit late coming down their street, they would be worried and keep sending the children out to see if he was coming. The stableman gradually got used to this new life, not that he had any choice, and he was grateful for whatever he was given: he never went hungry. The children's naughtiness didn't bother him, because he was a man of Vani and therefore especially fond of children. 'A child's heart is pure,' he thought to himself, and believe it or not, he found it even pleasant that he was entertaining so many children at a time. Neither did he resent the women's mockery: on the contrary, his heart swelled with pride to have so many cackling women inviting him up at the same time. If it didn't wholly match the dream of his youth, it did at least partly do so, and it was enough to console him. In short, everything would have been well, if the horses hadn't made his life hard. A horse that had been standing peacefully only had to hear the sound of his footsteps, or catch his scent to start fidgeting, then go almost rabid, rear up on its hind legs, break free of its bridle and gallop off, like a crazed blind man, through Vani's streets. When this happened repeatedly and the people of Vani were fed up with chasing and calming down horses, they told the stableman, 'Think of something, we can't go on like this.' After that the stableman began walking around with a child's rattle, which he shook over his head to let the city know, 'I'm coming, be prepared.' When they heard the sound of the rattle, the people of Vani rushed to tighten the reins of their horses, put sacks over their eyes, stroking the horses' necks with one hand as they did so. The horses no longer went mad as they used to, although they were still alarmed, and fidgeted and snorted.

So Vani's first beggar appeared. The people soon got used to him, and eventually bored with him, so that they even forgot him. Now only a few children, for fun, or gratuitously, by force of habit, would call out, 'Gelding!' at the stableman as he went down the street, nodding his head, before going on playing with their playmates. All this roaming the streets and sleeping under the open sky had entirely purged the stableman's body of equine smell and warmth which he had absorbed over the years, mixing with thoroughbred stallions and brood mares in the king's stables. The horses no longer paid him any attention and he could go approach them freely, press his nose to their flanks and breathe in as much as he liked the scent he adored.

The day that the stableman was being castrated and his bellowing could be heard in the throne room, Tsutsa giggled and said, 'Now we'll find you a wife.' Oqajado was startled, his mother's words had unexpectedly lit up his mind and shown him what he had hitherto tried in vain to see, what bothered him, saddened him, but what he tried to get used to, as he couldn't explain it. He had first had this numbing, stifling feeling in Crete, but now that was easier to explain, since he considered it to be nostalgia for a throne and was sure that as soon as he became king, his mood would lift. But that had not happened; even on the throne he still had this feeling. Now Oqajado was fearful: 'What's wrong with me, what do I want? I wonder what's happening to me.' He couldn't actually reveal it: how could he tell Tsutsa, 'Being king isn't enough for me, there's something else I lack.' So he was forced to bear this suffering alone, to be patient, reconcile himself to it, let it be part of his flesh and blood. Patience was all very well, but now he was tormented by curiosity, he wanted at least to know what it was called, what had caused him this suffering. He sat motionless and thought, every now and again touching his nose, because his mother had told him that curiosity made your nose as long as an elephant's trunk.

Now, however, Tsutsa had explained the riddle to him. Oqajado's suffering had a name. Bachelorhood was what was wrong with him, as his mother's heart had diagnosed and told him without a word. He understood the illness, but Oqajado also felt that it now required more patience. But why should he endure, when a medicine existed and nobody would be better at finding this medicine than his mother? The important thing was that Tsutsa was sorry for her son. At this moment Oqajado really wanted his mother to be sorry for him, to treat him with pity and sympathy, to worry and say something to comfort him, although everything was going to be comforting anyway. Whatever Tsutsa said to him, every word produced a tear from him, and he didn't hide the tears so that his mother would feel even more sorry for him. His mother would rush to comfort him, 'You've got to tell me what's happened, why have you dried your eyes?' But he wouldn't tell her the truth, he would act as though he were ashamed of his sudden weakness; he would reassure his mother, 'Why should anything have happened to me? I expect it was just a speck of dust in my eye.' But there was no hiding anything from Tsutsa, she would guess everything and would then help him. 'Oh dear,' she would say as always, 'Oh dear, I've made him cry, it's my fault he's crying.' She could say whatever she liked as long as she wished her sick child well and made him better. Oqajado couldn't manage any more without a wife.

'But don't blame me afterwards,' said Tsutsa.

Oqajado was incapable of understanding anything, his eyes were clouded, for once his mother's giggling had penetrated his switched-off mind. The saying goes, the smaller the man, the bigger the dream: in fact, what happened afterwards was all like one weird and endless dream.

By the time Oqajado's eyes could see again, he was married to a woman called Kama. The first feeling Oqajado had for his wife was fear. His wife's beauty was the source of the fear. The tender and spoilt Kama terrified anyone who saw her with her beauty. She radiated such an uncanny light that everything around her was enveloped in a freezing haze. Her light could reach into the deepest cellar and fill all the surroundings with the chill of the grave. This eerie light stunned both animate beings and inanimate objects. People tried to stay as clear of it as they could, they avoided the clutches of this light which deprived even the sleeping of rest. When they heard that the queen was coming, people covered their windows with rugs, filled all the cracks and openings with wax, but Kama's disturbing light penetrated everything and scattered shards of frost on whatever it touched. Fortunately, this frost and stunning effect did not last long, and wore off as the queen passed on. Eyes blinded by the light soon recovered their sight, and the sensation of an imminent and ineluctable end gushed out of people's ears, like water from a broken barrel. For some reason, Kama reminded the people of Vani of Dariachangi. They knew by tradition that Dariachangi had her own light, that violets and roses fell from her mouth and that wherever she walked the grass grew so lush and green that cattle disappeared bodily in it. Children could hang and dangle on Dariachangi's beams of light, as on a vine's branches,. Kama's light was different: it darkened things. In that momentary darkness trees withered, grass faded and fell flat on the ground like rags, birds fell from the sky, their hearts broken, the cattle in the paddocks bellowed and butted each other. But, fortunately, it was all over very soon. The queen's sedan chair had only to pass out of sight for the surroundings to recover their initial state; but people felt for some time afterwards their hearts racing and the freezing cold of the gloom that had come over them.

'I'm cold, Oqajado, I'm cold!' Kama called out to the ice-coloured mirror. This enormous mirror had come with her as part of her dowry; it now stood in the hall. The mirror seemed to make the cold even sharper, and Oqajado no longer knew how to help his wife. Ever since their wedding he himself had been constantly shivering, but nobody dared light a fire. Kama couldn't stand fire, she was mortally afraid of it and, in fact, if she only glimpsed it far away, she would immediately start to thaw like a gigantic icicle.

Everyone walked around the palace hunched, the floor was covered in hoar frost, the cold got into the walls and the outside of the palace was covered in frost. Kama spent whole days sitting in front of the mirror, complaining, 'When will the mirror let me in? I can't stand it any more, I'm numb with cold.' Kama envied the other Kama who lived in the mirror and talked from there with her double, who had been left outside and who could listen without end to the amazing stories the Kama in the mirror was telling her. 'Believe me, it's better here, there's no cold and there's no warmth,' the Kama in the mirror told the one left outside. The latter sat without moving in front of the mirror, waiting for the surface of the mirror to open up and for the long-awaited land to shelter her. Kama was afraid she might miss this fateful instant and be stranded outside for ever. Later, when Kama disappeared without trace, even Oqajado believed that his wife really had managed to get into the mirror. But he wasn't heartbroken: he had no reason to be. Kama had numbed his blood forever; the very mention of women angered him. If he spent an hour with her he would sneeze and his nose would run for a week. For a whole month Kama couldn't get out of bed, so thawed and weakened was she by being alone with her husband. Because she could no longer manage to go up to the mirror, she had it brought, framed in a block of ice, to her bedside and with sad, envious and ecstatic eyes she looked at it, gazing fondly at the Kama living in the mirror.

Oqajado missed his mother once he was married; he neither saw her nor remembered her. Where had she vanished to, he wondered. At first he was surprised, then afraid, hoping she hadn't abandoned him, and then set off to search for her. Tsutsa had locked herself in her room and lain down without undressing on her bed, wrapping a shawl round her head and pulling all the bedclothes in the wardrobe over herself. Her restless, bulging eyes were all that was visible, like a fox watching from its hole. 'I am your servant, king,' she called to her son, struggling to lift her blue-veined arm from under the blanket, and removing a hair that had stuck to her lip.

'I wish I'd never heard the word "wife",' groaned Oqajado.

'How dare you!' yelled Tsutsa.

Tsutsa knew that this day would come. More than anything she was afraid of women, but she was a woman herself and her instinct had never let her down. Ever since she had put Oqajado on the throne, she shouldn't have had anything to worry about, but she still had an obstacle, a treacherous enemy who was bound to appear and try to demolish the fortress that Tsutsa had cobbled together. That's why she never let her son's flat and motionless face out of her sight and, when Oqajado's brow became full of pimples, Tsutsa realised that the enemy was at the door. The enemy was powerful, one blow of his hand could annihilate everything she had accumulated over all this time. Oqajado just rolled his eyes in confusion, not aware yet of the enemy's treachery, but he had already licked its poisonous dagger-point, and his face would at times become so burning hot that he would empty a whole pitcher of cold water over his head. But the ice-cold water would hiss and evaporate, and the fire would go on burning. Then he would be overcome by an urge to flee; and to avoid fleeing, he would have the gates locked and would pace up and down his room. Only Tsutsa knew what the cure was; she also knew that she had to allow him some time in order not to lose him for ever. But Oqajado was not the sort of man to be allowed any freedom, especially in his present state, when the first woman he met could wrap him round her little finger, making him forget forever his mother and the throne just by whispering one word. Tsutsa wanted Oqajado all to herself, she had given birth to him for good reason, not to get him tucked up in women's skirts. To Tsutsa, Oqajado meant more than an ordinary son to an ordinary mother. Oqajado was another Tsutsa, an appendix, essential, without whom even Tsutsa could not be what she was and could never achieve what she had achieved. Oqajado was the only thing Tsutsa needed. Ahead of her was darkness, the darkness of an unknowable future, and Tsutsa was striding boldly through this darkness because fear and hesitation would mean death for her. What did it matter whom she met on the way, stableman or king, the main thing was that her marriage with the dark had a result, that it bore fruit and hadn't let down a woman fighting for the future. Oqajado was the child of darkness, not the usual pup which a mother remembers only until her eyes lose their cataracts and she can see the light. Light can be deceptive, whereas Tsutsa needed Oqajado permanently, because their unity, their inseparability brought forth a throne, a crown, a secure and carefree life. Either on their own had no value. So Oqajado should see nothing but his mother: even a blind man can see his mother. Tsutsa was capable, and nobody could stop her, of raising the son that their common cause required. She could achieve this because she wanted to, because she had no other choice.

But when Oqajado came to maturity, Tsutsa sensed danger: on the land that she had secured permanently a storm was brewing. A storm of passion which stopped at nothing and hit both hovels and palaces equally. Tsutsa knew how strong this storm was, but she somehow had to withstand it, had to make it abate in time and, if she could, exterminate it. Any other woman couldn't have taken over a life scarcely begun. Who had the right just to turn up and at no cost, without a fight appropriate the nest that Tsutsa had spent years making with her own beak out of reeds of dream and mud of sin? Tsutsa knew that there was nothing she could do about the storm of passion, it was beyond her, but at least she had a grip on her son. So Tsutsa got to work, spinning like a top, until she found Kama and felt reassured. Nobody could have found a more beautiful bride, no marriageable man would have rejected Tsutsa's choice. But Tsutsa had seen what was apparent to nobody else, let alone an inexperienced oaf, who couldn't look at a stick in a dress without getting excited. Kama's beauty was the beauty of coldness, isolation and barrenness. Tsutsa was overjoyed, for there was nothing in her son that Kama needed, and this would be such a lesson to her son that he would remember it to his dying day. Tsutsa would just help her son a little by convincing him that any and every dress concealed the same secret. Kama inspired Tsutsa with great hopes, so she told her, 'My beauty, my lovely daughter-in-law, I'm relying on you.' And when she saw her son's confused face, she became all jocular and chucked him under the chin, as she had always done. Oqajado blushed, avoided his mother's eye and muttered barely audibly, 'Do I push her over, or does she lie down by herself?' For an instant, Tsutsa was sorry for her son, she knew what she was letting him in for, she knew the state he would be in when he came back to her, but this was no time for a mother-and-son talk. She pushed him off encouragingly, telling him 'You'll work that out for yourself,' and locked herself in her room, because the cold that her son would soon feel had already got into her body.

'I'm cold!' Oqajado groaned again.

'Be quiet,' Tsutsa tried to calm him. 'I'm cold, too, but I put up with it for your sake. 'You've got what you wanted,' she went on a little later, because she was sure that Oqajado had no more to say. 'You got what you wanted. That's your wife. Thank God, you can't blame me for anything.'

Oqajado went back, downcast. His mother was right now, as always. Oqajado wanted to be with his mother, he felt better there; he dragged his feet, but he had to leave, for he was king and the throne was waiting for him. He could have brought the throne here and never left his mother's room, but the throne, unlike Kama's mirror, could hardly be dragged all over the place, could it? And Tsutsa wouldn't have permitted it. Because it wasn't possible. The throne couldn't even be moved, it had to stay in the same place so it didn't have to be looked for, so it was easy to know where to find it and he could always walk solemnly and gravely towards it. 'It's hard to be a king,' thought Oqajado.

'Just wait, there'll be lots of times you'll want to be with your mother,' Tsutsa shouted after him.

Life in Vani, diverted into new channels, gradually settled down: it got used to the banks and flowed down between them. Bakha the vintner was the same old Bakha, but he had a new worry: his wine no longer made people drunk, it stupefied them. He was sure that Hey-Boy was up to something, contaminating the wine, but he said nothing for the time being, waiting until he caught him at it before holding him accountable. Bakha the vintner found people unrecognizable: the people coming down the forty-steps of his cellar were different, they drank wine differently, standing up, gulping it down and getting tipsy quickly. 'Who are they, where were they before?' Bakha the vintner asked in amazement, but he still sat in his old majestic way on his favourite chair with the round-headed stick between his knees and his hands propped on top of it.

Bedia the fisherman was again surreptitiously measuring the distance between the boat station and the sea, just as surreptitiously extending his rope, which had now grown rather heavy, rubbing his neck like a yoke.

Bochia still carved cradles, the golden, crunchy and scented shavings coming up to his knees, and the woodpeckers which his foster-father had tamed now perched on him. He would stay as still as a tree until the colourful and restless bird pecked too hard with its beak. After sweeping up and bundling the shavings, Potola would carry them out into the yard to burn, only to find just as many shavings there when she came back in.

Black-eyed Malalo's reception room was seething, boiling over with life. So many people came and went along the path that Oqajado had blazed that she and her six daughters could barely cope with receiving their guests and seeing them off. At first glance, it appeared that nothing had changed in Vani. The city had acquired just one more wonder: Oqajado's palace, even when the air was scorchingly hot in the city, was covered with icicles.

That was how it seemed at a glance, but time, of course, had changed many things. Time had done its usual work. Time had its own agenda. It didn't show anything, it took no heed of anybody, it had no eye and no heart. It just passed, dragged on, unfeeling and powerful. Black-eyed Malalo battled on for a long time, she tried cosying up, she tried pretending, but got no results, except that she reinforced her beliefs in fighting and not giving in. True, old age frightened her so often, it kept jumping out and shouting, 'Gotcha, gotcha!' extinguishing all hope, but she kept her weapons up. The parrot, as aged as its mistress, cawed 'Hostess, hostess!' more often now, as if it too felt the passage of time and was trying to say as often as possible the only word it had learnt since it came to live with human beings. In fact, the parrot was warning black-eyed Malalo, repeating itself again and again, for this word was the only one that black-eyed Malalo fully and thoroughly understood. She had been captivated from the start by this word, and had adopted it, convinced that it had been invented for her, that nobody deserved it better than she, and black-eyed Malalo fell head and heels in love with it. She took it as her due, she got used to it. The visitors changed, but the word 'hostess' remained unchanged. So it would always be, if time hadn't turned against her, to oppose her. Now, even if the hostess paid a guest his weight in gold, he still would refuse to believe that this ugly woman, with swollen legs and fist-sized varicose veins attacking her calves like leeches, was once a svelte woman as bright as a bonfire and with the voice of a chalumeau. With every day, her guests became more polite and reserved, and black-eyed Malalo felt the distance between herself and her guests getting ever wider. But she couldn't let life ebb away so easily while she still breathed; she couldn't turn her back or shut the door on it. She would still go on being hostess for a long time, if not for ever, she would greet them and see them off; many times more she would undress them and dress them again, like a silly little girl with her favourite dolls. Had she wasted her time training the parrot that sparkled like a firebrand dipped in water? Had she wasted her time telling every dog and son of a bitch, 'Think of me as your hostess, do come again.' Everyone, everyone had to know that she was still the hostess, she first, and her daughters next, and that the country still had to reckon with her.

Black-eyed Malalo had really done so much to thwart once again old age standing at her door. What nobody expected happened: black-eyed Malalo had a baby, a seventh daughter. The girl was named Ino. The smell of baby filled the house and everything now took on the appearance of an ordinary home. Six daughters, with the same hair style, in the same dresses, but now rather weather-beaten, attended their mother when she gave birth. The birth of a child gave them a great deal of joy and enthusiasm, but it saddened them too. Their mother had got the better of them: even in old age their mother had succeeded in doing something they had lost the ability for in their youth. Black-eyed Malalo was more than they were and always would be one step ahead. They might now have become seven, but black-eyed Malalo was eight in number. Her totally unexpected pregnancy instilled into her daughters a belief in her superiority and omnipotence. A common roof and common profession brought them and their mother close, so that they treated her like a seventh sister: they would tell her, 'We're all the same,' but now they felt how much above them black-eyed Malalo was, not just the seventh, but the creator of seven. This tiny, grey-eyed creature would soon be like its older sisters; meanwhile it cooed happily, lying next to its all-powerful giver of sustenance.

Ino soon noticed the amazing similarity of her older sisters, with their same hair style and same dresses. It took her a long time to tell the difference between them, because all six bent over in the same way to look at her, talked baby-language and laughed the same way when Ino reached out for the beads dangling from their necks. Ino was happy, so happy that she couldn't tell daybreak from dusk. Day and night were equally rosy, peaceful and gentle. When she was learning to walk, her mother took her toddling to the parrot's cage and Ino laughed heartily when the puffed-up, yellow-eyed, black-beaked bird spun like a wheel on its perch. The cage rocked and rocked, and made Ino giddy, and she imperceptibly grew. In the evenings, the six sisters bathed, combed and dressed Ino up to show her to the guests. 'You know you have to say hello to everyone; don't make a face when you're given a present, don't let anyone say what a bad-mannered little girl we have,' the sisters instructed her, while she fluttered like a butterfly and couldn't wait to show herself all got up in her new dress to the guests. Morning brought the sound of her mother's and sisters' carefree chatter and peals of laughter. When she heard those sounds, Ino always stretched out blissfully, and then the warm, rich smell of milk would fill the whole house. With tousled hair, bare-foot, still sleepy and already hungry, Ino fluttered into the big room and looked with delight at her mother and sisters, until they noticed her. All of them had just washed and were elegantly combed, amazingly beautiful and lovable. Ino would go up to each one of them, quivering strangely, and stand on tip-toe to kiss their scented cheeks and foreheads. 'No don't, I've only just done my hair,' the sisters would shriek, pretending to be angry. But Ino was happy.

Icicles still covered Oqajado's palace. When the sun was high, children would cool their faces by knocking icicles down with sticks, then running off at breakneck speed before the guards could yell at them from the walls, although the guards, wearing felt cloaks, were themselves furtively breaking off the icicles and throwing them into the street. Now not a day passed without Oqajado looking in on his mother. Kama was thawing in front of the mirror, having now forgotten her husband. She rarely saw Oqajado in the mirror or caught a glimpse of him walking behind her, surly, his arms folded.

One day Oqajado went to see his mother and Tsutsa, sitting up in bed, gave him such an alarmed look that he was crestfallen: he realised some disaster must have occurred.

'What's happened, mother?' Oqajado shouted at her.

'The worst that could happen…' Tsutsa hummed to herself, rather than replied, looking round helplessly.

Then she fixed her gaze on her son again and looked at the flat and motionless face until a smile flitted over her lips. Oqajado felt a little reassured. 'You really were born under an unlucky star,' Tsutsa giggled uninhibitedly, but then she started coughing and couldn't get her breath back until Oqajado came running in with water.

'I've lost the use of my legs,' said Tsutsa, and after a short while repeated, 'I've lost the use of my legs!'

Oqajado was at a loss, but he felt relief, because he had been so struck by fear that the moment his mother opened her mouth some terrible dragon seemed to fly out of it.

'It's nothing,' Oqajado told her.

After this Oqajado carried Tsutsa about clasped to his chest like a baby. He took her for walks in the courtyard and carried her as carefully as if he was taking a bowl brimful of boiling water from one place to another and was afraid of scalding his feet.

'Don't trust anyone else to carry me, will you,' Tsutsa whispered to him. 'Anyone who wants to destroy you, will first put an end to me.'

Their close mother-and-son relationship was soon the talk of the whole palace. The women wanted nothing better: they burned with pity for Tsutsa and yet envied her happiness. 'Not even a herdsman, let alone a king, remembers his mother these days,' the women said when they saw mother and son going for a walk, and they dried their tearful eyelids on the hems of their scarves. 'Woman, she can say, "I've raised a real son!",' they silently paid tribute to Tsutsa, wrapped up in Oqajado's arms: for greater security, Tsutsa clung with both arms to her son's neck. Tsutsa really was a portable mother. She might have lost the use of her legs, but her mind was a healthy as ever, this mind could take the weight of both of them, mother's and son's, a fact that both of them knew. Oqajado had strong legs, but he couldn't take two steps on his own. Nature had got something wrong, left something out, when it failed to make one creature out of the two of them. Two heads and two pairs of legs were really more than they needed. Tsutsa's head needed Oqajado's legs, and Oqajado's legs needed Tsutsa's head. Which is what happened eventually. Nature had corrected its inadvertent mistake. Now Oqajado could walk more confidently, he could deal with regal matters more quickly and easily, he could understand more correctly, quickly and easily what decision Tsutsa had taken on any particular question.

One evening, while strolling in the palace courtyard, Tsutsa put her hand to her lip and said, 'There's a fairy tale I must tell you.'

Oqajado became animated, as excited as a child, and clasped his mother tighter. He loved fairy tales, but he knew his mother wouldn't tell him one just for nothing, or for fun: she was showing or teaching him something, or hinting at something. She had always acted in this way, and anything he knew of the world came from his mother's fairy tales.

'Once upon a time a king ordered a man to bring buffaloes with diamond hooves and golden horns,' Tsutsa began. 'These buffaloes lived in the sea.'

'In the sea?!' Oqajado exclaimed.

Tsutsa got angry: 'The diamond hooves and golden horns didn't surprise you, but you make a fuss about the buffaloes living in the sea… You must be really stupid if you think I'm interested in what surprises you and if I'll wear myself out for that.'

Oqajado fell silent: what could he say? His mother was right. 'True, buffaloes living in the sea are not worth making a fuss about,' he thought to himself, until Tsutsa's anger subsided and she went on with the tale.

'I shouldn't bother telling you anything!' said Tsutsa.

Then she asked him where she'd stopped, but without waiting for an answer, said: 'The buffaloes lived in the sea and only came onto land to drink water. Now you'll say that if they lived in the sea, then they could drink just sea-water, but if you didn't know before, then let me tell you now that sea-water is undrinkable, it's bitter and salty.'

'True,' said Oqajado.

Tsutsa continued: 'The man was unable to carry out the order, so he went to see a sorceress. You did the same thing once, so this man went to see the sorceress and told her, "If you can, set me on the right path." The sorceress wouldn't be much good if she didn't help a man who'd come asking for help. That's true, isn't it? A sorceress helped you, didn't she? So this man, too, wasn't left unhappy. "Can you find an ox hide and a bushel of nails?" the sorceress asked him. "I can," the man replied. "Then," the sorceress told him, "take an ox hide and a bushel of nails, an ox hide and a bushel of nails, an ox hide and a bushel of nails, cover the source with the ox hide, cover the source with the ox hide, cover the source with the ox hide, nail it to the earth with the nails, nail it to the earth with the nails, nail it to the earth with the nails."'

Oqajado's face broke into a big wide smile, because he understood why his mother was repeating the same phrases to him: he had to pay special attention to this part and memorise it. This was an old trick which she'd used many times. Oqajado couldn't wait to tell his mother, 'I've got it,' but he held back, because Tsutsa had gone on with the fairy tale:

'When the buffaloes come out of the sea, they won't find the water, they won't find the water, they won't find the water. They'll beg you, "Give us water to drink, give us water to drink, give us water to drink, and we will become your slaves, we will become your slaves, we will become your slaves,"' Tsutsa finished and suddenly fell silent, as if she'd fallen asleep in her son's arms.

'We will become, become, come, …ome,' said Oqajado, slicing up the last word as if that was what it was all about.

'Have you understood anything?' Tsutsa asked him.

Oqajado turned a deaf ear to her, as if he was thinking and didn't hear his mother's question. A little later he repeated, 'We will become, become, come, …ome.'

'You haven't understood a thing,' said Tsutsa and touched her son's jaw with her outstretched fingers.

A week after this conversation, guards were placed at the Greek's source, and an enormous clay toad was placed in front of the spring, and a price was set for water. Those who came to fetch water first had to put money in the toad's gaping mouth and then press their pitcher against the pipe. Children were now forbidden to splash about in the spring's tank, which bore the permanent imprint of Phrixos's and his four sons' palms.

'These things are happening on earth because we have forgotten the sea,' Bedia kept telling his wife.

Bedia couldn't rest any more, the enormous sea was slipping away between his hands, but the city thought he was mad and nobody believed him. They listened to him respectfully, nodded their heads and tried in every way not to laugh in this elderly man's face. Bedia had in fact come to resemble a madman. His eyes had turned white thinking about the sea's treachery as it prepared to steal away; the coil of rope round his neck was now starting to slip off his shoulders. The idlers who gathered in front of the shops found it hard to resist the temptation to put a foot on the rope's coloured ends and drag Bedia along; Bedia, however, noticed nothing because he was thinking about the sea's treachery and about the general misfortune which this treachery would bring about.

Bedia's wife was infected with her husband's anxiety. As soon as dark began to fall, she would throw a shawl over her shoulders and stand alone on the shore of the thundering sea, which was now some distance from their little hovel. She stood and watched, and Bedia couldn't work out whether his wife was wailing or singing, because the roar of the sea and the howling of the wind let just pathetic snatches of his wife's voice reach the hovel. 'Why did I let it affect that poor woman?' Bedia worried, as he stood on the threshold of the hovel. He called to his wife: 'Fine, that's enough, don't mourn for the wretched sea before it's time to.' But every day he became more and more sure that the sea really was retreating. And his wife's continuous wail reinforced that belief. Bedia saw his wife as a ghost, bending back and swaying in the sea wind: the sea seemed to be striking her, getting rid of an unwanted witness. It was as if the sea was embarrassed by this odd creature which was looking so intently into its soul, and that was why it dawdled and hid its face, because it felt that this woman's sadness and misfortune was greater than itself. The sea was even afraid of the woman, it was yelling at her, drenching her from head to toe, throwing sand in her face, saying, 'Leave me alone, I know what I'm doing.' But the woman stayed there without moving, not taking a step back, quietly wailing. Her voice made the sea more disturbed, it shamed it, weakened it and, angered, it beat its chest against the sharp rocks on the shore. 'That's enough, woman, you'll catch a chill!' Bedia would shout, and beat his own chest with his small fist, which was as hard as a cobblestone. Then he, too, would whirl about on the spot, as if joining a round dance, and accompany his wife's wail. Then he would be overcome by an itch and would stick both hands under the rough fibres of the rope and tear at his skin until there was blood, like dirt, under his fingernails. As he did so, he would cry out angrily, 'That's enough, woman, I can't stand any more.' But Bedia and the people of Vani had a lot more yet to undergo and endure, because this first mistake which they had inadvertently made and which nobody had paid attention to at the time, was looming larger with every day.

CHAPTER NINE

THE fishermen were pulling their net out of the sea: they had formed two lines and were tugging at the ends of the net with ropes as thick as a man's wrist. As the rope emerged from the water, it coiled like a snake around the front man's feet. 'Hey, pull! Hey, pull!' they urged each other on. Their work was more like dancing than heavy labour. They were all bending back at the waist, lifting their arms up in the same way. The net slowly approached the shoreline: between net and shoreline the water roared. Two boats were following the net towards the shore, and the boatmen herded the fish with long sticks. Soon the head of the arched net was sticking above the water, sliding up over the sand and folding as it spread itself out. The distance between the middle of the net and the shore gradually lessened. Suddenly a silvery moving mass was pulled out of the seething water, like a new-born island still shaken by underground tremors. These were the fish. The fishermen let out a shout of joy. Water was streaming out of the net, which had been dragged halfway out. Moss-green strands of seaweed hung from it like the sea's curdled blood. The fishermen rushed forward, up to their waist in the water and began throwing the fish onto the shore. Seagulls, too, came down for the fish, shrieking madly, flapping their wings and trying to get at the fish. The fish writhed and shone like boiling silver. The fishermen raised a terrific yell and uproar, grabbed their oars and somehow fended off the shrieking, howling, squawking robbers. But in a very short time one seagull, hungrier or bolder than the others, came back. For a while it sat a little way off on a sand dune and watched the bustling fishermen. The fishermen didn't notice the seagull. They had no time for it.

But Parnaoz could see it. Parnaoz was sitting very near, on the same sand dune as the seagull. Without thinking, Parnaoz picked up a pebble, but he didn't throw it. Somehow, being so close to the bird perturbed, even excited him. He sat there, tense. Either the gull didn't notice him, or it wasn't afraid of him. Parnaoz had never seen a seagull so close, or even sitting on the ground. He was even astonished, for they were always in the sky. The bird was sitting two steps away, scratching under its wing with its beak. Suddenly it hopped off, bravely broke into the circle of fishermen, grabbed a fish in its beak and was about to fly off with its loot when someone saw it and waved an oar at it. The gull let go of the fish, but flew off unharmed; it circled several times over the head of the fisherman who was holding an oar, shrieked several times and perched on the sand dune again. Parnaoz found it heart-warming that the gull trusted him. Fisherman and gull stared at one another. The fishermen was bending forward a little, holding the oar in both hands, standing as still as a statue. Soon, the seagull hopped towards the fisherman as if it wanted to test whether he really was a statue or not. The fisherman lost patience and waved his oar when the gull was still far off. The seagull flew up, probably unintentionally, for it then landed in front of the fisherman. Parnaoz was amazed and amused by the gull's boldness, while the fisherman just seemed stubborn: tension made his face sweat. The gull suddenly came flying up and hit him in the face so violently, that he, a big man, tumbled back and sat down on the sand. The gull shrieked, circled squawking a few times over the fishermen, whose enormous hands blotted out the sun, so that they could see this troublemaker of a seagull better. Then the bird vanished into space. Parnaoz breathed a sigh of relief, he too was sweating, and his arms which he'd pressed into the sand, were shaking. The pebbles in his hands had left red marks with a white centre. Suddenly he heard laughter. He looked up and saw Ino: he didn't doubt that this skinny, freckled little girl, who looked just like a goat kid, was Ino. Somehow Parnaoz remembered what a woman neighbour had said: 'The seventh one is still tiny: she's a goat kid.'

Before Parnaoz first saw Ino he'd heard that there was a wicked woman in their city, more witch than woman, who took away men's wits, then sent them to sleep and sucked out their blood. Her name was black-eyed Malalo; she sang all day, because it was her song that stupefied men, then their eyes were blinded and they forgot everything. She thought only about clothes and hats. Her daughters were left to grow up on their own, wallowing in bed all day, because they had everything on a plate. All the men in the city served these women, took away what belonged to their families and handed it over to them, because this witch was so wicked as to mix henbane into the men's wine and feed them donkey brains. All this Parnaoz learnt from the women. Various people came to Parnaoz's house, to borrow something or give it back, or just for a chat, but nobody ever left without mentioning the witch and her daughters. Parnaoz wasn't in the least interested in what the women said, but he couldn't help listening, because that's where he hung about. He didn't understand very much of what they talked about, but when they mentioned Ino, he became all ears, probably because Ino was the youngest of them, the littlest witch. She was a goat kid, not a witch, a white goat kid. She would become a witch later, when she grew up and, as the women said, came to look like her mother and sisters.

When they said this, their voices and their faces were such that Parnaoz was upset, as if he himself was in danger; but he was a child and never sad for very long, and he had Tsuga, the most beautiful and the most clever and most mischievous dog in the whole city. He didn't need anyone else. If he recalled Ino from time to time, it was because he had never seen or known what she was like and he was torn by his child's curiosity. He wondered if she really was as he imagined. This was an unconscious interest, palmed off onto him, forced on him: not awoken by outside forces. The older women's talk had given rise to this interest, not Ino herself. Ino was just a goat kid, nothing else, the only way Parnaoz could imagine her. Whenever Ino's name was mentioned, he could see a white goat kid. His curiosity wanted far more, it reached out further than a goat kid to the place where the goat kid's owners were. But they were so far off that a child's curiosity couldn't reach that far. That was what annoyed Parnaoz. His annoyance included the goat kid. 'If I ever come across her, I'll have to set Tsuga on her,' he silently threatened, when the women started whispering, or suddenly fell silent as if they had only just noticed Parnaoz. So Ino had a hold on Parnaoz's thoughts and imagination even before they met. Unawares, very slowly, imperceptibly she was accumulating in another child's heart and mind, like snow falling at night. But one day Parnaoz would wake up and see everything, as far as the eye could see, white with snow. Meanwhile, however, he had Tsuga by his side. Tsuga followed the endless run of days and nights barking: she barked at cackling hens and shadows quivering on the paving stones; Tsuga would fetch a stick that Parnaoz threw into the sea; Tsuga slurped rain water that was stored in Kaluka's barrel; if a spoon or a sandal went missing, or crockery was broken or a rug was torn, Tsuga took the blame; leftovers from dinner were kept in a copper bowl for Tsuga. The most joyful, noisy and unbridled thing was Tsuga's mischief; the saddest thing was Tsuga's eyes when she was punished. Very rarely a white goat kid happened to run into the yard where Tsuga lived and disappear for a while. Who knows for how long Parnaoz would have forgotten Ino, if he hadn't one day dared to ask the women why Ino should be pitied, or why she should be unfortunate if she spent the whole day wallowing in bed and getting anything she wanted, like her mother and sisters. Kaluka then answered, 'Women like that do whatever they fancy, they get fed on grapes.' But Parnaoz couldn't ask even Kaluka why it was a misfortune to wallow in bed all day and eat grapes. Somehow he was embarrassed, or rather afraid of a secret being revealed, casually exposed by adults. But the secret's dazzling nakedness allured, bewildered, alarmed him and even struck him dumb, because he sensed that it was important to penetrate this secret and not just circle round it. But he wasn't yet ready for that. Even if he were allowed in, he wouldn't have been able to see anything, like a blind man entering a treasure-house. His mind was not like a lamp which is deliberately lit in order to seek something; it was a bonfire accidentally lit by lightning. Parnaoz got accustomed to thinking about the secret and outgrew his childish naivety. Now he deliberately hung about the women in order to listen to their talk; he tried not to be noticed or to attract attention, because he felt he was doing something wrong by acting in this way. Clearly, the women didn't intend him to hear what they were saying; they just paid him no attention, took no account of him, because as far as they were concerned, he was still a little boy. If Parnaoz had dared to ask for explanations why this little girl was supposed to be unfortunate, his question might have been taken to be childish curiosity and naivety, they might have told him the truth or beat around the bush, or made this annoying child go away, 'Why are you hovering around here? Go and find something to do somewhere else.' But Parnaoz wasn't going to ask this, because it was the question he was afraid of: he thought the women would laugh at him or be angry with him, turn red and tell him to get out. Luckily, he had Tsuga with him: one whistle, and he could forget about the women and about Ino who had been turned into a goat kid by her magician of a mother.

One day, however, a misfortune happened which made him forget not just Ino, but everything. Tsuga fell into a latrine. The whimpering of the frightened puppy stirred up everybody within hearing. To his dying day Parnaoz wouldn't forget this pitiful, blood-curdling sound. The puppy cried out for three days, and all that time nobody could think how to get him out. A lit torch couldn't show anything except the pit's wet walls, covered with white worms. 'Kill it, for pity's sake,' said Kaluka. Philamon tied a knife to a stick with a bit of rope and stabbed at random into the murk several times, but clearly the puppy was not fated to die such a death. Philamon propped the filthy stick outside the hut. The puppy went on crying and crying, until its pitiful whimpering finally attracted a rescuer. 'If you knew how badly I need a dog,' said the rescuer. He appeared only on this third day, stopping at the gate to ask for water. Kaluka brought him out a jug of water. The traveller's clothes were in shreds, his sandals were broken and on his nose he had a big red wart the size of a bee sting; a stone the size of a fist hung from his neck on a tassel. When he spilled water on his chest, the stone instantly turned black. He drank for a long time. He set aside the jug, wiped his wet face with the back of his hand and repeated, 'If you knew how badly I need a dog.' Then he came into the yard and headed straight for the latrine. Kaluka followed him and tipped out the rest of the water as she went.

A reborn Tsuga nestled against her saviour's feet, but he kicked her away. He stood nearby and wiped his rags clean with fig leaves. Parnaoz didn't dare even call Tsuga, who had been brought out of the black maw of the latrine. He sensed that their feeling of closeness, of being inseparable, which three days before had seemed eternal, had now vanished. Because he had been unable to help his friend, he seemed to have no right to remind her of himself, or to ask her forgiveness. Tsuga in turn just gave him one look and went back to the pit from which Shubu and Philamon had pulled her rescuer. Before her rescuer had even set foot on the ground, she managed to lick his face several times. Smiling, the rescuer seemed to be looking for a stone. But Tsuga didn't run off: she lay down in front of him and whacked the ground with her tail. When he went out of the gate, the rescuer said once more, 'If you knew how badly I need a dog,' and left without a backward glance, quite sure that Tsuga would be at his heel.

After that Parnaoz remembered Ino more often, or rather, when he thought of Tsuga, he also remembered Ino, for some reason. His timid nature sought a comrade, and he recognized the moment a comrade appeared. Ino wore a red dress and red ribbons were woven into the little curls of hair around her ears. 'How ugly she is,' thought Parnaoz.

Their friendship lasted two years, just two years, until others' sins drove them out of Dariachangi's garden, and what seemed to be eternity was chopped up into ordinary days and nights. Only then did they realise that they were not alone, that Dariachangi's garden was not the whole world, but a small, almost insignificant part of the world, although nothing else existed for them over those two years. They smelled of apples, they had apple blossom in their hair, they seemed to have been born in that garden, at the same time, in each other's sight. The feeling of freedom made them giddy and bold; they imagined they were masters of the universe. Actually, they were free, because they sought what was similar, not different, in one another. If Dariachangi's garden really had been the whole world, they would have been completely happy. Like this garden, they would never grow old, and the district would have been full of healthy, golden-haired boys and girls. But they were not the first human beings, nor were they born for each other; they weren't meant to begin life, they were meant to continue or end life begun by others. Life needed them for itself, life intended these two pieces of wood for the fire on which it would warm its frozen hands. Their isolation was an illusion; not for a second had life taken its eye off these two happy children clambering through the trees like squirrels, shrieking with joy as they greeted the sea's foaming waves, roasting themselves under the sun and writing, then erasing, then writing again each other's names in the sand. Sometimes Ino squawked like a parrot, sometimes got down on all fours and called out, 'Look at me, look at me, I'm Tsuga.' Then Parnaoz could see Tsuga with her tail up, ready to leap at him. Sometimes they lay still, next to each other, looking at the sky: you'd have thought they were two green branches that someone had put in the sun to dry. In the sky, two lives ran in one channel, burbling between the clouds like a torrent strewn with apple blossom, to become one with eternity. But this too was an illusion, magic wrought by dreams, a sweet lie, the obverse of truth, because only in the sky could the reflection of two torrents, two different fates merge into one. On earth, however, each had their own channel, a different one traced before they were born, established and legitimized, and, like it or not, each would be muddied by the silt which had built up over the years in the channels.

At first they met by chance, and their meeting place was always on the seashore in front of Dariachangi's garden. Sometimes Ino didn't turn up for a whole day. In rainy weather both of them stayed indoors and it never occurred to either that you could meet in the rain as well. In bad weather nobody would let them out to bathe or to clamber in the soaking wet trees, but they could have thought of some other pretext to leave the house for just a minute for something that couldn't be put off. It would have been easy to run to Dariachangi's garden if Ino was waiting there, sheltering under a tree, drenched from head to toe and shivering as rain fell like big teardrops on the trees. This is what they did later, when they made trysts and vows that they would definitely come, as long as they were alive, whatever the weather, however obstinate their elders were. And standing under trees in a wet dress had its charms. They caught the elongated raindrops sliding off the leaves in their mouths, were pleased by their boldness when they got drenched, and laughed at everything. Every day they told one other the same stories, asked the same questions, but they were never bored because each day the old story seemed new. The same question took on more meaning every day, becoming deeper and more demanding. They wanted to know everything, they told each other every tiny detail of what had happened to them. Not that there was anything to tell: one's adventures were all linked to the talking parrot, and the other's to the dog that fell in the latrine. They exaggerated a lot and claimed fictitious qualities for the parrot and the dog, which they wouldn't have believed if they'd heard them from others. But they believed each other. They weren't fooled: they simply had an urge to believe. They were still too little to be disbelieving.

'If you miss her badly, then hit me with a stick and I'll turn into a dog,' Ino once told Parnaoz.

Parnaoz now loved life, found joy in everything, the fear of his own existence which he had felt since birth had vanished without trace. As long as he could remember, everyone covered their mouth and talked to him in a whisper, inspiring him with fear of the man to whom he was unconsciously, blindly drawn. Everything changed after he made friends with Ino. The sail-sized canvas no longer drew him as before. Now it was fear of his father that kept him sitting still on the three-legged stool, and impatient to get out of the twilit room into the bright sunlight where he would see Ino. The breeze wafted flowers from Dariachangi's garden, the shore and the sea were strewn with white petals. When it was time to go home, they reluctantly got dressed, raking up with their feet the clothes they had strewn about, spending a lot of time sorting whose was which. Ino put her dress on back to front, in order to take it off, turn it round and get dressed all over again. They thought everything was funny and laughed. Everything became interesting and they examined carefully a stick, a shell, a coloured stone or a dung-beetle as round as a big drop of tar washed ashore by the sea — everything that their foot or eye came across on the road home. When they were home they thought about each other, but this was so far a pleasant thought, a pleasant expectancy which allowed them the privilege of resting and sleeping soundly.

Parnaoz was alarmed and perturbed by Ino's remark that, if he missed Tsuga, he could throw a stick at her and she would turn into a dog. It reminded him of the danger of changes that were bound to come. Parnaoz could no longer relax. He went back to his shell of vague, fearful anxiety and hopeless weakness. Tossing and turning in bed, unable to sleep, Parnaoz sensed that Ino's remark had a different, greater meaning, was saying something else, but his hearing was not yet able to grasp this something else. He would have used his fingernails or a twig to open his hearing's blocked gates — more a mouse's bolt-hole, than gates, through which a terrifying, overwhelming fearful thing would break into his soul. He had no doubt that this would happen, but he still wanted to understand the name of this fearful thing, what it looked like, why it even existed and, if it did exist, why it was attacking him. The nights grew longer and dragged out. His room filled with spectres. Parnaoz loved Ino. He loved her and did not, could not know it. 'I'm suffering because I killed my mother,' Parnaoz thought. He was really suffering like a grown-up. The suffering was increasing, roughly and prematurely. 'I don't want to be born, don't give birth to me,' he pleaded in his dreams with his mother. But his mother smiled like Ino, shut her eyes and dimples appeared on her cheeks. 'No, no, no,' Parnaoz would wake up yelling as he was being born, but when he came to from his dream he no longer remembered whom he was yelling at and what he was saying no to. The sweat dried quickly, he could feel his legs getting numb with cold, but was afraid to lay his head on the pillow, as if the pillow were the source of his hallucinations. He sat there, his teeth chattering. He waited impatiently for daybreak, when he would see Ino and tell her everything.

But the moment he set foot out of doors, his night fears and hallucinations vanished without trace, losing their power in daylight, their credibility as well as their power. It was really hard to believe what he had seen, heard, felt and undergone in the night. From whatever he thought about, whatever visions appeared to him, his mind so far drew only one conclusion: Ino was in danger, or he himself was, rather than Ino, for one fine day it was very possible that she could disappear as had Tsuga. Parnaoz could imagine it all: someone coming, in rags, with a wart, like Tsuga's rescuer, and saying, 'I need Ino more,' and taking her away, in fact he could see Ino following this stranger. Parnaoz couldn't say a thing, because he was afraid of this man, or rather felt shy, embarrassed and even sorry for him. He couldn't help averting his gaze, because this man had inflamed reddish eyelids and dried yellow foam was coming from the side of his mouth. In the daytime, the hallucinations vanished, but the sensation of danger still stirred, like a fledgling nestling under his shirt. Parnaoz never revealed his fear and suffering to Ino: he felt in his heart that these were his fear and suffering, the tent which he had to sleep in at night, but fold up and carry on his back during the day. One thing was clear: he could not go on endlessly like this. Something would happen, in fact it was happening and, once it had started, it was bound to come to an end, good or bad. Ino was getting bigger every day, more illuminated and more inhibited. They still bathed naked, but now Ino was slower undressing and quicker dressing. She would suddenly grow thoughtful and, when she surfaced from her thoughts, would smile awkwardly at Parnaoz. Her gait had changed, as if her body bothered her, as uncomfortable as a new dress worn for the first time. Parnaoz was witnessing a miracle, the eternal miracle: in the body of a girl with curls round her ears a woman was awakening, the hostess of the world, the element that tramples on death. Amazed, Parnaoz watched, his heart pounding, desperately wanting to fall wounded on the spot, on the sand that was strewn with apple blossom, so that Ino would see his blood. No, nobody would let him have Ino without a fight; the reason she hadn't been married off was that this time in others' eyes was unimportant, it didn't count: she wafted a smell of flowers, not blood. The important part would begin when they were driven, like stray goats, out of Dariachangi's garden: when others saw Ino.

Could he know whom he was angry with, who planned to take Ino away from him? Ino was with him, sunning herself next to him, splashing about in the sea with him, running up to wherever he was. But he was resenting somebody, denouncing and accusing that person of all sorts of things, a person who probably didn't even exist. Parnaoz was like a bear sulking with the woods, while the woods stay quite unaware. Parnaoz was barking at bushes, like a frightened dog, he was once bitten, twice shy, and all because he was disoriented by the simultaneous pressure of his age and of love and premonitions. Now he ran out of the house at daybreak, his face showing he had not slept all night; nobody dared ask him where he was off to. Popina suffered other fears: she was sure that Parnaoz knew and understood everything, and ran away from her because he no longer liked being at home, he couldn't come to terms with his sister's dishonour. But he was too young to call the person who had dishonoured his sister to account, nor could he drag his sister by the hair. Those were Popina's thoughts and she was grateful to her younger brother for sparing her so far, for averting his gaze, asking no questions and keeping his anger to himself. Popina could no longer look him in the eye, she was ashamed, and most of all because of her younger brother, because she hadn't spared the time to bring him up and had forced him to swallow this humiliation without a word. Stunned, dismayed, aghast at her own misfortune, Popina paced the room aimlessly, unable to get down to anything and waiting, as if for death, for the day when she would have to reveal what there would be no point hiding.

Popina was wrong. Parnaoz knew nothing of his elder sister's misfortune. Every morning he was running away from his own source of pain, or running towards it, because that was the only path he had. Then he lay down yet again on the wet sand and waited. The calm, pacified sea lapped the shore, just loudly enough to be audible. But Dariachangi's garden was buzzing with life, every breath brought a volcanic scents and sounds of leaf and flower, ripe fruit and birds' cries. Parnaoz was lying face-down, waiting. His worries were now more solitary, and as sharp as an axe. After all, Ino might not be coming, she might be ill, or not be allowed out! The wait was hard, but he was prepared for it, for his intuition told him that waiting had to be his only weapon when battle began. Nothing else was to hand. He lay there waiting. Ino should have come. What could have happened to make her forget him? Nothing but injustice, a mistake, a misunderstanding could stop her: he was waiting for her as stubbornly, patiently and monotonously as the sand. One had to wait, the other had to come. It could be no different. It would really be a great injustice on the part of man and nature if things turned out otherwise. And she was coming. The hostess of the world, she who trampled on death, the answer and justification for waiting. She held her sandals in her hand and was paddling ankle-deep in water. It was easier to walk in water, or the sand would hurt her feet . The water swirled in her broad, deep footprints, wiping them away in a stroke, as if nobody should know her comings and goings, as if she had come from nowhere and only now been born from the marriage of sea and earth, or the mind of a waiting child. 'The water's warm!' Ino called from some distance to Parnaoz who was sprawling face-down and had no intention of getting up, for Ino was there now, with him, and he had only to raise his head to see her. Ino was coming ever closer and, wrapped in the beams of the morning sun, she dazzled him, like an idol emerging from a temple.

Then Parnaoz had a new fear. On the way to Dariachangi's garden, he looked around, avoiding passers-by, trying to pass unnoticed, as if the whole city were watching out for him, as if everybody was interested in where he was going. But even Dariachangi's garden turned out to be no safe haven, its velvety shadows couldn't hide their nakedness. On the contrary, it made them more visible, like a bonfire at night. And so, one fine day real life, noisy, sinful, coarse and ruthless, broke into their naïve world. It came to collect its kindling, because in its opinion the sun had made them dry enough to make a fire. The fire was hungry and had run out of patience: it was the only way to light up the ancient well-trodden path along which the eternally fleeing human race streams.

Ino and Parnaoz were sheltering from the heat in Dariachangi's garden. Again, their hair was wet. Two steps away, a lilac bush was in flower. Bees circled round the bush as if they couldn't find the gap that would let them into the bush. Suddenly they saw Shubu. 'Parnaoz!' Shubu called. He was standing at the edge of the garden, holding a gnarled two-pronged stick, and his beard, which reached down to his chest, was swaying in the sea breeze. Both Ino and Parnaoz were startled, as if they had done something very wrong and had been caught by a judge before they had time to destroy the traces. They hurriedly threw on their clothes and left the garden, their heads bowed.

'Where have you been, lad? Popina's given birth to a boy,' thundered Shubu.

He couldn't understand how he'd run home, rushed to Popina's room and kissed the wrinkled, red piece of flesh which was wriggling and howling in Kaluka's arms.

The father of Popina's baby was Philamon. Popina and Philamon were almost the same age. Kaluka had given birth first, followed by Marekhi. Worried by the imminent ordeal, Marekhi wouldn't leave Kaluka's bedside. She sat at the head of her servant's bed, asking the same question: 'What will I feel, how will I be, will I manage?' She did manage, but her fever didn't go down for a whole month, and she lay there half delirious, not speaking, but smiling, exuding the smell of milk, while her bared chest was covered in cloudy drops of sweat, like coarsely ground salt. So, in the early days, Kaluka ended up breast-feeding both Philamon and Popina together. Whenever they opened an eye, they saw each other. Things didn't change later. As time passed, they grew up in each other's sight. They went through the same troubles: after catching measles, they shared a bedroom. Kaluka decorated their room with brightly coloured ribbons, then put a lute on her lap, as if it were a naked baby, and for three weeks she never stopped singing. After measles came whooping cough and the children shared a bedroom again. This time Kaluka treated the illness with songs of praise and sweetmeats, but the lute was forgotten. Instead, they never fell silent all those three weeks, crowing non-stop and hoarsely like young cockerels. They were as used to each other's company as to walking, eating or sleep. They saw the same faces and objects every morning, they ate bread from the same oven, and followed in each other's footsteps. When they began to think for themselves they were surprised that one of them was the child of a lady, the other of a maidservant.

Later, Popina went to see her father and told him: 'I'm pregnant.'

Ukheiro had a weeping wound and Popina rebandaged it. Ukheiro's withered leg, covered with black and brown scabs, just trembled, then began shaking, perhaps with pain.

'I'm pregnant!' Popina repeated, holding a pus-soaked rag and staring hard at her father.

Women talk in that particular tone when they are afraid, in a tense, commanding and challenging, yet amazingly helpless voice. In fact, they are asking for protection and mercy, but they don't want to seem wretched and pitiful to their protector.

Ukheiro looked his daughter in the face for just a second. He was neither amazed nor upset. It is quite possible that he hadn't absorbed the meaning of what had been said, and couldn't perceive it in all its acuteness and vitality, because the day hadn't yet dawned for his sail-sized canvas, and so didn't yet exist in Ukheiro's chronology, and thus could not affect him. For Ukheiro there were two sets of time: current time, and resurrected time. Ukheiro needed resurrected time in order to suppress current time. This time was his own personal time, once it had been transferred and digested. The second time round it was easier to bear and to digest. Here he had all his kith and kin, and knew everybody and everything by name. And so he himself felt more relaxed and calm in resurrected time. He never thought of denying current time, which is obligatory and the same for everyone, but, like other people, he didn't keep up with it, he just encountered it and split it, as a rock divides a river's current, which then turns back to enter its dark and distant source. 'But time still passes,' thought Ukheiro, 'and doesn't give a damn about anything. The night I killed Two-Noses, Marekhi told me that she was pregnant; now her daughter's pregnant.'

'Women are meant to get pregnant,' Ukheiro said, his hand working on the flower embroidered at the end of a line.

Under the weight of his hand the flower became warm and tousled.

'Who by?' shouted Popina. 'Aren't you interested in who got your daughter pregnant?'

Popina wanted something to happen, for the ceiling to fall down, for the earth to open up and swallow her and everybody else. Or for her father at least to yell, smash something, raise his javelin, the way he behaved when he ran short of coloured threads. Popina knew that women got pregnant, but she couldn't accept the idea that her pregnancy was nothing more than a totally ordinary, insignificant and painless event. It didn't upset or anger, or even surprise anyone. She thought that what had happened to her was so loathsome and abnormal that, if she had told anyone about it, the world would collapse, her father would die and she would have dogs set on her or be stoned. In actual fact, nothing happened. When Kaluka found out, she kissed Popina's belly and said, 'God loves you.' Her father didn't even give a cursory look, as if she had brought him news that was out of date and therefore of no use.

'Your slave got your daughter pregnant,' Popina said in fury. 'Philamon! He dragged me into the shed, stuffed your coloured yarn in my mouth and pulled my dress over my face. The next day your daughter put Philamon, drunk and unconscious, in her bed: she invited him herself. Because a bed is better than lying on the ground. So he didn't stuff that damned yarn in my mouth and didn't pull my dress over my face!..'

Popina suddenly fell silent, and a little later she went on in her usual calm voice, 'That's the only way a woman can defend herself when there's nobody else to protect her.'

'Philamon, Philamon…' thought Ukheiro, and recalled Marekhi's first pregnancy when she rushed about in fright, muttering the same thing for nights on end, 'Oh if I gave birth before Kaluka, I'd be free now.'

Not long afterwards Popina fell ill. She had an attack in the bath, when she broke into a cold sweat and started shivering. Kaluka lifted her, still covered in soap, out of the bath like a baby and sat her on a divan. When Popina came to, Kaluka was kneeling in front of her, drying her feet. Popina smiled pathetically, because she suddenly felt again the bitterness of having no mother, and she had no other way of asking for comfort and help. Kaluka kissed her hard, shiny belly, where there were still drops of soapy water, like a large clay bowl that had been washed and turned upside down.

Ukheiro sat up in bed, raised his javelin over his head and shouted, 'Have Philamon come in!' But Philamon had fled long ago. Nobody knew what had happened to him. Ukheiro was informed that he hadn't left a message, or a trace. Ukheiro was furious and flung the javelin at the wall, getting rid of it for ever, as if he'd been saving it for this day and would never need it again. He was rid of it, and free. The javelin, once freed, whooshed like a dragon, split the wall and stuck for ever in the cleft. Its body went on quivering and humming for a time.

When the whole house was full of nappies and swaddling clothes for Popina's first-born, and there was no space left, they would hang the nappies and swaddling clothes to dry on the javelin shaft. Ukheiro paid no attention, because he no longer considered the javelin to be his; he no longer loved it or needed it.

Silence crept into the house. Everyone felt that they were wrongdoers and, at the same time, wronged. The baby was born without a father, in fact the baby's father was as much one of the family as any one of them. They thought that the cries of Philamon's baby would bring him back, that he would pluck up courage, ask for forgiveness, and everyone would be together again. But it seemed that Philamon had no intention of coming back: fear of Ukheiro had got to his flesh and bones and he was running away without a backward glance.

Giving birth had so exhausted and weakened Popina that she was unable and unwilling to do anything. There was nothing she wanted. She thought she would now just lie there, saturated with the smell of her milk and the baby, her head spinning with weakness, and strangely, incredibly happy and proud, a feeling which was very soon changed into ordinary unhappiness and humiliation. She was an abandoned, rejected woman, and her first-born urged and forced her to accept forbearingly, welcome and look the truth in the eyes, because she was no longer alone and no longer belonged only to herself: she had at her breast a piece of herself, her offspring, yet at the same time a new, utterly independent life, which was as demeaning, noisy and greedy as life itself.

Philamon's disappearance was still the talk of the people when they found out that black-eyed Malalo's daughter and Ukheiro's son had also run away. 'What are they running away for: have they heard anything we haven't?' was the current joke in Vani.

The news was a surprise, but the escape had been planned for some time. They started thinking about it when Shubu came looking for them in Dariachangi's garden and told them Popina had given birth to a boy. Parnaoz was already on the run that day, because everything he did was aimed at running away. The two of them had gradually got used to the idea and they found it as natural as any bud unfurling in Dariachangi's garden. Ino was ready for anything, glad in fact, and kept on repeating that they should go somewhere where even Shubu would find it hard to find them. Parnaoz saved up bread, took it up to the loft and put it in a coarse sack. It would be foolish to set off on such a journey without bread: who knew when they would reach a band of outlaws? It would be hard to find food in the mountains, they'd be lucky to find even shepherds, but they'd have to hide from shepherds, too, because even shepherds couldn't be trusted to let them go free: they'd drive them back with their flocks. Parnaoz's plan was simple: it was its simplicity that enchanted the two of them. They would go to the mountains and join the outlaws whom the city had been talking about for a year now. They would offer the leader of the outlaws a ham (Parnaoz already had his eye on a haunch, but he would have to steal it at the last moment so that Kaluka would notice as late as possible that it was missing.) The outlaw would be grateful for a real ham, which he must be missing. The outlaw would give them both refuge; Ino would do the housework, cook dinner, clean and sweep, while Parnaoz would help the outlaw go hunting and do whatever outlaws do. What more could an outlaw want? If the outlaw insisted on living alone, then they would build their own hut… next to the outlaw's, within hearing distance.

So they reasoned: they did the measuring, and the cutting. What they didn't notice was that their plan, which involved disappearance and isolation, depended on some outlaw, like a donkey on a stake to which it is tethered. The outlaw was at the heart of their dream: they had put him there themselves, because in the impassable remote mountains where they intended to go they would have nobody but the outlaw to rely on, an outlaw about whom the whole city told a thousand horrors, whether witnessed or rumoured.

At last the appointed day, or rather night, came. The cock had not yet crowed when Parnaoz slipped out of bed like a ghost, carefully shut the door behind him and crossed the yard. He shouldered the sack which he'd hidden the day before in Popina's dyeing shed, briefly spun round, sack and all, to mumble anxiously, as if half-mute, 'Farewell, my home!' and raced to Dariachangi's garden, where Ino was waiting for him.

It was not yet fully light when they noisily clambered like goats up through the stunted bushes of the foothills. When the sun's first rays hit the earth, they reached a cave. Undergrowth concealed the entrance to the cave so cleverly that, if you didn't know it existed, you would have had trouble finding it. Between the undergrowth and the cave there was a strip of green grass as verdant as if Popina had spilt her dye on it. They had been walking so fast that they were both in a sweat, and lumping the sack hurt Parnaoz's shoulder. The smoked ham had become as heavy as rock salt. They decided to rest here. Parnaoz threw down the sack and sprawled on his back. Ino quickly followed suit, and they both lay down on the narrow strip of grass. When they got their breath back, they took an interest in the cave. 'Let's take a look, at least,' said Parnaoz, sticking his head through the opening, before jumping back in fright. The spirit of the cave rushed out with a great flapping of wings. It was too quick for their eyes: they just heard a whoosh of wings, and black and red lines flashed in the air. Clearly, the cave sheltered some sort of birds, but these had been forced out, no less frightened than Parnaoz and Ino, yielding the cave to bigger creatures: the cave's soul had flown out, they thought.

Inside, the cave turned out to be quite extensive and high. Parnaoz stood on tip-toe and lifted his arm, but still couldn't reach the roof. Ino liked the cave.

'I'd love to live here,' she said.

Without further ado they started cleaning out the cave, as if they had already decided to lodge here. They didn't even mention the outlaw. First they took out the stones and boulders and roughly levelled the floor, then they made brooms out of broken branches and swept it clean, but there was so much dust in the cave that they rushed outside coughing, and lay on the green grass, watching for a long time clouds of red dust lazily coming out of the narrow entrance like some fabulous dragon which seemed to have ceded its lair to newcomers without a battle, a lair which it might have been quietly living in, undisturbed for centuries. Now the cave was their property, a refuge for their first bold plans.

The first day passed so quickly that they didn't notice. Parnaoz took some bread out of the sack, broke it in half and the two gnawed their ration of dry bread for some time.

Before they ran away everything had seemed different. Before then hunger and thirst did not exist, nor did dangers fill the night which was about to fall on the earth and take everything, including the little cave, into its bottomless maw. Jackals were howling somewhere. A rock that somebody might have set rolling, or which had broken off by itself, took ages to tumble down the mountain-side before it was swallowed up in the gorge. It had all looked quite different before they ran away: now they were sitting in a little cave and night was coming: in fact, it had come. They were now night-dwellers. The silence was tense, full of vague, mysterious sounds. Stars twinkled in the sky. The cave became even darker and hotter. They sat, clinging to one another, huddling in the airless dark, like a single creature, as if they'd come to earth all over again because they could find no other way to escape their ordeals.

'You see that star? It's my present to you!' Parnaoz told Ino, showing her a great blue star.

Ino couldn't take her eye off the star: she watched until her eyes lost their focus. Then she smiled and put the present in her heart. At that distance the star was just a glimmering blue light, but it suddenly turned solid and took on weight when Ino put it in her heart. She hadn't thought that light could be so heavy, that this glimmering spark might be too much for her heart and its pointed beams might scratch her heart's walls. The star pushed out of her heart her whole storc of revolving, rose-coloured air, and Ino was left gasping for breath. It hurt, but she found the pain pleasant and calming; she wanted to cry, and she smiled; she wanted to talk, but she kept silent, not knowing what she might say.

It was getting darker still in the cave. Like puppies waiting for their mother, they stuck their heads out of the opening and looked at the stars. The stars' multitude gave them courage, as if they were no longer alone, and they were part of this multitude. The stars were in fact flaring like flames and twinkling. Sometimes they even seemed to be laughing, and they hung in the sky like the apples in Dariachangi's garden. They were so close you thought you could put a hand out and pick one.

A week later, a bellowing herd of cattle, covered in dust and crowned with a cloud of midges, passed through the city. The clatter of hooves on the paving stones and the tinkling of cow-bells was deafening. The streets and alley-ways were permeated with the smell of dung and meadows. People couldn't come out of their houses until all the herd had passed, as if the whole city were covered in a torrent of mud. It was the herdsmen in charge of these cattle who said, 'We spotted some children in a cave.' After that there was no problem catching them. People caught them in the cave before they had time even to jump out. Not that they even tried to, for both were so starving after days with nothing but dry bread that they could barely lift their heads. They were lying in a corner, like puppies whose mother has died.

All that week Popina was distraught: 'It's my fault, I've caused their death. My poor brother was so ashamed of me that he ran away.'

When Ino and Parnaoz were brought back to the city someone yelled, 'They're bringing the outlaws.' Everyone came to watch, laughing and guffawing. The people of Vani had no intention of hurting the feelings of the boy and girl: they had no idea of the fire burning in their little hearts. But just a glimpse of these midget 'outlaws', who tried to join the 'band' a little too early, was enough to make one laugh. 'The ground is ready, all we need is the spade,' joked the people of Vani. Parnaoz walked with his head bowed, not thinking of anything, not even of Ino. He didn't even look once to see if she was being brought in too. He felt his head was swelling and buzzing unstoppably, buzzing and buzzing. Defeat had made him wiser. He tried not to stumble or fall down, to keep his temper and reach the end of the street, for anybody might find it amusing to watch him. Being defeated meant he had to walk with his head bowed, past people laughing loudly.

Ino was locked up out of sight and sound by her mother and sisters. They spread their wings over her like a mother hen, and didn't let her even show her face out of doors. Parnaoz was greeted at home with joy, embraced and kissed as if he hadn't been seen for a year. But there was reserve and caution even in this sincere joy. If anyone expressed their joy and happiness, others silenced him, 'Don't say so too loudly.' They were afraid of Ukheiro, not knowing how he would receive a son who'd run away from home, or, more generally, how the whole incident would end for his family. When Popina saw Parnaoz frowning and tight-lipped, she was more alarmed, believing that Parnaoz hated her and that she was the real reason he had run away. She recalled her childhood fear calling to her constantly when she lay stretched out on her back: her brother must be afraid of her because she was a woman. But Popina couldn't help being glad to see her brother, who in one week had burdened her with not just a year's but a lifetime's shock and doubt, sadness and regret. Popina caressed Parnaoz and fussed over him, though sensing that this was not the old affection of an elder sister any more. Rather, it was a wrongdoer's attempt to win forgiveness, the worship of a powerful senior by a weak junior. Parnaoz noticed the sudden transformation in his sister, and couldn't get away quickly enough to be free of these unpleasant embraces and kisses which only irritated and saddened him. Parnaoz was sorry for Popina, although he didn't know what there was to be sorry for in his elder sister. But instead of returning her affection he pushed her away roughly and said, 'Go and see to your baby, I don't need anyone to cuddle me.'

Popina hunched her shoulders like a dog that has been scolded, the smile froze on her stunned face, contorting it pitifully, so that Parnaoz was even glad when Kaluka told him, 'Your father is asking for you.'

This was the moment the whole house had been anxiously waiting for. They were all helpless, nobody dared to come between father and son. 'Let's hope that maniac doesn't go for the child,' they thought to themselves. Parnaoz would rather die than go and see his father, but after a disagreeable encounter with his sister he was now ready to enter a hungry lion's cage, let alone his father's room, as long as he didn't see Popina's scared and miserable face again. Kaluka's words brought Popina to her senses and she called to her brother as he went through the door, 'Don't be afraid, but don't go too close.'

Ukheiro was embroidering and didn't raise his head at first, as if he hadn't heard Parnaoz come in. Parnaoz was somehow touched by the peace and tidiness that reigned in his father's room: it reminded him of his dead mother and indeed, there was something motherly in a man softened and blanched by prolonged illness over the years, a man who handled a crochet needle with such female skill. This odd feeling stuck in Parnaoz's throat, like a rough stone ball; here, in his father's peaceful, darkened room he felt for the first time that he had done wrong, at least in the sight of this man, but he would rather feel a criminal than ask for pardon. He felt he had to resist. Parnaoz was now incapable of thought or choice. A quiver began in his ankles and soon reached his waist; Parnaoz pinched his thigh as hard as he could to stop the trembling.

Ukheiro raised his head and looked up in amazement, as if this was the first time he had noticed Parnaoz. Clearly he found talking hard, for he indicated with a wave of his hand, 'Sit down.' Parnaoz went up to the chair and sat down, very astonished by something, because he could no longer rely on his trembling legs. Ukheiro was again silent for a long time, until something like a smile formed on his lips. This smile only heightened Parnaoz's feeling of criminality. Ukheiro roughly put a hand on his face as if he saw his own smile in his son's eyes and didn't like it.

'What do you intend to do now?' he asked his son.

Parnaoz couldn't understand properly what his father was asking: at that very moment a convulsion seized him and bent his fingers. His numbed fingers automatically, painlessly, but obstinately stuck to each other and wriggled in all directions, like green branches held over a fire.

'It's time now you learnt a skill,' Ukheiro went on, surprised and a little annoyed by his son's silence.

'Forgive me,' Parnaoz barely managed to mutter, unable to do anything else.

Ukheiro frowned and he went back to his embroidery.

It was only when Parnaoz was coming out of his father's room that he remembered of Ino.

CHAPTER TEN

THE winds that blew from the sea brought to the city the fetid smell of rotten water. The shore had been breached and had changed colour: it had something alien about it. At times the sea reared up, roaring and spitting like a dragon dragged by its tail; at times it ebbed out quietly with a sigh and a groan. Downcast, Bedia kept uncoiling the rope round his neck, or rather freeing himself from its rough coil and hitting, trampling and pounding it with his feet until he was dizzy with tiredness. Relieving his feelings by beating the rope, he then shook it out, straightened it before wrapping it round his neck again, and then he moved off home like a snail into its shell.

Like a layer of smoke, the seaweed spread over the abandoned ground, more a mixture of earth and water than ground. Mouldy, musty bubbling pools, like incurable ulcers, beset its entire length. You'd have thought someone had dug up his detested enemy's decomposing corpse from its grave and left it there, thrown for the gulls to peck to pieces.

The women were picking the seaweed, hauling it away in sacks and spreading it out to dry in the streets in front of their houses. The sun made the seaweed shine gold and softened it nicely. The women insisted that their children slept better and had better dreams on mattresses stuffed with this seaweed.

Kaluka too gathered up enough seaweed for a mattress, drying it in the sun and putting her grandchild on the mattress. Everyone called the child Popeye, because when Shubu first saw it he said, 'Look at the son of a bitch: his eyes are popping.' The name was permanent.

Popeye was a healthy child: he grew in months as much as other children grew in years. He began to walk and talk at the same time. Every day he grew more like his father Philamon, but for some reason people avoided saying so to Popina, until she herself said, 'This brat is the spitten image of Philamon.' The other members of the family were glad: they took Popina's announcement to be a pardon for Philamon. After all, Philamon was kith and kin. If anyone said, 'I wonder where he is now,' Popina would instantly retort, 'Wherever he is, he'll still be the same fool as ever.'

Kaluka was grateful just for a mention, good or bad, of her son, but when the conversation turned to Philamon, she would get down to some task and not join in, although she was all ears. She never once mentioned her son in anyone's hearing; but nobody could see what was in her heart, nor would she let them. It was a matter between mother and son, just mother and son, and therefore not the business of any third person, no matter who. Kaluka wasn't offended when Popina called Philamon a fool, because she knew Popina had good reason. Kaluka had raised Popina as her child, too, and treated her equally, so her parent's unfailing instinct had always warned, or rather persuaded her, that Popina loved Philamon. Kaluka considered this to be a greater misfortune than the loss of her son. Philamon's disappearance was prompted by cowardice and ignorance; a human being had been a wholly innocent, undeserved victim. 'After me, Popina knows my son best,' Kaluka had always thought. But the two women had never discussed this topic, they understood each other without saying anything. When Kaluka lifted the distressed Popina out of the bath and when Popina, her lips turned blue, smiled wanly at her, then she decided that she would never ever leave her, she would kiss the dust on her feet if she could possibly redeem the crime of her cowardly and ignorant son. That is why Kaluka never went looking for Philamon. She no longer had any right to leave this poor woman whose doggy eyes pleaded for help and assistance; she was trampled on and demeaned by love. Moreover, as long as she was by Popina's side, Popina would not lose all hope of Philamon returning. She herself was convinced that Philamon would never ever come back. Fear strong enough to overcome love can easily make a man forget the path that led to that fear. Philamon was a part of fear, he dwelt in fear, and Kaluka in her heart of hearts blamed herself for giving birth to him as he was; and now she had to accept things gracefully, bow her head and endure her punishment without a word of complaint. And she endured.

They were equally heartbroken, and all the unspoken womanly warmth, tenderness, hope and love were directed at Popeye. The sharp-witted and restless Popeye became, from the day he was born, the master of two very loyal, eternal slaves. Popeye enjoyed his fortunate life, and gladly went along with it. He grew up cheerfully and loved getting in everybody's way. His cheerfulness was indefatigable, although many of his dreams remained dreams. But the only enviable thing about him was that he had no trouble forgetting each day once it was past, and he expected every coming day to be better and better. He was barely twelve years old when he was seized by a sudden desire to get rich and went to see the vintner Bakha, telling him, 'Let me marry one of your daughters.' Bakha the vintner was sitting on his favourite chair, with his favourite stick between his knees, his hands like roof tiles on the stick's rounded head, and his chin propped on the roof tiles. He took his time examining this blushing milksop who was offering to be his son-in-law, then asked him, 'I've got three daughters: which one are you asking for?'

'I don't mind which,' Popeye immediately replied.

Bakha the vintner again fell silent for a time. 'What odd people there are nowadays,' he thought, half afraid, half regretful. When the blushing milksop started fidgeting, he asked him again, 'What else can you do?'

'Nothing so far,' Popeye retorted. 'But I want to learn butchery.'

Bakha the vintner fell silent again, for just as long a time, but Popeye was impatiently waiting for his final word. He was thinking about butchery, pleased with himself for thinking up such a good idea, and he was more and more taken with it. Finally, Bakha the vintner granted him an answer: 'When you've learnt butchery, then please come back.'

'Then it's all agreed: thank you,' Popeye replied.

Popeye repeated to himself three times, 'It's all agreed, it's all agreed, it's all agreed.'

Popeye sent his grandmother to see Vani's famous butcher. Pushiani, the butcher, didn't refuse Kaluka, but a whole year, then another passed without Popeye ever picking up a knife or cleaver.

'Lad,' Pushiani told him, 'do you think butchery's easy?'

Pushiani was in fact such a master at cutting and sorting meat, that just watching him was worth your while. His apprentice watched him closely, not feeling the fragments of bone and meat flying into his face. Sometimes Popeye deliberately smeared blood on his collar to make a bigger impression on the women when he got home. 'Just like his grandfather, he likes blood,' Shubu would say.

Popeye would have become a fine butcher, had he not been put off by a dream. The dream so frightened Popeye, who was timid anyway, that he could no longer even look at the butcher's shop.

When Popeye was learning to be a butcher, the whole city was full of cripples. You couldn't go down the street without stepping on a bundle of rags, with a forehead, a gouged eye or an arm cut off at the elbow coming out and staring at you, like the head and neck of some hairless animal flapping in the air. These were war cripples. Vani, too, had taken part in a war that had broken out far across the ocean. 'An army,' came the message from the Supreme King, and even Oqajado hurried to comply: he wanted to repay his debt. Ships packed to the brim with Colchian warriors constantly sailed out of Vani's stagnant port. The same ships brought the cripples back, together with news of the war. Returning to peace, disabled, but still alive, lads used their arms, amputated at the elbow, to slide the bowls of wine, given in charity, to themselves, and they told endless tales, endless, endless. Perhaps they had pleasure, even took pride in frightening people with what they had to say. While the cripples had listeners, they no longer felt themselves rejected or singled out, for everyone, storyteller and listener, was the same. What difference did it make who was crippled by what, by the sword or by fear?

This would have gone on for some time, until one fine day they were all seized. The cripples vanished, but their stories remained.

The cripples' tales gave rise to Popeye's dream. In his dream Popeye was already a butcher, his dreams had at last come true and he'd attained the butcher's block, slashed by the cleaver blade, but human heads and feet fell off the block into his apron skirts.

As soon as he woke up, Popeye, as white as a corpse, ran to see Pushiani and announced, 'I won't come again, I've given up the trade.'

'Lad, if you knew how near you are to your goal…' said the butcher, genuinely saddened. In his opinion, Popeye was very nearly a butcher and needed very little to be able to carry on this trade, but Popeye was so riddled with fear that he couldn't be induced to stay; he felt sick at the sight of the butcher's block, slashed by the cleaver blade and polished by fat. For a while, Popeye withdrew from life: sick with fear, he needed to feel cosy and safe, to get warm in bed, sweat this accursed malaise out of his body, partly if not wholly. Now he sat for days on end in Parnaoz's workshop: the tapping of the hammer and snip of the cutters calmed him, absorbed him and enveloped him in dreams. Popeye had always disliked his uncle's occupation; even now he thought it no fit trade for a man, but in this jerry-built wooden shed he felt calm and forgot his fears, for his uncle had broad shoulders and a hammer in his hands.

Parnaoz had built his 'workshop' onto Popina's dyeing shed, and had hung his father's 'love letters' arranged across the wall; he sculpted dogs' heads from these stones. After his defeat Parnaoz had put up this workshop and henceforth he never let go of hammer and chisel, as if they were the punishment for his being defeated and he had to sit without lifting his head cutting up stone. Parnaoz conscientiously served his sentence. The inscriptions, dizzy with passion and loudly proclaiming love, scratched by Ukheiro's coarse hand, were gradually obscured, erased and annihilated by the chisel. As it slid over the stone, the chisel raised sparks and showered Parnaoz's eyebrows, eyelids and shoulders with grey stone dust. By now Parnaoz had sculpted several dogs' heads: they all looked like Tsuga. If Popeye had been old enough to have known Tsuga, he would easily have seen the similarity. Even now, Parnaoz was making a sculpture of Tsuga's head, as he had planned; there was not much left to do. He put down the hammer just for a second to wipe the stone waste from the back of his hand, and froze, his mouth agape with astonishment: he was looking at Ino. Parnaoz was perturbed; he looked with confusion at Popeye, then bent down to the sculpture and blew away the stone dust stuck between the eyes and the lips.

'I think I know that girl,' said Popeye.

That alarmed Parnaoz more: Popeye, his nephew, frightened him by accidentally witnessing Ino's secret incursion into Parnaoz's workshop. Ino had emerged from stone, had broken through it and at last got through to Parnaoz. But this meeting had a witness. No, nobody must know that there still existed a world where he and Ino could still meet as they used to. This world didn't have its own time, and it endlessly mixed up past days and events. On the other hand, it brought back to him the original clarity and animation of each day and event. This world was called thought, it was more invisible and inaccessible than a fairy-tale world, but Parnaoz was afraid of anyone being able to forbid, or rather confiscate thought. That's why he muttered in embarrassment, 'How could you know her, when she doesn't exist? I've invented her.'

Popeye didn't insist: he had come here for relaxation and healing, and nothing else interested him. That wasn't entirely true: a few things in this workshop did interest Popeye. For instance, he was anxious to know what profit could be had from carving dogs' heads. 'What would we do with so many heads now?' Popeye pestered his uncle, but Parnaoz only shrugged: he didn't know or care. To make some use of the time, Popeye began thinking: could there really be any useful profit in this hobby? He thought so much that in the end he had an idea.

'That dog's head has magic. It will frighten off thieves,' said Popeye.

Parnaoz looked at him with amazement. Popeye smiled and repeated, 'It's no ordinary thing: wherever you put it, a thief won't be able to come near the house.'

Now Parnaoz smiled.

'What's so funny?' Popeye said, suddenly angry. 'They sell anything at Vani market. So take it there, perhaps you'll find a sucker.'

Parnaoz would sell the dog's head, count the money and then hand the money to black-eyed Malalo, and black-eyed Malalo would take him off to see Ino, and the outlaw would greet Parnaoz and Ino with a fanfare and ask, 'Where have you been all this time?'

Parnaoz smiled bitterly. He had a bad taste in his mouth, but the seed of hope now persisted in growing, taking root in a rock: it would soon send up a shoot and become a big, rose-coloured flower. Wherever

Parnaoz looked, the flower was in front of his eyes. The allure was so great, so enchanting, that Parnaoz could no longer resist wrapping up the dog's head in canvas, putting it under his arm and hurrying off to Vani market. 'This dog's head has magic: it will frighten off thieves,' Parnaoz rehearsed on the way, because he sensed that any sucker, if there were any, would hand the money over only if he heard those words. He had barely unwrapped the canvas when he was asked, 'What's your price for the stone, lad?' Parnaoz was dismayed, but this was no time to sulk: 'It's not a stone, it's a dog's head, no thief will go near the house of anyone who buys it,' he replied. Because thieving was a novelty in Vani, everyone was very afraid of it: before that, it was unheard of to lock your door.

The dog's head was bought. As soon as the money was in Parnaoz's hand, he could smell fire and looked all round to see who had lit a fire in the middle of the market, but couldn't see anything; the smell pursued him all the way to black-eyed Malalo's house, as if he was carrying the smell. He didn't know how he got to this long-desired house, how he opened the heavy door without announcing his arrival, how he found himself in the cool and darkened room. 'Hostess,' he called, or rather someone cawed, and only then did Parnaoz see black-eyed Malalo. Black-eyed Malalo had put her bare arm on the table, an uneaten bunch of grapes lay between her half-spread fingers. She was asleep. Parnaoz saw a bowl brim-full of bunches of grapes, lying next to the bare arm. 'Hostess,' someone cawed again: black-eyed Malalo suddenly opened her eyes wide, as if she had deliberately been keeping them shut. When she looked at Parnaoz, she frowned. She had been holding a grape for God knows how long, and now put it into her mouth and split it with her front teeth. Parnaoz gave a start, as if splashed by the grape's juice. Then he plucked up courage and put the money for some reason not on the table, but on the floor at black-eyed Malalo's feet. Black-eyed Malalo moved the money with her big toe, as if counting it, and yawned into her bare arm, which lay on the table like a plump, long-tailed animal.

'I've brought you some money,' said Parnaoz, because he was sure that black-eyed Malalo had no intention of talking to him.

'That's right, debts must be paid,' said black-eyed Malalo, yawning.

In his heart, Parnaoz had rehearsed a thousand times what he wanted to say, what he imagined would excite and gladden black-eyed Malalo: 'What a day to celebrate! My youngest daughter has a faithful suitor.' In reality, things went differently. Parnaoz was struck dumb, in a daze, and forgot everything, while black-eyed Malalo yawned and split grapes with her front teeth. 'I've brought you some money… I've brought you some money,' Parnaoz repeated mindlessly to himself, and when black-eyed Malalo started speaking normally, instead of breaking into song, his mouth dropped with surprise.

'My girls are not getting married,' said black-eyed Malalo, suddenly standing up, or rather rising lazily upwards, like smoke from a bonfire of damp fallen leaves. She stepped across the money scattered on the floor and waddled to the door. Parnaoz couldn't help looking back where he had come in. No, there was another door which Parnaoz hadn't noticed, because it was hidden by a curtain. The curtain was embroidered with a mermaid, and when black-eyed Malalo drew the curtain, the mermaid vanished as if she had dived into the water. Black-eyed Malalo pushed the door with her flank, then opened it slightly and put her foot in the gap, indicating to Parnaoz that he should come. Parnaoz blindly obeyed her command, blindly went to the door and looked through the crack, although nobody had told him to. He grasped that this was the reason he had been summoned. Then black-eyed Malalo pressed her enormous chest on his cheek, and he quivered as if the mermaid was clinging to him. First Parnaoz saw the bowl of grapes, exactly as black-eyed Malalo had placed it on the table, then he saw a woman and a man. They were sitting at the table, tucking into the grapes. The woman sensed that a stranger was watching, looked up and in fright covered her chest with her hands. In fact, Parnaoz could hear no sound, the woman's face looked as if she had shrieked. The man, too, looked towards the door. 'I wonder who he is,' thought Parnaoz, as if finding this out was the only reason he had come. Black-eyed Malalo was laughing, Parnaoz could feel it on his cheek, which was pressed against her shaking chest. He had to fight for breath, as though the mermaid had dragged him under the water and he was now desperate for air.

'Why?' Parnaoz asked hoarsely, not knowing what he was asking, or whom, black-eyed Malalo or Ino.

When he came out of the house, he saw a fire. Children had made a pile of dead leaves and were burning them. 'That's why I was smelling fire,' Parnaoz said stupidly, gladly, like a man who has reached safety.

That same day he buried Ino. He went to the cemetery at night, dug a grave and in it put Ino's head that he had sculpted from his father's 'love letter', and then filled it with earth. The grave formed a hillock and he lay down across it. He was exhausted and his arms hurt. The night passed: he slept patchily, for whenever he dozed off, he dreamed of the mermaid. She stuck only her head and bare arms above the water, while her scaly tail waved about horribly in the water. 'Come on in, lad, I've got something to show you,' the mermaid called, and Parnaoz immediately opened his eyes wide with fright. When he was finally fully awake, the birds were chirruping, a donkey was braying somewhere, and someone had already heated up the bread oven and the smell of hot bread reached as far as here, the cemetery, where nobody needed it any more. But Parnaoz was hungry, and the smell of bread made him drool and wish he was home. He couldn't wait to get there.

After that Parnaoz came to Ino's grave almost every day. He came even though he was afraid, for he wanted to look after the dead, and Ino was one he mourned, or rather she was his now she was dead. He would first lie across the grave and talk, talk aloud, senselessly and endlessly, trying not to think of the mermaid so that Ino would not be afraid in the dark, under the earth. 'Greetings, greetings, Ino!' he would whisper, then shout, as he lay face down on her grave, and his face touching the rough surface of the earth, warmed by his own breath, filled him with a pleasant, although partly fearful trembling, as if it were a being, submissive and abandoned for ever, which shared his passion and pain. The surroundings were really intimidating. Bats swooped through the arches of the sepulchre, their dark shapes rushed about like lost souls, as if they were searching for the boy stretched out on the grave, so as to tear at his hair, gouge out his eyes and drive him away from their realm, because they wouldn't let this boy talk or come near to the newly dead. He covered the grave like a broody hen and sang. Parnaoz really was singing to chase away fear, to stop it interfering and to make it run away, its tail between its legs:

Scattered millet see-ee-eed…
Who but a chick picks up?

Parnaoz sang with a voice broken by tears, stretched out on the grave mound: he was sure that Ino was listening.

Everything had happened as it had to: his father's legs had to be smashed, Tsuga had to fall into the latrine, Ino had to eat grapes with some strange man and shriek when she saw Parnaoz; she had to be as afraid of the sight of Parnaoz as of death coming on a blue camel. Wasn't that all so? Everything died as soon as Parnaoz touched it, because before or during his birth he had committed the worst murder: he had killed his mother, life itself. 'I don't remember a thing, not a thing,' Parnaoz kept saying to his invisible judge, but what did it matter whether he remembered killing his mother or not? What would that change? He had committed the crime and there was more evidence to prove it than to deny it. The biggest proof was lying here in the cemetery: his mother's corpse, her remains. At first Parnaoz had rebelled against this terrible accusation, his mind could not accept or believe it, but he was shaken, his body distressed him, his body remembered something that had happened before he was conscious. He was like a man who was drunk the day before and, on waking, is afraid because he can't remember anything, but he senses physically that something is bad. Parnaoz, too, hadn't wanted to wake up for a long time, he fought and fended off awareness, hiding his head under the pillow for ages so as not to hear the sounds of a world that had woken up to daylight, sounds full of truth. He preferred Kaluka's lies to the truth. After all, couldn't he have been born motherless and come down from the heavens with the rain? A child's intuition let Parnaoz feel from the start that the only solution, if any existed, was hidden in this beautiful lie. He grabbed the lie with both hands. His mother did not exist, so she couldn't have died, Parnaoz couldn't kill his mother because he didn't have one. Unfortunately, only Parnaoz thought so; everything else around him, animate or not, asserted the opposite: for instance the little pitcher his mother liked to drink water from; the chair which she used to sit on; the sail-sized canvas in which her body had been wrapped and which his father was now embroidering; above all, his father — didn't the 'love letters' prove that his mother had really existed, breathed, walked, smiled and was much loved by the man who sent letters that heavy? Once Popina told him he had his mother's eyes. Parnaoz was horrified: he had not only killed his mother but robbed her, too. He shut his eyes when he drank water so as not to see his own eyes in the glass, he smashed the little pitcher, he stole the chair and burnt it, he sculpted dogs' heads from his father's 'love letters', for it then seemed to him that this was the only way: rebellion, intransigence, a rejection of everything that affirmed the existence of his mother. Parnaoz was a child then, and fought reality childishly, in vain.

In reality, he had been deported to this world to serve his punishment, because this was the only place to be punished, to atone for a crime: day by day, drop by drop, without end. This world was a place for serving a sentence, and there was no other world for him. If one did exist, he had to forget about it, like the world from which he had been deported, where he probably would have been happy, because he hadn't yet committed a crime. Everything that he had undergone and still had to undergo here was part of the punishment. Nothing here belonged to him, except what had now died, or vanished for ever. He had to wrap what his soul treasured in rags of thought to hide it from everyone, as a beggar hides his only gold coin, although it is of no use, because he is afraid of revealing it, in case it is taken off him: 'Who gave you that gold coin?' He had to stay silent, to stand aside, to bow his head in order not to lose what he had, what really belonged to him. His only duty was to serve his punishment: there was nothing he could ask for, but accepting the crime, rather than serving the punishment, was hard. The punishment even calmed him, distracted him, gave him something to do, but it made him permanently convinced of the reality of his crime. Now Parnaoz wanted nothing more than sympathy, someone else sharing his fate, because everyone had their own fate, path and punishment. Everyone needed sympathy. His father's legs were smashed; Tsuga had to spend a lifetime licking her rescuer's dirty feet; Ino had to eat grapes with a strange man; he had to break up stone with chisel and hammer. No, only by patience, submission and hope, hope that he would manage to atone for the crime. Really, his mother would forgive him! Parnaoz already knew that his mother existed somewhere, beautiful and happy; he also knew that her poor remains were somewhere here, buried in the same cemetery, in the earth, in as much dampness and darkness as possible. But every day his mother became closer, dearer and more indispensable to him, a mother he had never seen, or had forgotten at the moment of his birth when he was torn from her rose-coloured womb. His mother was like a dream forgotten at the moment of waking, vanishing without trace. Not altogether without trace, however, for she had left a heart-rending feeling of half-sadness, half-happiness, even if she had vanished, weightless and ethereal. But somewhere here there still was a small patch of ground bearing her name, permeated with her flesh and blood, hardened with her bones and exuding her scent. Parnaoz wasn't sure where this place, this little patch of ground, was. He'd never asked anyone, because he was too afraid, too shy: he felt that seeing him would disturb and distress his mother's remains. And what would he say when he went to see her, how could he, the murderer, ask her, the victim, for sympathy, however compelled, unaware, blind and ignorant the murderer might be?

Thus Parnaoz grew up, never having wept for his mother. Now he was too old to throw out his arms and legs and have a tantrum, and he would be a laughing stock if he did, but his nature, the other Parnaoz, invisible to outsiders, stood there like a child in floods of tears, bitterly, heart-breakingly, childishly sobbing at the door which his mother had shut for ever. Perhaps Parnaoz had chosen to dig Ino's grave near his mother's, so that his mother could see her child, her killer, suffering, so that she shouldn't feel, think or believe, above all not believe, that she could be forgotten. No, a mother, most of all a dead one, is unforgettable. It was his dead mother who inspired Parnaoz to bury Ino. It seemed that whenever he had something precious he had to consign it, like his mother, to the earth. Parnaoz was no longer a child, he couldn't be content with Kaluka's lies. He had to think of something else, he had to find a profession, as his father advised when he came back dismayed by his failure to become an outlaw. He had started his trade, he was working as a stone-cutter; all day long he looked at grey stone. He was paid for this job so that every evening he came back with a loaf of bread under his arm, earned by his own sweat. But stone was sly: it gave him bread, but it had its own aims. It kept him tied to one place, sucked him dry of thoughts and desires and turned him to stone, too. When he realised this, Parnaoz became somewhat wary; he saw when he looked around that a long time had passed, he couldn't recognize his native city: the temple was faced and the streets were paved with stone he had cut. The city was still called Vani, but Parnaoz roamed its streets like a stranger. A lot had changed, a lot had happened around him; Parnaoz had been hammering at stone for so long that he hadn't opened his eyes to see the changes that had occurred in his absence. Popeye had built himself a two-storey house and realised his childhood dream: he had married a daughter of Bakha the vintner, a woman far older and taller than him. 'If I ever find it too much, I can hang myself from my wife's neck,' Popeye joked.

Bakha the vintner asked Popeye when he saw him, 'Which one do you want?'

'The one with the biggest dowry,' was Popeye's immediate response.

'An older one,' Bakha the vintner told him.

'All three of your daughters are older than me,' said Popeye, still unabashed.

'I mean the oldest for you,' said Bakha the vintner.

'That's agreed, then,' replied Popeye and repeated three times to himself, 'That's agreed, then; that's agreed, then; that's agreed, then.'

Popeye celebrated his marriage in the new house. He laid on a banquet fit for a king's courtier. He worked for the king and was considered a courtier; he went every morning to the palace and came back from there every evening. That was enough for his enemies to go blind with envy. He may have blinded his enemies but, if you'd asked him what he was paid for, what his job was, he couldn't have answered. What he'd been told was, 'As you serve the king, you might be needed for anything.' But it was still difficult to explain what this 'anything' meant. He spent his first salary on a leather sack and all sorts of tools which he fancied might come in handy: he threw a knife, an adze, a machete, a saw, an auger and a plane into his sack, and cheerfully got down to fulfilling his duties, which were still vague and undefined, but all the more enthralling for that. But his job gave Popeye an equally vague fear. Fear, like an emboldened rat, crept over him mainly when he was about to go to sleep: it didn't take its red, motionless eyes off him until it had made him so anxious that he leapt out of bed like a madman.

The thoughts and hallucinations that Popeye had then: the whole palace seemed to be relying on him, but he couldn't understand what he was supposed to do, what was being asked of him; he didn't know how to act, which tool to pick up first. 'Give him time, give him time, let him have a think,' he thought he heard Oqajado's voice, and it made him only more confused, sweat more and roll his eyes pathetically; he was sure nobody would come to his aid, or dictate to him, because everyone envied him his promotion and they couldn't wait for him to lose his position. 'Give me a bit more time, I'll think of something in a minute,' he wanted to say, or rather bellow, but his voice failed him, his throat was blocked: the red-eyed rat had jumped down it. These torments lasted until dawn, but once it was daylight, he forgot them. The weight of the sack on his shoulders brought back his cheerful self-belief, and he pranced with pride when the city, alarmed by the jingling of his sack, watched the king's man walking casually, boldly like a commander, down the middle of the street. Jingling just as loudly, he entered the palace, not even glancing at the guards. Nobody knew what he had in his sack, although they all, the whole city, recognized the sound of the sack as the city had to hear it twice a day. Every morning and evening, whatever the weather, even if the heavens fell. Popeye spent the whole day roaming the palace with nothing to do, wandering to various places. He would pick at the bread in the bakery, sip the wine in the cellars, drop an obscene word or two in the women's quarters, until evening came. 'That's agreed, then,' he would repeat three times to himself whenever he was informed that he wasn't needed any more that day. Then he shouldered his leather bag and set off home, or rather to the dungeon that two women had dug to hide and bury their sins. But Popeye was not the sort of person to let anyone bury him alive. He had already understood everything and if he kept returning of his own accord to this dungeon of sin, it was because so far he had nowhere else to go to. Only when he built himself a house could he breathe freely and finally stand up straight, and be sure that he could openly show the loathing he felt for his mother and grandmother. Both mother and grandmother only served to remind Popeye that he was a bastard. This was his sole fundamental sorrow, which gave him no peace, and hindered him in his work, because he felt he could do more, and gain more boldly what was to be gained, if those two women had been less frivolous in their time. If only three people, himself and those two women, knew this story, it could have been endured, but the whole city knew he was a bastard, had known even before he was born, and this is what enraged him: that other people knew in advance what concerned only him. The origin of this truly irreparable injustice was these two women, his own mother and grandmother, because one had given birth to him and the other had taken to her bed the man, thanks to whom Popeye, the fruit of thoughtless, short-sighted urges, had come into this envious and mocking world.

When he built his house, he calmed down a little, he seemed to emerge from his dungeon and find permanent freedom. He really felt this when he first shut himself in his still damp, half-built house and stretched out on his back on the dirty floor, like a herdsman in the open fields.

'Now I have my own house,' Popeye, tearful and moved, whispered to the ceiling, like a herdsman revealing his secret love to the stars.

Before he married, Popeye slept in the bath. He did so for two reasons. Firstly, he was reluctant to unmake and ruffle his beautifully arranged bed, as big as a ship's deck. He had bought this bed and was especially fond of it, in fact fearful of even lying on it, in case he caused it any pain or damage. What he liked about coming home was looking at the bed, delighting in its grandeur and solidity, its tidiness, so that waiting for the anticipated pleasures and the anticipated journey would be even more intense and unbearable. The bed meanwhile patiently waited, like a ship docked in the port, for its first travellers.

Secondly, he slept little and thought a lot in the cold granite bath. He had a lot to think about, he had to use his head as well as his hands if he was to keep up with life. Popeye liked to think about his accidental father, and he always saw the same thing when he thought about him: Philamon, a rag around his thighs, running off into the bare meadow, with earth and gravel on his sweaty back, as if he had been lying on his back and had just been made to get up. 'Where are you running off to? Where? Why don't you look and see the life your son has?' Popeye called to his runaway father and smiled blissfully at Philamon running in panic into the bare meadows, aimlessly and without a backward glance. Popeye tried many times to imagine his accidental father, but never saw anything but the sweaty back of a man running away. Popeye longed for the runaway to turn round just once and show his face, because this was the face he wanted to spit at.

Popeye was a practical man and could spare no time to pursue a maniac. Time was passing, the world was seething and about to boil over: things could not be put off. Popeye would not allow any delays, once he had tried out something and, once he had a bee in his bonnet, he would put his heart and soul into things. One of those things was his marriage, a project started long before, but not yet finished, because his father-in-law had put off paying the money agreed until his death, saying 'It'll be safer for you like that.' Popeye was not amused by his father-in-law's 'caution', but he didn't dig his heels in, for he had done the most important thing by getting possession of a yard-long promissory note: it didn't matter where the money was for a year or two. Today or tomorrow Bakha the vintner had to make the journey to that land from which no man returns. He was human and however much he wanted, he couldn't be immortal. But the father-in-law sent wine for the wedding, and that put Popeye in a good mood, although he snarled at his beanpole of a bride, 'Don't think I'll put up with anything.'

The wedding went off well: the odd couple, so very unsuited to each other in age and appearance, put the guests in a festive mood. In fact, the bride was more like the groom's mother, than wife. Both tried to hide their age, one exaggerating, the other understating it, which made them both ridiculous. Popeye was highly excited and made everybody drink the wine his father-in-law had provided, and didn't stint himself. But he suffered worst, for he spent the wedding night slumped and nauseous in his wife's arms, cursing and swearing at his father-in-law, 'Never mind the money, I think that bastard of a skinflint has poisoned me.' All the same, Popeye allowed his wife to ruffle their waiting bed, the size of a ship's deck. In bed, too, they discussed money. Popeye worried all night, constantly removing the wet towel from his brow and spitting green fluid. Patu (the name of Popeye's wife) was more relaxed: 'My father's never told a lie,' she reassured her husband, and regretted only that her longed-for wedding night was spent largely being a mother, rather than a wife, to her vomiting husband.

Popeye was afraid to open his eyes in the morning, in case he found that Patu, unable to put up with his cursing and swearing in the night, had left the bed. Fortunately, she was still there, otherwise Popeye would have probably been heartbroken at ruining so stupidly by his own actions a business which he had taken so far. Patu was his promissory note, and that needed care and looking after, attention, affection and servility… until it was cashed. So he was patient and went to bed every night with Bakha the vintner's beanpole of a daughter, whose wretched nature was just as short of brains as she was of beauty, as if having a rich father meant she didn't need to have either brains or beauty. For now, Popeye had to put up with much else. His wife brought her mother as a dowry, saying, 'Until I get used to you, I'm afraid I'll be unhappy without my mother.' But Patu's 'getting used to' Popeye was extended for quite a time. Her mother took a liking to Popeye's house and found it easier than her daughter did to adapt to the new surroundings; Popeye smiled and tried not to have ill feelings towards his mother-in-law, for he had to be nice to her as long as the money was out of his reach.

Rachel, the mother-in-law, never missed a chance of lecturing the newly-weds: she got worked up every night, as if Patu was the first woman to go to bed with a man: 'Don't let him do what he likes, or he'll get out of hand, a man has to be kept in order from the start,' she told Patu. But Patu ignored her mother's talk, she liked being with Popeye and twirled around in front of the mirror wearing just a night-gown. Rachel persisted: she thought it her duty to give her still inexperienced daughter every single detail of her knowledge and experience.

'Your father never looked at anyone but me, because... Why are you singing, girl, is this the time for such things?' Rachel would shout, her patience exhausted when her daughter ignored her.

Patu kept singing one and the same song, not that she can be blamed: if she felt like singing, why not?

What else apart from dea-ea-eath
Will split apart our love?

Patu sang in front of the mirror and Popeye, who was nice, warm and already dozy in the deck-sized bed, had heard it for some time: he privately cursed his mother-in-law's nagging and his wife's singing ('one or the other') and longed to go to sleep so deeply that Patu could not wake him up again. Patu didn't care at all what her husband thought, whether he loved her or not, or liked being with her, or not. She, or rather what she felt and thought, was the only important thing. Patu took the enjoyment she had in the deck-sized bed to be her compensation, personally earned, for having endured so much, having kept her virginity for so long. Patu was now reaping the harvest, it was her celebration and everyone had to join in. 'My first-born, sweeter than my soul,' Bakha the vintner had once said when her mother had sent her, with her hair done and wearing a new dress, to kiss her father's hand. After that, Patu had never doubted for a moment that she was 'the first-born, sweeter than my soul'. Her child's soul was permanently impressed, as an article of faith, by her father's compliment, the first she had heard from a man. Then her mother helped to strengthen this faith. Whenever she and her mother bathed together, Rachel always gazed at her with delight and said, 'You'll be happier than me, because you have far more beauty spots.' Patu was convinced that Popeye stripped her naked in order to count her beauty spots. Sometimes, at such times, she would tell him, 'Look, I've got a spot here,' and Popeye would then lose all desire. Sitting on the bed, her head in her hands, Patu would twist her body one way, then the other so her husband could get a better look and count her beauty spots.

'What else apart from dea-ea-eath
Will split apart our love?'

She hummed and hummed, never stopping. In the morning she got up with those words, some time after Popeye had left, and every night she went to bed with those words, when Popeye was already asleep, or was drifting off. But, clambering up onto the deck-sized bed, Patu would first of all wake up her husband, and she had many ways of doing that: if tickling didn't work, she stuck the end of her plait up his nostril, and Popeye would finally be forced to open an eye. He finally became wide awake when Patu fell asleep. His mind would devise all sorts of sudden deaths for Bakha the vintner, all sorts of curses and magic spells, but neither curses nor spells had any effect. On one such night Popeye had a horrific realisation of how unbearable it was to lie next to a dim-witted woman, how hard it would be to get through even one more night.

CHAPTER ELEVEN

THE very next day Popeye went to see black-eyed Malalo. Nobody was surprised to see him. Popeye was well-known. As soon as she heard the jingling sack, black-eyed Malalo called to her girls, 'Whoever's free, bring the grapes: Popeye's coming.'

She said this because she knew Popeye only too well. The king's man would rather die that cross the threshold of black-eyed Malalo's door. When black-eyed Malalo first invited him in, he replied, 'I'd rather not, dear,' in such a tone as if he meant, 'How dare you propose such a thing to me?' After than he was never invited in, but he was greeted at the door with grapes, which they ate too, while he held a cut bunch, picking at it as if it was a corn cob, and telling bad jokes. But this time Popeye broke his habit. He smiled shyly at black-eyed Malalo, who had come to greet him, holding a plate of grapes for him, and strode straight into the house. Smiling, black-eyed Malalo followed her guest, because she realised instantly that something had got at the king's man to turn him into a gate-crasher.

'Oh, if only everyone wasn't busy!' black-eyed Malalo said with genuine regret and offered him the plate of grapes again.

Popeye took a bunch and arranged it on his hand with his tongue.

'All seven?' he then asked.

Black-eyed Malalo pushed the empty plate aside and burst into hearty peals of laughter: 'I've gone quite crazy in my old age; actually the seventh is free.'

Popeye wrinkled his nose. He didn't fancy at all black-eyed Malalo's skinny youngest daughter. He preferred her plump older sisters. When he was coming here, he was thinking about the six of them. Six at a time, because he couldn't single any out, so alike were they. He thought of them mostly in order to justify his behaviour: where's the harm, they're just plump girls. But he felt sorry for Ino, or at least upset by her, seeing this anaemic girl even angered him in some ways, as cattle with sunken flanks upset a thrifty peasant, regardless of whose they are. 'You don't feed her enough,' Popeye would tell black-eyed Malalo, as if he was angered, nodding as if he was really sorry for her.

'Hostess!' Popeye called to the reed cage; the parrot changed position on its perch and its yellow eye shone in fury.

'Is it true, it talks?' Popeye addressed black-eyed Malalo.

'It's asleep,' black-eyed Malalo answered, and she herself yawned.

What seemed most insurmountable to Popeye was coming here and revealing his desire, but both things turned out to be far easier to carry out than he had imagined. Both smiling, guest and hostess achieved mutual understanding. It no longer made sense to leave without finding out what he was being offered. Perhaps none of the six plump girls were actually free today. He was going to spend the night here waiting for stupid women, was he? Anyway, what was wrong with Ino? 'I might as well have a bit of fun,' Popeye finally decided and put the half-eaten bunch of grapes down on the table. He put his sticky hand on his chest. Host and guest, again smiling, without saying a word, set off in different directions. Black-eyed Malalo made a beeline for her armchair, while Popeye, his neck to one side, gently opened the door to Ino's room.

Popeye needn't have been so coy: he was wrong to think that the main problem was entering the house. Suddenly he became anxious, his heart raced, so that he was surprised and somehow alarmed at being locked up without forethought and unarmed, not so much in an easily available woman's room, where everything would go as he wished, as in the cage of some predatory animal. Now any unplanned movement on his part might have fateful consequences. He had imagined everything differently, before he got here. He never doubted that Ino, as soon as he freed himself of his sack and closed the door, would fling her arms round his neck. Nothing of the sort happened, for Ino didn't move and stayed sitting on the divan, bending forwards, tense, as if waiting for Popeye to get away from the door so that she could rush out of the room. Ino really was like a wild animal, the taut skin over her cheekbones had an ominous glow to it, her mouth was barely open, showing her razor-sharp pointed teeth. She breathed the air in so deeply that her fine, translucent nostrils merged together, and her flashing eyes looked Popeye not so much in the face, as in the throat.

'Hello, birdie!' said Popeye, his courage failing him, more to pacify Ino, as if she really would go for his throat if he didn't say something loving in time.

Popeye didn't expect such a reception. Ino had brought out grapes for him before. He might have been mistaken, but Ino had seemed glad to see him; she stood with her arms folded and looked at him with a smile as he clumsily picked at the grapes placed in his hand and exchanged banter with her mother and her sisters. And when Popeye said, 'It's nice being with you, but my job is better,' Ino would grimace pathetically, as if she was heartbroken, as if she didn't want him to leave. He noticed and enjoyed this, even if he didn't like Ino; but when Ino was there he made better jokes, was wittier, like an actor encouraged by his audience's support. Ino always took the part of an audience. She stood there smiling, not interrupting Popeye and her mother's and sisters' banter.

'When you're out of doors, you're brave. If you really are a man, come on in,' Ino's plump sisters would say to Popeye, laughing identically, in the same tone.

'Ha, ha,' laughed Popeye. 'Come on in… That's a good one, by God.'

Although he said this, he felt in his heart that the plump sisters were right, that he was braver out of doors: he found it easier to talk to a lot of women that to get into bed with one. One thing frightened him. If he was with just one he might not be able to control his desire, he would blanche, or his voice would fail. In short, he wouldn't be able to act as he should with these experienced women. And that one woman would, of course, tell everyone of Popeye's shame, and then he wouldn't be able to stand so boldly in front of this house, from which eight women, sure of his strength and superiority, came running at the sound of his footsteps. It was crucial to resist temptation, not to lose the superiority which only self-control could give. But he finally went astray, and Patu made him do it, Patu the beanpole who grudgingly gave him her all: her age, virginity and beauty spots. So far, Patu was Popeye's only woman, but he knew and felt that there was nothing special about his wife apart from her age and height. True, Patu often told him he ought to worship the ground she stood on, since she was older and taller than him. But Popeye was not such a fool as to be dizzy with happiness or to consider an older woman two heads higher than him to be God's blessing. Popeye only put up with his wife's 'merits' because of her father's money, but he found he could not stand the wait. Now was no time to settle accounts with Patu.

He regretted coming here, but regret was useless. He had to think of something if he wasn't to be made a complete fool of by this ugly woman. The trouble was that this ugly woman stupefied Popeye. He'd never experienced anything like it, his mouth went dry, his leg trembled as if the earth was quaking, his gullet felt blocked: he wanted to promise Ino something to make her gawp with amazement. At that moment he would have sacrificed everything for this woman if she would only let him come close, put her arm round him, lift her dress at least knee-high and bare at least her shoulders. If things had gone on like this for just a minute longer, Popeye would have perished, he would have collapsed, with his sack, on his knees, promised her golden slippers, a silk brocade dress, a bracelet and earrings. 'Scattered millet seed,' Popeye croaked, and was horrified at the sound of his voice. Ino shuddered. Her stony face quivered for just a second, but a second was enough for Popeye to catch it, to clear his mind and for his unbridled, humiliating lust for a woman available to everybody to give way to fury and hatred. 'Ha, ha,' Popeye laughed. Not an ounce of his recent emotion was left. He was the usual Popeye, sharp-witted, rational, practical. He summed up everything instantly and was celebrating his victory in advance, a victory far more important for him than stripping naked and subduing a skinny girl.

'Apparently, Ino, too, is older than me,' thought Popeye, smiling calmly and casually. His attitude to a woman who almost had him on his knees and nearly got a dress and slippers out of him was now like a well-fed spider's attitude to a dead fly that is nicely wrapped in the web and has been set aside for tomorrow's lunch. He had known Ino for a long time, but it never occurred to him that Ino was the same girl that Parnaoz had sculpted out of his father's 'love letters'. All Popeye had said was, 'I think I know that girl,' but his uncle Parnaoz had disabused him, 'How could you know her, when I've invented her?' Popeye didn't persist, he wasn't interested. He then had other things to think about, other interests. He had milked this subject until it had run dry. And he had at least helped Parnaoz sell a dog's head. Parnaoz told him, 'I sold it and paid off an old debt.' He wasn't interested either in his uncle's old debts, though he was upset that he didn't get a kick-back from a deal he had initiated. Then the girl's head disappeared from the workshop, but Popeye said nothing, although he suspected that his uncle had sold this head too. He kept silent, leaving it to Parnaoz's conscience, but secretly he was amazed, offended and angered not to be thanked. It was not so much being cut out of the deal as the injustice that distressed Popcyc. Injustice unsettled Popeye, and to him Parnaoz now was injustice incarnate. Ever since his eyes had opened and he'd looked around and seen the world better, his uncle had been going on about 'honestly earned bread' and 'decency', but had understood them in his own way, conveniently. He disapproved of his nephew, but cynically and without a qualm pocketed money he'd got thanks to that same nephew. He not only pocketed it, he reproached Popeye for it, saying 'You led me astray by sending me to the market.' Fine: by God, that was adding insult to injury.

And that was that, but Popeye had endured so many other injustices from his respectable uncle that he forgot about the stone heads. Then he started work: instead of encouraging and supporting the younger man, Parnaoz reproached him, saying 'It's finished: now you don't have any right to be angry if you're hit on the head, because you have to work for others to earn your bread.' He said so because he was envious of his nephew. Cutting stone is not like serving the king. Cutting stone was all Parnaoz could do, and he envied others their ability to do what he could not. Yes, he was envious, it was unfair because he also envied Popeye his house. At first Parnaoz refused even to honour him with a visit, he was too envious even to congratulate him and he frowned his usual frown. Popeye couldn't hide his resentment and hit back, so that everyone could hear, 'What's wrong, uncle, why look so miserable? We've moved hearths, but we're still kinsfolk.' Parnaoz only frowned more and persisted, 'Why make more enemies? Why did you have to go off on your own? We should have been satisfied with our poor lot: bitter or sweet, nobody could grudge us it. Nobody! If you don't believe that, then ask Popina and Kaluka, they'll say the same.'

But Popeye was no fool, he could see better. Nobody? Parnaoz was the first to grudge things, he counted every morsel Popeye ate. Even if he never said so, he didn't need to: you could see it. The way he would come in, the way he brought bread that stank of sweat, as if he were the world's provider. If the women were one minute late bringing him a clean shirt or fetching water to wash his feet, he would start a blazing row, just like his father, as if the world would come to an end if one wretched stone-cutter still wore his sweaty shirt or went to bed with dirty feet. No, he liked respect and even expected it, sitting with a god-like frown on his three-legged stool while Popina and Kaluka ran in and out with bowls and flagons. As if even a dog would eat the bread he brought, so rotten and so soaked was it in human sweat. And he sat there, puffed up and silent, demanding respect, attention and thanks, especially from Popeye, of course, because a piece of that bread, soaked in sweat, covered in stone dust and crackling under your teeth, was always broken off for Popeye. The bread failed to nourish Popeye: it shrivelled and weakened him, because he ate it with hatred, bile and under duress, because his uncle watched him eat it and smiled, expecting gratitude. Popeye had no father, he was born by accident, he was unforeseen and so he had excellent reason to be grateful to, and kiss the hands of someone equally accidental and unforeseen, but who was, luckily for him, a noble, respectable and generous patron whom the gods had provided for him free of charge so that he wouldn't be wholly abandoned. What would it have cost Popeye to say thank you? Parnaoz was no stranger, he was an uncle, his mother's brother. He was obliged to offer his nephew protection. But was that really so? Was nothing going on? Of course it was going on. For one thing, gratitude meant being reconciled to your fate, admitting you were accidental and unforeseen. Secondly and thirdly and for the hundredth time, Popeye was never reconciled to anything. He didn't consider himself to be lower than anyone or to have fewer claims on anything in the world. And he had proved it.

Firstly, he proved it to his kinsfolk, stupid women, and the stone-cutter Parnaoz. True, Parnaoz disliked Popeye's job and house, but if he lived ten lives, he would never be able to get either of them, because of his incompetence and, above all, his respectability. What would Popeye want with such respectability, it couldn't clothe you or feed you. That sort of respectability could only have bad consequences: it irritated people, it turned sweetmeats sour, and it was a senseless, baseless assertion of principles which life proved to be quite wrong. Popeye was a man, the whole city knew him, or rather shook with fear at the sight of him. Who'd dare grudge him his daily bread? Nobody! Nobody at all now. Not his uncle, who swore by his principles, avoided people and spent all day hammering at stone and steaming with sweat, like a donkey's saddle blanket. 'Sorry to disappoint you, uncle,' Popeye repeated angrily, because somewhere in the murky depths of his heart, despite everything, he had an uneasy feeling that his uncle was different, somehow unlike everyone else: that 'somehow' enrages him.

Parnaoz disapproved of Popeye's wife, too, because he didn't have one of his own. Popeye first thought that when Parnaoz frowned in his usual way and gave him a sermon, 'You're still young, you're ruining yourself for the sake of money, and making a fool of a woman old enough to be your mother.' But Popeye didn't give a damn about his uncle's sermonising; on the contrary, he was even more sure that he had made the right choice and decision. Well, was he supposed to marry a slut and carve a slut's head from stone? Would that be more respectable than marrying a decent woman? Fine: if that's respectability, Popeye would shut his eyes, stand aside and keep out of it: let Parnaoz marry Ino. Not just stand aside, but do all he can, not rest, not eat until it's a done thing. He'd sound it out now, and find out what Ino thought of his uncle, and then get down to business. He'd free himself for ever of any obligation towards his uncle, he'd repay kindness with kindness. Ha, ha: a fine couple, a stone-cutter and a whore, the son of a famous warrior and the daughter of a famous whore, a daughter who'd soon be as famous as her mother, if she put on a bit of weight, or at least padded out her dress with rags here and there. Then we can sit down and talk about principles.

That's roughly what Popeye was thinking as he stood like a pillar in Ino's room, quietly exulting, his eyes shining with pleasure. No other woman could have given him so much pleasure. But Ino spotted his sudden change of mood: now she was looking at him with amazement, puzzled that he was smiling like that, wondering if he was mocking her or rebuking her, putting on airs or showing that now he didn't think she was worth talking to. Ino was upset, she couldn't sit still on the divan; her eyes pleaded with him to utter something, anything, even abuse, mockery, humiliation, because in Ino's opinion Popeye had every right to do this. After all, he was Parnaoz's nephew: she wouldn't have thought that he'd come here to bed her, she wouldn't have admitted for a minute that Popeye would stoop to such a thing. No, Popeye had come to stand up for his uncle. If he was sparing her by saying nothing, it was because he was sorry for her or was too worked up to find the words which Ino deserved and which would have crushed her like a bed-bug on the divan. 'Say it, I deserve it,' Ino wanted to shout, but she sat there as if bewitched and did not take her eyes off her judge and the sack over his shoulder. Popeye was thinking of other things, his triumphant mind was soaring elsewhere. 'You've lost the dress and the slippers, birdie,' he rejoiced silently. 'Popeye's a hard nut to crack: never mind, I'll find you a husband and you'll have plenty of what you would never have earned: respectability and bread that stinks of sweat.'

'Parnaoz sends you his regards,' Popeye said out aloud.

Popeye was the only man who could bring Ino news of Parnaoz. Every time he turned up she was both alarmed and glad, because she secretly believed that Popeye had good reasons for coming, and was up to something, but she couldn't work out whether it was good or bad. She expected bad, rather than good, although not knowing tormented her even more. But she was grateful to Popeye for controlling himself and sparing her for so long, because she would have died on the spot if he'd brought her bad news about Parnaoz. Popeye came round like the seasons, the fifth season of the year, for everything around froze during his visits. In fact, everything vanished, except Popeye and the sack over his shoulder, and the free hand which held Ino's heart and ruthlessly, nastily picked at it, as if it were a bunch of grapes.

What Popeye said struck, but did not surprise or gladden Ino: she was just stunned. It took her time to make sense of what he said. She couldn't link Popeye to Parnaoz in her mind; she felt a muffled, rough blow to the back of her head; her expectant nature had a blissful sensation of pain. Again, Ino's face became stony, she stared at the ceiling, as if trying to recall if she knew anybody called Parnaoz, but she soon saw clearly, leapt off the divan and rushed out of the room so suddenly that Popeye's smile froze on his face. Popeye had no other business in this room: what he'd learnt was enough for the time being, but he was still annoyed that Ino had left him without even saying sorry.

'What right does she think she has?' he thought bitterly, but this was no time to make a fuss: a business he had impulsively set up now needed seeing to. Getting annoyed was helpful: he could weigh it all up better, and he had a lot to think about, a lot to sort out, to follow every thread and get to the bottom of things. Just one thing was certain to begin with: Ino and Parnaoz knew each other. Ino was the girl that Parnaoz had sculpted and then sold the statue without telling Popeye, pocketing all the money, although if there was any justice in the world, if his uncle didn't make up all the rules, some of that money belonged to Popeye. But this was no time to go into such petty details. He would find another way to prove he was right. What now had to be determined was whether Ino loved or hated Parnaoz. It needed time, caution, intelligence, cunning to establish this, for he was dealing with a woman: woman's love and woman's hatred are very similar. Mentioning the name of someone loved or someone hated could equally well make a woman leap up, as it had just made Ino leap up. He felt one thing, as painful as a boil or a splinter deep in his flesh: whether Ino loved or hated Parnaoz, this man, whom Popeye now relentlessly dreamed of humiliating and overthrowing, stood far above him. Even to Ino, Popeye was nothing but a client. Mentioning Parnaoz made her leap up like a madwoman, forget everything, including her duties, as if Popeye had shown her a dead toad. 'That's agreed, then; that's agreed, then; that's agreed, then,' said Popeye as he went clanking and jingling down the street, impatient to see Parnaoz. He wondered what his uncle would say: he couldn't wriggle out of it now by saying 'How could you recognize that girl when I invented her.' Let him try, that's what Popeye wanted so that he could chant at him, 'Liar, liar, uncle liar!' After that he would know how to act and what to say.

Popeye didn't and couldn't know that he was already playing a major part in Ino's and Parnaoz's lives by patching up what he himself had destroyed. Popeye's howl when he was a baby had driven Ino and Parnaoz out of Dariachangi's garden; they had been separated for good when Shubu informed them of Popeye's birth. What followed was just a pitiful and ridiculous struggle. Neither Ino nor Parnaoz were aware of this: nobody was, except fate, for Popeye was as ineluctable as fate.

Parnaoz was serving his punishment: he was cutting stone. He had only to hit the rough surface of the stone with his hammer for the roar of the city to disappear. All that remained was stone, a dreary uninhabited island, and he himself took on its colour, covered in stone dust from head to toe, using the hammer to chase away thoughts that threatened to drag him off the little stone island and plunge him into the sea of life. Life was unwilling to concede him even this little island, it besieged it on all four sides and splashed it with its muddy waves. 'Leave me alone. Can't you see I'm on my own?' Parnaoz would say to himself. 'If you want a quarrel, just give me one man, just one, and then we'll talk.' Parnaoz wasn't afraid of life: he was ashamed because he had been defeated. He had tasted defeat once, and he had managed once, but wasn't sure he would a second time, to walk firmly and calmly past a crowd of mockers. Thinking about defeat unbalanced him. He set to hammering the rough surface of the stone with crazed determination, as if he were trying to break into small pieces his one and only refuge. But the stone was strong, and human solitude made him stonier and gloomier.

Parnaoz knew what had happened: he knew that his crime was the offshoot, the continuation of others' crimes, and he himself was a part of the tree of these crimes that had rooted deeply, developed a mighty trunk and many branches: he was the crown and would be the first to feel the force of the wind and rain. Parnaoz looked up at the sky. However much the wind might bend him, or the rain press down on his neck, he would still find a way to keep his eye heavenwards.

He was afraid to look down, afraid to see the branch of which he was the continuation, the crown, because the branch was his father Ukheiro, the once famous warrior, his enemy's nemesis and his ruler's hope. The warrior was now lying on his back, embroidering in order to fend off the hostile truth. Ukheiro was fighting the truth, for the truth threatened to take away his friend's corpse; Ukheiro could not, as long as he lived, let it do that, he couldn't give in, because this corpse was his only proof that he had really ever existed, lived, walked, been called a man. That's why Ukheiro hid it under his sail-sized canvas, why his face remained stern, why he rejected life. Nobody was entitled to poke about in the rags covering the precious corpse; he was grateful to be allowed to keep the corpse and to howl to it, at least at night, about his sadness and helpless state. Parnaoz was sure that his father now understood how fate had made a mockery of him, by turning a famous warrior into a stupid child sent by one man to wreck another man's vineyard and then given a kicking as a reward, and such a kicking that he couldn't stand up again, because the man needed the stupid boy just for five minutes, just as a lust-crazed warrior is forced to say a few sweet nothings to a slut only until he is fed up with the sight of her. When Parnaoz thought along these lines, he was overcome with anger, he wanted to throw down his hammer, stand up tall on his stone island and shout: 'Stop mocking my father!' But when he visualised his father's sorrowful face, he bit back the words he was about to say, just as a guest, reluctant to upset the lady of the house, swallows, without chewing it, a piece of a nasty-tasting dish. 'Give me just one man, one man,' Parnaoz repeated senselessly and endlessly to himself, when he got back to his stone.

Parnaoz dreamed of another man who would neither tell tales about him or mock him. So far, this other man existed only in his dreams. And dreams were as different from reality as a chalumeau from a simple reed. The reed has to be cut, sharpened, to have its heartwood burnt out, holes bored in it, and even then you don't know if it will play. Popeye had let Parnaoz down. He was fishing in muddy waters: he didn't give a damn about anything else, which made him more dangerous than any stranger. Parnaoz's talks with his father led nowhere. Ukheiro took Parnaoz's complaints to be accusations, and defended himself, not letting his son get close. His beard tousled, his eyes popping, he fended off his son as the apostle of his worst enemy, the truth.

'You talk like this because you've never had a javelin in your hand!' shouted Ukheiro of the tousled beard and popping eyes.

'Father!' shouted Parnaoz, trying anything to stop his father's voice. 'Father! You talk as you do because you can't do anything any more.'

Parnaoz had no doubt that, if his father was on his feet, he'd be the first to pick up a weapon and teach him how to use it. Parnaoz couldn't handle weapons, in fact; nobody had taught him, and he had never held one. To him, Ukheiro's javelins were stakes from the derelict fence of a distant past: they provoked sadness and a vague pride, his whole childhood, as if he was looking from afar at forbidden fruit, because, apart from Popina, nobody dared lay a finger on them, for fear of Ukheiro. After Marekhi died, only Popina was entitled to scrub and polish her father's javelins. Parnaoz spent his time looking at the javelins until he forgot their importance. He forgot, as this was what his father wanted, for his father knew best how much sorrow and weeping could be caused by these steel-tipped shining sticks once someone picked one up.

'Even you are afraid of your javelins,' Parnaoz shouted.

Ukheiro really was afraid of these sharp-tipped, proudly burnished and temporarily, only temporarily motionless snakes. He was frightened because he had moved back and seen them from a distance. When he was holding one he didn't notice that their insatiable tips always pointed at somebody else, but when there was a distance between him and a javelin, he realised what they were, why they had been devised and forged. Fear forced him to be silent. But his silence instilled fear in others, above all in Parnaoz, because he didn't know how to use those javelins. If he'd ever handled one, he might have damaged himself, gouged out an eye, or sliced his throat open. If Ukheiro were on his feet, things would be different, Parnaoz would be a warrior, he would have been familiar with javelins from childhood and, at least, he would have relieved his father of them when Ukheiro came home.

'It's your fault if I don't know how to handle a weapon,' Parnaoz said, more calmly, although he was still angry.

Because Parnaoz was in the right, he was angry. Sometimes he thought his father deliberately behaved like this to stop him, his flesh and blood, from being able to correct his father's mistake.

'Can it be better this way? Did you really want your children?.. Say it, admit that you were wrong!' Parnaoz implored his famous father.

The unending dispute between father and son made Popina quiver like an aspen leaf. She could hear the words, but not infer their meaning. What she most feared was Popeye interrupting. She instinctively knew that what her father and her brother were arguing, or rather shouting about all the time was aimed against her son. The shouting made Popina feel this. Popeye must not hear this shouting, it must never reach his ear, otherwise… Popina didn't know what, and, lurking outside the door, she wrung her hands. Sometimes she listened to the street sounds. She was long reconciled to her fate and obligations, she had erased wishes and dreams from her heart long ago, and now had only one desire: that nothing should happen, that everyone should go on as they were. She had to look after three men, and all three were equally close and dear to her, so dear that every morning and evening she gave thanks to the gods for entrusting her with the care of these three men. Popina's thoughts and concerns were confined within the walls of the house and she would spare no exertions to see that everyone in the house showed one another love, calm and compassion: in her opinion, only calm and compassion and acceptance of fate could shield them from worse misfortune which was bound to happen, and was already happening, if they didn't come to their senses quickly and stop this endless quarrelling and shouting. Popina's unerring female intuition told her this, and she raised the alarm as soon as she heard father and son raising their voices. But nobody paid attention to her fears and premonitions. Or else (and she often thought so) men were born to cause misfortune to themselves, and to others. Popina had suffered from this fear ever since she was a young girl, from the day Philamon locked her in the dyeing shed and raped her. She didn't understand then, or now, why Philamon had done it. She had no explanation for this truly outlandish behaviour, except that Philamon was a man and brought misfortune with him. Popina feared misfortune most of all, and so she showed herself submissive to everything.

This attitude made life worth living and gave her the courage to get out of bed each morning. She knew she was a little insignificant creature, an adjunct to life with no right to her own thoughts and dreams, because she had to give them up for the sake of other people's thoughts and dreams. Anyone could trample on her if she was tempted by her own thoughts or followed her own dream, or longed for anything, even if she kept it to herself in her heart of hearts, secret from others. Being trampled on hurt; it was horrible, as she already knew too well; she tried not to think about anything or dream of anything, or long for anything, except peace and quiet, health and happiness for these three men. Popina feared men's innate strength, which demanded other's submission, not love. Love angered and irritated them; it left them feeling confused. All three men were close to her, her flesh and blood, but Popina still feared them and probably wouldn't have been surprised if any of them did what Philamon had once done. Fortunately, nothing of the sort had so far occurred, but that was not nearly enough to change Popina's beliefs.

When she heard the jingling sack, Popina rushed to Ukheiro's room to inform her father and brother, who were red-faced from shouting, that Popeye was coming; then she ran back to greet her son.

Popeye always came in with a smile, then looked all round as if he was expecting to see someone else there. This was a different sort of conversation between parent and son: unexpectedly broken off, searching with panic for a way out of the room, and making even more noise. Smiling, Popeye looked round at his mother. Lurking by the door, her arms folded, Popina shook her head pointlessly, as if trying to shake back a hair that had got into her eye. Popeye went on smiling and smiling, crowing with pleasure, for father and son, taken aback by his unexpected visit, were watching each other. 'Fine, that's how it should be,' Popeye thought triumphantly. Everyone, his grandfather and his uncle too, should finally get it into their heads that he was the king's man not Philamon's bastard, and had more responsibility than others thought.

This time, too, Popeye came in smiling, with no trace of the anxiety he had suffered. 'Has the cat got your tongue? Hello!' said Popeye, putting his sack down by his feet.

Ukheiro went back to his embroidery, leaving Popeye to Parnaoz.

'Tha-a-anks a lot,' Popeye continued. Then, after a while, he added, 'I'm not so bad as you'd like me to be, and not so good as I'd like to be.'

'Nobody here would like you to be bad,' Parnaoz replied, for some reason harshly and roughly, before leaving the room.

Popeye looked at Ukheiro, who was embroidering, his face calm, since he had got back to his own world where he could hear nothing. Popeye shrugged and picked up his sack.

He caught up with Parnaoz in the street, stood by his side and seemed to be resuming a conversation begun a long time ago. He said, 'There's no reason for you to sulk at me for walking with you, it's for your own good. Who knows what Patu's being told about me, I can't stop them talking. I do what I have to do.'

Parnaoz looked at him with amazement. But he didn't stop: he quickened his pace, as if he sensed danger and was trying to leave the area. He really did feel something like danger, unpleasant, worrying: he couldn't help being tense. He was seized with anxiety, his heart was pounding madly, as if he'd seen a snake slithering towards him. Popeye caught up with him again and put a hand on his shoulder. Parnaoz stopped. Popeye smiled from ear to ear, got as close as he could and looked round conspiratorially before gabbling in a whisper, 'I know everything, I've just come from there.'

'From where?' Parnaoz asked impatiently, although he knew what Popeye would reply.

'Ha, ha, from there!' Popeye repeated.

'I don't have time just now, we'll talk some other time,' Parnaoz suddenly speeded up and examined Popeye, as if their being together was something forbidden, dangerous and wholly unimaginable.

Parnaoz tried to get away, but Popeye again put a hand on his shoulder. 'What do you mean you don't have time?' he almost shouted, before immediately lowering his voice and going on in a whisper, 'What's the hurry, how long are you going to be like this?'

'It's none of your business,' thought Parnaoz, but said nothing aloud; he just looked in amazement at his nephew, as a child looks at a magician putting a guinea-fowl egg in his mouth and taking it out of his ear.

'Well, a girl should ask what's got you down,' said Popeye.

Parnaoz felt himself blushing, as if Popeye had said something obscene, as if he had discovered a disease Parnaoz had been hiding and now intended to make public. Parnaoz had no right to silence him, to put a hand over his mouth. He hadn't warned Popeye in time, 'I've got such-and-such wrong with me, but keep it quiet, you know what people are like, they'll make a mountain out of a molehill.' Parnaoz didn't trust Popeye, for Popeye had found out his secret and was now going to show no mercy, if only because he had not been trusted, and he had learned from outsiders what he should have learned at home, before other people. Popeye made Parnaoz feel ashamed, ashamed because he was standing there confused, helpless, dumbstruck. He had never ever thought before that what had happened between him and Ino concerned anyone else: the corpse of their love seemed to him to be buried so deep that he never suspected anyone could find it. But Popeye had found it, because it was buried badly, in a hurry, in a panic.

Parnaoz was like a criminal who is more ashamed of his judge than of his crime, because he committed the crime blindly, thoughtlessly, in a state of insanity, but only now has a just and noble judge helped him understand the consequences of his thoughtlessness, blindness and insanity. What Popeye had said implied that Parnaoz had deceived and betrayed Ino, had led her on and abandoned her 'there', a place which he undoubtedly ought to have rescued her from, as her only possible rescuer. Yet, for some reason, Parnaoz hadn't even lifted a finger when Ino was watching out, still believing, not yet despairing; but, instead of her only possible rescuer and protector, it was his nephew who occasionally turned up. Even that seemed very fortunate, God's grace to her, and she was ready to go on enduring more of the misery inflicted on her there by her mean mother and sisters. Just one warm word from Popeye would have restored the poor girl's courage, and she might really have believed that Parnaoz still intended to ransom or abduct her. But Popeye lied to her so shamelessly because he was embarrassed by his uncle, his principled uncle who lectured others not to fall as others do into the mud, because, unlike others, he did not think only of sating himself, so understood more than others and was therefore more responsible. Of course, deceiving a girl was no great deal, but Popeye was surprised, he did not expect this of his uncle and so was forced to deceive and flatter the poor girl every possible way to stop her changing her opinion of Parnaoz.

Parnaoz had no reason to be surprised or offended by his nephew's reproaches, because Popeye was only speaking out of a sense of justice; of course, Popeye would support Parnaoz all the way, if he didn't disdain his help. Popeye helped other people, gave them a hand, and it would be natural for him to stand up for his uncle. His uncle had the right to command him, for, apart from anything else, he helped bring Popeye up on his sweat-soaked bread and hand-me-down shirts. True, there were a lot of things about Popeye that Parnaoz disliked, but Popeye couldn't be accused of ingratitude. Popeye was quick on the uptake, too: he could understand and evaluate anything. His father rejected him, but his uncle had taken him on, put him on his feet and made a man of him. Now his uncle was entitled to roll up his sleeves and reap the harvest. One word from him, and Popeye would have gone through fire; he'd have snatched Ino from a dragon, let alone black-eyed Malalo, if Parnaoz asked him to, just asked, since he himself could not possibly be involved, he had to protect his good name, whereas Popeye didn't give a damn what people said about him. The main thing was to give uncle joy, retrieve for him what belonged to him, what was his, but what he had lost because of nature's injustice and his own high principles, his reserve or ineptitude. 'Just tell me, uncle. Ha, ha, snatching a girl's no problem,' Popeye told Parnaoz, who was only more embarrassed, and would rather die than talk about this with Popeye, who was at his side like a fellow-conspirator. But Parnaoz couldn't see anything, a rush of blood to his head had blinded him and made him quite as helpless as a blind man. Popeye's voice was jostling him, like a guide jostling a blind man, and he couldn't even cross the street without him now, or he would have stumbled into a pit, or a carriage would have hit him.

'Ino's dead. Ino doesn't exist as far as I am concerned!' he managed to mumble, as if pleading with an enemy, 'Don't hit me, spare me, you see I'm blind.' A moment's blindness seemed to Parnaoz to last a century, but Popeye's smiling face still upset him, as if that face blocked his vision and, if he couldn't see it, he could always feel it, like a dirty blindfold that had slipped down.

'Ino loves me, Ino is waiting for me, Ino is relying on me,' Parnaoz thought. 'No, that's impossible: Ino is dead. It's been a long time since I was last at the cemetery, I expect the grass has grown over everything. I couldn't pull the grass away, because… that's what I'm like, spineless and cowardly, I'm ashamed of my love, I'm frightened of being laughed at, of what people will say. Popeye wouldn't be frightened, he wouldn't retreat; he says himself that he doesn't give a damn what people say about him. You have to do the right thing by somebody, don't you? Yes, you do. So that others will see that you're right. I chose the mass of people in preference to one person, because I'm a coward: a coward of principle, whom nobody needs, because they already know how useless such a person is. That's why they let him stand aside and why they've forgotten he exists: they don't expect anything of him, because they've always been convinced he's a useless, but harmless animal. They were right to make him drop, as soon as he was shouted at, the bread that he'd taken without asking from the public store, because he didn't know the importance of that bread, didn't know that it belonged to everyone and he couldn't deal with it on his own. One shout, one scolding was enough to make him understand that. He stood aside at once, feigned death and even refused the crumbs that he probably could have got. He didn't actually refuse them, he just dragged off his share and buried it in the ground, like a greedy fox with its leftovers.'

'Uncle, what happened to the head you carved from your father's stone?' Popeye's voice suddenly sounded out. Parnaoz replied candidly, 'That head's been buried in the cemetery,' as if he were continuing his thoughts. But Popeye's voice brought him back to reality and, although his sight had not yet returned, he didn't dither, he marched down the street with his head stuck out, like a real blind man. 'Just give me the word, uncle, ha-ha, snatching a girl's no problem…' Popeye called out as Parnaoz quickened his pace.

A week later the castrated stableman came to visit black-eyed Malalo's establishment. This event caused great excitement in the house. The girls, dressed in velvet, assembled in the main room. What could be more surprising, interesting and entertaining for these women than a guest who was like a man in every respect, but was not a man. A visit by a castrated stableman was more inconceivable for them than a visit from Oqajado. They had heard what had happened to him, the story was as familiar as the talking parrot, but there was something else surprising. The parrot knew its place, he stayed in its cage, whereas the stableman had come to the very place where he had no business. All the women's faces suggested that they were little girls whom someone had given an enormous doll, no ordinary one, but a walking, talking doll which looked so much like a live person that it needed a lot of restraint not to touch it, or ask it something to see if it would answer or not.

In short, there was noisy excitement in black-eyed Malalo's establishment. The stableman was holding something heavy wrapped in linen. It was obviously heavy, because he kept using his knees to take the load, and the sinews in his neck were tense. The stableman raised his head, bared his crooked yellow teeth, and noisily snorted the air through his flared nostrils, constantly whinnying and stamping his feet. When the women's giggling began to die down, he asked, 'Which one of you is Ino?' The girls pushed forward Ino, as white as a corpse, and told her, 'You're in luck, he's chosen you.' He took the heavy object wrapped in linen in both hands and thrust it at Ino, telling her: 'Parnaoz sent it to you.' This made the girls burst into peals of laughter: they were in the mood to make fun of anything the stableman said or did: everything seemed laughable to them. Ino, however, was like a wild animal: she went for the stableman's hands with a predator's speed and mistrust, as if afraid the object wrapped in linen might be snatched from her. Not knowing how she got there, she found herself in her room. She sat on the divan, her knees trembling, her heart racing. She could still hear the stableman whinnying and the women giggling in the big room. 'Now let me go,' the stableman kept neighing, but suddenly there was such a shrieking that it was clear that the women weren't letting him go, clutching his coat-tails, so that he was forced once more to bare his teeth, whinny once and turn round, stamping his feet.

Finally Ino found the courage to put the object on her knees and carefully remove the linen. What she had in her hands was a round, grey stone, but she wasn't surprised, she almost expected it, as a harmless joke at her expense, and she smiled as she looked at the door, because her six sisters had just then burst into a peal of laughter. Then she put the stone on the table and stood up. She still held the linen in which the stone was wrapped. Her mind was empty, she just wanted to get out of the room, but somehow lacked the courage, she was shy of her sisters, without knowing why. She touched her quivering lips with her clenched fists and paced up and down the room. Suddenly she stopped and looked at the stone which had rolled onto the divan; then she cautiously went on tip-toe towards the divan, as if she feared waking a child asleep on it. She stared at the grey stone for some time. The stableman was whinnying in the big room, but Ino couldn't hear anything now except for the pounding of her heart. She felt as if somebody was staring hard at her all the time. She stood bewitched in front of the divan looking at the stone. She couldn't bear to look round the room and disperse the unpleasant sensation. Perhaps she was afraid to look because she was getting more and more convinced that she wasn't alone here. 'What's happening to me?' she said, trying to recover from this sudden stupefaction: but she couldn't recover, she didn't want to and, as if waking from sleep, she was reluctant, although some sinew or cell in her body was constantly raising the alarm and mercilessly, painfully dragging the rest of her out of this stupefying haze, like a small, razor-sharp hook dragging an enormous fish. Ino shrieked briefly, mutely. The grey stone on the divan was looking at her with almost living eyes.

She no longer had any trouble making out its other facial features: it was a head, a girl's head with curls of hair sticking out, carved in stone. 'That's me!' she thought and couldn't help putting her hand over her double, as if she no longer believed that it was made of stone. From somewhere in the depths of her soul a smile, sad and lifeless, suddenly came, just for an instant, but her face became animated, like a torrent sweeping down a rose petal. Now there really were two people in the room: herself and her head sculpted from stone by Parnaoz, the old Ino and the new, the happy and the unhappy, Ino who belonged only to Parnaoz, and Ino who belonged to the whole city. They stared hard at each other's face, as if whoever spoke first would be the loser. Ino put the end of her hair in her mouth to stifle the sound of sobbing in her throat. This sudden encounter had split her in two, she was simultaneously happy and unhappy: the little girl with the curls sticking out and the woman who'd passed through many men's hands. Ino fell to her knees and began kissing the stone sculpture of her head ardently, as if it had risen from the dead, or as if it were dying in her arms and all she could do was try to revive it with kisses. She wept burning tears. Her tears left blackish-grey marks on the stone, and dripped from its rough, hard cheekbones, as if it too was weeping Ino's tears. After crying, embracing and kissing the stone, Ino felt calmer and twisted the linen into a roll; then she whipped the stone head with it, with a wave of the arm so forceful that she shut her eyes in fear, as if the stone would crack and shatter into smithereens under the blow, and she would be buried by the fragments. But the stone did not suffer. Ino kept on hitting it until her shoulder hurt and her fingers were numb. Then she put the thrashed head and the ripped linen under the divan and left the room, her face implying that nothing had happened.

CHAPTER TWELVE

SHIPS still came into the port as they always had, although the water was no longer visible: rubbish thrown overboard, sticky strands of algae and yellow water-lilies covered the surface like wine-must. Only when an oar dipped into it, did a flash of water prove that the sea was still alive under its thick coating of filth. Now the fishermen had to make week-long trips far off-shore, and spend all day and night fishing, but they still came back empty-handed. If there were two or three small fish flapping their tails at the bottom of the boat, that made the unsuccessful fishermen even angrier. All they could now do was blame it all on Bedia, their former chief. 'He wouldn't rest until he'd made the sea really angry,' they grumbled as they listlessly rowed their empty boats. The nets, shiny with jellyfish, had become as useless as elderly cats. They trawled them to no purpose, but couldn't abandon them, their old loyal friends.

The city was waiting for a strange death: Queen Kama was thawing. Tents had been set up in the palace courtyard, as they had been during Phrixos's illness, but now, as then, the soothsayers and healers were at a loss: they had never seen such a patient, or illness. The queen was thawing, like an icicle brought into the warm. In fact, she was on a bed of snow, with a covering of snow, but was still thawing, draining away, slipping off as they watched. Mules brought snow from the mountains. Water streamed from baskets filled to the brim with bluish snow, but, as rumours from the palace had it, mourning would be declared any day soon. As she withered away, Kama's eyes grew and grew: you could even hear the stinging, blinding light pouring from her eyes. Every minute the servants cleaned the mirror's steamy surface, for the queen had not yet lost hope: she did not believe that the mirror would leave her outside and not open the door to her. She had a mattress and a blanket of snow, she lay on a pillow of snow, staring hard at the mirror. The mirror world, too, was covered in snow, and, in this still snowscape, the queen's eyes rested like two bright gigantic stars. Nothing else could be seen except bottomless, endless whiteness and disturbing emptiness. The Kama that dwelt in the mirror had vanished without trace. But the queen was thawing, and the bowl under her bed quickly filled with water. The snow brought down from the mountains permeated the palace with the smell of forest meadows and dry pine needles.

But even before the queen vanished, the city witnessed other wonders. Death made its first surprise visit to Bakha the vintner in his forty-step cellar: it slipped down and in so neatly past the rowdy drunks that nobody noticed: only three days later did his kin realise. Bakha the vintner's death was followed by the disappearance of Dariachangi's garden, so that for some time the city forgot all about the palace and its inhabitants.

Bakha sat dead on his favourite stool for three days and nights, his stick, from which he was never parted, between his knees, his hands like roof tiles on its rounded head, propping his chin, as if he was ruminating on the life he had lived. It was a long life, festive, noisy, tireless, dizzy in its mix of sweet and bitter, its uniqueness and its splendour. Bakha was made for jubilation, love, amusement. He'd lived like this until old age and weakness drove him down the forty steps. But his life began the day that he woke up in a vineyard, after his first feast, next to an unknown, but desirable woman. Above, stars looked at him, scarlet, as if reddened by wine. The breeze caught the tail end of a smouldering bonfire's smoke and sent the smell wafting down the alley-ways. Crickets sang their hearts out; the dry, warm grass purred like a cat by a stove. Their clothes hung on vine stakes and swayed with every breath of the breeze, as if they were continuing a dance which their exhausted owners had dropped out of. By their heads was a jug, plump as an idol, full of wine, and only the coolness of this jug, rolling on the grass like a drunk, alleviated the stuffiness of an August night. The bleating of a goat kid tethered to a peach tree was echoed by laughter from other couples, hidden, like them, in the shade of the trees. After that came an unbroken run of days and nights, laughter and joy, like the naked flesh glimpsed under the petticoats of girls in a round dance. Drunkenness led to love, love to drunkenness, unabated and inflamed. Not even his family could make Bakha forsake his one-day friends and one-night mistresses who appeared from nowhere and never ended, like the days and nights.

Bakha loved Rachel, and did so without restraint, but she was different — she was a wife and couldn't dance round bonfires like other women, if only because she might, if she followed in his steps, wake up one fine day in the arms of another man. Rachel wanted to be angry, but couldn't, because after a night out, Bakha would come home having forgotten a month's worries and expectation. 'Remember I'm your husband: all the rest shouldn't mean a thing to you,' Bakha told her when she tried, in vain as usual, to restrain her strange husband. Everything her husband lived by was strange to Rachel, strange and incomprehensible. She had a father and brothers, but had grown up without seeing a drunken man. Although they always had wine with dinner, and a jug of wine was the first thing they put on a dinner table, they took it away untouched afterwards, as if it were needed only to decorate the table. Rachel had grown up in a rich family and knew the value of money. How often she heard her women friends say, 'The city's full of Bakha's mistresses, he pays for the whole city to feast,' but what amused her friends didn't worry Rachel. She was worried by what enraged her father: where did he get the money from, and when he had it why did his son-in-law, her husband, so pointlessly, stupidly squander money earned by hard work and patience? Rachel was between a rock and a hard place: what her father disliked, her women friends approved of, even delighted in. They competed to be the first to run and gabble to Rachel about Bakha's latest adventure. 'A couple of days ago he was riding a donkey through the city with a whole suite of boys and girls,' they would tell Rachel, their eyes shining and mouths drooling, and would always end by adding, 'That's what a real man should be like, but my husband, you could skin him alive when he's asleep, and he wouldn't notice.' Rachel believed them and relished being the wife of a man everyone envied; so she held back, or rather did not break down over a husband as hard to handle and endure as Bakha, who squandered everything away from home and brought back only what his wretched companions had left over. In her heart of hearts, without telling her father, she shared her women friends' opinion of Bakha, which is why she didn't see their treachery. However hard it was to live with only half a husband, she preferred a fate constantly envied by other women.

What kept Rachel going was this belief, and when she had children and their crying filled the empty space left by her roaming husband, she no longer had time to think more deeply about life. When her father died, she clung more closely to her husband, at least in name a husband, because she was frightened of and unused to independence. But now her father's dissatisfaction infected her, giving her a sharper tongue and greater courage. But experience taught her that this was the only way she could keep up her family's and husband's reputation. Bakha came home to hear her grumbling and bitter words, as if what he couldn't find away from home was what drew him back. Rachel sensed this and never forgot to say something bitter whenever she saw her longed-for man. It was the only weapon that could somehow subdue this man. 'My father had men like you as his servants to wash his hands,' she scolded him when he cam back to relax. Bakha just smiled, stretched his limbs and smiled, tired and pleased. 'If it weren't for my father,' Rachel went on regardless, 'we and the children would all starve to death.' Not that there was any sign of her daughters starving, but Bakha still frowned and his mood changed, for the only thing that Rachel could really reproach him for was his father-in-law's wealth, although Bakha had different ideas, belonged to a different class of people and believed that people who spent money did as much good as those who accumulated it. People who made money needed people to spend it, just as a roof covered with snow needs a man with a shovel. So Bakha climbed onto the roof of life and scattered his father-in-law's money with his shovel. He was killing two birds with one stone: he was satisfying his own obsession and freeing his father-in-law's soul from the weight of all his money. 'Whatever a man accumulates is always oppressive and harmful,' Bakha said, and went on living as he had: he kept nothing. He was sure he wasn't taking anyone else's property, because his father-in-law was his children's grandfather, and grandchildren are the most entitled, moreover without asking, to take bread from their grandfather's pantry. The bread was also better off eaten by a child than by green mould or rats. That's what Bakha thought, but his wife's words still lacerated his heart, for he loved his children more than himself and if they had ever lacked anything, even for just a day, he would hire himself out as a porter or sell himself into slavery. But fortunately things never reached that point.

To avoid listening to his wife and poisoning his mood, he would lie on his back and pile all three daughters on his chest, and share with them equally everything he had. 'One has my soul, another my eyesight, the last my strength and health,' Bakha would nurture his children, who chirruped like fledglings on his broad chest, and they were all content, father and children. Only Rachel went on grumbling: 'All the wastrels one dead man is feeding!' Her face looked sour and her voice was so furious that she would without hesitation have eaten Bakha's soul, eyesight and strength and health, if it were possible. Time did what Rachel could not. Bakha's strength, health and eyesight gradually failed him, with every day he found it harder to keep up with his old wild, relentless life. He couldn't hold on to it, let alone keep up: he had to be a straggler, or give it up altogether. Bakha found it hard to surrender, give up, or forget. He couldn't for even one day forgo taking a look at life's thoroughbred legs, listening to its voice, warmed by wine and love. Bakha, after some contemplation, was still unable to adapt: so he tried cunning, and devised something. Life itself couldn't resist the temptation and met him halfway. Bakha opened his forty-step cellar and became Bakha the vintner, building himself an underground temple, a little refuge for a great life, and settled in like a god. 'Look after your hearts. Don't accumulate too much joy, or sadness. Hand both of them to me. My cellar is the treasury for your joy and sadness,' Bakha told his first customers, and after that life constantly went up and down the forty steps of the stairs, giving relief to the spirit and rest to the knees, rushing to meet new adventures with greater enthusiasm. Time passed, until one fine day Hey-Boy, now grown up and sensible, poured water into a barrel of wine, in full sight of Bakha.

'What are you doing?!' asked Bakha, amazed.

'What are you doing?' Hey-Boy mimicked him. 'Why don't you go upstairs and see what's going on?!'

'It's all over,' thought Bakha, amazed to have admitted so easily what he had been avoiding, resisting and hiding from for so long. 'It's all over,' Bakha again told himself, this time firmer and more insistent.

Bakha sat there dead for three days and nights on his favourite stool, leaning on his favourite stick; who knows how long he would have gone on sitting there if some drunk hadn't tripped against Bakha's round-handled stick. Recently, so many strangers had joined the company in the forty-step cellar, and many didn't know Bakha the vintner by sight, they thought he was a stray old man whom Hey-Boy had kindly taken in. True, Bakha the vintner did not deign to banter with the drunks, but his heart sank when he heard their senseless uproar, or when one drinker, trying to be kinder than the others, drained leftover wine into a bowl and handed it to him, clapping him on the shoulder and telling him, as if he were a pal of the same age, 'Drink up, old man!' Bakha itched to take his cornel-wood stick and smash in the head of this bullying host, but at the same time he pitied him, as a sick man so diseased that he no longer knew what he was doing. The drinker really did look sick, he didn't look at all like a man out to enjoy himself: he could barely stand, he was dishevelled and disorderly, his eyes were lack-lustre, they barely flickered, like ash-covered coals; he didn't speak so much as mumble joylessly, lifelessly, irritatingly, as if he had drunk poison instead of wine and was gradually succumbing, losing his speech and mind. Once Bakha used to open up at the sight of a drunk, and he also felt like a drink; now a mixed feeling of fear and pity came over him and he could not work out what had happened, whether the people or the wine, or both had changed. He sat there thinking, his head hurting and his heart saddened by this endless buzz and roar. Thinking like that, he gave up the ghost.

When they took his stick away, he rose up as if alive and about to go for the throat of his ill-mannered customer and say, 'How dare you?' But he instantly fell down on his face, like a felled tree. He crashed so thunderously to the ground that the cellar walls cracked, the whole cellar was filled with dust and the people, already tipsy on the watered-down wine, rushed coughing and spitting out of the forty-step cellar. The dust hadn't yet settled when Popeye came running down the steps, followed by Bakha the vintner's shrieking family. Popeye rushed straight to the trunk and, unable to find the key, broke the lock with his axe. His jaws hung open with amazement: he found the chest empty, but for one roof tile at the bottom, perfectly ordinary, exactly like those that covered the houses of Vani, red and shiny, as if it had just been rained on. The sight was so unexpected for everyone, that Popeye thought it might be gold cast in the shape of a roof tile, and even tested it on his teeth. But the taste of terra-cotta dashed that hope. When he inspected the tile more closely, he saw that it wasn't quite ordinary: it had an inscription. He kept turning it in his hand, so tormented by the tile that he finally lost patience and spoke.

'Son-in-law, now you know what sort of man you are,' said the tile.

Those were the exact words on the tile. Everyone who read it confirmed the fact. Full of spite, Popeye turned to the dead man, but by then Bakha the vintner's body had grown too big for the cellar.

'Look, he won't even let us have the cellar!' yelled Popeye, even more enraged by this new trick of his father-in-law.

Bakha was lying face-down, quiet and so gigantic that you'd have thought an elephant, not a man, had died in the cellar. Popeye instantly recalled the lessons he had as a child from Pushiani the butcher, rolled up his sleeves and hauled the carcase of his deceitful father-in-law out of the cellar piece by piece, like some worthless piece of old furniture.

Hey-Boy bought the forty-step cellar and all the barrels. Popeye also sold Hey-Boy the two-storey house and deck-sized bed when Patu gave birth to yet another stillborn baby. Popeye gave Patu no time to recover from labour: he parcelled up her belongings and handed them to Rachel, with a message, 'I'm handing her over: your daughter's been a partner to death, not to a husband.' Then he bought himself a hovel by the palace walls and moved in there. These events occurred later, after Parnaoz left for Crete.

Bakha's sudden death brought the city to life, gave people something to talk about and cheered them up. Bakha was responsible for this, as if his only reason for dying was to make a fool of his son-in-law. The relationship between Bakha and his son-in-law was, of course, common knowledge. Apart from Popeye, everyone believed the vintner to be rich, and they secretly envied Popeye as the imminent owner of these riches. They were normal human beings and took a close interest in everything, considering it their duty to get involved in anything that happened in their city. Popeye's story was especially interesting: he was one of them and had grown up in Vani, but had been singled out from the rest. The distinction was noticed from the start: they had always been intrigued by this boy with the slicked down hair and scraggy neck, who went as red as a poppy, with his precocious plans, his repressed fear and shyness, resolutely striding down the streets like a man with a purpose, looking urgently for a rich bride to marry and for a profitable trade to learn, as if making up for time lost before he was born. 'A fine lad,' the people of

Vani used to say, as dazed by his appearance as by the arrival of masked actors. But Popeye worked while they amused themselves. He toiled, he trained and gathered strength while his fellow citizens laughed and guffawed. One day the 'fine lad' became a man to fear, although all he did was never to deviate from his plan, conceived at the same time as he was, a plan which was considered fine and brave when he was a boy, because it seemed impossible ever to achieve. But Popeye achieved more than any of his fellow citizens, because he had no time to fool about or even learn how to behave. Popeye was thought to be a man to fear, but nobody could say why they personally should fear him. The impression just arose over time, and it was perhaps based on the nasty feeling aroused by the jingling of the leather sack that bounced up and down all day long on Popeye's back. That's why an awkward silence, like an admission of guilt, descended whenever Popeye appeared, like an angry nanny suddenly looking in on a roomful of naughty children.

Bakha's death and Popeye's disappointment gave Vani a special sort of unconscionable joy, as if they were all avenged, but the settling of accounts hadn't been wholly just. Popeye began to play the part of the wronged man, although his misfortune made people smile rather than sympathize. Making a fool of Popeye meant a lot: it was unimaginable, for it needed a very ingenious piece of trickery. Bakha may have died, but Popeye, especially when embittered, wouldn't let his death deter him: for days and nights the city awaited something spectacular. Everyone talked about the father-in-law's trickery and the son-in-law's deception. But this time they were let down and had to change their minds about many things. Something quite unforeseeable happened. Popeye's stoicism and magnanimity left everyone lost for words, it made them feel ashamed and very pensive. Instead of setting the dogs on his faithless and deceitful father-in-law's corpse and throwing his family into the street, Popeye had Bakha the vintner laid in a gilded sarcophagus, personally cut the plaits off his wife and sisters-in-law and sent messengers all over the city to invite people to the funeral. 'If poor Bakha had ten sons, they wouldn't have done so much for him,' said the stunned people of Vani as they stood in the deceased's courtyard like groups of freed prisoners, their arms folded, as if waiting for the right time to thank their liberator once more before they accepted the gift of freedom. In fact, Popeye really did look like a victorious general mourning the defeat of a worthy opponent and thus making his own might and nobility even more obvious.

Pushiani had slaughtered a whole herd of cattle: there was a pile of heads and feet by the bench where he was bent chopping up meat; he kept looking at Popeye, hoping his former apprentice would notice him. True,

Popeye hadn't taken up the trade, but Pushiani secretly felt that he had a hand in Popeye's success, for he remembered the little boy with the slicked down curls and the scraggy neck. It was a windy day; everyone's eyes were red from the smoke. Ash flew like bits of cobweb in the air. Popeye and Parnaoz were standing in the middle of the courtyard. They could hear Bakha the vintner's widow and family wailing in the house.

'They're weeping for themselves,' said Popeye with a smile.

Then he bent down, picked up a stone and threw it at a dog. The dog jumped up with a yelp, but did not go far; it crouched almost where it was, watching Pushiani's bloody hands. Pushiani laughed out loud, but even that did not make Popeye look at him.

'Who does that wretched cur belong to?' Pushiani began, thinking that he could now talk to his former apprentice, but Popeye frowned so severely that Pushiani was frightened and nearly hit his fingers with his chopper. 'Did it hit you, or didn't it?' he called to the dog, but his voice failed; he put his chopper under his arm, grabbed a jug of wine from the edge of the bench and took a sip: the jug, too, was dripping with blood.

'I dislike that man. I'll bet he eats live chickens, innards and all. Ugh!' Popeye said, spitting in Pushiani's direction; wiping his lips on the back of his hand, he went on, 'When he eats the head, he holds the throbbing carcase between his knees. This country's incorrigible, isn't it, uncle?'

Parnaoz hadn't heard, because black-eyed Malalo had just come in with her seven daughters. With a swish of her dress, black-eyed Malalo crossed the courtyard, adjusting the snake-like shiny pointed beads of her necklace on her enormous chest. Ino was the last in the procession. Popeye had spotted them and was looking with a smile at Parnaoz. 'That's all right: Popeye couldn't stop them coming to the wake,' he thought, but he felt himself blushing, his face burning. At first glance, there was nothing odd about it: everyone had the right to come to the wake, but for some reason he never thought that those women could possibly come here. However much Parnaoz pretended or deceived himself, they still existed, mixed with people and lived as others did, going to feasts and funerals. There was nothing surprising about that: why should they stay indoors, why should the city scorn them just because they'd kicked out a stupid boy? What had left an incurable open wound in Parnaoz's heart was old news for the city, no more than a childish prank; if anyone could have seen into Parnaoz's heart they would be open-mouthed with astonishment, even distressed, but they would consider him a fool. The girl with the curls, who had left her tooth-marks, like a mouse eating a cake, on Parnaoz's heart, had long vanished, or rather changed, taken on her final form, as the world required, fully formed and complete. Ino's death and burial was just the dream of a humiliated, heartbroken child, a desperate final act of resistance against nature and life, in an effort to hold on to what others felt no longer existed, what others no longer needed. However difficult this dream was to renounce, time had its usual effect, labelled, laid bare, revealed, or hushed up everything for ever.

Parnaoz knew, of course, that the real Ino was alive: the real Ino was the biggest enemy of his childhood dream, she could kill off the girl with the curls that stuck out, destroy, eradicate her, although Parnaoz imagined it would be harder to meet or see Ino than… to bring the dead one back to life. Yet he had never stopped waiting for her. After the day when he came for the first and last time out of black-eyed Malalo's house, he deliberately avoided thinking about the other, live Ino: he had devised his obsession with stone only to stop thinking about her, but over time he had never had such an agonizing, unbearable and childlike desire as he had for the sight of the second, live Ino, the lost Ino, whom he might now find it hard to recognize. Time had not affected the dead Ino. She was still the little freckled giggling girl with the red ribbons plaited into her hair, and it was this difference that allured Parnaoz, the difference between the dead and the living Ino; it drew him on, it excited him, it intrigued him, but he felt that his hope of meeting a transformed Ino was something treacherous implanted in him. Hope would lead to treachery if he really did meet the live Ino. The live Ino would deprive him for ever of the freckled girl with the curls sticking out, as it would of the stray goat kid that got caught up in thorns: they would drain from Parnaoz's mind and would be thrown out, or rather back and locked up for ever in the musty enclosure of past days, visions and feelings, which was their only real place. But the temptation was to big to resist, it was irresistible. Was it possible for this image of a girl, fixed in his memory, to be just the fiction of a feeble, ephemeral dream? It would be the greatest of misfortunes, because Parnaoz's existence would be called into question, would even become pointless and meaningless, if the pain which he regarded with his hidden, barely conscious pride as his distinguishing feature, his inviolable right and his banner, was after all a far-fetched invention.

Meeting Ino did not augur well for Parnaoz, but all his timid and passionate nature longed for this meeting and he was neither able nor anxious to work out what lay behind this urge: a desire to be disillusioned, the betrayal of hope or the magnetic power of misfortune. Popeye's magnanimity that day finally persuaded him that the encounter was inevitable. Ino really did exist, and what's more she remembered Parnaoz and still seemed to have hopes of him. But there was something else more important: not the confirmation by another man that Ino existed, but the other man himself. Popeye's behaviour that day both oppressed and inspired Parnaoz with its unexpected magnanimity, as if he had by sheer chance discovered after a lengthy intense search an object which was right under his nose, which had been overlooked, not lost, because he himself was confused, distracted and, above all, used to losing this object, yet couldn't help going on with the search, out of habit, and had the irritating feeling that after all this time he had got used to being without it, had forgotten the object's importance and purpose. What Parnaoz thought he had lost turned out to be Popeye, his own nephew, blood of his blood and flesh of his flesh. Popeye turned out, or could turn out, to be the other man whose absence so tormented Parnaoz. True, Popeye told him a lot of harsh truths and touched his soul's most hidden and sensitive place to the quick, but that was not the point: it was much more important that Popeye had shown sympathy, offered help, so that Parnaoz was aghast, blinded and had trouble taking in all that he had learnt from Popeye. When he did take it in, he felt not natural satisfaction or relief, but sadness, confusion and shame, as if an undeserved reward was being thrust at him, as if he were considered worthy of a reward he'd done nothing to deserve. He found it hard to refuse the person who was rewarding him, deliberately or not oppressing him with his generosity in offering such a reward. He needed it like the air, more than the air, and he now had to decide only whether to accept or refuse the undeserved, but needed reward. It was equally hard to express refusal or acceptance: both seemed equally attractive and loathsome, both smelled of temptation.

Fortunately, after this Popeye was no longer visible, as if he sensed his uncle's dilemma and was giving him time to think. Parnaoz couldn't imagine when and with whom, let alone his nephew, he would discuss Ino, but once he was on his own, he lay on a divan and took trouble to relive the conversation he had that morning: his heart warmed and swelled, a somnolent, tranquillising sadness came over him and he barely realised he was weeping. He smiled with childlike sweetness at his attack of weakness, and he was then like a child who has just quarrelled with a whole gang of local urchins and, worked up and steeled by his own smallness and weakness, stubbornly, angrily attacks the dismayed urchins, and then suddenly finds he has a protector whose sympathy makes him so happy that he cannot and will not hold back the tears that are flowing down his bloodstained cheeks. He wept for happiness, and because he was happy he wasn't ashamed to weep. Of course, much of what Popeye had said was disturbing, but just the feeling that his pain affected someone else, made them ponder, held their interest, was so pleasant, so rare and essential, that Parnaoz ignored the other aspect for some time, the smoke and flames of a warning bonfire with its soot and fierce heat. Very rarely, just for a minute, an alarming thought came over him, crawling like a lizard, that Popeye might go and see black-eyed Malalo and instead of doing him a favour put a spanner in the works. Parnaoz wasn't going to marry Ino, the thought never crossed his mind, because no woman was or would be more alien to him than Ino, and that girl with the curls sticking out had really been dead a long time and Parnaoz would never forgive anyone, let alone Popeye, for waving her colourful rags for the whole world to see. Now, however, Popeye dominated his whole being, as first love dominates a silly inexperienced girl who can't wait to run away and entrusts herself without reserve, blindly, to a beloved whom she has seen only once, has never properly talked to, but finds to be closer and dearer than anyone on earth; at the same time she senses that this step will upset her parents, stain and shame their reputation, but the choice has to be made, because both sides, parents and beloved, are stronger than she is. One side draws her with its destructive boldness, the other with its legitimate, accustomed, monotonous, but reliable peace and quiet.

Parnaoz could no longer rest, or get down to anything; he sat at dinner with clenched teeth, everything irritated him, he made such a fuss about trivialities that the frightened women huddled in a corner, not daring to answer back. Popina or Kaluka only had to mention Popeye for him to shut them up, as if they were Popeye's enemies, trying to disparage him in Parnaoz's presence. 'It's us who've been bad, us. We threw a man out of the house and we still reproach him,' Parnaoz shouted: at such moments he resembled his father and Popina couldn't help looking at the locked door of Ukheiro's room. But at night, lying on his back on the divan, his eyes wide open, comforted by gratitude, he dreamed of something happening to Popeye when only he could be of help. Only Popeye's friend Ino, the live Ino, poisoned his pleasure: while waiting for him, she was bedding most of the city, using his neglect to excuse her fornication. 'It's not Popeye's fault,' Parnaoz thought, 'that's probably what he's told and believes.' Tossing and turning in bed, Parnaoz took the same decision every night, to intercept Popeye at dawn on his way to the palace and tell him everything frankly, explain, to make the things clear before it was too late, so that he did nothing that couldn't be put right later. But the warmth and light of day made what seemed a firm decision evaporate like dew, and he assured himself that he could not just go and see Popeye, perhaps because it was now an urgent need to be near him, by his side. Parnaoz considered himself in Popeye's debt: he had to act first in order to prove his loyalty, to be entitled to approach him.

Frankly, Bakha's death pleased Parnaoz in a different way, for it gave him a pretext to support his nephew at a time of grief. All that time he stayed close to Popeye, never took a break, ran like a small boy on every petty errand, as if nobody else could do it, or not do it as Popeye wanted, in a satisfactory way. Parnaoz, covered in sweat and dust, got a nod from Popeye, who then gave him a big smile, took him aside and told him, 'You really mustn't, man: stop: I need you for something quite different.' He said it in a tone and with an expression that gave Parnaoz goose pimples; his innate childhood fear, foreseeing defeat and disappointment, reared its head, like a snake, in the darkest, furthest corner of his soul. Parnaoz blamed himself for being like this, for getting everything wrong, he was angry at getting worked up by a moment's mistrust; he couldn't help averting his eyes from his nephew's smiling face, as clean and shiny as a glass vessel, just slightly tinged by the pinkish liquid it contained.

When black-eyed Malalo and her daughters came into the courtyard Parnaoz was stunned: he intuitively sensed that something new and mysterious was about to happen, shaking and changing everything with its novelty and mystery. Parnaoz had a desire to flee, as he had a long time ago when Shubu announced Popeye's birth in Dariachangi's garden. He would actually have fled if Popeye hadn't been there to shame him. Now, for some reason, struck dumb in the middle of the courtyard, he was most embarrassed by Popeye, he would rather that the earth split open, thunder struck him and killed him on the spot than have Popeye see the women stride so boldly and provocatively across the courtyard, as if all the people here had gathered to see them, rather than pay their respects to Bakha. Parnaoz saw the guests at the wake, standing there with their arms folded and their heads lowered, come to life, get excited and start whispering. He had the impression that everyone was looking at him, as if he had brought the women here, and he felt that he had, because he secretly considered them his kinsfolk, dwellers in his thought who, thanks to his negligence, had been prematurely driven out for all to see.

'Well, they've come, have they?!' Parnaoz heard Popeye saying. 'I'd wouldn't be a man if I couldn't turn a wake for that son of a bitch into a wedding,' Popeye said, looking Parnaoz in the face.

'Whatever will be, will be,' thought Parnaoz, continuing after a short pause with a prayer, 'Let what must happen, happen, but soon, right now.'

'Why not?! They should be grateful we let them into the family,' Popeye exclaimed. He was talking in his ordinary voice, loud enough only for Parnaoz to hear. Yet it seemed like shouting to Parnaoz; his ears rang, but he couldn't silence his nephew. He stood there, his head bowed, sure everybody was looking at him. 'Now is not the time for this, now is not the time for this,' he repeated to himself, but Popeye would not let up: 'Our family is different, but my father-in-law deserved no better: he didn't leave a family to mourn him, he left only drunks and whores: here they all are. If you think I've spent all that money for that skinflint, you're very mistaken. I've spent a long time waiting for this great day, uncle…' God knows what else Popeye said. Parnaoz died several deaths, dying was sweet, but reviving was bitter, and when he finally came to his senses, he expressed surprise that the deceased's coffin had not yet left the house.

'Parnaoz!' Popeye called.

'It's my fault,' said Parnaoz.

'It's not going to rain, is it? What do you say, uncle?' said Popeye.

Parnaoz couldn't help looking at the sky… A chain of light, translucent white clouds ran across a clear blue sky.

'That bitch dared to talk to me about morality,' said Popeye. 'She said, "You were seeing that woman: how can you now marry her off to your uncle?" You understand. She's dragged me into that dirty business. Don't be afraid, I gave her as good as I got.'

'It's my fault,' Parnaoz repeated.

'It's your fault, of course it is. When a man your age doesn't have a wife, people can't be blamed for having their suspicions. Ha, ha,' Popeye laughed, then called to the butcher: 'How are things, Pushiani?' but didn't wait for an answer, turning back to Parnaoz, 'So I told your future mother-in-law, "Woman, I've got a wife and I'm expecting a child any day, so you help me sort my uncle out, that might stop his respectable family dying out without heirs." You know what she said to me?'

Just then the castrated stableman ran down the street: he looked as if he'd been attacked by a rabid dog. He was badly shaken, steaming with sweat as if wicked children had thrust a burning log into the nosebag he wore round his neck. When he saw the crowd of people, he tried to stop, but lost control and somehow flew into the air like a hen with its wings clipped. He was gasping with emotion, spinning like a madman and biting the air with his bared, crooked teeth. He clearly wanted to say something, but instead of a voice, his throat emitted a nasty roar. A sepulchral silence followed. Bakha's mourners and the stableman splayed in the street like a scarecrow stared at each other. But this silence and muteness did not last long. Suddenly everything seethed in an uproar, and almost the whole city cried out at once, 'Dariachangi's garden has vanished.' There was a tumultuous roar, as if a dam had burst its banks: crushing everything in its path, the crowd rushed off to Dariachangi's garden.

'I'm doomed,' thought Popeye, only now noticing that Parnaoz was no longer standing next to him. 'I'm doomed!' he yelled, this time out loud, and rushed, as if scalded with boiling water, in the wake of the roaring crowd. Fear gave him wings and a wolf's running powers, so he soon caught sight of his uncle's back. 'You lunatic! Philamon!' Popeye called out, but his voice was lost without trace in the crowd's uproar. As soon as the torrent of people passed out of the city they met Oqajado's soldiers. The soldiers were carrying loads of apples in their coat-tails, and were wearing crowns of apple branches, full of fruit, round their brows. The fist-sized fruit struck their sweaty brows as the branches swayed. They sang as they came. The sight of the roaring crowd, like a herd with no herdsman, and of their whitened eyes, alarmed Oqajado's soldiers, who emptied their coat-tails and got out of the crowd's way. Anyone who couldn't free his coat-tails or jump aside in time, was crushed by the crowd, trampled as it went on its way. 'Why are you doing this, people?' a soldier cried out, his ribs all broken, waving his limbs pathetically, like a beetle that has fallen on its back. Parnaoz found his feet sticking in the sand, he was stumbling, but still running ahead of everyone: he had to be ahead, to run faster, like a mother whose house is on fire with her children locked inside. Dariachangi's garden was Parnaoz's house, his childhood, his love, ideal and dream… everything! He didn't think so at the time, he wasn't thinking at all, he was rushing blindly, primitively through air as fleshless and as oppressive as an alarm bell.

Fear made Popeye run, but he wasn't entirely clear what was happening: his infallible intuition told him that this wouldn't be the end of it, the palace would get to hear of it, if it hadn't already, and then it would be too late to make excuses. He would be the first to be held responsible, and they would be right. Between ourselves, wasn't Popeye to blame for gathering so many crazy people together on this of all days, to pay their respects to a stinking corpse surrounded by all the drunkards and whores of the land, like flies, and his father-in-law, as well? Hadn't he chosen today of all days to take revenge on that impotent stonecutter who was running ahead of everyone like a jackal escaped from a trap, a man who was his very own uncle, too? No, he had to think of something, to try to show the palace, otherwise… he had no time to think now, he had to act quickly and sensibly, weigh each fraction of every minute, for any minute his entire future life could be toppled. Running made his heart pound madly: he caught sight of a piece of rope and grabbed it, like a man swept away by a current. He hung onto the rope. Popeye was so panicked by imminent danger that he couldn't see whom the rope belonged to. He just glimpsed the dangling end of the rope and his mind lit up: a rope was just what he needed to catch and tie up his fleeing uncle. It didn't matter if he succeeded or not, the main thing was that others saw him try to tie up his uncle. It had to be done before Parnaoz came to a halt by himself, before he reached Dariachangi's garden. He tugged the rope with all his strength and it spun Bedia round and round like a top, threw him to the ground and dragged him along for some distance until it was free of his body. Bedia, flung face-down on the sand, looked like a snail pulled out of its shell, both helpless and loathsome. The coil of rope that he had worn constantly for years had covered his whole body in ulcerating sores, leaving only here and there patches of live, sickly white skin, like quicklime dissolved in water and thrown onto a rubbish tip. Popeye kept running, picking up the slack loops of rope as he went, his eyes colourless with fear, fixed like claws on Parnaoz's back. Soon both were rolling in the sand. Popeye tried to wrap the rope round Parnaoz, but couldn't, for Parnaoz was stronger than him. Fear gave Popeye strength and daring, while Parnaoz couldn't understand what was happening, why a sobbing Popeye was embracing and kissing him like a demented child. Popeye was actually kissing Parnaoz's face, neck and shoulders, whatever he could reach, and they were both gradually getting entangled in Bedia's rotting rope. 'It's for your own good, you fool, for your own good,' Popeye mumbled, spitting onto the sand kneaded with his tears.

Everything calmed down as suddenly as it had flared up. What had to happen had happened: there was now no point running away. Both of them realised this at the same time; they now sat up on the sand, breathing heavily and staring one another in the eye. Popeye crawled back on all fours, freed his entangled feet from the rope, then quickly stood up, span round and headed back to the city. Parnaoz watched Popeye's departure for a long time: he left footprints like a mole's holes in the whitened sand. 'I should have killed your son, Popina, your son… Forgive me for that one thing!" thought Parnaoz, now deeply convinced he really would kill Popeye: he would get up, would follow his footprints, which showed in the whitened sands like a mole's holes, and dash his brains out wherever he caught up with him. Dariachangi's garden, or where the garden used to be, was behind him: he was sure of that even though he never once looked in that direction. He would rather die than turn his head so as to perpetuate the tiny drop of hope that still flickered weakly in his battered soul. Parnaoz sat down on the sand, as forlorn and pitiful as a father who has lost a son, who knew that his son had died, but wouldn't admit it, was in no hurry to see his dead son, not knowing how to face him: did he have the right to kneel down by his cold corpse? No, of course he didn't. If he'd been in time for the death bed, he might have done something, he could have poured him some water… The dead belong to the person in whose arms they give up the ghost. But Popeye had stopped Parnaoz, had bewitched him like a snake, had intoxicated him with venomous kisses and stolen his provisions for the journey. How could Parnaoz continue his journey now that he had nothing left? Popeye couldn't get far, his every footstep had turned into a real mole's hole, he would be found: but perhaps that was what Popeye wanted? Whatever door Parnaoz knocked at, he would be offered poison instead of water, he would have ash thrown in his eyes, dogs would be set on him and he would be pointed out to children: 'Look, this man killed his own nephew!'

The extent of the wonder stunned the people. Dariachangi's garden really had vanished. The bare earth was covered with shattered branches and withered leaves, branches with crushed apples, as if a herd of pigs had passed over the area. The sea, or the part of the sea once shaded by Dariachangi's garden, intensified the silence and emptiness. It appeared and became visible for the first time, strikingly bare, forcibly stripped and therefore repulsive. The crowd dispersed; no grass rustled, no bees buzzed. Bees, butterflies, birds and all, Dariachangi's garden had vanished, without trace and forever. Everyone felt they were being chastised, personally threatened by someone who had extinguished this enormous, timeless garden, like a candle flame, with one breath, with the sole purpose of terrifying them.

Meanwhile Bedia caught up with the crowd. He was like a phantom, naked, his hair and beard dishevelled. He stumbled all the time and wept like a woman: 'I've lost the sea, have you seen it anywhere?' Someone picked up the tangled rope and, rather than hand it, flung it at him as if throwing rags over a corpse.

CHAPTER THIRTEEN

THAT evening Popeye came. 'Popeye's coming,' said Popina; then the others heard the jingling sack. After the morning's tumult Popina's forebodings had not receded for a moment. A disaster had now happened, but that was something else, affecting the whole city; it did not frighten Popina who secretly longed very much for that disaster to be the end of it, not to strike anybody, at least in her family, her house, which, she was utterly convinced, annoyed everyone, especially after the cypress trees that Shubu had planted had grown tall, making their house more visible. This pair of cypresses could be seen from anywhere in Vani: people called them 'Ukheiro's javelins'. Popina had repeatedly said that they ought to be cut down: they were useless, trees of mourning, but her threats remained mere words. If anyone had taken an axe to the cypresses, Popina would have been the first to fall at their feet and stop them, because Popina was afraid of these tall, slender, pointed trees and believed that they housed souls which would become terrible dragons at the first blow of an axe, then fly to heaven and wreak vengeance on anyone who hurt and insulted them. 'Good, beautiful gods!' she lovingly and apologetically called the cypresses, watering their scaly limbs with hot steaming blood and walking round them with prayers and pleas until the chicken whose head she had torn off deflated in her hands like a burst balloon. The trees were silent, ignoring the woman fussing round their feet as they towered heavenwards, eternal monuments to incurable sadness.

Popina had never been so glad to hear the jingling sack, she calmed down straight away as if she had been waiting all day for that sound: it was the sound of her son coming back to her, and soon, in a minute, they would all be together. All Popina wanted was for them all to be together. It didn't matter if they didn't love one another, she just wanted them to sit around for hours, months, years, but together, under the same roof, close to one another. Popina knew that her son didn't love her, and why he couldn't love her, and secretly approved of him, always taking his side, because she was sorry for him, badly hurt by his parents, marked out from everybody else and laughed at by everyone. Popina saw Popeye through the eyes of her father and brother; she herself was blind to her son's faults and merits; had she been alone and not as intimidated by her father and brother as by the two cypresses, she might have considered herself to be a happy mother. How many mothers envied her, how often neighbouring women angrily told her, 'Why look so miserable when you have a son like that?' But Popina always felt downcast instead of glad, because the son who seemed enviable to the neighbours had only one feeling, hatred, and if he hadn't yet forgotten his mother existed, it was because of that feeling and a desire to show it. Popina didn't need others' help to see her son's hatred, nor was it a sudden revelation. She'd noticed, sought and found it right from the start in her son's eyes, voice, behaviour and heart, because hatred can be concealed in the heart like a hot brand in a rag. Popina was the mother of this hatred, she had given it birth, Popeye had brought it from her womb, like blindness, deafness, weak-mindedness or club feet, but what mother would kill a child because of a physical defect at birth, what mother hasn't been blinded by dreaming of a miraculous cure for her child that nature might grant one fine day which dawns and fades, and fades and dawns again without end, but only in a dream or in hope. 'One fine day' had led Popina astray, 'one fine day' had led her to believe her son might be cured, cleansed of his incurable disease and, above all, would forgive, forgive and forgive. But time was against her: the disease was getting stronger, it was growing, it was no longer hidden and couldn't wait to infect everybody and everything. 'I've doomed my son, Kaluka, my son; I'm a foul mother,' Popina complained to Kaluka, then her eyes stopped moving and she said in the same tone, 'My son doesn't need me, I'm expecting something,' and Kaluka would shudder.

'He hasn't got children himself, that's why. He doesn't know the value of parenthood,' Kaluka said deliberately loudly, more to hide her own emotion than to allay Popina's.

Popina was wrong on one point: Popeye had other feelings for his mother. Hatred was not the only one. For example, Popeye was grateful to Popina and, as time passed, this feeling strengthened, because he came to see Popina as the only gate for him to enter this world. He had grown to love this world so much that he was aghast at the thought of what he would have done if that damned Philamon had been able to bridle his lust and things had happened differently. Popeye gasped with fear when he imagined him being carried by Popina in a sack to the river, like a blind puppy, to get rid of Philamon's traces, committing a worse sin than fumbling with her own slave. He gave deepest thanks to the gods that this hadn't happened, not that Popina had any right to kill him, she was only obliged to give birth to him. Everything else depended on Popeye: whether he tried to put right something spoiled by others from the start, or not, it would either stay transplanted from one cowardly body to another and end up hopelessly twisted up, with its head beneath its knees, or it would succeed in being born, standing on its own feet and opening its eyes. Popeye managed more than that by discovering that everyone was similar, of the same kind: legitimacy or illegitimacy were just empty words, which someone tosses to the crowd like false coins and then bursts into laughter at the ensuing scramble. First of all, Popeye was grateful to Popina for giving him a chance to discover this. The discovery gave him a goal: now he had to prove to others what so far only he knew. He knew that everyone had the same birthmark of sin from their mother's womb, some on their face, others somewhere hidden. 'That's agreed, then; that's agreed, then; that's agreed then,' he kept repeating to himself, and then added with the gravity of a folk healer, 'We must be patient, let's wait and see, it's not hard to strip a man naked.'

Sometimes Popeye was even sorry for Popina, but his pity was simple, baseless, momentary, mixed with loathing. He felt pity for his mother as for a dead bird, only when he saw her. He seldom saw her. He came more often to remind his kinsfolk of his existence, lest they think he'd be as easy as Philamon to get rid of, to send away. No, Popeye's place was here, where he had business to attend to.

'Hello!' he would say as he came in, and, smiling, lower himself onto a chair. Like a rare visitor, or a man who'd come on a matter of some delicacy, he never stopped smiling. He sat on the first chair he found, put his leather sack by his feet, like a pedlar, and smiled. Popeye found it restful, entertaining, pleasant to startle so many people at once by turning up when least expected. They all looked him in the eye lovingly, spoke ingratiatingly and apologetically, too taken aback to know what they were saying. When Popina begged him to make himself at home, at least wash his face, for it was after all his house, he just shook his head to say 'no' and smiled, but this time in a different, reassuring, magnanimous way, like a king disguised as a commoner whom bad weather forces to take shelter in a poor old woman's hovel and who is glad, glad as a child, to pass unrecognized, glad that people don't realise who their guest is: or they wouldn't dare offer him a flea-ridden bed and mouse-eaten bread.

'I have my own house and home. You don't need to offer me all this,' Popeye said, smiling.

This time he had come unannounced. They had just had supper. Popina was carrying a pile of plates to the kitchen, but when she heard the jingling sack, she turned towards the door and stopped. She was hoping to seeing her son safe and sound. The disappearance of Dariachangi's garden and the panic that overcame the people had caused widespread destruction. It was the talk of the city. People also said that the first thing Oqajado would do was to punish his people for failing to keep order.

'Hello!' said Popeye. He immediately sat down on a chair and put his sack by his feet. He smiled his usual smile, but he was clearly in a bad mood. His cheekbones were hot and red. He sat and smiled angrily, biliously, bitterly, like a man slapped in the face, who doesn't yet know how to react: to swallow his anger and the insult, or to take instant revenge.

'You won't get into trouble, will you?' Popina asked, unable to hold back.

'What are you talking about?' Popeye asked, as if puzzled.

Popina suddenly became worked up, looked around for a free chair, and sat on it, still holding the plates: then she said, 'Well, about this morning's business.'

'Oh yes,' Popeye went on, looking at Parnaoz. 'Uncle was the first to run away.'

Now Popina also looked at Parnaoz. He was sitting there with his head bowed, looking at his hands, which were like pieces of rock, heavy and craggy fragments to be used as weapons in an emergency: they radiated a strength which might not frighten all who saw them, but did fill people with a disorienting sort of melancholic sadness, like fire or rain, because they were meant for labour, not for killing. Parnaoz hadn't expected Popeye to turn up after what had happened that morning: he imagined Popeye would try to go into hiding, run away and seek refuge as far away as he could, to stop Parnaoz carrying out the horrible plan he had hatched when he was grappling with him. Parnaoz was quite unable to put aside a plan that had suddenly come to him on the sun-baked sand, a plan singed by his own heat, lying in his soul like sand in a river. His whole body ached, buzzed and itched, as if he were a man walking into the sea for the first time. He had spent the whole day thinking about Popeye, the Popeye now before his eyes, and countless other versions: smiling venomously, sobbing like a child, with a face twisted in anger, or contorted in death. When the rumour spread that Oqajado's first act would be to punish his men, Parnaoz was worried, because Oqajado had less right than anyone to punish Popeye — no right at all, since the king might not even know of him, whereas Parnaoz loved him and, if he found the strength, would kill him, solely out of love. Parnaoz had other reasons to take this terrible step, but he intended not to settle scores with Popeye, as Oqajado would, but to save him. Changing and correcting Popeye was as impossible as making a spade out of air. The gods had made Popeye as he was and as long as he breathed, he would plough hatred, sow fear in the street, in the shops, among neighbours, in his own family, because he himself was fearful, always fearing everything, even his own shadow, because he didn't even trust that, he didn't believe that he too could have a shadow.

Parnaoz now knew Popeye. He'd grasped everything and his heart, ripped by Popeye's hook, bled with pity, pity and anger: if this morning's panic were to have unpleasant consequences for Popeye, then Parnaoz would be Oqajado's unwitting ally. If Popeye was punished, it would be only for having such an uncle. The uncle of a king's man should behave with more dignity and not run all over the place ahead of everybody like a boy water-carrier trying to be the first to fill his pitcher at the source and then run to a customer with fresh cold water. But that's a bad comparison: the boy water-carrier is doing his job, keeping a family, perhaps, helping sick parents, raising younger siblings on money earned carrying water, or he's working for himself, thinking of the future, when one fine day he'll put on new boots and a new shirt. But Parnaoz's running about in the morning was just senseless, aimless fleeing, no more than the crazed state of cattle panicked by an eclipse of the sun: it was for nothing, out of stupidity, for what was happening had to happen. It had happened, too: everyone had their own horseflies that made them run. Most people were drawn by the extent of the wonder, by an incredible spectacle; many ran because others were running. But the outcome was the same for everyone: a feeling of criminality, an endless wait for punishment and hatred of this momentary loss of control, an indelible stain arising like a boil on their eternal obedience. Now they considered themselves dupes for following the sound of someone else's footsteps, and they would themselves stone to death and take revenge on that someone if they had a chance.

Parnaoz was willing to take the blame for everything. That morning, when he had run towards Dariachangi's garden, he thought that so many people followed him because they sympathized with his misfortune and were offering him unquestioning, selfless support. His heart swelled with pride: people's sympathy gave him wings and, until Popeye put a rope around him, he didn't suspect for a moment that his pretext for flight was madness and stupidity, that his banner was sheer insolence, ripped up by the javelin of dismay, polluted by sick dreams and hallucinations. Who knew or wanted to know, why should they be interested in the spectres of two naked children, two mummies preserved in permanent sadness and regret, shrouded in stubborn stupidity and obstinacy? What did Parnaoz need them for? What rainy day was he saving them for? What did he hope for? For a profit? Like a boatman trading in drowned bodies hidden underwater in the sand, mutilated by the rocks and half-eaten by fish, until the grieving kinsfolk find them, recognize them and buy them back.

Parnaoz was ashamed; he looked down at his hands and waited to hear what Popeye would say, what he'd come to say. Parnaoz wouldn't have been surprised by anything he said, or rather he would have listened to it without demurral. Popeye had good reason for coming: he was in danger and the probable ordeal entitled him to say what he liked. If he'd said,

'I've come to take you away, because you're the real criminal and I have no intention of being held responsible for you,' Parnaoz would have followed him without a word. He would have offered him a hand just as promptly if Popeye had asked for help. Nevertheless, Parnaoz had not abandoned his plan; but at the moment he was preoccupied by a feeling of guilt and pity for Popeye. He looked at his hands and waited, knowing that Popeye had business to discuss; if he wasn't the first to speak, it was only because he himself needed to be calm enough to set out what he had to say, to choose his words: he was only human, after all.

'Uncle was the first to run away,' Popeye repeated.

Popina looked at Ukheiro's room, as if she feared approaching thunder. Then she smiled. 'I'm sitting here as if I had nothing to do,' she said to the locked door of Ukheiro's room, but she didn't get up from her chair, clutching instead the pile of dirty dishes closer to her stomach.

'Don't be afraid, it's all going to be all right,' she said quietly, timidly after a pause.

'It's all your fault!' Popeye suddenly shouted, slapping his thigh with his fist.

Popina couldn't help covering her face with both hands, as her mother used to do whenever Ukheiro was mentioned. She dropped all the plates and they scattered with a crash all over the floor. Even now Parnaoz did not move. Popina crouched down and gathered the smashed crockery in her skirts. The oil lamp flickered. A moth was circling the flame. Now and again a puff of breeze or the breath of people in the room blew the moth into the flame and it leapt back in panic, only to fly back instantly and carry on blindly and loyally with a giddy dance to its divinity, at the boundary of life and death. The moth could not leave its divinity, this tiny light, which seemed to be called up from non-existence by its dance and its circling; it needed its two days of life only for this, to see and be sacrificed to a beautiful, deceptive, enchanting and ruthless divinity. Crouched on the floor, Popina gathered up smashed crockery in her skirts. She was like the moth, drawn to her divinity and unable to make her feet leave the room where nothing good awaited her. Kaluka brought in another oil lamp, but it was still dark in the room, only separate parts of Popina's body were visible, shining and reddish, like skinned flesh.

'Don't quarrel, it's disgraceful,' said Kaluka, putting the lamp on a brick shelf.

'Spare us that, woman! You should have thought about disgrace at the right time!' Popeye snarled.

Darkness did not inhibit the conversation. All this time Parnaoz hadn't raised his head, but he could easily guess whom Popeye was addressing, his mother or his grandmother; but he knew that Popeye had come only to see him, it was with him that he had business. If he was going for the womenfolk, it was only to blaze a trail, to clear a path that would be straighter and firmer. Parnaoz waited patiently.

'Why are you sulking: is it my fault I was born a boy?' Popeye was saying. 'Fine, it's a pity I wasn't a girl: I could have seduced at least one man. How about uncle? It's a family custom! Why look for outsiders, isn't it better to do it with one of the family? An insider can keep up appearances, an outsider is different… Make one mistake, and you blot your copybook. Then what can you do? Just tell me one thing, Kaluka, if you remember, what was the so-called father of your son called, eh?'

Parnaoz breathed a sigh of relief: he hadn't much longer to wait, judging by Popeye's tone and behaviour. Popeye was fidgeting, as if he'd been tied to his hair and was trying to get free. Soon he got to his feet and stayed standing until he'd got things off his chest, slung his sack over his back and left, jingling and clanking, a room where three people's hearts were pulsing like the moth with the singed wings.

'Do you know why uncle was the first to run?' Popeye suddenly asked, then waited a little, as if warning his listeners to pay attention, for the important part was now beginning; smiling, he went on: 'Because Parnaoz doesn't like Popeye. Uncle doesn't like his sister's son, he doesn't give a damn about him. In fact, it's worse: he hates him. Didn't you know? Is this the first you've heard of it? How could you, experienced women, be so blind? Well, if Popeye had been a girl, then like his mother and grandmother he'd have a bastard sitting on his lap and when he heard the voice of his uncle who feeds him, he'd leap up like a dog, lick his hands and feet like a dog and even if his uncle is so worn out dragging stones around that he gives him a kicking, he'll still fetch him a clean shirt, make sure the water to wash his feet isn't too hot, and stare his only hope and protector in the face, expecting bread that stinks of sweat. Unfortunately, it didn't turn out that way, Popeye let his uncle down, his uncle who cares for others, and wouldn't let him show how kind and generous he is: that's right, isn't it, uncle? No, not altogether. Your principles, kindness and concern are just a cover for a useless clown, that's all, there's nothing else under that mask: a clown's uselessness and cowardice. You're afraid of going to bed with a woman, aren't you? Popeye's done everything better than you. That's been hard for you nice people to see, has it? Popeye's got a two-storey house that he built with his own sweat, because it didn't fall into his lap, like other people's. Popeye is in the king's service. He's a well-known man, he's respected, he's feared, he's got a wife waiting for him at home, pregnant too: that's quite a lot, isn't it? Can anyone, let alone uncle, his elder, be blamed for dying of envy, when all this time he's learnt nothing except banging away at stones; he hasn't even got the money to buy time with a whore, so he snarls like a vicious dog and stops other people eating their grapes. Tik-tik-tik, go on, woodpecker, keep tapping: people should stick to what they know. But stones don't even have worms, so how can you stave off hunger? Luckily you've got me. If you didn't, what would save you from starvation, eh? Envy, of course, envy. It's easy to envy somebody, but to build a house needs more than that, so does getting a woman pregnant… Something or other. But you can't do that, so let others get on with it, old boy! Are you too busy? I was right to say you're like a mean dog, it doesn't eat and it won't let others eat. It wants everything for itself, whether it owns it or not. Everything. I expect he knows, he understands what I mean. Uncle is a clever man, he's cunning, too, underhand. Don't think he's simple-minded. He can be angry, too, oh yes, if you knew how angry he gets. Angry and proper. Once I visited a whore, it was on his behalf, but he wouldn't forgive me. He got so angry, really angry and turned people against me, he thought, "He's here, so they'll beat Popeye up instead of me; I'll stand aside with clean hands and principles." That's true, isn't it? I expect he thought, "The king will kick out my nephew and that will keep him off other people's patches." Go on, deny it!'

Popeye suddenly raised his voice. 'Just ask him who he's going to marry; if that wretched garden hadn't vanished, you'd have a whore sitting here in the house. "I'm a maiden," she'd say. Every night she sleeps with the whole city and she gets up in the morning a virgin. But you only need one night to sell your belly, as if you were trying to catch up, or might not have another chance. No, I'm not quite right, that whore needs you as much as a blacksmith needs bellows with a hole in them. If you don't believe, then go and see her — I'll give you the money. Quite apart from anything else, what right do you have to bar a door that's open to everyone else? You were infuriated when I told you I'd come out of there, weren't you? Aren't I allowed to peep through that door? Of course, I'm your nephew, what will people say? I don't give a damn what people say. I go where I want, whose business is it? I want to live, and life is for anyone who can use it, who has any energy. Morals are for later, when we get old: at the moment what's mine is yours, what's yours is mine. What was yours yesterday may be mine tomorrow, and it will be. Nobody's allowed to get in my way, or spoil things for me just because my mother had me in the wrong circumstances, was in too much of a hurry and forgot a few things. And you, uncle, have no right, especially you, because my mother, among other things, is your sister, your flesh and blood. So what do I care who gave birth to me, one of you or both? To me the two of you are one person, the same people. And I'm one of you, although we can't get on with each other. That's so, isn't it? It is,' he answered himself after a pause and bent down to pick up his sack. He walked backwards out of the room, not taking his eyes off Parnaoz's hands, which all this time lay on their owner's knees as motionless as fragments of stone.

While Popeye was talking, sometimes his red hands, and sometimes his quivering jaw, nose or ear-lobe would leap out of the dark, as if chopped pieces of human flesh were constantly swirling in boiling water. What Popeye said frightened Popina most. Crouching on the floor, even smaller when frightened, she was trying furtively to creep away on all fours, to slip away from this sticky pool of hatred spewed out by her son, but the pool kept spreading, filling cracks in the floor, slithering like a shiny pack of horrible snakes, trying to get up her skirts. Popina wanted to flee, but her feet would not obey her; she wanted to scream, but couldn't open her mouth, as if it was all happening in a nightmare. Parnaoz still sat there motionless, like a witness; his heart overflowed with loathsome pity. 'No, we can't… we can't go on living like this,' he thought.

Popeye had unburdened himself and relieved his feelings, but he was alarmed by Parnaoz's silence, he intuitively sensed a new, greater danger, a real one threatening only him, directed at him, not blind, indifferent or random. Even as he talked, Popeye realised that he'd gone too far, leaping into an unknown river, crossing into alien territory. But he couldn't stop himself: the guard's silence and indifference enraged him, provoked him to an outrage, even though this guard had got ready in his coat-tails a whole pile of heavy, razor-sharp stones. 'He's luring you on, stop it, don't get any closer,' Popeye's second, always sober mind warned him, but Popeye could not stop now, he was in thrall to fate.

Popeye was so carried away by fear that he could drag himself home. 'Make my bed, I'm dying,' he called to his wife from the threshold and, barely undressing, got into bed. To avoid Patu's stupid questions, he immediately turned to the wall and plunged into thought. He had a lot to ponder. A lot had happened to him in a short time, and it unbalanced him and blotted out his innate feeling of fear. Was it really necessary for Parnaoz to know what Popeye thought of him? Did that lessen his power? On the contrary, Parnaoz was now in a stronger position, he knew what he shouldn't know: his enemy's identity and plans. Popeye had betrayed a secret, and not a simple one, but a decisive one which determined the result of the battle to come. Popeye had kicked this secret into enemy territory: nobody but a fool would do such a thing. Even a fool would have controlled himself! But Popeye didn't because… no, however angry he was, he couldn't call himself a fool: it was fear, that damned fear, that had thrown him. Only a step away from his prey, he was ambushed by a more powerful beast. In fact, Popeye couldn't be blamed for being afraid: you try not being afraid in his shoes!

Even the grass in the palace courtyard had withered, even the guards in their felt cloaks now had grey hair, and all Oqajado's guards were men who would tackle a bear single-handed. Courtiers, as white as sheets, were taking each other out of the palace hall as if they were casualties on a battle-field. 'We can't calm him down,' they said in a tone precluding further questions. This phrase was a whisper that ran through the whole palace like a dying man's convulsions. If there was even a minute's delay in finding the guilty person it is hard to say what the consequences of the loss of that lousy garden would be. The head of the palace guard had vanished, four women in the laundry room were drowned: whether they were drowned or threw themselves of their own will into the boiling water was never established; two servant girls were found hanged by their own plaits; there was a fire in the bakery and the substantial building was reduced to ashes so quickly that nobody escaped, but for one or two who were so badly burnt that they couldn't say, and nobody could tell, who they were. Thus nobody knew who had survived and who had not.

So Popeye can't be blamed for being afraid, it was a bad day, a great ordeal for him. Only his will power saved him. Today his life hung by a thread, as did his unique, irreplaceable treasure which could never be found again. When the rumour spread that Oqajado would first punish his own people for the morning's chaos, Popeye felt his courage drain away. He was hunched as if he was about to be seized, as if he was Oqajado's only servant, just because it was his uncle who was the first to run away, like the ram leading its flock of sheep, like a madman in fact. Everyone, not just Popeye, saw him. They were all saying that Ukheiro's son was running away. Nothing could be hidden from the palace, but how could the palace know that, more than anyone else, Popeye hated this mad epileptic? This is why he was hunched, shrunken, hiding in cracks in the wall and, if the search for the guilty person had lasted much longer, he could not have held out, he would have fallen at Oqajado's feet and said (if his voice didn't fail him), 'But I tied him up, what more could I do, one man couldn't overcome a whole city.' The truth would come out, wouldn't it?! If people saw Popeye's idiot of an uncle running ahead of everyone, they would have seen Popeye tying him up the stone-cutter.

Fortunately, the criminal was soon found: the king found him. Afterwards people hit their heads with their hands and said, 'Heavens, wasn't it the man who neighed like a horse and said, "Dariachangi's garden has vanished?"' 'Fine,' Popeye thought, 'other people forgot about him, but how could it happen that I forgot something like that? But suppose… No, the king's never wrong, but suppose he was this time? Then you'd deserve it, then you'd be liable? To say at such a time "I knew and I forgot," is the same as "I knew and I hid it". As if they don't know that you're guilty, too. Of course they know, but they've forgiven you because you didn't mean to do wrong, because they're more generous than you are. Because you will have to dedicate your whole life to redeeming this accidental crime, you have to prove that you're worthy of respect. Good, that gelded beanpole is in for a bad time, but what does that do for Popeye? He will never find peace, he'll never get over his fear which hounds him like the king's yapping lap-dog.'

The more he thought, as he stared at the wall, shivering feverishly, the more he was convinced that his father-in-law, the city clown and trickster, was to blame for everything. How could Popeye lower himself to the level of that corpse? It was Bakha, not his own illegitimacy that was ridiculous. Being a bastard was dictated by destiny, and however hard he tried, he could not get rid of it, but his own heart was his to command and direct as he wished. He would follow his heart. He would kill two birds with one stone: he would settle scores with his father-in-law and his uncle. If he got it right, it would be a really good idea. Then you'd see the laughter when Popeye raised his glass first in a toast and said… No, first he'd beg Parnaoz to do the honours and chair the feast, 'You're my uncle, so be our host.' Parnaoz would make a face, then Popeye would smile ironically and say, 'I must be mad, how can we possibly have the groom making toasts at his own wedding?' Then there'd be an uproar. People would start looking for the bride, but apart from black-eyed Malalo and her seven daughters there wouldn't be a single woman anywhere in sight.

But it didn't come to that: the cup slipped twixt hand and lip. He was in too much of a hurry to take revenge on his father-in-law and uncle: instead, he only made things worse for himself. One disaster overrides another, and that is what happened to Popeye: he had only himself to blame, and he was furious. He loathed his own body, flabby and sweaty like a bitch that has just given birth. It was as if he had dropped blind puppies too fast and felt horribly weak as they, the results of stupidity and greed, crawled over him and nuzzled his teats. The desire to humiliate his uncle and father-in-law obsessed Popeye so much that he forgot some elementary truths, such as that there is a time for everything, and events wait for time, time doesn't wait for events. It's a fact that poison taken at the right time tastes sweet. Popeye had forgotten this, he had carved the spit, but the bird to be roasted was still flying in the sky. He thought about it, and anger made him helpless. 'I'm dying,' he groaned like a man on his death-bed, but when Patu came running to his bedside he kicked her away, because Patu and his father-in-law were one and the same.

Popeye lost his mind the day Bakha the vintner went to a better world. 'You should be buried like a dog,' he called to his father-in-law, who had wasted all his years of expectation and made him the laughing stock of the city, and nearly taken him with him to death. That was the day when it all began. Today was the crowning day when Popeye endured fear and worry: it was surprising that he hadn't lost his bearings, that he was still alive. He'd escaped the wolf, only to risk falling into the jaws of a vicious dog. When a man survives a great ordeal, he becomes a lumbering oaf of a boy, he thinks a lion is a fly, that heaven and earth are both under his control. But it was still Popeye's fault. He knew whom he was dealing with. A man who smiles as he lies in his coffin is capable of anything. Frankly, though, what had he got to complain about? He lived to the sound of music, whatever he had he spent on his stomach. But he did look after his family by leaving them such a good working donkey that they needed nothing else. And that stupid donkey inherited what it deserved: 'Now you know what sort of man you are,' it was told, and had a broken roof tile and a yard-long promissory note hung round its neck, so that in the absence of the deceased nobody should doubt whose donkey it was. That's why Bakha was smiling, relaxing in his sarcophagus decorated with vine shoots. But if there was any justice, it was now Popeye's turn, and he was going to have his due. But the dead man's smile unsettled him, it intrigued him as an ominous and alluring puzzle. Popeye bent over the sarcophagus countless times, staring hard at his father-in-law's swollen face. 'I feel that vampire's got something more in mind for me,' he thought and regretted not following his first instinct and not tearing the yard-long promissory note into shreds and throwing it in the corpse's face for all to see. Perhaps Popeye should have done this, perhaps his precious wife's family had more tricks up their sleeves, but he preferred to sit it out, because his beanpole of a wife, his promissory note, had decided to get pregnant. Yes, Patu was pregnant and, when she produced a result, the promissory note might be cashed: at the third attempt, she might give Popeye a child. No bastard, a real legitimate child. True, he had built a lot of castles in Spain with his father-in-law's money, he always needed money, but in his heart of hearts he preferred having his own child to money, a child was now needed more, because only his offspring would prove that he was entitled to all that he had earned and had yet to earn: he had come to earth for a good reason, not by chance, as his enemies said: he was necessary, inevitable, because he could do everything, including, of course, multiply. Ever since Patu had been his wife, she'd given birth twice, but both times the baby was still-born. 'It's because your father won't pay his debts,' he told her spitefully. What infuriated him most was the waste of all that time he was compelled to spend in the deck-sized bed and, above all, the labour involved, unpleasant and forced.

The injustice of it is what drove him mad, because he was deeply convinced that unpleasant and forced labour ought to produce much more fruit for him, so that the labourer could forget about it, so that the labourer shouldn't come to dislike his labour. The opposite had happened: fruitless labour made time itself — precious, unrepeatable time — barren. Popeye was like a passenger on a ship who has either to jump into the water or wait for a long-awaited shore to come into sight. He had no other choices, but the shore was not visible, it was hidden by haze, or the ship had lost its way. In fact, the deck-size bed had creaked along like a ship adrift in a night of expectation, mystery and hope. The shore was still out of sight, although it ought to have appeared twice. His wife seemed to be in touch with death, even friendly with it: who would make up for the time Popeye had wasted? Nobody, if he didn't look after it himself. He had to cleave rocks, reach to the sky, twist himself into knots: that was probably why he attacked Patu like a maniac, as if she were a house wrecked by an earthquake where a child was buried, not a child, but his child. Sometimes Patu was infected by her husband's fear and distress, and she came to believe that her husband was right to reproach her. Patu sang to herself less and visited her mother more often. Her daughter's barrenness gave Rachel food for thought: 'Why can't my daughter give birth?' she wondered, but she, too, was helpless against nature's mysteries and tried not to look at her daughter's worried, pleading face. Patu looked at her mother with hope and reverence, as barren women look at the idol of the goddess of fertility. 'Have you been doing as I instructed you?' Rachel asked for the thousandth time, when Patu crouched at her feet; and when her daughter nodded to say yes, she couldn't think what next to do or advise a woman looking so desperately at her in a desire for motherhood. Popeye was getting nastier, more venomous and frightening every day. 'If you're on such good terms with death, then have your father taken off,' he yelled at Patu in her torn nightshift, as if she were a prisoner under interrogation. Hearing his wife's sobs only enraged him more: 'She's in advance mourning for all of us,' he thought.

'Sing! Why have you stopped singing?' he asked, his eyes white with rage.

Then he started rushing about like a caged wild animal, singing spitefully, hoarsely, mocking Patu: 'And what else apart from dea-ea-eath Will split me from your love?'

'How can I curse my father?' thought Patu, hunched with fear. One day she was so distressed and bitter, so fed up with everything, so sorry for herself than she blurted out: 'If I have to be in such a state, what do I care about father or anyone else?' That evening Bakha the vintner died in his forty-step cellar. If Popeye had known in advance what the death of that vampire would bring him, he would have forced him back to life, would have turned the world upside down, would have shortened his own life to add to Bakha's, anything to prevent the terrible consequences. He wished he didn't know Parnaoz, that he didn't have an uncle with stone brains and stone hands: if Parnaoz had to exist, why did he have to be his mother's brother, unless this unjust world was against Popeye? 'I'm dying, don't come near me, at least let me die the way I want,' he moaned, groaned and lamented, as if he were really dying, or were already dead and was to be buried in the deck-sized bed, as if it were a family tomb, together with his still-born progeny.

In fact, Popeye was being reborn, this time not from a silly, timid woman's womb, but from his own mind, tempered, experienced, well taught and made wise. This rebirth was painful, so painful that he confused it with death, and for a moment he was about to throw down his weapons, but the wall saved him, or rather a cricket in a crack in the wall: Popeye happened to see it and connect this little insect, as black as a plum withered on the branch, with the vexing sound that devastated the world. The cricket sensed a stranger's eye and fell into a despondent silence. The unexpected silence healed Popeye's mind. Drenched in sweat, drained of strength, he now lay quietly and smiled, as if he had reached the promised land which he had been longing for day and night, aided only by faith and fear. Ever since he was a child he had been afraid of crickets, for some reason he imagined the sounds they made were otherworldly: in summer they seemed to break through cracks that the heat made in the ground and then endlessly, indiscriminately cursed and swore at the living; they were invisible and as troublesome as the smell of a corpse left out in the sun. Popeye had never yet seen a cricket, which may be why he had such an image of them. Now he lay there smiling, astounded and ecstatic because the problem was so simple. 'Oh, so that's how it is,' he thought, drawing his first conclusions from his discovery. 'Ha, ha,' he laughed, 'If that creature were visible, nobody'd let it anywhere near them. Men are afraid of and settle scores with what they can't even see; anyone will take a knife to a big cow; the smaller you are, the easier it is to hide; and the better you hide, the louder your voice and the greater your value.'

'They mustn't be able to find you, ever!' Popeye suddenly yelled, and sat up in bed, then stuck his index finger in the crack and squashed the cricket, which, as an exposed spy, was now superfluous and worthless.

Before Parnaoz left for Crete, uncle and nephew met once more for a talk. Parnaoz got up at dawn and spent some time waiting at the Greek's source, until he heard the jingling of Popeye's sack. Once he saw his uncle, Popeye slowed down, but didn't halt, or stop smiling, although his face became tense, as if he had to avoid a lurking vicious dog on his way. The day before Popeye had put Parnaoz's name on a list of craftsmen being sent to Crete, so that he wasn't at all surprised to see him at the crack of dawn. Anything said in the palace always did the rounds of the city before the person who had said it. But Popeye didn't give a damn, because he was at that moment sure that he was doing the right thing for both of them, for himself and for his uncle. Nor should anyone else be surprised or amazed by Popeye putting himself out like this. If he'd been a craftsman, he would have enlisted, too, because, as he heard and realised in the palace, serving King Minos was every mortal's most sacred duty. And Minos, the Supreme King, had started building the biggest palace in the world and needed craftsmen. This had been announced, of course: Minos has ordered craftsmen to be sent and so, naturally, we should all pull our weight. What craftsman would back out if he were given such a chance to demonstrate his loyalty and his craftsmanship? 'Ha, ha, what a shame that I have an uncle like that, but I can't even handle a hammer,' Popeye said with a smile when a courtier clapped him on the back and said, 'You really are a fine son of a bitch!'

The moment Popeye appeared, Parnaoz realized that he'd been fooled again, ensnared again, yet again thanks to his own stupidity. 'It looks as if I'll never learn sense,' he thought, but it was too late to turn back, he was unable to endure one more day of agonizing thoughts after that fateful incident, when he had been deliberately torn apart for fun, as if by sated wolves, bellowing in his face as he lay sprawled on the ground. No, it was better to be duped like this than to turn back. Parnaoz was tormented by his own plans: it was his fault, for he himself had summoned it from the darkest cranny in his soul; now, as dangerous as a wild animal that has escaped captivity, he wouldn't let anyone near him and he didn't even want to look at the dark, damp lair from which he had escaped, thanks to his captor's negligence. Parnaoz tried but failed to put right his accidental mistake. The plan was blind, searching for the right path by scent, but it had sharp teeth and Parnaoz only had to let it go free for an instant, to release his bloodstained hands from its mouth, then nothing could stand up against its blindness and determination. Parnaoz hadn't changed his mind, he still thought that for Popeye death would be a blessing. He considered Popeye to be the most unhappy of men, because nature had endowed Popeye with glands that oozed poison, and however often he spewed it out, he would never fully purge himself: he himself was the source of the poison. But he was remarkably full of vitality: his arrogance, like a wooden club, blazed him a trail, for he sensed that brazen self-assurance was the best way to make others doubt themselves and believe that he was as necessary and indispensable as a snake or scorpion.

Popeye was the worm in the stone, a worm in crumbling stone, and thus a worthier heir to the land that Ukheiro's grossness had destroyed than Parnaoz who was no longer entitled to see this destroyed land, who had been stopped not just from caring for and ruling it, but even seeing it, so as to clear away its dust, tidy up the scattered stones and find a pitcher handle, infallible proof, confirming that under these ruins there really did exist a land which must have been his homeland. He wondered if Popeye knew all this. Probably he didn't, he couldn't know. Can a worm have a homeland? Worms appear when everything is over, and on what is of no more use to anyone. If Popeye knew this, in Parnaoz's opinion, he would have killed himself and spared Parnaoz the sordid plan which he now felt he must carry out. It was all he thought about: he devised thousands of ploys and means for killing Popeye, and agonized, because he still loved, or rather pitied him, and was loath to dispose of him. Thus he had no right to stand back and shut his eyes, or calmly watch the worm squirming on the corpse of his homeland. Popeye was a victim but he evoked no sympathy, because he was, even before birth, meant to live in this way and, worst of all, he could live no other way, his disease was congenital: it could not be sucked or rooted out from his body. Nature had borne him for this disease, to carry and spread it: Popeye was unaware, as the wind is unaware what plant's seed it blows from one place to another.

Popeye must have sensed the fear that he aroused wherever he appeared with his jingling sack and his smile, always as lovingly polished as a kitchen knife. 'If they've done nothing wrong, why should they be afraid of me?' Popeye thought, sincerely believing the whole world was populated by his personal enemies, by people who envied him and were waiting for his downfall. Naturally, he told his uncle: 'You envy me, that's why you hate me.' But Parnaoz felt there was nothing enviable about Popeye: however much he acquired, he would always be a pauper, for he didn't know how much he needed, or what he needed, and why: his acquisitions didn't strengthen him, as a harvest makes a peasant; they weakened him, as swallowing a rabbit weakens a python. Nature had foreseen this and therefore gave him poison glands: when digesting, he was as weak as a woman giving birth, and had to be protected by poison.

Such thoughts stopped Parnaoz from sleeping: he looked like a disinterred corpse. Until Popina knocked on the wall, he would prowl up and down his room as if the door and window had been bricked up and he couldn't find a way out. In the morning he was embarrassed when he saw Popina and ran out of the house without breakfasting, all the quicker to climb onto his desert island and break the stone's rough surface with his hammer — carving the wall-eyes and the chillingly razor-sharp teeth of his horrific plan. 'Men his age are like children, they can't go to bed alone,' Kaluka told Popina, who was upset by her brother's restlessness.

Popina agreed: she suspected there must be a woman involved, and sooner or later what she most feared would happen. Popina was afraid of Parnaoz's future wife. Whoever she was, goddess or whore, Popina would still kiss her feet, would love her, heart and soul, but what obligations would this wife feel, why should she put up with a dishonoured and rejected woman who had brought nothing but shame to her family and who was the reason why everyone in this accursed house hated one another? A sister-in-law would feel the same as her son who disliked her, and rightly so, because if he took his sister to his new house he would bring her sin with her, and it was enough that Popina's sin had already defiled one house. They kept her on here probably only out of respect for her father, though Parnaoz had never made her feel that he disliked living under the same roof as her. But who could be sure that he was just being guarded about what he said? He'd never said a kind word, or a bad word to his sister. Popina really couldn't remember Parnaoz saying a kind word and, ever since Popeye had appeared, she'd never seen him smile, either. So he'd never forgiven her. Parnaoz was one thing, his future wife another. A wife could do a lot. Perhaps that was why Parnaoz was in no hurry, he was sparing his sister, he was sorry for her, but he couldn't manage without a wife and he was suffering silently. Or else… Popina didn't want to believe what Popeye had said that day. The things men say when they're angry: father doesn't spare son, nor son father. Popina was well aware, she'd heard a lot, how often she'd been distraught, until she became convinced that this was just typical of men. Now she still believed that men acted like this to frighten her, they found horrible words to demean her, but a minute later they themselves remembered nothing. 'I'm in everyone's way, I spoil everyone's life,' Popina lamented through pursed lips. As frightened and startled as a trapped bird, Popina listened to Parnaoz prowling, unable to sleep, on the other side of the wall.

Parnaoz almost decided to tell Popina the reason for his misery and restlessness, but whatever words he might use to express that reason sounded so unbelievable and so horrible, that at the last moment he bit his tongue and just begged his sister, 'Leave me alone, I'm not in any pain, I'm not thinking of marrying.' How could he tell this poor woman that the reason he couldn't stay in bed was that he intended to kill her son? Popina was right in one respect: her constant questioning made Parnaoz realise that his thoughts of killing Popeye were just as relentless and painful as his thoughts about Ino. Parnaoz's plan was doomed to be abandoned, but he couldn't have been in more agony if he had actually killed Popeye. In his mind, Parnaoz had already committed murder, all he had to do was to drag out the corpse for all to see, or rather face punishment, because only punishment would give him peace. That's why he was overcome by a hitherto unprecedented anxiety, and why the rumour that shook the city about craftsmen being despatched to Crete gave him a stunning feeling of bliss. Parnaoz felt as if sentence had been passed on him personally: somewhere, far across the ocean, someone as cruel and just as a god had looked into a man's heart, read his mind and judged him. But there was another danger. It was possible that they misunderstood whom sentence had been passed on, or they understood but had despatched someone else instead, while they trusted in Parnaoz and hid him because he was Ukheiro's son and Popeye's uncle. So he did not delay and the very next morning got up at dawn to wait for Popeye at the Greek's source.

'Why do you want to go to Crete: who's going to take care of the family?' asked Popeye, spreading his arms when he heard his uncle's request. Privately he was thinking: 'The wretch really is off his head.'

'The whole country is going. I'll go and try my luck,' said Parnaoz.

'Listen, man; yesterday I was stung by a mosquito: it must have been a venomous one, it's left a lump the size of my fist under my nipple,' said Popeye, scratching his chest.

'You should have lanced it with the tip of a knife,' Parnaoz told him.

'Why use a knife? It wasn't a wasp that stung me, man,' said Popeye with a smile. Then he added: 'I don't mind helping you, uncle, but it's not very easy, there are a lot of people who want to go.'

Parnaoz stood by the Greek's source watching until Popeye was out of sight.

When the day came for departure, Parnaoz went in to say goodbye to his father. Ukheiro was embroidering, as if all this time nothing had changed, but Parnaoz was immediately struck by the way time and illness had broken and destroyed Ukheiro's enormous body. An emaciated, desiccated old man was now sitting up in bed, and when Parnaoz saw his father's thin slack neck, he felt tears welling up. Ukheiro smiled at his son, although he was still absorbed in his embroidery.

'By the time you get back I'll have finished it, and then we'll sit down and read it together,' said Ukheiro.

Parnaoz kneeled down by the bed and lifted his father's hand so he could kiss it. Ukheiro made an attempt to frown as usual, but for some reason he too was on the verge of tears: he didn't hide them, but openly wiped his reddened eyes, weakened by constant embroidery.

'Bring us some wine, Popina,' Ukheiro called to his daughter, and went back to his embroidery.

Parnaoz went on for some time watching his father's withered fingers bustling like gigantic ants over the sail-sized canvas. Popina clutched the jug of wine like a baby and wept silently.

When Parnaoz left his father's room he felt that he would never again be able to see this extraordinary and unfortunate man whose whole being, over the years, had been persistently devoted to a self-sacrificing effort not to break down, not to accept his misfortune.

And so Parnaoz never saw Ukheiro again.

PART THREE
PARNAOZ

CHAPTER FOURTEEN

A man's shouting brought Parnaoz to his senses. He'd heard the voice for some time, but paid it no attention, fending it off, slipping away from it, as a corpse lying at the bottom of a river slips off the hook dropped to drag it out. But the voice persisted relentlessly and, although it hadn't yet hooked onto the switched-off mind, it still broke through. 'I'm dead and Tsuga is howling over my body,' Parnaoz thought as he slowly regained consciousness, but once he was fully awake he couldn't remember anything, neither the disturbing voice nor his stupid thought. A tense, suffocating silence reigned all round. He was lying in the dark. His whole body ached. His limbs hurt and he was dizzy with weakness, as if he had come into the open air for the first time after a long illness. But the air was filled with dirty bird's down and smelled sour, like a derelict hen-house. The man shouted again, to Parnaoz's relief, as if he had impatiently been waiting, eager to hear just that voice. 'Nothing's happened to me. I'm lying down… like my father,' he managed to think before fainting again, but he didn't reach the bottom of unconsciousness: he'd stopped at some point half-way, branches had interrupted his fall. That was exactly how it felt: as if he was lying on branches and swaying with them. He was neither surprised nor afraid. When he opened his eyes again he saw a child. The child was sitting on the floor and watching him with amazement. They looked at each other for a very long time, until the stunned child merged into the dazzling light. Two days later Parnaoz regained his sight: the child was sitting on the floor as if it hadn't moved all this time, and his big, astonished eyes were watching him. Then the child's face trembled, his mouth opened, showing shining white teeth. Parnaoz couldn't help being infected by the child's smile, and his dry cracked lips burned.

'Mummy, the dead man's woken up again!' the child called out.

Now the child watched the door. He'd stopped smiling as he impatiently stared at the door. A woman entered the room. She was drying her wet hands on her apron. When he saw her, the child fluttered like a tethered bird and looked proudly at Parnaoz. The woman smiled: she was so strikingly like the child fluttering at her feet that Parnaoz was deeply moved.

'Thank God!' said the woman.

Parnaoz shut his eyes, this time deliberately, because he suddenly remembered everything and was embarrassed: the smiling woman who had thanked God for his survival; the child squatting on the floor, who had announced his survival to the world; the bed on which he lay. Parnaoz was embarrassed by his survival. What was the point of rescuing a man who had been sentenced to death by those who worked with him for ten years? He now remembered everything: it all came back the moment the woman entered the room.

He had been beaten, worse, he had been stoned as if he were a snake. The inevitable had happened. Isn't a man right to take a spade and smash in the head of snake lying in his path? Even if the snake hasn't poisoned anyone and has slithered out only to warm itself in the sun, everyone has to throw a stone. They are bound to do so, for even if the snake hasn't yet poisoned anyone, tomorrow it could easily bite a child whose parents carelessly left it sitting on the ground. 'I'm a snake, God, a snake!' Parnaoz thought with fear and loathing. All those ten years he seemed to have filled his comrades' hearts with poison and hatred: when they had no more room for his poison and hatred, they spewed it out again.

The ten years had passed. Parnaoz felt it, stretched out on someone's bed in a stranger's house. Time had passed, but nothing had changed, because the time itself was useless and pointless, part of a punishment, to be endured as an obligatory illness. For those ten years nobody had been interested in his identity. Even when he first arrived in Crete, nobody asked him his name, his overseers were only interested in his skills. When Parnaoz told them he was a stone-cutter, forty thousand men called out with one voice, 'Come over here, you must be one of us.' From then on Parnaoz merged into the forty thousand stone-cutters, forty thousand stone-cutters became Parnaoz, and these forty thousand, like Parnaoz's twins, ran together to the latrine, quenched their thirst at the same time and lay down to sleep at the same time, in order, when the overseers yelled at dawn, to leave their bunks of unplaned boards with regret and curses, and, armed with heavy hammers, to attack the rocks again, and work out their anger on the rocks. All day long they fought the stone, chopping and cleaving it, crumbling and shattering these immobile and unfeeling monsters which showered them with dust and sparks from their horrible mouths and guffawed, until humans, worn out by their hardness and obstinacy, could no longer lift their arms. Unlike the others, Parnaoz had a special relationship with stone: he loved it, dressing it with mysteries, filling it with memories: this was the only place where his real nature dared to come to the surface. Stone was Parnaoz's friend, a dumb and loyal friend who lifted him every morning out of the musty sea of forty thousand men and once more stopped him drowning. Parnaoz was indulgent towards his friend, always taking care where he aimed the hammer, first using his hand to wipe off the dust, then waking the stone before stepping into the virgin territory which he had cut in the rough surface. That was why his chisel slipped freely, with a passionate quiver and crackle, into the rock's veins, like a comb through a woman's hair.

Tsuga joyfully filled the whole island with her barking, she stuck her nose into every cranny and crack, she would sneeze and wipe her nostrils, covered in grey dust, on Parnaoz's shins. The island smelled of apples and of earth softened in constant coolness. 'Ino's a good girl, look, Parnaoz, what she's up to!' an invisible Dariachangi would say to Parnaoz and he would automatically look as the voice told him. Ino had risen from the sea and was running towards him. She held her arms out in front, and her upturned palms were cupped together. 'She's bringing a jellyfish,' Parnaoz thought, and smiled: Ino, on her knees in front of him, her voice mingled with tears, was sobbing, 'Look, Parnaoz, look what I've found.' Sea water was dripping from Ino's fingers, and a dead bee was stuck to her wet palm. 'Why did it fly so far… poor thing…' Ino was saying, then added: 'I expect the wind blew it away.' Then she lay down next to Parnaoz, wet and naked, startled and upset by the sight of the dead bee, but still as brilliant as the light. A sunbeam was tickling her nose and dimples appeared on her cheek. Parnaoz felt giddy, his eyes lost focus and he couldn't see anything but the light.

Finally he heard the stone-cutters' coarse laughter and came to his senses, gathered up his tools and reluctantly clambered off his island of stone. Now he could see only the stone-cutters' malicious eyes and hear their sarcastic, bilious talk. 'If you want, we'll light you some torches and you can work at night, too,' the stone-cutters would tell him: exhaustion made them look even more frightful and ruthless. Parnaoz felt in the wrong, he realised that he wasn't behaving according to their fraternity's unwritten rules; he realised that sooner or later he would be held to account, either to give up the dream, or… God knows, what forty thousand men's hatred would involve. But even forty thousand men's hatred was better than forty thousand men's mockery. He could hardly say, 'It's my way of doing things: I work extra time and get in your way so I can spend more time thinking about a skinny girl and a puppy.' But judgement day was approaching. Parnaoz sensed this, but what could he do, how could he atone for this involuntary crime that brought on the just wrath of forty thousand brothers? 'That man gets so much work done, so what the hell is wrong with you lot?' the overseers would yell when they came to inspect the work and found the other stone-cutters too tired to lift their arms, while Parnaoz felt aghast, speechless as he stood, head bowed, yet again depressed and dismayed by fate's treachery. When he got back to camp, falling like a rock onto his bunk of unplaned boards, he would stare at the rain-stained ceiling and listen to his forty thousand brothers groaning in their agitated sleep. The camp stank of sweat. The insects, emboldened by the vulnerability of sleeping men, rustled, screeched and squeaked. Freed of the weight of daylight, the world was ragged, broken up: it shone and bubbled like boiling tar. Everyone was lying in this tar, but Parnaoz was still alone, alien and superfluous.

So time passed. Crete was full of a mass of outsiders, and all of them sought in their own way to get used to, to merge with, to adapt to their new surroundings. Whether they had been brought by force or had come of their own free will, they all brought with them their own worries, desires and agonies; their eyes were too full of the dust and fog of the land they had left somewhere over the ocean to see other people's misfortune. Everyone mourned for their own dead, their neighbours' dead seemed to be merely sleeping. So Parnaoz did not give anyone insight into his heart. What difference would it have made? They would have silenced him and told him, 'That's nothing, why don't you ask about me?'

Now Parnaoz recalled his father more often: Ukheiro was like a hare at bay, forced to wait for the end, because all around the dogs are waiting, crouched, their tongues hanging out, for their master, so that they can give him, their provider, the pleasure of killing the hare. But the master takes his time coming; sure of the dog's vigilance, he prolongs his pleasure, humming, playing with his club. Didn't Ukheiro look from a distance like a heap of stones, a looted pedestal on which, instead of a name renowned for blood and bravery, treacherous fate had clambered and made countless mocking faces. So Parnaoz had nothing to tell apart from the story of a mangy dog and a girl. He was just a simple artisan, merely a woodpecker in stone, as Popeye said; what did it matter whether he was in Vani or Crete, if he couldn't build one or destroy the other. He had to go wherever the stone took him, he had to disappear, to get further from his father's house, so as without losing his patience to strike the hammer against the sacred stone which a mocking fate had made his pedestal.

That was how Parnaoz thought, and he nearly decided, like others from Vani, to stay permanently in this alien land, build a house, fence in a yard, plant fruit trees, so as to make it harder to abandon this country and, once and for all, accept fate like a man and say with a sigh, 'Even if I don't, then my grandson will eat the plums his grandfather planted.' But as time passed, thoughts of the motherland became more unbearable, his merciless memory kept bringing up something, so that he could no longer swallow or stop the tears blocking his throat. Memory, like a good housewife, never threw anything away, even the simplest almost insignificant detail. But every detail now had a foreign fragrance and aroused sadness and pity, like a baby's hand. Parnaoz no longer knew what to hold dear, what to keep in his heart: the three-legged stool, or the butterfly pinned to the wall; the rough white shell that lay in Popina's room and kept on whispering something when you put it to your ear, or the red-spotted bowl with the chipped rim, as if someone had nibbled it with their teeth when testing the strength or the taste. Parnaoz thought of these objects the same way as he thought of Tsuga and Ino, as if they existed only in his mind and had no other place. But one day something happened that finally convinced him of fate's irrevocability. Fate not only held the other end of the rope tied to Parnaoz's neck, it also held the stool, the butterfly, the shell and the bowl. Fate's rope had not got longer over the years, it had become tauter and it now pulled him back with more force towards the sacred stones, the pedestal, so that he, like a sacrificial lamb could be tied there.

The scaffolding was now being taken down from Minos's new palace, and its tall blood-red columns looked awesomely beautiful and oppressive next to the thousands of hovels and shanties. The workers had been called to dinner. Their tools, scattered in the marble dust, shone dazzlingly in the midday sun. Suddenly a worker fell off the scaffolding and crashed to the ground with such a noise that even those who had a bowl full of warm stew in their lap rushed forward. Parnaoz, too, ran up with the others. The dying man rolled his eyes, white with fear, pathetically, as if he was looking for someone in the crowd whose presence was now urgently needed, even hoped for. Parnaoz couldn't understand why he was drawn to the dying man, why he raised the man's head and put his ear to his mouth. The dying man was barely able to gabble, his voice was drowned in blood, but Parnaoz could make out his last words. 'What could your father do to me worse than this?' he gabbled: it was only then that Parnaoz recognized Philamon, Popeye's father, his brother-in-law by rape, a man frightened for ever by his own fiery passions and boldness and forced to flee for ever. 'Philamon, Philamon,' Parnaoz called out to the nothingness: Philamon was now dead.

For some time the dead man's head lay in Parnaoz's coat-tails, and tears streamed from Parnaoz's eyes, until the astonished workers forcibly dragged him away, Parnaoz was weeping for Philamon and himself. He felt as if his last compatriot had died and he understood for the first time how hard it would be to endure a longing for his lost motherland, that he would give up the ghost like this, too, and one day be unable to cope and would die, as birds die in the air, too tired to fly, exhausted before they could reach a branch or roof. Parnaoz also felt that the objects and faces accumulated in his memory had aged by ten years, and now looked at him in silent reproach. At night he dreamt of his father. For the first time in his life he saw his father standing. Ukheiro had come in to see him, holding a coloured thread, and told him, 'My thread is breaking and I just haven't been able to tie it together.' Parnaoz woke up thinking, 'My father's died.' The dream seemed to be a message from fate. If death had really taken Ukheiro, then Parnaoz was obliged to return to his homeland and, as the only man, look after his family. The feeling that he was needed gave him joy, and he thought of his kinsfolk differently: who knows, perhaps their home is in ruins, Kaluka will have aged and all the work falls onto Popina's shoulders. But he did not know what to think about Popeye, and so tried not to think about him. What business was it of Popeye's, how could he assume that Popeye would look after Ukheiro's household? He should do the right thing and live as was required of him, as befitted him, as others lived: accepting today, and hoping for tomorrow. He would support those dear to him, care for the sick, repair the tiles on the roof, fetch water, chop firewood and die a respectable death when his time came. Apart from that, he would marry as soon as he got there, so that Popina had someone to help her. He would have children so that he could do for them what he couldn't do for Tsuga and Ino, because of his childishness and naivety. That was what people called life, and he hadn't understood or noticed, until Philamon emitted his last breath and blood.

After that it wasn't long before the stone-cutters, angered by his diligence, intercepted him on his way back from work to camp, locked the door, flung him to the floor and gave him a terrible kicking. Parnaoz lay in a coma for two weeks, death hovering over his head, but fate seemed not to have doomed him. When he opened his eyes, he was lying in the house of a famous Athenian artist, Daedalus, but that was something he learned later when he could sit up in bed and hold a spoon.

'Can a human being have a motherland?' Daedalus would ask him as he sat by his feet, after coming in apparently just for a minute to see the patient, but so entertained by the conversation that he forgot to leave. His wife stood in the doorway, calling out, 'That's enough now, don't torment a sick man.' Their son sat on the floor, holding some fluff in his hand, looking at his father with his big shining eyes. Parnaoz apologized with a smile to all three, because he was sorry for them, though he couldn't have known why he should be sorry for them. Daedalus already had grey hairs, his face was wrinkled all over, although he was not old enough to blame the wrinkles on old age. But he had such lively and restless eyes, as if he had just opened them and was seeing everything for the first time. As restless as a child, he fidgeted all the time he was sitting down, and when he was walking he spread out his arms, bent at the elbow, like a bird running on the ground. If he were not so fond of talking, he would probably never have stopped walking, but he knew so much and was perturbed by so many things that he'd bored everyone with his talk so that they avoided him. But he needed a listener as a tree laden with fruit needs a prop. Even at night he did not relax: even in his sleep he argued and fought with and shouted at someone. It was his shouting that woke up Parnaoz, dragging him back to this world from a fortnight-long death. Very little of what Daedalus said made sense to Parnaoz. He thought this was mostly because of its strangeness, but he always listened attentively and was infected by his collocutor's emotions, and when he was at the gates of something mysterious, unattainable and magnificent, he was overcome by a feeling of bliss he had never before experienced. In this blissful haze he really believed that a statue might some day walk, or one fine day might open its mouth and say, 'Hello, how are you?'

'Motherland, motherland,' Daedalus said. 'Everyone looks for their motherland. We begin life blind and naïve, then, when we reach the age of reason, when our eyes finally open, we don't like it, we're afraid of it and we recall our motherland only when it's impossible to return to it, because we no longer remember the beginnings of our life which has merged with life in general and so has no beginning or end. We have lost our way wandering through endless corridors, and we move not according to our own desire, but because the need to move drives us as it will. And the need to keep moving is generated by the seed of fear and weakness, which is called hope. Hope is self-justification and deception, neither is much use or can help us in any way; hope just prolongs and makes its parents, fear and weakness, more or less bearable for us. Though hope is an inexhaustible source of the vital force which we use up as we wander the endless corridors. How does our wandering end? It doesn't, it has no beginning or end, its end is its beginning, its beginning is its end.'

Once Parnaoz was able to get up, their conversations moved to the courtyard. The courtyard was full of sculptures: the statues placed under fig and pomegranate trees really looked as if they were alive. Parnaoz loved to look at them, he sat for hours, dizzy with weakness, and saw, heard and felt the marble pulse and stir as it was warmed by the sun.

'They're as paralysed as my son,' Daedalus said in a voice that made Parnaoz's heart sink. What could he say to console this peerless sculptor and unhappy father, rewarded with a paralysed son by the mocking gods, who seemed to say, 'You are wrong to compete with us, you are wrong to take up our art, because, despite all your desires, your offspring are worms of the earth and have to crawl on the earth.' Daedalus understood this, his petrified seed made him upset, sad and rebellious. At times he said regretfully, 'My sculptures are beautiful, but they can't even offer you a drink of water,' and became so angry that he was ready to pick up his hammer and smash everything to smithereens if they didn't start moving, if they went on confirming his belief that his son, too, the big-eyed Icarus, was also chained to the floor forever, like a bowl catching rain water, which has to fill drop by drop with rain, or rather with sky, cut up into tiny pieces and brought down by the rain through the cracks in the ceiling. 'No, I shan't rest or stop until I attach wings to myself and fly up with my son,' Daedalus cried out, rushing round the courtyard as if he really was about to take off, as if he really did have wings. Parnaoz felt sorry for his friend who had tried everything on earth and now placed his remaining hopes on the sky. This hope kept him alive, awake, and was sustained by his endless talks. But Parnaoz kept having disturbing suspicions that imagining walking statues and flying human beings was slightly mad. Daedalus kept insisting, 'I have to fly, I have to fly, I have to fly,' waving his arm at the statues that peeped out from between the trees, as if they were trying to interrupt him, or jump on his feet and stop him flying. Parnaoz visualized Icarus blowing on a piece of fluff in his palm and watching with delight as it swirled through the air. He himself couldn't help looking up to the sky, but the sky was no longer visible: it was completely covered by ragged evening clouds. Then both of them remained silent for some time, as if even talking about flying made no sense when the sky was clouded. On earth, too, it was getting dark, and instead of statues only grey patches appeared here and there.

'Oh Parnaoz, Parnaoz, how can I help you, my friend?' Daedalus finally broke silence, only to mark the end of this particular conversation.

Parnaoz felt an nasty shudder run through his body; he felt overcome, overwhelmed that a soothsayer had marked him out, in a roundabout way, for a great ordeal which he would have to undergo sooner or later.

The cosy atmosphere of Daedalus's house calmed him instantly. Like any other family man, Daedalus re-laid loose paving stones, saw that the lamp didn't run out of oil, and sniffed the air with his eyes closed to guess what his wife was cooking for their supper. His wife sat by the window, knitting. When she caught sign of the menfolk she set aside her knitting and stood up to greet them with a smile, as if to tell them that here in her realm no sorrow could beset them. Then she called to the child that his father had come, but Icarus had already seen his father and crawled as quickly as he could towards him to embrace his legs and look up with his shining black eyes, as if his father were a magic tree and fantastic fruit hung from its crown. 'My son can only slide and crawl. But through the keyhole he sees all,' said Daedalus in rhyme, scratching the child, who was trembling with happiness, at the back of his head, as a master does when his dog greets him. Parnaoz felt tears welling up, and he promised himself that he would carry the boy about, show him everything and not let him ever be disappointed, although he didn't dare to go up and put his hand on the child's head. He wasn't entitled to intervene in this strange conversation between father and son. Without exchanging a word they understood each other and without forethought, guided only by instinct, they made the necessary movements to break the egg from which, like a golden chick, their allotted joy, sufficient just for them would hatch.

'I hope you turn into a quail for the hawk to eat,' Parnaoz heard Daedalus say much later: he was squatting on the floor by his son, telling him a fairy tale. His wife sat by the window, smiling as she knitted; not looking at her husband and son, she said, 'It's time you ate something.'

Parnaoz lived like this until he received permission to return to his homeland. He had never gone back to the camp: he wanted to avoid the wrath of the forty thousand brothers, deafened by the stone's loud laughter and blinded by its dust: that wrath had sentenced to death a man like them, a forty-thousandth part of them. His battered body still hurt, but he was able at least to help Daedalus by washing his brushes, diluting his paint, or holding the ladder for him. Daedalus was in the new palace, decorating the dancing hall of Ariadne, Minos's daughter.

'When I come into this room,' Daedalus told him, 'I can't see anything but a little girl. She's standing in the middle of the room, holding a pomegranate branch over her head and dancing. She twirls and twirls until she flies off.'

In fact, everything did twirl and fly about in the pictures the artist's brush painted on the walls. But one day that little girl was brought by her nurses to that room. The girl sucked her thumb and, stunned, even a little frightened, inspected the countless different fish and stars, the grove of flowering pomegranates and the little girls' round dance, the cat hunting birds, and the meadow flowers. The little girl's face looked as if she was heartbroken not to have her picture on the wall. She was the Supreme King's daughter, but she was frightened of growing up; despite her nurses' selfless efforts, her spirit resisted nature, and this girl of thirteen was more like a girl of six, as if she instinctively sensed what strange and terrible adventures were waiting for her after childhood. But in two years she would all at once make up for lost time and, without a thought, plunge into a sea of ruinous passion and sin. In two years' time she would be a deceived, abandoned and disillusioned woman, because she would make a choice between a foreign youth and her father, just as her spiritual sister

Medea had once made. She was born for great love and was therefore doomed, destined to be legendary, an exception, a rarity in the boldness of her passion and the naturalness of her self-sacrifice. Two years later she would come rushing into this hall and, just as stunned, frightened and abashed, she would gaze at the decorated walls, because the land that looked at her from these walls had stupefied her into believing that she too could fly. It would be hard for her to believe the opposite, and bare-footed, wearing only a blood-stained shift, she would start spinning in the middle of the room until she crashed down unconscious onto the stone floor. Both she and the brilliant walls would gradually calm down and then be captives of eternal stillness.

Finally the long-awaited day came and Daedalus personally handed Parnaoz a slender clay disc on which it was clearly written that he, a craftsman of Vani, Parnaoz, son of Ukheiro, was a free man and could return to his homeland. 'We've shown them!,' Daedalus kept exclaiming, but when he looked at Parnaoz, he came back to earth, felt dismayed and after a long silence, like a man come to offer condolences, murmured, 'Yes, brother: we all have our road to follow and each has to do it alone.'

Parnaoz waited impatiently for the day to come, but now the same feeling of disappointment came over him. He had been told he could go wherever he liked, that he was free, but however hard he tried, he couldn't feel or imagine this freedom. Every day that passed removed a part of his being and impoverished him, so that he had nothing left but that barren road. Parnaoz had already trodden that path so many times, that he could no longer feel it existed. Would returning to Vani change anything? Didn't he have to take with him that narrow, grey, unpaved road, always the same, that the same man had kept walking down? What sense was there, after all, in relocating that road if he himself couldn't change, couldn't find another way of coping with life? If Parnaoz had been able to live 'another way' then he would have to be reborn, a different woman would have had to give birth to him, in a different country, under very different stars and a different father would have to meet him behind that door which was so hard to open and which hid the secret not only of his conception but of his future life.

The little clay disc on which it was clearly written that Parnaoz, craftsman of Vani, son of Ukheiro, was henceforth free, could change nothing. He had to hang the disc round his neck, bundle up the presents he had bought for his kinsfolk, the two or three pennies he had managed to save, and set off once more on his travels. But this turned out to be no easy matter. The port of Knossos was, as usual, packed with ships, but they all seemed to have conspired, for not one was going to Colchis. For a whole day he and Daedalus exhausted themselves, but when they called out to a ship to ask where it was going and whether it could take one man, it was always in vain. For some reason the sailors standing by the railings were all in the same mocking mood, and made things harder for the now frustrated and exhausted friends. They sent them off in all directions, and one sailor told them, 'Why go to Vani, there's nothing but frogs there.'

Parnaoz was resolved not to go back, not to leave the port. What did it matter whether it was today or tomorrow that a ship accepted him, he was now a traveller, homeless, and his only thought should be to get out of here. Daedalus found it hard to leave his friend, but there was no point his waiting here any longer. They were more of a hindrance than a help to each other, because they had already parted, they were now inhabitants of different lands and were already used to being without one another. Now their being together was unnatural, because one had to leave and the other didn't. They themselves felt this, which made them more angry and more irritable, so that sweat streamed down their faces. 'This is all wrong, we should have asked first and then gone to the port,' Daedalus grumbled. Parnaoz, on the other hand, was sure that his friend was a hindrance, that his confused way of talking made the sailors want to mock him, and that was why they were being sent to and fro. 'If that's how it is, I'll go,' said Daedalus angrily. But before he left, he still smiled at Parnaoz, put a hand on his shoulder and told him in an unnatural, false voice, 'I'm not saying goodbye to you, because I'm sure we'll meet again this evening.' Then he laughed and added: 'In the end I'll make wings and in the twinkling of an eye I'll fly to Colchis to see you.' Parnaoz wanted to say some words of farewell, at least to thank Daedalus, but he stood there mute, watching the famous Athenian artist, a dreamer and a father of a paralysed son, elbow his way through the crowds.

That day a lot of ships left port, but not one of them had space for Parnaoz. Gradually people assembled, the port quietened down and was lost in the darkness. The gently rocking boats became gigantic shadows, merging with one another. The sea splashed gently on the shore. A dog ran along the deserted dockside, sniffed at a squashed pear and went on its way. He could hear the singing of drunkards in the distance, and he realised that it was now past midnight. A cold wind blew in from the sea, bringing the smell of smoke as the sailors lit fires on board. Parnaoz was dizzy with tiredness, his stomach rumbled with hunger and his teeth chattered with the cold, but he still didn't dare leave the port: he was afraid of the crowd, because he was now very much a stranger in this land, so strange, it seemed to him, that anyone might notice and start a row: 'What are you doing here?' Parnaoz saw the dog again: it was trotting back and carefully sniffing the paving in case it had missed anything the first time. Again, it stopped at the squashed pear. But it didn't touch it this time, either. Parnaoz couldn't see the pear now, but he remembered where it was. 'Tsuga, Tsuga,' he called to the dog. The dog looked round and, its neck still turned, ran off sideways. Parnaoz roamed about for a long time until dawn came, but the sky was so overcast that not a ray of light penetrated. Parnaoz squeezed in between some wine barrels, clutched his bundle to his chest and then fell into a corpse-like sleep. The drunks were the first to wake him: they were coming back to the ships, holding clubs and hitting out very hard at everything in their path. Every nook and cranny of the port echoed and repeated this horrible sound. It took Parnaoz time to wake up properly: he had the suspicion that the drunks had come into the port to look for him and would pulp him with their clubs, like the pear, if they found him. He lay without moving, not even daring to peep from between the barrels. When the drunks passed on, he went back to sleep, and when he next woke it was already light and the port was as noisy as ever. Now he worried how he could creep out unnoticed from between the barrels, for he couldn't stay there all day, could he? When he stood up he was a whole head higher than the barrels, but nobody paid any attention to him.

The first thing he saw was Daedalus running, like the dog in the night, to and fro and looking hard at the crowd. He was searching for Parnaoz, and had left the house to find out what had happened to him. That meant a lot, a great deal, to a man setting out on a journey, who, apart from anything else, now no longer felt alone nor found the port alien and frightening. Parnaoz felt like scattering the barrels piled up around him, breaking through and cleaving apart the busy crowd and embracing, better, falling at the feet of his friend who was waving his arms in the air to ask whether anyone had seen such-and-such a man. But nobody could understand him, they all shrugged and ran off on their own business. Only Parnaoz recognized whom those restless arms were designating in the air: his excited heart was filled with a vague, almost childlike sadness and pride. But Parnaoz held back, and when Daedalus chanced to look in his direction, sat down again among the barrels. He didn't poke his head out until Daedalus left the port. Daedalus spent some time doing the rounds of the busy, noisy port: clearly he could not find out anything for sure, and he hadn't come across Parnaoz. Could he have thought that Parnaoz, moved by his concern and loyalty, was sitting behind the barrels, biting his bundle to choke back his weeping?

The day ended without success. The one thing that Parnaoz learned was that ships from Vani were still on their way; God knew when they would arrive, or if they would arrive at all, for sailors disliked making predictions. 'Whatever Poseidon decides, will be,' they told Parnaoz.

Again the noise of the port died down, the area became deserted and Parnaoz once more saw the squashed pear. Ants were attacking it. Now the dog was due to come and Parnaoz waited eagerly, but today the dog failed to appear. 'I scared it off,' thought Parnaoz. The sun had risen and scarlet, sepia, smoky and black clouds raced after each other, as if frightened to be left alone in a sunless sky.

Parnaoz hadn't had a bite to eat, but he didn't feel hungry any more. He drank water several times and washed his face, too, because it was unbearably hot all day. That was all that Parnaoz remembered of that day. That night, too, he didn't dare leave the port, although he could have spent the night in bearable conditions in one of the cheap inns that had been spawned around the port and which had a damp mushroomy smell, too. Parnaoz had enough money, he would have preferred being in a dirty inn to lying on paving stones behind the barrels: at least he'd have somewhere to lay his head and wouldn't be so freezing cold, but the feeling of being an alien stopped him: if he left the port the feeling would become more intense and, in his opinion, wherever he went, he would be an outsider, would be the cause of some misunderstanding, they wouldn't even look at his money, they'd tell him they had no room or food for him, or, if they said nothing, would make him feel it.

Hunger and tiredness did their work by the third day and he was forced to enter the first inn he saw. Chia, the innkeeper, a bald man with a single wall-eye, saw the money in his guest's hand and smiled at him like an old acquaintance, seating him at the end of a long table covered with stains. The table was remarkably long: a horse could have galloped on it. Three men were sat at the head of the table, with a jug of wine before them: they were playing dice. They didn't notice Parnaoz coming in, and he breathed a sigh of relief as his initial anxiety and tension passed. But now he was worried that he had barged in for all to see at the end of the table. While he sat at the table he could not shake off his unpleasant forebodings, but they were not fulfilled. The only thing to be heard in the enormous room was the click of dice. Parnaoz tried not to look at the players, but, alarmed by the emptiness, his eye kept returning to them. Then he saw a wasp. The wasp was trying to find a way out of the room and was hitting the walls so hard that it was surprising that it was still alive. The innkeeper brought him roast meat, boiled chestnuts and wine, wiped the table clean with one sweep of his arm and asked, 'Where are you from?' 'I'm from Colchis, from Vani,' Parnaoz replied deliberately loudly, and looked boldly, or rather rudely at the players, as if they had sent the innkeeper to ask on their behalf where he was from. After three days without food, his throat had shrunk and he had trouble swallowing the meat. He chewed it for some time and swallowed, or rather forced down the accursed lump as best he could. He enjoyed the chestnuts, however: they were still warm and crumbled the moment he put them in his mouth. He washed them down with wine, thinking, 'The dog's sniffing the squashed pear now.' His body, deprived of sleep, easily gave in to the intoxicating strength of the wine, which filled him with lassitude and a hazy sleepiness, as if he had just had a hot bath. He couldn't understand when the room had become so crowded and noisy. All that he was aware of was that so many people had gathered round the table, laughing loudly, that it was hard to move, as if these people's hot sweaty shoulders were stuck to each other. A thick haze filled the room. Parnaoz looked towards the head of the table, but couldn't work out if the dice players or other people were sitting there. They ate, drank and guffawed, but seemed not to notice Parnaoz; yet Parnaoz was an outsider, occupying someone else's place and, if he hadn't been there, they would have been more relaxed. It was hard for Parnaoz to reach his bundle which someone's foot had pushed under the table; it was hard to break through the shoulders of his fellow-diners, find the innkeeper and, now almost asleep, find out where he was to sleep. The innkeeper took up a staircase, led him along a narrow dark corridor that smelled of dust and damp, and opened the first door with his knee. 'Lie down wherever you like,' he told him, and shut the door. There was one bed in the room, but it was big enough for ten men. A little window, cut almost at ceiling level, still shed some pale light and in this light glimmered a bed of unplaned boards, like an island of bliss. Parnaoz flung his bundle onto the bed, followed by his own body. His head on his bundle, for a short while he still could hear the racket coming up from the ground floor.

Parnaoz was wakened by the silence and an unpleasant feeling, as if a rat's little velvet paws had crawled over his face. Someone was lying next to him. 'A corpse,' Parnaoz thought for some reason and sat up in horror. His heart was pounding fast and loud. A woman was lying on the bed, more like a corpse than a person sleeping. She snuffled as she breathed, her teeth were bared and the whites of her half-open eyes were visible under her eyelids.

Parnaoz was quite sure that the bed was empty and he was alone in the room before he fell asleep. The woman must have come in later, and curled up without complaining next to a strange man because it was a special bed, meant for homeless tramps, and men and women were equal and the same, sexless as well as homeless, in this bed.

The sharp cold of dawn and thc deserted streets calmed Parnaoz somewhat. He remembered later that his bundle was still in the inn, but he was not going to go back there, even if the bundle were changed into pure gold. 'If they let her, it can be a gift to that poor woman,' he thought, not that he was any better off. Even if every ship was heading for Vani, who would take him there for no money, and how could he lay hands on the money so quickly? But something else worried him more. He was going mad because he hadn't bathed; he thought he was so filthy that people were coming out of their houses to look at the source of the smell.

Parnaoz soon found a sheltered spot near the port. It was still twilight and there was not a person around. The sky was just turning red. Long, ragged clouds were dispersing, torn up as silently and unevenly as wet paper. The wet coarse sand stuck, like badly milled flour, to his feet. Before undressing, Parnaoz looked behind him a couple of times, in case someone was watching him. He timidly entered the water, but it turned out to be warm. 'Don't be afraid, it's warm,' someone called to him from the sky in Ino's voice. When he was up to his belly in water he stopped, bent down and picked a smooth pebble from the water. The pebble suddenly became heavier in his hand, as if it reclaiming weight it had left in the air. He spent some time rubbing his body with the pebble and then put it back in the sea and swam in. The water, lazy and sluggish in the darkness, moaned as he clove through it. Swimming cheered him up, lightened his mood, clearing and cleansing it. When he was swimming back to shore he was sure that from today things would go better for him. It was colder on shore than in the water. He rubbed his body down hard with both hands and quickly got dressed: only when he hung his clay disc round his neck did he notice that his sandals were missing. He hadn't taken them off for four days. He'd gone to sleep wearing his sandals, he'd come to the beach in sandals, come alone and had met nobody, but the sandals weren't there, they'd vanished, flown away. 'Perhaps I took them off somewhere else,' he thought, seizing on this senseless hope, but his hopes shattered in his hand and vanished in space as he suddenly saw himself, bare-foot and penniless, setting off on such a journey. He smiled bitterly, like a hardened tramp. 'I'm a tramp, what else?' he thought and it frightened him: he ran everywhere like a dog, sniffing every stone and turning it over, although he was well aware that there was no point looking. He couldn't find his sandals anywhere, however hard he looked. Now he longed for someone to appear so that he could ask them if they'd ever heard of sandals vanishing. He fell to his knees in despair and struck the sand with his fist. The wet sand stuck to his hands like dough. The area was horribly silent and empty. Sitting here and pounding the sand made no sense. He leapt up and ran off to the port. The shore crunched as he left it. If there was anywhere he could go, it was only the port. Now fate had placed all his life on the worn-out paving of the port, and only here would his future be decided. As soon as he entered the port he saw the dog. It was crouched on its front legs, gnawing at something, and its eyes were rolling. 'Ah, that might be who took my sandals,' thought Parnaoz joyfully and ran towards the dog. The dog was scared and fled with its tail between its legs. As it ran, it kept its eyes on the bare-footed man who was looking at the fragments it had shredded with its teeth.

That night it rained, and Parnaoz, sheltering behind the barrels, dreamed of the squashed pear. The pear was lying in an irregular circle of its own juice, and ants were attacking it. Parnaoz picked up the pear and ate it and the ants, but, although eaten, the ants somehow crawled onto his body and stung his skin. He couldn't find these ferocious little insects; he got up and scratched, as if he had scabies. 'Serves you right,' Daedalus called out, leaping from barrel to barrel. Instead of arms he had two big wings, as if he had put on a Colchian shepherd's felt cloak. He flew up, flying all round the harbour and landed on a barrel. The fishermen were bringing their nets ashore and watching Daedalus at the same time, in case he snatched their fish. 'That was wrong of you, you could have taken my son for a walk at least,' Daedalus was calling, or rather bellowing over Parnaoz's head, and Parnaoz wished the earth could swallowed him up, his face was red with shame, but he acted as if he couldn't see or hear anything. Daedalus performed one more circle over the port and dived down on the net that was packed full of fish. Someone waved an oar at him, but Daedalus dodged the oar, laughed out loud and disappeared into the azure clouds. 'At least take me with you, don't leave me behind,' a woman said to Parnaoz. The woman's teeth were showing, as were the whites of her eyes under her half-open eyelids.

Parnaoz woke up. The rain had passed. There were small shiny puddles all over the port. He was lying in one of them, but he didn't feel able to stand, he had got used to the cold and the wet. He was lying huddled up, recalling his dream. He wondered with amazement why he had dreamed of this woman if, as he thought at first, the woman's face he had seen for a moment was only a mask hiding a face, a real face on the other side. The woman reminded Parnaoz of Ino, which is why he rushed out like a madman. He imagined that Ino must be living like that woman, forsaken and abandoned by everyone, all alone, sleeping who knows where and with whom! All day Parnaoz fought back and fended off the thought, but the dream would not obey him and a forcibly repressed and silenced thought kept coming to the surface. It also added Daedalus's paralysed son to Ino. Parnaoz's heart sank as he pictured Icarus. The boy's great big eyes reflected the piece of fluff, flapping up like a crane rising from the reeds in lakes separated by a ridge. He'd always intended to take little Icarus for a walk, but had never got round to it, never released him from the prison of sadness and solitude to which the gods had abandoned him at birth. Even while at the port, Parnaoz had many times mentally intended to carry out his promise, but everything was in chaos and he forgot himself, let alone Icarus.

Parnaoz was stranded in the port of Knossos for a long time. There was no sign of a ship going to Colchis, unless they were hiding it from Parnaoz and fooling him, for in that period he had become such a sight that nobody would have let him on board, or even accepted a jug of water or wine from him. Hunger affected him badly, making him go to all sorts of places, carrying luggage, washing down boats, collecting rubbish and even rummaging through it. Once he was nearly beaten up by the dockers for undercutting their pay; another time he was chopping wood in someone's yard and the axe split open the nail of his big toe. He made a gigantic pool of blood, and he had to clean the blood-stained logs in case the owner saw. Another time he was given someone's pig to graze. The pig had a clanking chain round its neck and shook his head so hard that Parnaoz's arms were nearly torn from their sockets. The pig had little red eyes and kept trying to bite his feet, probably drawn by the rotten rag on the toe which the axe had crippled. When Parnaoz leapt to one side, laughter exploded all round, although all he could see was the pig's snout. Then Parnaoz looked for windfall pears, but couldn't find any more there. 'I expect the dog ate them,' he thought angrily. The dog's treachery made him oblivious to everything else, the mockery and the hunger. He thought only about the dog, he imagined it lurking there at every step, he tried to lure it close, but the dog was wary. Several times he cornered it, but it turned out to be stronger, it had a slippery coat and it escaped from his weakened hands like a balloon. Parnaoz bit it, choked it, scratched it, squeezed its ribs between his knees, but failed to achieve his aim. All he managed was to get a mouthful of dog hair. The dog stood to one side, licking its ruffled hair flat, its melancholy eyes watching Parnaoz, panting and disappointed, as if to say, 'What can I do, human being? I'm in a bad way myself, but I'm not going to let you eat me.' The dog was clearly sorry for him, it licked his face, it nibbled at his hands, but never actually bit although it could easily have eaten, let alone bitten Parnaoz. The dog's magnanimity made him feel even weaker and more wretched, and, his mouth full of filthy dog hairs, he wept burning tears, like a child that has been thrashed. The dog crouched down nearby, keeping its eyes on him: it found it hard to leave someone it had got used to, and it preferred to fool about with a human being than roam about on its own.

Parnaoz sensed he was perishing. This was the end, and even the thought of getting back to Vani seemed like nonsensical tricks by jokers sending him all over the place on non-existent business. But instead of shouting in anguish and asking for help, he experienced a strange relief and bliss, as if secretly, unknown to others, he was eating forbidden fruit, deceiving everybody, and his own ingenuity and cunning made him giddy with joy. He couldn't wait to be found dead, for them to trace the smell to his cubby-hole behind the barrels and realise that they hadn't fooled Parnaoz, but Parnaoz had fooled them and got the better of them. Parnaoz had little left except a few rags, which he wore as if to make people laugh, and his clay disc that certified his freedom. Who knows how his story would have ended, if one day, finally inflamed with despair and helplessness, he hadn't heard a voice coming from the mouth of a god. 'Aren't you from Vani?' the voice asked him.

'Certainly, I'm from Vani, what do you want?!' Parnaoz exclaimed, only then seeing a man's amicably smiling face.

'Nothing: I'm from Vani, too,' said the man.

Parnaoz's mind saw the light. He grasped, or rather intuited that he was facing a heaven-sent saviour, and that his joy at the thought of inevitable death was nothing but foolishness, for he had never wanted so strongly, so greedily to live. He also felt that finally his torments and sufferings were reaching an end. He was no longer abandoned, he would be allowed on board a ship, would have a share of their bread, and would be offered water from their jugs, because he was from Vani, he had a motherland, he had a fellow-countryman who felt obliged to take care of him. As soon as Parnaoz climbed aboard, he broke off the disc certifying his freedom and threw it into the sea. Only the string remained round his neck: the dry fragments of clay fell down his shirt.

All the way from Crete to Colchis he was in a state between sleep and wakefulness. He didn't feel himself being pulled into a shadier part of the boat when the full force of the midday sun was baking him. The ship kept going, pitching over the crests of the waves and, its sides stained by sun and salt, it clove the wine-coloured sea from island to island.

When he had recovered a little, Parnaoz also took up an oar. He stared hard at the boundless spaces. From time to time flesh-coloured land would poke up, its head shrouded in white sea mist, and move closer to the ship. 'Land ahoy!' a sailor would call to the land they passed on one side, and only then did Parnaoz notice the forests with their clearings, the gardens and plots fenced in with wattle, and the people working on those plots. It was still along way to Colchis. Parnaoz didn't know how long he had lain unconscious: nobody told him, and he didn't ask. He had the feeling that what had happened to him before had happened in a dream, and he had only just now awoken from this bad dream. A strong wind laid his chest bare, brought tears to his eyes, and he cheerfully put his weight to the oar handle, because this was the only way he could repay the care and concern shown him. Boundless space was wide open before him, over him was the eternal sun, and the powerful wind's warm downy hands tried to snatch him up. Everything pleased him, made him feel so carefree and happy that he dared not utter a word, he sensed that his voice would not obey him and, like a forest dweller excited by spring, he emitted just one continuous sound. He was happy, but did not share his happiness with anybody, and couldn't force it on anybody, because this was a happiness of the body, the jubilation of life restored which couldn't cross the boundaries of one being. It was not infectious and it could not multiply. But Parnaoz was smiling constantly and his lips, cracked by the salty wind, were pleasantly sore. This smile was more like the spreading of roots that had survived a crippling drought and now found themselves suddenly in well-watered soil. Parnaoz was not aware that he was smiling. The oarsmen used their eyes to point to the smiling Parnaoz and took care dipping their oars, as if they were afraid of scaring off a bird that had perched on the edge of the ship.

Parnaoz was smiling like this when the oarsman sitting next to him stuck out his arm and said, 'Over there, Absyrtus's islands.'

So far nobody on board had spoken Georgian and Parnaoz couldn't help being startled. No, it wasn't an illusion: the oarsman sitting next to him really did say in Georgian, 'Over there, Absyrtus's islands.'

Parnaoz's gaze followed the oarsman's extended arm and he saw far away a narrow scarlet strip of dry land.

'Absyrtus's islands!' he too repeated.

Suddenly his heart started racing, as if he were obliged to make a speech to the people. From this point, their sea began, or rather at those islands, their ancestors' stormy path ended. This was as far as the heat of their death-dealing passions, reflected in blood, had taken them.

'It was Absyrtus's blood that made that land so red, because he was killed by treachery,' said the oarsman, noisily wiping his nose on his sleeve. He went on: 'All glory to the man that fathered him: he splashed his own blood in his enemy's face when he had no weapon left.'

All night long Parnaoz thought about his father. The closer he got to his motherland, the surer he became that he would not find him still alive. Yet it was now that he needed him, now that he wanted to talk to him, because he had now understood many things. He now knew what Ukheiro was afraid of, why he kept his lips sealed and why he forbad his son to pick up a javelin. No javelin could put right a wrong it had done. The wrong was too big, it was enormous, and silence and compliance only made it grow and become more treacherous. 'My father was trying to spare me, to warn me,' though Parnaoz, and Ukheiro's naivety and kindness aroused in him pity and anger equally. Ukheiro had done what he set out to do, he had begotten a son, but, nevertheless, he had done a worse evil. His son could only bring misfortune because he was the seed of a defeated, mocked, crippled and frightened man. His father's guilt was passed on to his son, but it would be far harder for the son to accept and endure it, like hereditary syphilis.

One day the wind brought the smell of a marsh. 'We've arrived,' the oarsmen shouted as one, working the oars more cheerfully. Then Parnaoz saw an eagle flying above the ship, almost as high as the clouds, flapping its wings like well-carved oars. Parnaoz followed the eagle's flight and far away, in the milky mist, he saw black, jagged mountains. These were the peaks of the Caucasus. Now they really had come to the motherland. The oarsmen dropped their oars, mingled and kissed each other and, as excited as children, started a round dance on deck. The ship, left unsupervised, turned round and round, swayed like a drunk and knocked the dancing oarsmen against each other. Parnaoz, leaning overboard, twisted his neck as the Caucasus now towered in front of him, now hid behind his back.

'The Caucasus, the Caucasus, the Caucasus!' he shouted, constantly wiping away the tears which either emotion or the wind produced, so as to get a better view of the black, jagged, resplendent and majestic dance of the mountains which drew the ship towards them by some invisible cable. They too were attached by the invisible cable to the Caucasus, and they were glad to feel this eternal, fate-decreed captivity which was for them the same as freedom, because everything here was as familiar, close natural, ordinary, comprehensible and bearable as their parents.

'The Caucasus, the Caucasus, the Caucasus!' shouted Parnaoz, his whole body leaning overboard, trying to touch the sea with his hand: from its murky green depths a shoal of jellyfish emitted light, like a drowned constellation of stars.

CHAPTER FIFTEEN

THE ship did not sail into port. It passed Vani by and went up the ever-flowing river. When the oarsmen saw that Parnaoz was surprised, they laughed and told him, 'You really don't know anything, the Cretans must have kept you shut up in a wine jar.'

Ships avoided Vani's port like the plague: they were afraid of getting permanently stuck there. Where ships exhausted by distant journeys used to rock on the waves, there was now a long stretch of sand banks like a sleeping dragon, surrounded by green bubbling water. Only small boats dared to slip in and out between these dunes in order to snatch from the mouths of that sleeping dragon the remains of reckless or inexperienced ships. A vulture now perched and groomed itself on the top of a mast sticking out of the sand.

The marsh that overpowered the ever-flowing river had made the river banks dangerous. Parnaoz waded through waist-high water and climbed out wet from head to toe. Sunburnt children with swollen bellies greeted him with yells, besieged him and started washing him down, but Parnaoz pushed them away because he had nothing to give them. The children, disappointed and annoyed, painfully lashed this penniless traveller once or twice, as if by accident, on the shins with wet willow switches. Who knows how much time they had wasted waiting for him? They then turned their attention back to the ship, but nobody else disembarked. It slowly rowed upstream: until it disappeared from sight, the children shook their fists, threw stones and mud, whistled and swore at it so foully that Parnaoz broke into a sweat. He felt ashamed for the ship's crew and for the children, as if they had come out onto those musty banks just because of him. He had disappointed so many children all at once. The children, of course, didn't care whom the ship was putting ashore, where the travellers and cargo men came from who landed in these inaccessible marshes, as long as they didn't go home empty-handed. Parnaoz now stood with his back to the river. He dared not even wave to show his gratitude to the ship whose oars were now cleaving the current, as if all they wanted was to get away from the children's abuse, anger and hatred, which pursued them on both banks like a pack of wolves.

The children soon quietened down, after running about a little more and getting even muddier: they didn't give Parnaoz another glance. To them he was a thoroughly worthless and useless object. Then they got into single file and set off to the city on a path which they alone knew. That knowledge very occasionally got them the money to buy themselves a treat. Today they'd been unsuccessful, but shouting and cursing had given them such relief that their eyes shone with satisfaction; like a band of warriors they proudly strode across ground that the water had softened, contaminated and made treacherous. Parnaoz followed behind them, but soon found out that he would be walking alone. He had only to get close for the youngest of the children, the smallest, a boy with the biggest belly who had golden hair and blue eyes, to bend over, grab a fistful of mud, throw it at him and then catch up with his fellow warriors. Parnaoz dawdled, not wanting to be treated to even worse language by the children who had decided to mete him out just punishment. He would somehow find the way, he had plenty of time, he was so anxious that in any case he wouldn't reach the city before dark. He spotted an object the colour of a tree trunk covered in moss and sat down, but this odd object could not bear his weight and bent, or rather collapsed, sighing like an animate creature as it did. Parnaoz fell back, found his arms up to the elbows in earth and only then realised he had sat on an animal-hide body-bag. This was the sort of bag his ancestors had buried their dead in before hanging them from trees. He felt fear and revulsion and stood up, flailing his arms, as if the bag's remains, disturbed by his carelessness, were trying to grab him. He ran from this place, stumbling and plunging in the stagnant water. Panicked frogs leapt on each other's heads and vanished in the pools which were covered with leaves of a vitriolic blue.

It was getting dark when he reached Vani. He cleaned the mud off with a stone and waited for the wind to dry him a little. The city didn't seem to have changed at all. The streets had been repaved; in one street there was a wooden mallet covered in dried mud apparently left behind by the stone-cutters. An old Greek woman was sitting at a street corner selling pumpkin seeds. The old woman watched him pass.

Parnaoz was heading home, or rather his feet were taking him home, because he was completely destitute, stunned, no longer worried or glad, as if he were going home tired after an ordinary day's labour and nobody would be surprised to see him. But when he saw the still crowns of the twin cypresses and the lizard-coloured roof he was rooted to the spot and his knees gave way: he felt as weak as if he had only managed to get up after lying ill in bed for a whole year. He felt dizzy; his arms waved feebly in the air. Fortunately the street was deserted. Nobody saw him.

When he had recovered a little and was more or less calm he realised that he could not go in: he could not drop in so casually on a family he had not seen for ten years and which might not even exist any more. Over that time anything could have happened: what right did he have proudly to enter a house of whose fortunes he had heard nothing? It was quite possible that total strangers might open the door to him and say, 'Who are you looking for, who's missing you?' He decided that first he'd find out what had become of his kinsfolk and then go home, if he could. The house was temptingly near, the cypresses's silence was inviting, as if they were waiting for him to make up his mind. Parnaoz turned back, walked all the way to the city walls, passed the wooden mallet with dried mud stuck to it and the old Greek woman trading in pumpkin seed, who again watched him pass. He then knocked at the door of the hovel at the very edge of the city. An old woman looked out of the hovel, shading her face with a trembling hand as if she had come into the sunlight, and leant her other hand against the hovel's door, to prop up her aged, weakened body.

'What do you want?' she asked after a pause.

'Mother, would you give me a roof for the night?' Parnaoz asked her.

The old woman smiled and answered, 'How do you know that I keep open house?'

'But don't leave me outside…' he replied, somehow worried, as if the old woman were refusing.

The lady of the house was weak and alone, hence the strong smell of damp and dust which permeated the whole hovel. At first sight, though, the hovel was perfectly tidy and clean. But this was superficial: it was a misleading tidiness, typical of any old person living on their own, and it evoked both sadness and revulsion. The moment he set foot inside, an overwhelming smell of damp and mould hit his nose, but he said nothing for fear of offending the old woman. He cautiously sat down on a rug-covered divan. The divan creaked.

He looked round the hovel. There was a handful of ash in the stove, as if the old woman had thrown her combings there. A large, copper-framed mirror, cracked right across diagonally was propped over the mantelpiece. Next to the mirror was an empty cage. The cage's former inhabitant's droppings and feathers were permanently stuck to the reed perches strung inside it. In a murky corner of the hovel Parnaoz then spotted a goat standing still and silent: he was as glad of the sight of this living creature as if he had walked all this way just to see it. The goat was looking askance at him, then, like a man reassured, it nodded several times, as if to say, 'Yes, that's how it is,' and bleated.

'Damn your hide!' the old woman exclaimed.

Parnaoz smiled. There were droppings the size of olives around the goat's back legs.

'Damn you!' the old woman repeated, adjusting her headscarf which was slipping.

Parnaoz sat and smiled; he was suddenly very tired: sleepiness was shutting his eyelids and luring him in. It was a mermaid, not sleepiness: it stood in transparent water, thrusting out of the water its bare arms which shone in the moonlight, and it smiled at him. Parnaoz smiled and swayed, as if standing in cool transparent water, the tips of his toes just touching the bottom, while pulses of water impelled him towards the mermaid. But the mermaid turned to fire and flickered like flames. In a shower of sparks she slowly, imperceptibly withdrew. The old woman had lit the stove and, her sleeves rolled up, was kneading dough in a trough.

'Now I'll ask about our family,' Parnaoz thought, trying not to look at the dough stuck to the old woman's crooked fingers. He felt that he badly needed to remember something, sensing how easy this something was to remember if he made an effort to overcome the drowsiness, but he was unwilling, reluctant and, above all, afraid, without knowing why. A loud banging came from the bottom of the dough trough as if the woman was working out all her anger on one fistful of dough.

'If you want to do a kindness…' Parnaoz began, but the old woman wouldn't let him finish.

'A kindness? I want to die, man!' she yelled, silencing Parnaoz.

She carefully put a ball of dough the size of a vulture's egg into the glowing embers which she had poked, and went on: 'I expect a kindness from you: you have to kill me, because you're the only one who can.'

'Mother…' Parnaoz tried again, but his tongue failed him, he didn't know what to say. One thing was clear: he had come to stay with a madwoman. In any case, he had to be well-disposed to and reckon with this mad old woman. 'Why did I have to choose this hovel?' he thought. The old woman was squatting by the fire, bashing the dough in the glowing embers. She didn't even look at her guest, as if the guest might use the opportunity to creep up behind her and, as she squatted by the fire, stove her head in. Very soon there was a smell of fresh bread in the hovel. This smell put Parnaoz at ease. He picked out himself from the embers an ash-covered lump, blew on it and played with it, as if it were a ball, so as not to burn his hands. They both laughed. Then they sat opposite one another and ate the bread. The old woman dipped her bread in water to cool it and clumsily gnawed at it with her toothless gums for some time, then took the softened and shapeless lump from her mouth with trembling fingers and rolled it in her cupped hand. Parnaoz tried not to look at her, swallowing his bread without chewing so as to finish his ration quickly.

'Being human means being patient,' said the old woman.

Parnaoz looked up at her. The old woman stared at him in the face and her eyes shone as if she really was happy to see him, to tackle the ash-covered bread with him.

'I wasn't always like this, I had my time, too. I've had quite a few men clinging to my skirts like thorn bushes,' she giggled and covered her mouth with a trembling hand.

He couldn't help staring at her, as if she had told him something he had to remember. So it was. He had for some time realised who she was, but he resisted this knowledge, as if that might make any difference.

'When I was a girl I was famous,' the old woman was saying.

'What's your name now?' he asked, his voice quavering.

The old woman noticed his perturbed state, and she fell silent for some time, as if to spare her guest's ears. Then she uttered a moan and said, 'Now I'm a guest in this world.' Then she got up, took the empty cage off the mantelpiece, swung it and called out three times, 'Hostess, hostess, hostess!'

Black-eyed Malalo had waited for this day a long time. She was sure she would definitely live to see it, she wanted to, because her unwisely squandered life deserved its day of judgement. Today, the day that Parnaoz turned up, had to be the day of reckoning. After her daughters had thrown her out of the house, she had found plenty of time for regrets, but without Parnaoz she could not take her leave of the deceitful and ungrateful world that had aged her, weakened her and made her, everyone's hostess, dependent on others' charity. Parnaoz was the only man capable of killing her. She understood that, once she was on her own and began looking at the world through the cracks in her hovel. Weakness enlightened her mind and made apparent the wrongs she had deliberately done to her own daughter and to the strange boy whose eyes had been enlarged by love. Black-eyed Malalo was then on her feet, afraid of nothing and really thought herself to be the world's hostess, although she still remembered, as if it were yesterday, her first and last love, which vanished like a hallucination, leaving her with a parrot cage instead of a flaming torch in her hands, a love she felt compelled to pursue until she herself came to loathe it. In fact, if there was any justice, she was more entitled to it than any woman, because she had received and asked nothing but unhappiness from love: and she wouldn't ask, as long as she was allowed to have love and was given time for it. Nor could anyone know the value of love better than her. When she looked at her love, her bones ached, her heart palpitated, she was like a thrifty hostess whose guests are recklessly, boldly spinning her priceless vase in their hands. No woman could have looked after her love better than she did, because she had felt only a premonition of inevitable evil fortune coming from love. And as long as she could see her love and she knew he was next to her, she had never rebelled against this feeling, because it was generated constantly and endlessly within her. But he, her love, his head slightly bowed, his lips parted in a smile, struck dumb by desire, looked at her with depressing calm and contentment, as he carved a stick with his knife that glinted in the sun. Black-eyed Malalo was blindly, recklessly drawn to him, like the sea to the shore, so that she could blissfully, with death-like bliss, just once more fling herself on his obstinate locks of hair, his lips which were like a bright fresh wound, his chest as strong as a fortress wall, and the knife which quivered like a living thing and gleamed in the sun's rays, like a naked boy in a waterfall. Then this splendid vision faded, only too soon. It was as if mortal eyes could not bear for very long its splendour and heat. It did not fade so much as simply steal away from black-eyed Malalo: on the day before their wedding he brought her a present, a black-beaked, yellow-eyed parrot, saying, 'You couldn't want a better companion,' as he handed it to her and departed, oppressively calm and carefree. Black-eyed Malalo turned a deaf ear to the truth: she didn't believe him, she put on iron sandals, and took up an iron stick in one hand and the cage and parrot in the other and set off to find her love. Many times she was deceived, many times she mistook a likeness for the real thing, because so much searching had blurred her vision and she lost her ability to recognize things. Finding the 'beloved' with great difficulty, black-eyed Malalo nurtured him, became his doormat, licked the saliva from his mouth so he wouldn't run away, so he'd stay with her for longer, just lie down or sit down in her room and by being there justify a woman's faith that he really loved her.

When they parted, black-eyed Malalo even put money in his purse, moreover in such a way that he wouldn't notice, or know anything, finding out only when the woman was no longer with him. The 'beloved' delighted in letting her deceive him, shutting his eye with pleasure, turning round at the right moment to lace his sandals when the woman was stuffing money into his pocket. He didn't care who filled his purse, or whether he felt the weight of the money in the woman's presence, or later, on his way home. Of course, every love of black-eyed Malalo, sooner or later, ended in failure. Either her eyes opened first, or the 'beloved' took leave of his senses and, depraved by a bed that cost him nothing and by money acquired so painlessly, brazenly showed his greed and impatience: 'Since you've got money coming in,' the roguish 'beloved' would begin, 'what are you going to do with it? I suppose you take me for a donkey, do you? I'm becoming the city's laughing stock.' 'So what, so what?' black-eyed Malalo would croon, wrapped in her pink clouds of illusion. 'People can say what they like, people can say what they like.' It took her time to realise what her 'beloved' was getting at, or she didn't want to realise, because she felt best in her pink, cool and velvety clouds. But eventually she had to stick her head out, because the cloud was artificial and airless. 'You pig! You pig!' black-eyed Malalo yelled when she was back on earth. The 'pig' was striding down the street by now and beating himself in the chest very hard with his fist, like a man who has been unjustly insulted or a peasant whose vineyard has been cut down by hail.

This went on for ages. Black-eyed Malalo suffered bitter disillusionment many times, until at last she became immune to love, turned nasty and became an ever-vigilant enemy of anyone who still did believe in it. Men, equally crude, impatient and confused, succeeded one another like ghosts, days spent with these men were indistinguishable, and black-eyed Malalo hated all of them, and hatred's rough cold hands changed and crippled her soul as well as her body. Now vengeance was everything for her. Vengeance and survival, because she was permanently convinced of life's treachery. Her provocative gait, her bold remarks, her sudden inflammatory smile and her ceaseless singing served only to control a world that was out to trample on her. She hated this world and was at war with it, she mocked, belittled, tormented and polluted it, because that's how the world had presented itself to her. She had no intention of getting to know it, she wanted only her own unhappiness, and the world had torn that from her grasp and instead had burst in on her, coming in to her room with its muddy feet and, as monstrous and helpless as a naked man, got into bed with her. Black-eyed Malalo was at first intimidated by the world's splendour, but soon realised how useless it was and, carrying out her duties, was able to laugh at it and belittle it. The world was big, but more submissive and easier to tame than any one man, or rather her first man who had bloody lips and pawed the ground like a race-horse. He was bound to run away, because he could; but the world couldn't run away, it had so many feet that they tripped each other up, it stumbled and had to cling to everything so as not to fall. It needed someone to look after it, to govern it, for it was as light-headed as a youth and as feeble as an old man. 'Hostess, hostess, hostess!' shrieked the parrot (or rather, love) in its reed cage, and black-eyed Malalo laughed and wept and wept, because the world that watched her was both lamentable and laughable.

When black-eyed Malalo found out about her youngest daughter's love affair, she was horrified. An enemy, which she thought annihilated and defeated once and for all, had revived, was sending out shoots and becoming so brazen as to insinuate itself, feeding on her flesh and blood in order to get the strength to attack and ravage her once more, as if what one human being had suffered at the hands of this enemy was not enough for it. The enemy was powerful and sly. Black-eyed Malalo had to root it out promptly and thoroughly, if she wasn't to lose all she had gained from fighting this powerful, sly enemy. Black-eyed Malalo did in fact respond in time and, this time, she won, but the consequence gave her no joy: it depressed and upset her, as if it were the death of a child she had been entrusted with by a neighbour. But she didn't grieve for long at the time, she believed she had acted rightly, because Ino was her daughter and love would bring her nothing but unhappiness. Remorse came later, becoming unbearable when her older daughters threw her out of the house, telling her, 'Clear off, don't scare our customers off.' Only then was she fully convinced that she had committed a sin which could not be expiated, and she was being punished by the gods for it. This sin now obsessed her. It was her reason for living: the sin refused her the right to die because death would free her of sin and would give her rest. 'If you really love and pity me, stone me to death,' she beseeched Ino.

After her mother was driven out, Ino too left her sisters. She was sorry for her mother and wondered how she would manage on her own, but black-eyed Malalo dug her heels in and told Ino, 'Why should you bury yourself alive? I can't have you staying just to give me a drink of water.' But Ino still wouldn't leave her mother: whenever she had free time, she dropped in to see her. While black-eyed Malalo tore her hair and wailed: 'Why are you being so kind, why don't you smash my head in, snake that I am?' she swept the hovel clean, aired the bedding, made dinner, then heated water and forced her childishly obstinate mother into the tub. Her mother was small and weighed nothing, and the sight of her exhausted, pallid body with its blue veins both touched and gladdened Ino. Then they ate together and for a time they were both happy. 'Do you want me to bring the mirror?' Ino asked her prettily combed and well scrubbed mother: black-eyed Malalo dismissed the very idea of a mirror and both of them laughed heartily, like mother and daughter. Ino never came empty-handed, she always brought a dress or a headscarf, slippers or a blouse. Black-eyed Malalo was in despair, distressed that her daughter, who was so deprived, was bringing her things, but at heart she was glad and her face lit up like a child's when Ino unpacked a present for her. But black-eyed Malalo no longer wanted for anything, telling her daughter, 'I don't deserve the clothes I have,' and she put the presents in a separate trunk. She opened the trunk only when she was alone: she spread an untouched dress on the bed, put her brand-new boots at the foot of the bed and a still folded headscarf at the head, then wept for herself like a hired mourner.

'Poor black-eyed Malalo, the child you ruined has brought you things, how she loves you, how well she's treated you, get up and look before the grave takes your eyes away.' Sometimes Ino caught her mother lamenting: then she pleaded, 'Now, now, please, what have you got to cry about? As long as I'm alive, you won't want for anything.' These words made black-eyed Malalo even more upset and she banged her forehead hard against the edge of the bed until the skin was grazed and her face was covered in her decrepit blood. Ino could barely tear her hysterical mother from the bed, wash her face, put a cobweb on her grazed forehead and tell her all sorts of silly things, true and false, until she had recovered and abandoned her lament. Black-eyed Malalo listened with bated breath to her daughter's tittle-tattle, her face gradually grew calmer, as if what her daughter was telling her intrigued her. But just when Ino was sure that she had calmed her down, Malalo would ask: 'Why have you forgiven me?' She asked in such a tone that Ino felt weak, as if she too were about to cry and sob with her head buried in her mother's lap. 'What is there to forgive? You're my mother and I do for you what you did for me.' But black-eyed Malalo shook her head stubbornly and insisted, 'Why have you two forgiven me, why didn't you and Parnaoz smash my head in?' Ino was so pleased by the mention of Parnaoz's name that she didn't interrupt this time and, as long as black-eyed Malalo wailed and lamented, she kept her head in her lap and, imagining Parnaoz coming out of the sea, shivering with cold, her heart was filled with happiness. Black-eyed Malalo was the only person on earth she could talk to about Parnaoz. They mentioned him almost every time they met, and kept telling each other what they knew about this boy, always so surly and kind-hearted, whom they both recalled as if he were a fairy-tale hero.

'I opened my eyes and there was Parnaoz,' black-eyed Malalo was recounting yet again how she first met Parnaoz.

'The same day?' asked Ino, as if she didn't know or hadn't heard this.

'Yes, the same day,' replied black-eyed Malalo, continuing, 'He looked so terrified, it was hard not to laugh.'

'He was embarrassed, not afraid,' Ino said, standing up for the little boy. What she said secretly to herself was, 'He wasn't afraid or embarrassed, he loved me and was looking for me.'

They had heard about Parnaoz leaving for Crete, but they never doubted that he was bound to come back. They both expected him, for they felt that he was the only person entitled both to punish and to forgive them. The more time passed, the weaker black-eyed Malalo became, the harder it was to bear the waiting, and the more she longed for death, since she and the world were now at odds with each other and no longer needed one other. In any case, not a drop remained of her prolonged and happy-go-lucky hospitality. Huddling in the hovel of old age and weakness, black-eyed Malalo recalled her love again, his head slightly bowed, his lips parted in a smile, mute with desire, looking at her with oppressive calm and contentment as he carved a stick with a knife that glinted in the sun. She recalled him, but instead of an evil, inevitable unhappiness, she experienced a vertiginous, calming bliss and contentment, because in her imagination only this contentedly smiling man, as restless as a horse or divinity, could extract her from the locked prison of the world where he had once imprisoned her. That was the sole reason for this man or divinity to exist, but black-eyed Malalo could no longer remember his face, and when she thought about him she always visualized Parnaoz. For her, the two of them had become one person, an eternal creature which every woman saw in different guises but perceived in the same way. Black-eyed Malalo understood too late that she had expelled the goddess of love from her establishment and done so because she was sorry for her daughter, or rather envied her because that day she had become convinced that waiting was pointless, that time had rushed by to the sound of a parrot's endless shrieks. Now the shrieking parrot was all she had to prove that love had existed for her, too, a love which now, after so many years of futile searching, shone in her own daughter's eyes. Black-eyed Malalo felt jealous. Jealousy made her spiteful and confused, it broke and aged her prematurely. Her sin was getting larger and larger, like a ship coming closer to shore. This ship was to bring the man who would judge her and pardon her, who would give her permission to die and let her slip away without regret from the murk of this world, as empty and as unprofitable as the cage with its dried droppings. And now her waiting was over. Her judge was sitting before her, calm and merciful.

'Oh, Parnaoz, Parnaoz!' black-eyed Malalo almost groaned: he wasn't at all surprised at being addressed by name in this stranger's hovel, because he was now used to the idea that this hunchbacked, tiny old woman with no eyebrows and a broken mouth was once the famous black-eyed Malalo, whose singing people from other cities used to come to listen to, people who would not hesitate to pay a whole year's earnings for a bunch of grapes from this beautiful woman's hand. In Parnaoz's imagination, too, there had never been a woman more beautiful and powerful than black-eyed Malalo. There was a time when he too would have stood before her, his knees trembling with fear and his lips sealed with anxiety.

'Mother, old mother, how are you?' Parnaoz asked, still anxious.

'Now you can kill me!' said black-eyed Malalo.

'What are you saying?' exclaimed Parnaoz with genuine amazement. 'This is no time to die!' He inspected the hovel as if he had left the elixir of life there ten years ago and was now trying to recall where exactly he had put it. Then he saw the goat again. The goat had white eyes, ringed in red, and was screwing them up as if trying to remember something.

'If you want to live, kill me!' said black-eyed Malalo. She forced herself to smile and added, 'Good guests should know when to leave.'

Black-eyed Malalo was ready to die. Her waiting was over. Here in this little hovel, apart from the guest, nobody and nothing was stopping her. This last visitor would soon be off, and she would be alone on her bed with its wobbly legs, she would turn her back, shrunken by old age, to the hovel's mouldy emptiness, and would cuddle up forever to death, the most powerful and loyal of men that she had ever met in her life's long path. She saw death again: in the darkest corner of the hovel his cold, ice-coloured eye shone, enlarged by desire, but black-eyed Malalo wasn't in the least frightened. On the contrary, like the leader of a caravan who has completed all his preparations in good time, she was overwhelmed by a deep sense of peace. Or a bride, rather than a caravan leader, who has let the last day of her maidenhood slip by unnoticed while she is busy getting dressed for her wedding.

'The master has come!' said black-eyed Malalo.

It seemed to Parnaoz that she meant him, and he looked at her in amazement. Black-eyed Malalo was looking blankly somewhere beyond him, the light in her eyes had gone out, and in that one moment she really was like a dying old woman. For some reason he recalled Philamon, looking up with reddened pleading eyes, irrevocably frightened by the death which had suddenly befallen him. 'She's dying on me, too,' he thought with a shudder. 'I'll do it on my own, on my own,' she gabbled as she let Parnaoz lead her to her bed.

'I thank you, gods, for sending someone who will look after my poor Ino,' said black-eyed Malalo, and lay across the bed.

She had shrunk so much that you would have thought someone had put a bundle of dirty washing on the bed. Parnaoz looked in amazement. 'Sending someone who will look after Ino,' she had said, as if he had come to Vani for Ino's sake, but the mention of Ino alarmed him, as a housewife busy chatting to a neighbour is alarmed when she remembers she has put milk on to boil over the fire. Black-eyed Malalo was worried, she feebly threw her neck back, her eyes had an ominous shine and she moved her lips, cracked and unnaturally taut, like a rabbit's. But Parnaoz could no longer make out anything of what she was saying, although the dying woman was obviously addressing him. Several times she asked him: 'If you're really Parnaoz, why don't you kill me?' He was overcome by pity for this unfortunate woman, and watched over her, his arms folded. What should he do? How could he help? He had to stand there and wait. No, he had to go, because leaving was his only obligation. He felt he wasn't needed in this hovel where there was room only for death and the dying. His being there prevented a marriage, the only thing that would bring the dying woman relief. The only thing that held him back was the dying woman's momentary lucidity, but this lucidity made the ending more terrible and heart-rending. He felt that he would have new griefs and new sins on his conscience. Whether he now left black-eyed Malalo or not, he would be in the wrong, and this sin was allotted to him by fate, which had brought him so far and made him turn back from his home so that he could commit it. Now he had to choose what would be better for black-eyed Malalo. For her it was better that he should leave, because his presence was prolonging her life, and prolonging her life only meant prolonging her suffering.

He bent over the bed, kissed the dying woman's sweaty forehead and told her, 'Perhaps you should sleep, and I'll bring you a healer in the morning.' As it said it, he knew he would neither bring a healer nor find black-eyed Malalo alive again, even if he had the courage to enter this hovel. He was lying, deceiving a dying woman, and he hated himself… Suddenly black-eyed Malalo extended her hand like a hook as he bent over the bed, and grabbed his neck; with a strength unimaginable for a decrepit, dying old woman, she drew him towards her. Parnaoz's neck hurt, and he was repelled.

'Swear to me that you'll look after Ino,' groaned black-eyed Malalo, breathing a hot, death-like vapour into his face.

'I swear to you,' he replied without hesitating, more to calm the dying woman so that she would quickly let go of him and not breathe that hot, sticky vapour over him. At the time he did not take on the full import of his words, he just felt, in fact was, compelled to reply on the spot, as he did. Black-eyed Malalo let go of his hand and he couldn't help shuddering as if some part of his body, whose existence he had not suspected hitherto, had suddenly been amputated by an axe. He had left the hovel when he heard black-eyed Malalo's voice.

'Ino loves you!' she called.

Parnaoz went next to the cemetery. To his astonishment, the grave where he thought he had buried the stone head of Ino was easy to find, but, as he thought, it had been neglected and was overgrown with grass. He tore up the grass, dry and as sharp as a knife-edge, and it then looked more like a grave. His slashed palms throbbed pleasantly, he felt at ease and cheerful. Then he lay down on grave he had tidied, as he did in childhood, and put his lips to the earth, dried up with the heat and crumbled, exclaiming, 'Your mother's died, girl: your mother.'

And, lying on the grave, he fell asleep.

In the morning, setting off for his father's house, he realised that Ukheiro was no more. The house was empty, as if his father had left it so for his son. Not that Ukheiro had ever walked round his own house, for he was confined to one room: but while he lived, the whole house was charged with his silence, everyone was hushed, waiting for one of his sudden rages. Now the tense silence and expectation had vanished, replaced by an inexpressive emptiness. The emptiness had waited for Parnaoz, and he had to fill it: his time had come.

He entered Ukheiro's room and the first thing he saw was the low three-legged stool on which he had sat for hours, months, years, without uttering a sound, holding his breath, watching with delight as the sail-sized canvas covering his father's shattered legs became more and more colourful. Now the canvas had been folded in four and was placed on the bed, like an enormous book. The last javelin Ukheiro had thrown was still stuck in the wall, but now grape-juice sweetmeats were hanging on it to dry, dusted with white sugary powder. He tore one down and bit into it. 'I made them,' said Kaluka joyfully and clutched him to her breast.

'When did he die?' Parnaoz asked her.

'Who? Your father? Five years ago,' Popina replied, smiling at him.

Popina didn't know what to do for her brother. Sudden joy had so stupefied her that she flew rather than walked, fluttering about, in a hurry to show him everything which, in her opinion, he must be glad to see.

'Come and see your bed now… You remember this chair? Look, the pitcher you broke…' Popina kept twittering, not noticing that her brother was standing still, slowly, diffidently chewing a dry piece of sweetmeat. Suddenly Popina clapped her hands 'Actually, black-eyed Malalo died last night. You remember her, don't you,' she asked him. He nodded.

This was all in the past for Parnaoz, apart from anything else, he had brought this death and, if he'd been delayed or met with some hazard, black-eyed Malalo would still be alive. He was her unwitting killer, and when Popina said, 'Black-eyed Malalo has died,' he shuddered like a murderer who didn't think that the corpse he'd hidden would be found so soon. 'Perhaps somebody saw me last night,' he thought, now genuinely afraid, because he did not know how he could defend himself if anyone pointed the finger at him and accused him of murder.

'From today I'll lie on my father's bed,' he said, as if no better or safer refuge existed in this world. 'I don't need bedding, I'll cover it with this,' he said abruptly and put his hand on the sail-sized canvas.

Popina's smile froze on her face: she hunched her shoulders, as if she were feverish, then threw back her head, as if fending off an annoying wasp; then she smiled again, but differently, pallidly, sadly, and said, 'Certainly, whatever you like.'

Only then did Parnaoz pay attention to his sister. Popina had aged, her hair now had long white streaks, her face had shrunk, the skin on her neck was chapped and slack, as if she had not just lived, but endured or survived over the last ten years. Parnaoz was touched. He put an arm round his sister, pulled her close and sat her on his knees. 'How are you, sister, how is your life?' he whispered into her ear and kissed her temple. His lips felt the vein pulse and for some reason he felt even more sorry for her. Popina realised that her brother pitied her, his sympathy softened and weakened her, and she put her head on his shoulder, like a sleepy child taken into somebody's arms. Kaluka put the bent fingers of her left hand on her cheek, propped the elbow with her other hand, bent her head a little to the side and, her eyes full of tears, looked at the siblings' affection, like a sick woman looking at a tree in blossom.

CHAPTER SIXTEEN

THAT evening Popeye and Ziara came. Ziara was an orphan raised on charitable neighbours' leftovers and hand-me-downs. Before she met Popeye, she would spend a night with one neighbour, the next with another, because everyone took turns using her as domestic labour. She was a tiny woman: she could have hidden under a buffalo pat. Wherever she was sent, she would take someone's child by the hand, thinking that this would make her look less ugly. Her neighbours were sorry for this silent, but deft girl and were so used to her that they felt something like love for her. Ziara loved everybody, considered everybody to be her family, so that, whoever she was with, she would always cheerfully get down to work. When the city was still asleep, Ziara was on her feet and busy, seeing to the cattle, fetching water, then taking a long-handled broom and sweeping the veranda and the courtyard, singing as she worked. 'It's daylight,' people would say when they heard Ziara singing.

Ziara first saw Popeye in the street, or rather she first heard the jingling sack: this strange noise made her turn towards the street and left her permanently astonished: Popeye was coming down the street, his head high, proud and majestic. It was in this district that Popeye had chosen a small remote hovel where he moved in straight away, as soon as he had sold his two-storey house to Hey-Boy, and had handed back to her mother his two-yards-tall spouse, that friend of death Patu. For the time being, Popeye preferred to live like this. Lately, so many various troubles had happened to him that he himself was surprised to have survived them all intact. He had become the talk of the city, and tongues never stopped wagging, but this was his fault: he had overstepped the mark, got carried away and pranced about too early. Everything that happened to him was thanks to his father-in-law and uncle: his own family had turned against him, although it was the city that blamed him for his father-in-law's death and his uncle's emigration. They said he had chopped up his father-in-law like a cow, he had sent his uncle over the ocean, and there he was like a sore thumb in his two-storey house, they said, begetting still-born children. God knows what else they were making up or would make up about him, if he hadn't moved out in time. The city gossip still didn't die down, although they needed something else to talk about.

What was important was that the palace was silent. It still opened its doors to Popeye and paid him his salary, but this endless gossip might well have annoyed them and they might not have put up with it any more and one fine day they might have asked, 'Who is this Popeye, after all?'

That was what his enemies wanted, hoped for, and they couldn't rest until they squashed this particular cricket against the wall, should it ever, just for an instant be stupid and cowardly enough to crawl out of its refuge. Now he had better stand aside and play the innocent. He had to avoid his house and the wine cellar, because both got on people's nerves, and that was why people had turned against him. But if a king's man were seen in this wreck of a hovel, wouldn't that stop people gossiping? Now would they stop talking? 'Well, would you believe he's got nothing but a frayed rug and a jug with a broken spout?' No, his enemies wouldn't rest, they wouldn't let him off so easily, but they'd have to bite their tongues. At worst, they'd laugh at him: 'How are the mighty fallen!' But Popeye could cope with that: mockery was nothing to be afraid of. He could take care of everything, put everything right as long as he had the right to carry his leather sack. Nobody could take that right away, not even Oqajado, for whom could the king trust more, who could serve him better? In actual fact, he was considered as just another ordinary employee in the palace: Oqajado probably didn't even know he existed. But in the people's eyes, Popeye represented the palace and exuded the smell of royalty. Tomorrow they would start chatting about something else: what had to pass would pass and Popeye's star would shine in heaven once again. People would be outraged about a dead father-in-law and a missing uncle only while the news was fresh, but they had to take account of the living man, whether they liked him or not. Popeye knew that and so put up with his life in his mouse-ridden hovel. 'That's agreed then; that's agreed then; that's agreed then,' accompanied the jingling from hovel to palace: he was now planning to get back his two-storey house and the forty-step cellar, too.

When he was told in the palace that he could go, that he wasn't needed any more that day, he set off for the forty-step cellar, descending the steps as if they belonged to him again and he had come to inspect. 'Hello, how are things, you haven't added any steps, have you?' he would remark to Hey-Boy, and then count every single barrel, stroking the rounded sides of some, tapping some with his fist, checking the hoops on others, like a careful, thrifty owner. Hey-Boy somehow considered himself obliged to invite Popeye to sit down and then personally offer him a dew-cold jar of wine, as cool as a woman's arm. Later, at midnight, Hey-Boy and his boy waiter, whom he called Bakha, would have great trouble getting Popeye, drunk on his free wine, up the forty steps of the staircase: they pointed him in the direction of home, and gave him a push, as if launching a raft into the water, and Popeye would sail off, swaying over the rapids of his drunkenness, following his instinct, as a raft follows the current. Trying to break through the fences, dogs barked at him. 'The butcher's had another skinful,' grumbled the people of Vani, woken up and alarmed by the row, as they turned over in bed. But Popeye went on, staggering, yelling to spite his enemies. 'Long live our king!' he called to the heavens and cursed the dogs tearing at the fence and their owners, dead or alive. But the nearer he got to his hovel, the worse his feelings of loneliness and abandonment became. Nobody was waiting for him there, neither friend nor foe. There was just one bed, one jug with a broken spout and one frayed rug. Sometimes he lay on top of the rug, sometimes underneath it, depending on the weather. He opened the door with a kick. 'Damn whoever built you!' he cursed the hovel, and threw himself onto the bed without undressing. He could never forget the advantages of the good life. But time was flying by at fabulous speed, or dying, like an oil lamp brought into the wind: suddenly finding himself in the dark, Popeye could now only think and dream of a good life. These thoughts and dreams were lacerating him. He lay there, his eyes wide open, on his bed of loneliness, and thought and thought, but his thoughts got him nowhere: they had neither flesh nor bone, neither scent nor taste. He was thinking about what he had thought about before, and even acted on, but had, in the end, given up. Now Popeye had new grounds for thought. He realised this later, when he was more or less used to his new circumstances. He thought about Ino: he choked with rage, his mind clouded over, thinking of the moment of weakness which this ugly, skinny girl had caused him. Only Ino made Popeye feel inferior, if just for a minute, but for that instant Ino had dominated him. He let her do so, he almost kissed her feet, offered her slippers and a dress: worse, he had even sung to her. The singing infuriated him most, his ears still rang with his own rasping voice, and gave him no peace. He thought about her as someone flogged thinks about the flogger; but one night he woke up in a sweat, drained the jug with the broken lip in one gulp, then ran the length of the city and, out of breath, turned up at Ino's door. When he got his breath back he gruffly barked out, 'Marry me!' as if he was passing on someone's message. Ino frowned at first, then gave way to laughter, finally got control of her voice and told him just as gruffly and scornfully, 'You're completely out of your mind.' Popeye turned back without a word: even before he'd come out he knew that his nocturnal visit was going to end like this.

Ino's refusal convinced him once more that more haste meant less speed. There was a time for everything, and sooner or later the right time would come. He had to wait, and so he did. Every morning he slung his sack of tools over his shoulder and went down the street jingling towards Oqajado's palace. The blood of the people of Vani froze when they heard the noise, they herded in their children who had come to the courtyards to play, they locked their doors and waited with trembling hearts for this unpleasant jingling to fade. The only person glad to hear this sound was Ziara. She liked it because it announced the coming of Popeye. When she heard the sack jingling, she would get excited, her heart would start pounding, she would tidy her hair, smooth down her dress, turn her back to the street which Popeye would come down. She raised so much dust with her long-handled broom that she was covered from head to toe and invisible to Popeye. 'I'll drop dead on the spot,' Ziara thought, as he came down the road, proud, head held high, like a ram leading its flock. He didn't even know she existed, and he would have taken no notice of a dishevelled girl whose dress was burnt looking after someone else's fire. But Ziara thought that Popeye had eyes only for her, that he patrolled this street morning and evening to see her and, stirred by a vague happiness and fear, she couldn't settle all day, until the jingling of the sack came back. Her world had shrunk, so that just the jingling of iron and sweeping up dust were enough to fill it. However late he returned, she could not get to sleep and lay down on a kind neighbour's veranda, waiting for the longed-for sound which marked for her the onset of night and allowed her to sleep. Until then she didn't even yawn or feel drowsy, however tired she was or late the hour. From one jingle to another jingle of the sack Ziara got on with her work or slept. This sound was her sun and her moon, because she loved Popeye. Love so emboldened her that what would never have crossed her mind seemed now the most natural thing in the world. 'Never mind, he'll have to bend down to kiss me,' she thought as she swept the yard or carded wool. Love changed her ideas, gave them new colour, made them more cunning. In her thoughts she did whatever she wanted, said 'Good morning' to Popeye as he walked down the street, called to him and waved at him, then she would enter his hovel, sweep it and clean everything; she would meet him at the door when he came back, curtsey and wish him good night. He would bow in return and respond to her greeting. So in her thoughts they were good friends.

These thoughts finally made her so light-headed that they took her over, and one fine day she really did slip into Popeye's hovel. She didn't need to look closely to see that everything was filthy. She clapped her hands and rushed around, as if she were joining boys and girls dancing. Coming here was not just right, it was necessary. Didn't she clean other people's houses and yards? If Popeye had been at home she would, of course, have gone back: an unmarried girl couldn't visit a strange man. But who knew better than Ziara when she would or would not find Popeye at home? Soon it was all so clean that you could have eaten off the floor. Afterwards Ziara went every day to clean Popeye's hovel and was so used to her new duties that she entirely lost her feeling of fear. She held a broom in one hand if she was beating the rug, and sang as she did. As tidiness is more obvious than filth, Popeye soon noticed the changes in his hovel; if he was sober, he held back, not wanting unnecessary fuss; if he was drunk when he came home, he swore and cursed loudly so that the neighbours would hear, 'Who's interfering in my house, who comes here tidying things up; I've never asked anyone to. If I catch them at it, I'll break their ankles and then let's see them creep into other people's places and poke around in other people's trunks!'

'You've no reason to swear at us,' the neighbours said the next day. 'If someone really does come, and they are human, then keep a look-out and catch them.'

Popeye did keep a look-out and caught Ziara. She was wearing a sleeveless dress and when she threw back her hair with the hand that held the broom, so as to see who had come into the hovel, Popeye was struck by the sight of her black armpit: he pressed her against the door.

Dishevelled, her face contorted, looking even uglier, Ziara ran out of the hovel: only then was Popeye struck by what he'd done. He spat and rubbed his lips, which were imbued with and swollen by Ziara's virgin lips. Imagining her dishevelled face poisoned his mood, horrified him and, whatever he thought about, he couldn't forget the sight of her exposed, blotched breast and her viscous eyes. He paced the hovel for some time, but couldn't resist the temptation and set off to Hey-Boy's cellar. The momentary passion that had flared up for just one moment in his body, like a gale blowing through a room with no walls, was enough to change him, to awake his conscience. He now differed as much from the Popeye who, with his sack over his shoulder, walked to work like a ram, as Ziara differed from Ino.

Ziara was very soon in the grove of the departed, lying on her back on the boggy, softened earth, looking at the leather body-bags swinging in the breeze, at the few remaining trees, unable to feel the damp and the cold penetrating her, as they did the earth. She was happy and unhappy at the same time: it seemed to her that now she had to lie down forever, to become part of the marsh, be overgrown with moss, covered with fungus and mould and wait. What for, she didn't know and could never understand, because the inevitable had happened, she had undergone what had to be undergone, and it was so unimaginable and so divine that she didn't think it could be repeated, or that she could ever repeat it. Then she clearly heard Popeye's voice, which she had never heard before, and couldn't help lifting her head. In her imagination he could have had no other voice. Popeye seemed to be calling to her, the voice repeated several times, 'Get up, or you'll catch cold.' But Popeye at that moment was in Hey-Boy's cellar, banging his fist on the table, and yelling, 'Long live Philamon, my father! A real man ought to have a few bastards to show for his life!' Hey-Boy smiled and nodded in agreement.

The damp and the cold were, in the end, too much, and Ziara started to shiver. She clung to the hallucinatory voice like someone sucked down in a quagmire clinging to a branch of a wing-nut tree. She sought a pretext to go home, or rather to Popeye's place. She knew she would go back, for if she didn't see him, she'd die and be left for all time in this marsh. 'He can beat me,' thought Ziara. 'If he wants to, he'll beat me, if he doesn't, he won't.' The thought became obsessive: 'Perhaps Popeye is looking for me: I've left him and run away, as if what happened was his fault. God knows how worn out he is looking for me.' But in her heart of hearts she very much wanted to live, for Popeye to see her and take her in, even if he chased her out with a stick like a stray goose, in front of everyone. She thought for so long that she ended by believing Popeye was racing around at breakneck speed, looking for her. Then she thought it time to leap to her feet: she galloped off to the hovel, without even shaking down her dress. You'd have thought she was a scarecrow that the wind had blown out of a vineyard to flap through the air at will. When she got near the hovel, she was overwhelmed by fear: how could she show herself to Popeye, what would she say to him? But she plucked up courage and peeped through a crack: the hovel was empty. She breathed a sigh of relief and strode in. Now she was sure that he'd gone out looking for her. She sat on the bed, not meaning to stay, just to get her breath back, until Popeye returned. She'd run a great distance without a rest, and her legs throbbed. The sack of tools was lying on the bed and she realised why her back hurt so badly when Popeye had laid her on the bed. She touched the sack very gingerly, but it still jingled, like a wild animal growling in its sleep. She smiled at the sound and suddenly felt sleepy: it was night time for her. She moved the sack to the head of the bed and laid her head on it.

By now Popeye had bored Hey-Boy's last customers with his endless babbling, arguing, and forcing wine on them: they put up with him because they were afraid of him. 'Are any of you cleaner than me, eh?' remonstrated Popeye, and when they tried to calm him by answering, 'We're all the same,' he raised his voice even louder, and he yelled at them, 'Don't argue with me!'

He was hopelessly drunk, but wouldn't let go of the glass, although he couldn't take any more; he belched when he tried to swallow any wine, spilled it over himself, but persisted in calling for more: 'Everyone's got to drink to my father Philamon!' Finally they succeeded in luring him up the cellar's forty steps, sent him on his way, and then they all ran off in different directions.

'So you've left me, have you? I'll make you sorry!' Popeye bellowed to the sleeping city, and wended his way, staggering home to his creaking, decrepit hovel. When he entered and saw Ziara asleep on the bed, he was as glad as if a dream had finally come true. He even sobered up, sat at the foot of the bed and bent over to put a hand on her thigh. Ziara squirmed, stretched out and opened her eyes. Popeye had another human being next to him, as real, live, fragrant and hot as freshly baked bread.

'Hello, birdie!' he said to her lovingly.

In his drunken state and in the dark, Ziara struck him as no different from any other woman, but when he opened his eyes and saw on his numbed shoulder her face, washed out in the cold first light of day, staring at him in fear and reverence, his loathing and anger came back. 'Right, clear off!' he roared at her and, before she could get out of bed, he flung her off as violently as if he was smashing an empty pitcher against the wall. Ziara could barely get up, and, not saying a word, slipped out of the hovel. But she didn't go far: where could she go, when her spirit was in this hovel? Love had made her stubborn and obstinate: she did not forsake her duties, she went on sweeping, tidying, doing the washing, cooking and then, sitting on the bed, her hands on her lap, she waited for him to come home. She was not afraid of beatings or death. Death at Popeye's hands was bliss, and she never showed any desire to escape daily thrashings. To her mind, everything was happening as it should, as Popeye wanted, and whatever he wanted meant more than life to Ziara. Anyway, what did Popeye's beatings matter? Wasn't he then touching her? What did his scolding and cursing matter? They belonged to her, they were addressed by him to her, to nobody else. They were together and it didn't matter what this togetherness might be called. Seeing Popeye come home, drunk and bestial, gave Ziara genuine joy. 'Hello, birdie,' he would call at the gate and go up to her, his arms spread out, as if the woman timidly sitting on the edge of the bed with her hands on her lap, waiting for him, was one woman, and the woman whose head lay on his numb shoulder in the morning was another. He loved the first one, he was glad of her, because he needed her as a cat is needed in a house ridden with mice; he loathed the second one, because she was superfluous, like a fifth leg on a horse. Ziara soon understood and even accepted the difference: from the moment Popeye went to sleep to the moment he woke up she considered herself the happiest woman in the whole world; her head lay on Popeye's bright white shoulder and his alcoholic breath and hot vapours blew into her face. 'I wish he were so drunk that he never got sober,' she dreamed, as she lay there with bated breath, looking at him as a child looks at new boots at the head of its bed, boots which to be put on in the morning and proudly shown off, creaking and squeaking, to his playmates.

As time passed, the two of them got used to living together like this. At night they wore themselves out cuddling and caressing, but in the morning Ziara, hurled against the wall of the hovel, just like a smashed pitcher, ended up in pieces on the ground, yet, by some magic, instantly became whole again, with not even a crack to show for it. Full of energy, singing as she worked, she began tidying up the hovel. Popeye, his sack slung over his shoulder, strode to Oqajado's palace, jingled for all the city to hear, proud, challenging and striking, like a ram leading its flock.

Before the women had time to discuss Ziara's adventures, Parnaoz instantly realized who she must be and greeted her like an old friend.

'Just ask her what her family was called,' Popeye told him, his eyes indicating Ziara.

But Ziara didn't wait to be asked and said, 'My family were farmers, but my belt is Kama's.' Popeye burst out laughing and scolded her, 'Shut up, you stupid idiot, if the king heard that, he'd show you Kama's belt!' Ziara's face turned red with happiness, she even seemed pretty, bowing her head and waving her little legs in the air.

Popeye had barely changed at all, he did not seem to have aged, but constant drinking had made his face puffy and his neck even scraggier. When he first came in, he greeted everybody coldly, as drunkards tend to when they're sober. Parnaoz thought he must bear a grudge, and rightly so, since Parnaoz had wanted to kill him. But when wine was brought, Popeye cheered up, became talkative and invited everyone to dine. 'If we don't speak, this wine won't say a thing, even it we sit here till morning.' Ziara sat, her head bowed, next to Popeye, and whatever he said, she smiled, as if they had agreed to this in advance.

'Stop now, don't drink so much!' Popina said anxiously. 'Parnaoz has been travelling, drink some other time, the wine won't run away.'

'You'll be the death of me!' yelled Popeye, 'Don't tear the breast out of my mouth.'

'He hasn't changed,' Kaluka said to Parnaoz.

Smiling, Parnaoz looked Popeye in the eye: he was glad not to have killed this scraggy-necked, puffy-faced man. What difference would it have made, what would it have put right, weren't there lots of Popeyes? Parnaoz would only have added one more senseless, futile sin to his sins.

'It's all temporary, it's all temporary. I own your weight in money, but that's not the point,' Popeye was saying.

Parnaoz meant to say that what happened wouldn't cause trouble to anyone, that now he was back he would stand by Popeye, but he was embarrassed. He thought that if he said as much, the women would think he was drunk and gone soft in the head. 'I'll tell him later, there'll be time,' he thought. Just then, something brushed against his leg and a dog barked under the table. He wasn't frightened, but couldn't help moving back on his chair and looking under the table. Ziara was there on all fours, smiling and barking at him. Popeye banged his fist on the table and laughed out loud. Kaluka and Popina smiled: Parnaoz realised that this was familiar entertainment. He felt very sad, not knowing why.

'All right, stop it, you stupid idiot,' Kaluka called to Ziara, who was still barking under the table.

'Let her bark, let her bark!' shouted Popeye.

'Shubu's come,' said Popina.

Ziara's barking and the mention of Shubu reminded Parnaoz of his childhood. Popeye tore the head off a grilled fish and put the whole head in his mouth, then he picked off a piece of bread and dipped it in salt. Shubu was now in the doorway, holding a pronged stick, and his snow-white beard covered his chest. Parnaoz didn't know how he came to be next to Shubu. He could feel the beard, it smelled of wet flour, and Parnaoz was weeping with joy. 'Forgive me, Shubu, forgive me, I never remembered you all those ten years,' Parnaoz mumbled, his face pressed against this clean fragrance and whiteness: he was sure that from now on they would always be together, loving one another.

A whole month passed without Parnaoz leaving the house. He lay motionless on his father's bed, staring at the ceiling and recalling his life so far. Popina was heartbroken to see her brother stretched out on their father's bed, when he had only just come back; she thought that Ukheiro had come back to life, so much did Parnaoz resemble his father. 'Get up, I beg you, don't just lie there,' Popina pleaded. But Parnaoz was so tired and so much longed to rest, to enjoy the family's scents and cosiness that, for all his respect for his sister, he would rather die than get up from a bed steeped in the smell and warmth of his father's body. He could feel his father, and that wrapped him in a pleasant and safe haze, as if he had gone back to the distant and mysterious cosmos from which he had once upon a time come to earth. He could live peacefully in this haze, because nobody could use Ukheiro's infallible javelin and popping eyes to drag him out of it. During this month he got up only once, when black-eyed Malalo was being buried and the funeral procession passed their house. When Kaluka called out, 'They're burying her,' Parnaoz stayed for some time lying motionless, finding it hard to leave this haze, as pleasant as sleep in the morning. He kept deceiving himself, saying 'It's still early, no need for me to hurry, in the time it takes them to get to our house I can get up ten times over.' After that reassurance, came 'Look at the time! I was too late when Kaluka said that Malalo was being buried.' But when he finally took it in, he leapt off the bed like a madman: he might just catch sight of Ino in the distance. Black-eyed Malalo's seven daughters, however, all had their faces covered in black mourning clothes, and the seven were so alike that, had black-eyed Malalo had come back to life, even she would have found it hard to tell them apart. But one of those seven women in black was Ino, and if Parnaoz couldn't see her, Ino could see him. That in itself was great happiness.

Who knows when Parnaoz might have left the house, if he hadn't had a dream? The dream made him forget his tiredness and got him off the bed. He dreamed of his parents. He had never actually seen his mother, but he didn't doubt for a moment, in the dream or afterwards, that the beautiful young woman who came in to see him with Ukheiro was his mother. Both his mother and Parnaoz behaved as if they saw each other every day, neither was surprised, and neither groaned during this sudden encounter. Ukheiro had put a hand like a lion's paw on the shoulder of this beautiful woman who looked as if she ought to be his daughter, rather than wife. Not that this was surprising, either: his mother had been very young when she died and so would always be young in dreams, too.

'I dreamed last night that our parents came and reproached me for not coming to see them,' Parnaoz told Popina in the morning.

'Our parents?' she asked, or rather shrieked.

'Yes, mother, too…' he said. 'I've got to go.'

'Where?' she asked, utterly taken aback. 'Where do you have to go?'

'To the cemetery,' he replied.

'Thanks be to God!' Popina breathed a sigh of relief.

He and Popeye went to the cemetery. Parnaoz had wanted to go alone, and insisted he had to find his parents' burial place by himself. So Popina, who had got herself ready well in advance, had to take off her street clothes and stay at home. Popeye bumped into Parnaoz at the door and, as soon as he found out where his uncle was going, announced that he had managed to get a day off work solely to accompany Parnaoz on his walk there. Popeye had been drinking and Parnaoz was reluctant to say no to him. But his mood was spoiled: things were no longer going as he had planned. This drunkard, whose birth had once brought him unbounded joy and whom he later wanted to kill, seemed to exist only to ruin everything Parnaoz did. After ten years nothing had changed, for they themselves hadn't changed: Parnaoz still walked as timidly and nervously by

Popeye's side, feeling that Popeye was forcing him along, because he really did not want to go to the cemetery any more. Their visit today would be nothing more than the usual dutiful visit to the departed. But Parnaoz had ascribed far more importance to this day. For one thing, this was the first time he was going to meet his parents and talk to the dead. This was such an extraordinary, mysterious and pure occasion for him that nobody could share it, or was entitled to share it. For another thing… this was the day that Parnaoz had finally returned to the motherland. Today he would be sure that he had a motherland, that the land in which his parents' remains were at rest really existed.

Of course, Popeye had a point: nobody could stop him visiting his grandparents' grave, but why did he feel such a desire today of all days? Was he doing this deliberately, to spite Parnaoz, or was it his goal to spoil and poison the first tryst between a son and his parents, to witness and spy on everything and stop the dead parents telling anything to their son but not to him. This is what Parnaoz thought and feared; he was ashamed in fact to be demeaned by such thoughts as he went to receive his inheritance from his parents. The jingling of Popeye's sack reminded him of the invisible and eternal shackles he had worn since he left his mother's womb. The dead relied on him, they left in his trust a tiny plot of ground filled with their bones and purified by their blood. They needed someone to look after them and they were right to chose to summon their son to show this care; but they hadn't even considered whether their son was fit to do so. Death had made them forget many things, had made them see things more simply, and made them more demanding, for in that eternal dampness and darkness there were no difficulties, obstacles or pain, since nothing ever happened there. There was no jingling of the sack, and no voice of a world forever lost, the voice of the living, evoking nothing but sadness, regret and memories of better things.

Summer was more noticeable in the cemetery. The heat had burned the cypresses, singeing and spoiling their evergreen foliage with scarlet spots. The grass was so withered that it broke at the sound of footsteps and released tiny puffs of pollen. There was a multitude of insects and reptiles, and a constant rustling and stirring in the bushes. But the most amazing thing was that Parnaoz had dug Ino's grave almost right next to his parent's mausoleum: they were virtually neighbours. This had been wholly accidental, and you could see the hand of fate in it. When they passed Ino's grave, Parnaoz bent down and picked up a dead branch from it. Popeye laughed and told him, 'See to your parents' grave first.' Popeye knew that he had come across Ino's grave, but Parnaoz was not interested in how Popeye had come to know where it was. He no longer cared.

Popeye was standing by a small mausoleum, and Parnaoz realised that this was his parents' eternal resting place, which Popeye had guided and accompanied him, or rather treated him to, as if he were showing a foreign visitor his estate. Popeye stood like a host by the mausoleum, giving Parnaoz a smile of invitation. Midges swarmed in the mausoleum as well as outside, but it was cooler there.

'My grandfather was a good man,' said Popeye, sitting down on a lizard-coloured gravestone.

There were two such gravestones next to each other in the mausoleum. One bore Parnaoz's mother's name, the other — his father's. Parnaoz shuddered, as if he had caught a chill: that was all he felt. Popeye took off a sandal and shook it against the gravestone.

'My grandfather was a good man,' he repeated, putting his sandal back on; then he continued, 'He hit me with his belt once.'

'Is that why he was a good man?' asked Parnaoz.

A large black and brown grasshopper crashed against the gravestone so hard that it sounded as if a stone had been thrown by someone. The grasshopper's long dry legs scrabbled on the stone's rough surface and it got a hold. It sat there for some time, turning its head.

'No, that's not the only reason. He was just a good man,' said Popeye.

Parnaoz thought he might see the sea if he stood on the gravestone. Popeye laughed. Unsurprised, Parnaoz asked, 'Why are you laughing?'

'When I was asleep he took the blanket off me and kissed all the bruises his belt had left. I was amazed and wondered if he'd gone mad, but I kept mum, I played dead. After that he always stared me in the eye. I pretended that I was very hurt. In fact, I wasn't bothered at all, it didn't even hurt,' Popeye laughed again, a false, superficial laugh, and went on: 'What sort of father wouldn't beat his son?'

Popeye was telling a brazen lie. In any case, Parnaoz knew that Ukheiro, however much he loved Popeye, though he might be annoyed enough to want to thrash Popeye, was unable to get up and take a look at the sleeping boy. Moreover, Popeye had called Ukheiro his 'father'. Either he was mixed up because he was drunk, or he was making fun of Parnaoz, as if Parnaoz were a stranger and he, to pass the time, to be polite, was telling him about the family. Perhaps he was accusing Parnaoz, subtly rebuking him for being indifferent and disrespectful to his father, because he had abandoned him for ten years, at a time when he most needed someone to care for him and help him. In any case, Parnaoz found himself standing by the mausoleum like a stranger and meekly listening to his nephew's blathering: his nephew had more rights here than he did. Popeye disported himself and sat casually and boldly on the tombstone, like a king on his throne. And Parnaoz could not tell his parents apart, not knowing who lay under which stone.

Parnaoz left the mausoleum and found the area to be unfamiliar; he automatically looked up at the heavens. Lightning flashed across the sky, followed by thunder: grey shadows covered everything. The statuary scattered around then froze still. For a moment Parnaoz was reminded of Daedalus's courtyard. The memory flashed like lightning in his mind. Popeye came out of the mausoleum and stood next to his uncle. Both were now looking at the sky. Black, reddened clouds, like smoke rising from a monstrous bread oven, had silently and imperceptibly piled up over the city, like legions of treacherous enemies. There was another flash of lightning, as if someone powerful and invisible had just ripped a golden thread stitched across the edge of the clouds. Torn open, the clouds roared, and the first heavy drops splattered down on the grey, drought-stricken earth. Suddenly there was such a burst of rain that they were forced to go back into the mausoleum. The rain showed no sign of stopping; instead, it grew heavier, and soon a steely, opaque wall of rain pressed against the mausoleum door, and the air inside became stuffy. Popeye sat on the gravestone where he had sat before; Parnaoz thought that Ukheiro must be under this stone.

'Nature doesn't want us to separate,' said Popeye.

In fact, Parnaoz and Popeye had never been so close or so alone. Popeye was right: nature had seen to it that they were close and alone, had pushed them together, huddled them in a mausoleum besieged by rain, forced them finally to get to know one another. One was the victim, the other the executioner. Nature had appointed Popeye as Parnaoz's executioner, which was why Parnaoz had been unable to kill him. Had he done so, then life's and nature's laws would have had to be broken and the victim would have had to do the executioner's job, and that would be an unimaginable injustice. Much that they had considered, measured and established a long time ago had now to be radically altered. This alteration required time, time and energy, which nature or fate had already devoted to this task and would not devote again. How could they find the time or the energy and, if they did, who would be so foolish and frivolous as to exert themselves twice for the same task, why make the executioner the victim and the victim the executioner, just because the victim preferred it that way? It was up to the victim to see to any changes. The victim was not ready for that, or not up to the job. The victim knew it, but knowing it diminished and depressed him further. If his executioner, with the sack over his shoulder, boldly marched to the city, that was the victim's doing, the result of his cowardice, timidity and incompetence. If the victim had only been a bit stronger and bolder, that jingling would never have been heard in the streets of Vani. He had only to overcome his softheartedness for a minute, to stop caring for a minute what the city would say, to forget his conscience for a minute in order to be rid for ever of that vague fear and the humiliating feeling of an uncommitted crime. But if he had been capable of doing that, he wouldn't have been a victim. Popeye, on the other hand, was a genuine executioner, from birth, even when Parnaoz held him in his arms, dying of fear in case he dropped or hurt him. Popeye was always stronger than him and it made no difference if Popeye didn't yet realise this: sooner or later, he certainly would realise it, and then go into action, waste no more time, in fact make up for lost time and not fuss about with a predestined victim who could never get away.

'Do you remember wanting to kill me?' Popeye asked him. Parnaoz did not deny it, as if he was waiting for such a question: he replied, 'I did, but I couldn't kill you.'

'Because you were too afraid,' Popeye immediately responded.

'Yes,' Parnaoz assented.

'Well, I wouldn't have been,' Popeye went on, challenging Parnaoz, and kicking his sack as if he was scaring off a dog crouching at his feet.

The sack yelped, just like a whipped dog.

'What do you want from me?' asked Parnaoz.

Popeye said nothing; he listened to the sound of the rain in the mausoleum. He seemed to be giving Parnaoz time to think whether he understood what he was asking. Parnaoz did understand, but it was now too late. Asking that question meant admitting Popeye was strong and superior. That question had arisen over the years, in order to erupt today, at his parents' mausoleum, in Parnaoz's most vulnerable place, and it erupted through ooze and rock with torment and suffering, dazzling with its sudden light and freedom, unaccustomed to that light and freedom, and therefore utterly unable to go back.

The silence went on for a long time and distressed Parnaoz all the more. He would rather have Popeye slash his throat here on his mother's and father's graves than sit here, his head drooping, like a man humiliated. He thought for a moment that he was mistaken and that he had once again hurt Popeye's feelings for no good reason, but before he had properly formulated this naïve thought Popeye gave him a conciliatory smile and said something that made Parnaoz want to stay in the mausoleum forever.

'We can go and see Ino after we leave here,' he said.

'Liar!' Parnaoz yelled and swung his arm hard at Popeye. It is hard to say whether Popeye saw his arm and dodged it in time, or whether he had ignored him and happened to bend down to pick up his sack just when Parnaoz meant to strike him.

'Ha, ha, I've roused you, haven't I?' Popeye laughed. He lazily stood up, slung the sack over his back, left the mausoleum. Jingling as he went, he set off down the muddy path. The sack had quickly got wet and dark.

Parnaoz had been deceiving himself all this time: there was just one Ino, known to the whole city. Thinking about a girl whose curls stuck out, and looking after her grave was mere childish stupidity. Ino was alive: while she lived, no grave could hold or stop her. This was as sure as the death of his parents now lying under those stones. It didn't matter which stone lay over whose heart: the stones were equally aged, grey and rough to the touch. It was no good pretending, he had to face the truth and have the courage to admit, at least to himself: 'I've failed to save just one skinny girl, let alone the world.' The truth was hard, it conceded nothing, it had no pity, it wouldn't tart itself up for you, it didn't care if you liked it or not. It was up to you to accept it or not, to reconcile yourself with it or rebel against it. But it wouldn't be ignored or spurned, for it existed and had its place, and a visible one, too. Of course it was visible: what else? Parnaoz's eyes hurt, and his head felt light. The goddess of truth was as naked as nature, bold as the wind, penetrating as the rain, determined as the sea and lethally beautiful. Parnaoz had to fall on his knees before her. He had to kiss the dust on her feet, hit his head against the earth and sing hymns magnifying her. But where could he hide from love? Forsaken by everyone, how could he forsake her? How could he drive her out of his soul when she, dragged in the mud and cursed, had no other refuge?

Parnaoz rushed out of the mausoleum and set off down the path at a run. The wet, slippery path slithered under his feet, as if he were running down the back of a living dragon. He was glad of the rain for giving him a chance to be drenched, and went running into it. As he ran, he could barely contain himself on the wet path. Once or twice he nearly fell over His arms were now up to the elbows in mud, and he could not help spreading his fingers apart. The wet bushes and thorns, bent under the rain caught his feet, clung to his clothes, as if their last hope were slipping from their hands. Parnaoz went on running, seeing nothing, feeling nothing, but holding out his muddy hands, his fingers spread out, as if he had to break through a wall or wanted to show the world: 'Look, the rain has knocked me over and covered me in dirt!' He arrived home at a run, entered the courtyard, grabbed Popina's spade which was propped against the dyeing shed and, still running, turned back. Now he was running with a spade, clutching the handle with his muddy hands, as if he were chasing someone he meant to kill, or were running at breakneck speed to save a vegetable garden which the rain had flooded. Again he passed the row of shops and workshops; again people sheltering from the rain watched with indifference this man, drenched from head to toe, running past, brandishing a spade. They were out of the rain and did not need to make a run for it. Someone called out, 'A thief in the garden — smash his head in!', but Parnaoz didn't even hear this. When he reached Ino's grave, the rain had stopped.

'The grave is mine, it's nobody else's business,' Parnaoz thought, and plunged the spade in. The rain hadn't soaked the earth: only the top layer was wet. Parnaoz, still drenched, suddenly broke into a sweat and the sun, which was now shining, made him steam, like a bonfire doused with water. The clods of soil he turned had dry, friable earth attached in clumps to the downy grass roots. He dug without lifting his head, getting into the trench from time to time. For the second (in fact, the third) time, he stood first up to knees, then to his waist and soon up to his shoulders in an open grave. Either Ino's head would appear or the spade's edge would strike stone. His shoulders ached, his palms throbbed, but he wouldn't rest. He recalled that he couldn't have dug such a deep grave: when he buried it, he himself wasn't tall enough. Then the grave was shoulder-deep and he recalled that, when he got out, he had his elbows on the edge of the grave. But Ino's head wasn't there. Parnaoz dug frantically, although there wasn't enough room to wield a spade, he kept hitting the sides of the grave and tearing his tendons. The pile of earth around the open hole kept falling in, raining down on his head, sticking to his sweaty shoulder-blades. The smell of earth and rotten roots made him feel sick. The grave had been robbed. Parnaoz was now sure of this, he'd suspected it before he began digging. In fact, he began digging to convince himself for once and for all that Ino's head had escaped captivity. Who knows what it had cost her to bribe a gravedigger and escape. 'Yes, but why would Popeye want to rob this grave?' Parnaoz wondered later. It was very hard to explain. 'I suppose he sold it,' he thought, unable to think of anything else, although he was aware that he was deliberately thinking this, to get round a riddle that in his tired state he couldn't and no longer wanted to solve. Popeye had also urged, in fact persuaded him that Tsuga's head could be sold.

Parnaoz flung the spade out of the grave and sat down on the bottom, wiping his face with his throbbing arm. 'We've wasted all that effort, brother,' he said, despondently, and levelled the earth with his hand. There was no point sitting there, but he was so tired that sitting in the cool grave brought him ineffable bliss. He lifted his head and saw the sky. 'Daedalus, Daedalus!' he shouted to the sky and then continued silently, to himself, 'If you're my brother, just teach me to fly, how to fly out of here.' He was finding it hard to get out of the grave. He couldn't get a grip on the crumbly soil. His whole body was worn out by this futile running and labour. Finally, he somehow clambered out. He sat on the edge of the grave and shovelled the earth back with his feet. Suddenly a bird perched in the lilac bushes and whistled. He became alert, as if it was unimaginable for a bird to perch and whistle in a lilac bush here in the cemetery. He stretched out his neck, trying to catch sight of the bird, but couldn't, although he could hear the whistling. He picked up a hard dry clod and threw it into the bushes: the bird fell silent, but very soon began to whistle again. The human action had either annoyed or encouraged the bird, and now it whistled without stopping, at the top of its voice.

'It's cursing me,' thought Parnaoz.

After the rain the world was shining, laughing in its primordial beauty, showing neither tiredness nor age, ready to begin everything again, to give birth, to create, to kill and destroy. Perhaps it was now, in this one minute, in the conjunction of muddy earth and baking sun, that so many different sorts of seeds sprouted, so many shoots, worms and insects broke through fibres, cocoons and eggs to emerge in the sunlight, where each had room to spread their limbs, to swim, to turn, because just as many were leaving the sunlight, dying, being washed up, rotting, and taking their place in the cycle of death and life, but in a new form, changed by the eternal transformation, coming back to earth after a myriad of years, transfigured when their turn came. But after a myriad of years their duty would be the same: to live and die, to die and live, and so on without end. However small and insignificant their being or disappearance, if they left the magic cycle of life and death, they would hinder something, and this hindrance, even momentary, would destroy the perfection of this world and the next. So even an insect was not entitled to disappear without trace. Each creature must leave behind its likeness, and until it has created that likeness, it may not die, because death counts as rest for it. So, on passing over into death, it can wait with its arms folded to be supplied with new vestments and a new mask and to be called: 'Arise, your time has come!'

CHAPTER SEVENTEEN

'I have to marry,' Parnaoz told Popina one day.

Popina dried her hands on her apron and sat on a chair. Steam was coming from her reddened hands.

'What did you say?' she asked, almost in a whisper, because she had suddenly lost her voice.

'I have to marry,' Parnaoz repeated. 'She'll help you in the house.'

'She'll help me?' Popina asked in the same voice, coughing several times as if a dry bread-crumb had got into her windpipe.

'What makes you so surprised? Can't I?' Parnaoz asked in turn.

He too found it hard to speak.

'Me surprised?' said Popina with a sob, and only then did Parnaoz realise she was weeping.

The woman that Parnaoz was destined to marry was Tina. They knew one other as small children, Tina lived in a house across the street, opposite theirs. That was all they had in common: they met every day, but barely noticed one another. Like any child, Tina preferred others' yards to her own. She sat for hours in the fig tree that Shubu had planted, hidden in its shaggy leaves, singing at the top of her voice until her mother called her from across the street, 'Get out of there, you little nuisance, we've got our own fig tree.' But Tina preferred the other fig tree; fear of her mother made her, however, come down. Her face red from singing, her shoulders chafed, she sullenly left the yard. Sometimes Tina squatted in front of Kaluka, pestering to be allowed to use the pestle and mortar. 'We've got our own mortar, you little nuisance,' her mother called across the street, but Tina preferred the mortar which, like a magician's chalice, wafted out dizzy scents and, when it was pounded, sounded just like her heart. When Kaluka tipped ground coriander or walnuts into a bowl, Tina always licked the mortar clean. 'Why don't you play with our little boy?' Kaluka would ask and Tina would shrug and answer, 'I can't, that's why.'

'Why can't you? Is Parnaoz a bad boy?'

'All boys are bad,' replied Tina.

'Oh dear, Tina, Tina… You should live as long as I've lived,' Kaluka laughed.

If Popina was present at the conversation, Kaluka would wink to Tina and tell Popina, 'Have you heard, my girl? Tina will marry our boy.'

'Nothing of the sort,' Tina said.

'Really, Tina?' Popina asked, as if she believed what Kaluka had said.

'Nothing of the sort!' Tina repeated, on the verge of tears.

Tina was fond of both women, because they paid her attention, talked to her as if she were their age, sometimes thrust an apple into her hand or tipped some hazel nuts into her lap. Her mother scolded her, but Kaluka and Popina smiled and told her to come again; her mother always stopped her doing things, as Tina said, 'she was getting under her feet,' and grumbled all the time, 'Will there ever be a man as awful as you, so that I can get rid of you and rest?' 'Nothing of the sort,' Tina would think, not daring to answer back. As time passed, instead of becoming closer, Tina and Parnaoz became estranged, and soon stopped greeting one another, as if they were really strangers, or disdained their childhood acquaintance. Tina stopped coming to see Kaluka and Popina and if she came on some neighbourly errand, she did so only when she knew Parnaoz was out. Gradually her mother stopped cursing and swearing at her. The family of a marriageable girl quietened down, held its breath and prepared for the encounter with destiny. Kaluka and Popina were really fond of Tina, whom they had watched grow up, and kept reproaching her, 'What is it girl, what have you got against us to make you give up on us?'

'Nothing, Auntie Kaluka, nothing, Auntie Popina… Quite the opposite…' Tina mumbled, blushing as if she had just stopped singing and had clambered out of the fig tree.

When Parnaoz departed for Crete, Tina started visiting the two women more often. If her mother needed her, or friends called for a stroll round the city, they would first visit Ukheiro's house where they were sure to find Tina. Three women of differing ages sat in the main room, little suspecting that they had more in common than shelling beans, stringing garlic or boiling damson sauce or grape juice. Kaluka and Popina liked all that Tina said or did, but it is hard to say whether Tina's nature was so perfect, or they saw only the good in her because they loved her. By this time Tina had got to know these two equally unhappy women very well: they hid their unhappiness with truly heroic resolve and stubbornness, trying to make the best of it, not seeking happiness elsewhere. They didn't like washing their dirty linen in public. They treated Tina as one of the family, they were used to her, fond of her. Once Tina lifted her dress to show them a grazed knee, telling them she'd fallen in their yard: both women were thrilled to see her slender, thoroughbred legs. In no time at all Tina had become a woman, and Kaluka said, quite disinterestedly, without any hidden agenda, 'Do you remember how angry you got when we said you'd marry Parnaoz?' Tina smiled and quickly lowered her dress, as if Parnaoz had come into the room. Popina sighed, 'I wish that could be so, then I wouldn't be losing a brother.' This exchange brought the women closer, and they mentioned Parnaoz more often, as if this was the only subject to talk about when Tina was there: Popina kept sighing, 'I wish it could be so.' Neither asked Tina whether she agreed for it to be so, as if all three had already come to an understanding on the question, and now the sighs and endless dreaming were a way to put right something that had gone wrong. So none of them noticed when and how they started playing 'happy families'. Now they had a family question to resolve; Popina kept telling Kaluka, 'Let's wait and ask the bride.' The 'bride' connived at this and enquired as keenly about Ukheiro's family as if she were Parnaoz's wife and he had asked her, 'Well, you're a woman, so while I'm away, you support my folk.'

All three, not just Tina, knew that Parnaoz might never return or would be already married when he did return: there were plenty of examples of that in Vani. But they all kept their end up; all three, in their safe refuge of female faith and hope, helped each other to live and wait. Tina liked being called the 'bride' and was used to this unreal status, she felt obliged to think all the time about Parnaoz as a loyal, principled husband whom fate or misfortune had sent far away for a long time and subjected to a cruel ordeal. Tina even dreamed of Parnaoz. In her dreams they acted and talked like a real couple. Parnaoz asked her about his family, enquiring about each one, and always told her when he was leaving, 'I'm grateful to you; I'm in your debt for your loyalty and respect.' In the morning, Tina, excited by her dream, in casual house clothes, ran across the street and Popina and Kaluka were as excited by her dream, as if Tina was bringing them real messages from Parnaoz. Then the women started interpreting the dream and again agreed that everything would be as they wished. 'Did he ask about me?' Kaluka asked for the tenth time, and Tina again replied, 'Yes, about everybody… Then he kissed me and told me he was grateful and in my debt.'

When Ukheiro died, Tina put on mourning, although she had never seen her 'father-in-law'. She bustled about right until the burial, spinning like a spinning-wheel, and she gave a dinner three times for the whole city. So many people came to Ukheiro's funeral that if you'd thrown a plum down, it wouldn't have hit the ground. People kept coming, more and more of them: whether they knew Ukheiro or not, everyone wanted to see a man who'd managed to live bedridden so long, without killing himself or going mad. People now came as if to see a champion who won a glorious contest and whom you could come and see even if you didn't know him personally, because it was not his person that was important, but the victory which he had won and which had made him famous. Tina managed to look after the bereaved and all the housework. Housework is unending when there is a deceased member of the family in the house.

People who came to offer their condolences were met by Tina, Popina and Kaluka: in vain Tina's mother scowled and made signs at her to come out, 'Why are you here, what business is it of yours?' Her mother didn't know that her daughter was a bride in this house and was only acting as a good bride should. People, who, like Tina's mother, also knew nothing, said, 'What a girl, such a good neighbour! These days your own child wouldn't do so much.'

Ukheiro's death had made Parnaoz indispensable to the family: it needed a man… Shubu looked after the estate; Popeye occasionally looked in, but only to quarrel, grumble and distress his mother and grandmother more. 'You threw me out, you got rid of me, and now you can't manage without me,' Popeye would say venomously and the women were lost for an answer, so shaken were they.

Popina walked about, her spirit killed: what could she do, to whom could she tell her grief? Kaluka might see any complaint as a rebuke, for while Popeye was Popina's son, Kaluka had given birth to Popeye's father. Without saying anything, Kaluka knew what was burning Popina inside, and she didn't deny her sin, because if she hadn't given birth to Philamon, she wouldn't have conceived Popeye. It was a great sin, great enough, if allowed, to play with the lives of these two vulnerable women, who were tied to one another by one rope, so that both could be manipulated at the same time. That was why a third woman, utterly free of their sin, even ignorant of it, was equally dear to both of them. Tina was their redeemer. The closeness, or rather the purity and ingenuousness of this third person was mortar in the wall of their patience, which had cracks appearing here and there and was in danger of collapsing. This wall could not be allowed to fall yet, not because life was sweet and the two of them would find it hard to leave this world of their own free will, but because they were still needed in this world, at least in this house, where people died or whence they fled, but where nobody was now born. Did they have any right to leave as long as an ounce of hope remained that life might again set foot within these walls? They were women and they had no right to leave. Tina was that ounce of hope which they clung to like drowning men, and they were so inspired by a desire for survival that they believed Tina really was the sister-in-law, that Parnaoz was bound to return, because there was a wife waiting for him at home, and once again the smell and cries of a baby would fill this doomed house.

'You're so beautiful today, our bride!' Popina told Tina, who was glad to be called 'bride' and 'beautiful' by Popina.

Tina had her task and goal, and pursued her goal doggedly, patiently, like grass seed under a paving stone: the grass will eventually break through the stone and crack it and send its green, velvety shoots through the cracks. Tina had decided to be Parnaoz's wife when Kaluka, pestle and mortar in her lap, jokingly said, to pass away the time, 'Like it or not, I have to marry you to Parnaoz.' What the adults then thought was a joke was no joke to her: even then, she believed that it would happen sooner or later, because she wanted it to. It didn't matter that Parnaoz hadn't looked at her, had disdained to play with her and wouldn't even eat figs she'd picked. When Tina herself had picked them! Hidden in the fig tree's wide, shaggy leaves, she ate one and put another in her skirts for him. She sang a song for Parnaoz, and made her voice as shrill as she could so as to remind him of her existence, to warn him that she was there in his fig tree. The wide shaggy leaves made her body come out in spots, but she put up with that, because she could kept a closer eye on his every step. 'I know, I know, I kno-o-ow everything,' she sang and yelled at the top of her voice, until her mother scolded her from across the street and told her to come down, her arms grazed and stung. She really did know everything she needed to know about Parnaoz to stop him doing anything silly or getting lost. The main thing was that he shouldn't get lost, whatever else happened. Tina was sure of herself and never took to heart Parnaoz's indifference, which might have made anyone else give up any plans they had. Tina fought, she knew that she had to get Parnaoz, like her daily bread, in the sweat of her brow, by patience, as her father kept telling her when he lifted her fist which she had raised to her mouth and asked, 'What are you eating?' Tina would answer straight away, 'Your sweat.' Her father would smile and say, 'Remember, bread has to be earned in the sweat of your brow and with patience.' Tina repeated that to herself and for some reason she saw Parnaoz as the bread.

'You know, father, Parnaoz has got a dog,' she chatted to her father.

'So what? Haven't we got a dog?' asked her father, surprised.

'Dogs die before people, don't they?' Tina persisted, and her father was suddenly bored by talking to a silly girl, because he hadn't grasped what she really wanted to say.

Tina was thinking about Tsuga: when she heard Tsuga's yapping and Parnaoz's laughter, she couldn't help smiling and thinking how long Tsuga could go on yapping if nothing happened and the dog died naturally, with oozing eyes and hairless flanks, like the dog they used to have until father brought a new one home. Her father had to bring a new dog after they found the old dog one morning dead in the yard. Tina loathed the old dog because it had worms wriggling in its nose. 'It's served us a long time,' her father said at the time. 'But how long has it served us?' Tina now wondered, for Tsuga showed no signs of dying.

Death bored her: she was starting her life, getting more beautiful, frivolous and cheerful by the day. And Tsuga was the only creature that Parnaoz now heeded. Tina hated Tsuga, but never revealed her hatred to anyone. Wherever she went she praised the dog, saying what a wonderful dog they had, as if she, Parnaoz and the dog were the best of friends.

Parnaoz must have heard of these remarks, because once, quite unexpectedly, Parnaoz took notice of Tina, even stopping to say, 'You know, Tsuga was frightened by a frog yesterday.' Tina took a great interest, listened with a radiant expression to the whole story: a green, pop-eyed toad sat in front of Tsuga, its puffed-out throat bubbling as if it had a mouth full of water, and Tsuga trembled from head to toe until Parnaoz punched her and said, 'What a coward you are.' Then Tsuga cheered up and barked at it, as if to say, 'What are you doing there?' and rolled the toad over like a gall bladder. Tina smiled, laughed and kept her eyes on Tsuga while Parnaoz was telling her all this; meanwhile Tsuga was brushing against their legs and spinning like a top, chasing her tail.

Later Tsuga fell into a latrine and Tina celebrated her first victory, although she never let anyone know. In fact, for three days she stayed at the latrine, begging everyone, 'Help her, I'm so sorry for her.' At night, sitting up in bed, she listened hard to hear if Tsuga was still whimpering. When a rescuer threw out Tsuga, covered in filth, Tina was at first frightened that he wouldn't take away that filthy animal, but when the rescuer's equally filthy arms appeared from the pit, Tina was sure that Tsuga's fate was decided. She had got rid of her first rival, had her first victory, and success made her cleverer and more serious. The battle was just beginning, and she would have contests with a rival harder to remove before final victory, when she persuaded Parnaoz, too, that he belonged to Tina, that there was no other course of action for him. 'By patience and sweat, by patience and sweat,' Tina sang to herself.

Tina fought many small and great wars, overt or covert, on the path she had chosen in childhood. She never lost heart, and never tired of keeping an eye on Parnaoz, lurking behind the fence, crawling on her belly. She had often grazed her knees or elbows, torn her dress and had a thrashing at home, but she bore it all without a word, because she was fighting and she knew what for. Once, when she and her playmates were at the Greek's source filling their water pitchers, a hook-nosed girl put her hands on her chest like a grown woman, and said, 'That Parnaoz thinks a lot of himself.' Everyone, including Tina, laughed, but her laughter was different, just a mask to hold back her anger and not make the others laugh even more. As she laughed, Tina plotted how to punish the hook-nosed girl who folded her arms like a grown-up woman and took

Parnaoz's name in vain. Tina filled her pitcher and set off home, but she didn't go there, she hid in an alley-way behind a stone wall and picked up a cobblestone. When the snub-nosed girl appeared, Tina threw the stone and smashed the pitcher she was carrying on her shoulder. The poor girl was soaked from head to foot, and left holding just the handle of the pitcher: she went down the street, sobbing. Tina caught up with her and told her, 'You were babbling away like a grown woman just now, now you're snivelling like a baby: aren't you ashamed?' Then Tina adjusted her pitcher on her shoulder and set off home.

The friendship between Parnaoz and Ino alarmed Tina somewhat. Ino turned out to be harder to get rid of than Tsuga. Tina hadn't seen Ino before, although all the boys and girls of Vani knew each other. Then someone said, 'That girl's called Ino, she's the daughter of a wicked woman,' and whispered into a neighbour's ear. Tina lost interest. She now knew her rival's name, and that was enough. It can be said that during all their friendship Tina never took her eye off Ino and Parnaoz. They were thus never alone, but when one boy, also at the Greek's source, said for all to hear, 'Ino and Parnaoz run about naked in Dariachangi's garden,' Tina was dismayed, as if this was the first she had heard about it and hadn't seen it with her own eyes. First of all, she lost her temper with the boy, because it was none of his business and he had no right to see, even by accident, what concerned only Tina, was only her business, or rather hers, Ino's and Parnaoz's. This was the first time Tina showed any weakness or lack of foresight: she had thought that she would wait for a day or two and then cause trouble, but she couldn't control herself and scratched the boy's face, already ugly with fear and amazement, so badly that when the boy's mother heard children yelling and came running up, she couldn't recognize her son and asked, 'Where's my boy?'

Tina fought. It's hard to say whether she loved Parnaoz or not, but clearly she was fighting to have him, and the feeling, if we call it love, that he aroused in her grew far faster, cleverer and more cunning than Tina herself did. Even then Tina was cleverer than other girls her age and, above all, already knew what she wanted and, still more important, knew how to get what she wanted: by sweat and patience, so that nobody felt like rebuking her for it or depriving her of it. Thus not even Parnaoz's and Ino's friendship made her despair: Tina had to endure much that others, especially a girl her age, would have meekly turned their backs on or forsaken, in order to seek new amusement which would give them only pleasure, particularly as their immature, still growing and always changeable nature was unused to patience, calculation and foresight. But patience gave Tina more pleasure than anything else, she could patiently put up with anything that patience could get for a human being, she could endure indifference, humiliation, hatred, love, betrayal, loneliness, pain and, believe it or not, her own self. This feeling of patience, its greatness and endlessness spurred her, rather than depressed her. She sped along towards her final goal like a ship with the wind behind it speeding to port, when this good wind is the only force left to get it into port: all the oars are broken, and the oarsmen, starving and thirsty, are all unconscious.

When Ino and Parnaoz ran away from home, Tina's mother gave her such a bad time as if she were the instigator of this flight and were about to follow Ino and Parnaoz. 'Is this why I've been working myself to the bone?' she yelled, while her husband tried to calm her, 'Leave her alone, woman, she's still wet behind the ears, what does she understand?'

'Nothing of the sort!' Tina wanted to say to her father, but she was in her seventh heaven because her mother was cursing her instead of 'them' and must sense that 'they' and Tina were inseparable and bore equal responsibility for everything.

As Tina's intuition told her, 'they' were soon found and brought back. Even if they hadn't been found, they would have been brought back at some point, because they hadn't left properly: a greater part, the essential part of them, without which they would find it hard to breathe and walk, had remained in Vani, forgotten in their haste, or else, one sillier than the other, they thought they could manage without it. Quite wrong, I'm afraid. If not, it would be Tina, not they, who turned out to be silly. But she wasn't silly, because she managed to be patient. She allowed herself, though, to go off quietly and inspect the cave where they proposed to live without her. Tina found the sack in the cave: there was a haunch of ham and ten dry loaves in it. Tina nibbled at just one loaf and picked a piece of meat off the haunch: she took her share and left the rest as they would have left it if they'd stayed. 'Look, what silly children,' Tina thought. 'I'd have kept going and going until I dropped unconscious to the ground.'

A long period of Tina's patience was over, if not completely. She had won this battle, on her own, without other's help: she therefore felt that her victory was ten, or a hundred, or a thousand times more pleasant. That night she went to sleep so calmly and deeply that she didn't even twitch. Her worried mother came in twice to see that she hadn't run away.

First Tsuga, then Ino vanished like last year's snow. Nothing else seemed to stop Tina from taking hold of Parnaoz, saying for all to hear, 'He's mine, I got him with sweat and patience,' but the job wasn't done: there was still something dividing Tina and Parnaoz, and until that something vanished, she couldn't consider him won. Unfortunately, Tina didn't know what she still had to endure, but every fibre of her being felt, but could not see, its existence, as if she had suddenly lost her wits and sight, or her wits and sight were not, for the time being, enough to spot this 'something', to name, define and destroy it, or just get rid of it. Fighting with no rival and no bloodshed was hard; it was a dreary struggle and Tina grasped that a new patience was beginning. She had to overcome, or else everything would be thrown away.

Time still passed, albeit more slowly. Tina's all-transforming, devastating strength was transforming and devastating her. The moon, as if to spite her, always rose in her window and her nature, expecting a great transformation, even when asleep, worried and distressed her. Tina was wholly in thrall to and permeated by the moon's mysterious and all-embracing power, so, constantly turning over in bed, she seemed to be embarrassed by the moon and hid her face from it. But the moon was everywhere, and whatever position Tina found in bed, wherever she looked, her small untouched breasts, as hard as stones, shone in the moonlight like unripe oranges. In the darkness that reigned all round, the moonlight struck her face like ruffled yellow foam. Tina had new feelings: she grew, she matured and anxiously watched her own body's growth and maturing, as if the house where she had lived so carefree and fearless had been entered, or crept into, cautiously, furtively, on tip-toe, by someone she didn't know: those cautious, furtive footsteps alarmed and frightened her, because she sensed that the visitor was up to no good. Anyone with good intentions doesn't come in like that: he calls from a distance, he warns, asks permission to enter and Tina would have time to think whether to let this stranger into the house where she had so far lived alone and felt at ease. Now she felt helpless, for the first time feeling alone, yet there was no sense raising the alarm, nobody would come to her aid. The visitor would sneak in and she would shut her eyes, give in to him, yield up room, in fact become one with him, one being, one new being which would still be called Tina, but would no longer be entirely the former Tina, as bold and shameless as a boy, yes, a boy. Nature had drawn a line under her 'boyhood' and from tomorrow she could no longer perch in the fig tree, singing for all the city to hear. A woman was awakening inside Tina: she didn't know how to receive this visitor, how to treat this alien creature with customs and qualities other than Tina's and would change Tina rather than follow her bidding, for the visitor was stronger, nourished by Tina's blood, and took up more room in her being.

Of course, the household noticed that Tina had become a woman: they immediately started getting a dowry together. They no longer thumped her on the head, they stopped scolding her or making her do housework, as if she had become an invalid, not a woman. Tina did seem to be ill, her parents fussed over her, kept her out of cold draughts, and mollycoddled a girl who had run about barefoot, rain or shine, who climbed trees and who was toughened by diving into the ever-flowing river or the sea. Her parents' excessive care both amazed and pleased Tina, and yet did not, but she did not resist, as a patient bemused by weakness does not resist a nurse who only wants to save the patient, to bring him back to health. Tina also wanted to recover quickly and go on with the battle at any cost: she sensed that what was going on was meant to give a sense and a name to her longstanding goal and plan, and to make it clear and understandable not only to her but to everyone. Of course, there was no point carrying on the fight in the old way, but new ways would be found if she stayed calm and patient, even though patience was now harder to sustain: her feet had grown, but she still had the same sized boots.

The family, Tina, her father and her mother, were all expectation; but, unlike Tina, the parents were waiting more anxiously, nervously and vaguely. They were waiting for someone, anyone at all, it seemed, as long as it was a suitor for Tina: they didn't want to have a marriageable girl in the house too long, or else the neighbours would 'talk' and be sorry for her. They were most afraid of Tina's neighbours, but they had another fear, harder to surmount: their daughter might run out of patience, not hold out any more, and, one fine day, suddenly get out of bed with a swollen belly! Then they'd see the neighbours' joy. They would really be disgraced and all the pains and hopes to see Tina happily married would be in vain. Dazed and wearied by her awakened femininity, Tina slept at night like the dead, whereas her parents slept fitfully, whispering in bed until dawn, as if they were hatching a plot against their daughter. Like conspirators, they measured, cut and stitched plots, made and unmade plans to ensure that their only daughter, their only comfort in old age, the only fruit and proof of their life, should be decently married off. But could they really trust a girl who was sweating with the heat of an unexplained fit of passion, throwing the blanket off herself, baring her chest, and with lips that shone bright like a still bleeding wound, murmuring hymns, wordless and senseless, to passion? Anyone could understand such utterances and would be as shocked by them as by a murder or a suicide.

Yet one day, before Parnaoz left for Crete, a suitor for Tina did appear. The family was relieved, their hearts soared, they forgot all the agonies they had been through and received the people who wanted to become relatives by marriage with marked dignity and pride. Tina's suitor was the boy whose face she had scratched with her nails at the Greek's source and whose mother had then been unable to recognize him. Now he and his mother sat down with Tina, not knowing how to get round to the subject. The woman picked at the end of her headscarf and smiled at everything. The lad blushed deep red: he felt hot and couldn't stop looking out of the window.

'Please help yourselves to food and drink, the fruit is from the garden,' said Tina's mother.

'Thank you, dear. Don't go to any trouble,' said the lad's mother.

'Tina picked them,' Tina's mother persisted, as if everything depended on whether the fruit was eaten or not.

The woman picked up a plum, wiped it with her palm and bit into it, or rather just skinned it with her front teeth, and released the sour juice. Then she elbowed her son, shaming him into taking a plum. The son was looking out of the window: he refused so loudly that he was frightened by his own voice, put his hand to his blushing forehead and smiled.

'Well… we… this business… in short…' the lad's mother began, to be interrupted by Tina's mother, 'This year's the first time it's fruited.'

Both mothers laughed and apologized simultaneously.

Tina's fate seemed to be decided, both sides said what they needed to say and reached an understanding. Now it was up to Tina. Both mothers looked at her with the same pleading eyes. The lad was looking out of the window again, but Tina sat there calmly as if that was her only duty, as if she had been asked just to sit there, be present and listen, or not, as she wished. 'We're embarrassing the girl,' said the lad's mother. The lad sighed, as if he had been holding his breath all that time. 'Sorry we couldn't give you a better reception,' Tina's mother apologized.

The lad and his mother hadn't reached the end of the street when Tina caught up with them. They were talking about her, in fact, but were not expecting at all to see her now. They were both so flushed with embarrassment after such a difficult, but obligatory visit that they looked as if they had been to the bathhouse, not to see a family.

'Tina, my child!' shrieked the lad's mother.

Tina was looking vaguely somewhere over their heads, as if she had with difficulty rehearsed what she now had to say and, if she saw anything or anyone, she might lose concentration and get it wrong.

'If you really become my husband, while I'm alive, while I can still see you, while I still have teeth in my mouth and nails in my fingers, I'll tear the flesh off your bones,' she said.

Mute with fear, confused, mother and son left, almost at a run.

A deal that was virtually done was thus suddenly wrecked: Tina's parents didn't know what to think, how to explain the irksome silence and inactivity of their daughter's suitors. Why should they disdain Tina and, if they did, why had they hidden this disdain, why didn't they say at the time that they didn't like her, that they'd changed their minds? Raising people's hopes is no light matter. Or were they playing a trick? Did they hold some old grudge, revealed only now? But Tina's parents hadn't offended anyone, had they? 'Not anyone?' they asked each other for the tenth time: the man spread his arms and shrugged, the woman looked him warily in the eye. Tina's silence made them even more depressed: they felt pity for their spurned daughter. 'There's no reason to cry, she isn't dying,' Tina's father told his wife, but added without any conviction, 'We'll have so many oafs like that one knocking at the door that we'll have to beat them off with sticks.' They said nothing to Tina: they could not even bear to offer her words of comfort, because it seemed to them that if they started consoling their daughter, then things would go so badly that consolation would really be needed. Apart from them, the whole city knew about this failed match. The mother and son who'd been frightened off by Tina had hidden nothing, and their story had warned off others: young bachelors mentally crossed Tina off their list, because the last thing they wanted was to be the talk and laughing stock of the city. Tina's parents realised that they could expect nothing good: week after week passed and soon they would be standing at the door not with sticks, but with their necks stretched out, begging passers-by to come in and at least take a look and not be so blind.

Tina fought on. She couldn't hear her parents' lamentations or the jocular remarks of Vani's inhabitants. She had won another little battle, but final victory was still a long way off, she had to be constantly armed as well as patient and had to scrub and polish daily, as her mother scrubbed and polished the pots and pans, because she would need things not for one day, but for ever. Patience was really Tina's only weapon, and even she had no idea how long she would need it until she finally won, or how long it would last. 'I'll hold out, I have to hold out,' she said when she heard that Parnaoz was travelling to Crete. Really, she had no right to wait for him, but she didn't and couldn't reconcile herself to losing Parnaoz, because the one thing she could never do was reconcile herself. So she endured. She sensed that the journey to Crete was Parnaoz's last act of resistance, that it would end in defeat, because he was running away from his real protector and seeking a non-existent friend. Only she, the real protector, could save him, while a friend could only wreck him. Parnaoz did not yet know this, he was leaving in order to find out and he was sure do so, because a time would come when he needed someone to look after him. Do waves know what shore they will break on, whether it will be rock or sand? Yet they cannot wait to reach the shore to break, disintegrate and be annihilated for the sake of a moment's contact, for which they were born somewhere in the dark frozen murk. A friend is either a wave, or a rocky shore, either perishing himself or letting you perish. That is his power and beauty, an eternal power and ephemeral beauty, for every new couple, every new rocky shore and wave, brings with it a peculiar, unique beauty. A protector is different: she is a sandy shore, and neither perishes herself nor lets you perish. Her heart and mind are in the right place; both do only what nature has obliged them to do. Nature, not fate. Her heart pumps round, with a peasant's thriftiness, just three litres of blood and her mind guards that blood like a watchdog, for it knows that every drop is needed, like a hereditary treasure buried in the earth for centuries and never dug up or touched by anyone, for that buried treasure is the foundation for the strength, fame, past, present and future of the whole race. There are no rainy days for this race while the treasure remains buried: so the race may easily suffer losses, have much to endure, but it will not perish as long as it has this wealth underfoot.

Tina had her buried treasure, and her foot stood securely on it. Parnaoz's departure for Crete naturally perturbed her, but it could not shake her. She stayed standing upright. Anything could happen to Parnaoz when nobody oversaw him, but whatever happened he was sure to return, because he had a protector. He had to realise this as soon as possible, for only that realisation would save him, would calm him and convince him that she was the only shore, a refuge rather than a house, where he would be inviolable: he would have a protector by his side and not a friend as frivolous as himself, a wife and not a silly naked girl.

Parnaoz was bound to come back. It didn't matter when: Tina would hold out to the end, because time was unimportant for her. The goal was the important thing, and without a thought she sacrificed everything else to that goal, time, too, of course. When you know that you're expected somewhere, you don't have to go, you can choose whether to go or not, it's up to you and, however disappointed the person expecting you may be, they can't altogether blame you, because half the blame is theirs, for they, or their expecting you, may be the reason why you'd rather not go. But it's different when you don't know who's expecting you, who is enduring your absence. No, Parnaoz was bound to come, he had no right not to, because he didn't know that Tina was expecting him.

After Parnaoz's departure Tina started to visit Popina and Kaluka more often, so that before Parnaoz returned she could get used to her designated place, a place no other woman could occupy. This was Tina's place and the other women of the family silently assented to this, or rather convinced themselves, because they needed to: Tina not only warded off their loneliness, if loneliness can be warded off, but gave them faith that things were not yet over for them. Tina was a young woman, undefiled, unbroken, full of hope and good cheer; she was beautiful, too, and had thoroughbred legs. Tina took into her skirts a third of the beans to be shelled and of the garlic to be strung, and sat between Popina and Kaluka. She had known since childhood that here, under this roof, between these walls she had to shed real sweat and permeate the whole house with its smell, as conquered earth has to be permeated with blood. In fact, when Tina saw Parnaoz again (on the day that black-eyed Malalo was buried) she felt with all her soul that the battle was over. Parnaoz stood by the gate, Tina looked through the window of her room, as the funeral procession passed between them like a sluggish, lazy river whose water is totally covered with broken branches and flowers. A heavy wooden sarcophagus swayed as it moved at the head of the procession; in the sarcophagus lay the mother of seven daughters, a refugee from Babylon, and hostess to the whole city. Seven women in black followed the sarcophagus, and one of them was Ino, but this meant nothing to Tina, now that the battle was over and Parnaoz huddled by the gate, like a defeated warrior, pale and at a loss, for his fate now lay in the hands of a conqueror who would decide whether to kill him or let him live. Tina felt as if she was able to stretch her arm over the street and pick Parnaoz up like a chick and show him to everyone, as the booty of her endless, unlimited and deliberate patience. But she held back, preferring to wait until Parnaoz called for her himself.

'Am I surprised?' Popina sobbed: now Parnaoz saw she was crying.

'No, Popina, no…' said Parnaoz lovingly. 'I didn't mean to put it like that. What's so surprising about my getting married?'

'Surprising?' Popina now smiled and her wet face shone.

'Dry your tears,' Parnaoz told her.

CHAPTER EIGHTEEN

THE family had new food for thought and talk. And for alarm, too. Parnaoz may have decided to marry, but would he marry the woman they had chosen? There were plenty of others, he might choose some other woman, and may have returned just for her. This woman might be a foreigner whom Parnaoz had met over there, conquered and was now only waiting for her to arrive, having come first himself to warn his family, so that they would not be unprepared when the foreign woman came. Popina and Kaluka had all kinds of thoughts. And Tina had vanished somewhere, which worried them most, because they now felt that they might have misled and strung along a poor girl who for all those ten years had truly believed these two feeble and powerless women, or two vicious, selfish old women imploring everyone, grimacing like beggar-women, making people sorry for them, women desperate to put on mourning clothes for their sins and unhappiness. That's what they wanted Tina for. They were getting her ready, and if they had carried out their plan, Tina would have, without hesitating, meekly, even gladly, swept up a third of their sins and unhappiness just like beans to be shelled or garlic to be strung. They would have ruined Tina, but they were preoccupied with saving themselves. Was that why Parnaoz couldn't say all that he wanted to say? Would it have been easy to say, 'I'm marrying, so would you please go because there can only be one mistress in the house.' That may be why he asked Popina, 'Why are you amazed?' In fact, why should she be, what was so amazing about a new wife not wanting to live with her husband's relatives, however well she gets on with them? Every woman wants her husband and family to herself, and not to be told off for lying down when she fancies, for serving fried food one day and letting her family make do with dry bread the next. If a sister-in-law visits, then she's a guest, but if she comes to stay, she's a pest.

This is how the two women, plunged into thought, discussed and argued. Clearly, their assumptions were not wholly unjustified. Parnaoz might well have got involved with some shrew whose first concern would be to throw his family out of the house. 'While they're still here, I can't be a proper wife,' she might say. There were many examples of that. Or, as Popeye once said, there was a woman he meant to marry, but he was too ashamed to say so, and that was why he kept putting off the wedding. One way or another, Popina and Kaluka would only get in the way. It was Parnaoz's house and, after all, he could bring into it whomever he wanted.

Everything had to be sorted out as soon as possible: the two women knew that one superfluous woman, let alone two, is the hardest thing to bear.

Popina took Ukheiro's sandals, almost never worn, from the trunk and went to see Parnaoz.

'Try them on, they're your father's,' she told him, as she squatted by his feet.

'The sword?' Parnaoz asked.

'What sword?!' said Popina in amazement, looking up at her brother.

'My father's,' said Parnaoz. 'Didn't he leave one?' he asked her a little later.

'I don't know anything about that,' Popina said anxiously, looking round the room as if there must be a sword somewhere. The only weapon in the room was the javelin, still stuck in the wall, still with white-powdered grape-juice sweets hanging from its handle. Ukheiro's other javelins had long ago been sold as stakes for Popeye's vineyard. A year after Ukheiro died, Popeye had taken the javelins. 'There are a few things in this house that belong to me,' he said, and left.

'What did you say?' Parnaoz asked again.

Popina shook her head.

'I knew it!' said Parnaoz.

Someone was chopping wood nearby. They both listened to the sound of the hatchet. Then a cock crowed. A scorpion froze on the ceiling, above their heads. 'It'll fall down any minute,' Parnaoz thought, but he didn't move, a strange wanness came over him, taking over his whole body like an illness. He didn't want to alarm, burden, obstruct, or artificially disturb his sister by prolonging this mysterious minute, filled by the sound of the axe, the cock's crow and the scorpion's frozen shadow. It seemed to be a final minute, deliberately dawdling so that everyone could finish what they had to do: the hatchet splitting the wood, the cock crowing, the scorpion spewing out venom, and the bereaved brother and sister mourning their orphaned state. Parnaoz sensed that this minute was dawdling for his sake, so that he had time to see, take in and familiarise himself with everything that had existed so far, but that he either couldn't or wouldn't notice because he didn't want to believe that real, eternal life is comprised of these simple sounds and objects, such as the sound of an axe, the crowing of a cock or the shadow of a scorpion frozen to the ceiling. He too was a simple creature, not entitled to rebel against that simplicity; he was a component part, as insignificant and at the same time as essential as anything else. He too was essential, inasmuch as he was proof of the precision of current time, at this moment: this was no small matter, because this one moment was one minute not just for Parnaoz but for the whole universe.

Popina was thinking about their father, or rather the day before he died. She was reminded of that day by Parnaoz's odd question, 'Didn't my father leave me a sword?' That day Ukheiro did leave his children something in fact, but not a sword. But Popina couldn't understand what her father was getting at. Later she forgot, because she had never been interested. That day Ukheiro called for Popina. She thought that one of his wounds must have opened so that the bandage would have to be changed. When she entered the room, everything seemed strange: she immediately grasped why. Ukheiro was not embroidering, he had laid his hands on the sail-sized canvas and was staring, his eyes popping, at the wall. He didn't turn his head, but he asked who it was.

'It's me, father,' said Popina, taken aback. She hadn't expected that question.

'Who's there in the big room, I meant,' Ukheiro asked her.

'Ah yes,' said Popina, calmly. 'Nobody, just Tina, our neighbour.'

'Forgive me!' said Ukheiro and Popina was again startled and confused: she looked hard at her father's face.

Something was bothering Ukheiro: he wanted to say something, but couldn't say it, couldn't let go, as a child can't let go of a toy, not because he grudges it to anyone else, but because he doesn't trust others, doesn't believe they'll look after it, not drop it and break it, while he loves the toy, goes to sleep and wakes up with it, cuddles and warms it, and can even pass his own warmth and smell to it, breathe life into it, animate it. He shows fear and mistrust, because it comes to life only for him, and for others it remains an inanimate and unfeeling object, a toy. Doesn't it break the child's heart when his playmates call him stingy, turn their noses up at him and won't let him near them any more, not wanting him or his toy? But now it is more dangerous to lend anyone the toy, because children with a grudge might now deliberately or vindictively break it and smash it to pieces in a minute, to show the price of spurning their friendship for the sake of a toy.

Popina understood nothing, however; she looked at Ukheiro's face in confusion. She saw but couldn't perceive anything, because the face had been familiar since childhood.

'You and Parnaoz, forgive me…' Ukheiro continued.

'Father…' Popina began, but Ukheiro interrupted her, or didn't hear her, and continued, '…for everything. You and Parnaoz, so tell him when he comes back. There's no other message, none.'

'Would you like me to change your bandage?' Popina asked.

'No, I'm all right now: go!' said Ukheiro.

Now Popina suddenly heard herself say, 'His beard was tangled with bits of thread. Tina and I picked them out one by one.'

'Why didn't he wait for me to come back, why?!' said Parnaoz.

How could Ukheiro have waited for Parnaoz? Was it up to him when he died? He hung on for quite some time. After the battle of Vani, when a fateful accident chained a man of his stature to his bed, he never stopped dying. During that time his turbulent life, after countless wounds and sores, quietly leaked away, like wine from a cracked wine jar. Just before he died a child could easily have picked him up, whereas when he was wounded ten men could barely carry him to Vani's city walls. His family did not notice, because it all happened before their eyes. What should they have thought: when they needed wine, that they would find the wine jar empty? They thought the wine jar was soundly sealed, but life was leaking away, streaming out and vanishing senselessly and without trace into the ground.

'Why didn't he wait for me to come back, why?!' Parnaoz repeated.

Popina went on recounting how she brought him dinner and found him lying on the floor. 'No, I didn't see father, the canvas was lying on the floor. I wondered where he'd gone to, I was astounded, and when I bent down to pick up the canvas, I saw his foot, then I knew, and it wasn't hard to see: he'd slipped under it.'

'It was loneliness that killed him!' said Parnaoz.

'Tina's a good girl,' Popina suddenly said and then fell silent.

'Yes,' replied Parnaoz, in fact talking to himself.

It was not long afterwards that Tina entered Ukheiro's family, this time forever. A new woman was busy around the hearth, a hearth she had long been fond of, had thought and dreamt of. She was now its lawful mistress: that hearth would now want for nothing, it would never go out; she would work for all the world to see, her face red with happiness and the reflections of the hearth. Tina felt on her very first night that their bed would be a place only to fulfil conjugal duties, not for oblivion, for death-like bliss. But for her this alone meant a lot and she assented to it.

'Are you asleep?' Tina asked.

'No,' replied Parnaoz.

'Perhaps you're not comfortable?' Tina asked again.

Parnaoz put his hand on her breast. Tina froze. Parnaoz felt as if someone was watching them, as if the whole city could hear the slightest rustle they made, as if… he was lying in somebody else's bed, doing somebody else's duty and being shamelessly deceptive: his hands and all his body repeated, or if they couldn't repeat, at least imitated the movements of this 'somebody else', to stop a woman blinded by the darkness and passion from realising that fate had put him in her bed, instead of the 'somebody else'. Tina fought like a wild animal caught in a noose. Somewhere, dogs were barking. In the morning, as soon as Parnaoz opened his eyes, he heard Tina's voice. 'See to the pots, Popina,' she was calling. The whole house filled with reassuring bustle and fragrant, appetising vapours.

One year later the house was full of the squawks and wet nappies of a newborn baby. Now, instead of grape-juice sweetmeats, rags and swaddling clothes were hung out to dry on Ukheiro's javelin. The baby had hardly opened its eyes, but the house already seemed too small. Every day they tore up old dresses, aprons, headscarves and shirts to make swaddling clothes, but this tiny, wrinkly-browed and angry creature messed them all up; three women, their sleeves rolled up, spent all day long washing, mangling, hanging out and ironing rags with faded leaf and flower patterns. Parnaoz would leave the house, bent double, like a man defeated, so as not to be caught by the washing lines or not to get his feet entangled in his baby's acrid-smelling soaked rags. He smelled the same, and walked the street both extraordinarily proud and embarrassed.

They called the baby Ukheiro. Tina immediately declared, 'Call him what you like, it makes no difference what his name is.' She did so not just to please her husband and his relatives, but because she really didn't care what they called this new force, this new mortar strengthening her fortress walls. The baby's birth gave Tina greater rights and importance. Popina and Kaluka looked at her adoringly, as if she were a goddess who had performed a miracle in front of them. No miracle could have been greater: the ceiling seemed to be higher, the walls to have retreated, the cradle to have blossomed and birds to have started chirruping over it. Bare-breasted, smiling carefree, Tina happily dandled the baby on her mighty fleshy thighs, which her dress could barely contain, fitting her so tightly round the lap that it seemed about to tear, like two buffaloes roped together and driven in opposite directions. Tina was as simple, bold and kind as a goddess; she loved and pitied the people made happy by seeing her; she could go on sitting endlessly like that, entertained and entertaining others while the baby bounced up and down in her lap, crackled like a flame, slithered like a fish, but unable to get away.

For Parnaoz everything seemed to be over, or rather Parnaoz no longer had the right to live as he used to, whether he wanted to or not; he had to stop raking over his father's and, consequently, his own wrongdoing and to renounce for ever putting those wrongs right, for he was no longer on his own. He had a son, helpless and mute, and therefore he had to take him into account, to care for his happiness and future, he had to purge himself with this feeling of a new duty, just as a slate is cleaned with a rag so that new words can be written on it. Everybody has already learnt, or copied out, the words previously written on the slate, so they now have to be rubbed out and new ones have to be written if the mind pursuing knowledge is to make any progress. But was marriage a step forward for Parnaoz? It didn't give him that feeling. On the contrary, he forgot what he used to know, he lost what he used to have, and instead he had a family round his neck, and the family demanded so much of him, so many hitherto non-existent petty things now had to be dealt with that he had no time left to think properly about the changes which had come to his life. Getting up at dawn, he came home in the evening, his arms trembling with exhaustion, it was all he could do to take off his shirt, stuck by sweat to his shoulder-blades; after washing his feet he was enveloped in steam and dozed on a chair, snorting like a horse; but in the morning he got up promptly, without a thought, to lay street paving again, to re-lay floors, to cut out stone baths. The more jobs he had, the more eagerly he worked, because he was no longer serving a punishment for a crime he had not committed, but raising a child and serving life.

As before, Shubu supported the family. The vineyard and corn field, which had been given to Ukheiro for bravery on the field of battle, still existed, but gave a smaller harvest with every year, apparently ageing, like Shubu, although he didn't let age get him down, or give the vineyard and field any rest. He still walked erect, his gleaming white beard, a proof of immortality, down to his chest, but the years had taken their toll. He now seldom came to Vani, although it was only two hours from Ukheiro's estate. He lived in a hovel built in the vineyard, with a donkey tethered nearby: that was all. Until harvest time when he hired labour, there was not a single person to speak to, and Shubu spoke only to the vineyard and the donkey, as if they understood him; and, amazingly, they did.

Shubu dug, manured, pruned, and embellished the vineyard, and at night lay down next to it to warm it with his body, as if it were a sick wife suffering from the cold. Days and months passed, and loving toil gradually made the vines sprout yet again; soon little light-green leaves, like handkerchiefs clenched in a fist, sent out tendrils. The shoot grew as big as a man's hand and produced little green wart-like beads. This was the time when spring rains, like Dionysus's followers, came running, laughing, cackling and yelling, over the land. The vineyard was full of lizards and frogs. The wart-like beads grew every day and swelled with light-green fluid and light, especially light, for these beads were lit up at night and attracted thousands of different midges and other insects. At the end of summer, the beads changed colour: they were now the colour of light and their skin was so taut that it seemed it would burst if a finger touched it, or they might stick to the finger like drops of honey. When Shubu took a bunch in his hand his heart filled with paternal joy and pride. In autumn the vineyard turned red and sad; the bunches, packed full of sun and earth, were in pain, like the breasts of a woman about to give birth, pressing out the milk from her swollen, broadened nipples. The vineyard was in labour, it had to bring forth new fruit from its loins, torn by birth pains. The vineyard needed to recover, to rest, although, neither asleep nor awake, it had already passed into twilit drowsiness that comes over a woman who has given birth. It was then that Shubu hired a labourer. Each vine produced a basketful. Bees hovered round the grapes that were bursting with their fullness; the bees were intoxicated and hummed a monotonous drunkard's song. Shubu threw off, almost at once, the weight of all his years, as the vineyard threw off its fruit, and like a light-headed young father he didn't know what to do with himself. His sets of twins sat in baskets and wailed deafeningly, demanding to be housed, asking for more and more attention.

When Shubu learnt of the birth of little Ukheiro, it took years off him. He spoke lovingly to the vineyard, as if it were his elderly wife, encouraging her, 'We're not old, woman, you can see we're still useful.'

Tina was happy because she had all that a woman could want. The feeling of victory was stronger every day. Naturally, she didn't mind whether Parnaoz loved her or not: she wasn't so silly as to dream of that. It was important that Parnaoz bore the title of husband, that he was with her and always would be, whether he liked it or not. That meant a lot in itself: she had never aimed to gain more from her constant struggle. Whatever she couldn't achieve, she would let time achieve, time and forced proximity. Tina knew Parnaoz well, as well as the district where she was born and had grown up. She could with her eyes closed imagine him from top to toe, she could guess in advance what he would say or do, and she also knew that his soul was so full of love and loyalty for the unattainable, invisible and non-existent, that it had no room left for her. 'So what? What I have is enough,' Tina thought as she curled up in bed. 'I'm happy and my happiness is big enough both of us. My flesh should feel and experience what my soul feels and experiences; the main thing is that, so long as I have a living soul, I don't let my husband and child want for anything,' she thought, and she was right in her own eyes, she was entitled to happiness, having shown such single-minded firmness in realising her childhood dream. She could, of course, have got married earlier and been just as happy with any husband, but Parnaoz was not just a husband for her, he was, by chance or on purpose, a touchstone for Tina to test her will, dignity and abilities on. He was a foundation stone, which she had dragged alone, unaided, step by step, inch by inch, to the open foundation pit so that she could build her future life on him. Her ideas, if only because of their proximity, inevitably generated similar ideas in Parnaoz's mind. He thought roughly the same and felt sorry for his wife, who was striving so blindly and recklessly for happiness, cobbling up a nest out of nothing, as a destitute girl cobbles up a dress so as to keep up with her friends when they go dancing. Parnaoz also felt that he was essential to the happiness which his resolute brave wife was seeking; but he felt the weight of the castle in Spain which obsessed his wife as she sought happiness. Now he was obliged to endure and carry without dropping an irritating weight, because someone, namely his wife, the mother of his son, his partner in life, required him to. Fate was mocking Parnaoz. The happiness he gave another person was false, imaginary, but he had to endure, stay quiet, because one end of the rope was round his neck and the other round Tina's wrist. The rope was Ukheiro, their son.

Once Parnaoz came home and saw the little boy in the yard; the boy was sitting on the paved path, holding an apple in both hands and smashing it hard on the paving. Apple juice stained the paving. Parnaoz was moved: an image of his forgotten past seemed to be resting in the courtyard, in the still noonday heat, as frail and brittle as a new shoot on a branch, but empowered to hold him responsible for letting down, forgetting and then summoning up the past again. Parnaoz felt paternal: his blood warmed up, his bones softened, and he was flustered as if some danger threatened the boy who was squashing an apple on the paving. 'Why have you been left on your own?' he wondered and looked all round. 'A-a-ah,' called the child. Hens were raking the ground by the fence. A fruit tree's slender leaves cast shade like a fishing net over the child and the yard. Parnaoz bent down and cautiously picked the child up. The boy stroked Parnaoz's cheek with his wet hand and Parnaoz was even more touched, so weak and small was the child's hand, so alive. The boy's warmth and frailness took away his strength; he took him carefully, timidly to the house. He had to open the door with his knee and, in that pose, his knees bent, he froze to the spot when the door opened by itself and the three women, Tina, Popina and Kaluka, greeted father and son with a smile: 'Oh, our menfolk have come back!' Taken aback, Parnaoz smiled, not knowing which woman to pass the child to, for none of them showed signs of taking the boy from him. The child was in no hurry to go to the women; he put an arm around his father's neck, holding a squashed apple in the other, and scowled at the women, as if he had found someone to protect him and was now going to settle scores with them. 'Look, just look at the way he takes respect as his due,' the women laughed; then they deliberately frowned and put their hands on their hips, saying to the boy, 'Why are you scowling at us? What have you got against us?' Parnaoz had understood the women's pretence of anger and smiled with embarrassment. This was the way that a lion is lured to a live goat kid, and the lion, encouraged and appetized by the kid's bleating, walks with grave, regal steps into the trap.

A child is the most reliable measure of time. His daily growth is proof of your daily ageing and decline. The child's gains are your losses, and the closer a child gets to anything, the further you withdraw, as though you were tied to one another on opposite spokes of a wheel and the wheel, without your noticing it, turns. Dawn for the child is dusk for you.

'God, how life has flown by!' though Parnaoz.

Indeed, a lot of time had passed, for that is time's main quality: it marched on its path, uncaring, cruel and business-like. It didn't care who, or what it walked over, what it squashed, what it shattered, on what it left the permanent imprint of its bare soles, as long as humanity did not die out, for it constantly had to destroy and crush whatever human hands and mind endlessly created, as if humanity thought, 'I've done it for me, for my posterity,' so that the sight of the ruins of humanity's handiwork and ideas might convince posterity that it has got where it was meant to get: to its father's house.

Time also affected human souls, as the moon affects the elements. Time's ability to affect things is so natural and therefore so imperceptible, that the human eye has found it hard to follow, and changes in man's surroundings or his own being, which he perceives mostly in times of momentary alertness, appear to be inevitable, because they happened without his being aware of them.

So it was in Vani: it was a normal city and normal people lived in it.

One day, in Vani's most remote street, Bedia was found dead. The coil of rope had by now grown so big, so heavy and so tangled that, finally, tormented by old age and by a secret that remained unrevealed, Bedia was suffocated in its colourful coarse coils. Bedia lay there like a fly choked in a spider's web. The spider had sucked out all his blood and left bits of cobweb all over him. Bedia was found by children. They easily recognized him, although only the crown of his head and his heels were visible in the tangled coil of rope. Bedia had long been known as the city madman and the favourite target for the children's mockery, like the stableman of Æëtes and then of Oqajado.

‘Bedia’s coming, it’s Bedia’s dragging the sea on a rope,’ the children shouted, standing on fences and walls, greeting with a hail of stones and yells the old man, swallowed up from head to foot by pieces of rope of various colours and sizes, all tied together. Bedia really was a weird sight, like a hedgehog standing on its hind legs. His body had become rounded, covered in spines, wound in endless layers of rope, whose colourful coils swayed as he walked, like snakes emerging from a snake’s nest.

‘People, the sea is deserting us, people!…’ Bedia cried to the streets, his voice cracking, his body sweating, eaten up by dirt and rope hair, repulsive and ridiculous.

Bedia was found by children, who took hold of the ends of the rope and dragged it down the middle of the street. Bedia’s corpse wasn’t damaged, as it was thickly, safely wrapped in tangles of rope: you would have thought that jackals had dug a mummy out of its sarcophagus and exposed it. Wrapped in rope, Bedia covered the streets in dust; people, brought out by the children’s shouts, crowded round him, coughing and sneezing. Yet Bedia’s death upset everyone: gathered around his corpse in the middle of the street, they all had the same painful feeling that Bedia and his colourful coil of rope were inseparable and necessary, even if tiny, parts of their city, without which the city would lose its specific, characteristic aura. They could no longer see Bedia going down the street like a hedgehog on its hind legs and trying to scare people with the news that the sea was receding., although the sound of his cracked voice had made everyone smile and put them in a mood for fun. In that way, Vani was like any other city. Every city has its madman, for it needs one, especially a harmless one that doesn’t throw stones, but stops in front of you so you can turn and look at him, be amused and glad. You can’t spend all your time thinking about business, worrying yourself sick, not sleeping at night, can you? If you don’t let your hair down occasionally, you too could go mad. But as long as you enjoy having a madman around and his every word and action seem funny, you can rest assured.

The Vani madman, who had replaced the stableman and who would probably soon have his own replacement, now lay in the middle of the street, like a mummy dragged about by jackals. Everyone felt sorry, they all remembered the happy moments over the years, the surprise gifts of a peerlessly generous man. The city was grateful to Bedia, but unable to express or demonstrate its thanks: it was too tongue-tied, and had too many hearts and tongues: it feared saying something stupid and looking ridiculous in turn. Bedia was unique, but now dead, useless and quits.

Bedia’s wife then arrived, picked up a rope end and dragged him off homewards. She went round their hovel with the corpse and stopped at the door. She turned to the corpse and told it, 'Say goodbye to your house.' When she was sure that her husband had finished saying goodbye to the hovel, she picked up the rope again and dragged the corpse to the sea. The sea was now a long way off. At first the corpse bounced over the pebbles left by the receding sea, then it slid over the sand and slithered over the muddy ground, leaving a wide trail through the sprouting water plants. Finally it floated off into the water; but this was not yet the sea, it was marsh water, dead, airless, foul. Her head bowed, the woman went on, like a pack animal, stubbornly wading through the water. At first it came up to her ankles, then it got deeper; her dress was wet to the knees, she was tired, her hands were chafed and hot. The corpse had become much heavier. The water didn't accept it or float it, but splashed, turbid and muddy, as the head of the corpse clove the surface. But the woman went on. Now she was knee-deep in water, and her dress was wet to the waist. It was hard going, she stumbled, she took rapid breaths; from where her neck joined the base of her skull a sticky torrent of sweat flowed down her spine, and made her whole body itch. The woman went on, cursing angrily with all her heart, she cursed the sea and the corpse: half sinking in the water, it seemed to catch on the underwater roots and resist her. The rope had become taut, covered in mud, silt and slime, and long strands of thickened mud, softened by the spring sun's rays, hung on it like icicles. 'Just the same for me, never properly dead or alive,' the woman thought. Her dress was now wet to the chest and its fraying fabric revealed her emaciated body, disfigured by age. 'Never properly dead, or alive,' she repeated persistently, half angrily, half regretfully.

Suddenly she halted and there was such a silence that she looked round in amazement at the corpse. She could hear only the sound of her own breath. Icicles of mud were falling off the slackened rope with a splash, a dragonfly, as light and translucent as a flower, perched on the corpse. The woman got her breath back, then turned round and headed for the shore. The corpse described a broad, bubbling circle and tautened the rope again. The woman gradually quickened her pace, running rather than walking, frantically splashing through the area, infuriated by her own lack of foresight, trying to trace back as fast as she could the random route she had taken, like a pupil crossing out a misspelled phrase before mocking schoolmates and a stern teacher notice. She stopped only when she reached firm ground. The corpse had turned into an enormous clod of mud, barely resembling a human body, like the beginnings of a statue, but the woman could no longer see that: she was tugging the rope with all her strength and the corpse slowly, agonizingly came ashore, like a net full of fish. The woman abandoned the half-landed corpse and fled back to her hovel. The corpse was left alone, indifferent and unfeeling. Here and there, long strands of water plants lashed at it. It lay there, unable to feel or see or hear its wife drag the creaking boat. The corpse didn't care: it had turned into a monstrous clod of mud and didn't care what God moulded out of it, or whether He moulded anything at all.

The woman dragged the boat down, then went behind it and put all her weight against it. The boat clove the wet ooze, dipped down and its prow bobbed up and down in water, as if it had suddenly come to life; the rest of the hull rolled and listed with a grating noise on the land. The woman kept her hand for a time on the stern, as if she were calming a living creature and not letting it topple over into the mud, then she went back to the corpse and with an effort got her hands underneath it and lifted it up. Clods of mud fell off the corpse, it became lighter, but it was all she could do to carry it to the boat. She pushed the corpse head first into the boat, while the exposed legs stuck out overboard, but she paid no attention, put her shoulder to the boat, cursing and pleading, as if it were a mule that had dug its heels in. Mud splattered over her face, her whole body shook with tension, her feet were ankle-deep in sand; she kept slipping. With great difficulty, stumbling and creaking, the boat slid forwards. At last it was floating on water and the woman felt relief. She lay with her belly on the edge of the boat and pushed at the ground with her feet. Now she was covered in mud from head to foot. She lifted up her lower garments as if they'd come from the washing trough; muddy water streamed from them. She stood up in the boat and pushed an oar against the soft sea-bed. Before it got to the open sea, the boat kept sticking in reeds. But she pushed ahead, the water gradually getting deeper, and when the oar could no longer touch the bottom, she realised that she was now at sea. Now she used the oar to row. The waves came one after the other, passing under the boat, and the woman held her breath.

This was the first time she had been in a boat on her own. She had always been afraid of the sea. She was first afraid on her wedding night when Bedia, to the guffaws and roars of the drunks, put her in a boat and rowed her out to sea: the wedding guests stood with burning torches on shore, sending them off with singing. The woman could not see a thing, she was sitting with her back to the shore, unable to breathe, pitching up and down in the air, as if she had been put on an invisible swing. She could hear only the splash of the oars and the sea's uncanny sighing. 'This is my real home,' her husband was whispering to her. Now her husband's legs were sticking overboard, coiled in mud-encrusted rope, as if he had been disembowelled. 'He was always yours, because he always loved you, only you' the woman murmured. She was talking to the sea and the sea every now and again suddenly sighed in reply, as it had on her wedding night. The man's death had brought the woman and the sea closer: he had been husband to her, but lover to the sea. Time had cooled passion and reduced any capacity for jealousy, and now they could chat calmly, without emotion, like elderly relatives. 'He couldn't drink wine any more. If he had just one glass, he'd spend all night tossing and turning as if he had a fever. He didn't want food any more; if he really missed it, he'd ask me to cook him something, but at most he would only nibble at a piece. In the end he was completely out of his mind, I had to follow him about, as if he was a tiny child, and then he goes and dies in the street…' the woman mumbled, as if she had come to leave a child with a relative and was telling her about its misbehaviour.

This was the real sea now, mighty, rough, and bottomless; the shore was almost out of sight, just a narrow flesh-coloured strip lying under a bright white cloud. The woman began to worry, she was agitated, and stood up in the shaking boat, crying out loud, 'Goodbye, husband!' as if calling for help, or as if her husband would understand. Then she caught the oar on the corpse, and the enormous clod of mud fell with a loud splash into the water: first, a foaming pit formed, but it soon closed up and a brown, swishing stain took its place; soon this stain faded, melted away. The corpse, washed and cleansed, floated on the surface. Every piece of rope was restored to its original colour, and became even slacker, as it swayed slowly, sluggishly, lifelessly, like some sea animal's limbs.

The woman was dismayed: she hadn't expected this: she immediately grasped an oar and rowed the boat towards the floating corpse. The corpse resembled a strange animal, garish, with many feet, that had died its own death in a chasm of the sea and had only now floated up to the surface so as to show its beautiful colours to the world.

The woman pressed the oar against the corpse's chest and sank it, but it slipped off the oar like a swollen balloon and floated up again. This recurred several times. The woman did not know what to do next: all around her stretched nothing but endless water and monochrome space; in the middle was her boat and a floating corpse wrapped in colourful ropes.

'What do you want, you wretch? What?!' she yelled.

Then she sat down in the boat, hid her face in her mud-covered lap and burst into sobs. The sun had dried her back and bleached her dress. But she sobbed her heart out, bitterly, like a child lost in the forest. There was nothing around, nothing but empty, steely, monochrome space. The boat and the corpse revolved in the same orbit, caressing, clutching and evading one another, as if they were out at sea to play, for fun. But the woman had no time for games, she had work to do and had to summon the strength for it, whatever it cost her, even her life. 'Help me, we have to bury him. You wanted him when he was alive, why do you refuse him when he's dead?' she bellowed to the sea. Anger made her eyes pop out, exhaustion made her face shrunken and stony. The sea would not accept the corpse, it threw it back, it refused to take it into care. The woman thought this very unjust, shameless: for as long as she could remember it had done its best to take the corpse away from her, it almost broke into the house, every night it stood, shamelessly refusing to move, at the door of their hovel and call, whisper — who knows what it had in mind? — as long as that corpse had breath in it, and the strength to get up on its own from the woman's bed in order to go off with its other love. Now the sea was refusing, for it had no need of an inanimate corpse; but the woman would not give up, now she wouldn't move until she got her own way.

The woman bent down over the water, grabbed the end of the rope, knotted it to the stern and rowed towards the shore. The rope joining the boat to the corpse tautened again, slithered out of the water, sent slivery droplets everywhere and shone. The upright tail of a big fish ploughed the water for about ten metres, like a plough making a furrow in the earth, and then vanished into the water. The woman didn't see the fish; her head bowed, she was working the oar. Two puddles of water slid up and down at the woman's bare feet like a flat cold-blooded invertebrate. The woman ignored them, too; she had other things on her mind and kept looking anxiously at the sky: she had to get everything done by nightfall. She had to see with her own eyes the corpse sink, settle down, this time forever, in the walls of the house which it had striven to reach all its life and where, it might well have moved long ago, if its earthly wife had not shown such stubbornness and had never let herself give up restraining it.

As soon as the boat's bottom scraped the sea-bed, the woman leapt out and ran through the knee-deep water. It took a long time to reach proper ground, to choose a suitable rock and drag it back to the boat. Then she went out to sea again. The sun was already setting, the sea's surface was flecked with white crests chasing each other: in a word, as her husband used to say, the sea had 'spoiled'. The boat rocked all the time. The flat round stone turned out to have two black eye-like holes running diagonally to each other. It was like a fossil, or rather a stone carving of a jellyfish: the woman sensed its bewitching gaze overcoming, stupefying and numbing her. A whole day had passed and she hadn't had a bite to eat or a drop to drink; her arms were fit to break; pain, hot and sweaty, had settled in her shoulders and, whenever she moved, it throbbed in her heart. At one point she fainted with the pain, but, to her own bafflement, it brought her round again. She never thought of resting or even giving up this absurd back-breaking toil, because she herself did not think it absurd: in fact, she was sure that the gods had given her life so that she could do it. It was her task and only she could carry it out. Whatever it cost her, she had to commit to the sea her husband's corpse, in fact an entire heritage which he had acquired by constant meekness and subservience. Perhaps the sea's insatiable heart would now be sated, appeased, and would look kindly on the land which had angered it just because of one wretched husband and wife. The woman had always feared the sea. Although she was jealous of it all her life, as if it were not the sea but the widow next-door, she never said anything bad about it. When she was young, she praised it at dawn and at dusk, she crowned its crested waves with flowers and kneeled to beseech the sea to treat her husband well, to send him back home unharmed, to release him for a little while: a wife, especially a young wife, had no right to demand more. Her husband smelled of the sea, his lips tasted of the sea, but the wife still stayed silent. Not daring to stop her husband, she woke him herself so he wasn't late going to sea. Left alone, she felt like the maid-servant of her husband's mistress, washing her feet, combing her hair, holding up the mirror for her while she dressed up to be more beautiful when she met the husband. The wife bore this without protest, since she was afraid of the sea, constantly afraid: to her mind, the sea would not forgive her marrying this man whom the sea needed for itself. And it didn't forgive her: first her husband went mad, then he gave up the ghost in the street, like a stray dog. But even the dead husband didn't belong to her, the sea had to take him from her so that it saw with its own eyes, to be quite sure that death had taken the man who had gone mad for love of the sea and had even tried to tie it down.

That was what his wife thought, using her teeth to try and free the rope tying the corpse to the boat's stern. The taut wet rope had become even more knotted and would not yield, it slipped from her mouth and made her gums bleed. The salt water burned her chapped lips, but she sucked the rope as if she was dying of thirst, and tore at it. The boat, left without oar or helmsman, turned round and round, taking the corpse with it, but the corpse was describing an ever bigger circle, leaving a wider wake on the surface. The rope would not give in or break free, as if had not been tied on by the woman a few hours earlier, but was an offshoot of the boat, an inseparable part that could only be separated by cutting. But the woman had only her fingernails and teeth. Her nails were already worn down, blue and soft. Her teeth had no effect, but she still desperately gnawed at the rope, like an old dog at a bone. Her mouth kept filling with salty and soft liquid which made her nauseous and, hanging her head overboard, she coughed like a consumptive.

In the end, the rope was freed. The woman wound the loose end of the rope round her wrist. She was breathing loudly and feeling dizzy, for the boat never stopped spinning round, and the ever heavier corpse was pulling her in, twisting her arm, tightening her muscles as if trying to drag her overboard or to escape from this stubborn woman's hands. The woman caught her breath and then went back to work. Now she was bending backwards. Her feet pressed against the side of the boat as she tugged on the rope. The rope lashed from side to side as it came aboard and coiled at her feet. The corpse struck the side of the boat. Now the boat and the corpse revolved together round the same axis. The woman smiled bitterly, biliously as she clasped with both hands the muddy rope, which could slip away at any moment. She had exerted herself for nothing: she had left out something. The stone was at the other end of the boat: squat as an idol, utterly unconcerned by the woman's plight, its tiny black eye-holes merely stared hard at her. But the woman could not be angry with it or curse it, because it was now for her a sacred stone, a gravestone. The woman had to think of something: just sitting there was pointless, for the stone wouldn't come to her and she couldn't reach it from where she was. The two were rooted to the spot, the stone by its own weight, the woman by the corpse's. The woman passed the rope between her thighs, slackened it a little and crawled towards the stern. The rope sensed that it was free, tensed up, gathered strength, quivered, slipped over the edge of the boat and flung the woman onto her back. The woman felt a terrible pain in her thighs. Blood rushed to her brain, her old bones came apart like dogs scalded with boiling water. The rope applied yet more pressure, as if it meant to cut off her legs at the groin. Pain made her forget the rock and the corpse. She instantly let go of the rope as if she had touched a snake. The rope slipped with a rustle into the water. The woman managed to catch sight only of its frayed end and then heard the splash. 'It's got the better of me,' she thought, stupefied. She lay there looking at the sky. She felt no more pain, only the palms of her hands throbbed, but she was afraid to move or look at her flayed thigh, as if the pain had not abated, but was lurking at her feet, watching her. She lay as if dead, outwitting the pain. But how long could she lie like this? She had to return home! But it was a long way to the shore. The rope had slipped from her hand with enormous force, but however deep the water, it must by now have reached the bottom. The woman no longer expected to see the corpse, but the moment she sat up she caught sight of it, garish and sprawled out. It floated some distance from the boat, as though watching it in case the boat tried attacking again.

This time the woman found it easy to row up to the corpse and pick up the rope, as if the corpse had accepted its fate, or was tired of this senseless game of hide-and-seek. Now only little crested waves constantly splashed the woman's face as she bent over the edge of the boat: the corpse offered no resistance, calmly waiting for the rock to be tied to its chest and then, after a push, going away. The corpse slowly sank: it was visible for some time, until the darkness came up from the sea and enveloped it. The woman watched the sea for some time, waiting, but the corpse did not reappear. Then a scarlet sun, its light softened with honey, set over the sea. The woman sat down to the oar and headed for the shore, although she had no idea in which direction to row: she rowed on, because she was desperate to reach her hovel. An overwhelming, apparently never-ending tiredness came over her and she felt nothing else, neither hunger, nor thirst, nor her flayed thigh.

CHAPTER NINETEEN

BEDIA was one of the very few old inhabitants of Vani who had been alive in the 'good old days'. But in Vani, as elsewhere, nobody believed in the existence of the 'good old days'. They were dismissed as an old woman's invention, a dream to console them for their old age. 'When we get old, we'll say that, too.' they said, though they were secretly a little afraid lest their old age might be so tyrannical that they might be nostalgic for today's dog's life. But they tried to put on a brave face and went on living as before. Life was blind, heartless and harsh: in its leaky leather bag it carried two puppies, one white, one black, one called laughter, the other tears. Life picked out of the bag the first one it laid hands on, but life itself sat baking in the sun, warming its old bones and blinking its cataracted eyes.

Parnaoz, too, had accepted his fate: in fact, in his heart of hearts he was even content with it. He had a family, his son was growing up, the cockerel crowed on his fence, work went well and his roof tiles shone in the sun. But in the depths of his soul doubt had arisen and settled, like a lost traveller on a rainy night whose flesh and bones are absorbing another family's warmth and who is thinking, 'It's better here than at home.' 'Accept it, fine, but just ask yourself whether you're entitled to it or not,' the doubt appealed to him from a dark cranny in his soul. Only its steely eyes glinted in the dark, but Parnaoz was afraid other members of the family might notice and begin asking who it was and what it wanted. Parnaoz did his best to hide it, trying to patch things up because he was no longer alone, or rather he no longer belonged to himself. Time had changed many things and cooled many things down; it had scattered like ashes everything by which Parnaoz had been living. Now he approved of his father and when he saw three women forcefully undressing little Ukheiro and putting him in a bowl to wash him, he appreciated big Ukheiro's stubborn silence. The smell of the baby's pink body, as it bounced in the hands of the three women looking after it, lit up the whole world like the dawn, intoxicating it, touching its heart and teaching it patiently to accept everything. But doubt kept sniggering; the sniggering reminded a horrified Parnaoz of fate's treachery; a premonition of inevitable misfortune raised its head again, snatching the hammer and chisel from his hand and making him go back home, as if some disaster had happened in his absence and the only question now was whether he would find them still alive when he got home. But as soon as he heard little Ukheiro's voice, he would go back to work when he got to the gate.

'A-a-agh,' little Ukheiro would cackle, and hearing this absurd voice, Parnaoz was willing get down on all fours and bark like a dog, bellow like a cow, cluck like a hen and roar like a lion, so long as nothing hurt or happened to this pink creature, trustingly crawling in the sun, still as pitiful as a blind man and as vulnerable as a cripple. 'Without hesitation, without hesitation!' Parnaoz would retort to the doubt lurking in a cranny of his soul when it upset his mind still more with malicious questions. 'Suppose one fine day little Ukheiro fell into the latrine…' doubt kept devising new horrors, and Parnaoz kept silencing it. 'Without hesitation, without hesitation,' he called out, and couldn't help walking faster, for doubt could call up countless horrors that might happen to a small child.

One day, doubt's vicious sniggering blighted Parnaoz so much he stumbled hard against a stone and yelled out loud, hopped quickly to a wall and sat down. The pain pursued him and wouldn't let go, standing over him like an attack dog. Parnaoz was drenched in sweat as if someone had poured dirty dish water, or greasy bath water over him. The wound on his big toe, that he had once split with an axe, had opened again. He clutched the painful toe in his fist. Blood oozed between his fingers. Parnaoz cursed, and only then saw a woman standing by the gate across the street, watching him with a smile. 'I've seen her somewhere,' he thought without reflecting, and was then abashed when he imagined what he looked like, a child, or rather a tramp, squatting by a wall, covered in sweat from his woes, grimacing with pain. The woman smiled; he made an effort to smile back apologetically, and tried to get up. Now the woman laughed out loud, in peals of laughter. Parnaoz felt angry, or rather dismayed to see his plight an object of mockery to this unknown woman, but awareness of his helplessness alarmed and confused him so that he was unable to speak. He set off for home, hopping along the wall like a hen with a broken leg.

'Wait,' called the woman.

When Parnaoz failed to look round, she ran across the street, caught up with him and confronted him, her arms akimbo. She was wearing a dress open to the navel. Her wheat-coloured dewy skin filled the cut in her dress like light in a mirror. Her half-exposed breasts moved up and down as if the earth would collapse if they stopped for even a second. He tried not to look at her, but she laughed again and now he recognized the voice. Startled, he became tense, as if this voice asked, or rather forced him to remember something. 'No, I can't remember,' he thought, his mind struggling. The woman looked at him in amazement. Her eyes expressed pity and sympathy. He found it hard to believe that this woman had laughed so merrily just a minute ago. The woman's slightly prominent lower lip quivered and the first tears were about to well up in her face, worn out by secret cares. She worried him and again he tried not to look at her. But she kneeled down in front of him and cautiously put her palms on his dangling foot, as if she was putting them under a waterfall.

'No,' Parnaoz yelled out loud; when the woman looked up in surprise, he remembered everything. He forcibly tore his foot away from her and, despite the pain, struck the ground with it so hard that dust rose up. The woman's face, wreathed in dust, was all the more pitiful for her forced smile. A person smiles like that when they aren't believed, when they get mistrust instead of the trust they deserve, or rebukes instead of thanks.

'Leave me alone!' said Parnaoz.

'Don't I even have that much right?' asked the woman.

'She's making fun of me,' he thought.

'You were hopping about so touchingly,...' she started to say.

'What's that to you?!' he responded angrily.

Five minutes later Parnaoz was sitting in the woman's room with a bandaged toe. She cleaned the wound with a rag soaked in vinegar which stung his flesh and made his toes clench: she laughed again. 'Why do you laugh at everything?' he asked. 'Because it suits me,' she replied.

As soon as he came in, Parnaoz was struck by the bed, unnaturally large, clean and empty. He could see nothing but the bed, although he sat on a chair, with his head bowed while she bandaged his toe. The woman was so preoccupied with what she was doing that she seemed to forget about him: only his sore toe and she herself existed. She existed only to soothe the pain, wrap it up like a child, or rather a doll, and she cuddled the bandaged toe as if it were a home-made doll, cooing to it happily. Then she got up reluctantly, as if the doll's real owner had suddenly turned up, folded her arms and told him, 'Now you can go.' He did up his sandal and again caught sight of the bed, a woman's bed, but as cold and oppressive as a sarcophagus.

The woman was happy: she didn't hide it, her face expressed everything, like bonfire flames reflected on a bystander. She felt as if she had been waiting all her life for this moment, because she believed that it existed, that it was inevitable and, above all, had never doubted that she deserved it. In her opinion, every creature had the right to a moment of happiness, however terrible or insignificant the creature might be. Could she have coped with life if she weren't convinced that even she wouldn't be forgotten or abandoned or left destitute, when the time came to distribute those 'unique' moments? Had she done less or suffered less than others to be left high and dry? No, she mustn't be left high and dry, fate could do as it liked — she could be rebuked, mocked, be dragged about by the hair, but she had to be given her due, what was there for her. She didn't care whether others liked or disapproved of her, supported her or spurned her. What was the point, really, of being as naked as light, a nakedness which puts everyone in the mood for jubilation, or of dressing up in garish rags like a clown, just aiming to entertain people and make them laugh. She felt with all her being that she was entitled to this one minute which, above all, would be serve to prove that she was human. Apart from that, she had something without which any woman would be worthless and repulsive, whatever career she pursued. She had her own star, given to her by a little boy, as silly as she was. Her heart, protected by the points of this star, burned constantly. Who would have thought that this leaf-size light, quivering like a leaf, could turn out to be so weighty, so tireless and inexhaustible? At first she was almost afraid that this exposed light, which lit and fired her whole being from inside might be exhausted and go out; but when childhood became a dream-like memory and everything was called by its real name, she realised that the star would stay fixed in her heart until the little boy came and asked her to give back what he had childishly and ignorantly given her. How distressed she would be, how she would blush, how weak she would be at the knees when she imagined this boy coming, this surly boy who drew dogs for her in the sand with a dry stick, who picked apples for her in Dariachangi's garden, who competed with her in swimming, who threw a jellyfish, as flabby and slippery as boiled starch, at her naked body. 'Give me back my star,' the boy would say. 'The star? Give it back to you?' she would answer in confusion, trying to wriggle out of it now she was a mature woman, tempered by life, who'd been through a thousand men, but, confronted by this tiny surly boy, she became a child again, as silly, naïve and pure as she used to be. 'Is that why I gave it to you?' the boy would reproach her, sticking out his hand as if it were that easy to grab a star which was forever fixed in her heart, cemented by her heart's blood. 'But you gave it to me!' she would fight to the last moment to keep the star, but the boy would be stubborn and respond roughly, 'I didn't give it to you for that reason.'

But the woman was happy, boundlessly, madly happy just to see the boy again, to hear his voice: demanding and angry, as hurtful and pitiless as a cane, the boy's voice reminded her of the stick which the boy had refused to hit her with at the time. Pain sobered her, cleared her mind and made her clever and cunning, too. 'It's your fault, why didn't you hit me with the stick?' she blamed him in her joy at finding so unexpectedly a reason to justify herself. 'Why didn't you hit me, why?! Now I'm not going to give you back the star, so we're quits,' she would say to the downcast boy. The boy would be amazed and his expression would change, he hadn't thought the woman would remember everything, but now he'd recall the wrong he had done her: then amazement would give way to despair and he would withdraw his hand and hide it behind his back. 'Quits, quits, quits,' the woman would cry in joy, and spin in front of the flabbergasted boy. As she spun, the years would fall away, like brightly coloured petticoats from their torn hooks. Gradually, she herself waned, ever smaller and more naked until she became the same size as the boy. The passed years lay at her feet like dropped petticoats, and she had only to step over them for her and the boy to run again, arm in arm, to the sea-shore or to Dariachangi's garden, or to the cave, but stepping over the petticoats was difficult, impossible, because they were piled up as a barrier higher than the eye could see.

The woman was distressed, she rubbed her eyes, but even her woman's mind could not devise a way of crossing over the pile of past years. 'You're a boy, you climb over,' she called to the boy, but the boy was running off without a backward glance, at breakneck speed towards the stagnant sea, to Dariachangi's garden which had long ago vanished, and to the cave like a dragon's open maw which had devoured their whole life's supply of provisions: a dozen or so dry loaves and a smoked ham. The boy would run off alone without her, but without the star, too. The woman was left with the star. She put back on the past years that resembled brightly coloured petticoats, and waited, sure that the boy couldn't manage without the star and would, sooner or later, come to see her. He would come, but possibly she wouldn't recognize him. Thoughts are one thing, life another. Thought keeps what no longer exists for life. During that time, probably, the boy would grow up, change and resemble the men who constantly visited the woman's room. But the woman still waited and didn't lose hope: lo and behold, she was right! She now knew for certain who was sitting in her room. There was no question of any mistake. True, time had left its mark on Parnaoz, too, but his eyes had lost none of their glow, they were still those of a boy who made her a present of a star, not a skimming stone or a coloured pebble, but a real star.

The one minute of happiness which the woman had waited for so long, turned out to be so protracted and unbearable that she did not know what to do, how to draw it out or to fill this soul-stifling time that shackled her. 'Why doesn't he go?' she thought, distraught, because it didn't enter her mind that she was just a whore to this man, and if he had the desire and enough money for his family not to notice, she would have to satisfy his desire without a word of protest. That was the reality. The rest was the fantasy of a frivolous mind, meant to make a fool of the woman and convince her that the star she was given was in her heart to be cherished. Yes, but why did they single out that man, why did they think him a fool, why should he remember a star he had given away when he was a child or remember to ask for it back? No other man would hesitate to give a whole constellation to a woman he is alone with in her room.

The woman laughed. Parnaoz looked at her as if he hadn't seen her before. She was smiling ironically, her arms akimbo.

'Would you like me to lend you a stick?' she said, pointing to a corner with her head.

Parnaoz suddenly noticed a round-headed stick: it reared up in the corner like a snake and shone, as if dipped in pitch. It even seemed to sway a little. But it was Parnaoz, not the stick, that was giddy: the whole room seemed to be turning upside down and he thought with the calmness and contentment of the dazed, 'I'll smash that stick over her head.' But she was talking in a provocative gabble, swallowing her words, but still achieving her aim. He turned pale, his jaw began to quiver, distorted with loathing and hatred, as if someone invisible had slapped mud in his face. That was what she wanted. She had suddenly found a means of self-defence: she sensed that the sight of the round-headed stick had infuriated her visitor. She used all the means at her disposal to stop him having the same desires as the men who came to see her. She made herself loathsome, devised countless foul things to say to make him leave sooner, as pure, unsullied and inaccessible as he was when he came in: she put the stick between her legs, laid her hands over it and propped her chin on them, watching, inspecting him. As she spoke, she laughed nastily, angrily, falsely, as if offended that her joke had been ignored. The nasty, angry and false laughter helped bring the listener back to his senses.

'It's no business of mine,' thought Parnaoz, knowing full well that he was deceiving himself with this reassurance, to stop himself smashing the stick over the head of a woman telling him so shamelessly how old men stinking of urine and stale sweat stripped her naked and looked at her, since that was all they could manage. He may have thought it was no business of his, but he had never felt so acutely and painfully before that this woman's fate and misfortunes were his business: this woman stood for all women as far as he was concerned, for his mother, sister, beloved and wife. He was unable to offer filial, fraternal, friendly or even conjugal loyalty to this unique woman, because he had been for her an inattentive son, an indifferent brother, a foolish friend and a cowardly husband. So he had no right to smash a stick over her head. Quite the contrary, he should fall at her feet, beg for pardon, or swallow his pride and clear out, fly to the warm, cosy nest which he had shamelessly put together for himself, and there he could forget for ever, to the sound of his squab's chirruping and his wife's cooing, that a room ever existed where the victim of his neglect, indifference, foolishness and cowardice was to be found, as horrific as a dead man stolen from the cemetery and brought back to life, yet at the same time pitiful and harmless, like a hand-reared wild animal.

'Then another man, the old man's son-in-law,' the woman persisted, 'pawned this stick with me. You don't have anything you want to pawn, do you?' she suddenly shouted.

'It's all over, and that's just as well,' thought Parnaoz as he stood up, but the pain tore at his foot and he had to support himself with both hands against the chair he had been sitting on. The woman suddenly froze, as if the same pain had struck both of them at the same time.

'Now you can go, actually,' she said after a pause. 'It's good that it's all over. You should be more careful when you walk in our city streets…' she said in a calmer voice. Her face showed little dimples as she smiled.

'Thank you very much, but I'll do without the stick,' said Parnaoz, turning towards the door. Then something happened which neither expected, which left both incapable of further pretence or desire. The sound of Popeye's jingling sack was heard in the street. The room became airless; they could both hear their hearts pounding. At the same time they looked at one another, anxiously, unhurriedly, then the woman put her index finger to her lips, silently ran to the door and slid the bolt. Coming back was hard for her: now, for the first time, she was embarrassed by Parnaoz as if he couldn't have understood where he was until Popeye turned up. She had cleverly hidden from him, in fact herself forgotten, that people came to this room not just to get back a star they had given in childhood, or to have a sore toe bandaged. The woman's shoulder began to tremble. Her weeping was silent, accompanied by trembling shoulders. Parnaoz went up to her and put his hand on her head. He had a lump in his throat, he had never been so unhappy. Leaving her and staying in this room both seemed unbearable to him. He wanted to speak her name, shout and roar it for the whole world to hear, but he didn't dare, he was ashamed and afraid of being discovered here. In any case, he was ready to be turned into a lizard, a spider and to crawl for ever into a crack in the wall, because he was horrified by the very thought of Popeye with his sack over his shoulder, standing in the courtyard, looking at the fruit tree, as if that was why he had come, as if he didn't know who was there, who was trembling like a hare behind the bolted door. If Parnaoz had been a real man, he would have stopped the woman bolting the door, he would have told her, ordered her to stop crying, but as for Popeye… he couldn't be seen by Popeye, he couldn't say a word to him, he would rather die here in a whore's bedroom. The woman had noticed and had bolted the door for his sake, she had shown him mercy, had spared him, protected him from danger, felt sorry for him: that was why she was now weeping: she never thought there existed anyone who needed her pity.

Time dragged on, ever more sluggishly, so that a second seemed to last a century. They were too afraid even to move, as if they no longer had the right to do so. It seemed they would have to stand there like that, because fate and destiny had now devised this as their punishment. Popeye was standing on the other side of the door, waiting for the will power of the prisoners in that room to fail, for them to realise that there was now no point in hiding, for them to open the door to him and confess with a conciliatory smile that they were just as lustful, depraved and shameless as he was, as everyone was, but that others were better than them, since they weren't hypocrites and took what they wanted openly, satisfied their desires openly, without shame. They were no longer entitled to justify themselves, and they didn't even know to whom. Who would believe that they had locked themselves in this room out of childish purity and naivety, and not for the purposes this room usually served.

What right did Parnaoz have to yell at Popeye in the cemetery, 'You're lying!' Wasn't his lie even worse? He was just a bare-faced liar. He was lying now, lying to himself, for, as time passed, the longer he held out in that room, the more dirt the two of them, he and Ino, would be in: they were the only couple in the whole land who had no right to be together in that room. It didn't exist as far as they were concerned, it mustn't exist if the aura of eternity, purity and reality were not to be stripped from the little boy and girl who had really existed, loved each other and believed that you could make a present of a star, turn into a dog for one another's sake and make a life with an outlaw. Such childlike faith and love were, perhaps, the foundation of the land, enabling it to survive and not be destroyed. The land stood on the shoulders of two children, a girl and a boy, and on faith and love, and they were now a woman and a man shut in a room, in fear of being witnessed, taking away those two children's last inch of territory, their last foothold. The woman and the man both felt this, because they were the creatures of those children, or rather the surplus, useless burden shed by those children. They were taking away each other's past, their safest refuge, where they could shelter when they were exhausted and trampled down by life, not only shelter, but be renewed, purified and restored, for the past smelled of apples and had the wings of a quarrelsome seagull.

Outside, the seasons passed, trees blossomed, became laden with fruit, withered and were stripped bare, and the wind blew the dry leaves in all directions, then snow covered everything and only one black spot remained still in that boundless whiteness. The black spot grew larger, took on human form with a leather sack over its shoulder, but it was going nowhere. It or he didn't want to go, and wasn't going, however many times the vault of the sky turned. He would stay here, outside the whore's hovel, for only here could he prove that everyone was the same and nobody had any right to look down on him, reproach or blame him for anything, because others, in fact everyone was like him, everyone was besmirched with sin from their mother's womb, and if they hid the fact, they did so only because nobody had thought of catching them at it, they had just been taken at their word. He wouldn't move an inch until he had witnessed, or proved what he already knew, but had no proof of. Now, at the cost of his patience and what had seemed to be a waste of time, he would have the proof.

CHAPTER TWENTY

In Vani, constant, tiresome autumn rains set in. People shut themselves indoors. The city drowned in mist, a gigantic cloud hovered over the city, like the exhalation of God. Here and there you could see the naked crown of a tree or part of a roof, like wreckage of a ship sunk at sea. The sticky, thickened air carried no sounds, the cockerels crowed as if they had sore throats, the dogs' barking barely reached the house gates. Oil lamps flickered. The quince-coloured light made everything look more alien and inhuman.

Parnaoz was also confined by bad weather, but he was afraid to be at home, as a traitor is afraid to be in the camp which he has been plotting to betray. He could not bear to look at the fire or at his wife: after meeting Ino, he was even more unshakably sure that the thread Tina had used to bind them together was weak. It wouldn't need much time or strength to break that thread. All he had to do was to stop resisting the invisible voice whispering in his ear, 'Get up, why pretend? Why deceive others, why deceive yourself?' Then everything would be turned upside down. The voice irritated Parnaoz by telling the truth, but it augured badly. 'Why pretend?' it might say, but he couldn't pretend, however much he wanted to. The skinny girl with curls that stuck out, whose naivety and purity had for so long given a sense to Parnaoz's existence, had vanished without trace, had stolen away from his memory, like a bird flying out of a cage, and her place was taken by a woman who had been through every door in life and looked through every crack, had been the prisoner of a thousand men and the overseer of a thousand men's sarcophaguses. But Parnaoz loved this woman. Pretending was senseless now, but had he ever pretended? No, he had been struggling all this time. It no longer mattered whether he had struggled well or badly, the point was that he had struggled, fought off, resisted and barred love, afraid of its depth, its secret chasms, its abyss covered with corpses and pearls. Parnaoz had been struggling with the sea, a sea of love, and all his life he had been plunging about in seething waves, like an empty clay jar sealed with pitch. But all his life he had felt the moment was imminent when the pitch stopper would be dislodged, or the jar's bottom would crack and it would no longer hold the dormant passion accumulated over years of patience. In the end it would surface, like a wild animal rabid with tooth-ache, blinded by the light, as weak and ignorant as a newborn baby, doomed to perish, but already prepared to perish, which would make it frightening, for intimations of inevitable death would fortify and embolden it, rather than make it complacent.

This passion was Parnaoz's distinguishing feature: it could no longer be hidden, any more than the toe that Ino had bandaged. Tina never asked what had happened to him, or who bandaged him, because asking would have been foolish. Tina didn't speak up until she rebandaged the toe. Her hair, parted in the middle and combed straight down, shone; Parnaoz felt he had done this woman wrong, he was destroying her, or had already destroyed her, because her voice, smell and bodily heat could fill only the house, not his heart. The love that belonged to Tina was as shrivelled as overwintered garlic bulbs, empty, put away. But he could not and would not say as much, as if this woman with her hair combed down was not his wife, but a guest who was overstaying her welcome while the host kept on laying the dinner table and making the bed, because hospitality obliged him to. 'I shouldn't have come home,' Parnaoz thought.

He felt as if he had been brought here, to his motherland, to his father's house, under false pretences. The reason he felt like this was that he used to think and see things differently before he came back. If he hadn't been allowed to come back, he couldn't have stayed away, he'd have stolen a boat, made friends with pirates, or would have crossed the sea with neither boat nor friends. Everything seemed different abroad. There he never doubted that Ino was waiting for him: he even thought she would meet him at the port, put her arms round him in front of everybody and announce an end to their sufferings and torments. He never enquired how Ino might find out the exact day and hour of his return. Or was she supposed to spend ten years standing all the time in the port?! Well, that was what Parnaoz wanted and longed for. He was so far from the motherland that he only remembered the good things. Now, he was sitting here in his own house, like a genuinely foreign sailor, feeling that it would always be like this, he would never lose this feeling of alienation, even though he was surrounded by his kinsfolk, while his own flesh and blood was crawling on the floor, grabbing anybody and anything in his attempts to stand up and be like a human being. Parnaoz found it heart-rending to watch his son, to leave him as a hostage in his own family, and if he broke the conditions imposed on him by fate, he would first of all be sacrificing this pink creature. Parnaoz also suspected that the women who handled little Ukheiro were spiting and humiliating him by treating the baby harshly and roughly, deliberately feeding him until he choked and, instead of making a fuss, panicking everyone; they were laughing, clapping the boy on the shoulder-blades and telling him, 'Ugh, you useless child.' Then they'd look round with a mocking smile at Parnaoz, as if to say, 'Do you still doubt we're in charge of your soul?' Then they'd give the baby another slap as soon as he had recovered, 'You should be ashamed of yourself, look how you've frightened your father.' Parnaoz really was frightened, until he heard his son get his breath and voice back. His blood curdled; he too held his breath. But the women casually threw the baby like a puppy from lap to lap, once he was bloated, and his face smeared with porridge and minced apple; they just laughed if he fell sprawling to the floor or hit his forehead on a paving slab. When Parnaoz rushed forth like a madman, the women yelled at him, kicking out like children: 'What's wrong with you, why the panic? If he doesn't fall over, how can he grow up?' Shubu once told Parnaoz, 'If you hang a child's guts on the fence, it will still shoot up.' Day and night he hoped that was true.

Little Ukheiro was like any child his age, weak and silly, but unaware of either his weakness or silliness. One minute he wept bitter tears, the next talked absolute drivel, and cuddle up to everybody and everything, even if they had just hurt him, directly or not. He was learning about life, and these rapid, constant changes of mood helped him to adapt to life's equally changeable sweetness and bitterness, warmth and cold, softness and roughness, on which his future depended. If he came to hate the floor he banged his forehead on, he would never be able to walk on it. But he would have to walk on the floor, his head held high to see the sky, whose light soft fingers gently stroked his neck while he crawled on all fours. So he had to endure pain and learn to accept it. Little Ukheiro lived as nature dictated: pain was essential, it gave him knowledge needed for life. But now and again little Ukheiro had to put up with wholly unforeseen, useless pain, therefore all the more heartbreaking. His mother would suddenly pick on him, pinch him hard, or dig a spoon mercilessly into his mouth and shout, 'You're all the same!' He was taken aback by pain and surprise, but could only burst into tears. He didn't even understand what his mother was saying, but understood that they were not words of affection and not a lullaby. His mother would never use that tone to say, 'Clear off, you jackal, get lost!' Not that those words made sense to little Ukheiro: he didn't know what a jackal was or why it was disliked. But when his mother said this, her eyes became so loving that he forgot to free his hand from the swaddling clothes and to shake the rattle fixed to the head of the cradle. He smiled happily and proudly as he imagined the jackal being chased away, and went to sleep with that smile. His mother's sudden bursts of anger upset him: they were such a misfortune, that he couldn't take them in or stand them for long: he couldn't help looking for someone to rescue him, or rather comfort and distract him. His father served this purpose, always turning up in time, as if summoned, to cuddle him and lick his tear-stained cheeks. Then his mood changed to one of laughter and play; he tried to lick his father's cheeks, and although the stubble scratched his tongue, he would just spit and stubbornly cling to this face that was as hard as stone and prickly as a rug.

If little Ukheiro couldn't understand, at least Parnaoz knew why Tina lost her temper with the baby. This fabulously patient woman sometimes lost control: she dragged the baby so roughly, or pinched him so hard, that the pain tore her own flesh. But she couldn't help it, she thought she'd go mad if she didn't let her anger loose on the baby because of the endless waiting, of this artificially concocted family and, above all, of her unrequited, still unacknowledged love. To the very last moment Tina hoped that her patience would be rewarded differently, and that Parnaoz, at least, would settle down in the depth and splendour of this patience and would realise that such patience had come at a high cost to the woman who loved him and whom he didn't love, that he would just once put a hand on her differently, if only as a horse is patted when it wins a race. But things went in the opposite direction: Parnaoz was becoming more of a stranger every day; saying the most simple, banal words was getting harder every day. They both thought first about what they would say and how, or whether they would say anything at all. Tina suffered because Parnaoz was again distant from her, belonging again to someone else, even though he lay beside her as a husband every night. Their married life had elements of compulsion and rebellion in it, as if the two of them were trying to shed a burden foisted on them. This unwanted closeness and the obligation to be together had its effect: Tina lay where she had to, where her place was and she tried or did not try, as she wished; her hot body still took on a magnetic power in the dark of the night and silently attracted everything masculine in their room.

Parnaoz was in torment, resisting this eternal, divine force, but in the end went to her, like a thirsty man to a spring, inflamed by his suffering and by an inhuman ecstasy. He went because he could not do otherwise. There was only one escape: he should have fled the room, the house, in fact, and abandoned everyone and everything forever: his father's grave and his son's cradle. It was a big sacrifice, horrifyingly big; the only reason to make it was that he didn't love his wife. Rather, he loved someone else and would always do so, even if he lived ten lifetimes, even if he was hanged by the feet, disembowelled, buried alive, plunged into boiling pitch. But for that other person, he might not have even wondered if he loved his wife or not. Like other men, he would probably have grumbled to his wife only if his dinner was late or she'd forgotten to cool the water to wash his feet, or had gone to borrow salt from a neighbour and stayed there gossiping and chatting until evening. Tina had done nothing wrong, she hadn't forced her way into the house: he had invited her, brought her in, for he thought differently then and didn't care whom he brought in, whom he married. Then he was looking for a refuge, a hiding place, somewhere to hide from Ino, and he refused to believe that no such place existed, in this world or the next. Tina was doomed, but innocent. Tina was a bird that had chanced to fly into the rickety hovel of his life and, instead of letting her fly out again, or showing her how, he had thrown her food to peck at, warmed her by the fire and got her used to him, and she was now, out of fear, unable to stay alone in the hovel.

Tina deserved nothing but respect, for she understood everything and still put up with it, for his sake and for the sake of his rickety hovel, in order to give the family a semblance of the smell of a wife and baby. She now displeased, in fact irritated Parnaoz; he rejected comfort and respect, because he had none for her, who was alone, abandoned by everyone, perishing and causing him to perish. Her patience most irritated Parnaoz: it shackled and inhibited him, made him hate himself and her. He would rather she shouted at him, quarrelled with him, called in the neighbours, threw him out of the house. But if she had acted like that, she wouldn't have been Tina, and it would have been easier for him to relate to her and speak to her. Tina could behave in no other way, patience was her strength and her weakness, it was all she knew and she clung with both hands to this all-conquering and all-defeating force; she was suffering and making someone else suffer. But she wasn't his main obstacle.

In the end, sooner or later, they would have made one another see that staying together was absurd, stupid, nasty and cowardly, as they didn't love each other. But Tina was the mother of a child, of little Ukheiro, and he was not just a child, but Parnaoz's last hope. When he heard his carefree cackling, his heart was rent with ardent pity, he mentally knelt down to ask forgiveness for begetting him, for he was sure that he could not do what his father had achieved: he couldn't hide from his son that he was born a slave and would die a slave if he were as deliberately deaf and obtuse as his father and grandfather were in mistaking treachery to the motherland for self-sacrifice. Little Ukheiro had to find a different path and to know the truth from the start, as soon as his ears and eyes were opened and he could stand on his own two feet. However much his father loved him and pitied him, he still couldn't keep the truth from him: telling the truth was his only obligation, for which the gods had created him: he had to discover the truth for himself, unaided, and then pass it on to his son, implant it. This didn't oblige him to live with Tina, but abandoning Tina meant abandoning little Ukheiro, and a son who grew up without a father might not trust a man who was only there for his conception, not for his upbringing. Upbringing was more important. Little Ukheiro had gradually, from the start, to get used to the truth as he did to walking, as a snake hunter to snake venom. Ino was different: she belonged only to Parnaoz and, whatever her life, she would always be his alone. His son wouldn't. So he couldn't abandon him if he wanted sincerely to fulfil his main obligation, speaking the truth. For that reason he couldn't take a step which would settle and clarify everything and make life more bearable. 'You blame it all on your son,' an invisible voice called to Parnaoz, and he, too, sometimes believed that this insistent voice of truth was just the result of his cowardice and timidity, a lying, invented voice justifying his cowardice and timidity. 'You're worried what people will say when you leave a pearl of a wife and child and go off with a whore,' the invisible voice went on accusing him: he leapt out of bed like a madman when his thoughts froze at this point.

Tina would turn over to face the wall, slowly exhaling as if asleep, while he, as if sick with fever, an innocent prisoner on trial, repeated, 'No, no, no,' not knowing how to deflect this stifling, demeaning accusation, which was as merciless as the truth. 'It's not Ino's fault if I can't sort out my life,' he argued with the invisible voice, although he sensed he wasn't being totally honest with himself. His life was filled with thoughts of Ino, like a pomegranate with seeds, and everything that happened to him, good or bad, was because of Ino. He blamed her, although he couldn't say how she should have acted, what she should have tried to do to put their lives right. Had he made any efforts in that direction? He had tried to buy the girl with the money raised from selling one lousy dog's head: instead, he should have been a highwayman, or a pirate, or tunnelled into the king's treasury and laid the entire country's wealth at the feet of black-eyed Malalo: black-eyed Malalo had a better idea of Ino's value than he or anyone else did. Wasn't Ino worth all the wealth of the country? Wasn't it worth for her sake, to save her naïve smile, becoming an outlaw? Burning down cities and drowning in blood anyone who stood in the way? Of course she was, but he was incapable of becoming an outlaw, thief or murderer. He had almost kissed black-eyed Malalo's feet, treated her as if he were her child, when he should have smashed her head in, at least spat at her, because, greedy and unfeeling, as merciless as a dragon, aged by lovelessness after passing through the arms of a myriad of men, she was what stood between him and Ino. But she was right and Parnaoz wasn't, because she knew the value of Ino. In any case, black-eyed Malalo had her own path, her own accounts with the world, she tried to make everyone resemble her and live as she did. What did she care if some people disliked her free and easy way of life? Why should she yield her daughter to someone, when she needed the daughter herself and knew her value better than that someone? She wasn't going to yield her up unless Ino was removed by force; if that someone was a little boy, why didn't he fall at his father's feet and tell him 'I'm dying, help me'? Perhaps Ukheiro would have sold all he had so that his son needn't suffer. He could have tried. But no, Parnaoz couldn't ask his father for help, his father couldn't even walk, he spent all day embroidering without a break, and only a baby's wet nappies hung from his javelin. Parnaoz therefore chose the easiest way out: running away and blaming everyone else.

'Why didn't she kill herself?' Parnaoz had wondered. 'Why should she kill herself? Perhaps she even liked that life. Didn't her mother and sisters live like that? Who showed her a different life or gave her a choice?' Parnaoz should have killed Ino or himself, but he couldn't do that, it was beyond him.

Tina never asked questions and took no part in these burning passions which nature, the gods or fate had fired in her absence, before she was born. She just existed, like an underwater rock, breaking the waves that rolled over her, whether she wanted to or not. Tina deserved nobody's anger or hatred, her only crime, if a woman can be charged with it, was to have married Parnaoz, to have wanted to be his wife. In fact, on their wedding night she told her husband, 'I badly wanted to be your wife, but now I'm not surprised or even glad.' She never thought for a moment that by being his wife she might bring him only torment. Quite the opposite, all she wanted was to make him happy by caring for him, giving him attention and loyalty and, if necessary, sacrificing herself. She thought she herself was happy: she had the husband she wanted, he was the father of her child, she had a family and nobody in that family thought of limiting her rights, or looking down on her, or treating her with suspicion, because she gave them no cause to: she worked hard and kept watch on everything around her, like a warrior guarding his commander's tent. But there was one thing Tina didn't know and couldn't foresee: one person's happiness is not enough for two persons, happiness can't be shared. She realised that later, but still put up with it, because that was all she could do. She was guarding what she had acquired, in the same way as she had acquired it. She swallowed many bitter tears, the tears of a rejected woman, many nights she spent awake, her eyes wide open, but in the morning she was still the same Tina, a cheerful, hard-working, affectionate, proud wife and happy mother. Nobody knew how desolate and pitiful Tina's bed was: instead of conjugal caresses, two utterly alien bodies, even at a moment of greatest intimacy, could not forget their alienation; they didn't give themselves to one another, they submitted; they satisfied not emotion, but irritation, since their togetherness was imposed by accident, not an inevitable necessity. Woken up suddenly, Tina pleaded in vain with her husband to give her time, to let her come round, but no sooner were they fully awake than they parted again. Tina understood this later, when her female intuition told her why her husband forced himself on her: by doing so he was suppressing the truth, his passion was aimed at an entirely different woman. So every move he made was painful, humiliating and punitive. 'Give me time, let me come round,' Tina might say, but she had every reason to know that her husband wouldn't give her time to come round, any more than a small band of outlaws would give time to a caravan camped and asleep at the side of the road, because the band of outlaws didn't know how much resistance the caravan might put up, if they were worth robbing. But the band still attacked, because they had no alternative: their cave was full of bones they had gnawed, and any failure or reluctance to act by their leader could be the ruin of this little band, could scatter it and destroy its faith in its leader and success.

Inevitably, Tina sensed this, for she was not the woman her husband's rebellious flesh was seeking. Parnaoz knew only one thing: whether he got together with Ino or not, he could never accept not being with her, or any substitute life offered, or anything from life. His very existence would be oppressive and unbearable for anyone linked by fate to him, whether as wife or son, nephew or sister, because a fundamental mistake was made at the very start by hiding from him what he needed to know as much as he needed to know his mother, or rather his mother's grave. In this case, not knowing was a sin, an irreparable evil: there was only one way to put that evil right: to go back to the past, the cave, humanity's first shelter, via ancestral graves, stepping and crawling over them, and beginning life again, not just one's own, life in general, when nobody knew what freedom was, as everyone was still equally free. This evil had a horrible aspect: its victim didn't know he was a victim, and so lived not as he should or would if he had been given the necessary knowledge.

Parnaoz had found the knowledge by himself, unaided, and many things had been destroyed and distorted for him; he had been set apart, against his will, from others. The world in which he existed had been exposed for what it was: it was split into two, he found himself in one half, everybody else was in the other half. The second half hadn't noticed yet, but it would eventually notice his apartness, and would seek out the reasons for it; it would be unable to take them in and this was likely to make it quarrel with Parnaoz, trample him underfoot, crush him and get rid of him, rather than follow and trust him or mess up the life they had arranged merely for his sake. In Parnaoz's opinion they were all ignorant, cowardly and meek sheep who were only too glad to be fleeced of their surplus wool and didn't care who wove a shirt from that wool. They were naked, but unforgiving to anyone who saw their nakedness. This was typical of all the rest and, all in all, it simplified, rather than complicated life. Nakedness made people alike, took away their sense of shame, emboldened them: this boldness was their only wall, although they couldn't grasp the fact, to save them from complete annihilation, but it made their existence loathsome and deplorable.

Of course, this hadn't come about instantly or by itself. Far away, in the palace of Knossos, it was devised and decided in the Supreme King's mind. Minos knew that lies, not the sword were the tool to conquer a people: lies and inertia. The noose which Parnaoz had felt since the day he was born was the end of the rope which Æëtes's faithful guards had used to tie him up and get him out forever from his native city. No illustrious general could have done what Oqajado had done, however many legions he had and whatever weapons he armed his legions with. Oqajado had entered Vani under the banner of the legitimate heir to the throne; the banner was held high by Æëtes's opponents, men of Vani who loved their homeland and were ready to die for it. For them the battle was a battle for justice, for the sake of the country: it never occurred to any of them that a more devious, farsighted enemy would, with their help, forever deprive them of their motherland. Many died a hero's death on their native soil in the battle for Vani, and accepted death with gladness as worthy sons of the fatherland who could no longer choose between life and death when the motherland's life was at stake. Now they lay, forever misled and duped, in a mass grave dug by Oqajado. They had one great advantage over the living: they'd never know how badly they had been deceived, they'd never suffer pangs of remorse at the sight of boys they'd raised to manhood. The survivors' lot was dismal beyond measure: either they had to put a brave face on things, pretend to be fooled, and enjoy their rewards, or they had to hide their weapons under babies' pissy nappies and, like girls awaiting bridegrooms, ruin their eyesight doing crochet.

The choice was made long ago: it was now too late to bite their nails. Truth was clothed in lies, like a wolf in sheep's clothing trotting freely among a flock where the shepherd has been ousted. The sheep were happier without their shepherd, because he walked about with his crook, stopping them from falling down chasms or scattering, while the wolf agreed to anything, they could do as they liked, go wherever they fancied, nibble the grass when they liked and come back to the flock if they wanted, or not come back at all; if a rock got their head or a razor their belly, nobody was counting them, nobody would come running after them with a pack of shaggy dogs. The wolf enjoyed more trust because it walked like them on four legs and was clothed like them. The shepherd had always been a stranger and had now become even more of a stranger, once they could not hear his warning shouts or the shrill sound of his chalumeau. The sheep, happy with their animal freedom, grazed right up to the edge of the abyss. The wolf sharpened his teeth, for there would soon be meat and bones in abundance. 'What's up with you? What have you got to worry about? You left the flock in time, didn't you? You decided not to be a sheep, you wouldn't touch your share of the grass and thorns. Well, grass and thorns aside, you just got scared of being smashed to pieces like the rest of them, since you prefer your own skin to the flock's skins: the flock has everything in common, including death…' Parnaoz needled himself, sometimes suspecting he might be blaming his weakness, his profligacy, on others, thus sinning even more. 'But why,' he wondered, 'do others live happily with their families, working, rejoicing and dying, according to the rules; why is it only me who sees misfortune and ordeals, however hard they are to detect? Perhaps my father was right: what could he tell me, when he had nothing to tell?' These thoughts made him suffer more, he was becoming guilty in everyone's eyes, but the feeling of guilt made his existence absurd and useless, rather than frightening. Then why was he prolonging his life? Because he couldn't reconcile himself with what he'd lost, or so that he could tell his son the truth? But what was the truth? How did he know if the truth was what only he considered to be true? He might be committing an even worse crime: deceiving and ruining his son. Perhaps silence and acceptance were the only paths that the gods allowed a human being, perhaps he was not on a path allotted to human beings, had totally lost his bearings and was therefore alienated from the world around him? 'It may be so,' he concluded, his head aching, and retreated to his shell where he could once more try to explain the inexplicable and ponder the imponderable.

CHAPTER TWENTY-ONE

It had been raining non-stop for a whole week, but the house was pleasantly, drowsily warm. Water boiled in the pot over the fire. The women boiled water to feel more comfortable, and the bubbling, steaming pot made the room cosier and more friendly. Everyone was enveloped in a dewy haze. Voices and movements took on the sluggishness and softness of underwater creatures, and an eerie, fairy-tale mystery. 'Popeye is coming,' said Popina. Very soon the others heard the familiar jingling that gradually broke through the sound of the rain as it came towards them. This voice roused Parnaoz from his thoughts: he heard little Ukheiro cooing, the pot bubbling and the women calmly chatting. Ziara came into the room, with Popeye's sack over her shoulder; she put the sack down by the door and covered her face with her wet hands.

'Popeye will be here any moment!' she said, smiling like a baby whose face has been washed.

Popeye followed in Ziara's wake and made straight for the fire. Pools of water appeared on the floor tiles. Ziara stood by the door again, smiling awkwardly. 'What are you staring at? Come and stand by the fire,' Popeye called to her. Steam came off him in puffs: only his hands, stretched out to the fire, were visible. Ziara joined him by the fire, trying not to step in the pools he had left. But this was not easy, for Ziara had short legs and his stride was three times longer than hers. She hopped from pool to pool, rather than walk: it was such a ridiculous spectacle that nobody could help smiling. Popeye whinnied, let Ziara disappear into the steam around him and then asked the women, 'Do you know what my spouse wants most of all?' Not waiting for an answer, he went on, 'She wants a baby, and says why shouldn't she, she's as good as anybody else. The things she wants! Ha, ha…' He whinnied again, Kaluka put two pairs of slippers by the fire. Ziara quickly took off her wet boots, then her stockings and put the slippers over her bare feet. 'Come on, change your dress, too,' Popina invited her, but Ziara shook her head, looked at Popeye and smiled, probably thinking how ridiculous she'd look in someone else's dress, whoever it belonged to. Ziara was shorter than any of them.

'What did you say you wanted?' asked Popeye.

'I want a baby,' replied Ziara without hesitating.

'Do you hear that, Tina,' Popeye appealed to the women and then turned to Ziara: 'Just tell us if you deserve to have a baby.' His voice was ominous, and he was clearly looking for an argument.

'Ziara, come and join us, it's warm here,' said Tina.

Dry and dishevelled, Ziara trotted out of the cloud of steam like a little animal. Popina handed her the baby and she suddenly plucked up courage, sat with the women and dandled little Ukheiro on her knee. She seem less tiny and ugly with a baby in her arms. Ziara knew that and, feeling grateful, her face shining, she kissed the top of little Ukheiro's head. The women began chatting. Popeye was still in a cloud of steam, his red hands sticking out likc boiled crabs. Parnaoz was sure that Popeye was watching him and smiling sarcastically. He knew what brought Popeye here in this downpour, and why Ziara had come too. Popeye had been jubilant all these past days at knowing such a great secret. But what did he actually know? Only that Ino had bandaged Parnaoz's sore toe. Anyone would have acted as Ino did in the circumstances. Yes, but how had he chanced to get into trouble outside Ino's house? How did Parnaoz know that Ino lived there? Secondly, what business was it of Popeye's where Parnaoz chanced to get into trouble? It was nobody's business, and people should have the decency to keep out of it, or else… Or else, what? What are you threatening? If nothing had happened, why is your heart missing a beat, why are you afraid to look at the cloud of steam, as if it were not a cloud, but a dragon in the form of a cloud that has crept into the house and will turn back into a dragon at any moment. It crouches in front of you and smiles so that you will drop into its maw, rather than see its smile any more. No, so as to block its throat, stifle its voice and stop it saying what it has come to say. He's been bullying that wretched Ziara, spending a week coaching her to say here, 'I want a baby, I'm as good as anybody else.' Of course she is. If you have a baby, you won't go gallivanting about playing hop-scotch all over the place, and scowling like a money-lender when you're at home. Quarrel outside, and be forgiven inside, that's what you're up to. But you can't fool Popeye's eyes, and he won't let you fool anyone else, your wife or the other woman. Are you trying to kill two bird with one stone? When you're with your wife, you want to be with the other one, when you're with the other one, you run back to your wife, as if the dead have risen from the tomb and are chasing you.

No, that won't work. You have to drop one of them, forget one of them for good. Or perhaps you're hoping that she and Tina will come to an agreement and you can lie down between them? You're nothing but a coward, a coward! No, you're a mouse, a tiny little mouse trying to drag off two walnuts at the same time, but it can't and the cat catches up with it and roots it to the spot with its bewitching eyes. Any moment now the cat will come out of the cloud of steam and kick the mouse around wherever it fancies: everybody will die laughing. Then they'll grab hold of your tail, when you've fainted with fear, and throw you on the dunghill with a wave of the arm. You can be thankful if they go no further and the cat lets them throw you on the dunghill. Cats like the taste of mice, and know that mice like playing dead.

Those were Parnaoz's thoughts when Popeye emerged from the cloud of steam, sat on a chair facing Parnaoz and put his sunburnt hands on his thighs. 'If he mentions Ino, I'll kill him,' thought Parnaoz. Popeye uttered not a word, just placing his hands, fingers outspread, on his thighs; then he got up, went to Ziara, took the baby from her and came back to the chair with little Ukheiro. When the baby saw Parnaoz, his face lit up with joy, he snorted, his pink mouth dribbled and he stretched out his hands. Parnaoz was reluctant to take the child from Popeye, who sensed this and smiled, turned little Ukheiro's face towards himself, put him on his lap and bounced him several times. 'Horsie, horsie, horsie, whither shall we gallop?' Popeye exclaimed. Little Ukheiro suddenly forgot Parnaoz, laughed with all his heart and enjoyed the bouncing; it made him breathless, and he put his chubby little fingers up Popeye's nose. Parnaoz tried not to look, he felt himself getting irritated, his skin turning prickly, as if Popeye was rousing him to anger, 'Horsie, horsie, horsie…' Little Ukheiro snorted blissfully, spraying silvery bubbles of saliva, and splayed his limbs as if he would fly off if Popeye let go of him. Popeye deliberately played with little Ukheiro under his father's nose, as if to say, 'You're the child's father: what right have you to think of anything else?' One more minute and Parnaoz would have leapt up, torn the baby from his hands and then… he didn't know what would happen, but if the game, meant only to provoke him, between a simple baby and this snake of a man didn't stop right now, something had to happen. What most enraged him was that Popeye was making a fool of little Ukheiro, pretending to enjoy playing with him. Parnaoz could not signal to Tina to take the baby away: she was busy talking to the women. He didn't dare call out, not trusting his voice, which might show his hidden anger and anxiety and attract everybody's attention. The women went on calmly talking, happy to be together under the same roof, close to one another, when such peace reigned all round. They wanted nothing more; they had no worries.

'Don't torment the poor thing!' Parnaoz exclaimed, unable to put up with any more.

Even then, the women ignored him, or possibly failed to take in what he had said in such unnaturally weak and throaty, quavering tones. He felt ashamed and held his tongue. As usual, he now felt he was blushing painfully, sadly and anxiously. 'Ha, ha…' Popeye laughed. Popeye was sitting very near, so must have heard what Parnaoz said and caught the hidden emotion. He got up and dropped the baby into Tina's lap. Tina looked up with a smile, handed the baby to Ziara and went on talking. Popeye returned to his chair.

'That's life,' he said.

'What did you say?' asked Parnaoz.

Popeye did not answer; Parnaoz didn't persist. They sat quietly, listening to the women. Little Ukheiro had calmed down in Ziara's lap. It was raining outside. If Popeye meant to say anything, now was the time to speak. Peace and quiet reigned all around. Popeye propped his elbows on his knees and stared Parnaoz in the face.

'Are our women keeping anything from us?' said Parnaoz, more to stop and silence Popeye, to make him bite back what he was about to say.

Popeye had nothing good to say, but what he did say was so surprising and unimaginable that Parnaoz's jaw dropped with amazement. The constant rain, the atmosphere of peace and quiet in the room, and playing with the baby may have put Popeye in the mood for frank conversation, but he could also have set a new trap and planned new treachery.

'Uncle, suppose someone were to shout out one day, "People of Vani, stop being slaves," what would you do?' he asked.

The reply had to be immediate, or Popeye would laugh out loud and say, 'What are you afraid of, we're not among strangers, if I can't say it to you, who can I say it to?' So Parnaoz replied straight away, 'I'm with everybody else.' Even if he'd thought first, he would have said the same.

'What do you think everyone else would do?' Popeye asked again, sliding closer on his chair to Parnaoz.

Now Parnaoz pondered his answer, but Popeye went on, 'Of course they'd take whoever shouted that and smash his head in. You'd do that too, wouldn't you, uncle?' Popeye pestered Parnaoz, who had turned pale.

'I don't know what everyone else would do…' said Parnaoz evasively, and then felt that he'd been defeated: this defeat was more significant than his others, because he couldn't say in his nephew's presence what he considered to be the greatest truth, what withered and festered in him, like dirt left in a wound by a careless doctor.

After this conversation he was even less able to relax. Deliberately or not, Popeye had shown the absurdity of everything that he had worried about for so long, seeking non-existent ways out, trying to rake about in something finished and forgotten; he had failed to see that it was as difficult and unimaginable as sending out to graze cattle which had been slaughtered and flayed. He had begun so many difficult tasks on his own, ill-equipped, that he had made himself and his isolation objects of mockery, for in the people's eyes a man who eats alone is pathetic, and who fights alone — useless.

Popeye had said that Parnaoz wouldn't do what everyone else would do: smash the head in of anyone who dared to shout out, 'We're all slaves; I don't want to be a slave any more, so kindly sacrifice yourself and your families for my freedom.' Popeye's truth was more bitter and so more authentic: it held water. What Popeye said implied that Parnaoz hadn't stood back from life, but that fate had singled him out. It had abandoned him, a man so embittered by solitude that he didn't notice how much he was roused to envy and rage by others' complacency. His envy was mixed with shame, and it clothed him in garments unseemly for his rank. So he was a spectacle to everyone, like a garishly dressed clown roaming the streets to draw in the crowds to a show. Popeye was right: Parnaoz wouldn't act like everyone else: he couldn't smash the head in of someone who might be himself (as Popeye suspected). 'One more thing,' said Popeye, 'a white donkey is disliked by other donkeys: they fear it, in case their owner picks on them for not being white, too.' After a pause, Popeye went on, 'What's the point of one man having principles, when it's better not to, since they only get in everyone's way.' Parnaoz understood that he was considered a man of principle, and that was his worst crime, it made a white donkey of him, he stuck in everyone's throat, poking into other people's affairs instead of seeing to his own. Popeye didn't say all this openly, but what he implied and what Parnaoz inferred was that if everyone minded their own business things would be all right. In fact, how much better off everyone would be if Parnaoz didn't exist, or if he was like everyone else and kept at least one stone ready to throw at any truth teller. Parnaoz assented to much of what Popeye said, he listened attentively, fearing their tête-à-tête might be interrupted. 'I hope the women have forgotten about us,' he thought occasionally, and only this thought stopped him from listening to Popeye more calmly.

'If you live with wolves, you have to howl like a wolf,' Popeye was saying. 'That's an old proverb, and even if you could add a new one, the old is better than the new, because it's tried and tested and more reliable. When a man has a job to do, he puts on his old clothes; his new clothes are for show, to put other people's noses out of joint.'

Parnaoz kept listening, amazed that he was taking in Popeye's words without demurral or protest. But deep down inside nothing changed: his spirit, like a meadow in the wind, might be swayed and ruffled, but it wouldn't shift: the breeze couldn't move it. Parnaoz felt as if he was on the verge of a great transformation; he had only to take one step to find himself in a totally new world, new at least to him, where, as a legitimate inhabitant, he would find lasting peace and the right to enjoy everyday life. But he could find no way to take this seemingly tiny step, although his entire being was ready for it, desperate for it, like a sick man who suddenly has hopes of a cure and now depends entirely on his carers. It is vital that his carers don't get fed up with him, that they spend one more night, running about fetching his medicine and taking out his chamber pot without being revolted.

He couldn't blame Popeye, who was ready to help Parnaoz if he was on the road to recovery; Popeye spared no effort, he came up with all sorts of proverbs: 'A foreign crow has laid a black egg; A woodpecker keeps pecking, but nobody sees the hole he pecks; If you eat someone's bread, you must brandish his sword; I don't believe a cricket can lay an eagle's egg.' But Parnaoz was not destined to take that fateful step, for patient and carer had conflicting interpretations of the same words. That may be why Popeye, his patience exhausted, told Parnaoz, 'If a fish comes ashore to graze grass, it's finished, it ends up in the fisherman's net.'

After this, they all sat down to dinner. The women had worked hard, as if this were a feast for important guests. With four women in charge, the whole house was in a festive mood. They laughed loudly, offering each other dishes before anyone could stand up, 'Why get up? I'll bring it to you.' They made sure that they all enjoyed themselves, and for the time being really loved one another. Ziara kept little Ukheiro at the table in her lap and, whatever was served, asked if a baby could eat it. 'Let him down, it won't hurt him, he's used to crawling,' Tina told her, but Ziara held on even more tightly to little Ukheiro, as if someone was trying to snatch him from her. Tina's remark reminded Parnaoz of Daedalus's paralysed son; he worried lest his son, too, might not be able to walk. He could clearly see Icarus confined to the floor, his big, astonished eyes staring at a piece of fluff fluttering through the air. This vision so alarmed and bothered him that he couldn't stop himself asking, 'At what age do children learn to walk?' There was no reason why his son should be like Daedalus's, but he was fearful, seeking misfortune everywhere, as a blind hen looks for wheat, for, as Popeye said, he enjoyed his own unhappiness. Those were his thoughts as he worked out his son's age. Little Ukheiro was now one year old. But he was unlikely to be a late walker: the women would have noticed before, they understood more about babies than he did. He calmed down a little and called to Ziara, 'Put him down, look, he's stopping you from eating.' Ziara clutched the sprawling little Ukheiro even harder to her lap and said, 'Oh dear, no: I love him, he's my baby.'

Kaluka brought in a chicken stewed whole and put it in front of Popeye. He threw a handful of salt onto the steaming bird, saying, 'Chicken, chicken, it's all your fault: Now you're cooked, here's the salt,' and tested the knife for sharpness. For some reason, everyone became alert, silent: they watched Popeye's hands. He scraped his hand with the knife blade, looked at Parnaoz with a smile and said, 'Your knife's blunt, uncle.' Then he got up, went to the door, kneeled down by his leather sack, stuck his arm up to the elbow into the opening and fiddled about as if he was extracting a live snake and trying to grab it by the neck. The sack started jingling. After a short while, a long, pointed knife, shaped very like a live snake, flashed in the air. 'That's what you call a knife,' said Popeye, coming back to the table. Only he and Ziara ate the chicken, except for the wings: nobody else touched it, although the two of them urged everybody that it was a beautiful chicken and well stewed. Popeye offered Tina one wing and Parnaoz the other, saying with a grimace, 'You should eat each other's wing, so that neither of you flies away.'

When Popeye and Ziara left, the house became dead quiet again. It was hard to talk, as if people after a longstanding quarrel had got together, but found nothing to say, since they had been at odds for so long that they were alienated from one another. Tina took the baby off to bed. Popina and Kaluka cleared the table, as if someone had died at dinner because of them. Parnaoz stayed sitting at table, drinking, but the wine had no effect, it didn't do what he required of it; he wanted to get drunk, to stop thinking about anything, to lose consciousness, to faint and be dragged out like a corpse and be put to bed, as insensitive as a corpse, if that was his place and he had nowhere else to go. Parnaoz was not meant to sleep in that bed, he could pretend no longer, his hypocrisy had sickened and humiliated him enough. Popeye had cut off his retreat, had removed his last chance of seeing the meeting with Ino as a dream, a nightmare, non-sensical fantasy. He had imagined the day he met Ino would be different, he had portrayed it differently, although he didn't believe that such a day would ever dawn. It had dawned, and night had fallen on it, too.

Night had fallen a week ago, for all eternity and to his shame, without hope or trace. On that day Parnaoz had let his last chance slip out of his hand, his last chance to justify himself, to redeem his wrongdoing and to reveal his real true nature. That day Parnaoz lost Ino, finally sacrificing her: that was the day he should have taken her, dragged her from a room besmirched by a thousand men's depraved passion, and together with her have started the endless path to take them back to the past in real time, to the little cave: there they could have lived as human beings once lived, bold and free, relying on themselves, fearing wild animals and loving the sun and, above all, sure that they would wake up the next day together by the embers of an undying fire, warmed by its eternal heat, like puppies against their mother's belly. But this was a dream, a futile dream: whatever Parnaoz thought, however much he dithered, in the more enduring and firmer half of his heart he knew he would never do this, even if the day he met Ino were to recur ten or a thousand times: it was no more real than all the other days typical of his nature. This day was his in particular and he had to live with it. And he had lived with it. He had pushed Ino away, turned his back on her for ever and rushed to be with his family, because outside Ino's room, or burial place, lurked a rogue desperate to be pally with Parnaoz. Parnaoz took fright, and then he too became a rogue, a traitor, a shameless hypocrite. As Popeye later explained to him, that made him like other people and entitled him to live with them, but he lost forever something quite unique, since there was no replacement. He had lost the right to dream and to love. He had wanted both rights, but wouldn't lift a finger for either or make any sacrifice. How could wine help or even affect him when his mind was so soberly, slowly, tortuously and painfully opening his eyes as wide as the sky, and his inner eye could see Ino, her shoulders shaking with weeping and her bee-coloured head drooping sadly, like a flower snapped off by a herdsman's whip. Parnaoz longed for Ino, more bitterly than he longed to see his dead mother, more agonizingly than to return to his lost motherland: Ino was the only woman who could replace both his dead mother and lost motherland. He had never felt so ill with longing for her; his whole body sensed that she was lost forever, departed and never to be seen again.

He was not aware of leaving the house: nobody stopped him, nobody asked where he was rushing off to, as if the others sensed that nobody was now entitled to remind him of their existence or show him any attention. He was free, he now belonged to nobody or nothing except a suddenly conceived plan. It didn't matter at all what this plan was, important or not, ruinous or salutary, attainable or unattainable. What mattered was that it existed and could influence him.

He was running by now, the darkness shone like molten pitch, sticking to his body and hindering it. He was bent forward, his hands covering his face to fend off the rain: he was determined to forge on. There was no end to the city, as if it too was like the darkness, or rather pitch, dragging out, lengthening and sticking to his heels. The dogs sheltering in the yards barked half-heartedly, just for show, so that their owners would hear: their canine instinct told them that this man, out of breath, was no threat to them. Perhaps they were encouraging the man caught out in the rain, 'Don't be afraid, this is still friendly country, you'll find somewhere to shelter.' Parnaoz kept running, his head and shoulders cleaving the rain and darkness. The narrow, empty streets were like tunnels from which the paving, lit by the drizzle, came running towards him. In the light that came through the windows golden streams of rain seemed to oscillate, as if the goddess Diana were lying supine on the roofs, her hair hanging down. 'I'm running like a lunatic through the city,' thought Parnaoz, amazed that he hadn't reached open country. He was so tired he could barely breathe; he was wet through. But he could still feel the rain running down his neck. Suddenly he recalled Daedalus, or rather had a vision of him, a black figure trying to grip the wet roof with a flap of wings the size of a shepherd's cloak, calling to him. 'Why can't you understand that the end is the beginning, and the beginning is the end, the end is the beginning,' Parnaoz repeated endlessly, pointlessly to himself as he ran.

When he left home, he was not yet quite sure about his plan, he sensed he ought not to resist it, they would get acquainted later as they travelled. But as soon as the first drop of rain struck his face, his mind became clear and he saw the little cave again when he and Ino, running away from home and hoping to find the outlaw, had once sheltered with nothing but ten dry loaves and a ham. They were bolder then and nearer a goal which after so many years ceased to exist. But the cave was still there, it had held out, thanks to two children's provisions; the two children's dream, like an irritated oyster shell, had turned it into a pearl. Night clutched it in its hand and, every now and again, would open its hand to show, excite and attract Parnaoz. Blindly, at random, he traced his way there, the sand and pebbles crunching as they slipped under his feet, he flailed his arms to break through the spreading bushes whose wet, supple branches mercilessly struck him in the face, as if the rain and the darkness had angered them and made them attack this lonely man holding out his arms to them, clutching them, because he had to climb higher to where he supposed his refuge to be, the treasury of his hope and dream. Somehow he had to get there, and he would, since he was human and had no choice. After drudgery, torment and much disappointment, undergoing countless ordeals, escaping from years of captivity, he would see a treasure which, in better times, he had hidden for a rainy day. Buried treasure had enabled him to hold out; knowing this had saved him from being trampled down and killed by life. Now it was important not to lose his way and find the treasure untouched. Much time had passed since he had taken the treasure up there and entrusted it to the earth, thinking he would never need it.

It was easy to find the cave: he didn't even have to search, as if he had come straight to it, led and guided by his heart. But as soon as he saw the cave, he felt weak at the knees: a demonic, non-human, non-existent intuition told him that someone was there. The feeling he experienced couldn't be called fear, but it was like fear, shackling him, extinguishing all enthusiasm, making him feel duped. Nevertheless, he entered the cave, like a prisoner who has come to ask for mercy, bent double and prepared to accept the unexpected. He had to enter, even if a she-wolf were to leap on his face or a snake coil round his neck, or an outlaw's dagger stab his belly. When he stood up straight he saw two yellow spots, as if the spirit of the cave had opened its eyes at the sound of a man's feet. The spots suddenly vanished and Parnaoz felt a terrible blow in his chest: he could not at first think what had happened, it seemed that, blinded by the darkness, he'd bumped into the cave wall, then he heard the clattering of hooves and the two yellow spots flashed in another corner of the cave. He calmed down: some harmless animal was sheltering in the cave, and it had been startled by the arrival of an alien visitor and was about to leave, assuming that the alien visitor would let it and would back away, just for an instant, from the exit. Parnaoz's chest throbbed, rather than hurt, but it was getting hotter and hotter, as if Kaluka were putting a hot brick wrapped in a shawl on it, as she used to do when he was a child, shivering after running about in the rain or splashing about in the water. He didn't realise he was blocking the exit: the cave was getting more airless, the animal's acrid smell was accumulating like lukewarm water in his mouth and nostrils. The animal was still agitated: it rushed about, its hooves clattering over the cave floor, it was breathing loudly. Parnaoz backed away from the exit and sat down, or rather let his back slide down the rough wall: he was too tired to move. A blast of cold air came into the cave, running round it like a hound, rubbing its damp haunches against everything. It was still raining outside. Abandoned to itself, the rain ran chattering down the stony slopes. The inhabitant of the cave calmed down, huddled in a corner and fixed its two yellow spots on Parnaoz. 'It can see me,' he thought. Then there were more yellow spots mingling with one another, glimmering, and Parnaoz fell asleep. In the morning he was woken up by a goat's bleating: the goat was standing over him, watching him with its big, watery, red-rimmed eyes.

Outside, the rain had stopped. The floor was covered in goat droppings. Parnaoz was sitting in them, his whole body aching, his clothes had dried to his body and rubbed against his skin, making it hard to move. Then he saw pieces of rotten rag and a white ham bone, the remains of his and Ino's provisions. He stretched out with pleasure as if he had woken up in a house he had long wanted to be in. The goat bleated and he smiled. Everything around was touchingly familiar. The goat kept bleating at him as if demanding money for the overnight stay.

'Hey, old girl, this is my house!' Parnaoz told the goat.

The goat was overdue for milking, its swollen udder would no longer fit between its legs. It had produced so much milk that it dripped from the swollen, reddened teats. The white, fatty drops splashed onto the floor and left a pool the size of a hand. Finally, Parnaoz saw the goat's predicament and crouched down anxiously at his rear legs. He gingerly laid a hand on its hard, swollen udder and the first stream of foaming milk spurted onto his knees. Its sinewy, stubborn teats kept slipping out of his sticky fingers. Anxiety made him sweat all of a sudden. The rough, inexperienced male hand hurt the goat's udder, but the pain was nothing compared to the bliss of having all that milk released. It stood still, so as not to hinder its inexperienced milker. The milk spurted out as it was released: first it gushed onto the milker's knees, and then onto the ground, where it made clouds of milk that bubbled as they mixed with the dirt, changing colour as they sought a way out of the cave. Parnaoz was up to his ankles in milk; the smell of milk and a cloudy vapour rose over him. He knelt in the milk and put his mouth to the udder: a powerful, penetrating stream splashed into his eyes, blinding him, but he managed to control it and noisily gulped it down. His whole face was smeared with milk. 'How can it hold so much milk?' he wondered, for both he and the goat were now up to their waists in milk. The milk had found its way to the exit and was slowly meandering in pulses out of the cave, emerging into the sunlight, rolling down the slope at breakneck speed, carrying its magical warmth and smell as far as it could. But there seemed to be no end yet to its source. The goat's generous bounty surprised and gladdened Parnaoz: it seemed divine to him, for the goat stood there with a god-like calm, only occasionally looking at the man crouching by its legs. Then it gave a series of bleats, pulled its shrunken wet udder from his hand, as if he had been holding the teats for fun, waded through its own milk and left the cave, followed by a stream of milk.

Soon the cave floor, the white ham bone and the pieces of rag were visible again. A few puddles of milk were left here and there. Parnaoz had never felt so glad, as if the goat's milk had healed all his ills: as if he had never had any ills in need of healing, as if he had been born in the cave, raised by the goat and could now emerge into the sunlight for the first time. He was still anxious, and his heart still fluttered, for he did not yet know what he would find outside the cave. All he could hear was a bird whistling, and the bird had such a calm, resonant and pleasant voice that a world which had such voices in it could not possibly be ugly, evil or dangerous. This world was bathed in goat's milk and probably exuded an intoxicating smell of milk; the verdant meadows were dotted with flowers and scarlet-coloured bees buzzed around them; the meadow had been ploughed by a man, whose naked children, as beautiful as the flowers and busy as the bees, followed him; the children clutched to their bellies baskets full of the seeds of corn, goodness, love, peace and wisdom. This was the world as Parnaoz saw it in a cave permeated with goat's milk: for some reason he recalled his father's sail-sized canvas, but now that gave him joy: he was glad at the resemblance of the world seen from the cave to his father's handiwork. This resemblance proved that Ukheiro had seen the same world, or at least wanted such a world to exist. So the two of them turned out to have the same eye and desire. That meant something, if only that two were better than one, more believable, and so another might tomorrow join them, if that other man actually existed and was now listening to the bird whistling. Three men are already a people.

Parnaoz boldly came out of the cave. The goat was nibbling at the new grass. It lifted its head when it heard his footsteps: only then did he realise he had seen this goat before and recall where and when. It was black-eyed Malalo's goat. He hadn't expected that. If fate wasn't mocking him, why then had black-eyed Malalo's goat taken shelter in this cave? 'I suppose it's possible…' Parnaoz began to think, but stopped. Not even Ino would have known of the goat's existence; even if she had, how could she have found time to look after it? Such thoughts were silly, but led to a thought that was harder to dismiss and which gradually, with every day, took hold, becoming sweeter and friendlier, assuring him that the gods were making him the goat's herdsman, to cleanse it of its ancient sins and show it the attention and care which he failed at various times to show his loyal dog, the girl with the curls that stuck out and the paralysed boy. The gods were just and kindly: they wanted to teach Parnaoz. He should be able to watch over one goat if he really meant to start a new life.

Parnaoz forgot his house, lay on his back on the cave's stone floor and followed his own amiable idea. It explained, expounded and proved to him, with the credibility of a man who had died and been reborn countless times, that it would not be at all amazing if Ino came up here one fine day. 'Does a stone thrown into the sea vanish, to be lost for ever? No, it does not vanish, nor is it lost; it simply disappears from sight because it sinks in the water. But someone may dive into the water and bring up the stone which we thought was lost for ever,' said the friendly idea. Parnaoz was so pleased and excited by these friendly words that he could not stop listening to them, lying stretched out in a hollow created by the weight of his own back. It was incredible that things were happening just as the friendly voice said, but its words were a fragment of the rope of hope which anyone in his state of mind would not hesitate to clutch. He found it hard to let go of this rope, but he had to, at least for a time, because down below he had a growing son and the boy needed support until he had learnt to walk and stand up straight.

The family had long ago noticed that Parnaoz had gone feral. Tina was as busy as ever in the house with pots, pans and the hearth, but the fire blazing in her heart horrified Popina and Kaluka. They were both women with experience of bitter rejection, icy solitude and life's thorns. Tina was unhappy, and felt forsaken by fate: her destiny had been decided by two foolish women for their own advantage, because they needed Tina more than she needed them. They never asked Tina if she consented to be their sister-in-law, nor did they ask Parnaoz, although he was away at the time and they didn't even know if he would ever return. They had duped a girl who had come as a neighbour, praised her, indulged her and lured the bird into the trap by calling 'bridie, bridie!' Now Tina turned out to be the unhappiest of the three women: she had a husband, but lived a widow's life; she made a bed for two and went to sleep alone, if she slept at all; she was forced to work in the family like a woman who enjoyed a husband's affection, lest others guess or realise what a tiny insignificant, demeaning, yet hard-won place she occupied in this family.

Parnaoz, as well as the women, sensed this: he felt sorry for Tina and tried to be as attentive and forbearing as he could towards her; but he felt that these efforts were inevitably futile, because his heart was not in them: he had left it in the cave with the half-wild goat, and he couldn't wait to finish work and run up to make sure that the goat was safe and sound. Until he got to the cave, he was as anxious as if he was late bringing medicine to a lonely sick mother. As soon as he left the city, he was seized with forebodings lest he fail to find it, or a wild animal had attacked it; but he had only to look into the murky the cave, and two yellow eyes would flash and he would hear a familiar bleating. 'Keeping the home fires burning,' he would say with a feeling of gratitude, then lie down in the hollow the weight of his body had made. This is how Parnaoz lived: after the day that little Ukheiro perished he virtually never left the cave, until Oqajado's soldiers dragged him out, more dead than alive, unconscious, feeling nothing.

Life had fundamentally changed in the house: the women had no heart for it. As soon as they got up, they argued whether to visit the cemetery or look in on Ziara. Ziara was now pregnant, a reason for them to visit her every day. They barely noticed little Ukheiro growing up as fast as if he sensed he had little time allotted for him on earth and had to hurry if he meant to grasp and understand anything, if he didn't want to leave the world as ignorant and naïve as he was when he entered it.

One day Tina put little Ukheiro on his feet, turned him to face Parnaoz and pushed him from behind. Parnaoz was sitting at the other end of the room, staring, as if bewitched, at his son staggering towards him. It didn't occur to him to get up and offer a helping hand. He sat without moving, overcome not by fear but by an impatient, urgent and disturbing expectancy. Little Ukheiro safely got to his father and put his outspread hands on Parnaoz's knees. 'He can walk,' thought Parnaoz, looking at his wife. Tina watched him, her eyes full of tears, looking like shattered panes of glass. Tina's tears made Parnaoz shudder: they were tears of joy brought on by seeing her son's first independent steps, and of mourning. She was weeping for her son's leaving: her son was leaving her forever, and she would be alone. Parnaoz managed to utter the words, 'Congratulations: our baby is becoming a man.' Tina smiled, dried her tears on the back of her hand, and said, 'I'll need to wait a lifetime for that.'

A minute later Tina laid her head on her mother's lap and sobbed like a child. Her mother was carding wool. 'What's happened, you poor thing?' she exclaimed, shocked, running her hand through Tina's hair and forcefully pulling her face up from her overheated lap. Strands of wool stuck to Tina's wet cheeks. Not wanting to alarm her mother even more, she made a great effort, explaining as she sobbed, 'It's nothing, mother, nothing: little Ukheiro has started walking.' Her mother was dumbfounded. Like any elderly person, she could quickly and easily prepare herself to hear about and endure any misfortune. If Tina hadn't responded promptly, she would probably have said, 'What can you do, child? What will be, will be,' because her instinct was to soothe her daughter, rather than make a pointless fuss, especially as she didn't know what misfortune had struck her poor daughter. Tina's words were like a bucket of cold water over her curiosity, which had awaited or demanded something unusual. 'Get up, don't spoil my wool,' she growled at Tina, and shook her skirts. Tina was still sobbing, straightening her hair which had fallen over her face, and smiling awkwardly, to hide from her mother that she found it hard to get up: in fact, she couldn't get up, she couldn't feel her legs, as if below the waist she had only cold, numbed emptiness. 'Suppose I can't stand any more?!' she thought in terror, but she didn't give up trying: she knew she could overcome if she was patient and didn't let it show, so that her mother wouldn't realise. Otherwise there would be such an uproar that the whole world would come running. 'What's happened, what's the fuss about, can't mother and daughter just sit carding wool?' Tina said to calm herself, looking with a smile at her frowning mother.

'Since I'm sitting here, let me help you,' said Tina, picking up a flock of wool.

She had no more time, it had run out, like grain from a mill hopper: all that remained was to sew up the top of the sack and sling it over her back. What had to happen, had happened, and it had happened as she wanted. It was nobody's fault, was it, if everything seemed enchanting and easy to reach from the swaying fig-tree branch? Tina had carried out what she had aimed to do and nobody could now blame her for sitting at her mother's feet, carding wool. But didn't the thwarted dream, the utterly wasted patience and the lost time need to be defended and justified? No, a time for a new battle was dawning for Tina: a time for vengeance, and she would be equally ruthless to anybody who failed to understand her, or appreciate the good in her, or thought that she would put up with anything. Sitting with bated breath at her mother's feet meant defeat, that she accepted her fate, admitted that she was helpless and in the wrong. But it was too late for Tina to make a confession, and she no longer was entitled to take the blame, since she had so far deliberately turned a blind eye and a deaf ear in order to win time, to take a step forward, to reach the disfigured corpse of her love and assure herself that it really was a corpse, and the corpse of her love. Others might delude themselves, misidentify or even invent things, just to frustrate Tina. However hard it might be, it was better to see with her own eyes and expel from her heart the hope and doubt that tormented her: 'Too bad, if I was misled; too bad, if I deliberately turned a blind eye.'

She had now turned her back on everything: the dispiriting path and the sight of a once beloved corpse. But even a corpse needs taking care of: the corpse was the only person that Tina had to bury. She was its closest relative and would give it a decent burial, with plenty of tears and sacrifices. Even if her mother hadn't said, 'Go away: why are you sitting here? You've got your own wool to card,' she would still have got up and forced, with her usual stubbornness, her numbed legs to raise her, and would have opened the gate to Ukheiro's yard, as she used to, with the casualness of a proud wife and happy mother: her real life was the other side of the gate, and it was not over yet. It still lacked something small, insignificant but necessary for it to have the right to end. That 'something' existed only inside the gate. When she took hold of the handle, her heart quivered as it did on the day that she became wife to Parnaoz. 'Here it is, my house,' she thought then and now as she entered the yard. Coming up to the house, she turned back, picked up a broom leaning on Popina's disused dye-house and swept the dry leaves from the paved path.

She had no intention of changing or correcting anything: she had in fact firmly decided to wait for the end, whatever that was. Intuition told her that something extraordinary was about to happen which would shake and horrify everybody. Finally, the temple would collapse, the temple of patience, built with the stones and mortar of stubbornness. She had grown up and been formed by that temple's walls, but the childish naivety and dreams that were its foundations had gradually taken on another role. If she could lure Parnaoz into this temple, then it could be for them and their children a most mighty and permanent refuge. She had done the impossible, but the temple hadn't fulfilled its purpose. It had become a lime kiln, a prison, a morgue… Tina must have left something out or put too much in, or failed to take account of something, but it was too late to put that right. Either the temple stayed as it was, or it fell apart altogether, and it was falling apart. She was now used to the idea, but neither heartbroken nor remorseful: she felt an inexplicable joy waiting for the crashing of collapsing walls, and was impatiently trembling, like a child watching a tree being cut down and desperate to see the swaying, quivering tree come crashing down to earth to the sound of branches being smashed.

Tina's expectations affected the other members of the family: they all had forebodings, all worried in their own way, for they could not put a name to what was in store for them: they did not know what it meant. Not knowing alarmed them more; they avoided each other's gaze, they built up walls between one other, in order to get through the day somehow, a day that seemed to be against them, and to go to bed on their own, each on a separate island of darkness and silence, where nothing but thorns grew, but where there was no rest until dawn from the deafening, unrelenting howls of the jackals.

Popina went walking to the cemetery more often, never missing a day. However much housework she had, she preferred to be there, as if work could wait, but the dead could not. 'I can't help it, I dreamed of them last night, father looked so awful that I spent all night crying, something bothers him, but I couldn't understand,' she said in explanation. In fact, something bothered her and she couldn't work out whether the worry came from home or was a foreboding. She seemed to be better able to deal with an expected misfortune if she was close to her parents. Her dead parents had become more of a support than her living relatives, because misfortune could only come from the living and to the living. Popina recalled her deep-seated fears; she looked everyone in the eyes with alarm, she tried to please everybody, because she did not know from whom and to whom misfortune was coming, a misfortune which her premonitions confirmed every day. She didn't forget the twin cypresses and bathed their rugged bases with blood. By caring for and serving everybody, she hoped to win over the gods and keep the family intact. What else could she do or was she capable of? At most, of telling her parents of her woes, and even there she was reluctant to tell everything, she only hinted at what hurt and embarrassed her, deliberately, so as not to upset or distress her parents too much. When she swept out the mausoleum and watered the paving stones, sitting on a rock, she would smile as if she really could see her parents, and she would begin to talk to them, softly, systematically, listening to her own voice so that she could soften or correct anything that slipped out which might displease her parents. Her parents listened attentively. She tried to make every word as pleasant and acceptable to the dead as possible.

The day that little Ukheiro learned to walk, Popina ran to the cemetery. She made everything sparkling clean, sat on a rock, laid her hands in her lap and said, 'Congratulations to both of you: today little Ukheiro started walking.'

'He's a big boy now,' said Popina's voice, warmer now; her tongue loosened. 'He's cut his first teeth. And there's nothing he can't say. The other day Shubu brought some blackberries from the vineyard, and looked him in the face to ask him, "Do you know why you're called Ukheiro?" He didn't stop to think; he said, "Because my grandfather was called Ukheiro, grandfather was a warrior and I'm going to be a warrior, too." We nearly died laughing. Shubu's promised him a dagger. No need to be frightened. Not a real one, a wooden one. "If you're always such a good boy, I'll carve you such a good dagger that will be the envy of Prometheus himself." After that we couldn't keep him away from Shubu. "I want to go with you and watch you carve the dagger." It was all his mother could do to get him off the donkey.' (Popina laughed out loud, visualising Tina tugging at Ukheiro who was squatting on the donkey.) 'O-o-oh,' Popina laughed and groaned at the same time, and then suddenly became gloomy. She sat silent for some time, frightened and hunched, as usual. Then she shook her head, as if to throw back the hair that had fallen onto her face, and said, 'God forbid that he should be as unhappy as you were.'

Today, Popina could neither show her parents mercy nor pretend to them: she would speak frankly of her fear and even reproach them outright. She had no choice, she still relied on her dead. They may have died, but they remained her parents and had to help her from the other world, and offer her advice and comfort. Popina was sorry for the dead, but even sorrier for herself. They were in the earth, true, but they were together at least, and that was a great relief, their great advantage over Popina. She had a brother and a son, but they were both total strangers to her, she was afraid of both of them, for one was born without a father and was thus doomed to be looked down on, while the other was a permanent burden to her. Popina may have been the only person who thought like this, having persuaded herself that she brought her brother and son only scorn and misfortune; she made her life wretched with this imaginary crime, because she had no inkling of how men thought. Thanks to her strange and frightening father, all men were strange and frightening to her. Nobody frightened her as much as her father, because he was always dead to her: he had died when her mother died but, unlike her mother, her father was one of the angry dead who had been left unburied so as to frighten and oppress the living. Even so, she couldn't be held responsible, being a child; and her father was covered up with the sail-sized canvas in which her mother had a little earlier been shrouded. Popina's frightened mind perceived and took in many other things wrongly, and immutably. Although much time had passed since then, nothing had happened to change her mind or dispel her former beliefs. Weren't Philamon, Parnaoz and Popeye just as strange and frightening? 'It's your fault, father, your fault!..' Popina said aloud, and her blood curdled just at the thought of daring to accuse a dead man; but then she decided to unburden her soul completely, to gain a little relief. She forced herself to laugh and went on, 'You men see everything the wrong way round: you don't want what you've got, and you don't know what you want. As time passes, my brother is more and more like you. You'd be like that if you could get to your feet. I'm sorry for Tina: whatever happens, she is somebody else's child, why should she share our misfortune?.. She doesn't know how to win my brother's heart; her family is everything to her, she thinks of nothing but her husband and son, she has no time to run and see her mother. Can't a man say a kind word to his family? Why can't he? Tell me why not. Who else can I ask? And there's my son, he scowls at me, as if… doesn't he have the right to scowl? We deprived him of a father, by making him run away. He kept running as long as he had breath in his body, but why should we have it in for him, what could we have against him? That your daughter should have had a better husband, is that it? No, father, anyone is better than us. Someone has cursed us, we carry the sin for something, and we're too confused to notice that there are other people living, apart from us. Why should we ruin other people's lives? Everyone has something to be glad of: they have guests, they have both trouble and delight. But who comes to see us apart from Popeye and Ziara? And now Parnaoz has become just a visitor. I'm not complaining for myself any more, who needs me, but am I the only person alive? I should have been buried when my mother died: I should have been buried alive. Why did you leave me, mother, why? Aren't you sorry for me, at least aren't you sorry now? You should have taught me something at least: didn't you know where you were abandoning me?! If you hadn't betrayed me, perhaps I might have had a day's happiness, perhaps my son wouldn't be poisoning everything around him. My son is poisonous, mother, he has snake's venom under his tongue. How can he live like that, who can possibly care for him? He's the child of sin, that's why; he's my son, that's why I'm sorry for him, sorry I gave birth to such a child. He's a snake of a man, mother, a snake of a man. Tell me what I should have done, where I should have run to, now that I can't run away! Running away is for men, every man runs away, they all have running away in mind. That's true, isn't it, father? I bet you wish you could have run away. Because you couldn't, so you withered up, that's what drove you mad. But why did you have Parnaoz when you were both dying? Parnaoz is more unhappy than me, than me or you, father; he's your son and he's like you, but his heart is broken, and that's why he hasn't been able to do anything. A day or two ago Tina couldn't stop herself telling him, quite rightly, "What can I do? There seems to be no way out, I can't stop you any more. You can blame yourself for whatever happens to you, you don't want a wife or a son, you're deceiving yourself, you force yourself to hang onto us, because you know and you're afraid of what is going to happen to you without us. Otherwise, why do you torment us, or yourself for that matter? What had to happen will happen, and the sooner the better." That's what she said, father. Your son couldn't say a thing, he sat there hanging his head. It really hurt me, I nearly yelled out, "Don't believe her, Tina's hurt and doesn't know what she's saying." But I was tongue-tied, too. Because Tina's right, father, isn't she? Answer me. What do I do, how do I help Parnaoz? Your son is perishing, your son!'

Popina's tears were flowing, as if she'd buried her parents only the day before, as if she had been orphaned then and was full of self-pity. All she could do was to pull at her dress with her fists, as if she couldn't be calm until she'd torn and ripped it. She shook her head several times as if displeased or dissatisfied by her dead parents' advice and instructions, even though this advice came from her own inflamed mind.

'I know that nothing will do any good, I know that this is our fate, but do we just stand there with our arms folded?!' Popina lamented.

Talking to her parents nevertheless made her calmer, as if she had shed a burden as bitter and harmful as bile. The words she had spoken took her out of herself and gave her relief. Popina stood up, smoothed her dress down and said, half jokingly: 'When you were alive, nobody dared talk to you; now you have to listen to me, whether you like it or not.'

Leaving her parents' mausoleum, she was like someone escaping from a trying, obscure dream: by the time she got home there was nothing left, she couldn't even recall what she'd said. But she was sure that she was returning after talking to them, but nothing had changed: her doubts and her fears remained. 'The two of them are making fools of me,' she thought when she got home. 'They nod yes to everything I say, but don't help me at all.' Popina was thus just as perturbed and confused at home as before, but yet more distressed by her own weakness and the indifference of the dead. 'Perhaps life is better there, and that's why what's happening to us doesn't bother them,' it occurred to Popina, as she quickened her pace, trying, as it were, to catch up with her thoughts and not let them tear her to pieces. Life went on: even she had no right to leave this world whenever she wished, however enchanting the picture she had of her parents' life in the other world. Apart from anything else, there was little Ukheiro, and a pregnant Ziara. She had her joys, the gods were not altogether angry with her.

Popina had deliberately kept the story of Ziara's pregnancy back from her parents, she was frightened the gods might jinx it and scorn her premature joy. In fact, she was joyful. When Ziara gave birth that would change a lot of things, above all it would change her wretched son. As a mother, Popina felt, without saying so, how Popeye suffered from being childless, how it intensified the venom and how that venom was choking him. Popeye needed a child as medicine, it would cure him of the venom, or give him an excuse to run away. If everything went smoothly, he would leave a replacement for himself even if he did run away. He was a man and, one way or another, Ukheiro's blood ran in his veins, at least in part, enough to give him no peace. Popeye knew that a lot depended on Ziara and he was being so nice to his wife that the neighbours had begun to gossip about it. Popeye took a look at his home, had the hovel re-roofed, the courtyard fenced in and even bought a donkey. Ziara was embarrassed riding a donkey through the city: tiny as she was, she looked even smaller, hanging her head as she stared at the donkey's mane. Smiling, Popeye led the donkey and deliberately jingled his sack louder to make everyone pay attention. One day he even took the broom from Ziara's hand and swept the hovel himself, saying, 'If you give me a live child, I'll stop hitting you altogether.' Popeye knew all this, because Ziara hid nothing from her mother-in-law. 'He said that to me yesterday, he did this and that to me,' she would blurt out. Popina knew why her son was being so indulgent, why he fussed over Ziara, whom attention and pregnancy had made plumper and prettier. Ziara had to give Popeye a pretext for running away.

That's what Popina thought, because in her opinion men had children so that they could then run away, as if the bawling of a newborn baby was some mysterious, longed-for sign announcing their time, as a cock crow announced the dawn. Popina believed that only after that sign did men begin life, a real man's life, with no sense, with nowhere to lay their head, with no women, as fast and free as the wind. The day that dawned when their offspring bawled meant the end of their obligations, and the start if their last day, belonging only for them. That's why they lost track, why they couldn't even end the day peacefully, they couldn't die decently: they didn't die, they perished and took others with them, since perdition was as inevitable for them as liberation, although they didn't have enough time to realise that. Instead, it was the women who understood, not just Popina, but any woman. Tina was right to tell Parnaoz, 'I can't stop you any more, and whatever happens to you, you can blame yourself.' Tina knew what would happen to Parnaoz, so did Popina, and so she was angry with Tina for letting him go so easily, for giving up on her duties: in Popina's opinion, if a man's duty was to run away, a woman's was to stop him running away with her last breath, to fall at his feet, to cling to him, even if the doomed man was kicking her. Either endure, or cope, because that was a woman's duty, that was what God made women for.

Popina had not told her parents all this, and she had distorted many things. Of course, Popina always took Tina's side, she sympathized with her and backed her up, but the day that little Ukheiro learnt to walk, Tina's fury and ruthlessness horrified Popina. She thought it was so unexpected and so wrong that she could not for some time make sense of what was happening and, her jaw dropping, she stared at her sister-in-law. Tina was dishevelled, her dress was twisted, her face was as red as if she had been riddling wheat on the threshing-floor. Parnaoz was sitting with his head bowed. Popina pitied her brother, and couldn't stop herself exclaiming, 'Don't believe her, she doesn't know what she's saying.' But Tina was saying what had been building up inside her for years; the words that came from her lips had a mortifying effect, for they were the words of an embittered woman who had run out of patience. 'Why should I envy Ziara?' Tina was saying. 'Why do I have to be singled out when husbands take their toads of wives for donkey rides. Anyone who doesn't like the look of me can drop dead, you can all go hang yourselves for all I care.'

Parnaoz sat their, his head bowed: in fact, he was watching little Ukheiro: pitifully hunched, stunned and frightened, the boy looked now at his father, now at his mother, like everyone's favourite toy accidentally snapped in half. Like all small children, little Ukheiro had his own arithmetic, where two and two always made three, himself and his parents. That was as far as his arithmetic went, or needed to go. Three was for him the clearest and yet the most magical number: indivisible and unchanging. Doesn't everyone calculate the way that suits them best? Why shouldn't a child have his own arithmetic? 'It's all very deviously arranged,' thought Parnaoz. 'If you want the good, you have to shut your eye to the bad. One follows the other. Either you turn your back on both of them, or you have to hug both of them: they're both like wilful, badly brought up children, you only have to pay the slightest attention to one, and they'll both get onto your lap, because they won't get in each other's way, they have a prior agreement to share everything like brothers.' That's why he was as he was, unable to do anyone any good, because he couldn't do anything bad. He couldn't get rid of the mark of the criminal, whether he were washed in goat's milk or human blood. He would always be like this, nothing could change or transform him, even if he learnt something, it would only come in handy in the next world. If a man gives anything up, he does so forever, and whatever he chooses has likewise to satisfy him forever. You can't possibly have it both ways, either good evil, or evil good, joined and concocted by force, and therefore horrible, bloodless, lifeless, a fire with no spark, no good for cooking or heating.

That was the sort of fire in his family hearth, and Tina could not have been more right to douse it with water, stamp it out with her feet, because no fire at all was better than this sort of fire. He was no good at pretending: they had seen through and understood his deviousness and thrown back in his face the sand which he had tried to pass off as twenty-two-carat gold. He was a criminal, not because he didn't love Tina, but because he didn't give her the means to put up with him, because he'd made her life a pointless, futile waste of time. But he'd dropped himself in it, too. If he'd wasted Tina's time, Tina had deprived him of any way of justifying himself. If he now had no family, how could he tell his son: 'I suffered for your sake and I was silenced for your sake?' It was good that it had happened this way, good that what had to happened eventually had happened in time. Everyone had to do what they could. A stone-cutter has to carve stone because he's learnt how to carve stone and knows nothing else or, if he does, has to forget it, because knowing too much is always a hindrance, wears your arms out, dims your eyes and threatens you with countless other things, but gives you nothing: it's surplus knowledge, and that is harmful. A human being needs no more knowledge than he inherits, like a house or a weapon, a bed or a kneading trough.

Those were Parnaoz's thoughts: he recalled his father who had died five years ago. He pitied his father and had a childlike longing and impatience to hold some object that had been in his father's hands. But getting up now would have been a shameless act: at this moment nobody needed him as much as Tina did. He could still endure this day, drag it out, but Tina couldn't. Tina's patience was exhausted, a patience which once seemed to be inexhaustible. But however incomprehensible and unexpected the end of this patience might be for Parnaoz, he had no right to stand in her way, because a scarlet-coloured flower, after being buried for so long, was finally plucking up courage. But he could see how colourless, destitute, simple and ordinary this courage was making Tina. An ordinary woman now stood before him: she had lost all patience because of ordinary unpleasantnesses, and had no idea that there were worse unpleasantnesses in the world.

'She'll make the child hate me,' thought Parnaoz, but he still stayed sitting on his chair.

CHAPTER TWENTY-TWO

FIVE years passed after that day. Now Parnaoz went no further than the gate of his house, as if that were the end of the world; even then, he was reluctant, for he was embarrassed in case the neighbours saw him, and he felt like death while waiting for little Ukheiro to be brought out. But his desire to see his son was so strong that he couldn't and wouldn't resist it. This desire was like a rope round his neck, dragging him finally to the gate, like a nervous beggar who hardly dares stretch out his hand and, if he does dare, has to wait for someone to bring him a piece of bread, however humiliating and unbearable the wait may be, because he's so famished that he couldn't get to the end of the street without that bread. Parnaoz stood and waited, he would rather wait than call out, although he was sure the whole district was watching this man lurking at his own gate like a beggar, having come to ask to see his own son. It was such an odd spectacle, arousing so many different emotions, that nobody could be blamed for peeping from behind their curtains. 'They can watch me as much as they like,' Parnaoz reassured himself, for he couldn't turn back without seeing his son, who had become as precious to him as a gift of bread: hard to renounce, a substitute for all other food, found by chance and therefore making him quiver with awe. After all, some other beggar might have got there before and there'd be no alms left for him. 'If you knew how badly I need a dog,' Parnaoz recalled, while waiting at the gate, the words of the man who rescued Tsuga and now, after so many years, he understood their sense, understood the man with the torn sandals and the stone round his neck who climbed down the latrine pit without hesitation or revulsion.

Parnaoz never knew in advance if his son would come out with him or not, because it was quite likely that little Ukheiro might be bored going out and coming back on the same path with the same man, even if that man was called 'father'. Do fathers really have so much time to walk and talk with their children? They were forced to do so, they had run away because they had no home where they could ignore each other and yet be together, never talk yet say more than now, during this forced walk. Their meetings were identical, the greedy brush of monotony tried to paint the little particular space that nature still left for them, but they couldn't do anything differently, or even imagine things differently; yet they went down the streets together, frightened and excited like conspirators: they felt they were infringing something, or intending to, and the feeling of some inexplicable crime brought them closer together. In fact, they were committing a crime, because they intended to detach their father-and-son relationship, a direct, connecting sinew, from the complex and persistent organism called a family. But this sinew had no real independence, it was an offshoot, branch, continuation of an even older sinew, and inextricably entangled with similar, related sinews.

'Shall we go for a walk?' Parnaoz would timidly ask, and when little Ukheiro looked up, his eyes gleaming with joy, he finally calmed down and his feeling of alienation and powerlessness vanished, and he boldly led his son into his past. There was a lot in his father's past that amazed little Ukheiro. He couldn't imagine that earlier, almost yesterday, where there was now an impassable stagnant marsh, the sea had lapped, boats had sailed on it, competing to be the first to arrive at Vani's port. The sea still existed, but had retreated so far from the city that only its steely reflection could be occasionally glimpsed when the wind bent back the reeds. You had spent a whole day wading through snake-infested bogs, and with a good guide, to get to the sea. The fishermen's quarter still existed and still bore that name, but nobody now pursued that ancient calling: they had turned their backs on the sea and now wandered the upper city looking for casual work. The wives and daughters of former fishermen made reed mats and baskets instead of fishing nets, and followed the menfolk to the upper city, bringing their handiwork to sell. Their tiny boarded houses now stood half in water and, if they needed to borrow salt or fire, they visited each other by boat as far as the upper city, because the water was dangerously deep. There was often an uproar at the very edge of the district when they spent a long time looking for a child or elderly person who had fallen into the water, the search was always in vain. Gradually, people got used to it. They believed that the constantly bubbling marsh and its evil glow was a monster released from the netherworld to choose its sacrificial victims. This was better than the monster swallowing everyone at one go. A former fishermen would put his family in a boat with a rotten hull when he brought home their piles of baskets and rolled up mats; instead of an oar, he used a long punt pole which he pushed against the treacherous soft and silty marsh bed and propelled the boat. Charon seemed to be taking the souls of the dead to Elysium; moonlight reflected on the marsh's surface made those sitting in the boat look like the dead, so silent and motionless were they, as if they were being rowed to a mysterious and sweet land of death, instead of home.

It was just as hard for little Ukheiro to imagine that a large apple orchard had grown by the sea, and that anyone who wanted could eat the fruit of that orchard, as long as they didn't break any branches, or else Dariachangi would die and the garden would vanish, and that happened because someone forgot Dariachangi's testament, passed through the generations, like the secret of the herb of immortality. Dariachangi was so beautiful that people were said to eat by the light she shed.

What his father told him was quite unlike the fairy tales that the three women took turns to tell him. Those fairy tales had the same tenderness and lightness as the three women, and were all identical, all with equally happy endings, because they were meant to send a child off to sleep and not to peep into life's locked trunks. His father's tales so excited little Ukheiro, as if they had happened to him and he were remembering them, trying to recall something he had experienced and undergone, not hearing them for the first time. The city as it was when his father was a child was more enchanting and familiar to him. He never doubted that he himself had run through the city's streets, had picked an apple in Dariachangi's garden, had gone to the noisy port to see foreign ships and taken Tsuga with him to somersault over the hot sands. All this had happened when he and his father had been one person and had everything in common, saw the world through the same eyes and heard its voices with the same ears. Sometimes little Ukheiro felt as if his father had fallen silent and he himself was going on with the story: he had only to shut his eyes tight, and the sea, Dariachangi's garden, the quarrelsome seagull, and Tsuga rolling in the sand would all be back in place. That is perhaps why he would ask his father, 'Remind me again,' instead of 'Tell me.'

'When I grow up as big as you, I'll have a house in the marsh,' little Ukheiro said once.

A leaf had stuck to his grazed knee; when they were coming back from the cave, he hurt his knee when he tripped over a dry root and fell. 'The women will kill us now,' said Parnaoz. Little Ukheiro leapt up nimbly and smiled at his father, but found it hard to take his hand off his painful knee. Parnaoz pulled a leaf off an alder tree and put it on the knee, 'Hold it there and it'll soothe it for you.' Little Ukheiro found walking hard, because he had to keep putting his hand out to hold the leaf. Then the leaf stuck to the clotted blood and he forgot about it entirely.

What his son said alarmed and amazed Parnaoz: 'When I grow up as big as you, I'll have a house in the marsh.' Little Ukheiro understood more than he seemed to, or was right for him. Parnaoz knew that a child's mind had an acute perception of everything it is offered, but what little Ukheiro was offered was more than enough to arouse the child and his tender mind, like a smouldering bonfire which needs more and more kindling so as to scatter the embers, blaze forth in full and light up as far as it can the darkness all round it. Parnaoz brought all the kindling the bonfire needed, but interfered no further. It could let its flames blaze wherever it liked: in other words, let him draw his own conclusions if he was now capable. What alarmed Parnaoz was that he hadn't thought this day would come so soon: he was amazed as well as alarmed, though there was nothing so amazing or unnatural in little Ukheiro's words. No longer content with the land, the sea had left, the marsh was actually moving ever closer towards the city. Nothing could stop this squirming, sluggish, creeping disaster. Soon not just their house, but the whole city would be covered in the marsh's dribble. The city was smaller and older than the marsh, and too weak to do battle with this young monster. Every hour the monster grew bigger, spewing poison from its toothless maw, darkening the sky with its damp vapours and haze, weakening, rotting and exhausting any remaining human beings with its blank, frozen eyes. Little Ukheiro was right. He was already working things out, thinking, but a thought born before he was conceived, dragged over a thousand paths, scraped on a thousand walls, hidden and hushed up in a thousand different ways, was still hard to deal with or endure for a sparkling clean, pure soul, which had never been touched by a bird's foot or a flower's petal.

This didn't matter when he was with his father; his father's presence gave the thought the aura of a dream, made it pleasant and turned the mood jubilant; but when he was alone, the thought became ruthless, angry and cruel, it wouldn't leave him alone or let him come close, as if his childish age irritated it, as an orphaned grandchild irritates a grandfather who is sick, a grandfather, weakened by old age, left with nobody but this tiny child, but able to understand that the grandson can't look after him, however much he may want to, for he is too small: neither the medicine or the boiled nettles he offers can be trusted. Little Ukheiro sensed as much and he devised everything he could to be with his father for longer and to get home as late as possible. Parnaoz, likewise, was reluctant to part with his son, but the time to go home had suddenly become imminent. 'I expect all three of them are standing by the gate,' he thought, and he could immediately visualise Tina, Popina and Kaluka standing, their arms folded, by the gate, reassuring one another.

'Let's go, the women will be worried,' he said, and little Ukheiro no longer objected, although he kept repeating all the way home, 'But they know I'm with you, so what is there to worry about?'

At the top of the street Parnaoz said goodbye to his son: those were the hardest moments for them. Both had the feeling that they would never be able to meet again, as if they were parting for ever, but they hid this from one another and said not what they wanted to say, but what would speed up a parting that was so difficult and depressing for both of them. 'Well, run off, I can see that you can't wait to get to bed.' 'Won't be long,' and many similar meaningless parting words were said by Parnaoz to his son; then he stood watching little Ukheiro go down the street and his heart was filled with both sadness and joy, for little Ukheiro had shared his father's experience: the bitterness of forced parting and the joy of expected reunion. That alone made life worth living. It was what little Ukheiro needed, and he was happy. This happiness kissed with lips of fire, took one's breath away and left the taste of blood in one's mouth. Before he got to the house, little Ukheiro looked back several times to the top of the street where his father stood stock still and gradually vanished from sight in the dusk, but he could still make out his facial features. 'Don't hang about, go,' the spectre would signal to him, waving his hand, finding it hard to stop himself running off towards him.

Little Ukheiro had his own thoughts, secret, hidden from everyone, even his father. A thought occurred to him when his father took him up to the cave and showed him the hollow in the ground where he lay. 'I've taken my father's house away from him,' thought little Ukheiro, suddenly pitying his father: luckily the goat was there, otherwise he couldn't have stopped himself bursting into tears. Little Ukheiro started playing with the goat to hide his face, which was quivering with the tears he held back.

'Well, this is where I live,' his father said.

'I know you live here,' thought little Ukheiro, who pretended to be preoccupied playing with the goat. 'You used to live where I live now. We can't live together even here, because I will live here when you move somewhere else.' So it seemed that father was yielding his place to son, as if the house where Parnaoz used to live and where little Ukheiro lived was just a plank floating in the sea and this plank wasn't strong enough for the two of them, and one had to give it up for the other, so that they didn't both perish. If that was so, then Parnaoz was right to yield up his place to his son. But was it so? Were they really both at sea and was grandfather's house really just a rotten plank? Of course, it was hard for little Ukheiro to make sense of all this, but he had to grasp it somehow, for this was his thought, conceived within him, unprecedented, not refined or orderly: it was an offshoot of the great thought inherited from his father.

Life went on as usual, quite uninterested whether little Ukheiro noticed it, whether his intuition kept pace with it or not. 'Stomachs can't wait,' Kaluka said every morning, tying the end of her headscarf to close her mouth as she started kneading the dough. Popina swept the house, and Tina aired the bedding, beating the rugs hard with a cornel stick.

One day something happened that nobody expected, which perturbed, confused and frightened the whole city.

The city had just gone to sleep when two men came in through the city walls. Both were bald. Their heads shone as if covered with golden bowls. They both wore short tunics, and their sandal laces reached up to their thighs. They were brothers, one called Fear, the other Horror. They strode boldly and casually, as if born and brought up in the city. 'Are we on the right road?' asked Horror. 'We've already arrived,' replied Fear. Without knocking, the brothers opened the very first gate and went to the window of the hovel, where a light was burning. 'Say what you like, there's really nothing better than spying at people's windows,' said Fear. The brothers looked in through the window. There were four people there, a man and three women. The man had his back to the wall and was looking vaguely into space. Two women dressed in black sat next to one another on a divan, their hands on their laps, keeping a careful eye on the third woman. The third woman was wearing an old shift with a torn hem; she had slippers on her bare, swollen feet, and was pacing up and down the room. She was pregnant and seemed younger than the other two women, but labour pains contorted her so that she looked like a woman a hundred years old. She was a little woman, with short legs, and a monstrously large belly: you'd think her belly could carry her about at will. An oil lamp flickered on the table, mercilessly flashing distorted, weirdly lengthened shadows of those in the room onto the ceiling and walls. The restless candle flame only half-lit the objects and people, so that objects and people seemed to stand in a marsh covered in spots of light. The brothers knocked at the window and then ran off. The pregnant woman was Ziara, the two women in black next to each other on a divan were Popina and Kaluka; the silent, motionless man by the wall was Popeye.

At midnight Ziara gave birth to a still-born baby.

The next day Tsutsa told her son and provider, on whose shoulder she perched like a trained magpie, to look out of the window: she told him, 'Can you see what's happening in your kingdom?' Oqajado couldn't see anything special. In the palace courtyard, next to the stable, was a pile of manure, an old javelin propped up a washing line, and smoke was rising from the bakery. 'They're baking bread,' thought Oqajado, but he kept his eye on the courtyard, because he knew his mother wouldn't have brought him here without good reason and so was giving him a probing stare as if to say, 'Can you understand anything, or not, my son and provider?' Oqajado was meant to notice and understand something: that's how it had been as long as he could remember, and so it would always be. 'How long must this go on?' Oqajado mentally lost his temper with somebody, and suddenly felt how fed up he was with it all: what was the point of this absurd torment, why did he have to rack his brains to understand what his mother had already understood? She should say it outright and put an end to it; they were alone now, just the two of them, mother and son; the third person for whom Oqajado was somehow forced to strain his head had some time ago set off for the other world, or rather she had moved into the mirror, and got her own way, denying her husband even a means of burying her, as if her husband had been incapable of doing the decent thing by her. Instead, Oqajado had laid a bowl of water to rest in the family mausoleum. What else could he do? He had to give her some sort of funeral. That was all that was left of Kama. Nothing gave Oqajado so much pleasure as Kama's disappearance. When he saw the bowl of water lying in state in the hall, his spirits rose, he felt that his real reign was now beginning, untrammelled by any obligations, unlimited and unrestricted, because there, in water as turbid as tears, the bejewelled crown of his kingship was floating. So he had the people weep and mourn for a whole year, while the palace was covered in black mourning cloth, becoming so dark that you couldn't go anywhere without a flaming torch.

Later he laughed at the memory of the darkened and airless palace, and at the game devised by his mother to torment him: it did torment him, or rather exhaust him, until he found out where Tsutsa was hiding as invisible a cricket, somewhere that Oqajado had to seek on all fours. 'Follow the sound, you silly boy,' she would cry. What else could Oqajado do than follow the sound? But it always misled him, and when it seemed to him that he had caught his tormentor, then he heard Tsutsa's mocking chirruping from a completely different direction. His mother couldn't walk, but she could slither like a lizard. After Kama vanished, a longed-for peace and quiet settled on the palace. He was bothered neither by plaintiffs nor petitioners; they had all the time in the world for debates and games. Who knows how long these carefree sweet days would have lasted, if Tsutsa hadn't chosen today to set up yet another test of her son's observation? Oqajado stood by the window; half of his face was burning from his mother's probing stare. He felt how fed up he was with everything that he understood and that his mother would make him understand. He felt his shoulder, on which his mother perched, becoming as numb as the driver's seat on an ox-cart. 'If I throw her off and break her neck, that will finish it,' Oqajado thought, but Tsutsa was impatiently flapping her wings like a magpie: she had seen a weird creature like both a child and an enormous bird. It had fallen into the palace courtyard, and for all its frantic efforts could not fly off. It desperately ran up and down, flapping its wings, almost taking off, but immediately crashed down and sprawled in disorder, its wings grounded, sweeping the courtyard. 'Attaboy! Let's catch it!' Oqajado was about to shout, but Tsutsa stopped him, telling him,

'Don't think for a moment that it's a bird: it's the stableman's grandson.' Oqajado found his mother's words so incredible that he threw caution to the wind, leaning his whole body out of the window.

'What are you doing, wretch?' shrieked Tsutsa, adding after a pause, 'Though you've got good reason to jump!'

His mother's shriek both sobered and frightened Oqajado: it made him open an eye he had hitherto kept closed, and suddenly persuaded him that he was witnessing an extraordinary event, that an unforeseen danger had appeared. The stableman's grandson had grazed his knees on the cracked paving stones of the palace courtyard; there was something very alarming and horrifying in the helpless fluttering of this child who had tied wings onto himself and was now like a wild animal caught by the leg in a snare, prepared to gnaw through its own bone in order to escape the snare.

'The whole city is like this. Nobody wants to stay with us any more!' Tsutsa yowled.

'Nobody wants to stay with us any more! Nobody wants to stay with us any more!' Oqajado repeated to himself, his blood rushing, not his decrepit, sluggish blood, but its ancestor, his blood's ferment seething like fermenting wine in his veins, making him forever restless, unable to settle, never sober. It made him promises; it had made him pick up a stone to smash his father's head, for it promised him something worth shedding his father's blood for. And Oqajado had sacrificed, or rather severed it with a stone: one end was tied to the central pillar of the royal stables and, however hard he pulled on it, any step he took towards his goal would always hang in the air, the short rope of blood pulled him back. Oqajado suffered until a soothsayer opened his eyes; then he hadn't even thought nor did his hand shake. With just one blow of the stone he squashed the rope of blood like an ant. He then let out a yell of triumph at the sight of his father, tied to the pillar of the royal stables, his head smashed in, giving up the ghost, writhing and trembling. After that he had no trouble reaching his goal, he got what he was promised and for many years had so cherished and enjoyed with his sensual body that it even bored him.

But this certainly didn't mean that Oqajado was ready to give up his throne or forget all the old enjoyment, the self-sacrificing loyalty or the wife who had withered and aged in his arms. No, even he was not so witless or unjust as to turn his back on his one and only real, legitimate wife in old age. He was born for that woman and fated to live and die with her. Kama was only an addition, she was his real wife's dowry. That was why she melted away, drained and vanished; his real wife was as eternal as a goddess and, if she aged, she did so only out of respect for Oqajado, so as not to distress him, as he himself was elderly and feeble. She didn't want him to be full of envy at the sight of a young wife. This wife was called reigning, the throne, crown jewels, the palace, the country, respect, fame, wealth, pride, dining and sleeping undisturbed. Did it matter if Oqajado was a tiny bit fed up seeing every day the same face with make-up decaying in its wrinkles, its eyes oozing pus, barely able to see, but still open, because a regal nature's eternally youthful, eternally desirable splendour yet again flashed out from the shrunken cracks that her eyes had become. The rays flashing out from these shrunken cracks governed Oqajado's being, as threads control a puppet. They both knew very well that when Oqajado dangled from the rays of light coming from his wife's eyes, he would stop scratching his nose or forehead and start scratching the back of his head or putting his hand on his belly. 'Now sho-o-ow me our e-e-eye,' his wife, breathless with laughter, would say with difficulty. Oqajado would also laugh, because the ray would switch to his wrist and pull him in an entirely different direction. That was how they behaved, what they called royal entertainment, but they could also be downcast, and this, too, was royal, regally enchanting and splendid. It looked more like a dancing game for a swineherd and a goose-girl.

Oqajado would put his hands behind his back and patrol corridors of silence and emptiness, which made the sound of his slippers more silent and inhuman, since this sound was part of them, their banner of solidarity. His heart filled with pride as he walked, like a child sent to the shops for the first time, feeling his parent's gaze and anxiety pleasantly tickling the back of his neck, 'I hope nothing happens to hurt my little boy.' Oqajado could feel the entire country's gaze, anxious and distressed, bemused by the sight of the king strolling alone. The country was dying of anxiety, but still couldn't penetrate the king's mind. Oqajado would only knit his eyebrows harder, slow his pace and feel quietly jubilant: 'Got you there: sorry to disappoint you, try and guess then, if you're so clever.' There was nothing to guess: if a man strolling alone wore a crown, that was enough for everyone to look at him with envy and awe. But now some lousy grandson of the stableman had taken a dislike to being here, to gawping at the king. Fine, by God, but why did he stroll down the corridors, why did he endure this hopeless sadness and misery if there were no more spectators, if everyone had suddenly made a move and flown off. 'Where the hell are they flying to?' wondered Oqajado, feeling with his old well-worn intuition, as well-worn as his behind from sitting on the throne, that he was facing the throne's most treacherous enemy. And his mother wouldn't have made all this fuss for nothing.

Tsutsa didn't have her arms folded when she confronted this new enemy, but she was too was beset by thoughts and had to ponder things as deeply as possible. Conspiracy, treachery, rebellion, poison and daggers were old enemies of the throne, so old that they could now hardly be called enemies: they were so familiar and intimate with one another, that they couldn't be anything but inseparable. In any case, they needed each other. The throne always knew where they were, what they were up to, when they could be expected to appear: the throne would really be unworthy of its status if it overslept and let them overthrow it. Basically, their relationship was limited to this: the throne must not forget about their existence and must always be on the alert, while they had constantly to be at work around the throne, waiting for an opportune moment. This was a sort of game, a royal game which made both sides, the throne and aspirants to the throne, more cunning, and heightened their state of alert.

The stableman's grandson was a quite another matter, utterly unimaginable and therefore unforeseen, a monstrous bird sauntering or flying in from some other country. 'You won't get away with it, brother,' Oqajado was now getting round to thinking. In fact, what was going on? If people learnt to fly then neither the throne or its occupant would be worth anything. He might as well stick his head up to the heavens and huff and puff from up there until he was bored with it: who would listen to him or fly to be on his lap? No, Oqajado had to do something before that happened, before people learnt to fly. 'Are those wretched stablemen out to kill me?' he said in sudden fury. How dare a snotty-nosed stableman's offspring spurn Oqajado, how dare he take a dislike to being here: would he be better off elsewhere? Of course not. He was born like a frog in filth and now he'd be swallowed up in filth. Before he'd properly finished thinking this. Oqajado scented filth. He was amazed that the smell seemed to come with the thought. He curled his lips and inspected the hall. Plaster was peeling off the walls, lying on the floor like clumps of powdered, dusty paint; the paving was loose, with pools of water forming here and there: Oqajado couldn't help looking upwards. Bats were hanging head-down from the ceiling. Cobwebs hung like a demon's handiwork. No matter how much they tried, no soothsayer could now say what was once depicted on those walls. Patches of mould, like monsters released from the underworld, were attacking the walls, eating at them, stretching and swelling the walls, and now slept soundly among the remnants of human beings and animals. Oqajado laughed, because on one wall just one human foot was pursuing the rear of a wild boar.

'Why are you laughing? We're doomed!' Tsutsa yowled: so far she had been still and silent on her son's shoulder, giving him time to think.

'What are things coming to here?' Oqajado wondered and reached out for a black piece of cloth hanging from the window frame like a banner of malice. But he couldn't get hold of it, the fragment was stuck to a nail as a souvenir of the year's mourning that Oqajado had declared out of respect for his wife. Afterwards it must have been blown about by every gust of wind, but Oqajado hadn't seen it before. The fragment of mourning cloth reminded him of Kama, and Kama reminded him of the mirror. A century had passed since he last looked at the mirror. Inspecting the palace had put him in a bad mood and alarmed him, too: 'Perhaps I don't exist any more, either, and someone else is walking these corridors in my place.' He felt bodily drawn to the mirror: his body remembered where it was, or else he might never have worked out or grasped that this ash-coloured, or ash-covered object was a mirror. It was covered inch-thick in dust, cracks like wriggling wrinkles had formed in the dust while it had been hidden away and neglected, as if a swarm of hideous snakes had slithered over it. Oqajado wiped the surface with his elbow and stared as if looking down a well. From the mirror's bottomless depths a dishevelled face slowly climbed up and showed its features: it was bedraggled, its eyes were sunken from fear or lack of air, it was dirty through and through, flaccid and decomposing, belonging to a weird creature as frightening as it was pitiful, ridiculous, loathsome, wrathful and wretched. The loosely hanging mouth revealed bare gums, dry mucus stuck to its nose, but the eyes shone furiously as if the creature were angry, as if someone had dared to bother it by summoning it from the abyss of the mirror. 'This is some catastrophe,' thought Oqajado, and couldn't help covering the mirror with his open palms, as if trying to send this strange monster back down. 'So this is who devoured Kama,' Oqajado tried to shout, but he bit his tongue promptly, because a sniggering Tsutsa had perched on the monster's shoulder, too. He smiled bitterly, and biliously. The familiar sniggering enlightened him, once again made him understand what had to be understood and see what he now most needed to see, what made his hand twice as heavy and as long. 'So that's how they see me,' he said angrily, very angrily, as if looking at an obscenity scrawled by someone beneath his name on a latrine wall, instead of his image in a mirror. Now it was easy to understand, too, why the stableman's lousy grandson had tried to flee the premises, why he had flayed his face by jumping from the palace to the manure heap, flying with wings cobbled together out of chicken feathers and old rags.

'My grandmother told me that if a chicken flies over the fence, you can consider it gone forever,' said Tsutsa.

'Chickens shouldn't fly over the fence!' said Oqajado, pleased that he had found it so easy to draw a conclusion from what his mother had said.

'You're right, you're right, bless you, son.' Tsutsa applauded, and flapped about with joy, horrifying Oqajado, who thought, 'If she starts flying, too, then I'm as good as finished.'

Oqajado's eyes were open and his ears unblocked: the flapping of wings shook the whole palace as if people had decided to make off with it. Naturally, it would take Oqajado only a moment to squash this brazen child, but his experience of the throne told him that one victim demanded yet another; blood might frighten ten people, but it would arouse one person to fight back, so that this person would then have to be pursued and bridled. No, the matter had to be solved bloodlessly. Does a chicken that flies over the fence always have to be slaughtered? Suppose it's a good layer? Then it shouldn't be slaughtered, it should have its wings clipped, and then it can be allowed to run free and cluck as much as it likes when it's about to lay, but the egg stays this side of the fence.

The imminent danger suddenly made Oqajado alert and wise. Hitherto he'd been different, he'd had no reason to be alert or wise. He even liked his mother telling him the same thing three times over. What was he thinking of, what was he trying to do? Was it that easy to get into the mind of a king? That was what a mother was for: to think when her son couldn't. No, he couldn't say anything against his mother, Tsutsa was a fine, brave woman and picked up the signs of danger in good time. Today, after all, she had taken him to the window: and it was just as well she had, for it would never have occurred to him to look out of the window, he was so bored and fed up with everything, but, with all due apologies, this was a different sort of laziness and boredom, aimed only so that his one and only eternal spouse, could see and say, if not out loud, 'My man is tired.' The chickens really thought they could fly over the fence and do as they liked, mess up the country with their louse-ridden feathers and make the palace look like a chicken run, bringing in lice and feathers. But Oqajado wouldn't be Oqajado if he didn't look after his hens: looking after hens is no big job: all you have to do is catch one, put its head under your arm and personally pluck the wings which the henhouse-girl has carelessly let grow too long, so that the hen forgot it was a hen, got an appetite for flying and thought it was a hawk. 'It's a good thing my mother reminded me about the hens,' thought Oqajado and firmly resolved to get down to business without delay. First of all, of course, the stableman's grandson had to be punished.

The stableman's grandson did in fact deserve priority: firstly, he had been learning to fly in front of the king; secondly, he was nearby, within the palace walls, and was easy to catch. Moreover, he would lead to others, he would blaze the trail. Oqajado did not hesitate much longer: he immediately ordered four stakes to be placed in the main courtyard, for the stableman's grandson to be stretched over them, wings and all, and to be flogged with leather straps soaked in water until he realised what he was, a stableman's spawn hatched in a dunghill, not a bird.

The swish of straps and the child's shrieks filled the city like boiling pitch. It suddenly fell deadly silent, as it became all ears. People hoped that it was an illusion, but the lashing straps carried the shrieking child's shredded flesh and blood over the palace walls. Blood and bits of flesh splashed in everyone's faces. When the walls sent the ripped wings wafting through the air, like a heated bread oven wafting hot ashes, they all understood the point: the palace was warning them, giving them for now a subtle threat: if they didn't come to their senses promptly, then there would be no difficulty in bringing the leather straps over the wall, too. Everyone began looking for their children, everyone somehow imagined their child lying under the lash. That night nobody in Vani, except the children, had a wink of sleep. 'My heart tells me it's bad news, woman,' men groaned, and the women had no words of comfort for them, either. Only the children totally ignored the palace's threat. Next morning the city was full of winged children They cobbled together wings out of any conceivable material; dresses and headscarves vanished from trunks, as if taken by fanned flames; bags, in which selected feathers and down had been collected for months to stuff pillows, were emptied. The piece of mourning cloth on the palace window frame still flapped. Children ran down the street whooshing and yelling, as if their yells would add to their strength and really lift their light bodies into the air. Nobody listened to their elders' calls, pleas and warnings; the shrieks of their thrashed playmate only inspired and emboldened them. This did not look like a game: it was more than a game, it was provocative, irritating. It came as no surprise to the children's elders when Oqajado's soldiers suddenly rushed out from every nook and cranny and fell upon the children with swishing leather straps. Children's howls followed the noise of the straps in a blood-curdling sound which hung over the whole city. The adults straight away tried to protect their children: 'Leave it to us, we'll punish them,' they pleaded, bitterly distressed by their children's wrongdoing, for even they weren't totally convinced of the children's innocence. But nothing could now stop Oqajado's soldiers. Children, bent double with pain, were crawling over each other, trying to hide in cracks in the walls or under stones, but even here the swishing leather straps got them, and the whistling tips left yet more wide bloody stripes on their ripped clothes and bodies. The air became stifling: it was saturated with sweat and blood, and the feathers took a long time to float down to earth.

Nightfall more or less restored the city's usual atmosphere. Only the lamp lights started to flicker a little later, more timidly, nervously, as if someone might start flogging them, too. On the roofs of some houses a cat wept like an orphaned child. In the middle of the street a dog crouched and barked at the moon: someone threw a stone at it with a curse; with its tail between its legs, the yapping dog hid in the shadow cast by fig-trees overhanging a wall. Then the heavens came into view, suddenly full of stars. But on earth, where the cool of the night brought down mist, everything turned dark blue. The darkness sighed like a living creature. Not a squeak came from the houses, as if they were plague-stricken.

The twin brothers patrolled the city again: both were in a good mood and chatted uninhibitedly. 'I can see that we're going to be staying in this city for some time,' said Horror. 'Does it matter where we happen to be?' responded Fear. They both laughed, or rather thundered, and the city, like a snail that has been disturbed, withdrew deeper into its shell.

The city was in a reflective mood, wondering what it had done wrong, but unable to shed an unpleasant feeling: it didn't know what to call it, how it had befallen them, why it wouldn't go away, why it forced them, like an insistent drunkard, to recall something. The people had forgotten something without which they were not entitled to leave their homes. They now felt and grasped this, but their memories, for all their efforts, go them nowhere, opened no doors, like an angry wife determined to punish her sozzled husband — he might be standing outside the door, but can't understand what he's done wrong, why nobody will open the door to him, assuming it is actually his house. He is incapable of turning back, he can barely stand, the world is spinning and, unless he stays close to the wall, he'd never find it again. But he knows in his heart, and a drunkard's unerring instinct confirms it, that he has come to the right house. But the sepulchral silence reigning in the house and this accursed darkness arouse a twinge of doubt in him. If they'd just open the door just a crack, enough for him to catch the smell of his family, then he could be sure of everything, the familiar smell would restore his senses and he would run around like a faithful hound, licking people's hands and faces, and then others would recognize him, because he would have their scent.

People began examining their consciences: they felt as if they had come to the cemetery, but had left the deceased at home. Now they were looking at an empty grave, puzzled why they had come here, what to do with this empty grave. Although they examined their consciences, they found nothing. They strained themselves, they recalled anything at all that could be recalled, perhaps they accidentally recalled the most important thing, that pulled them back into the past, like a faithful dog pulling back a blind man who is standing by a cliff. Returning to the past turned out to be no easy matter; especially as they had got to this point without looking back. They never thought that they would have to turn back: if they had, they would have marked their trail. At the time they were interested in the road yet to be travelled, not the road already travelled. The latter belonged to the dead and was part of the world of the dead. The road yet to be travelled was theirs alone, inaccessible to anyone else as long as they were there. Later, it wouldn't matter if not a stone was left still standing. But things weren't entirely like that: they could no longer go off without a backward glance, they had to tread the ground and not move on, scratch the back of their heads and curse fate for not having made any provision for this. 'Some disaster must be happening all over our city,' they wailed, and dug their heels in, like a horse sensing danger underneath a wooden bridge, ignoring its master's whip and loud curses. They were now both the horse and the rider, a rider demented by anger and a horse wise to danger. Who would come out on top, who would get his own way? The rider felt turning back would be shameful: how could he say, 'I was too scared to cross the bridge?' The horse would rather drop dead on the spot than put itself and its master in danger. 'Gotcha!' the danger hiding under the bridge calls to the horse, who whinnies, turns his neck and bares his yellow teeth, because that is his only language; but this is enough to make its master doubtful, thoughtful, even frightened. Now pride would decide everything, whether he follows the horse's mind or his own, but as the horse has already sown doubts, he too begins to think differently: it wasn't so much crossing the bridge that bothered him, as turning back. He himself wanted to turn back, and if he made the horse dig its heels in again, he would do so only make a retreat look less like running away. Later, he knew, he would blame the horse and make fun of it for its stubbornness and cowardice. He would blame everything on the horse, and the horse would accept the blame, for who was going to question the master? They would laugh and tell him, 'No, brother, if it's like that, you shouldn't get on that horse again.' 'That's what I'm saying, aren't I?' he would reply, and that would be the end of the matter.

So the city turned back to the past, and they remembered the old men warming themselves in the sun, forgotten by death itself. There was a feeling that it was possible that these elderly people recalled what other citizens had forgotten, or what they hadn't asked about at the time. They made these cob-webbed ragged elderly people sit among them, put into their trembling hands bowls filled with watered-down wine, and implored them, pleaded with them, shouted down ears blocked by time, 'What's happening to us, have you ever heard of anything like this?' The elderly were alarmed and distressed by this sudden attention and blankly rolled their pus-filled, eyelash-less eyes: they couldn't understand what these strangers wanted from them, why they were being given wine, more than half of which spilled onto their chests and their numb knees. 'Good luck to you, children, what you're doing is very noble,' they lisped, smiling a decrepit, feeble smile at everything, and nodding. Their aged intuition dictated this response: they nodded in approval of anything, since agreeing was the only action they could take, and their constant head nodding kept up a link to a life which had become just a continuous, cosy haze for them. But they couldn't have yielded anything, because they exuded a smell of colostrum and piss, which gave their last days the same aura as their first. So they had forgotten everything, thanks to the cunning of the elderly or the kindness of nature: they had been freed from memories of the life they had lived, so that they could now pass over into death without fear or sophistication, just as they had come into life.

The people quickly became convinced that they could salvage nothing but head-nodding and confused smiles from these deaf old persons, these sacks of bones warming themselves in the sun, unable to see anything but shadows. Then almost everyone suddenly recalled Bochia, the burliest but most innocuous of men. The reason that it took so long to think of Bochia was that he had stayed exactly the same as when they had first seen him. A lot of time had passed since then: they had grown up, matured, reached Bochia's age, but no such changes were noticeable in Bochia, as if time had passed him by, ignored him and thus failed to age him. This exception should have been astounding, but nobody had yet taken any heed of this miracle, simply because everyone was used, from the day they were born, to Bochia as he was, unchanging, eternal, innocuous and kindly. Bochia was an inseparable, vital part of their city; his stability and sameness made life more reliable and longer for others, Bochia was rarely to be seen in the streets. But nobody questioned or worried about where he'd gone to, as if it were impossible for anything to happen to Bochia: before they were born, they had been told, Bochia existed, always the same, the same age, width and height, just like the statue of a god, or rather an actual god who, because of some crime or at his own insistence, now lived with human beings and tried to be like them, hiding his godhood so as not to cause fear or be forsaken. Bochia had achieved all this, but, but he still gave people cause for doubt, to be more alert and attentive. Whole generations had passed away around him, the earth was packed tight with the dead, but he went on in his workshop without stopping, sitting in golden piles of wood shavings, or stood beneath trees while woodpeckers perched on him. He had only to stand under the trees to feel a wave of calmness, whatever worries he might have: his blood rushed youthfully and he longed for his sleek Potola. Possibly his real soul resided in these trees, and so time could not diminish him. More amazingly, Potola took on her husband's eternal youth, health and love of life. Even now their family was alive with the sound of creaking cradles, while most of the brothers and sisters of the latest baby in the cradle were already sleeping their eternal sleep, sated and tired after lengthy lives unmarred by illness. If the people of Vani searched hard and enquired deeply into their roots, they probably would all have turned out to be related, so long-lived and unending was Bochia's and Potola's posterity.

Bochia told the people of Vani, gathered in front of his house, the story of the flying ram: he told them how this ram brought through the air a little boy, whose country had pursued him with a knife and who could find no better refuge than Vani. He told them how the people of Vani, moved by the foreign boy's fate, stood up and interceded for him, ensuring that the boy who had flown here would not feel a stranger in their houses, or be afraid: in the opinion of the older inhabitants, a frightened child could never make a good friend or a good family man.

A lot of water had passed under the bridge since then. A lot had been forgotten, but Bochia still had a strong feeling of happiness to come which the sight of the little foreign boy had aroused. True, life had given the lie to this feeling, everything took a turn for the worse, but Bochia still couldn't get rid of the feeling, which stayed with him like the smile on the face of a disillusioned man.

Memories carried Bochia away: even a lie told by a man of his age was believable. The people were stunned; they gawped as they listened to him; they were reluctant to move, afraid lest these miraculous visions that Bochia's story evoked vanish and flutter off into the air like colourful butterflies that waft the scent of roses and cover the land in golden powder. As Bochia talked, he too was amazed how everything took on a fairy-tale wonder and enchantment, things that hitherto only he had known, that had been permanently deposited, together with countless other memories, in the depths of his heart and, perhaps, had thus lost their colour and meaning, like grandmother's wedding dress. But now, brought into the sunlight, taken out of the trunk, aired in the breeze, in front of so many curious grandchildren, it not only recovered its original softness and lightness, it reanimated its owner's intoxicating virginity, the quivering as her wedding was prepared. People's hearts swelled with pride, they choked on belated tears, and an equally belated regret distressed them, because they had so easily and casually forgotten such a fine, beautiful grandmother whose grave they could no longer find, if only to clear it of weeds and sit just for a minute at her feet.

Bochia could not know what evil he was doing, or else he would have killed himself, assuming that he was able to die, rather than blurt out such rubbish, giving people cause to dream and raise their eyes to the skies.

That day Bochia spent a lot of time under the trees, but he utterly failed to recover his good mood. At first sight, it seemed that nothing could possibly endanger Bochia and Potola: their innumerable progeny was in every way normal, none had grown wings, none was trying to peer at the heavens. Other worries now beset Bochia: he felt that he really had spent a long time on earth, he had stayed far longer than a man is meant to, but all that had suddenly been erased. It had been driven out somewhere in the chasms of non-existence by the swishing leather straps and the howling of thrashed children. Bochia stood beneath the trees, seeing again the basket with handles from which, God knows how many years ago, he had lifted his foster-father, naked and as soft and fluffy as a cloud. Bochia too was now as empty as that basket and was slowly getting even emptier, for he had lost for ever the smell and warmth of babies, both gone with the wind blowing freely through his rickety walls.

Even Potola couldn't relax that night, turning in bed like a roasting spit, as if she were in a stranger's bed, somewhere she was unused to. Potola could not live without Bochia, she didn't know how to live without him, because, as long as she could remember, he had always been by her side; she slept next to Bochia and woke up next to him. Her day began with Bochia as did her night. Dawn and dusk came for her when Bochia decided, when he said, 'It's dawn' or 'It's dusk.' She understood nothing of this world other than Bochia. This was not just for a long time, but always, and always was the only word that denoted time for Potola. Now a crack had appeared in Potola's time, it had broken like an eggshell, and a black chick was lying outside it, the one night in Potola's life which she noticed, because she was alone, without Bochia. What could be done with this chick: who could get it back into the broken eggshell? Still wet, with slimy down sticking to its body, it seemed to oblige Potola to raise somebody else's chick. No, Potola didn't want this night, she wouldn't be able to get through it even if help eventually came and it ended. But how could it end without Bochia, if she didn't have him next to her? Potola was in torment: she dared not call to her husband, and she was afraid in case Bochia was sleeping peacefully and had forgotten all about her. She struggled with herself, she didn't want to believe that Bochia could so easily forget his wife who would sweep the house ten times over for fear of his unbridled passions, would do the washing all over again, clothes and crockery, so that her husband wouldn't see her sitting idle. Was it possible for such a man as Bochia to sleep peacefully now? No. Potola would rather die or have her heart broken. So she dared not leave the room, and her excited mind kept seeing Bochia's shade wandering in, but Bochia's shade had not even crossed the threshold, it was hunched by the door, like a sulking child. 'What's happened, you aren't ill, are you?' Potola called from the bed. When Bochia didn't answer, she ran towards him and came up against a locked door, instead of Bochia. 'Wake up, wake up, wake up,' Potola now yelled out aloud, banging her fists on the door. But not a sound was heard from Bochia. Barefoot, pounding her fists, her throat hoarse with shouting, Potola clutched the numbingly cold door and wept bitterly, for a long time until night's darkness began gradually to fade in the room and the dawn light cast everything in a blue light. Then she heard hens clucking and unbolted the door, but even then did not leave the room; she went back to the bed, put her feet, frozen from standing on the stone floor, into slippers and wrapped a shawl round her shoulders. 'Why am I shaking like an old woman?' she thought for a second, and went into the courtyard. Bochia had made a bed under the trees, but hadn't got into it. He'd lain down on the blanket. When Potola got near, her jaw dropped with shock: Bochia's corpse, shrunken, wrinkled and yellow with old age, lay on the bed. Potola automatically looked up, as if some fruit had withered on the stalk and fallen down.

CHAPTER TWENTY-THREE

THE twin brothers locked the people in their houses. Vani was like an uninhabited city. You'd have thought a magician had turned everyone, men, women and children, to stone, or that they'd all upped and fled. The sepulchral silence was broken only by the spurting and splashing of the torrent, as thick as an arm, of the Greek's source. The city was abandoned to the brothers who strolled carefree and casual through the streets. Every now and again, if anyone dared to poke their head out of a house, the brothers stamped their feet at that person, who would immediately make himself invisible. Bushes that were once trimmed and beautifully cared for now sprawled untidily; ivy and bindweed now crawled over the streets like a swarm of reptiles; grass cracked the paving; the mortar in the walls dried up, and decrepit blood-coloured lichen took its place; rows of bracken and horse-tail could no longer resist the pressure of their rampant fellow ferns and invaded roads and paths; nettles grew lush in the shade of the stone walls; moss covered the well-handles like green smoke; spiders wove webs between houses, across streets; hungry cattle broke out bellowing from their sheds and roamed the streets; poultry quickly abandoned their nesting places and now laid eggs wherever they fancied. The brothers had lots of entertainment: they collected eggs in their coat-tails and threw them at each other; they rode cows at a gallop; they dragged pigs about by the tail, making them squeal and squealed themselves like pigs; they plucked hens alive and sent the naked hens rushing round the city like messengers of death.

Anyone with his nose pressed to the window could see all this and be heart-broken, for everything would have to be started again from scratch if he ever went outside and wasn't left to rot in his locked house, like his exhalations and his thoughts. But no human being worthy of the name could stay so inert, arms folded like a corpse. Fear and Horror had conquered the city, but he had to accept this, because he could endure anything except the destruction of all he had worked for. There was no time to waste. The cattle would have to be domesticated again, the poultry cajoled back to their old nesting places, the weeds cleared, the long shoots of ivy and bindweed cut back by spade and axe. 'I'll make them wish they'd never been born, I'll wipe them out with spade and axe,' people began planning, and mentally saw the blazing bonfire on which the freedom-loving weeds would burn, pleasantly filling the land with peace and soporific smells. People lived for that smell, they now longed for it and their tongues itched, for so much to say had accumulated over this time. No, things couldn't possibly continue like this, nor would they. The country was not cut off from civilisation, the truth was looking for a way, the wrongdoer was being traced and would be punished, and the honest toiler would be avenged for his thrashed children and would once again walk behind his all-providing ox and plough the fields. Again, people would visit the neighbours not just to borrow salt or fire, but to see how they were, what they had to eat and drink, what clothes and hats they were wearing. Otherwise, what was the point of living if you didn't rub shoulders with people like yourself, if you didn't come to dine with them and got them talking? No, things couldn't possibly continue like this for long. If not today, then tomorrow good weather had to come, it couldn't be put off any longer. If not today, then tomorrow people would come out of their houses and would smile at the world like a neighbour who is friendly again. Tomorrow would be better, for by tomorrow everything might be sorted out, there was no sense hurrying when danger was about. Just one more day you could bear to live like a wolf.

But these expectations were thwarted. People's ears still heard the swishing of leather straps, when new information struck the city like thunder: the son of the stone-cutter Parnaoz had crept up onto the dome of the temple, spread his arms like wings and leapt off. Soon the whole city stood by the temple in confusion, now looking up at the temple dome, now staring at the place where little Ukheiro had crashed to earth. 'You'd have thought that he had actually flown,' witnesses were saying. Their faces were blank with fear and anxiety, their voices trembled, as if they themselves had only just survived a terrible ordeal.

The earth had noticed in time a child's body soaring into the sky and had stretched out its mighty arms in such a way that little Ukheiro just spun round once in the air and dived headlong to the ground, making a noise as if he had brought the sky down with him.

Tina was washing up at the time, but every time she put little Ukheiro's bowl into the water, the water turned as red as blood.

Parnaoz was laying paving in the lower district, and when he came running to the temple the pool of blood had already been covered with earth. Here and there one of little Ukheiro's hairs was stuck to the damp earth. Silence and emptiness reigned all round, as in the lair of a lion that has just eaten. Nobody would have thought that just a short time before there had been such a whirlwind here. The sun's rays bounced off the temple walls and struck Parnaoz's eyes. He turned his back on the temple, sat down by the pool of blood covered in earth and passed his hand cautiously over the wet earth, as if he was afraid it might slip out of his hand. The coolness of the earth penetrated his whole body; he put his wet palm on his face and blew on the hair stuck to his fingers. The stream of air made the hair twist and soar upwards. Quivering and spinning, it flew over the temple, swerved to miss a flock of birds, passed through thin clouds and headed towards the sun. Propping himself on the ground, bending back, Parnaoz watched the hair until sunlight and infinity blinded him. The day that Parnaoz was born, his father had sat exactly like this on the battle-field, dazed, his legs crushed by the wheels of a chariot.

Tina did not tear at her face or make the earth quake with her laments. She was ready for disaster, for she had never stopped expecting it. Since the day that little Ukheiro began to walk, her forebodings had never ceased for a moment, but she never asked for anyone's advice or help. Who could have helped her? What had to happen had happened. As time passed she began to doubt more and more if she had acted rightly. Perhaps she was herself to blame, she had done something wrong: she had pangs of remorse and she felt distressed when she saw pity and sympathy in her son's eyes. When little Ukheiro first saw his mother in tears, he himself burst out crying and said between his sobs, 'Don't cry, I'll grow up and be your husband.' After that day Tina did not cry in her son's presence, but little Ukheiro was still aware of everything and understood more than he should have. This confused, worried and frightened Tina, because, apart from anything else, she knew that she had done her son wrong by giving birth to him for her own reasons and purposes. At the time she couldn't foresee her son's future, for she had only just won the battle and was giddy with victory: all she thought of was how to consolidate that victory. She had conquered the territory, but it now had to be assimilated, the walls had to be replastered, the roof changed, the divan covered with her mother's rug and her childhood dolls arranged on it, so that she didn't feel an outsider and others didn't notice that she was, either. She needed a child, for it would best confirm her belief that she had fought a just cause and deserved to win what she had. At the time Tina could not have thought differently about a child who did not yet exist, who had only just been conceived in her mind before it appeared in her womb. When she gave birth, Tina's plans faded without trace and no longer interested her, because suddenly, against her will, she had something bigger to care for. She loved this little warm cooing creature more than herself, and forgot the hopes she had placed on it. She didn't even think about whether she was entitled to them, whether she was right to plan this, even if she had the right to have a baby. She had known from the start that the man who was to become the baby's father didn't love her and gave no sign of ever loving her in the future. But the child loved both mother and father equally, and could never have made a choice between those two fires: he had to spend all his life in their ruthless heat and be burnt to ashes by them. But Tina couldn't have foreseen this, because she had lying next to her living proof that she was right: its little hand felt her breast as it half-closed her sleepy eyes.

In reality all this was merely a malicious joke. The gods had mocked Tina, who in her obstinacy had failed to understand them until her son's blood spurted into her face. Little Ukheiro's death finally sobered Tina, convincing her that all her life had been the result of her own dream, incapable of withstanding the passage of time or the changes of the weather. She had apparently nurtured in vain the fruit which needed so much toil and patience to produce, and which the tree of her stubbornness and patience had finally brought forth, only for the first gust of wind to crash down and squash on the pavement, for the whole city to see. Did she never once doubt why the gods had so graciously granted everything she had expressed a wish for? Didn't she have reasons for doubt? Of course she did. How many times had she held in her hand an empty husk instead of a corn cob? Happiness had often, very often, tickled her neck with its chubby paw, but every time she reached out for that chubby paw, she found her hand empty. But at the time Tina was more worried that others might notice her disappointment. She would freeze instantly at the prospect of loud laughter, she thought that everybody would look at her hands as if she had taken something that wasn't hers, although she herself felt the same way, which was why she had these thoughts, and tried not to lose face, always following the path she had chosen since childhood with more pride and defiance after every defeat. What did it matter if she was taking something that wasn't hers? For one thing, why did it belong to somebody else, by what right? Why wasn't somebody else doing more to protect their property? They weren't lifting a finger to protect what Tina intended to take, because it really belonged to someone else and always had done: the gods had given it to someone else and however much Tina fooled around, she couldn't scratch out the brand, stamp or sign that fate had marked it with. The gods had given Tina patience only as a cat is given a ball of yarn: the cat is supposed to amuse itself, not actually hunt, but to play at hunting. Finally the gods got bored constantly playing with her and put an end to the game at a stroke. Now let others try, if they feel like it, to change the fate which someone has set out and decided before they were born. Everything was over for Tina, the mill had run out of grist, and all she could now do was fill her sack with wasted time, sling the sealed sack over her shoulder and set off home. Tina staggered into the street as if she really was carrying a heavy sack on her back, and, wearing a dirty, sweaty shift, she felt how tired she was of a life as pointless and endless as her patience.

Parnaoz lay down in the cave, not thinking about, or waiting for anything. He sensed that he had very little time left, that he now had no time to do anything. What was left for him to do? Little Ukheiro had said, and even done, it all for him. His son had brought out into the open and shouted out everything that had pained and tormented Parnaoz, what he hadn't accepted and yet hadn't been able to do battle with. His son had outdone him, which was the most important phenomenon in his life: his son had outdone him and thus justified his entire life; his son had crushed him underfoot, overthrown him and annihilated him, and thus restored his faith in victory. How long this faith would hold out was not important: the main thing was that with this faith Parnaoz could leave the world.

Little Ukheiro's death removed Parnaoz's eternal lack of conviction, eternal dithering and eternal feeling of fear: like a poisoned animal, he had now finally spewed out the venom that life had stuffed, quite openly, into his mouth by force at every step he took. This had taken so much time and such enormous sacrifices that he felt emptied, rather than liberated. This sensation of emptiness made him giddy and sit so gormlessly by the earth-covered pool of his son's blood.

Parnaoz was now dead, he felt, and constantly felt that, since he was liberated from everything and everyone, from his own being, but there was nothing in this freedom that any living man could resort to. This freedom was death, it brought with it a shroud permeated with the smell of worms and roots, and it murmured, 'Nobody dies without my being blamed for it.' He waited impatiently, with a child's eagerness, as if death were bringing a sackful of presents. It seemed that only one more step was needed for him to see everything anew that he had lost for ever, that he had consigned to the earth. He hadn't thought that the end could be so desirable. If death had changed its mind, he would have reached out himself for a shroud, as a sleeping man reaches for a blanket that has slipped off, so as to cover up his flesh and the goose pimples raised by the otherworldly cold. The end was the beginning, and the beginning the end: Parnaoz had arrived at the point where he had entered the world. He lay like a babe in swaddling clothes; his soul rejected everything that had ever happened to him. It was all really like a dream that is hard to remember, and he found it easy to believe that he was a babe in swaddling clothes. He was swaddled so tightly that he could hardly breathe, his limbs were numb and he was drenched in sweat, but he nevertheless lay without moving. 'I have to. Mother's never wrong, she knows about raising children,' he thought, and his parched lips sought the goat's udder. He drank the milk mainly in the hope of washing away the hair that stuck to his palate. Of course, the hair was imaginary, but nothing could remove this worrying sensation. His palate, scratched with dirty fingers, hurt and bled, but the hair wouldn't go away; instead it seemed to grow. Parnaoz got angry with the goat, as if it was the goat's fault that the milk wouldn't wash away the non-existent hair. He bit the udder and forced it away, but the next instant he was anxiously calling to it, 'Mummy, mummy!' The worried goat was standing over him and bleating, and watching him in amazement with its wide, watery, red-rimmed eyes. But when Parnaoz, in a fit of anger, punched it hard between the eyes, it rushed out of the cave with a clatter of hooves; just for a tiny instant it stuck its dazed head through the cave opening, and then it disappeared forever.

'But where's Popeye been all this time?' Parnaoz wondered, suddenly recalling his nephew. He had forgotten, in fact, that he expected to find Popeye here: they had agreed a tryst here, so that nobody would interrupt a private conversation. Today it would all come out into the open, and his heart raced strangely as he waited for his co-conspirator, but he still huddled, so that Popeye wouldn't be struck by the sight of his feet sticking out of the hollow.

'How are you, uncle?' said Popeye, rubbing his hands as if he was a hungry guest looking at the table laid for dinner.

Parnaoz said nothing, pretending to be asleep, not because he was afraid of Popeye — quite the contrary, what had he to be afraid of? — he simply had nothing left to say to him; he now remembered that they had already told each other everything, and many times too. He was even bored with it, no longer interested. Now only one thing bothered and dismayed him: he was now longer than the hollow he lay in. 'Why? How could that happen?' he wondered with amazement. Blood was rushing from his exposed legs to his head, his legs had pins and needles. Ants seemed to be crawling over his swollen, frozen legs. Where had these ants come from? They had eaten him before, at the port of Knossos, together with a squashed pear. The image of that squashed pear and the ants made Parnaoz nauseous. If he were going to rest properly, he had to fit into the hollow, obligingly curl up and make himself smaller, diminish: didn't everyone act like that, and why should he be any different? How many times did they have to repeat to him? If others could do it, why shouldn't he? Was he inferior? Popeye was a kinsman, but even a kinsman doesn't like you sticking your smelly feet in his face. Parnaoz was trying, curling up in all sorts of ways, but his feet still stuck out of the hollow as if they deliberately, provocatively wanted to be seen by everyone. The hollow was clearly too small: he couldn't possibly have suddenly grown longer, the very thought was preposterous: can stone submit so easily to a human being? He was well aware of that, he'd done nothing but work with stone. It was dark in the cave, for Popeye had his back to the entrance which in any case let in only a tiny chink of pale light. 'He's offended, I've offended him again,' thought Parnaoz, but almost immediately a fragment of hazy space enclosed in a distorted circle reappeared, and he heard Popeye's voice. 'Are you in agony?' Popeye asked him and, as was his habit, sniggered nastily, like a man who has given advice which someone distrusts, and then sniggers only to prove immediately that he is right.

'Now why don't you say who was right? Ha, ha…' Popeye giggled, and Parnaoz's blood curdled. Popeye was right. Did he realise what that meant? Parnaoz sighed, sweated, so tense that he nearly tore his muscles, but he still couldn't get his feet into the hollow. Popeye crouched down by his feet, watching him carefully, like a man who knows what he is doing, as a sensible and experienced peasant looks at a diseased fruit tree. No, he was not just going to leave alone a tree which instead of sending out fruit buds has suddenly developed yellow stalks, dried bark and has only to be touched to collapse into dust. The tree needs treatment: it can't be allowed to go on standing and be utterly unlike its fellow fruit-trees bowed down with buds and ready to produce fruit once more, to do conscientiously their duty for nature and men. Eh man, think of all the sweat that man produced to make one lousy tree flourish; if every tree were as barren and degenerate as this one, what could he do? The gods and nature have decreed: a tree exists to bear fruit, to be like the next tree, not to sprawl untidily all over the place and think it's better than the others. Growing too high won't do a tree any good: it will just suck up others' share of water. And why should it? What have the others done to it? Other trees stand with their heads bowed and toil, yes, they toil, they are weighed down with fruit, while this second tree, stupefied by its height, stares at the sky and forgets all about its duty.

'Anything excessive is bad,' said Popeye, crouching by Parnaoz's feet. 'The reason you're in agony is that you don't fit that hollow. You're too long, lo-o-ng. Ha, ha… so we have to…'

'No!' Parnaoz shouted, because he now knew what had to be done to make him fit the hollow, to give him rest, to put an end to everything.'

'Damn you…' Popeye laughed, as a kind grandfather might laugh at his grandchild's foolishness. 'You really are stubborn, oh dear, oh dear!'

Parnaoz could hear the sack full of tools hitting the stone floor: his last hope drained away. He hadn't noticed the sack at first, even wondering why Popeye had left home without it, but he blamed himself for such a naïve thought. Was Popeye the sort of man to forget his tools and thus put himself to double the trouble for one job? Parnaoz was very mistaken if he thought that. Popeye knew his job, and knew it well. If Parnaoz had known his job that well, things might have turned out better, at least in part. Now it was all in vain: Popeye had won and, as he had won, he was in the right. It was all over, anything else was stupidity. 'Stu-pi-di-ty,' Parnaoz spelled it out. Popeye and his profession were ancient. Parnaoz was born yesterday by comparison, he was just his crazy friend. Really, who on earth would have thought of anything so stupid? Sorry to disappoint you, Daedalus, but if flying were that easy, who would stay on earth, I ask you? Men are meant to carve stone and build houses, make roads. That's how it has been and will be. 'I wonder if it will always be like that? Always?' asked Parnaoz, this time aloud. Popeye replied instantly.

'Of course, of course, what's got into you, my dear bloke? I've said it before, and I'll repeat: always!' said Popeye, raking through his open sack as if he intended to pull out a live snake. There was a nasty jangling of iron from the sack, a saw blade flashed in the cave's slightly pale darkness, as if the darkness had laughed and bared its teeth.

'A man has to fit the hole provided for him if he wants a peaceful life. Nobody has any right to get up and tell him, "You live in a hole!" Whose business is it if a man feels fine in that hole and, before he goes to sleep, whispers to the gods, "You've given me all I need, nothing needs to change." But if he wants… But you yourself sense how uncomfortable it is to lie there, don't you?'

Popeye's last words were accompanied by the screech of the saw. Parnaoz fainted, from fear more than the pain. Almost immediately he woke up, amazed that it was all over so quickly. Popeye had gone, and he himself… he was holding his breath with anxiety and shame. How right and kind Popeye had been. Whatever Parnaoz thought of him, whatever he accused him of, however angry he was with him, he had nearly… 'No, I'm grateful, gods, that it didn't happen that way.' It was enough that he had committed a loathsome act, his son's blood was torment enough, Ino's misfortune was sufficient cause for him to beat his head against the wall, and Tina's curses would finish him. Hadn't all three fallen victim to his foolishness? What did he have against any of those three? Was the origin of these evils really hidden, it was where the dog's head, Tsuga's head, was buried. As for him, his whole life was just pretence, he had laid his hand on others like a thief picking others' pockets, when he himself had a snake hidden on his person. 'Thank you, Popeye, thank you. And if you can, forgive my ignorance. Things are much better as they now are.'

Parnaoz really now lay at ease in his hollow, as if he were in a bath of pleasantly warm water, purposefully, to prolong his pleasure, fighting off drowsiness. 'You're a cunning devil, Parnaoz, cunning, because you love the good life. Why not, why not,' Parnaoz repeated aloud, emphatically, sensing his face turning red with both shame and pleasure, as if he were a girl kissed for the first time by a man she can no longer live without.

'Scattered millet see-ee-eed, Who but a chick picks up?' Parnaoz sang, splashing his palms on the water, which was now up to his chin, although he was well aware that it wasn't water, it was his own blood, gushing from his amputated legs, pouring out like water from the pipe, as thick as an arm, of the Greek's source.

Little Ukheiro's fatality gave the palace cause for reflection: at least one hen had managed to fly over the fence! Mind you, it had cost the hen its life, but the fence, reddened with its blood, was a warning to the other hens, and made them race about clucking.

The hens' racing and clucking was nothing terrible or hard to deal with. A dead fox was hung over the fence and that stopped everything: but were what the palace considered to be hens really hens? Were hens ever known to kill themselves? No, this death had another meaning, and Oqajado could not fail to take heed. And Tsutsa was mewling, 'Now we have to show courage.' It didn't need much wit to realise that mother and son were involved in something bad. For some reason Oqajado recalled the day he entered Vani: to be precise, he could see as clearly if it were now the pallid face of the man who, with a javelin piercing his throat, called out from the roof of his house, 'Long live Ææëtes!' Oqajado's memory made him shudder, he was horrified that today of all days he recalled this man, the only man in the entire city who without thinking, hesitating or being afraid, in front of everyone, chose to die rather than recognize Oqajado as king. Today this had recurred exactly. True, his soldiers had hacked the man to pieces, but they apparently couldn't kill him off completely, for something of him was left, the blood at least which had persisted all this time in the earth, had spread underground in order to burst forth today and turn the paving of his kingdom red.

'If only he had simply fallen, or my soldiers had finished him off. But jumping off is a catastrophe,' Oqajado worried, feeling how much he feared and loathed this dead child and with what pleasure he would, if he could, bring him back to life so as to kill him with his own hands.

God knows how long Oqajado would have worried, or his obsessive mind would have fixed on this one point, had Tsutsa not come to his aid.

'What can you expect of a stupid child? It's his guardian who deserves death,' said Tsutsa, giving her son a testing look.

'My mother is a great, a gre-a-t woman,' thought Oqajado, and set off gravely, unhurriedly along the path his mother had indicated. He was now off not just to defeat the throne's greatest enemy, but to show the Supreme King what he could do. Today was a splendid day in Oqajado's life, today he would prove that he was worthy to wear the royal crown which Minos had personally put on the head of a man who was then a flat-browed, pimply youth. This youth now had grey hair, half of which had fallen out, but time had added more than it had taken away. Time had given him the ability to defeat everything and crush everything, and had rewarded his persistence, his endurance, his indifference, his tenacity, his blindness and deafness, with the cloak of eternal life. Time was satisfied, because Oqajado had never ever hindered its steady flow. Even today he wasn't hindering it, because in order to dominate this day, he was making every effort, carrying his mother in his arms, a woman who was as heavy as a rock and who repeated everything three times. Oqajado celebrated his victory in advance and imagined himself standing before Minos, the Eternal King, King of Kings, Parent and Multiplier of Kings. But he did not go pale with fear, nor did he go weak at the knees: he looked the King in the face as an equal and in allegorical language, as befits real kings, told him of the plans he had made to win today's battle.

'Listen, we were sitting there eating, and we decided, casually, let's see if a child or a dog has crawled under the table.' 'A child or a dog?' asks Minos. Oqajado laughs, 'Wait, don't confuse me. It was dogs, but there was a child mixing with them. Whose wretched brat, I don't yet know. Anyway, sir, the table was rotten, the child tripped up on it and accidentally, or on purpose, knocked off a leg, and pulled the whole table with all the food crashing down onto him. We all rushed out, he'd ruined our banquet. We don't know about the child, we're shaking ourselves down, all fussing about: someone shouts out, "Where's that child come from?" We had a look and what do we see? There's a dead chick lying there. "The dead child's been sneaked onto the dinner table," the people all shriek and rush out through the windows and doors. I was left there by myself with the dead child: I couldn't go, I'm king and host, too. I don't need to tell you that a king even in someone else's house is the host. I'm standing there, thinking. The guests have run away, but they're still watching me, wondering what I'm going to do. It's no joke, people have come for a banquet and something awful is happening in the family. If you don't finger someone for it, who's going to take the blame? After all, it's got to be someone's fault, hasn't it? They can't all be blameless, can they? The guests won't dare say anything against me, but I can hear them murmuring that I'm the host, so I ought to find the person responsible. Now, I'll bet you're wondering how I found him? I swear on my mother's life that Tsutsa didn't tell me. Why should she? Let's begin with the guests. They were there, but they couldn't have seen with their knees what was happening under the table, could they? Like you, they probably thought it was a dog. Why should they bother about a dog, we'd just sat down, pouring wine, cutting meat, passing round the bread or the salt. You're right, we could pick on one of them, but isn't there a more likely criminal? I'll explain it all right now. I'm making a bit of a meal of it, but now I'll cut a long story short. Who killed the child? The table did, of course. But the table's not the criminal. You know the saying, it's the last straw that breaks the camel's back? That's how it was. The table may have been rotten, but it was standing all right, it would have taken the weight of the food if the child hadn't grabbed hold of it. The child wouldn't be very strong, but just a little bit of strength was too much. So, at first glance, the child turns out to be the criminal. But, would you believe it, the child isn't the criminal, either. You can't expect a child to have any sense, it's his guardian who has to be killed, the child's parent. Apart from anything else, shouldn't he be looking after his child? Call himself a parent?' Oqajado finished and put his hand on his heart, which was swollen with pride. Then he knitted his brow in his usual way and yelled, 'Whose child is it?'

Popeye found it hard to swallow his saliva. At one point he decided not to speak out, even if cost him his life, but he immediately got angry and told himself. 'Well, why did you come running here? If you wanted to be killed, they'd have come for you anyway.'

The news of little Ukheiro's death was a call to action for Popeye: he was like a traveller lost in the desert, despairing after futile roaming about, who suddenly hears a cock crowing. He realised that he was saved, that this time, too, he had escaped jeopardy, because this time he was innocent. Why did he have to get together with Ziara, why did his wives have to produce dead babies, if this unjust world hadn't got it in for Popeye? Little Ukheiro's death reassured him a little: it was far more significant than the birth of a stillborn baby, which could easily be a gift from the gods to mock a father who longed for progeny. There was nothing surprising about that: the gods would think of anything for the sake of a good laugh. After Popeye had driven the women out of the house, he kept thinking about this as he lay on his back on the divan, the divan of sin, looking at the ceiling and smiling bitterly at the gods' joke. 'I understand, I've understood it all,' he would call out aloud; now he was upset that he had spent so much time and strength to no good purpose on that scarecrow Ziara. The thought of Ziara made his skin itch and he put the water on to boil so that he could wash again, in the middle of his hovel, but hot water could not soothe his fear-ridden body. He lay down and pondered. He had a lot to ponder. Someone had only to whisper into Oqajado's ear, 'The man who earns his bread from you is begetting dead babies, instead of defending you,' and it would all end with Popeye being abandoned by the whole world to his fate. In fact, he had so many enemies that he shouldn't be surprised if this was how things went. When the city was full of winged children, he became more alarmed, and more convinced that the end was imminent. He was convinced that the children deliberately ran about near his hovel, deliberately shouted at him so as to show others where the chief criminal was hiding. His crazy mother and grandmother had made such lot of noise and fuss that they had attracted everyone's attention, as if they were utterly heartbroken. They weren't at all heartbroken, they were jumping for joy, because they thought they were now beyond reproach: having a dead child is far better than having a bastard, isn't it? Popeye lay there, seething. He lay there, and listened with an animal's relentless hatred to the swishing of leather straps, like a fox, its knees weak with fear, at bay in the bushes, listening to the barking of the hounds. But a fox had nothing to worry about: it had four legs and could easily run, unlike Popeye who was huddling like a frozen cricket in the cracked wall of his thoughts and constantly imagining someone's thumb coming to squash him, coming closer and looming larger. Popeye believed he was a criminal, or rather that since he had been dragged into the palace, he wouldn't be surprised if someone blamed him for this child's game playing at being birds and said, 'Your dead babies have caused panic among the people.' The leather straps were swishing, every nook and cranny was being rummaged, every hole was being investigated, and Popeye's flesh hurt, burned, disintegrated. The swishing of straps died down sooner than Popeye expected, but the silence became harder to bear and it was imbued with a smell of danger, because Popeye knew by experience that this silence meant not the end, but a new start for the main goal: to find the guilty person. The guilty person couldn't have got far or hidden properly. He was lying in his hovel, and anyone you cared to ask could point it out for you, because everyone, from one end of the city to the other, recognized Popeye as easily as they recognized a three-coloured dog. As long as confusion reigned in the city, there was at least an ounce of hope that he could survive, that they might forget him, but now, in this regal silence, everything that had sunk and been suppressed during the confusion was surfacing again. Isn't it a calm sea that washes ashore those that drowned in the storm? In short, it was obvious that all roads were blocked and, like it or not, Popeye had to accept his fate. But little Ukheiro's death gave him new cause for hope. Now it was a matter of urgency: there were now two criminals instead of one, and if the palace saw, as Popeye did, that there were two, then there would be no difficulty choosing. How could his premature baby that only flickered into life for an instant be compared with Parnaoz's son? Why not? Obviously not! 'Are you telling me that you can't see the difference between the two children? There's a big difference, you can't fail to notice it. One was born dead; the other tried to fly, it was alive and it killed itself, because its daddy also had his head in the clouds, like the rest of his tribe. He did all he could to dupe his son. Ask me about all this, I know more than anyone. Who would beget a son just to destroy him? You can't expect any sense from a child, a child is stupid, and the parent has to be held to account; a parent has to pay for the pitcher if his naughty child smashes it. As far as my own baby is concerned, it isn't even certain that it's mine. Why would I beget a dead baby, do I look as if there's anything wrong with me? How do I know? Don't ask me, ask Ziara. Women are wretched creatures, there's nothing they won't do to a man.'

Such thoughts gave Popeye courage. Now it was important for others to think the same way and quickly disarm any hands pointing at him.

'The child is my uncle's. He's a waste of space, no use in the family and no use outside it!' said Popeye.

He'd started, so he had to finish, there was no point holding back, and there was no way he could help Parnaoz: he had to speak before he was silenced, before people were fed up listening to him and shouted, 'Clear off, we've understood everything.'

'His father was a famous warrior, the slave and humble servant of your father, and then yours,' Popeye told Oqajado. 'His name was Ukheiro, and he was worth a whole army. But he couldn't look after his son: how could he have, when he needed looking after himself, he'd lost half his body when they brought him home, a chariot ran over his legs. His son learned to be a stone-cutter and all he did was spend all day hammering at stone. I shouldn't speak badly of my own uncle, but he was never normal, my poor mother and my aunt took a lot of trouble over him, protecting his good name, keeping it all in the family, but they were wasting their time.' (Popeye suddenly sensed that he was talking about Parnaoz as though his uncle were dead, but this encouraged, rather than dismayed him; he was sure he was doing the right thing, the dead were beyond help, and the living needed to be saved, he was one of the living himself.) 'It seems to me that he must have been fed on donkey's brains,' Popeye went on. 'After that he always had his head in the clouds, he would stand there like a donkey, watching the sky. Sometime I would call him, sometimes my mother or our Tina, and he would finally come to his senses. Ha, ha, not really come to his senses, like hell he would: he'd give us the slip and find a cosier place. Well, in a nutshell, he wouldn't rest until he destroyed his own son. The boy was a lovely child, chubby, but as wilful and bad-tempered as his father. God knows where the hell the father learned to fly: he'd go on about it, saying I've got to teach my son, too. First I'll teach my son, then I'll teach the others. I didn't believe the rubbish he was spouting, I just told him not to expect anything from me and to hold his tongue, or else I would personally tell the king everything. But do you think he'd listen?! Once I even waved a stick at him, I meant to break his ankle, but he flew off and dodged it…'

Tsutsa whispered something to Oqajado, who raised his hand, silenced Popeye and asked, 'Is this the first time you've been here?'

'I've been in your service for a long time,' Popeye smiled, as if to say, 'How could you forget?' But secretly he was dying the death: 'Suppose he asks me what I do, what do I tell him?' But he soon calmed down, because the fear flashing through his mind had enlightened him and suddenly he felt with his whole being, with every sinew, bone and every lobe of his brain, that they had been paying him money with this day in mind, as if they had known beforehand that this day was bound to come and would give Popeye a chance to render the appropriate service to his master, who had all these years been stuffing his purse with money, too much money in Popeye's view, since it came to him with no effort at all. Now it seemed too little. The service he was now rendering was worth far more, he was helping Oqajado to find another criminal, no ordinary one, not a petty thief, but a man who was a danger to the country. What's more, this man was his uncle, his mother's brother, and that should be taken into account, too. By exterminating the criminal, you exterminated the crime, and that was a great deed, because the existence of such a crime cast a shadow on the throne and whoever sat on it. 'So that seems to be why they wanted me,' thought Popeye angrily. 'Well, kind sir, if you needed me so badly, why did you rate me so cheaply? If I'd known, I'd have named my own price for my goods.' Now Popeye looked more boldly and rudely at Oqajado, but the king could no longer see him, his royal mind's eye was like a flaming torch seeking the little cave in which the enemy of his throne was lurking.

When Popeye was on his way here he was thinking only of saving himself, but things had taken a turn so that perhaps something else could be saved. Nothing could in fact now save Parnaoz: even if Popeye took it all back, who would believe him? No, Parnaoz was a dead man, and all that he lacked was a burial, if, of course, he was thought to deserve consigning to the earth. Popeye, however, was still in this world, and Parnaoz ought to remember well how much a man needed in this treacherous world. 'I can't believe they're not going to give me anything!' thought Popeye and deliberately adjusted the sack slung over his shoulder so that its jingling brought Oqajado back to earth and made him notice Popeye. 'What can I do, uncle, it's my job?' he mentally apologized to Parnaoz, and to the three present: he smiled at the throne, Oqajado sitting on the throne and Tsutsa, perched on Oqajado's shoulder.

'Dismiss the man, why detain him?' Tsutsa told Oqajado.

Oqajado looked at Popeye with amazement, as if this was the first time he had seen him, as if this scraggy-necked man with the slicked down forelock and the sack over his shoulder had just crawled out of the earth. 'What more does he want? We've said all there is to say,' Oqajado turned to his mother. Tsutsa gave Popeye a look, smiled and told him, 'I'd give you a ring, but it's a souvenir of my husband, so I'd rather not.'

Parnaoz was quite unaware of being brought out of the cave, taken through the entire city so that everyone had a chance to see the enemy of the throne and throw ash in his face and spit at him, or even curse him. But, to the palace's surprise, people's lips were clenched as they watched with fear and sympathy this tortured man being dragged by Oqajado's soldiers down the street like a bundle of kindling. Parnaoz couldn't hear the quiet lamenting of the women or see the men's pallid faces, his weakened mind had taken him to his childhood and he thought he was back in the days when he had been an 'outlaw' for a week and was striding sullenly among his laughing fellow-citizens, trying only not to stumble or fall down, or lose his temper, just to get to the end of the street and let everybody see him and enjoy the sight of a boy defeated. In fact, there really was no great difference between that day and this one, except that one was the beginning of the defeat and the other the conclusion. The time that had elapsed between them had been a waste, an empty husk which had hung on the tree like other walnuts but, unlike them, contained an empty space instead of a kernel.

Two iron rings had been hammered into the tower wall; ropes as thick as a wrist had been pulled through the rings and their slack ends swayed over Parnaoz's head like rearing snakes. Parnaoz lay under the tower wall, and a soldier, kneeling on one leg, poured water from a goatskin onto his face. The square was packed with people. The tight-lipped women hummed like bee-hives. Helpless sympathy made the men drop their jaws. The blazing sun ruffled its wings like a phoenix over the shining roofs, and its burning exhalations stupefied the people even more. Their eyes half-blinded by the light, everyone stared at the sun, hoping for something from it, as if the sun really were the phoenix and could bring back to life the man sprawling under the tower wall and snatch him to a place of safety. Suddenly someone shouted, ‘Look, look!’ and from the dead-calm sea of people Parnaoz’s drooping head floated up, followed by his arms, which had ropes tied around the armpits, and were spread out like wings, and finally his whole body: from head to foot, as limp and lifeless as a rag. The soldiers, who were tugging on the ends of the rope tied round Parnaoz’s armpits, were out of sight, and the impression was that Parnaoz was rising up by himself. His flayed back left a wet, blackish trace on the wall’s rough surface. Even now Parnaoz was not aware of anything: he had lost consciousness when he was on the ground, and he swayed quietly in the air as unfeeling as a chopped off branch.

All night the soldiers kept a fire burning and dozed off in turn, as if anyone would come to steal this stiff dead branch. There were two of them, one fat and squat, the other tall and gangling; one was nasty, the other kindly. One genuinely slept when it was his turn, the other pretended to be asleep, because it seemed to him that the man on the wall was calling out, ‘Give me a drink of water: are you human?’ ‘Can’t you hear anything?’ he asked the other soldier, but the other soldier could only hear the impassioned crackling of the fire and the croaking of the frogs. By morning they were both in a vile mood. One was upset by the fear and pangs of remorse he had endured, the other by interrupted sleep and by watching over a troublesome fire. One stretched his limbs and looked up, and stayed frozen in that position, bending backwards, with his arms outspread, as if a sudden attack of lumbago had made him leap up. ‘He’s died, do you see, man, he’s died!’ he called to the other. The other was went up to the dying fire and doused it with his urine. The thick layers of ash over the embers hissed as they sent up white smoke. ‘What do you mean he’s dead, can’t you see his eyes are shining?’ he responded to the first soldier. ‘There’s nobody to close his eyes, is there?’ the first soldier answered. ‘He’s not dead, I said,’ the soldier by the fire insisted, and jerked upwards as if he was adjusting a load hanging on his back. Then he bent down, picked up a stone and said, ‘Well, if you don’t believe me, just watch.’ The stone struck the wall close to Parnaoz and bounced aside. The first soldier couldn’t help screwing up his eyes. ‘Hey, hey, hey!’ the stone thrower called, and when the man roped to the wall paid no attention to his shout, he too began to have doubts: ‘I think he must have died,’ he said, and began looking for another stone. ‘Wait, wait: it’s my turn now,’ shouted the first soldier, thinking privately that he wouldn’t throw so hard. They then took turns throwing. Neither of them hit the mark, for one was in a hurry in case ‘that midget’ beat him, while the other was distressed every time he threw a stone: ‘What have I done, why did I even pick up a stone?’ In the end a stone did hit the target: which of them threw it wasn’t clear, but it hit hard, because the whole body of man hanging in the air shook, and his head slumped to the other side.

Pain brought Parnaoz back to consciousness. 'I've been sleeping standing up, like a horse,' he thought as he got off the wall. He had taken only a couple of steps when he saw the twin cypresses, then his eye caught sight of the fig tree with its arms leaning over the fence like a woman waiting: his heart quivered, for he had come to his father's house. 'How close my house is to this place!' he wondered, and couldn't help looking back, but he could see nothing but bare, overgrazed meadows, except that he felt sure that he was being watched. He couldn't take his eye off the meadow and kept on looking until he noticed a gigantic clay toad between the bald hillocks. The toad was crouching in open country, watching Parnaoz. 'It can follow me as much as it likes,' he thought, and opened the gate. On the paved path in the courtyard Daedalus's paralysed son Icarus was sitting, holding an apple and squashing it on the paving. Hens were cackling by the fence. The child and the whole courtyard were wrapped in shade, as in a net. When Icarus saw Parnaoz, he threw away the apple and held out his hands to him. The child's tooth marks on the apple looked like an inscription. Parnaoz bent down, but before he picked Icarus up he took one more look at the courtyard, as if he had come to abduct the child. The child was overjoyed and fluttered like a bird in his arms; Parnaoz found this heart-warming, he felt he had done a kindness and there was nothing to fear. Nobody would have stopped him taking the child away: in fact, they probably expected him to do so, they knew why he had come and had deliberately placed the child in the courtyard. 'Shall we go for a walk?' Parnaoz asked, but he found the words as hard to say, as if he were telling a woman 'I love you' for the first time. As soon as they left the yard, Parnaoz was crestfallen: the marsh had come up to the gate. 'It's my fault, I've left it too late,' he thought, but said aloud, 'Look, you can see there's nothing outside your yard to get excited about.' But Icarus seemed not to have understood what he said and bent his body, like a rider on a horse that refuses to move. Parnaoz didn't want to disappoint the boy and took a careful first step, looking for a firm and safe a place to put his foot. Immediately, the marsh retreated, like the darkness when lit up by a flare. The boy fluttered again and Parnaoz boldly followed the marsh's retreating path. Where there had been marsh, trees pushed up their crowns and soon whole trunks rose up from the ground and, before their eyes, a boundless apple orchard was laid out. 'Here we are, Dariachangi's garden!' shouted Parnaoz and he was rooted to the spot with astonishment. Dariachangi's garden was verdant in the sunlight, it wafted intoxicating scents, it flowered in some places, ripened fruit in others, and here and there the fruit was already falling off the trees. Like gold dust, a swarm of bees hovered overhead; far off, as far as the eye could see, the breeze carried away the blossom. A white goat kid came out of the garden: when it saw the man and boy rooted to the spot, it bleated, leapt up with joy and turned back into the garden, as if saying to them, 'Why are you standing there? Come here, it's better here.' Then the sea sighed on the other side of the garden, bent the crowns of the trees with its mighty breath, and the infinite azure sky made Parnaoz giddy. This fabulous spectacle excited Icarus, he couldn't stay still, he fidgeted, bent forwards, as if he was about to go off, in fact fly off, without Parnaoz, and follow the breeze like the apple blossom. But Parnaoz held his arms more firmly, as if he feared that the boy really would fly off and succumb to temptation. 'You're hurting me, let me go!' Icarus said, losing patience. 'No, I won't let you go anywhere!' Parnaoz answered in sudden agitation.

Then he kissed the lobe of the boy's ear and whispered to him, 'This is how the world is going to be.'

'Isn't it already like that?' asked Icarus, surprised.

'Well yes, it is, and it will always be!' Parnaoz told him.

also available from the Garnett Press

Д. Рейфилд, О. Макарова (ред.) *Дневник Алексея Сергеевича Суворина* (*Dairy of Aleksei Suvorin, the 19th C. Russian magnate, in Russian*). 1999, pp xl+666.
ISBN 0 9535878 0 0 £20.00

Donald Rayfield (with Rusudan Amirejibi, Shukia Apridonidze, Laurence Broers, Levan Chkhaidze, Ariane Chanturia, Tina Margalitadze)
A Comprehensive Georgian-English Dictionary, 2006. 2 vols. pp xl + 1727.
ISBN 978-0-9535878-3-4 £75.00
(*a few seconds [8 replacement pages inserted in volume 2] are available at £55.00)*

Peter Pišt'anek, translated from the Slovak by Peter Petro. *Rivers of Babylon* 2007. pp 259. ISBN 978-0-9535878-4-1 £12.99

Peter Pišt'anek, translated by Peter Petro *The Wooden Village* (*Rivers of Babylon 2)* 2008. pp 206. ISBN 978-0-9535878-5-8 £11.99

Peter Pišt'anek, translated by Peter Petro *The End of Freddy* (*Rivers of Babylon 3)* 2008. pp 206. ISBN 978-0-9535878-6-5 £13.99

Daniela Kapitáňová, translated from the Slovak by Julia Sherwood *Samko Tále's Cemetery Book* pp 130. ISBN 978-0-9535878-9-6. £8.99

Nikolai Gogol, Marc Chagall *Dead Souls,* a new translation by Donald Rayfield, *with 96 engravings and 12 vignettes from the 1948 Tériade edition* 2008. pp 368. Limited to 1500 copies, large format, art paper. ISBN 978-0-9535878-7-2. £29.99

Donald Rayfield *The Literature of Georgia — A History*, 3rd revised, expanded edition. 2010. pp 366. ISBN 978-0-9535878-8-9 £25.00

forthcoming in 2013:

Otar Chiladze *Avelum* (the fifth novel by Georgia's greatest modern novelist)

second edition of D. Rayfield, J Hicks, O Makarova, A. Pilkington (editors) *The Garnett Book of Russian Verse. An Anthology with English Prose Translation*

all prices plus postage at current rates

to buy our books from Queen Mary Online Store: ***go to*** **https://eshop.qmul.ac.uk**
then click **Product Catalogue,** ***then*** **Books,** ***then*** **Garnett Press Books,**
or contact: *d.rayfield@qmul.ac.uk*
or write to:
Garnett Press, School of Languages, Literature and Film, Queen Mary University of London, Mile End Road, London E1 4NS, UK